THE PERAMBULATIONS AND PEREGRINATIONS OF PETER POLLACK

GREGORY KASTNER

FUNNY BUSINESS PUBLICATIONS LLC

ISBN: 9781522006770

Funny Business Publications LLC

18516 236th Avenue Northeast, Woodinville, Washington 98077

First published as Amazon Kindle ebook January 2015, ASIN: B00RYC33P6

First paperback edition September 2017

Recut, reglued (and 13.26% funnier, guaranteed) 2nd edition September 2019

Cover photos ©Gregory Kastner 2001, 2013

Chapter plates ©Gregory Kastner 1996, 2000, 2001, 2013

Cover design by Drew Kastner

To my parents

With special thanks to Drew, Michelle and those who showed
me the way along the way

Contents

War of the Pigeons

As the airplane lifted and beneath me the earth fell away, so did the ache in my heart. For the past three years, I'd been living without purpose, hating my inability (or my cowardice) to change that and feeling lost. So I'd freed myself. From responsibility, career, trying to impress my father.

Would traveling slake my thirst for something more? Change me, show me the way? Did a place for me exist? People who listened, who cared?

There had to be. At least I had to try.

But I've forgotten my manners. Introductions must be considered. Who I am, where I come from, where I'm going, my hobbies, favorite ice cream flavor, times I've been chased by a spotted hyena, preferred form of reincarnation, intense dread of agricultural economists - you get the idea.

The name's Peter. Peter Pollack. Age: twenty-four. Height: five foot nine inches. Weight: one hundred fifty-six pounds. Hair: brown. Eyes: blue. Shoe size: 9, though sometimes 8.5, or even 8. Distinguishing features: light freckles across the nose, cheeks and forearms, scarred left middle finger where I once did furious battle with a supermarket shopping cart, black metal-framed oval spectacles, undeniably lovely ankles (but in a masculine way, I assure you). Occupation: unemployed accountant.

Wait, let me explain. Sure I'm an accountant, but I'm interesting. Hand on my heart, pinky swear (you must learn to trust me). I know. Some (most) claim our species can't be interesting (especially those unemployed) and dismiss us thus. (They say we should never ever breed, either. Ever. For when the gene doesn't skip a generation – the sight is not in the slightest bit pretty.) The only professions less appealing: morticians and divorce attorneys. And often the cliché is frighteningly true. Nothing's duller than a man who counts the croutons in his Caesar salad every day to make sure he received the same as the day before (and the day before that (and the day before that)). But I'm different. (The ice cream and hyena will come. Be patient.)

Firstly, the company I resigned from wasn't your typical accounting firm. Yes, it had computers, a seldom cleaned coffeemaker and dark, sinister cubicles where men went missing for days at a time, but those are only the superficial accoutrements of the trade. A clear representation requires delving deeper. You must learn of its inhabitants and their secrets. If you have the stomach for it.

In his rush to finish his meals, Bass tended to spew half his food back onto his plate because he took too large of bites. He was always nervous when he wasn't working because he knew they wanted him to be and he was always nervous when he was working because he knew they wanted him to work faster. Even microwaving every one of his less-than-cardboard-flavored meals in the office kitchen for years didn't save him enough time. He was often seen hopping impatiently on one foot and then the next as he flipped through some unwieldy monstrosity of a file while waiting for his pepperoni hot pocket. Invariably he would snatch the snack free early and choke it down half frozen back at his desk.

Flounder picked his nose copiously and liked to shake everyone's hand three to four times per minute of conversation, frequently interchanging both habits to an alarming and frightening degree. He bitterly hated his job because he could not pass the Certified Public Accountants examination and he bitterly hated anyone he worked for because they had. Every six months when Flounder failed the examination, he vowed never to re-take it and burned all of his expensive, self-purchased and non-firm reimbursed study materials in what he hoped to be a spectacular but was really just a barely shrug-worthy bonfire in the parking lot which, nevertheless, usually earned him a fire department citation. Then, according to formula, followed a ridiculous amount of alcohol consumption of questionable quality, karaoke in a hotel lobby and/or late night supermarket lacking both a microphone and stage, and projectile vomiting onto an occupied police car or super huge, super unforgiving ex-Ultimate Fighter. Five months later, he resumed studying, having wasted the interval in denial.

Salmon trusted no one, never spoke to anyone except in the men's restroom of all places (possibly he was equally garrulous in the women's restroom, but, me not in the habit of frequenting said venue…), and did all the work himself despite being a senior manager. No one had ever seen him leave the building or even seen him in daylight (probably a good thing considering the unnatural bluish-white shade of his skin). Ever. When we arrived in the morning, when we left at night - Salmon was there. He worked with his office door shut and never smiled at anyone. Rumor was he had a cot hidden underneath the stacks of files in his office – among those who thought he slept, that is. I'm a sick man: I tried to make friends with him.

I tried to befriend Bass, also, but Flounder was just too sick and twisted for me to handle. A man that fond of his snot is not a man whose hand I want to shake on a regular basis.

Okay, maybe I haven't dispelled your negative preconceptions of accountants with that less than appealing description of my co-workers, but I promise things will get interesting. You'll laugh, you'll cry, you'll feel absolutely nothing at all.

Two Germans getting completely blitzed on cheap Greek beer occupied the seats separating me from the window. They kept buzzing the stewardess to request the pilot to do a loop-da-loop. At first she smiled and answered no, small children were on board the airplane. Not satisfied by this answer, the Germans persisted, offering bribes. Their supply of alcohol was cut off, but they had brought their own; the air soon reeked of Jägermeister. When that ran out, they resorted to cherry-flavored cough syrup. They tried dragging me into their schemes and plots but I kept telling them I was from Trinidad and Tobago and in love with an albino elephant named Fred. They laughed at first but, upon my unvarying repetition, began to plot my assassination in German. I then passed a note to the stewardess asking her to season their salads generously with cyanide. (She declined, saying it violated federal aviation regulations. But I knew better: my second cousin worked security Thursday afternoons at LAX.)

Luckily the Germans passed out over New York and I could relax (or as close to relax as one can when cramped in one position for hours with a metal bar digging into the small of one's back and the latch of the folding table on the seat in front of one broken and the seat attached to it constantly seesawing up and down as its occupant adjusted its position between bouts of prolonged flatulence). I settled back (well, sort of sideways and only until someone else headed to the bathroom and elbowed me in the ear passing by) and was reaching for my guidebook to backpacking in Europe when I realized I'd left it inside my luggage.

I have problems. I forget things. I always pick the slowest moving lane in traffic, the supermarket, wherever. (I make the mistake of queuing behind the little old lady with frizzy red hair taller than her in the express lane when five people with full carts occupy all the other lanes. She will demand three price checks on bananas and swear there was a two-for-one special on toilet paper advertised and not given. Then she complains with a surfeit of detail about the degradation of today's society before opening her *coin* purse to pay the cashier. Sometimes she drops the money, sometimes she doesn't. Then she will be short as in not even close and will ask the prices of all her items again and again, trying to decide what to return while ranting that in her day a loaf of bread only cost a nickel (which must have been like 274 million years ago before dinosaurs ruled the earth and amoebas were king). When I finally get to pay, people who arrived at the grocery store three hours after me are at home having eaten dinner and watched three episodes of *The Partridge Family*. Then the cashier will have to go on a break or the cash register won't have change or the credit card scanner will malfunction. Always. Every single time I go to the grocery store. Before work, after work, at midnight. A society of old ladies must monitor my every move, ready at a moment's notice to cut in front of me at the supermarket line and exacerbate my pain. Sometimes I think it's the same old lady following me, stalking me like I'm The Road Runner and she's an even more determined but less furry Wile E. Coyote.) Wanting a chocolate chip cookie, I receive sugarless oatmeal raisin. Chili cheese fries, carrot sticks… You understand.

"Actually," the stewardess said to me, "I lied about the cyanide being against aviation regulations." Glancing left, then right, she added in a conspiratorial tone, "We just ran out. College football players on the last flight. And one rather rowdy agricultural economist." She winked, then hushed my laugh with a finger to her lips.

I returned the gesture.

What did I expect to find exactly? I'd spent my whole life waiting, as if what I really wanted hadn't begun yet: when I got this or when I got that, could I then be happy. Only I didn't get those things. I don't mean to say that my life had been just a long string of disasters (subject to interpretation), good things happened to me. But never the epiphanies I expected. I kept telling myself that love or success could only intensify my own internal happiness, not create it, but when neither came…

As a child, the adult world fascinated me. The mysteries of the universe, its infinite varieties of life and not yet discovered possibilities– filled me with wonder and an overwhelming curiosity. Each day I woke eager to learn more, absorb more – I made endless lists of books to read, movies to see, music to listen to. And to fix its imperfections or what I perceived its imperfections. One lifetime wasn't enough. And always this idealization of love, a companion of the soul. Someone sweet, accepting, supportive. Tomorrow it would start. Tomorrow I would fix it. Tomorrow.

And life kept moving on. I wanted to be happy. I really did, but I couldn't, I didn't feel that way. What I had, what I was, was not enough. Having a job, being healthy – I wanted more. What exactly, I wasn't sure. Part of this trip was to find that out.

Once at Net, Block and Tackle (a California Limited Liability Partnership or CA LLP for short), I had a moment. Not what I sought, but close, real close. It showed me how to look, but not where. So I thought I'd try looking somewhere else: Europe.

This will not be a story filled with beautiful damsels in distress, of heroic deeds done in battle, nor of political upheavals in the unending struggle for human equality. No, this story will tell of hole-punching misfits, broken adding machines and summations run amok. This is an accountant's story. This is Alan's story. But on a larger scale this isn't just one man's story, but every man's. Every man seeks his place in a world full of confusion. As did Alan Albacore.

The day Alan stumbled into my life was a cathartic event for me, a cataclysmic occurrence of epic proportions. It opened my eyes to the utter absurdity of my chosen profession but also brought joy and, dare I say, bliss into my dismal existence. It was awesome.

On a Monday much like any other, the Los Angeles sun shone brightly, the office was awash with the aroma of freshly brewed coffee and the clattering sound of adding machines filled the air. I was shoving aside the wall of files surrounding my desk cubicle to get my third cup of coffee that morning, kicking staples and acco fasteners every which way in my struggle to break free, when he appeared at the other end of the hallway. Dressed in a suit much too large for the left side of his body and suspiciously missing a button, a dwarflike man was approaching from the other end of the corridor. His tie was too wide, his socks didn't match, and his hair was combed in every possible direction hair could go and a few ways it couldn't. He fumbled down the aisle like an inebriated panda bear with a gorgeous smile that consumed half his face and 3/7 of his collarbone. He was ridiculous, moronic and quite possibly the most beautiful sight I have ever seen in my entire life. (I say that now after visiting the beaches of the South Pacific, the mountains of the Himalaya, and the fjords of New Zealand and I mean it. Nor am I homosexual. Certain works of unique beauty in the world just transcend sexuality and Alan Albacore was one of them.)

It was a love affair of sorts. For the two weeks I knew him, not an hour passed without Alan doing something that captured my imagination and affection. Just when I thought he couldn't possibly come up with anything new, he would wear bright yellow tennis shoes to work or try to sharpen his pen in an electric pencil sharpener. The enormity of his unique gift still boggles me... I never saw him exert any effort to do these things, they just came naturally. He was beautiful, just beautiful. And when they fired him

(They fired everyone, even people who had never worked for them. My uncle received a letter of termination from them in the mail and he was a plumber in Wisconsin.), my heart ached like never before.

Alan had a presence about him, an aura of the immortal. As if he could transform you, elevate you. Clarify your folly of worldly pursuits. You never wanted him to leave. But then they fired him. No, they didn't kill him, but for me it was the same. He walked out of my life never to return. Our time together was oh so fleeting... I'm a better man to have known him: stronger, more appreciative.

Alan's ineptness as an accountant exceeded the sublime. Bad wasn't the word, no such word existed. People keen to collect unemployment insurance making genuine efforts to screw up couldn't even approach Alan. Simple tasks most people did unconsciously Alan made a travesty of. He transposed numbers, double counted subtotals, misspelled prepositions. He hole-punched work papers crookedly and then put those little plastic enforcement rings over, not around, the holes. And not one page was hole-punched in the same crooked manner as the one before it. He inputted people's Social Security numbers (multiplied by their weight and number of children over the age of three) as their salary income. He spilled every single cup of coffee he drank. Not some, not a lot – every single one. (He tried drying the files under the hand drier in the men's restroom until one caught fire. Then he just used paper towels. He brought extra rolls from home.) He talked to himself (during meetings, in crowded elevators, in toilet stalls), but rarely to anyone else. He sang at his desk when clients visited the office. He brought joy to my heart.

His downfall came as all great men's did: at the hands of a woman. Samson had his Delilah, Paris had his Helen, Alan had Cassandra Carp. Some (me) might say Cassandra was the epitome of evil, that she was a cruel and wicked person lacking even a molecule of human kindness, that the magnitude of her malice and misanthropy defied measure. Others might just say that she was an accountant.

Unlike other tragic affairs between men and women down through the ages, Cassandra and Alan's was devoid of sex. Luckily for Alan, I might add. Not that Cassandra was ugly, which she was to an extreme and startling degree, or that she was vicious, which she was to an extreme and startling degree. No, I mean to say or I guess I should say or maybe I shouldn't say or... (I'll stop.) As my department's manager, Cassandra had hired Alan temporarily for the income tax return season. Why? To taunt, humiliate and degrade him. She mocked him to his face, to his colleagues, to his superiors. Did it boost her ego? The world is full of spiteful people who loathe the surrounding world and when they see something innocent and peaceful they must destroy it: the cynics, the bullies, the murderers. Alan had no conception of reality, but he was happy. How could anyone wish to destroy that smile of his?

My last memory of Alan is him fleeing Cassandra's office with cheeks flooded by tears. Yes, he'd shredded a file by accident. Yes, all 845 pages of it, including laminated inserts and floppy disk backups. And yes, he'd called the client a communist. But who hadn't? Did that justify maligning his worth to the world? It's bad enough being an accountant, but being an awful one? You must seriously re-examine your reason for existence.

Outside the airplane's windows, the sun was rising again. Through wisps of dissipating white clouds, lush green coastline peeked into view. England! Where Arthur formed his Camelot, where Shakespeare penned his plays, and where Hitler finally failed.

One of the Germans awoke with a belch. With bleary eyes he peered out the window and focused unsteadily on the Tower Bridge. "Holy shit, Franz! We're in fucking England. Again."

His compatriot jumped two point three kilometers above his seat (I do realize the comedic value of metric system metaphors is highly controversial and is banned on three continents). Then, through one slitted eye that winced upon opening, Franz glanced out the window before recoiling at the light. "We got on the wrong plane, Hans. Again." He clutched wearily at his skull, attempting to massage the grey mass encased therein to no avail.

"We were drunk. Are drunk."

"Who is?"

"We is. You. Me. Us is. Drunk."

"I have to pee."

"Who doesn't?"

I said, "I don't."

"Who asked you? Who asked him?"

"Not me. Not I. Neither of us."

"How about me?"

"Not you either. I distinctly heard you not ask him if he had to pee."

"Good. Wunderbar."

"Not good. Not wunderbar. Nein. We're in England."

"Schiesse."

Hans asked loudly, "Anybody got any heroin?"

I said, "I don't. Have to pee or have heroin, that is."

The airplane landed. The English may be known for their politeness but I've never seen anyone so anxious to exit an airplane before. There was shoving, shouting, and legend held a couple of insurance claim adjusters were trampled.

"What'll we do?"

"Drugs first. Think later."

"I knew we were stuffed when they wouldn't do the loop-da-loop."

"Fucking English."

A swarm of English bobbies tackled the two Germans as they entered the airplane terminal. "Fucking Nazis."

"Wait!" Franz shouted. "I have to pee!"

Steel-tipped leather boots silenced him.

I slogged through customs in a daze. *"How long are you planning on staying in the United Kingdom?"* "A couple of weeks." *"Will you be seeking employment?"* "No." *"Do you have any money?"* "Yes." *"How much?"* "Three point two million." *"Dollars?"* "No, yen." *"This is no time for humor, son."* "Obviously." *"This isn't the States, you know."* "Obviously." *"Possibly you don't want to enter our country."* "Not at all. I'd love to spend my time and money here. All three point two million yen of it." *"I think perhaps we shall search your bag."* "Go ahead. Some of the underwear is even clean." He made a mess of it, obviously. Had to. But finally he let me go. (After he'd derided my hat and knee-high tube socks, of course.)

Europe! Years of waiting but never expecting, of hoping, of wanting to see the world... All over. A joy suffused my whole body that I hadn't felt in... maybe forever. How crazy I must have appeared riding that train into London: smiling like an escaped lunatic, my hair pointing every which way and a couple of others, a giant orange backpack propped between my bare white knees and a pair of ridiculously heavy mountain climbing boots adorning my feet. They were all headed toward their dreary jobs in their dreary suits with their dreary faces, but, me, I was going places. Bliss, unadulterated and unequaled, oozed from my every pore. I had finally *fucking* made it. I cherished each quaint, brick-roofed house, each factory smokestack, each tree (be it pedunculate oak, almond-leaved willow or common whitebeam, I didn't care), that passed by the open windows of the train as it emerged above ground outside the airport. I would have cherished the ants and beetles, too, if I could have seen them. I was giddy, just giddy.

It crashed to a halt, of course, but you knew that already. Weren't you paying attention?

I went straight to the hostel I had chosen as the most central to London's tourist attractions near the British Museum, priding myself on only having to ask for directions once. (Well, twice.) Full. I asked the greasy-haired clerk if he knew any other hostels with vacancies. "They're all full," he said and immediately picked up the phone. My "But--" drew a wave of dismissal. The English are polite?

I returned to the Underground entrance, beginning to feel the twenty-four hours without sleep. From a payphone, I called every one of the hostels listed in my guidebook. *No vacancy. We're completely booked.* Panicking, I started on the Bed and Breakfast's. A hotel in London would destroy my budget. I envisioned a long string of similar disasters, meeting no one and wasting all my money on accommodations I couldn't afford. Hair fell from my head and what remained grayed. Englishmen began to surround me to delight with laughter at my misfortunes. The last B&B. The phone kept ringing and ringing. And ringing. "Hello?" Success!

Sort of. Leaving the Underground at Victoria Station, I trudged through the London streets failing to find Warwick Way. Everybody drove on the wrong side of the fucking street and did their absolute best to run me down (Jaguar, Peugeot, bus(!)(double-decker!!)). Twice the *LOOK RIGHT* painted across the ground at every crosswalk saved me. I was cursed at, spat at and told to fuck off numerously. It gave me kind of a warm, fuzzy feeling knowing people were the same kind of bitter the world over. But can you really judge an entire country by its taxi drivers? Or by its hostel clerks?

I got lost. The streets didn't go straight and intersect at right angles, but spread out like claws, crossing each other at acute and obtuse angles and sometimes neither. Every possible permutation of the seven changes of direction from the station to the B&B I made. I went left when I should have gone right. I went right when I should have gone left. I explored dead end alleys, fell in manholes, detoured through people's gardens. I could not find the way. This did not bode well for the travels to come. Not well at all.

Whenever I went someplace new, I would circle. Like a lammergeyer scavenging in the Alps. All was part of a highly refined technique I had perfected over the years of having absolutely no sense of direction. (Navigating a swimming pool could give me trouble.) If I found my objective after the seventh pass, I considered myself lucky (my life to date average = 8.217 passes). And parking is a whole other story.

Eventually I located the B&B – I'd been in bigger and less crowded telephone booths. On the way I'd gotten directions from a young guy working at a new hostel with plenty of vacant rooms. I promised to go there the next day. Meanwhile I got to stay in a room so small the door only opened halfway on account of the bed being in the way. A bathtub emitting glacial melt was down a flight of stairs narrower than most tightropes. (Sisyphus had nothing on me and my trials and tribulations getting my pack up said stairs. But I won't detail them because I'm like that sometimes.) The mattress was three feet long, one foot wide and stiffer than an elephant's handshake. The closet held half a shirt. The room had no sink, no mirror, no television set, no clean towels and a blanket ideal for use as tracing paper. A bargain for forty dollars – such a sum in the United States would secure a clean motel room complete with all those missing things as well as a private bathroom spouting hot, soothing water, a coffee maker and unlimited ice.

My fellow denizens belonged to the elder population of the female species, all on the vertically challenged side and reeking of scented hairspray. Loud, demanding and each wielding giant umbrellas despite the gorgeous weather, they frightened me into my room with relentless offers of tea and biscuits (American translation: stale crackers) they'd brought from home.

Downstairs in the community "room," an Australian couple in their late forties were watching soccer. I sat down to relax, having shrunk my nether regions to the size of a garbanzo bean a few minutes earlier in the bathtub's Arctic sea waters.

"A Yank," the man said to my squeak of a hello.

I laughed politely. "That I am."

"We've been to America. Grand Canyon, Disneyland, Hollywood. You from Los Angeles?"

"Near there."

"All Americans are from Los Angeles."

"It is quite crowded."

"Horrible nightmares: the freeways. Yes? We've been to South America, too. Buenos Aires, the Pampas, Rio de Janeiro. That was last year."

"The year before, dear," the wife said.

"Was it? Nasty place, London. Always raining. Not today, of course. But otherwise always."

"Rains a bit," said the wife.

"Second time in Europe for us. Last time with a tour. Cost heaps, it did. This time we're on our own. Have a guidebook and everything. We were just planning where to go tomorrow. See?" He held up the same guidebook I had. "There are some really cheap places to stay outside of Oxford. Dirt cheap. Cost almost nothing. Not sure what we'll see, but they sure are cheap. Right, dear?"

"Yes, hon."

"Next year we're going to the Orient. Don't like the Orientals myself, but it's much closer, you see. Takes twenty-four hours on a plane to get here. With layovers, mind you. No direct flights. China, isn't it, dear? That's where she wants to go. They all ride bicycles apparently. Must be something to see. All those bicycles, I mean."

"Sorry, I'm going to dinner."

"Right. Staying here long? No? Bye then."

I wandered down the road in search of victuals. The sun was draining from the London sky, dabbing the sides of the houses with syrupy hues of orange and bright red. I found the nearest pub listed in my guidebook, an attractive spot named the Slug and Lettuce, and dipped inside.

"Hello," I said to the bartender. The patrons, mostly elderly gentlemen in suits, reclined around the room on polished oak chairs reading the evening newspapers. No one was talking.

A questioning cock of the eyebrows.

"Irish stew and a pint of... Boddington's." My subsequent comment on the night's pleasantness was met solely with a nod and further raising of newspapers behind me.

On my way up to my room, the Australians: "Wasn't raining, was it?"

"No--"

"Rains all the time here."

"All the time," the wife seconded.

I continued up the stairs.

Searching for my toothbrush, I discovered why my backpack had seemed heavier than expected while trudging around London earlier that day. My mother had added a couple of things when I wasn't looking. The first was a Jumbo Value Pack of Extra-Thick-For-Your-Protection Disposable Toilet seat covers holding one thousand in assorted vibrant colors. An attached note reminded me to:

1. Always use them!

2. Always use two at a time!

3. Always, always, always carry an emergency reserve in your daypack for short excursions!

Taped to the even more unusual second item was another note:

I knew you wouldn't take this on your own, but you need it, Peter. For my sake and for my peace of mind, please, please use it on all public transportation. Pity your poor old mother who worries about you and loves you very much. Mrs. Pike's boy went away to Europe last summer and they pumped sleeping gas into his compartment. Robbed him of everything and committed unspeakable acts upon his person.

It was my great uncle Herman's gas mask, a remnant of his World War II military service.

First the shots, now this. I'd had inoculations for yellow fever, typhus, tetanus, diphtheria, meningitis, polio, hepatitis A, hepatitis B, small pox (specially ordered), mumps, measles, German measles, Japanese encephalitis, cholera (only 10% effective), influenza, and even rabies. With ever larger needles. For twelve hundred thirteen dollars and six cents, not including tax. My mother made me promise to start a course of malaria prophylactics and had stocked my medical kit with antibiotics, clean syringes, splints, slings, braces, a water purifier, a snake bite kit, a bee sting shot and an intravenous drip. I'd had to promise to buy pepper spray when I arrived after numerous phone calls to the airline confirmed and reconfirmed the pressurized air capsule was disallowed. Bulletproof vests were never mentioned and I didn't bring them up. All for a trip to Europe, not the Amazon or the heart of the Congo.

I forgot to tell you that just before the Germans, this happened: over the intercom, the pilot said, "Folks, we have kind of a funny announcement to make. It's a message for one of our American passengers embarking on his first trip overseas. Peter Pollack, your mother said she loves you and that you're absolutely not to forget to buy your pepper spray when you land."

Jet-lag, self-doubt, and a pair of amorous neighbors of advanced age but surprising stamina kept me awake until a few hours before dawn.

It got better. Much, much better. But not all at once. It took a while.

The hostel was the first step. I spent most of the next morning waiting at Victoria Station with a few other bedraggled backpackers for a van to take us to the converted university dormitory, aptly named the Eurotower. Inexpensive travel is not for the impatient. In the time I was to spend waiting to check into hostels or catch trains, Magellan circumnavigated the globe, the Egyptians built two of the pyramids, Richard Remora earned seventy-five billion dollars, and the Chicago Cubs won two World Series. (*Editor's comment: Please note the final part of this metaphor pre-dates 2016 and was funnier then.*)

"Amazingly quick service around here, don't you think?" I said to a fellow backpacker.

He shrugged and went back to scratching himself. Apparently I'd interrupted him.

When the van finally did come I got to sit under two Swedish girls. Not next to, nor between, but under. Normally I would not complain, but these girls weren't quite on the light side. Far from it, to tell the truth, the whole truth and nothing but. This and the driver's fondness for hairpin turns and screeching his brakes whenever possible made my first real view of London through a haze of unwashed blonde hair and pain, lots of pain. To my astonishment we arrived, but they had to revive me with a defibrillator and a double dose of epinephrine.

The elevator took three months to appear and could fit only me, my pack, and a gorgeous Austrian girl inside. Absolutely no room at all remained for the two six foot tall Scandinavian swimmers. None.

Pushing the button for the eleventh floor, the pony-tailed brunette said to me, "Now the fun begins." My room was on the twelfth floor.

"Uh-oh."

"Worse than that."

"Worse?"

The rattling began.

"I see what you mean," I said.

"Oh, she's just getting warmed up."

The rattling escalated into a shaking. We crept past floor four.

"Dare I ask?" I ventured.

"I wouldn't."

The shaking became a thunderous quaking. I felt like... something that rattles a lot. You know.

The seventh floor came and went.

"Almost there."

"We should be so lucky," she answered.

"Um."

"Right."

The ninth floor came... and went. So did the tenth, eleventh (!), and twelfth (!!).

"Um again."

"Right again."

"Does it ever stop?"

"Only on fourteen. And only after it's gone to sixteen first."

"Mind of its own."

The quaking worsened.

"Would you hold my hand?"

She laughed. "It'll get better in a minute."

"Promise?"

"You have my solemn oath."

The doors opened at sixteen and three drunk Spaniards tried to get in.

"Sorry. We're trying to find my contact lens."

"You're wearing glasses."

18

I closed the doors. We descended.

"Here comes fourteen."

"Remember: get out quick." She emphasized her words with a nod.

"I'll remember. Unless I forget."

"Our lives may depend on it."

"Our?"

"You're blocking the door."

The doors opened. I dragged my pack out into the hall. "We survived."

"That's the rumor on the street." She smiled at me and headed towards the stairwell.

"Wait. You staying here long?"

"I'm checking out to meet my sister in Paris in a few minutes. Bye." And then she was gone.

I didn't trip descending the stairs to the twelfth floor.

As I opened the door, my eyes were drawn to the enormous hairy gut of the scantily clad man occupying the top bunk. Wearing only a pair of threadbare white jockey shorts, the balding forty-year old man blinked wearily at me behind a pair of green plastic framed spectacles. Then he licked his thick lips with a tongue smaller than the Golden Gate Bridge. "I'm Andre," he said in a muddled accent. After scratching the one part of his body I could not see, he extended his hand.

I took it, I'm not sure why and if I could take it back... (Later I would berate myself with a too loud "WHY?" and cause people in the Amsterdam train station to look uncomfortably away.) "Peter."

"You are from the United States? Los Angeles?"

"Actually... Yes."

"I am from Belgium. Are you a student?"

"No, I work."

"I am a chef."

"Are you traveling?"

"I am staying here." His meaty hands gestured towards all his worldly possessions: a tiny radio, a bottle of shampoo, a couple of old magazines. "I had a restaurant in Brussels, but my wife, she took it. She took everything. She is a bitch. A fucking bitch. I cannot go back to Belgium. So I live here. I work here. I am a chef. Not the boss. I was the boss in Belgium. I owned my own restaurant. I made everything. Soufflés, pate foie gras, everything. Now I make fish and chips."

"Oh."

"Here is cheap. London is fucking expensive. I see lots of people come and go, but here I like. Here is nice."

"Oh."

"I want to go to America someday. Hollywood. Yes."

"I must go now."

"Where?"

"The Tower of London."

"That is okay. Yes."

European cities are funny. One city block will be the financial district teeming with men in business suits. The next will be an old church or castle infested with tourists in obnoxious shirts, golf visors and many pocketed shorts bulging with maps, cameras, and guidebooks. The businessmen will be grim faced and carrying briefcases and umbrellas. The tourists will be gorging on ice cream, talking much too loudly, and photographing everything - flagpoles, statues of people they've never heard of, some rock where Napoleon once ate his lunch. Both will be in a terrible rush. One to get back to his desk in his cramped office with poor lighting and a squeaky, hemorrhoid-inducing chair - the other to the next attraction listed as "a must" in his guidebook. Were they so different?

The Tower of London was like this. Flanked on one side by the financial district and the other by the River Thames, the castle grounds were overwrought with the world's wanderers.

"We have to hurry."

"Honey, stand next to Jimmy."

"Mommy, I'm hungry."

"When's the bus leave?"

"Is there film in the camera?"

"What the hell is he saying?"

"We have to get to Westminster Abbey by three."

"Mommy, I have to pee."

"Where do we buy tickets?"

"Where can we change money?"

"Mommy, I'm bored."

"We have to hurry."

Sometimes bad beginnings bode the most wanton tragedy imaginable. Other times: no. My job at Net, Block and Tackle was not among those other times.

Driving home at sunset the night before my job interview at Net, Block and Tackle, my car got a flat tire. No, listen. I lived with my parents at the time near the top of a mile high mountain, thirty miles up a twisting one lane highway from the nearest city. Rock slides, fog and weariness kill a few people there each year. (For a while, turnouts were nicknamed for the person who'd met their untimely end there: Courtney's Curve, Winston's Wiggle, Debbie's Drop. Then that stopped. Not enough turnouts.) Rarer than call boxes for help are good Samaritans. Not having a jack, I had to find one or the other. Of course I walked the wrong way, choosing up. Half an hour later I realized my mistake and, not wanting the most treacherous and narrowest portion of the highway renamed Peter's Plummet, I started down. Wait. You'll love this. I'd put my regular lens glasses on my car roof while switching to my sunglasses before getting in to drive home. Five miles later, I realized I'd left them there. I went back to search, but no luck. So now I had a flat tire in the impending darkness and could only see out of my prescription sunglasses.

But my trials didn't end there. Wearing my dark sunglasses and driving with my high beams on, I pulled out after the tow truck that had helped me change the tire. Of course, the spare went flat after a quarter mile. As I steered into a turnout (which I couldn't be sure existed until I'd left my car with the yellow hazard lights flashing and walked up to it), I watched the tow truck slowly ascend the mountain curve after curve, oblivious or indifferent to my honking horn and blinking lights. Luckily I'd gone far enough that I had to walk down the middle of the highway to return to the call box as the road had no shoulder, only a flimsy guardrail protecting a five hundred foot drop. I wanted to cry, but crying wasn't allowed in accounting – it would get the working papers all wet. I only got hit by two side-view mirrors and one foot run over by passing cars (finishing off what the road's gravel had left of the new dress shoes I'd bought with my remaining graduation gift money). Even doubling back for the bright pink capuchon from a college Mardi Gras party I'd left in my trunk hadn't helped with the visibility-to-drivers factor, but it did earn me some very comforting and vociferous heckles (until it was swept off by a rather close black Cadillac into the darkness only to reappear a moment later in the talons of a raven flying away).

"Roadside assistance."

"Hi. I just called an hour ago because of a flat tire. My spare went flat, too."

Then the most compassionate *Oh, no* I'd ever heard. I wanted to marry that woman.

"Can I just call my dad this time?"

"Of course. Your voice sounds familiar. Did you blow a radiator last week?"

"Welcome to my life."

"No, thank you."

"I hear that a lot."

Another flat tire plagued my drive to the interview the next morning. And it snowed. But I got the job. Some might say that was the worst part.

The interview began: "Did you have any problems getting here from… Lake Arrowhead?"

Beefeaters, retired members of the British armed forces dressed up in fuzzy black hats and bright red uniforms, led the Tower of London tours. Speaking loudly, they recount in lavish detail the minutiae of the bloody tortures and murders committed within the Tower's walls. Treachery, incest, and patricide all draw big laughs. The bloodier, the better. Nothing drew crowds like the French guillotine.

Will Bergen Belsen become a joke's punchline in 2319?

The Tower juxtaposed different architectural styles from William the Conqueror onward – Gothic, Roman, Tudor – all were represented. Hangings were conducted in one spot, beheadings another. The latter was apparently *the* way to go. Get hanged, your family's social standing suffers for generations. And to be poisoned, burnt at the stake or drawn and quartered – well, no one and I do mean no one, respected you.

Listening in the chapel to the Beefeater recount the tale of Lady Jane Grey, the inevitability of fate struck me. Queen for a brief seventeen days before being beheaded, she probably did not even understand why. How quickly it can turn on you. And how quick it goes. The last three years had flown by. I was so glad I'd come. So glad I'd stopped waiting for life to come to me. I'd done the right thing.

Dreading a return to my room and the furry primate entrenched therein, I meandered through the London streets. Stepping away from the tourist center, the city became quiet. It was mid-afternoon, everyone was inside working. How could they stand it with a great wonderful world aching to be explored just outside? How had I?

Could I go back?

Tired, when a columnar monument dedicated to the lives lost in the Great Fire of London in 1666 offered me a seat, I took it. Inside a caged room no bigger than a broom closet, a hunched over man sat on a creaking stool collecting three pounds from tourists wanting to climb to the top. He sat there all day every day whether they came or not. When he saw my disinterest, he shrugged his shoulders and returned to his book: *Crime and Punishment* by Fyodor Dostoevsky.

Los Angeles. The city of angels. Home to Hollywood, the Dodgers, and Beverly Hills. A city absorbed in its own greatness, brimming over with enough ego to fill three universes (and a galaxy to spare). A city where superficiality reigned, anything went if you had money and nothing did if you didn't. A city forged by man's need to escape the drudgery of their own lives. A city engendered by lost dreams, hidden desires and discarded morals. A city full of metal, glass, sunlight, smog and not much else. A city constantly rebuilding itself with bigger skyscrapers, newer malls, and more hideous apartment high-rises over the ruins of the old. A young city without a history of conflict, without a tale of struggle. A city without a past and no future. My home.

European cities had that past. But it could be overwhelming. People had been struggling to survive here for thousands of years. They had persevered through wars, fires, and plagues. They had created Western culture and brought us civilization. With it had come slavery and nerve gas and Adolph Hitler, but also medicine and art and literature. And beer. We mustn't forget beer.

I returned to the hostel.

Hair was everywhere. In all his bulging, shirtless splendor, Andre awaited when I returned to my room. Still perched upon the top bunk, he lay splayed out in a decadent pose with both legs spread wide and far. He'd put on pants, thank God, but still the pair of tight-fitting black jeans accentuated the girth of his ass to an alarming and frightening degree. So much so I couldn't respond to his "How was the Tower of London?"

"Good. Great!" I croaked, then shouted, as the ability to vocalize words returned.

The door opened behind me and I was saved. Not by a ballerina from Brussels, damn it, nor by a model from Milan, but by a red-haired Scotsman wearing bright green hiking boots with red laces. "I'm Stephen." He shook my hand firmly and then that of the Belgian.

"Peter."

"Andre."

Stephen dropped his bag on the only open bunk (below Andre) and asked me the time. "Four thirty."

"That late already? Fancy a drink?"

We were in the nearest pub in three minutes and twenty-six seconds.

"To be candid," I told Stephen once we'd found a place to sit and consume our frothy pints of Ireland's finest, "the thought of spending a night in the room with all that fur frightens me."

"A good looking one, though, isn't he?"

"Absolutely gorgeous."

"I think he fancies you."

Out came my beer in a bit of a splutter. "Fucking hell."

"I fear for you, mate."

"So do I."

We ordered dinner. "I'll have the steak," he told the bartender. "But no vegetables. Not even if it comes with them. I don't care what you do with them: throw them out, feed them to the homeless, secret them home in your wallet, only don't give them to me. I'm a strict carnivore, I eat nothing but meat. Not weeds. Flesh. Carcass. If you give me a vegetable I'm apt to be ill. So don't. Give me a vegetable, that is. Potatoes, fine, but nothing green."

"Got it, mate. And you?"

"I'll have the salad."

"Where in America are you from? Los Angeles?"

24

I nodded. "You?"

"Scotland. St. Andrews."

"Golf."

"Golf."

"So you're traveling?"

"I'm just meeting my girlfriend. She gets back from Italy in a few days, so I thought I'd have a look around London beforehand. Yourself?"

"Traveling six months, though I've just started."

"Out of university?"

"I work. Accountant. You?"

"Studying to be a translator. Right now I'm concentrating on Arabic."

I knew there would be trouble when Stephen's steak arrived with a piece of parsley on top. Shock seized the Scotsman's features. Then a searing flash of hatred embroiled with loathing and spiced with burgeoning wanton violence. Twice he gagged on his words before: "What the fuck is this? I said what the fuck is this?"

"Looks like parsley to me, mate," the bartender answered.

"Did I not expressly request no greens whatsoever on my plate? Did I not?"

"Like I give a shit," the bartender said and walked away.

Uncomfortable silence.

"There are disadvantages to a country where one does not tip for a meal, I guess," I said.

Stephen looked at me blankly. I thought he might try to strangle me or, at least, maul me a bit. But he just smiled. "The English are such wankers."

"In the blood, is it?"

"Something like that."

"You think Andre is in love with me? I mean, can you form genuine feelings for someone in such a short time?"

"If the way he was looking at you isn't love, I don't know what is."

"And my chances of keeping the relationship strictly platonic?"

"Doubtful. Highly doubtful."

"Do you suppose, well, he wants to roll all over me?"

"That was my impression."

"Poor me. Poor, poor me." I finished my beer. "Shall we move on?"

The next barkeep was refreshingly female. "What'll it be, loves?"

"Pint of Guinness. Two of them. One for him and one for me. Or one for me and one for him. In either order."

"One for you and one for him or one for him and one for you?"

"Or vice versa."

The dark-haired girl laughed. "Out for a night of it?"

"Absolutely."

"American, aren't you?"

I gave her the old narrowing of the eyes routine. "You're one of my accounting groupies, right?"

"Uh, no."

"She's a hard one, mind you. Tongue of fire and eyes to match. That hurts, you know." I laid my right palm over my heart. "Right here. Rends me to the core of my being."

"You'll survive."

"Possibly, but only with years of therapy. People will pass me on the street and say *Look at that man with the devastating good looks who looks so sad. What malady do you suppose ails him*? And the answer will be this stunning English barmaid broke his heart."

"Tragic story redolent of histrionic melodrama and a joke taken way, way too far and beyond. Brings a wholly imaginary and bound to stay as such tear to my eye." Away it went with a brush of her ring-less hand.

She placed the two pints of beer in front of me and held up six fingers. Stephen and I paid her. She turned to Stephen, "Are you American as well?"

"Scottish."

"He doesn't like vegetables."

"He doesn't? You don't?"

"Abhor them, really."

"I'm a vegetarian."

"Well, take how you feel about meat and apply it to vegetables instead. Then you'd have me."

"With red hair."

"With red hair. One mustn't forget the red hair."

"Hair's important. Hair's the thing," I interjected.

She gave me back the eyes narrowing routine. "Who asked you?"

"That guy slumped over the bar singing into his armpit."

"With the perfect pitch?"

"Guy next to him. Crooning in Yiddish."

"Have a good time, lads." She left for the other end of the bar.

"Wait!"

"What for?"

"Foiled by the Yiddish joke! Again," I said.

Stephen comforted me, "You've always got Andre."

We tried getting another beer, but, alack and alas, 'twas not to be. She sent over the other bartender, a man with hair in all the wrong places and none in the right ones, to serve us. As an added reward, he even spilled some stale beer on my trousers while wiping off the bar.

"What the hell happened back there?" I asked Stephen on the way to the next pub. The London night was brisk and oddly quiet.

"Some birds fancy you, some don't. It's nothing personal. Just how it is."

"And I've always got Andre."

"But don't take him for granted or he may just slip away, also."

By the time Stephen and I were back outside the Eurotower, it was later than it had been before and earlier than it later would be.

The pallid grey building stood silhouetted against the London sky. Freckles of yellow light peered out into the night, shadowing the world's displaced roaming within. A slight buzz penetrated the darkness.

"What's that noise?" Stephen asked.

Could... No, it was too horrid to contemplate.

The buzz grew louder. My fingers began to tingle.

"The bar?"

The hair on the back of my neck rose on end. "It's higher up."

"Higher?"

"The twelfth floor."

"It couldn't. It can't. Not possibly."

It could, it was.

The sound grew. Swelled in a crescendo with seemingly no end. Built exponentially in a towering din. Windows rattled, walls shook, plumbing squealed. Andre's snoring had consumed the building.

People stood in the lobby gaping up dumbfounded.

We didn't take the elevator. It wasn't safe.

"Open the door," said the Scotsman, struggling to keep afoot.

"You open the door."

He gulped once and did so. His whole body began to shake along with the doorknob. Then he leapt inside. I followed him reluctantly, biting my lip to staunch the screams.

Stepping inside the room was like entering the belly of some enormous beast. Anything not tied down rattled around freely like a barrel full of rabid raccoons flung from the top of the Eiffel Tower. Toothbrushes and old newspapers pelted me from all sides.

"That bastard!" Stephen shouted. "That fucking bastard!"

"What?"

"I knew he was a wanker. The first time I'd laid my eyes on him. First impressions never lie. Never."

"What?" I found my bed and lay down.

"Something should be done. Complaints filed in triplicate."

"Absolutely," I said and rolled over. I went to sleep instantly.

Another noise woke me at six o'clock: silence. But it didn't last long. Soon Andre was up and banging around. Everything in the room that beeped, chimed or rang and I do mean every single, solitary, individual fucking thing, he made beep, chime or ring. Alarm clocks, bicycle bells, dinner cutlery, hair dryer: everything. He sought out each in a lumbering, clumsy manner that allowed him to stub his toe every other step and fume "Merde!" At first he kept the lights off, but abandoned that approach to the other extreme most thoroughly.

"WHAT THE FUCK IS GOING ON?" Stephen shouted in a decidedly vociferous manner.

"I can't find my keys."

"Who gives a fuck?"

"I think they fell behind your bed. I must get them."

"No... NO!"

Suddenly a wave of densest dorsal fur engulfed the Scotsman as I was made privy to the sight of the largest butt-crack in the Northern Hemisphere. I watched in horror as the Belgian chef slithered ever so slowly up and down Stephen's bed, fishing futilely for the missing keys with his meaty paws. All the Scotsman's muffled pleas and prayers availed him not. The room went grotesquely silent. Not a squeak, not a whisper could escape the deluge of sheer mass that was Andre. I wondered what would be left of the Scotsman. A very flat person? A mere stain? I dozed off.

"Got them!"

By the time I'd opened my eyes, Andre was gone and I could hear gasping alternating with dry heaves from the next bunk as Stephen sucked in much-needed air. I turned to the window.

Pale sunlight, diffused through the morning haze, seeped precariously into the room, as if testing its way cautiously through the

29

dreariness. Dark silhouettes of trees loomed across the horizon among the monolithic rectangles of steel and glass. The day seemed less than anxious to begin, less than anxious to infuse warmth on the slumbering earth and its confused and desperate denizens. But the sun refused to be dissuaded from its task, continuing its endless journey across the heavens, and the struggle continued. But for me, it brought hope. Today. Today.

The Scotsman was trying to speak. "Nearly... suff... ocated."

"So I noticed."

"Help. You could have."

"I thought you were enjoying it."

"Fucking... Americans."

I sat up in bed and rubbed my face in my hands, trying to wake up. Nearly seven o'clock on my last day in London. I had to get moving.

Stephen was looking in his wallet. "Those beers were dear. Very fucking dear. In Scotland you could get a pint for half as much."

"Oh?"

"Not much else to do in Scotland but drink. No jobs to be had and not much hope for the future. No economy but farming. How rich can you get on sheep and pigs? And the fucking English own all our oil. They have to keep us dull-witted somehow, so they give us beer cheap."

"So there is an upside."

Stephen didn't laugh. "Americans are all cocky like you're the best in the world. At least you're given a chance. In Scotland you can work your ass off your whole life and get nowhere. We don't have the industry or the technology. And it's so fucking cold most of the time. That's why so many Europeans want to go to America. For the opportunity. Where else can you get rich showing off your tits on television? Everyone's got a chance. Here the people with money have had it forever and aren't about to start sharing. No one else gets a shot. Our country isn't growing like yours. No one idolizes our sports heroes or wants to buy our products."

"But unless you're the best in America, you're shit. You have to be good-looking, the star athlete, the one with the most money. If you aren't or aren't trying to be, you're considered a failure. You mustn't just get by. You must be the best. Or you're ignored, even ostracized. Teachers favor the better-looking or smarter ones, parents push their children to win at sports, women desire men thirty years older than them with the Ferrari and three story mansion."

30

"At least you have a choice. You can better yourself if you want. In Scotland you can't."

I nodded and reached inside my backpack for my towel. "I have to shower."

I only have a few memories of my grandfather. One is the way he played pinochle.

Pinochle is a card game played by a pair of two-player teams. Each team bids against each other the minimum amount they think they can score at one deal of the cards. The highest bidder wins and must score at least the points bid or be penalized by that amount. The game is played to one hundred and fifty and the average winning bid for a hand is about thirty-three. Between the ages of seven and thirteen I played three thousand games of pinochle with my family.

Despite the opening bid being twenty-five points, my grandfather always started with:

FORTY!

Always. Whether he had a great hand or a terrible one. Occasionally,

FORTY-TWO!

and once

SEVENTY-SIX!

Never anything less. Laughing, my relatives would concede the bid and down we would go. (Unless my father was playing, also. Then father and son would bid to eighty-six by fours while my mother laughed. Games would end with scores of negative two hundred seventy-five being the winning tally.) And my grandfather always insisted "Let the young man play with me," before ruffling my hair affectionately. "Only if you promise not to bid forty, Grandpa. I want to win this time." "I promise, Peter. We'll win." Five minutes later:

FORTY!

Once I fled the room screaming in frustration (At eight, nothing was more important in the world than winning to me.) and it turned out he had all the aces in the deck (an extremely rare hand worth one hundred points). After I found that out, I never doubted him again. We lost the next sixty games in a row.

My other memory of my grandfather was his fear of heights. Or rather his deep-seeded paranoia/all-consuming obsession with. From nightmares about ladders, he would wake up in the middle of the night screaming, the bed sheets wrapped violently around his body and his brow bathed in sweat. My grandmother had to sleep in another room after his flailing arms broke her nose twice in one week. Bridges, skyscrapers, even staircases terrified him. The first words he uttered when he saw our house in Lake Arrowhead were: "Bessie, do you see that roof? Do you know what a fall from there would do to your pancreas?" "What?" I asked, aged six and ignorant of what a pancreas was. My grandfather puckered up his dry, cracked lips and made a wet raspberry. I remember the back of my knee trembling violently with the sound.

Ironically, my grandparents lived in an eighteenth floor apartment. With a balcony. Whenever we visited, my grandfather would shout, "Bessie, keep him away from the window. (It was shut and locked and fifteen feet away.) Oooooh! He could fall out! And it's so far down! Bessie! Young man, get back here! Young man!"

I couldn't go up open staircases. I tried closing my eyes and holding my mother's hand, but it just wasn't in me. Not until my grandfather was dead five years. Five years. And he lived until I was thirteen. My father loves to visit Arizona's Grand Canyon, but he can't go within twenty feet of the edge. My grandfather ingrained that fear into him.

Why travel? To tackle life with the same recklessness that my grandfather played cards. To disregard my future and live for the pure joy of it. To shake off the dread I'd had since forever of not doing the right thing. To experience new sights, new people, new cultures. To see how other people lived so I could decide how I wanted to. Most of all, not to look back fifty years from now and say I should have tried something else. Not to be afraid, of heights or anything else.

My grandfather was also an accountant.

Stephen and I took the Tube to Piccadilly Circus and walked across to Trafalgar Square. Nelson's Column towered above a ground carpeted with pigeons. Squawking and pecking each other furiously, the dark-breasted birds battled for the breadcrumbs hordes of tourists fed them. Pigeon shit was everywhere: on the manes of the lion statues, on the park benches, even on poor Nelson's nose. Horatio's reward for saving thousands of Englishmen's lives by defeating the navy of Napoleon was having his likeness defecated upon by filthy birds for eternity.

I turned back at the entrance to the National Gallery. Big Ben, the enormous clock adorning the face of the Houses of Parliament, loomed at the edge of the morning mists. It was going to rain. The Australians would be pleased.

Two weeks before beginning my job at Net, Block and Tackle, I called my eighty year old grandmother.

She answered the phone with no introductions, no exchange of greetings: "They're still there." Her voice was a cracked conspiratorial whisper.

"Who?"

"They're watching me. Waiting for me to leave the window. Biding their time. Patient bastards, they are."

"Who, Grandma, who?" I tried to remember the phone number for the Santa Monica police department. Gang members? Burglars? Congressmen?

"You know who. The goddamned pigeons!" Nelson wasn't the only one to suffer insult and injury from the rats of the sky.

"What pigeons, Grandma?"

"I'm gonna get those pigeons. Kill 'em. Kill 'em all. Those pigeons are bastards. Bastards. Look at 'em up there. Think they can beat me. Think they're better than me. Well, I'll teach them a thing or two. Demonstrate who they're dealing with. I'm not to be toyed with, you understand. Not at all. When I'm through with them, they'll be finished. Finished, do you hear me? Finished."

"Now, Grandma, don't do anything rash. You don't know what they want. I mean, there's no way to be one hundred percent sure, right? And you don't want to do anything you might regret later. Just hold on."

"You're laughing at me. But I'm telling you the truth, I tell you. They're out to get me. Five o'clock in the morning they start in on my balcony with their chirping. Chirp, chirp, chirp. Oy, it goes right through my head. No more. It ends now. Where's my broom?" She set down the phone.

"Grandma! Grandma!"

I heard a sliding door open on the other side of the line. Then screams, curses, chirping and lots of banging. Bang! Bang! (See what I mean?) Then a long, long silence.

I began to worry. Had the birds turned on my grandmother like in

33

that Alfred Hitchcock film? What would be left of her: some feathers and her skeleton picked clean, possibly one hand clutching a mahjong tile? Or would just her eyes be pecked out, a living reminder to the rest of us not to mess with the lords of the air?

"They always run when I go after them. If only they would wait, I'd show them. Oh, boy, would I show them."

"Show them what, Grandma? I'm not sure I like how that sounds."

"Just you wait, this isn't over. Nowhere near. I have not yet begun to fight. They shall feel the fury of my wrath. Oh, yes, they will."

Her husband dead, her children grown with children of their own, my grandmother's one true passion in life became the birds that had taken up residence on her deck porch. She stalked them like a big-game hunter, creeping around her apartment in the early hours of the Santa Monica morning with a broom clutched tightly between the arthritic fingers of her right hand. Her feet encased in pink slippers of the fuzzy variety and her dentures sometimes in, sometimes out, my grandmother was ready for battle any time of the day or night. To catch your prey, she told me, you have to be prepared for that mistake, that tiny miscalculation or lapse in judgment by your opponent that may come only once. And then you have to act. With violent, unmerciful swiftness. This was war, damnit. To win, you have to be willing to go farther, further and more fully than the opposition. And my grandmother was willing.

Another call, this one at three a.m. "I didn't hate the pigeons at first, you understand. They just wouldn't compromise. At the point of no compromise, what alternative course is there but violence? If neither side is willing to capitulate, physical conflict must ensue. I've tried reasoning with them, but they're just birds, what do they understand? Stupid, stupid creatures. So they must pay, Peter. They must pay." Click.

The pigeons became my grandmother's arch-nemesis. She readily accepted all the responsibilities included with such a title. More so: she embraced them. If you do something, she said, do it right. Having an arch-nemesis isn't all fun and games. It requires hard work and determination and hatred, lots of hatred. You must put in that extra effort that some people just aren't willing to give, fight that additional hour no matter how tired you are or how forgiving you may feel at any given moment. Yes, you must hate and hate some more. And then, my friends, you must hate a little bit more.

For months my grandmother kept her vigil. She would call me at work and say: "Three inches, Peter." "Three inches, Grandma?" "Today it was only three inches." Did my grandmother have a boyfriend? "I missed him by three inches. You know the one. The bastard with the lazy left eye. I could almost taste his blood." I could visualize her on the other end of the

34

telephone line: grey hair disheveled, one joint of her thick spectacles hanging askew over an ear and panting for breath. Never had I seen anyone move as fast as my grandmother when she spotted those pigeons on her porch. Olympic sprinter, my cousin Michael when he heard the words *free food*, the Millennium Falcon: none could move as fast as my grandmother on the hunt. Except those pigeons.

Until my grandmother bought the flypaper. It was a red letter day, a turning point in the battle. The pigeons had gained the upper hand in the weeks before the event. The squabs had become full-grown, allowing them to harass my grandmother in shifts. She'd begun to lose hope, her morale was low. She seemed listless and uninterested when I called her. Only television barely held her attention. And then she bought the flypaper on the Home Shopping Network.

"I did it!"

"Did what, Grandma?"

"I got those bastards!"

"Who, Grandma? The pigeons?"

"Who else but the pigeons, you dimwit! I used flypaper and the babies stuck to it. Then I dumped them over the side with the broom. They're dead, Peter. Dead. Oooh, you should have seen how mad the parents got. It was delicious, Peter."

Before the pigeon conflict, my grandmother had begun to give up on life. Her health was failing, every other week she was in the hospital for an operation. Her stomach allowed her to eat only very bland foods. Her eyes had gotten so bad she could no longer read. She never went outside and rarely did she even get dressed, complaining no one ever visited her so what was the point. But the pigeons changed all that. A spring came back to her step, a glint to her eye. The birds had resuscitated her. Her appetite improved, she got dressed up on the weekends.

When nothing else works, hate often keeps us going. Not love. It's a sad commentary on the human race, but it's true. The Germans rising out of the destitution following the first World War to form the murderous Third Reich proves that. Would this hatred corrupt my grandmother? Or could she control it?

We weren't in the National Gallery thirty seconds before Stephen confessed to me, "I'm not one for museums."

"I sort of like to take my time."

"Right. Where you headed after?"

"Westminster Abbey."

"I'm not one for churches, either."

"Maybe I'll see you tonight then."

The first and most dangerous species of museum visitors is the tour group member (or T.G.M.). Avoid the hordes they migrate in at any and all cost. Passing through pre-Colombian art exhibits in a blur, they swallow whole any who dare cross their path. Schoolmarms, Zen Buddhists, lone museum concierges: all can fall prey. Never let your guard down. Always remember and never forget: TGMs can appear from nowhere -- if you're not prepared, you're lost. Individually they may be the nicest people in the world—a soccer mom or yoga instructor--but in a group, they have no mind of their own. They have only thirteen minutes to visit seven rooms to see twelve "masterpieces" before lunch starts if they're going to stay on schedule, and they're going to stay on schedule. No one can stop them. Not me, not museum security, not even God. No one.

Identifying characteristics of TGMs:

1. Always shouting: "Ethel! Take a gander at this here baby Jesus! I reckon that's about the most damned beautiful thang I ever saw!" "Wilfred! I'm going to the bathroom! Don't let the bus leave without me!"

2. Complaints about the nudity: "Why isn't anyone ever wearing clothes in these here paintings? I've never seen so many breasts in my life, Wilfred! It's disgusting!" "I know, Ethel! I'm going to the bathroom! Don't let the bus leave without me!"

3. Wearing of funny hats and/or shirts

4. Bloodshot eyes

5. Constipation from sitting on buses all day

6. Touching the paintings, then taking flash photographs of the paintings to finish off whatever their sticky hands haven't: "Ethel, take a picture of me and this here nymph! Then I'll get one of you! Hurry now, it's almost time for lunch!"

7. Elbowing/shoving/cutting in line

8. Constantly hungry despite getting three bland and/or greasy meals daily (sustenance supersedes sights sometimes)

Be careful and maintain a safe distance. Keep a stout cane or umbrella handy for the purpose of fending them off (or ideally: a well-sharpened sword). Have no qualms about resorting to violence (the only effective way of dealing with their kind). And never, ever feed them.

Closely related to TGM's, more first cousins than brothers, are those who feel obligated to visit museums because their guidebook tells them to. Harder to spot because they don't travel in packs, don't be deceived by their politeness or being in less of a hurry. They are just as deadly as TGM's, possibly more so. To them, vacationing has become a job. Eiffel Tower: check. The Louvre: check. Big Ben: check. If you're not careful, they'll convert you. The pleasure of traveling has disappeared for them, it has now become a competition to see who can see the most sights in the least amount of time. Unable to relax and appreciate the beauty around them, they must squeeze every last drop out of the short time allotted to see these things. The highlight of their trip is their return, when they can tell their colleagues all the things they've seen. To them, the competition never ends.

Hardest to identify is the third class of museum visitor. Nearly extinct in the most popular museums because of the predatory nature of the first two classes listed above, they are a rare find. Not only do they stay out of your way, often they enhance your experience by interjecting an obscure rumor about the artist's parentage or an ancient scandal about an exposed appendage. Characteristic behavior of their kind includes standing at odd angles, chewing an earpiece of their spectacles and saying "Hmmm" a lot.

Positioning myself in front of a painting by Renoir, I attempted to attract one of the latter variety, hopefully of the female persuasion. My legs askew, I removed my spectacles. Then I commenced to chew and hmmm. Hmmm and chew. Sometimes I chewed, sometimes I hmmmed, sometimes I did both. Time stood still, time moved forward, but time did not go backwards. It may have considered going backwards or it may not have, but it didn't. Go backwards, that is. Unless it went backwards and I went with it, rendering it impossible for me to perceive its passing in an independent fashion.

My bait: a painting showing a crowd of people carrying umbrellas. All of their faces were turned except that of one girl. The rest of her face was expressionless, but her eyes held all the world's sadness. They were Belinda's eyes.

I found another painting.

Choose carefully. You may have to talk about this particular piece of art for quite some time so "Gee, what pretty colors" probably won't cut it. "Wow" might, though. Pick a subject with a touch of melancholy, but nothing morbid. Severed heads and still lives of dead rabbits are a definite no-no. Show you're a sensitive guy and can appreciate the pain the painter is attempting to portray. Virgins being led to their death are good, ditto dying fathers. But don't go overboard like weeping openly.

My next choice was a self-portrait of Rembrandt. His tired, worn out face reminded me of my grandmother.

Within seconds, the exquisite looking concierge had sidled up to me with a concerned face. "Are you choking? That noise you're making with your throat. Not the one you just made, but the one before."

"I was contemplating. Am contemplating, if you don't mind."

"It sounded like choking."

"I wasn't. Choking, that is."

A Japanese tourist who had nothing better to do than help ruin my afternoon joined the conversation. He'd travelled almost twelve thousand miles for the privilege. "Sounded like choking to me."

"Well, I wasn't."

"Let's ask that gentleman over there."

"Keep him out of it. Can't you see he's on vacation?"

"I don't mind. I thought he was choking, too."

"So did I."

"Look, who asked you?"

"Don't talk to my wife that way."

"I was talking to you."

"Don't talk to me that way."

"Why not?"

"I don't like the tone of your voice, sir."

"So?"

"Perhaps we should settle this outside."

"Hold on a second while I get my Uzi submachine gun." I left the room.

He didn't follow.

No moody, debauched women flocked. It just fucking rained.

The National Gallery was a defeat, but there were many more battlefields to behold. Europe was awash in them. And none would escape the spectrum of my resolve.

Westminster Abbey.

Mottled shafts of crimson and tangerine light filtered softly through the stained glass windows, leaving pools of cool grey silence scattered throughout. Figures pious and serene stood outlined against a white heaven offering hope and comfort in a world with neither.

This was England. This was Henry VIII, Charles Darwin, Isaac Newton, William Shakespeare. This was where kings had been crowned and great men buried. Poets, soldiers, kings: this was what we were. This was history. Out of the darkness, this is what we had become.

I wandered in awe of it all. Life had become a little more real for me. What I had only learned of in books was now tangible. These people had walked the same ground I was on, had breathed the same air I was breathing. These people had made a difference. It offered me hope. People did succeed in their dreams. Individuals could change the world. I could succeed. I could change the world. I could be happy.

Couldn't I?

The young man with short-cropped black hair leapt down from his bunk to shake my hand.

"Peter."

"Kim."

"Where you from?"

"I... Nippon. Japan. English?"

"American. California."

His face broke into an infectious smile. "Good. Good."

"On holiday?"

"English no good. Wait." He reached behind him for a pocket-sized dictionary. His dark eyes lit up when he found the page he wanted. His smile widened (and never lessened). "Yes. Before work."

"How long?"

"Wait... Year."

"Wow. Where else besides England? France? Russia?"

He nodded that he understood. He showed me a world map on the back of his dictionary. His finger circled the page.

"Everywhere?"

"Yes."

I pointed to India.

"Yes."

I pointed to Chad.

"Yes."

I pointed to the middle of the Indian Ocean and smiled.

His smile got even bigger. "No."

"Very good." I gave him the thumbs up sign. "What work do you do?"

"Wait..." His smile faded. "I work father shop..."

Stephen came in and nodded at us both.

"This is Kim. He's a Japanese porn star."

"No shit?"

"No shit. He was just showing me the size of his member. First of the Ten Natural Wonders of the World. Rivals the Amazon River in length." I spread my hands apart.

"Is that all? Never seen a Scottish member, have you?"

"I sorry. No understand."

"It's nothing. Parlay vou Francais? Hablas espanol? Sprechenzie deutsch?"

Kim shook his head to all three of the Scot's questions. "Japanese... Only."

"Balls of steel on this boy."

"And hung like a woolly mammoth," I added.

"Fancy a drink?" Stephen asked me.

"Absolutely."

"Kim, get your coat. We're getting you pissed."

"No understand."

Stephen clapped his hands briskly twice. "Happy hour starts in five minutes, lads." He beckoned Kim down off his bed. "We are about to engorge ourselves with alcohol, Kim. Besot one's person with a surfeit of inebriating concoctions. Get pissed out of our fucking minds. Give me that." Stephen snatched the dictionary from Kim's hands and pointed to the appropriate page to emphasize his following words: "We go downstairs. We drink and we drink and we drink. Get shit-faced utterly to the extreme and beyond. Puke our guts out. Vomit. Blaghhh. Good fun. Get your fucking coat. And bring this. We're getting you an English shag, too, Kim."

"Shag?"

"Insertion of your penis in a vagina or other appropriate orifice of the female anatomy."

"No understand."

"A fuck, Kim." Stephen demonstrated with a grind of the hips.

Kim laughed and donned his coat faster, putting the right sleeve on the left arm, then the left sleeve on the right arm followed closely by the left foot in the right shoe and the right foot in the wrong shoe. Stumbling occurred, pandemonium ensued, furniture grasped at and lost, arms flailed, noses tweaked, gasps expunged, entanglements both amusing and fraught with pain transpired. Doorknobs were turned the wrong way, slabs of wood attached thereto were pushed when they should have been pulled, thresholds were crossed by numbers too great and minds too few. Then, suddenly, the room was riveted in silence.

"Is it happy hour yet?"

A sigh, the second in a series. The bartender reluctantly checked his watch. "Two minutes."

A pause. Not a long pause, but a pause, nevertheless. "Is it happy hour yet?"

"Ninety-eight seconds."

Accusing whispers of rampant alcoholism spread out behind us through the trampled and bloodied we'd gone over, under and through to be first and foremost at the bar. "Is it--"

"Yes, goddamnit, yes!"

Slapping his five pound note down on the bar, Stephen called, "Ten Carlsbergs, please."

"You don't have to buy me beer."

"I'm not. Those are for me, lad."

One beer. Two beer. Three beer.

"Father's shop. What sell there?" I asked Kim.

Kim's face reddened. "Six."

"Six?"

"Six. Book. Cinema. Payboy. Penthouse."

Beer spluttered everywhere. (Shoes? Yes. Pants? Yes. Other places? Yes.) "Oh."

"No like. Must. No yen."

"Oh."

"Hello."

"Jesus!"

"No, Andre." The girthy gustatore handed each of us two more beers.

"Jesus!"

"No, Andre."

I wandered off to talk to a blonde with two eyes, two ears and some hair.

"Go away."

"Friendly sort, aren't you?"

"Fuck off."

"Why don't you tell me how you really feel?"

"You again."

"Yes. This is Kim."

"Hello, I Kim."

"He can fuck off, too."

"Kim is from Japan."

"I can see that."

"Kim is an actor in motion picture films of a pornographic nature back in Japan. His penis is very large. He is very good at fucking off."

"Leave me alone, you asshole."

"I think you are the most beautiful woman I have ever seen. I long for you tragically."

"Get fucked." A drink came splashing in my face.

"How refreshing."

"She gone."

"How sad. Ever been in love, Kim?"

"No."

"Keep it such, Kim. Not worth the pain."

Stephen handed me a new beer. "You certainly have a way with women."

We spent the rest of the night in the hostel bar, too drunk to go anywhere.

Sunshine snuck in through the curtains and screamed savagely in my face.

Stephen opened an eye tentatively. "You going?"

"Bus leaves in two hours for Edinburgh."

"If you want to wait five minutes, I'll go with you to the station."

As Stephen and I somehow, someway escaped the elevator (with our packs!), Kim came in from the street carrying a baguette and his daypack. "You leave?" he asked. "Together?"

"I go to Scotland now. Stephen and his girlfriend go tonight."

"No stay?"

"No stay."

Kim's smile disappeared. "Take photo?" Kim handed his camera to another backpacker in the lobby. "Please?" Then he stood between us and wrapped his arms affectionately around each of our necks. Stephen rolled his eyes at me behind Kim's head and I shrugged. Kim shook my hand and then Stephen's, his eyes misty. "Thank you for the drinking and the puking."

We laughed. "Good luck, Kim."

"Very nice to me. Most English: no. Hate Japan. Not you. Good men. Thank you."

I slapped Kim on the shoulder.

"Where next, Kim?"

"Ireland. Get pissed." He smiled, but his eyes showed fear. Fear of being on his own, fear of having to go back. Fear that this was all he got. He was trapped in a life he didn't want. And so was I. Or was I? Didn't I have a choice? I didn't have to go back. Or did I?

"Goodbye, Kim."

"Goodbye, Peter. Goodbye, Stephen."

"We've got a few minutes."

"Watch my gear?" Stephen inclined his head towards the restroom.

"Of course." The question startled me. But then we were going in opposite directions. Anything could happen.

Stephen returned. "Here's my phone number in St. Andrews. If you're up there next week, maybe we could have a drink… What's your surname, by the way?"

"Pollack. Yours?"

"Starling. You okay leaving Andre?"

"I'll get over it. In time."

"You're still young."

"Exactly."

"How long you staying in Edinburgh?"

"Just a few days, I think."

"Well, if I don't see you, have a good trip."

"It was cool meeting you."

"Likewise."

"This is the London-Edinburgh express. There are no scheduled stops. We will be merely pausing for petrol around noon for five minutes. You may step outside but stay near the bus. When we're done refueling, we leave. We wait for no one. I will ask you once and only once to board the vehicle. Once. It is against the law to consume alcohol, use drugs or engage in sexual intercourse aboard this vehicle. Disobedience will not be tolerated. Any rowdy misbehavior and you will be escorted off the bus by the authorities and incarcerated for a jail term up to five years. Regulations do not allow passengers to speak to the driver while he is piloting the vehicle. Obey these regulations. We should arrive in Edinburgh at approximately five o'clock. Our bus company is not liable for any delays if the bus breaks down or is involved in a traffic accident. That is all."

And that, friends, neighbors, and children of all ages, was London.

An Accountant in Paris

Someone was banging at the door. "Peter! You have to get up! Now!"

I sat up sharply and hit my head on the wall lamp. Pain, pain and more pain. "Fire. There must be a fire." I rolled out of the metal cot, hit my knee on its corner and nearly missed the nightstand with my left eye. Aaagh! Ehhhh! Must hurry. Not panic. Die if panic. Remain calm. Must find glasses. Oooh, the wall. And my toe! Fucking cold. Put on shoes. Wrong foot but no time. No time. Where are glasses?

"Peter!"

"Coming!" Again find nightstand with toe. No time! Maybe have to jump out window. But on third floor. Maybe live with every bone broken in my body. Eat through straw rest of life. Blink eyes once for yes, twice for no. Better than cooked like a Thanksgiving Day turkey. So cold for a fire. Lost feeling in my toes. Frostbite or has pain numbed all my nerves? Spots, purple and green, swim before my eyes. Smoke inhalation sickness. Drop to floor. Aaaagh! This time a table is the culprit and my shin the victim.

"Peter! Now!" More banging.

Crawl to door. Must breathe shallow. Keep face to carpet. At door.

Which opens into my nose just as I arrive.

Choking back blood, I shout, "Fire! Time we have, how much?"

Garbed in a faded blue dressing gown with a frilly lace collar and embroidered frog wearing spectacles near the bottom hem, my grandmother hovered above me silhouetted by the kitchen light, a mug of coffee clutched tightly in one hand and a lemon Danish in the other. "What fire? There's no fire. And don't bleed on the carpet."

No fire?

"What was all that banging around in there? You better not have broken any of the furniture. You hear me? If you're going to be staying for a while, you have to keep quiet. This isn't the mountains where you can't be heard over the animals. The neighbors will complain. And why are you wearing your trousers on your arms?"

"Fire."

"I told you there's no fire. Oy! What am I going to do with you? You're going to be late for work! Quit bleeding on my carpet and get dressed."

"Work?"

"It's five o'clock already. Get going."

"Work?"

"Are you going deaf as well? Yes, work. Time you earned your sustenance in this ungenerous world. Get up, up, up!"

I only had three and a half hours to get ready to drive sixteen miles.

Emerging into the Santa Monica morning two hours later, my left eye now an attractive shade of violet with lemon swirls, smarted sharply. My toes were a dull throb. My nose, well, my nose was not good. And I'd cut myself three times shaving. In short, I was a mess. A perfect day to start a new job.

But the trials had just begun. Later I would reminisce on that moment and say "Oh, those were the halcyon days wrought with bliss and a surfeit of contentment. Life still filled me with its limitless joy."

I turned the corner and then began The Suffering. My recently-purchased, newly washed and waxed automobile, all decked out in new tires, reworked radiator and vacuumed interior was noticeably absent from the place I had left it the night before. It was not underneath any of the nearby

48

trash can lids, it was not lurking behind any trees, it was not hiding in anyone's driveway. It was gone, lost, elsewhere.

I ran up and down (down and up) the street. I screamed obscenities. I kicked a tree. I wished for the car back. I prayed. I kicked another tree. The pain returned in my toes in an extreme and unrelenting manner. But, alack and alas, all was for naught.

The police officer looked up from a great pile of manila folders on the desk in front of him. More folders crowded the ground behind his chair and still more folders overstuffed his desk's drawers. "Yes?" he asked with the saddest voice in the history of mankind.

"Someone stole my car."

"Lucky me." He reached behind him for a new manila folder weighing three and a half tons.

"I want it back."

"Don't you all. Are you sure it was stolen?"

"Yes."

"Do you remember where you parked it? Are you sure?"

He was not writing down any of my answers, nor was he listening to them. He was counting the number of paper clips on his desk. There were six. One, two, three, four, five, six. "Were you drinking the night before? Forget you lent it to a friend? Did you lock the car? All doors? Did you leave the keys in the car? Do you have the keys with you? May I see them?"

"Why?"

He looked up. Sort of. I handed him the keys. "Do you have more than one set?"

"Yes."

"How many?"

"One."

"One?"

"Yes, one more than one. Also known as two."

Then came The Glare. "I think it's lunchtime."

"It's barely eleven o'clock."

"It's definitely lunchtime."

"Please. I've been waiting three hours to report this and it's my first day of work for a new job."

"Government regulations require me to take a one hour lunch break every eight hours of regulation pay."

"Wait. Where is your supervisor?"

"At lunch, also."

He didn't. Wait, that is.

"You."

"Also known as Peter."

"You."

"Right again."

"You're still here."

"And my car still isn't."

He shook his head in disbelief. I considered mentioning the ninety-seven minute lunch that started at ten thirty, but instead went with: "Can we finish my report?"

He sighed for about six hours. "Yeah, yeah, yeah."

"Good."

"Do you still have both sets of keys?"

"Oh, yes. When are you going to start writing this down?"

This sigh lasted nine point three hours. Then he stared at the desk for a long time. "You're sure?" he said to the folders before him.

"Of what?"

"Someone stole your car."

"Yes."

50

"And you want to do the report?"

"Yes."

"Why?"

"Why?"

"That's what I said."

"I don't understand."

"Your car won't be found. They never are. Ever. And then I have to do all this paperwork. I hate it, I just hate it. It haunts my nightmares, it's all I can think about. I come to work every day and it's there. I go on vacation and it's there. It never goes away, it never lessens, it just grows and grows. I became a cop so I could help people and all I do is fill out these stupid forms. In fifteen years the form hasn't changed. Not one word, not one comma, not one punctuation mark. Nothing."

"I'm sorry."

"You're not. You don't care. No one cares. All you want is your car back."

"Well..."

"And you won't get it. Back, that is. And now both of us will be miserable. You because you won't have your car and I because I must do this pointless paperwork. Will that make you happy? Will it?"

"Very much so."

There. A black obelisk towering above its surroundings, enveloping all in its shadow. Naively defying the heavens by its vastness of its denizens' mortality. Beneath its sleek, unblemished walls, teemed an army of humanity's greatest minds mostly engaged in meaningless, repetitive tasks in a stifling environment, able to see sunshine and breathe unfiltered air only on their allotted coffee breaks and deprived of a sense of purpose to their lives. It didn't look much like a prison, but it was one nevertheless.

"My name is Peter Pollack. I start work here today."

"Poor you." Short red hair, impeccable makeup, diamond-stud earrings.

"I'm sorry?"

"For your sake, for your sanity, I wouldn't."

"I don't understand."

"Heed my warning, for it will be your last. Preserve your humanity. Turn from here and go. Nothing but pain and heartbreak lies within these walls. Save yourself. This place will destroy you like it has all your predecessors. You think you'll be different, but you won't be. There is no escape. Leave, abscond, flee."

"You must be in charge of welcoming new employees!"

"Jest, if you must. Two years ago I was like you: bright-eyed and hungry to take that proverbial bite out of life. But this place corrupted me. Everyone here will betray you. Some from the start. Others will try to make you their friend beforehand. They will use you to the utmost and then spit you out, a dry husk of your former self. Today is my last day and I promised myself that if someone came through that door I would try to save them the pain that I had suffered. But I can see it is useless to try. Everyone must learn for themselves."

"Where are you going?"

"Bolivia. I've joined the Peace Corps." She picked up the telephone and uttered my name into the mouthpiece. "I won't be back. Truly."

"I believe you."

"Some people spend their whole lives saying they are going to change and some do it. I'm going to do it."

"Good for you."

When you imagine the devil, you picture a dark and sinister creature with a hook nose and warts who's fond of riding a broom in her spare time or a devastating, long-legged redhead with a malicious heart of the deepest ebony. You don't envision a five foot tall Chinese woman with a limp and enormous hair who stumbles a lot. You don't anticipate bad teeth and worse gums, a deviated septum and a beer belly. Cassandra Carp was all these things and much, much more. She wore nice suits if she had weighed thirty pounds less than she did. She wore expensive French perfume by the gallon. Unsightly green things always filled her teeth after lunch. All these I could have lived with, perhaps even grown fond of, for it's a person's anomalies that make them interesting. But. And that's a big *but*, mind you. Humungous. Gargantuan. Really, really large. *But* for her utter lack of remorse, her cruel void of human compassion. These things I could not abide. Perhaps they were the product of her looks, but they were still there. "Audrey? You're still here? I thought you quit." Her uneven jaw curled into the grotesque caricature of a grin from which one rotten black tooth scummed with lipstick

52

peeked through.

"I am. I did."

"Peter? I'm Cassandra Carp." We shook hands. "I'm sorry to hear about your car."

"So am I."

"Was it insured?"

"Not for theft: it was old."

"That's too bad. Unfortunately you've missed the first day of training. For your sake, I hope you can catch up. Ha, ha. Come with me."

Fool that I was, I did.

The bus passed through lush green fields partitioned by low stone walls and inhabited by sheep that looked like sheep, walked like sheep and may have smelled like sheep (I didn't get close enough to tell). They could have been British secret agents disguised as sheep, but I doubt it.

"Unbelievable," the New Zealander sitting next to me said. "I came halfway across the world to see sheep. My father owns sheep. I hate sheep."

"But these are British sheep."

"A sheep is a sheep is a sheep. Don't let them fool you."

"Who?"

"Them."

"Oh."

There were other variations, of course. Eight hours of them.

Oncoming dusk blotched the Edinburgh sky with pools of obsidian gray. Tenuous streaks of copper and maroon weaved sinuously through their midst, casting amorphous creatures of light across the roofs of the city's blackened structures. Rising against the bleak heavens, the castle kept watch over a hibernating metropolis atop a verdurous hill.

I crossed a cobblestoned bridge to the hostel, passing along wet, deserted streets and breathing in the chilled air. Little mirrors of light, remnants of the clouds' dissipated fury, dotted my path. No one was outside, the shops were closed. It was Sunday.

Upon reaching the Edinburgh bus station, the driver was fuming with disappointment. Only three passengers had been lost along the way, a record worthy of only shame in the eyes of his colleagues. One had been a victim to a restroom break at the time of refueling and a couple of backpackers had strayed too far into a field for a cigarette (sadly, my seatmate was not of their number). Perhaps if the driver could have run over one of their feet while shutting the door in their faces, it would have been enough, but they jumped back in time. His meager tally of casualties would bring nothing but ridicule and disgrace. No longer would his children be able to hold their heads high in school, no longer would his wife be able to patronize the local shops. The name Flanagan had lost its place of respectability in the eyes of the Scottish transportation community.

"Do you have any rooms?"

"About twenty of them."

"I meant available."

"No."

"No?"

"No. But I do have some beds if that's what you'd like."

"That's what I'd like."

Upstairs.

"How is it here?"

Long silence from a great bush of grey hair and a long flowing beard flecked with black. Then: "I don't understand."

"You don't speak English?"

Pause. "I'm Canadian." Pause. "Yes, I speak English."

"Have you been staying here long?"

"Why?"

"Is this anyone's bed?"

"I don't know."

"Are you traveling around?"

54

"What?"

"Skip it." I threw down my pack.

"Why do you ask so many questions? What matter the answers? Will you judge me if I say one thing instead of another?"

"I said skip it."

"I arrived today. I leave tomorrow. I went to a castle. Or I didn't. I'm going back. I'm not going back. What does it all mean? Why must we go back? Why must we do anything? I travel because I do. That's all. One day I'll die surrounded by strangers. Maybe tomorrow. Maybe tonight. What business is it of yours, these questions you bother me with that disturb my peace?"

Downstairs.

"Can I change rooms? There's a lunatic up there."

"Define lunatic."

"Madman, maniac, person of the deranged persuasion."

"Could you be more specific? Think: scientific method. Detail actions. The orator should let the listener derive his own conclusions once the pertinent facts and circumstances of the case have been presented. That is, be exact in your descriptions. If you wish to cast inauspicious vituperations upon someone's character, at least have the decency to be precise in your reasons thereof."

"Just give me another fucking room. Bed."

"Can't be done. All the rooms have been taken. Beds, as well."

"Twenty minutes ago, you said there were plenty."

"That was then, this is now. One must not plan the future by what occurred in the past."

Of course, the bastard snored. No way he wasn't going to.

Cassandra's tour of the office on my first day at Net, Block and Tackle was brief. "Your cubicle is over there. You have three pencils, one of them red for referencing, a two-hole-punch, a stapler, two pads of accounting paper, a computer and an adding machine. Your supplies are your friends. Guard them with your life. Especially your red pencil. I'd take it with you everywhere. If you make it to lunch, I'll show you where the restroom is."

I laughed but Cassandra didn't. What little of her charm existed was strictly reserved for the clientele. One did not joke with the underlings. The time wasn't billable. "Spend the morning using the tax program tutorial. Your first two days will be spent entering test cases onto the computer. Don't miss anything." She turned and left.

In a moment, she was back, "And never let me catch you using a blue pencil. They are reserved for the use of reviewers. There is to be no debate on this matter. None. If you should somehow get your hands on one, however impossible this may be, surrender it to me at once. At once, do you hear? They are kept under a strict lock and key and forbidden to the hands of the unauthorized. Violation of this rule is grounds for immediate dismissal." Then she was gone.

The cubicle housed four desks, two of which weren't empty. Dual grunts greeted my hello. Neither person even turned around. I sat down, turned on my computer, and opened the test booklet.

Once I glanced over at my neighbor and saw him covetously eying my red pencil, which had rolled precariously close to his side of the desk. I quickly picked up the writing utensil and placed it in my breast pocket.

Upon finishing two hours later, I wanted to put the test case in my binder for later reference. "Excuse me, do you have a three-hole-punch I could borrow? What's so funny?"

"You think it's so easy, finding a three-hole-punch? Do you honestly believe you can waltz in here and have one placed at your feet just like that?"

"I don't understand."

"I've been here three years and I've yet to see one. Every once in a while a rumor of one's existence crops up, but there's never anything to it. I know, I've tried. Perch in auditing allegedly has one, but when you go to auditing no one's ever heard of Perch. Show them an employee list and they'll tell you he's at a client. One Wednesday I spent six hours looking for one. Each time I thought I had it cornered… A three-hole-punch? Ha! You'd have more luck finding the Holy Grail."

But that was only the beginning of the insanity.

At twelve o'clock sharp, Cassandra appeared bearing reams of paper so voluminous they towered above her coiffure, an achievement of rare and epic proportion.

I gulped (not in a profuse and unabated manner though I certainly considered doing so and, later, regretted it profoundly). "Is that the next test case?"

"No. You must sign these papers."

"All of them?"

"Each and every." Down they came with a resounding crash upon my desk, making one leg of which sag under the considerable weight.

I leafed through the first few pages. "What are they?"

"Waivers of legal liability. They protect Net, Block and Tackle (a California Limited Liability Partnership) from any and all possible litigation in connection with your employment. By signing these documents, you hold the firm inculpable for bodily injury inflicted by coffee spills, power failures, power surges, atmospheric carcinogens, earthquakes, fires, floods, tornadoes, tsunamis, lightning bolts, riots, alien invasion, homicidal co-workers, defective furniture, paper shredder accidents, venereal disease contracted from a co-worker, client or company toilet seat, falling structural components of buildings and paper cuts. You will find the list to be all inclusive. If, however, you should think of something we've missed, please let us know and we will amend the documents accordingly. You must finish completing the forms before leaving today. You will not be paid for your time spent signing these forms. They are considered a term of your employment."

"Um... Okay."

"Each and every page must be signed twice and initialed once in black pen and in front of a notary public. Mr. Marlin here is employed for just this purpose. He cannot be bribed." Cassandra pointed to the man standing behind her. He was a slump-shouldered man in his late forties with a drooping gut and rotten teeth. His eyes were bigger than peanuts. Barely. He stank as if he'd bathed in orange-flavored soda.

"I'm Mr. Marlin. I cannot be bribed."

"Um... Okay."

"When you're finished with the waivers, we'll get you started on doing tax returns." Cassandra left. It was a view I would begin to enjoy more and more over the next three years: that of Cassandra going away. I didn't appreciate it then, for the experience was still new to me, but, a few days later (not weeks, not months), the sight grew akin to ecstasy.

Leaving the building, I tried to make friends.

"How are you?" I said to a new face.

"Metaphysically, spiritually, bodily? Or did you want a canned and terse reply of good?"

The second face was worse: "Why the fuck are you talking to me? I mean, why the fuck are you talking to me?"

My second day at Net, Block and Tackle was no better.

First came the bus: a strange, mysterious trip among the city's lost souls. There was a lugubrious clown besotted with cheap rum who endlessly quoted and compared the differences in the novel and movie version of *One Flew Over the Cuckoo's Nest.* There was an emaciated, soft-spoken grandfather in suspenders and wire-framed spectacles who shouted the words "FUCK YOUR MOTHER UP THE ASS!" every thirty seconds in between telling you about his six grandchildren who played electric guitar in the Los Angeles Philharmonic. But this is not their story. It's mine. If they want their story told, they can damn well write it themselves.

Then followed my return to my office cubicle where I found my desk stripped clean. Every paper clip, rubber band, pencil, acco fastener and plastic hole punch enforcement had been taken. My stapler, too. Even my chair.

When my first attempt went unheeded, I repeated, "Excuse me."

She looked me up. She looked me down. She sighed. "Is there anything I can get you?"

"A chair would be nice."

"What happened to the one they gave you?"

"Someone took it."

"Took it?"

"Pilfered, purloined or pinched it. Made off with it to sell in the black market of eastern Nicaragua."

"Are you sure someone didn't just borrow it?"

"They *borrowed* my stapler, too. Permanent like. Ditto my red pencil."

"See if it turns up."

58

"I tried that with my car. It didn't. Turn up, that is."

"See if it turns up."

"How am I supposed to work?"

The telephone rang and was to her lips in a blur of motion that surely transcended the speed of light. Out came the mouthed words: "I'm on the phone." Ten minutes later, she was still telling her mother about her Hawaiian vacation.

For three days I did tax returns standing up. I complained to coworkers, I complained to Cassandra, I complained to the copy machine repair man. Finally I gave up and brought one of those plastic folding lawn chairs from home to work on.

Then the hazing began.

I spent the morning of my second day in Edinburgh writing a postcard to my parents. A statue of Sir Walter Scott corrected my grammar and helped with the bit about the Japanese porn star.

Dear Mom and Dad,

Am now in Edinburgh. Seen lots of sheep, met a Japanese porn star and been to church. Museum police are searching London frantically for me, but, so far, I have eluded them. Stole the Rosetta stone in my backpack. It's kinda big, but I manage. Am traveling disguised as a cross-dressing Chinese architect named Jose. Rains all the time here. Haven't met anyone named Fred yet.

Love, Peter

For three years, Queen Elizabeth's army laid siege to the Edinburgh Castle. For eleven hundred days, men, women and children lived in the same cold, desolate rooms. They stared at the same dark walls, breathing the same stagnant air. Death threatened every day. Their world was a few hundred square yards. They were cramped together watching their food slowly dwindle away, watching their lives dwindle away. There was no hope of salvation. Winter came and went, came and went. Their captivity continued. Then, one day, their leader surrendered himself and was executed. Their struggle was for naught, but they were alive. And no longer free.

America was different. Free. Wasn't it?

Who were my fellow travelers? A generation adrift. They knew they had to change their lives, to get out. So they were here. Independent, free of responsibilities. And living on three dollars an hour wages, eating spaghetti sauce from a can (pre-BPA awareness), and watching American movies in the group living room. They worked in pubs, smoked marijuana and got drunk every night. But fear shone in their eyes. Of having to go back. Of their insignificance. Of the pointlessness their lives were to become. Still, they were all happier than any accountant I had ever met. No one was trying to outdo each other. Would it last?

"You just get in?"

"Last night. Kind of a dump, isn't it?"

"What do you mean?"

"It's filthy. The showers have no hot water. I saw a cockroach larger than a Volkswagen in the bathroom."

"People are very friendly here. It's a good scene. You're looking at things all wrong."

"How long have you been here?"

"Six months." Threatening five feet but not very aggressively, my fellow American possessed breath that could wipe out the entire Albanian army. A globe of kinky black hair encircled his ever present gap-toothed smile and prominent yet not intrusive proboscis. His clothes were a startling array of yellows, reds, and a pea green. A book on astrology peeked out of the top of his leather satchel.

"You studying here?"

"Just taking a break, man. Plenty of time for that later... I'm Franklin."

"Peter. From Los Angeles."

"San Francisco. Haight-Asbury."

"Never would have guessed."

He smiled. "A few of us are going to try this Scottish folk dancing thing tonight. Wanna come?"

60

"I'm not much of a dancer."

"None of us are. You should come. It'll be fun."

"Um. Sure. Sounds good."

"Meet here about six. We're gonna get a couple bottles of wine beforehand if you're up for it."

"Absolutely."

Seven of us stood outside waiting for the bus. The setting sun burnished the city's chimney stacks, storefronts and ironwork in a lather of peaches and cream. The sounds of civilization percolated through the air: the whir of car engines, the shuttering of galvanized steel doors, the tumbling of locks, the shouts of children. I drank in the myriad sights, letting Edinburgh sink in. In one pocket I held a map of the city torn from my guidebook and in the other, an entire bottle of red wine. Or a third of one, anyway. The remaining two thirds lay at the bottom of my stomach.

"The bus can only fit four of us," the blonde girl from Ohio said.

"You go. It's all right."

The bus pulled away.

"Want to wait?"

"Not really."

I downed the rest of the wine bottle in a flourish. "Fuck it. We'll run."

We ran. Three miles. I was wearing my hiking boots and was quite drunk. My two companions wore tennis shoes and starred on their respective high school track teams. I nearly died.

"Join me?" Before me stood a Scottish woman in her late thirties with short black hair wearing a white blouse and a blue woolen skirt.

"I'm not much of a dancer."

"I'll show you... Your left foot first. Now your right."

"Sorry about the boot."

"That's okay. Really fast now."

The room spun before my eyes as she twirled me around and around at dizzying speeds to the beat of the drums and bagpipes on stage.

The Scottish families easily accepted us as their own: inviting us to dance and speaking of American politics and our version of football during rests.

My life had been spent in fear. Fear of failure, fear of rejection, fear of embarrassment. But now I was dancing, wretchedly to be sure, with total abandon. My companion's gentle brown eyes and effervescent smile assured me I wouldn't be laughed at. Not even when I trounced her with my boots. Which I did repeatedly much to my chagrin. No greater comfort in this world exists than to be accepted for who you are, regardless of your age. Yes, I knew I would never see any of these people ever again, but what was new for me was that I no longer cared what others thought of me at that moment. I felt free. And confident for the first time since Belinda. A kind-hearted woman enjoyed *my* company. I could be myself, let go. Whether strangers approved of or laughed at me made no difference.

"Thanks for inviting me, Franklin."

"No, man. It's karma. Do good for strangers. Everybody does: soon there are no strangers. It's what traveling is all about, man. Spreading the love."

The next morning I took a bus to St. Andrews for the day. I walked along the coastline and dipped my bare feet in the icy black waters of the Atlantic. Then I had homemade ice cream in a waffle cone while visiting the ruins of the St. Andrews castle. (Mint chocolate chip – there, you know my favorite. And I didn't forget.)

(By the way, as for sorbet, I once had a four week dalliance in 1983 with raspberry coconut, but the passion faded and we both moved on.)

The dancing had infected me with a new carelessness. And I wanted to relive its freedom.

"Read anything else by him?"

"This is the first." Dark brown hair swept back over one ear with black horn-rimmed spectacles and a lissome figure, she was reading *The Stranger* by Albert Camus. Wearing faded blue jeans and a dark brown sweater, she sat alone in a bedraggled, brightly-patched chair in a corner of the hostel.

"*The Fall* and *The Plague* are also good, but I like that one the best."

She chewed her bottom lip. "Uh-huh."

"Staying here long?"

"For this summer, yes. I just graduated from high school. You?"

"Passing through… Want to go dancing? I saw this ad for a reggae group performing tonight at Haymarket Square."

"I don't know. How much does it cost?"

"Only two pounds."

"I can't afford it."

Seriously? "Don't worry, I'll pay."

"Um... Give me a minute." She went upstairs for her jacket.

"I'm Peter."

"Sara."

Our warm breath made white clouds in the street's chill night air.

"So what did you do today?"

"Worked. I clean dishes in a pub."

"You going to travel later?"

"No, I'm saving money for community college next year."

We arrived at the building. I paid and we went upstairs to a high-ceilinged loft with hardwood floors and brilliant white walls. The band was still setting up its instruments so we sat down.

"Aren't you at least going to see the rest of Scotland?"

"I bought a one way plane ticket here from Indiana. I've got to save enough to fly back. And I spend a lot at the Internet cafe chatting with my boyfriend back home."

"Boyfriend?"

"We've been seeing each other since I was fifteen. I didn't think I'd miss him as much as I do."

"How long have you been here?"

"Three weeks."

"Can I ask why you came to Scotland, Sara?"

"I figured I should see the world before Scott and I get married after we graduate. I want to get my Masters and he wants to work for his dad. By then, he thinks we'll be ready. Then we're going to have two kids, a boy and a girl, and live in this house near his parents. He says he's all over Jane. That was his girlfriend before me. We're perfect for each other."

Then, relief: the band began playing. "Hey, let's dance."

"I'm not sure I want to."

Would Sara wake up one day wishing she'd tried something else? Explored more possibilities, lived a life less planned? I couldn't live like Sara, but then Sara probably couldn't live like me. Who was to say whose path was better? You have to do what you think will make you happy.

"You know why I love him?" She'd followed me onto the dance floor. "My boyfriend? Because his favorite movie is *The Beauty and the Beast*."

"Oh."

"He's so cute."

I did some rampant head-banging to the mellow reggae music and drifted away.

The first song ended and Sara was there. "Scott's a Sagittarius. So am I. That's why we're perfect for each other. Jane was a Leo. No one ever gets along with Leos."

"I'm a Leo. People get along with me."

The second song started. "You've got a piece of food stuck in your teeth. Scott strongly believes in proper oral hygiene. Brushes three times daily. Flosses twice."

In the future I would be more particular about choosing my

companions.

The hazing started out slowly at Net, Block and Tackle, but, over the ensuing months, escalated in both caliber and frequency. Near the end, it was all-out warfare.

When Cassandra finally did show me where the restroom was, the lights were shut off when, shall I say, I was in a most indelicate position. Wicked laughter declined my half-desperate "Would you be so generous as to re-illuminate the room?" I finished as well I could, spewing vituperation indecent to repeat, and, in my hurry to leave, slammed headlong into my department head entering the darkened room.

As I apologized, two fellow tax staff snickered with triumph from a nearby cubicle.

Nothing was sacred to my oppressors. Pencils were glued to desks, crank telephone calls of a staggering and unrelenting quantity inundated my extension, flyers announcing various medical procedures performed upon my person to change my gender or magnitude of my manhood were circulated throughout the office. Chairs were dismantled, coffee was filled with salt, desk drawers were nailed shut. My keyboard was reprogrammed to type in Cyrillic and then Mandarin. Family portraits were defaced, personal phone calls were recorded. Every day was war.

My next encounter with the partner in charge of my department was again among the upright liquid waste receptacles. I had been avoiding him, fearing our inauspicious beginnings would agent my ending (out of sight out of mind type of thing). Not that I didn't like him, he just frightened me.

Barrington Barracuda was of medium height and medium build with a face suffused by the effects of years of alcohol abuse. Beneath thinning curly red hair was a grinning, leering letch of a man, constantly talking of the size of his penis or your penis or whoever's penis happened to be in the general vicinity. He was equally willing to discuss breast-size should the conversation take that turn. I liked him immensely. He was the only sane person there.

"New here? Who do you work for?"

"You."

"Paul, is it?"

"Peter. Peter Pollack."

"Right. From Wyoming."

"Lake Arrowhead."

"Right."

Our next meeting occupied the same venue.

"Peter. How's Wisconsin? Isn't that where you're from?"

"Lake Arrowhead, actually."

"Right… Is your cock really so big that you must put your tie up like that when you piss?"

"Truthfully…"

"Knew I hired you for some reason."

"The female secretaries appreciate it, also."

"Fucking water's freezing."

"I wouldn't know. I do the more sanitary wrap around."

Variations of this conversation continued for the first six months of my employment. Sometimes Barrington remembered my name, but never where I lived. So I started telling him I was from Bulgaria and my parents were killed by Mongolian nomads masquerading as door-to-door vacuum salesmen. He began to like me a lot more.

The day I left Edinburgh for Belfast, it rained. The road to Stanraer ran along the Scottish coast, but a cover of clouds let me see none of the Northern Channel. At Stanraer, I boarded a ferry to Belfast.

The ferry was the largest boat I'd ever been on with its slot machines, duty-free shop, cafeteria, restaurant, music lounge and pub. People went to sleep everywhere, even in the middle of hallways. I found a place to sit and there I sat.

"Trekking around, are you?" Round face, round spectacles, small mouth, small moustache. Walking stick with the head of a hawk. "Good to do it when you're young. You won't regret it."

"I hope not."

"Of course not. A man needs experience. Nothing better for it. Did it myself when I was young. When you get to be my age, you want the memories. Sow some wild seeds. Done my share in my day. Would have regretted it if I hadn't. How long you been gone?"

"Only a week."

"And how much longer?"

"Six months, I think."

"The world?"

"Just Europe."

"Good. Good. Whereabouts in America are you from?"

"Los Angeles."

"Ah, Hollywood. Crazy town, isn't it?"

"That it is."

"You going back?"

"I'm not sure."

We arrived in Belfast ten minutes before the hostel closed at ten o'clock. Worried I wouldn't make it, I paid a cabbie three pounds (after haggling him down from twenty) to drive what turned out to be a hundred yards to a windowless, squat building resembling a post-apocalyptic bomb shelter with barbed wire, an intercom system, and a high iron fence defaced by graffiti.

"What do you want?" the voice crackled over the intercom.

"I called earlier about a bed for the night. The name's Peter Pollack."

Long pause.

"Hello?"

The fence's electric lock buzzed and I went inside.

The gate shut behind me but the door in front of me did not open. Still just the voice: "Let me see your hands."

"I'm sorry?"

"Your hands. Let me see them."

I showed the peephole my hands and the wrists that came with them. "I forgot to wash after dinner."

"Open your pack on the ground in front of you."

"I'm sorry?"

"Do you want in?"

I did as the voice asked.

"Slow! No sudden movements." With panic: "What's that white thing?"

"Tube socks. Keep my toes snug and toasty."

"What's under that jacket?"

"My AK-47 assault rifle."

"That's not funny."

"May I come in now?"

Numerous door locks clicked. Clacked. Back and forth. As if which way to turn them was confused a number of times. Then: "Make sure to wipe the dirt off your feet."

The caretaker was a smallish woman in her late thirties with the face of a really unattractive iguana. Her glasses had lenses larger than the ones they put in the telescopes to look at Saturn. And her frizzy brown hair absorbed all the light in the room.

"Did you wipe your feet?"

"See?" I lifted one foot and then the other.

"It's twelve pounds a night. No credit cards, no personal checks, no travelers cheques. Cash and nothing but. No bills over fifty pounds in denomination. No IOU's, no collateral. The money or the door. Take it or leave it."

"Has anyone ever adequately complimented your adorable personality?"

"Men are scum. You are a man. Therefore, you are scum."

"Now you're just flattering me."

"How many nights will you be here?"

"One, thank you."

"That will be twelve pounds."

"Do you accept personal checks? Just kidding. Here you go."

"Room six down the hall. Take the bed by the door. Return the sheets to the office in the morning. Check out time is nine thirty sharp. This time is not negotiable."

"Good night."

"Lights out in twenty minutes."

"Do I have time to shower?"

"Lights out in nineteen minutes."

The hostel was actually quite clean. I dropped my pack underneath my bed and went to the community bathroom to brush my teeth. When I came out two couples sat in the hallway reading tourist guidebooks.

"Hello," I said.

"You're American?" She had short dark hair with luminous blue eyes. Rapturously beautiful. "We're Swedish. Are you staying in Belfast long?"

"I'm going to Dublin tomorrow."

"Yes, there's nothing to see here. But you shouldn't leave Northern Ireland so quickly. It is very beautiful. Don't waste your time in the big cities like Dublin. Big cities are the same everywhere… We're going camping along the northern coast. There are some beautiful steppes and cliffs. You've heard of the Giant's Causeway? And go fishing if you can. It should only cost you a hundred dollars American a day. It's really worth it. We just came back from sailing for a week."

"I'm not sure I have the time, but thanks for the advice."

They were right: I soon tired of the cities and the constant drinking. But then I didn't know it. So I went to Dublin the next day.

I was leaving the printer room when an admonitory voice stopped me: "What are you doing?"

"I'm sorry?"

My accoster resembled more of a robot than a human being. Immaculate hair, perfect teeth, impeccably cut navy blue suit, designer tie perfectly aligned. Not a button, not a hair out of place. Ate, breathed, probably even shat accounting. Could recite word for word any obscure subsection of the Generally Accepted Accounting Principles on demand. He obviously came from one of the big school's accountant assembly lines, he still had that new factory smell to him. "What are you doing?" he repeated.

"What does it look like, resemble, appear to be?"

"Don't fuck with me. I've been here two years, three months, six days, five hours, fourteen minutes. I don't have to take shit from any rookie fucking junior who doesn't read the clearly posted signs. If you choose not to follow the rules of this firm, I'm sure they can find another peon quite easily to replace you." He pointed. A greeting in large green letters. Letters all capitalized. "PLEASE REFILL TRAY AFTER USE."

"But I just printed my timesheet. Nothing else. It's one sheet of paper."

"So you want someone else to replace your paper for you? Everyone carries their own weight here, it's a unified effort. We're a single team working for a singular goal."

"To be an asshole?" I walked out.

There were other signs. Above the coffee maker: "Don't spill." Doorways: "Beware intersecting traffic." Elevators: "Please do not jump in elevator." Toilets: "Please flush." Cubicles: "Keep our office clean." "Please recycle." "No running in hallways." "Do not lean against walls." "Smoking is strictly prohibited." "Refrain from spitting."

Sadly and tragically, but not necessarily upsetting, there was no "Please don't stab your co-worker in the back." Apparently there was a "Smile and the world smiles back" until an incident ensued. That was all the information I could get and obtaining even that morsel cost me two pumpernickel bagels and a non-fat, extra-foam double cappuccino from Larry's Patisserie.

At the end, when I knew the war was lost, I tore down the signs with a passion. Not only were they replaced but they grew in number and diversity tenfold. But that must wait. All will come in due time.

"Peter. Take a seat, please." Barrington was not smiling. He finished reading a memo in his hand and then looked up at me. "Do you like working here?"

"I do."

"Do you think you fit in?"

What the fuck was going on? "I think so."

"No problems then, no complaints? We treat you well?"

"Yes."

"Then what is all this about not wanting to refill the paper trays after you use the printer?"

"I'm sorry?"

"Don't play stupid with me, son. Everyone's got to help each other out here. If you want to remain with this firm and this is a decision you will have to make, you must be willing to do your share. Now do you want to remain employed here?"

"Uh, yes, I do."

"Well, if I get any more complaints like today, you won't be. Are we clear?"

"Yes."

"All right. Now don't waste any more time on this. Let's all just move on. You have a bright future here, Peter, don't blow it."

"Thank you."

Bass told me the good news: "You're going to be working with Sigmond."

I was terrified (and though I didn't pee my pants, I *so* wanted to - even just a little). Sigmond Sturgeon was the madman of the office: a loud, obnoxious beast of an accountant with a mouth large enough to devour most breeds of poodle whole (and easily any of the ducks native to North America). He drove fear and abject depression into the most stalwart of college interns. Some lasted days, other hours, one an entire sixteen point three seconds. All left screaming. His pock-marked visage, scarred by craters and pits more appropriate to a World War I battlefield than to a human being's face, haunted the dreams of would-be CPAs--he truly was the dark side of accounting.

A loud thunderous shout echoed through the cubicles, shattering glass picture frames and cosmetic mirrors in its path: "HEY, YOU FUCKING IDIOTS, GET IN HERE!"

Bass shook his head. "You know Sigmond's why the building has no rats? Eats them all."

My mouth had gone dry and the back of my knee twitched violently. I toppled from my chair into a pile of files, tweaking my spectacles from my nose and cracking a lens.

Bass did not laugh. Sigmond Sturgeon was no laughing matter. In times past, men had ingested cyanide or begged death by firing squad to avoid working with him. One USC graduate had even lit himself on fire.

"BASS! WHERE THE FUCK IS THE NEW MEAT?"

"You'd better get going."

"BASS!"

I moved towards Sigmond's office. People I'd never talked to before shook their heads in pity, even the secretary who'd refused to help me get a chair.

A pizza box shot out of his office, tumbling end over end across the putrid blue carpet. The cardboard inside had been licked completely clean, not even grease stains remained. "ENOUGH DAWDLING. GET BACK TO WORK, YOU SONS OF BITCHES."

A flurry of white shirts and striped ties stampeded from the office, nearly leaving me trampled in their wake.

Few escaped alive, less unscathed. Gritting my teeth, I entered the den of the Beast.

"Who are you?" Up close, his face was even more hideous than I had imagined. Possibly his ugliness fueled his hatred or maybe he was just an asshole.

Behind him on his wall hung a jewel encrusted golden scabbard holding a scimitar. I later found out it was frighteningly real and kept frighteningly razor-sharp - could cut through nine redwelds holding files averaging 296.31 pages in width. Rumor was it had once belonged to Genghis Khan. (When asked a few weeks later why he had a real scimitar in his office, without a hint of a smile he responded "The better to chop your toes off with, my dear" before he nonchalantly moved on to the pitfalls of taking the home office deduction. A similar-type response once had when an intern asked why he kept a full length sledge hammer under his desk: "The better to smack you upside the head, my dear" resulted in her hospitalization for three weeks when she ran full tilt from his office into the floor's copy machine. Months later, people were still grumbling about having to go to the 27th floor to make copies until the 26th floor machine was fixed – to be fair, the elevator did stick between those floors a lot and always made a hideous creaking noise when making the trip that threatened such a recurrence. Her grade? Apparently an incomplete.) Among his office's decorations was a stuffed Pel's fishing owl, a Kori bustard and a Pygmy falcon (the world's smallest raptor) – all with glass eyes that seemed to follow you around the room, though one of the bustard's was hanging slightly and, even more intimidatingly, out of its socket.

"Peter. Peter Pollack."

"You're the new one, eh? Take off that bib, wipe the milk from your chin and come in. Don't sit down, I've got work to do. So do you. That pile over there: that's you. Review last year's files for an hour and come back. One hour, mind you, not fifty-nine minutes, not sixty-three. Sixty minutes. Three thousand six hundred seconds. No more, no less. If you're one second late, I'll know. One fucking second. Don't need a watch." He swiveled around in his chair and picked up the phone. "Wrasse, fucking get in here! What do you mean you're not fucking done? Hold on. Pollack, what the fuck are you waiting for?"

I needed the job. I needed the fucking job. And with the paper tray incident I figured I couldn't complain. "Do you know you've got a slice of pepperoni stuck to your left cheek?" I bent over to retrieve the files.

Sigmond wiped the remnants of his pizza away and started dialing another telephone number.

I left.

Two minutes after I returned to my desk, the phone rang. "Pollack."

"What are you doing?" Sigmond.

"I was trying to work on your tax return. Then the phone rang."

"Where were you?"

"Where was I? In your office about five minutes ago."

"No, I called you right after you left. You weren't at your desk."

"I went to the bathroom for Christ's sake."

"Good. Bathroom breaks are billable. But not excessively. You can pee once every three hours. Now get back to work. I'll see you in fifty-four minutes. And Pollack?"

"Yeah?"

"When I give you a project, you work for me. Me and only me. You don't put it down if Cassandra, Barrington or Almighty God himself asks for your help. If there's a giant earthquake, if the Chinese army invades, if a madman comes into the office and shoots everyone on the nineteenth floor, you finish my project. Even if he gets you in the leg. When I've got you, you're mine. You understand? Mine. Anybody complains, you have them talk to me." He hung up.

Twenty minutes later, the phone rang again. "Pollack."

"What are you doing?" Sigmond.

"I was trying to work on your tax return. Then the—"

"Good." He hung up.

On the bus south from Belfast, a young boy with a punk haircut, eyeliner and wearing a black leather jacket stood up to give his seat to a woman in her sixties boarding. "Well, thank you, young man. What is your name?"

"Matthew Murre."

"Where are you from?"

"From Blackrock, miss."

"Is your mother Margaret Murre? I'm going to call her and tell her what a nice young gentleman you are."

A filthy, smog-ridden city. Dublin. I'd left Los Angeles for this? Maybe the Swedes were right. Maybe I should see more of the countryside.

A stroll along the putrid River Liffey to the hostel while passing cars belched gasoline fumes in my face. Behind a bar, the dormitory room had twenty beds spread over two stories connected by a spiraling staircase. Loud music and no one sitting alone. Starting over again. But such an opportunity. Not many people get such chances. Not my parents, not my grandparents.

Don't waste it in self-pity. Loneliness is a small price to pay to see the world. Something would come up. Think positive and let it happen. But not with gasosaurus breath. I went into the bathroom to brush my teeth.

"Traveling alone?" asked a cute red-haired girl at the next sink. "Do you wanna go have some beers with my three friends and me?"

See what I mean? "Sure."

"We leave in like twenty minutes. Meet outside near the bar."

"I'm Peter."

"Candy. From Canada."

At the pub, Candy went off to talk to some locals, leaving me with her friends. After the first few polite questions about where I was from, where I was going and how long I would be at it, the three girls' conversation quickly turned to home: how their boyfriends were doing, who was marrying who, who had a new job. Two weeks away but with another six to go, it was as if they had never left. A myriad of new experiences beckoned, but they sat together night after night, missing them. Sticking to what was safe. Like ordering chocolate again at the world's largest ice cream parlor.

Near two in the morning, Candy got us free tickets to a club from someone she'd met at the bar. I took one look at the besotted Wednesday night inhabitants stumbling drunkenly into one another's arms while fighting to keep their eyes open and their legs upright, and left.

Sleep. But.

"Two people are in my bed," I said.

"Shhhh," the bed next to mine said. Well, not the bed. Beds can't talk.

"Hey, get out. This is my bed." I shook a leg.

"Shhhh!"

"My bed. Not yours. Out." No movement. No signs of life. Nothing.

"Shhhh!"

I dug through my bag for my flashlight. Disgruntled turning over and sighing spread throughout the room. Knife, no. Well, maybe later if the flashlight didn't work. Guidebook, no. (They never put useful phrases in the book anyway. Examples: Get the fuck out of my bed, it's three o'clock in the morning, I'm tired, I'm half drunk, I paid for this bed and you didn't.

Actually I heard that's just one word in Inuit, I really want to find out what it is.) Flashlight, yes. Click. The occupants were two Japanese boys, not a drunken couple as I first suspected. "Out! Now!"

"Shhhh!!!"

Pulling feet, I sent their heads to the floor with two loud bangs. Japanese curse words ensued. I stepped over the two aching victims and beneath the sheets. Ten seconds later they tried to join me. Aiming for only soft parts, I fended them off with fierce kicks that caused more moaning.

"SHHHH!!!"

The Japanese boys disappeared.

An hour later they returned. This time I needed the knife.

At three forty-nine, an American guy entered the room with an Australian girl. First, they slammed the door shut. Second, they tripped over thirteen people's backpacks. Third, of course, they tried to get in my bed together. When that option proved unavailable (I used the knife first this time), they moved into the bunk bed above mine, stepping on each and every one of my extremities (plus an ear and an elbow) climbing up. Just as I had returned to my dreams of the proper way to present a cumulative effect of a change in the accounting method in a consolidated corporation's financial statements, a battle commenced above me. After many whispered protests of a variety easily imagined, she was suddenly running topless around the room with the American chasing her ("No, I really like you. I respect you," in a drunken, slurred voice). A chorus of three Italians serenaded the girl with "You are… Very Nice!" every time she passed their corner of the room. Dirty socks, bus schedules and aluminum cans rained down on the amorous pair from above. Swiss army knives, Leatherman tools and sharpened mascara pencils were drawn. Violence of a most heinous and explicitly detailed manner was threatened. The girl left, slamming the door on her exit. The American returned to bed, making sure to step on all of my toes but carelessly missing two of my fingers during his ascent. And then, of course of course of course, he snored.

Thirty-eight minutes later, the Japanese boys tried to climb into my bed again. I killed them both.

Four sevenths of an hour after that, the American fell out of the top bunk. He opened the connecting bathroom door twice into his nose, each time slamming the door shut. I was just about to start laughing when he turned, stumbled my way and vomited on my feet.

At six zero three the next morning (approximately fifty-six and a half minutes after I'd finally finished cleaning my feet), the rustling of plastic bags began. By the third wave of packing at seven o'clock, I'd had enough.

As I sat up to let a lovely English girl with dark hair and a very healthy chest feel the fury of my wrathful tongue, my neighbor held up a restraining hand. He smiled and said to her, "So when you come to a hostel room, you throw everything out of your pack all across the room. This requires a complete repacking in the morning. In said morning you rustle every plastic bag in your gear six times thoroughly (not five, and certainly not four). The bags use nothing but the absolute loudest plastic possible, it's even laboratory tested to reach at least 186 decibels. Then you find you've forgotten to put something at the bottom of your pack and pull everything out again. You repeat this process at least three times. And you work in shifts with your friend, as soon as one is done, the other starts in. People like you infiltrate the hostels spreading unrest and insomnia everywhere, starting at six a.m., sometimes even earlier, and continuing on into late morning. Then when the ruckus has died down and a bit of quiet has settled upon the place, your colleagues, whom we haven't met yet but will surely do so shortly, arrive to check in and chuck their gear all over the room."

The girl laughed heartily. "Too bad I chucked that bubble wrap in Limerick. I could have reached 212 decibels."

He laughed back. "Look at all your stuff. I mean, how many bottles of lotion do you need?"

"First off, they are not all lotions. This is a face wash, this a body wash and this a *combined* shampoo slash conditioner sure to give your hair that luxuriant shine so coveted by models, actresses and female vocalists the world over. Notice how I emphasized the word *combined*, meaning it's *combined* to save room and weight."

"And the other six family value sized bottles?"

She stuck out her tongue and threw the loudest plastic bag at him, "Take that. It's a gift."

"You shouldn't have. Really. This is so sweet. I'll cherish it always, never shall it leave my person. I hope to be buried with it. Or in it. And every time I gaze upon its magnificent splendor, I will remember Dublin and the few moments we shared together. And what moments they were. You're too good to me, truly." His eyes welled up and a tear did spilleth across his cheek.

With and only with both our help could she shut the top of her backpack.

Ten minutes later, a tin whistle awoke me.

"Couldn't leave without my best effort," the lotion girl said to my neighbor.

"What?" he said, doing all the usual things people do when they've been blasted awake by a whistle two inches from their eardrum.

She suddenly kissed him on the forehead. "Take care of my plastic bag." She turned and left.

He winked at me. "Don't give a shit, my boy. Don't give a shit."

I spent the day visiting Jonathon Swift's church, Trinity College, and St. Stephen's Green. That night the Japanese boys were reincarnated in the form of a fat, drunk Italian with halitosis who also tried to sleep in my bed. This time I needed rope, a five thousand pound planetary winch, three crowbars and two Finnish hockey players to pry him away. Friday I left for Galway.

Verdant countryside traversed by a thin black ribbon of highway. A bleak gray sky broken apart by sheets of rain. Fenced country houses atop rolling hills. More sheep.

Galway was a college town with many pubs along its cobble-stoned streets. I spent two nights there and then headed south. I visited Blarney Castle in the early afternoon, getting my first and only fifteen minutes of Irish sunshine, and then went to Cork for the evening. Despite the hype, the Blarney stone wasn't much of a kisser. Too cold and frigid for my taste and none of the tongue.

Two feet (possibly 1.64) outside the bus station, a lovely Irish lass with depthless blue eyes asked me, "Do you need some help?"

"The hostel is two blocks over?"

"Just turn left there. Do you need anything else?"

"No, thank you."

"Good luck."

Idiot. No, forget it, she was just being nice. Walk. Walk. "Do you have any beds available?"

Upstairs. "American?"

"California."

"Malibu. I've got a house on the beach."

"Lake Arrowhead."

"Cool. Go for a couple of beers?"

Street. Rain. Pub.

Pay for two Guinesses. Find table. Sit.

"What do you do?"

"Work for the FBI. Or I will when I go back."

"Bullshit. You're what, twenty years old?" He was a typical American fraternity boy: backwards baseball cap, Kansas Jayhawks sweatshirt, blue jeans.

"Twenty-one. But I'm serious. I graduated high school at fourteen. Then did eight years of college in four years. My buddies in the fraternity would go out drinking and me: I'd just stay at home and study. Didn't even have time for girls, just studying."

"What?"

"Yeah, really worked my ass off. But it's what I wanted. Get out there in the real world. Do something. Help people. Make a difference."

"Sure."

"Finish up, buddy. We got a lot of drinking to do tonight. I go to work in three weeks and it's no more playtime for me. Just crime fighting. So this is my last blast of fun."

"I gotta go to the toilet." I left the pub through the back exit. An insincere prick is an insincere prick, even in Ireland.

I caught the ferry the next day to Cherbourg, France where I spent the night in a cheap hotel. Not even the rats and cockroaches could keep me awake.

Train station bound the next morning, another backpacker caught up to me and asked, "Going to Paris? Know any places to stay?" He was maybe eighteen, with short black hair and freckles.

"I was going to a hostel near the Louvre for 110 francs a night.

About twenty-two dollars."

"Way over my budget. Very expensive."

"Not for Paris. And it's near everything. You got a guidebook?"

"Nah, I'm trying to save money."

"Join me if you like."

"Cool."

"Let's go wait for the next train."

We sat in the morning French sun, the saffron light warming us and illuminating the surrounding verdurous countryside.

"Traveling long, David?"

"If I don't run out of money, two months. I've only got a thousand dollars."

"That's less than twenty dollars a day."

"Sixteen dollars and sixty-seven cents actually."

"Most hostels will run you more than that."

"And I've already spent two dollars on croissants for breakfast this morning."

"What will you do in Paris?"

"I don't know. Maybe just walk around."

"You're not visiting the Louvre and Orsay? They're two of the world's best art museums. Or you could climb the Eiffel Tower."

"All cost too much. I'd rather just look around and keep traveling."

"Why are you here?"

"My grandfather bought me a ticket to Europe by cashing out his life insurance early. He said he wanted me to see all the things he never could."

"But what will you see? You can't go to Paris and not visit the Louvre."

"Maybe Jim Morrison's grave. You know: lead singer for the Doors.

I heard the graffiti around it is pretty cool. Cemeteries are free, right?"

The train arrived. We picked up our packs and boarded.

Two other American guys shared our train compartment. "Play hearts?" the tall blonde asked.

"Sure."

"You guys traveling together?"

"We just met five minutes ago."

"Been to Paris before?"

"No."

"Staying long?"

"Maybe four days."

"Just the weekend for me. Sounds expensive."

The blonde glanced at me quickly. "Great place, though. Lots to see."

"But it's like twelve dollars to get into a museum."

"How many times do you visit Paris in your lifetime?"

"I've got to make my money last."

The other guy said, "Why don't we deal?"

The first hand I shot the moon. "I knew you were doing it, but I couldn't stop you," the blonde said. "Well done."

"Where are you guys headed?"

"Spain. We're just walking around today: we've been to Paris before. We've been studying abroad in Italy for three months."

"Sounds fantastic."

"It was. Are you headed there as well?"

"Yeah, I'm traveling around Europe for six months."

"Not Morocco or Turkey? With six months, I'd definitely go to either of those. European cities all look the same after a while. You get sick of churches, castles and museums pretty quick."

"I'll see how it goes."

Later, as the train conductor returned my train pass and passport, the blonde's friend said to me, "Your surname is Pollack? You're Jewish?"

"My father is."

"Are you going to visit Auschwitz?"

"No."

"It's really horrible what happened there. Everyone should go. Seeing the piles of shoes and hair... The statistics become real, attain substance."

"I think making a concentration camp into a tourist attraction where candy canes and popcorn are sold outside the gate demeans what happened to those people."

"No, there's no entrance fee."

"The message is still: *Look what we did. We're sorry, we shouldn't have.* But somehow it did happen. Hitler didn't kill all the Jews. His soldiers did and the people let them."

"It's so people don't forget."

"They already have. Rwanda. Serbia. Neo-Nazis in the States or Germany. Making a spectacle of people's suffering at Auschwitz won't change that."

"I don't agree. Even if the effect is minimal, any tool that might stem future or current ethnic hatred should be used."

"Maybe you're right. I don't have all of the answers."

The train stopped. "You sure you don't want to join us, Peter?"

"I'd like to go to Spain. But I'm thinking of going north first. And I'd like to hang out here a couple of days. Thanks anyway."

We shook hands and they stepped outside the compartment. David and I followed.

And then, suddenly, there I was. An accountant in Paris.

Failing to Thwart the Evil Army of T-shirt Vendor Clones Before a Holland Trip of Much Consequence

As David and I were leaving the Gare St.-Lazare, a T-shirt in one of the kiosks caught my eye. Bright green background with giant fluorescent orange letters heralding *PARIS ROCKS!!!!* above the Eiffel Tower, *Mona Lisa* and the Arc de Triomphe. It was the ugliest thing I had ever seen. I *had* to have it.

"Do you speak English?"

The rather large (with hair that matched) woman smoking a cigarette dangling from the corner of her mouth answered contemptuously, "What size?"

"Ah, you spied me eying that beauty. A piece of work, that is. Stunning." She made no comment. "What size should I get, do you think?"

"How can I know all the sizes people should wear? I do not know what size will fit you. I will never know what size will fit you. I will never care what size will fit you. Now choose. Or go away. I do not care which. Only do it quickly and then leave me alone."

I immediately wanted to be hers and only hers. Throwing heed, caution and prudence to that proverbial wind, I proposed, "Would you like to roll all over me?"

"I shit on your face. I fuck your mother—"

"Is that a no?"

She reached below the counter for a pair of scissors. "Off. They come off."

"You won't reconsider? About the rolling over me part, I mean." She was climbing over the counter when I fled.

"Did you get the shirt?"

"Love got in the way. But my lesson has been learned. Wait here."

My father would never forgive my not getting him the shirt. He is a bit of a collector of *fine* apparel. My mother does not agree with my father's definition of *fine*, however. Quite strongly. After being married twenty-five years to the man, she refuses to walk with him in public. She pretends he is a stranger, keeping at least thirty feet in front of or behind him. Not that most people would blame her. His cardinal rule: never dress for more than ten dollars (shoes excluded). And the challenge is: how low can he go. He prefers loud bright colors: tropical shirts, plaid trousers, even once corduroy socks. But if it's a question of price, he will sometimes sacrifice that spectacular *Mindy Macaw Love Songs Around the World Tour* tank top for a less conspicuous *My Grandson Is A Yale Graduate* sweatshirt. And matching colors is never a consideration. What is saddest, he has a rival at work: "Three dollars for that shirt! You got ripped off! Look at these shorts! One dollar sixty, including – yes, I said including - tax." When I haven't seen my father for a while, he shouts at me as I enter the front door: "These are new socks! How much? Two dollars! I hope you're joking. Do you take your old man for an idiot? I would never pay more than one dollar for a pair of socks. Never. And they'd have to be argyle at that price." If my sister and I try to ignore him, he pesters us until we answer, laughing all of the time.

Arriving at the next kiosk, I did a double take. The woman behind the counter resembled the other saleswoman exactly. Rotund figure, thick curling mustache, hairy mole the size of Pittsburgh underneath her left eye. Even wore the same much too tight camisole. Had I uncovered a conspiracy, an evil army of T-shirt vendor clones fiendishly bent on world domination? Were they just twins? Or did that slovenly exterior conceal a superhero physique so fast the human eye, or rather my eye, could not register its movement? Maybe it's safer I never found out.

"I'd like that T-shirt."

"What size?"

I took a deep breath and answered, "Medium."

Finding the hostel in Paris was not so easy. None of the streets we passed were on my map.

"Excuse me." The stockbroker kept walking. "Ekscuse eh moi." The hairdresser ignored me. "Pardon me, madame, do you speak English?" The mother of three looked up from applying her lipstick, said "Yes" and crossed the street without looking back.

"Must be my new deodorant," I said to David.

"I'll try... Could you help us?"

The man stopped. Looked us up, down, sideways. Sniffed the air. "If you're going to visit my country, learn the language." Kept walking.

More attempts, more failures. Then: "What the fuck is wrong with you people! Can someone please fucking tell me which fucking direction is the fucking Louvre?"

The man at the newspaper kiosk behind us suddenly said in perfect English, "Six blocks that way."

"Merci."

It wasn't six blocks that way. Not that it surprised me.

"Bon jour," I said to the hostel's receptionist when we arrived two hours later. "Do you have two beds? Du couchette, oui?"

She shook her head. "Don't try to speak French. Your accent is deplorable, your punctuation is atrocious, your vocabulary is worse than horrid. I studied French in school for twenty-two years. I wrote papers, I read masterpieces of literature, I was coached in the nuances of articulation. And when I learned your language, I did the same. I spent two years at Oxford to master it. I probably speak better English than you do. Don't think you can skim your guidebook for five minutes and speak fluently our beautiful language that has taken thousands of years to perfect. It insults our intelligence."

"Oui. I mean, yes." I was really going to have to get used to the service overseas. "Do you have two beds, then?"

"At the top of the stairs. Six flights. Take a look and then come back."

"Where's the elevator?"

"This isn't the Ritz Carlton."

"I suppose not."

The first floor. Legs a bit wobbly. The second floor. Legs more wobbly, knees aching. Third floor. Legs screaming in agony, best to amputate and end excruciating pain. Fourth floor. WHERE THE HELL IS THE MORPHINE?

The pony-tailed brunette from the London hostel elevator appeared around the next corner. "Almost there," she said with a smile, obviously amused at my pain. "Only twelve more floors. Maybe fifteen."

"No elevator," I gasped.

"I know. Sucks, right?"

"Need air. Must breathe. Help."

"You don't look seventy and yet…"

"Oxygen. Call am…bu…lance." I collapsed to my knees.

Concern flooded her flawless features as she put a hand on my shoulder. "Are you all right?"

"Dying. Need mouth to mouth resuscitation. Quickly."

David stepped closer to me. "I had CPR classes last summer."

"Not you. Her. Much much prettier."

She stepped back, laughing silently. "Sorry, but I've got a train to catch." She moved David to face me. "I think you're in good hands."

"Must have mouth to mouth resuscitation. David has cooties."

She turned and kissed David on the lips. "Now so do I," she said and then was gone for a second time, out of my life.

David was grinning stupidly.

"Come on, Romeo." We continued upward.

A typical dormitory room awaited us: stained walls covered with flaking paint, creaking bunk beds fabricated of glorified cardboard, mattresses harder than Iraqi tank armor, and all perfumed with the lovely aroma of dead rat.

"Don't put your pack there! That's my breakfast."

"Oh, sorry," I said, looking futilely for a place on the floor not occupied by dirty clothes, empty coke bottles or grease-stained food wrappers. Nor did I want to disturb the stegosaurus-sized ants busy playing Parcheesi.

"That's my dinner! Where are you fucking guys from?"

"America," David said enthusiastically. "He's from California, me Illinois."

"New Zealand. Do you guys want to see the fucking Eiffel Tower and all that shit?"

"I was just gonna relax..."

"Fucking come on. You can fucking relax when you fucking go home, man. Get your fucking camera and shit."

I went, despite my misgivings. After visiting the fucking Eiffel Tower and the fucking Arc de Triomphe (with a mad fucking dash through six fucking lanes of fucking traffic in order to take a fucking photograph), I walked back to the Place de Concorde by myself.

Paris was beautiful in the setting sun. The yellow facades and rooftops of the first arrondissement turned a burnished gold as daylight faded. Avoiding the cacophony of rush hour traffic, I lost myself in the winding side-streets. An eerie calm reigned over the strangely deserted sidewalks as families raced home to spend those few precious hours life had allotted them to be together. Slowly, webs of charcoal blue stretched across the firmament imbuing the city with silence and mystery. The sun simmered as a scarlet froth on the horizon as the sky bled to black. And then street by street, house by house, all was infused in man's self-created radiance. The jungle of bright neon lights in harsh artificial colors turned me to the stone pathways of the placid Seine. Among the dark corners and shadows, lovers secreted themselves for passionate exchanges. Feeling lonely, I returned to the light, drawn to the purplish glow of the Luoxor Obelisque.

As dusk succumbed to night, quiet settled upon the Place de Concorde. During the French Revolution in 1789, it was not so. For five years, the square saw the execution of over three thousand people by guillotine. The revolution promised to redistribute the wealth from the ruling aristocracy. Give France a new face where birthright lost its relevance. All men created equal with equal chances. A noble pursuit to end aristocratic oppression. Yet eighty percent of the people executed during the Great Terror were peasants themselves. And less than ten years later, when the lure of world domination beckoned along with riches purloined from other countries' oppressed, the French willingly ended their democracy so hard fought for by electing Napoleon emperor. Was it possible to change, to better ourselves or did other people's greed, even our own, always prevent that? Could I change my dissatisfaction with a life of accounting or would I slip back into it when I returned? Would money tempt me back? The enticement of something known and familiar?

I could have bought a private jet with built-in Jacuzzi and an island to fly it to for the price of a meal in Paris. After searching for an hour, I finally found a restaurant with one item on the menu I could afford and went inside. The price was the same as my hostel bed, but I figured I had to eat out once in the world's most renowned city for cuisine. When the waitress told me my choice was nothing more than two minuscule slices of rather unappetizing salami, I had a baguette from a street vendor instead. (I had to make the money last and Mom had promised me a Thanksgiving sized feast any time of the year upon my triumphant return.)

Back at the hostel, I stopped momentarily to watch the news on a small television set behind the lobby desk. A shrunken man in his early sixties with long white hair and spectacles joined me a few minutes later and asked me something in French.

"I speak only English."

He regarded me up and down for a moment. "You are American student?" He spoke very quickly with a heavy German accent.

Not wanting to go through the Standard Q&A, I said, "Yes."

"Which school? UCLA?"

"Yes."

"I was a professor there. I also taught at Oklahoma, Harvard, Stanford, and Michigan. I taught everywhere. But now I am a dying old fart. Do you know what a dying old fart is?"

I laughed. "Yes."

"Good because that is what I am. Once I taught physics to the world, teaching the secrets of the universe, but that is all over now. I was married two times, that is also finished. One, she left me. The other, she died. Now I travel all the world spanking the monkey as much as I can before I die. Do you know what spanking the monkey is?"

Again I laughed. "Yes."

He clapped a clammy hand on my shoulder. "That is good because that is what I am doing. Good luck in your studies, young man." He disappeared up the stairs.

Much to my chagrin, the professor occupied one of the beds in my dormitory.

The next morning I visited the Louvre, one of the world's most famous art museums. From when construction began in 1546 to the middle of the nineteenth century, each succeeding French monarch added his own wing to the building. In total area the former royal palace was over forty-eight acres and held thousands of works of art. Art aficionados spent months inside. David said the glass pyramid outside was cool and went to the Tower Records store in the underground mall instead, claiming penury.

By avoiding the most popular rooms, I spent most of the day alone, awestruck by the beauty surrounding me. How much love and loss can be conveyed in a downcast eye, a grasping hand, a supplicating lip. Striving to perpetuate those moments of inexpressible perfection and to share them in a new and different way with others. To show the splendor in the quotidian: light trickling through an open window, the mischievous twinkle in a child's eye, the longing in a forsaken lover's face. To capture the sublime moment for eternity: a tragic battle or a saint's selfless sacrifice. Men and women's efforts at immortality by excelling at their craft and expressing their rage at the world's distorted sense of justice within the confines of a painted canvas or sculpted marble. Each person has his own favorites, something that connects with them personally. Mine were the unwavering determination in the headless sculpture *Winged Victory of Samothrace*, the realization of what she had lost in the face of a sculpture of Eve after she'd eaten the apple, and the burgeoning of civilization and an end to the anarchy in the four thousand year old code of Hammurabi.

How could I achieve immortality? What could I create?

Did it matter?

There she was: the future Mrs. Pollack admiring a *Madonna and Child* by Van Eyck. Long, flowing blonde tresses with refulgent green eyes.

I joined her on the cushioned bench. A moment later I took off the glasses and firmly inserted ear piece in eating orifice to masticate. "Ahem."

"Yes?" A sweet, trilling voice. And in English!

"Don't you think—"

"My feet were just tired."

"Right. So were mine."

"They aren't anymore. Bye."

"Right. Bye."

She just needed time.

The phone rang at work. "Pollack."

"Fucking get in here." The line went dead. It was Sigmond.

I walked... Well, no, I jogged, or rather sprinted, towards Sigmond's office. I'd just given Sigmond my first completed tax return to review. Everyone avoided eye contact in the hall. Was this it?

When I arrived, Sigmond was finishing a phone call with: "WHAT KIND OF FUCKING IDIOTS DO I HAVE WORKING FOR ME?" before slamming down the receiver so hard the desk underneath cracked.

Sigmond looked at me. I looked at him. His enormous black eyes bored into my very soul, draining it of everything good and bright and joyous. The back of my knee began trembling again. Perspiration dampened my shirt (which, like all my apparel, my mother had triple reinforced all the buttons of without my asking). Then he opened his mouth and asked in a calm tone, "Do you like to work, Peter?"

Was I getting warned again or fired this time? "I... Uh, yes."

He reached onto the desk in front of him for a nectarine. He rolled it over in his hands three times and then shoved the entire fruit into his mouth. He chewed three times, his brooding eyes never leaving mine, and swallowed effortlessly: stone, stem and all. Then he said: "Good. That is fucking good. Because I'm going to work you to the bone, the marrow and beyond. You're going to live, breathe and eat accounting. You're going to go to sleep and dream accounting. But actually you're not going to sleep, you're only going to work. Go home now, fuck your girlfriend, call your mother and get a sun tan. Because on Monday, you're mine."

"Where's Bass?" I asked Cassandra a few days later.

She looked up from her desk with suspicious eyes. She gripped her blue pencil as if she'd like to pierce me through the heart with it. "Why?"

"Sigmond asked me to have Bass explain the fixed asset depreciation program to me."

"He's gone."

"Gone?"

"His employment has been terminated. He was stealing supplies."

"What?"

"Yeah, he thought we wouldn't notice." Her cruel, deformed lips formed into something faintly resembling a smile. "You see, the average working life of a ball point pen for a tax accountant is twenty-four working days. It's a well-documented figure. Statistical variances caused by changes in barometric pressure, temperature, and altitude are all accounted for. As are faulty tips and variations in ink volume. For the past two years, Bass has been getting a new pen every eighteen working days. That's six point six seven extra pens he's taken from the company. Even graciously allowing him to lose one pen a year still leaves four point six seven pens he's stolen from the company."

"Um..."

"I know what you're thinking. That's about seventy cents, right? But it's not the magnitude of the loss that concerns us, it's the principle behind it. Where does the theft stop? We could easily debit his compensation for the amount, which we did plus a processing fee on his final paycheck, but we cannot allow behavior of this kind to continue. We are in the business of handling people's money, we must give the impression we have zero tolerance for theft."

"You're not prosecuting?"

"That's up to the legal department. I've submitted a report encouraging such a course of action."

"They fired Bass," I said to Sculpin at lunch. Sculpin worked in the mail room. He was not an accountant. Whenever lunchtime approached, every accountant in the office would disappear. No one wanted to chance leaking personal information that could be used against them in the future to another staff member of lower rank. And I was as low as they came. But Sculpin didn't care, so I ate with him.

I'd met Sculpin on my first visit to the file room. He'd asked, "First day? You can always tell by the hunted look in the eyes." When I smiled, he'd added, "Welcome to the Eighth Circle of Hell. And before you ask, the Orange County office is the Ninth. Circle of Hell, that is. Though a lot of people argue it's Sigmond's department." When I laughed (with pain) and told him my name, he'd said, "Tomorrow I'm going to get fired. If I'm lucky."

Biting into a French fry, Sculpin said, "I know, I was downstairs when it happened. They had security drag him out. Got him over the head with a blackjack."

"A blackjack?"

"Uh-huh. He was just reaching for his pen. They said he'd stolen enough and clobbered him. When he resisted, they tried throwing him out of the window, but the glass is bulletproof and practically unbreakable. Made a hell of a noise, though."

"Bulletproof?"

"For snipers. Can't open them either. Prevents suicides."

"Over a pen."

"Six point six seven pens, actually."

"How did they know?"

"They monitor everything. Everything. Your keycard when you check in and out of the building against your timesheet. Supply lists. Call home when you say you're sick to make sure you aren't off on vacation. Read your e-mails, listen to your voice mail. Compare the fax machine dialed numbers against employment agencies and competing accounting firms. Use a private detective to investigate you before you're hired. They leave no stone unturned. If you spent a week in detention for trash-canning somebody in the sixth grade, they know it. If you make money for the company, great, if not, they will bear down on you with an unmitigated fury."

Wrasse appeared one night around the corner of my cubicle. His tie was loosened crookedly and one of his suspenders hung halfway down his bicep. Beneath a mass of black hair disheveled by nervous hands, Wrasse's haggard eyes glowed with fear. In a raspy, frightened voice, he said, "You're still here."

I shrugged.

"Sigmond?"

"Who else?"

"What are you working on?" He tried to read the file in front of me.

I closed the file. "My sinister plan for world domination."

"Funny. Stop working so hard. You're making the rest of us look bad." I smiled, but he didn't smile back. "I mean it."

"What?"

"I heard you asking Sigmond yesterday for another tax return at eight o'clock. You don't ask for more work at eight o'clock. You go home."

"What?"

"We've got things how we want around here. Don't fuck with us, man. We'll finish you."

I was paying for my second car in six months, my college tuition loan installments had begun and I'd had to buy over a thousand dollars' worth of clothes for the new job. Cassandra shot me dirty looks every time I left the office before her, even after nine o'clock. And now the staff were complaining that I was working too much. I couldn't win.

"You won't believe what happened to me last night," I told Sculpin while delivering a tax return to be mailed. "Wrasse threatened trouble if I didn't start working less."

"You've got to watch it. They'll do things to you."

"What? How?"

"They'll frag you, man. File clerks especially. Piss one of them off and they'll lose a file for days. Throw it in the garbage. Other staff will sign you off on crappy work. Invade your files and fuck them up with your forged signature on them. Hack your computer and screw up your tax returns. This place is a battleground, son."

"How come no one has ever fragged Sigmond?"

"Oh, someone tried once. An intern named Cod. The next day he disappeared without a trace. All they ever found of him was a fragment of his favorite tie behind the water cooler. Had teethmarks in it. Human teethmarks."

I'd thought my worries were over when Sigmond gave me his blessing for my work. I'd thought wrong.

My progenitors,

Am now in Paris. Seen more sheep and had a crepe. It was chocolate. The crepe, I mean. Mailed you one. Tried to ride on top of the train, but they wouldn't let me. Nor would they let me jump from the top of one car to another. Told them it was always a dream of mine, but no. Insurance policies, government regulations, blah, blah, blah. The French are so uptight. Got kicked out of the Louvre for dripping ice cream on the Mona Lisa. Chocolate again. Still haven't met anyone named Fred.

Love,

The son

Those who spawned me,

Paris is no city of love. Whistler's Mother wouldn't go out with me no matter how many times I asked. Neither would Manet's Olympia, despite her marked lack of attire. Looking at her, you'd think she was out for a good time, right? Prude in the nude, I say. Visited the catacombs and got lost, but met some really friendly skeletons who showed me the way. Didn't visit the Sewer Museum as it smelled like shit. Accidentally walked on the grass in the Luxembourg Gardens and got shot at. Fucking French. Tried to steal a giant chandelier from the palace at Versailles, but I needed a bigger coat. Was so angry I tried to knock over the Eiffel Tower with my foot. It wouldn't budge. A policeman asked me what I was doing. More shooting. But Degas' spectral rendering of the Knight of Woeful Countenance has inspired me to defy all those who stand against me and I trudge onward to the Land of the Waffle. Still Fred free.

Love,

The primary offspring

The day before I left Paris, I decided to visit the Sacre Couer. After the usual detours, I turned a corner and there upon the steps leading up to the spindled white church he was: my mortal enemy. His appearance was deceptively innocent: gleeful gulps of laughter spilled from his lips. His soft blue eyes twinkled with bemusement. A worn gray beret covered his rough-hewn white hair. But draped along his outstretched arms with creased palms facing upwards into the limitless abyss, were dozens of pigeons. I turned and ran all the way to the Metro station.

Brussels was another mad, bustling city full of people in a hurry. But behind a white picket fence, the white-framed yellow house was a haven amid the urban pandemonium surrounding it. Travelers congregated in the enclosed, grass-covered courtyard to swap stories in lavender lawn chairs before round glass tables. I was immediately invited to join in their circle and passed a large jug of burgundy.

As darkness descended, a group left for a light show in the Grand-Place, a half hour's walk away. Bottles of beer carried in pockets were shared as we sat on the cobble stoned square and watched the spindled towers and arched windows be illuminated in an array of bright colors to the tempo of classical music.

Back at the hostel, I fell into a conversation with an American girl wearing a red beret over her short brown hair. She was in her late twenties, but her deeply tanned features lined with age and worry seemed much older. I'd seen her unsmiling face during the light show and thought maybe I could distract her from her troubles. "You came from Paris as well," I said. "I loved the tranquility of Monet's water lilies. Sitting before them was very peaceful, very serene."

"Art doesn't really interest me anymore. It's all been done."

"Done?"

Her sad blue eyes showed no life when she talked. "I studied art history in school. First the Renaissance painters, then the French Impressionists, then the Cubists and the German Expressionists. I've seen it all and it bores me. Once you understand the style and the techniques, where is the interest? The enjoyment?"

"Why are you here?"

"I'm doing a bike tour around Europe for charity. But everywhere is always the same. The same misanthropy, the same intolerance, the same greed that always eventually turns to violence. Nothing new, nothing interesting. I've traveled the world and now I'm bored with it.

Relationships are all the same: interest at first and then, after a year, once you get to know each other, starts the lies, the cheating, the disinterest. Jobs: always the same bullshit."

No one said anything at the table. At home nor would I. But here: "You haven't earned the privilege to say you're bored with life. Men younger than both of us gave their lives on the beaches not far from here so you could sit there a free woman. Children in Bosnia or the Congo would love your dilemmas. I know you're on vacation and all, but your disrespect for their struggles and sacrifices pisses me off."

Everyone was silent. I'd created a disturbance. You're supposed to nod and smile, no matter what people say.

I was tired anyway, so I stood up and went to bed.

"When is the next train to Amsterdam?"

"Leave one minute. There."

"Where?"

"There." Again I missed exactly where the ticket cashier was pointing, but when I turned back around he was talking heatedly with someone else in French. One of the trains began to pull away. "Merde," I muttered (in adopting the local lingo) and ran to catch it. Obstacles of velocity-challenged elderly persons and ferine toddlers in stroller-like chariots assailed me. Dodging, ducking, hurdling and hopping, I gained my objective with a last gasp of energy. I tripped up the stairs and bloodied my lip on a conductor's muddy shoe but I made it. My struggle, however, was not over. The train was full. Squeezing and shoving between very unsympathetic other travelers, I found all the seats taken in car after car. Then, midway through the fourth compartment, I spotted an opening. But something drew my eyes to the other end of the car. A business man with harried eyes and disheveled coiffure, his lemon tie jostled askew and his white shirt creased by struggles similar to mine had seen the seat as well. Our eyes locked in mute battle. Neither of us was to be denied, this was obvious. He shoved through a pile of pink hatboxes and a birdcage with a singing canary while I desperately tried to maneuver between the oft-shifting limbs and multi-buckled hand valises of a flock of sleeping nuns. Somehow I persevered but then was stymied by an architect's collection of metallic cylinders. Defeat loomed large when a smirk on my opponent's face drove me over the edge. No longer would I be the victim. Brow-beaten by my bosses, discarded by my sister, abandoned by the love of my life: no way was I letting this cocky punk win. I changed to an aerial assault, hopping from the back of one seat to the next in a feat that defied all preconceptions of my own clumsiness and a couple of the laws of gravity. By half a stride, I claimed victory. I raised both arms in triumph. Then, I knew, "Is this train going to Amsterdam?"

"Other direction: Paris."

I got off at the next stop.

For the second time in fifteen minutes, a train official appeared. This one seated himself opposite me and nodded.

"Just a minute." I reached inside my money belt to find my Eurail train pass. Nine hundred eighty-three dollars and twelve cents for a thin piece of paper that tore quite easily and smudged each time you fingered it. If lost, I was screwed. It could not be replaced. I was prepared to maul, maim and murder to keep it. I hid it under my jacket, tucked-in shirt, trousers and underwear against my skin inside two zippered compartments (one locked with a tiny combination padlock) in a plastic Ziploc bag. "Sorry." The man mumbled something incoherently as I continued my search. Somewhere among the passport, credit cards, travelers' cheques, plane ticket, ATM receipts, emergency cash and lengthy record of my disease inoculations I found its green paper jacket. Then I spilled the remaining contents of my money belt all over the train compartment floor. I quickly scooped things up and promptly dropped them again when a staple plucked my thumb. Then I handed it over to the elderly gentleman and tried to stuff the contents of my money belt back into place, folding all the papers that should not have been folded and bending all the things that should not have been bent.

When I glanced up sucking my thumb, the train official was not inspecting my Eurail pass. Instead he was holding it precariously near the open window of the compartment by a mere two fingers at their very tips as one would a piece of very objectionable refuse. With his left hand he was opening his worn leather wallet. My pass waved gently in the wind, threatening to abscond from the premises at any moment. If necessary I would pull the emergency brake, Dutch prison cell or no. The official fumbled through the wallet for a moment with his left hand before finding he needed his right hand's assistance as well. He transferred the paper into the clench of his somewhat clean teeth. "Don't…" I stuttered.

The words of my travel agent came flashing back: "Take very good care of this pass, some ticket agents are very particular about its condition. Won't accept it unless it is in mint condition, claiming fraud. A smudge, a tear, a coffee stain: any of these can land you in the middle of nowhere at three in the morning as you are unceremoniously thrown off the train. Take it from me, I know. Once I was deserted on the train tracks in the Belgian countryside twenty miles from the nearest village. I had to sleep in a hedge. It rained and I got chased by two dogs and one really mean cat. In the

98

morning I got robbed. They took everything except my Eurail pass. Said it was worthless in its condition. No stains, no smudges, only the top left corner slightly, and I do mean slightly, dog-eared. So I walked barefoot and without a jacket to the next village and tried to catch the next train to Brussels. They wouldn't let me on. Oh, it was a horror. Guard the pass with your life."

"Please…" I pleaded as he adjusted his bite. The official found what he was looking for and handed it over to me: a worn, folded piece of white paper tooth-marked around the perimeter and one corner missing. Above much French writing, a photocopy of his picture adorned the paper's upper left hand corner. In the photograph, the official wore pajamas and a big goofy grin, much like the one he was giving me now. Was he propositioning me?

Everyone in the compartment was laughing.

A slender, brown haired beauty explained, "He's not the conductor. He's, how do you say in English, not right in the head. They let him wear the uniform."

I snatched at the Eurail pass in the man's teeth. He recoiled and the paper floated to the ground between our feet. He tried to grab it, but then so did I and we bumped heads. Both of us pulled back to rub the injured area and then tried again. Cranium met cranium. Laughter echoed in our ears. As I reached for the errant paper a third time, he refrained. But. Oh, yes, there had to be a *but*. *But* a man from the corridor entered the compartment at that moment and stepped directly on the paper and my hand in the process. I made with the appropriate sounds and let go. Out went the pass into the corridor where all the windows were open. No! Yes. No! Yes. I sprinted after as the paper dodged left and right to elude me. I knocked down two soccer players, an electrical engineer and a grandmother of six in the chase. Unkind words in Dutch echoed after me down the corridor. As the paper threatened to pass into the space between cars I dove. And caught it. Yes, it was smudged and bent in three places and was now adorned with two attractive footprints, but I had it. I had it!

"Whew," I said and looked up, smiling.

No one was happy for me.

Applause, however, greeted my return to the compartment. I smiled and took a bow. Then I tripped on my daypack sitting back down and dropped the pass neatly out the window as we were crossing a river.

I said fuck about forty-five times.

The girl said, "It was valuable, this paper?"

"Nine hundred eighty-three dollars. And twelve cents."

"And not insured?"

"No."

"I'm sorry."

Fifteen minutes later, the girl asked, "You're from the States?"

"California."

"And you are traveling around Europe or studying here?"

"I was traveling."

Her vibrant grey eyes studied me for a moment. "Can I ask you something about American politics? I'm curious to know who you want to be the next president."

"Well, I'm mostly liberal, but I think they're both crooks."

"So you prefer the Democratic candidate over the Republican?"

"I suppose."

"No leader is perfect. He might please you, but he not someone else. Or vice versa. I think you just have to choose the candidate who will do the best job."

"I agree."

"Traditionally, Democratic presidents are much more generous to impoverished foreign countries incapable of self-sufficiency. If the Republican candidate wins, a lot of very poor people around the world will suffer."

"But most of those countries' governments are so corrupt that hardly any of the money reaches those in need. You have dictators with million dollar homes in the Caribbean driving Rolls Royces and their wives own ten thousand pairs of shoes. Meanwhile, half the populace is living in mud huts, dying of cholera and subsisting on rice and polluted drinking water."

"But some of the money does reach those in need. Even if it's fractional, wouldn't you rather have nine children starve to death than ten? When you see someone needlessly suffering, don't you want to help?"

"Of course."

"There's a responsibility that comes with being the most powerful country in the world. My country is not so rich, not so powerful. Yours is: with the strongest army, the richest treasury. You have the potential to do such good. Also: the opposite. Just think: for maybe the first time in history, a democratic country is the most powerful. Combine that with modern technology and people don't need to starve anymore, they don't need to die of diseases that have been wiped out in the first world countries. But people have to want to help others and contribute. Some do, most don't. I mean, how much of your population even votes?"

"But why us? Why must we save the world if these people can't even help themselves?"

"Because you can. Most of these people are not educated enough to help themselves. You can't think of the world as us and them. Think of the world as one people, one race. No person should suffer because they were born the wrong color or in the wrong country. Instead your country uses its power to keep bloodthirsty dictators like Noriega or Marcos in power. They involve themselves in places they shouldn't. To prevent communism, whatever that is. Thousands of innocent people have lost their lives through your intervention."

"I know that. But we're hardly the first country to exploit our power: Spain, Britain, Italy, even Holland all did the same. I may not agree with our policies, but what can I do? Most of the intervention is done to protect American corporate interests overseas. The American people don't want innocent women and children to be killed in Cambodia or Guatemala. They just don't know what's going on. Corporate interests control most of the media. The conflict in Vietnam is proof of that. When television was given free rein to show whatever they wanted, Americans were disgusted with what they saw their servicemen were doing in Vietnam and pressured the government to withdraw our forces. The Gulf War was totally different. The media was completely blocked out, fed video tapes by the government of missiles hitting buildings. It was like watching a video game. The reality of death was gone. None of the innocent people being bombed was ever shown. In today's world of international mergers, only a handful of companies run the media. Everyone is owned by somebody else. Well, they're not going to run stories against their interests, are they?"

"But don't some people know what's going on and want to change it?"

"Of course. But it gets complicated. Big American corporations generate a lot of jobs and tax dollars. If you hamper their interests, Americans lose jobs and the government loses funds. Jobs mean votes. Also, it's very expensive to run a political campaign in the United States. Without television advertising, you don't get elected. Who pays for these campaigns? Indirectly, big corporations do. And they don't do it for nothing. But no

101

country has honest politicians. All the legislation in the world won't stop man's inherent greed."

"But don't Americans care that these corporations utilize inhumane working conditions and keep ruthless dictators in power?"

"People rarely see things unless they are right in front of them. For the most part, I don't think they care, either. It's just how things are. Everywhere, not just the United States. Most people have enough problems in their own lives, it's hard for them to care about babies in China or single mothers in the Sudan. Their wife is cheating on them, they just lost their job, their daughter is pregnant, their son is on drugs. They don't have time to worry about the destruction of the rain forest or another civil war in the Congo. They're happy enough if they have a job and their kids remain in school. Don't get me wrong, I think most people are good, but they have short attention spans for misery. People get behind saving the polar bears or curing AIDS for a while, but when the problem doesn't go away or feels like it never will, they want to turn to something easier."

"Democracy doesn't work if the people don't care what is going on. If they don't know what they're voting for."

"You're right. And democracy's power is fading. Governments won't run the future, corporations will. And corporations are answerable to no one. CEO's rarely keep their jobs for more than a couple of years. Profit is their only motive. They'll destroy a protected forest if the profit exceeds the environmental fine. People don't invest in the stock market to support humane causes, they want the biggest return on their money. Otherwise they'd buy a new car or a bigger house. So corporations have one and only motivation: to show profit. If they don't, investors spend their money elsewhere. More and more companies are hiring temporary employees without medical or holiday benefits, using employment at will contracts, firing long term employees for cheaper, younger ones… Nothing's personal anymore. All that matters is making more money."

"So we can own bigger houses, faster cars, flashier clothing. We buy what television and movies and magazines have programmed us to want. And we need to work harder and longer to get these things. And we treat each other worse because of it. I don't think anyone is happier because they own a Mercedes instead of a Toyota. And still the people in India starve. Because no one wants to sacrifice the Mercedes for the Toyota to help those less fortunate."

I nodded. "Survival of the fittest. It's a cruel world. If you want anything in this life, you've got to get it for yourself. You can't expect help from others."

"You sound like you've given up."

"I just don't think you can change people's minds. I think it takes a lifetime to make a small difference. Call me selfish, but I can't live my life as a Mother Theresa or Mahatma Gandhi. I have to live for myself. But I do what I can. Help when I can. It's not much, I know, but at least I try."

"I guess that's all you can do. But I still think Americans are more out of touch with the consequences of their actions abroad than most. You're such a violent, unforgiving people. Everyone owns guns."

"They actually hand us one at the border when we leave the country. Tell us to watch out for those war-mongering Dutch people." I smiled.

She smiled back. "You joke, but murder is glamorized on your television shows and in your movies until people are anesthetized to it. The reality, the finality of it is lost somehow. And you still have the death penalty which most of Europe has outlawed as inhumane and cruel."

"I actually agree with the death penalty."

"But it's conclusively proven that the death penalty does not discourage crime and is certainly no cure."

"I don't care about discouraging crime. I believe in punishment. An eye for an eye. If someone deprives you of your loved one, why should they be entitled to live a long, fruitful life, even in prison? They didn't give their victims that choice. Life is the most precious thing we get and we only get one."

"Most criminals are victims of their environment. They come from violent homes and often were molested as children. We can't blame them for their crimes. If you were in their same position, you might commit the same crimes."

"So who do we blame? Lots of people must deal with hardships and adversity. I'm tired of people not taking responsibility for their actions. People blame television, their parents, an ex-lover for their problems. Anyone but themselves. Most people, except those truly sick in the head, and you're not going to convince me every criminal is, at one point make a cognizant decision to do wrong, to go against their innate sense of what is right and what isn't. They choose themselves over society. Yes, your mother beat you and your father molested you, but you still knew it was wrong when you shot your girlfriend for cheating on you. You chose the first time you used the needle. You chose to surrender and must pay the consequences. Is it my responsibility if someone chooses to give up on life? Because I chose to be a good citizen, should I have to carry the weight of those who chose a criminal path? You must have the strength to not perpetuate the wrong done to you. Yes, it's hard to do something different when all your friends are joining gangs, committing crimes, but it is possible to quit. Many people have. We must stop making excuses for the weak minded criminals and force them to face their difficulties without committing more crimes. Turn the other cheek, I guess. If you steal something as precious as life from someone, what right have you to its privileges and rewards? If you don't respect the rules of a society, the human race, can you be allowed to pollute it?"

"But where does this eye for an eye stop? If you can't forgive, you end up with another Palestine, another Bosnia. World War Two was a product of Europe not forgiving Germany for World War One." She looked out of the window. "The next town is my stop. I'll explain to the train conductor what happened to your pass. Where are you going?"

"Amsterdam."

"I'll be back." She left the compartment. When she returned two minutes later, she said, "It's no problem." She stuck out her hand. "It was funny to have met you."

I shook her hand. "Likewise. And thank you."

"Good luck." And then she was gone. But I didn't want her to be.

I turned to the window and noticed for the first time the dark windmills spinning in the brilliant sunlight among waves of endless grass unfurling across the plain. Beneath straw hats, weary-eyed farmers driving tractors along rows of tilled brown earth watched us pass. Women in bright skirts rode bicycles over winding country roads lined with beech and ash. A peaceful place: Holland.

My successes with women number a torrid three-day love affair with a visiting distant cousin from North Dakota at the age of four which ended with unfulfilled suicide pacts and long bouts of gushing tears as her tyrannical parents tore us apart by returning to Bismarck, a markedly feisty Fedex delivery woman who amorously assaulted me delivering blue curtain rings to my parents one summer afternoon in 1986, and Belinda.

I was inept, fumbled my words, sweated profusely, lacked confidence. Drinking helped my confidence while harming my elocution, but I rarely got beyond introductions and never got a chance to spout my well-rehearsed line of: "Come on, you can go out with an accountant. Something to tell the grandkids about. They'll say, *Really, Grandma? You were so brave.* Epics shall recount your courage, passed down by word of mouth from one generation to the next. Moreover, I promise not to sing and only do one dance number: a little Swan Lake ballet bit over in no time at all. The abridged version. Three, four hours, tops. You don't even have to laugh at my witty repartee."

Once I actually got to ask: "You have done me a disservice, fair lady. Capturing my heart with the luminous aspect of your eye and your oh-so-enchanting smile. Could I contract a reverse repurchase agreement for liquid consideration, that is: may I buy it back with a drink?" But she had a dying grandmother to attend to or a boyfriend living in Greenland spying on penguins for the Secret Service, I forget which. She'd only stepped out to the dance club on a Saturday night for a minute to get some air.

I really liked: "Infuse my tortured soul with your unfettered joy. Become my beacon of bliss on this abbreviated path of darkness called life. Accompany my enamored soul for victuals this Friday next." but she didn't.

So, after three months of trying the Los Angeles bars, I gave up. I went to movie matinees on the weekend and read books. Then work took over my life.

I wanted to say all these things but they didn't let me. Be my girlfriend. Let me love you. Adore you. Feed you candlelit dinners for two. Rub your aching feet, serve you soothing cups of chamomile tea and bring you bouquets of freshly cut, long stemmed roses. But only was met with looks of "I'd rather be shot, stabbed, drawn and quartered than talk to you."

"Sorry, but I heard you speaking with that girl. Do you mind if I tag along with you to Amsterdam? I always seem to get robbed there on my own." Curly brown hair framed thick lips, a large sunburnt nose and dull black eyes struggling to stay open. He wore a leather vest, a bright red shirt and blue jeans ripped at the knees.

"Always? How many times have you been robbed?"

"Just four, but it's like a big pain in the ass. I keep having to get a new passport and the embassy doesn't believe me and all this shit."

"Just four?"

He counted on his fingers to make sure. "Just four."

"But how did you get robbed?"

"Oh, always at gunpoint."

"Jesus. Is Amsterdam that dangerous?" I envisioned masked men greeting me at the train station with bayoneted sub-machine guns and demanding my dirty underwear and half-empty tube of toothpaste. Not a pleasant thought. Some of my underwear I was quite fond of.

"Yeah, well, yeah. Fucking treacherous, man."

"But then why do you keep returning?"

"For the smoke, man."

I was obviously dealing with someone on the highest echelon of the evolutionary ladder. "How exactly did you get robbed?"

"I told you, man. At gunpoint. All four times. Well, three of them. The other time I'm not too sure. I was on acid."

"But were you in the hostel, outside the train station, wandering a bad neighborhood?"

"The first time I was a bit drunk. I'd just gone out for a few quiet ones, you know. Well, maybe more than a few, but can't a man have a drink without fearing for his life? I ask you truly, what is the world coming to? I probably shouldn't have walked home alone, it being four in the morning... Like six guys with guns started chasing me. One even had a bazooka, I think. So I had to give them my money."

Don't laugh. Don't laugh. "And the second time?"

"Well, I was kinda high. But still—"

"And the third?"

"That time I admit I was just stupid... Dangerous fucking city Amsterdam. Gotta constantly watch yourself. Let your guard down and they can sense it. Smell weakness, they pounce. The fucking Dutch are nothing but a bunch of fucking thieves."

As the train was rather full of Dutch passengers, I tried a new subject, "You came from Paris?"

"Yeah."

"You sound disappointed. Get robbed there, too?"

"Yeah, I mean, no. I wasn't robbed. But there's not much to see in Paris. I went to the Ferrari dealership. That was cool. But other than that, I needed to get out after a couple of hours."

Thankfully the Amsterdam train station was only five minutes away.

When we discovered we'd left it going the wrong direction, my companion said, "What kind of fucking country are we in? Why don't the signs just say in English which is the exit and which is the entrance? I don't speak Dutch, ninety-nine percent of the world doesn't speak Dutch. Who can read those signs? The Dutch are so fucking stupid."

Three point one seconds later, I lost him. I turned around and he was gone. I didn't mind.

A chorus of "Marijuana, cocaine, heroin" from street touts followed me through a labyrinth of coffee shops crowded with wasted American tourists. I kept a firm hand on my wallet and feared for my dirty underwear.

The hostel was a beautiful old building facing a canal. "Do you have any beds available?"

"Yes. Please register in here... You're American? You should be proud of your heritage."

"I am, thank you."

"I mean what I say. You live in a very great country. I remember when your army liberated my village during World War Two. They saved us. The Nazis were horrible. Your country saved us."

As I ascended the stairs, I decided to go out and get drunk. Fuck the Eurail pass.

I stepped inside the hostel room and there he was: ashen face, floppy blonde hair damp across his forehead, one hand clutching his stomach. Tall and ridiculously thin. Little did I know then that he would change my life. "Are you all right?" I asked.

"Just a bit of food poisoning, I think. Been shitting all day."

"Sorry to hear it. You from Canada?"

"Vancouver. States?"

"Yeah. You're reading *Catch-22*. Best fucking book ever written."

"I like it."

"Look, I was gonna go out now..."

"I'd better not. Don't think any girl would touch me right now. I smell like pooh."

I laughed. "See you tomorrow."

"Uh, maybe I'll have one beer with you. Maybe help clean me out. I've been sitting here all day."

In the lobby, my friend from the train was checking in. "Dude, that was so uncool ditching me like that."

"I didn't ditch you. I turned around and you were gone... Why are you covered in garbage?"

A banana peel hung from the back of his collar and mustard colored spaghetti decorated his hair. "I almost got robbed again. I told you to watch out for me."

"What happened?"

"This guy offered me some smoke for a real good price and led me into this sidestreet. His buddy was there with a machete. Not just a knife, a fucking machete. I ran, but they chased me and I hid in a garbage can to escape. I could have been killed."

"Dude, that sucks. Try waiting five minutes next time and buying your drugs in a coffee shop." I walked out and the Canadian followed me.

"You traveling around Europe?" he asked me.

"I was. Not sure any more. I lost my Eurail pass this morning."

"Lost it?"

"I don't want to talk about it. What are you doing?"

"Working on my history doctorate. I'm on my way to Prague to read some of the original documents and learn Czech. But first I thought I'd have some fun... Oh, no."

"What?"

"I gotta go."

"What about that Lord of the Burgers?"

"I have a travel motto: always shit someplace nice."

The Canadian darted into a five star restaurant on our right. White tablecloths, piano music and a maitre d' wearing a tuxedo. Shoving bus boys, brain surgeons and tax attorneys left and right, he made straight for the restrooms through the heart of the dining room. "Sir, you can't—"

I stood behind, laughing.

"Would the gentleman like a table for dinner?"

"No ingles."

"The gentleman must be mistaken. I overheard him speaking to his friend in English."

"I'm just waiting for my friend."

"I could give the gentleman a table where he could wait for his friend more comfortably."

"The gentleman would rather wait for his friend."

"Would the gentleman like a cocktail while he waits?"

"No, thank you. The gentleman will just wait."

"Maybe just a Coca-Cola? Isn't that what all Americans drink, i.e. the proverbial beverage of choice?"

"No and no."

"The gentleman is aware that the restrooms are for restaurant patrons only? This is not one of your McDonald's or Burger Kings, you know."

"Really? You don't serve Big Macs here?"

"Nor Whoppers, nor French fries, nor milkshakes."

"So the food sucks?"

"If the gentleman wishes not to partake in the splendid cuisine served in this fine dining establishment, the gentleman is kindly requested to vacate the premises. Immediately. Forthwith and without delay."

The Canadian emerged from the restroom and smiled in my direction. Three steps later, he quit smiling and retreated at a run clutching his stomach.

"The gentleman is not sure he completely understands."

"Leave. Now."

"What are you saying exactly?"

The upper lip of the maitre d' quivered but his eyes twinkled with delight. He'd found his arch-nemesis: me. "Brom, Brecht!"

"What do you mean the food poisoning wasn't your fault? Look at those cockroaches! And there goes another rat—"

Onto the pavement was I deposited with an unpleasant kick in the backside and a huge grin on my face.

Five minutes later, I heard another voice inside the restaurant, "Unhand me, sirs. Can a man not shit in peace? Have you no sense of decency, of common courtesy, no compassion?" The Canadian tumbled into the street beside me.

"Hello."

"I see you've been causing mischief, mayhem and twelve types of trouble in my absence."

"I got bored. Did you get to finish?"

"Actually, it was quite funny. Them being trapped outside the stall while I blasted away. I think one died of gas asphyxiation."

"Yeah, an ambulance passed by earlier."

"I don't think I'm up for the drink."

"Tomorrow then."

Back from my morning shower, I noticed my friend from the previous day's train occupying a bed adjacent to mine. Cradling an empty bottle of vodka, he was passed out on top of his sheets with his money scattered everywhere.

I told the girl standing nearby: "He said he's been robbed just four times."

She laughed and then said with an Australian accent, "Yeah, well, I've been robbed seven." Slender with shoulder length brown hair and a feline face. Piercing blue eyes and wide red lips. A small diamond nose stud. Not tall, but nice. Very nice.

"Are you going for the world record?"

"Keep your fingers crossed."

"How does that work exactly? Seven times? Is Amsterdam really so dangerous?"

"Every three weeks I'm robbed. You can set your watch by it. And it's mostly from other travelers, people I've been hanging out with. You have some laughs with people, do stuff together, you think you can trust 'em. And then they rob you. I didn't mind the Panamanian pickpocket, he was clever,
110

he did it with style. But the others…" She shrugged. "I think what freaks me out more than anything is the thought of someone wearing my stolen dirty underwear. Or even worse: later emailing me photos of him wearing it."

"And having to shop for all new clothes, trying on shoes and everything was really rough, right? Don't girls hate that?"

She smiled. "Exceedingly rough."

"What are you doing today? I mean, besides getting mugged, of course."

"That's not until after lunch. Before then, I'm pretty free."

"Want to go to a museum?"

"Why not?"

"I'm Peter. Peter Pollack."

"Emilia Emu."

"Like your national bird."

"You know why it's our national bird? Because it can only move forwards, not backwards. Like me." She smiled. "Actually I saw one move backwards once. And it wasn't an ostrich or a nandu, so don't go there."

"I wasn't going to and I'm totally not even thinking about possibly lying regarding such a course of action."

Fifteen minutes later we were walking along the canals to the Rijksmuseum. "So you're traveling, Emilia?"

"But I'm kind of stranded now. Need to earn some money. Getting robbed constantly hasn't helped my budget much."

"I can imagine. What do your parents say when you tell them you've been robbed again? And again? And again?"

"At first, my mum freaked out and wanted me to come home immediately. I think she knows I can handle it now. The last time I told her, she let out a long, loooonnng sigh and then finally said, *Again?* She never asks for details anymore, just where to send the money. Says she knows all the credit card company and bank phone numbers by heart now. American Express refuses to sell me any more travelers' cheques. I've been blacklisted. By American Express. Can you believe it?"

"The shame, the disgrace. You've got some nerve showing your face in public and how you live with yourself has got me completely and utterly flabbergasted."

"I think I've spent half of my trip in police stations and the other half waiting for money. Wanna hear something gross?"

"Lay it on me, baby."

"In Nicaragua, I ran out of money. All I had for the weekend was enough to buy a giant box of macaroni and cheese from the market. Back at the hotel, I discovered maggots inside. I admit it freely, I cried. My first tears in seven robberies. But I was hungry. So I washed out the maggots and cooked the macaroni anyway."

"That was gross."

"I warned you."

"It's a bit early in our relationship for such startling, personal revelations."

"The price you pay to be in the presence of *She Who Is Emilia*." A smug smile with playful eyes.

"Did you say Nicaragua?"

"I was bartending there. Pretty cool, huh?"

"I bet you've got some stories to tell."

Emilia did *The Nod*. "Oh, yeah."

"So how many fights each night did you break up?"

"On a slow night, it'd be just two or three."

"In between delivering babies and performing Heimlich maneuvers on choking patrons, of course."

"Of course."

"And you had to leave because you were scaring off all of the clientele?"

"I swear I thought he was picking up that beer bottle not to drink it, but to bludgeon the man next to him. Drink beer in a bar? Come on!"

"Right. What's he complaining about? His arm will heal in a couple of months."

"And that limp? There are people without legs, for Christ's sake!"

"But you are sorry about chewing off his ear. You have to admit you got a bit carried away on that one."

"Now look who's being gross."

"Never ever ever. Ever."

"Keep that up and people will think you repeat yourself."

"Never ever ever."

"Ever?"

"Yep."

The museum.

"How many?"

"Two, please."

"Twenty-five guilders."

"Student discount?"

"No."

"Senior discount?"

"You are too young, do not be foolish."

"Foolish discount?"

Inside, Emilia handed me her share of the money.

We wandered among the Rembrandts and Vermeers.

"The pear doesn't seem real to me."

"That guy looks depressed."

"Wife put a knife in his back."

"*Now* the painting makes sense."

An hour later, Emilia said, "I want to ask you something."

"Absolutely not."

"What do you think about sharing your toothbrush? Let's say a girl has just spent the night at your house. Not having hers, she wants to use your toothbrush in the morning. Do you let her?"

Was she asking what I think she was asking? "Of course. You?"

"Totally. I mean, you've just shared the most intimate of intimacies with that person. How can you tell her, *I don't want you using my toothbrush*? It's unconscionable."

"Indisputably."

"I had this boyfriend in Costa Rica. He wasn't really my boyfriend, but we were dating for a while. Anyway, he wouldn't let me use his toothbrush. I didn't like that."

"So you killed him."

"Well, he was a bit stupid. It's all right to the kill the stupid, right?"

"The ugly as well."

"For sure. And don't even get me started on the crippled."

"Waste of space. Black people as well."

"Indians, too. And Seventh Day Adventists." We both smiled. "Oh, and I almost forgot. Accountants. Exterminate 'em all."

"Watch it."

"You're an accountant? I'm sorry. I truly am. From the bottom of my black, uncaring heart."

"Just don't let it happen again."

"And let me tell you something else. The Latin lover thing. It's a myth."

"Bad?"

"Oh, yeah."

"Have you considered giving pre-sex briefings? You know, hang a poster of yourself naked on the bedroom wall. Then, using a pointer, say *I want you to hit here and here and certainly don't neglect this area*. Afterwards, even before the cigarette, present a post-coital wrap up. *Okay, you've still got to work on this bit. But this was much better.* Use constructive criticism, of course. Always tell him he did something right."

"That's an excellent idea."

114

"Do you want to go to another museum?"

"I'm a bit museum-ed out. Especially at ten dollars Australian a pop. But I've been wanting to rent a bicycle ever since I got here. Join me? They rent them back at the hostel."

We left the museum for the street outside.

"I was thinking," I said.

"Dangerous."

"They should make a movie about you. You're the polar opposite of Butch Cassidy and the Sundance Kid. They went to all these different countries and robbed people. You went to all these different places and got robbed. In the last act of the movie as you tried to get home with all your belongings, you'd be victimized by little old ladies, blind children, nuns. Even the airline stewardess on your flight home would short change you for your drinks."

She laughed and then said, "Travel six months in Central America and see how well you do. Where are you headed next, by the way?"

"I'm not sure, actually. Yesterday I lost my Eurail pass and now I'm a bit stranded."

"You weren't robbed by any chance?"

"I don't want to talk about it. But I wasn't robbed."

"Sure you were. How much does it cost to replace?"

"Nine hundred eighty-three dollars. And twelve cents."

"You could almost buy a round-the-world plane ticket for that. Mine was only seventeen hundred dollars American. Do you have the money?"

"I guess."

"And the time?"

"Yeah. But—"

"I mean, I don't know what you're looking for on this trip… Europe's nice and all, but to really see how other people live, you must see the Third World. It'll open your eyes. Different cultures, different attitudes. And it's much cheaper to live than here. You should go to Asia or Africa. Europe's like the States. If I were you, that's what I'd do."

"I'll think about it."

"I'll give you the name of a student travel agency here in Amsterdam when we get back to the room."

"Excuse me," a new voice said.

Our accoster was a gaunt black man with haggard eyes and a white beard. He was dressed in filthy rags and a broken brimmed Baltimore Orioles baseball cap. Needle marks lined both of his wiry arms. "I heard you speaking English. I'm American, too."

We walked around him, avoiding his eyes.

"Can you help out a fellow American with a couple of guilders? Dollars, even?"

Emilia hesitated, but when I kept walking, she followed.

"What the fuck is wrong with you?" he shouted, pursuing us.

I turned to him. "I'm sorry, man. I can't do it. I can't help you kill yourself with drugs."

He spat in my face. "Motherfucker," he whispered.

"What the hell?" Emilia held my arm and he ran off.

I wiped my cheek and we continued moving.

The beggar ran to the end of the deserted street and then turned back towards us. "Give me some money, you greedy fuck. Give me some fucking money!" We walked on. At the corner of a new cross street, he grabbed my arm and repeated his demand.

"You've got to be kidding. You just spat on me." I jerked my arm away and he spat at me again.

"You fucking..." I charged with raised fist, intending only to scare him off. He spun from my feint and then suddenly stopped an arm's breadth away. He reached into the back of his trousers with his right hand.

I saw a flash of metal in his hand and then his eyes were looking down the street at an approaching policeman. He turned and ran.

"Why didn't you give him the money?" Emilia asked, her eyes tense.

"My father was an alcoholic..." I shook my head. "I should have."

"He had a knife."

"I know. I'm sorry, Emilia... Do you mind if we sit down for a few

116

minutes?"

"Let's get back to the hostel first."

We walked in silence for a few minutes.

"I warned you about the robberies," Emilia said at the hostel door.

I laughed. "So you did."

"Still feel like renting a bike?"

"Let me just fix my mascara and I'll meet you downstairs in five minutes."

"You'd better. I'm not going anywhere with you looking like that."

"How do I look?"

"Absolutely ravishing, darling."

I blushed. "How sweet of you to say."

"You're sure about these bikes?" I asked. Weighing four tons each, the rusting bicycles were made sometime near the end of the Bronze Age. And I didn't trust their ponderous back pedal brakes.

"We'll be fine. Come on. You've got a map?"

The cobble-stoned streets along the Amsterdam canals made for a bumpy ride. But what was worse and what I was not prepared for was their narrowness. And then ten minutes from the hostel, a white Mercedes Benz with a radiator grille the size of New Jersey hurtled straight at me from the other direction. To my left threatened a drop of six feet to the green canal water. Buildings lined the right. Large black metal stanchions carved a narrow lane for vehicle traffic between pedestrian walkways on both sides of the road. Emilia dodged adroitly between them and I could hear her humming some maddeningly joyful bicycle riding song up ahead. But I couldn't slow down to follow her. Despite screeching horribly, my brakes did not reduce my speed. The Mercedes passed Emilia. Accelerating. I could smell the engine exhaust and see the panic in the woman's face as she realized my mangled remains were going to ruin her car's paint job. Emilia turned up ahead and started shouting at me. I could read the Mercedes license plate number now, but seemed to have no way of stopping it getting closer. This was how I was going to die. Then the horn in the Mercedes sounded and I jerked my arms to the left with all my strength.

I'd made it to a crossroad spanning a bridge. I shouted in relief as I felt the hot breath of the Mercedes on my back. Not thinking, I kept going. At the top of the arching one lane bridge, I saw the black Saab heading right towards me at sixty-three times the speed of light.

I darted through the stanchions on the bridge, jarring the back tire, but narrowly missing the grille of the black Saab. But my front wheel hit the bridge railing and stopped dead. I did not and plummeted into space.

"Amsterdam is not my town," I said three minutes later as I sat dripping next to the canal. I was shaking, but the water wasn't cold.

Emilia laughed with tears in her eyes and touched my arm. "Well, you're never going win the Olympic gold medal with that somersault technique. A five out of ten. At best."

"I know, I know. My arms were all over the place." (Little did we know, such jokes would become hopelessly antiquated with a new gymnastics scoring system.)

"You're okay?" she asked tenderly.

I nodded. "I think I'll go home now."

We collected the bikes. "You don't have to go with me," I said. "I mean, you paid for the bike, you might as well use it."

"I'll walk you back."

After a couple of minutes, I asked, "What do you want to be when you grow up?"

"I'd like to be a travel writer for the Lonely World guidebook."

"How will you submit your expense report?" I held up an imaginary piece of paper to read the tally. "Okay with the taxis. The meals are reasonable. What's this rather large robbery expense?"

She slapped my arm playfully. "Shut up. What do you want to be?"

"Television stuntman is out of the question, isn't it?"

"I reckon."

We crossed the last street and arrived back at the hostel.

"Think I'll get my deposit back?" I asked, shaking the now square front wheel.

118

"I don't know. You scratched paint off the fender. See?"

"Half?"

"Probably two thirds."

"So, you wanna go for a drink tonight?"

Emilia studied my face for a moment. "Do you believe in God?"

"No."

She turned her head away. "See that bench? I had the most spiritual conversation of my life there two nights ago."

Amsterdam was definitely not my town. "And where is he now?"

"His job started today in London. He's got an Australian two year working visa. But I told him I'm not ready to stop traveling yet. I want to see a bit of France and Spain first. But we'll meet again. I know it."

"You've known him long?"

"Just a couple of days actually. We've never even kissed. And he answered the toothbrush question wrong."

"Well, I'll go have a shower."

"See you later."

"I'll be at a bar called Dansen bij Jansen tonight if you want to come by."

"Sounds good. Oh, the name of that travel agent is in the book on my bed if you're interested."

"Thanks."

At nine o'clock, the blonde-haired Canadian from the night before appeared. Emilia had not been back to the dormitory. "Ready for that drink?"

"I was sort of waiting for this girl…"

"You didn't set a time? Always set a time. 'Tis my cardinal rule."

"I did tell her about this bar in the guidebook."

"Let's go, then."

"Well…"

"If she doesn't come back, you waste your night."

I nodded and picked up my jacket.

In the bar.

"What's your name, anyway?"

"John Jay. You?"

"Peter Pollack."

"You ready?"

"For what?"

"The two over there by the pool table – probably German – or the English birds in that corner – they look easy. Which should we take?"

"Well…"

"Look, if your friend shows up, it's not hard to extricate yourself. In the meantime, it's just talking."

"Let's take the English."

He smiled. "Always remember and never forget, no one gets out alive. But first a bit of the liquid courage."

John ordered two shots of peach schnapps.

"Peach schnapps?"

"It's my national drink. Come on, for luck."

We drank. I turned towards the girls.

John said, "We still need one for courage."

"We just had one for courage."

"That one was for luck. This will be for courage."

"Right."

"Hello."

John grabbed a man passing the table. "Have you ladies met my friend Ludwig? He's a heroin addict. I'm helping him quit."

"My name is Richard."

"Observe how his affliction has affected even the memory of his name. Heartfelt sadness consumes me. This is Peter. He's a drug dealer. He's trying to sell Ludwig more drugs. We're sworn enemies. To the death. And beyond. I hate him. I hate you."

"I'm sort of indifferent," I replied.

"You're a terrible man, terrible. Where are you lovely ladies from?"

"London. You're Americans?"

"Don't insult me. I come from The Great Land. I'm Canadian, for fuck's sake. He's American. Another reason why I hate him. By the way, I hate you."

"I'm sort of indifferent."

"Where are you from, Richard?" Inexplicably, Richard hadn't left. Behind a frothy pint was an enormous grin.

"I'm from Wales."

"Beautiful country Wales." John grabbed the next guy to pass by. "This is…"

"Douglas David Drake."

"Douglas David Drake. He's a heroin addict as well. I think, deep down inside, we're all heroin addicts. Even those who aren't, are. You know what I mean? Hey, look over there!" John pointed to the left and turned his head sharply to the right. "They're heroin addicts as well."

The English girls were laughing. "What's your name?"

"John. Most people call me John."

"We'll call you John then."

"Not very original."

"What are you doing in Amsterdam, John?"

"It's funny you should ask that. Peter and I were just discussing something completely different. You see, we work together."

"When you aren't hating each other."

"That's just a hobby. The rest of the time... Should we tell them, Peter?"

"I'm sort of indifferent."

"Can he say anything but *I'm sort of indifferent?*"

"Yes," I said.

The girls laughed.

"So we work together as..." John started.

And I finished, "Janitors for the CIA."

"Right. I'd nearly forgotten. It seems so long ago."

"Yesterday by my last reckoning."

"Right, long ago. An era lost to the ineluctable march of time peopled by a simpler, gentler generation not preoccupied by the superficiality of physical beauty or intent on the accumulation of wealth. When love of family and your fellow man weren't just catch phrases but tenets you lived by."

"Can Canadians work for the CIA?"

"That's top secret, highly confidential information."

"You could tell us, but you'd have to kill us?"

John sighed with admiration. "Brains and beauty."

I said, "We're going to need more schnapps."

"Indubitably so. Ladies?"

"What he said. Tenfold. Please."

"I'll get them. While I'm gone, explain to our lovely companions how messy secret agents are and how hard it is to clean up after them and all."

As I stood waiting to be served, a tall Australian with a dirty, broken wide-brimmed hat that drooped over his eyes said to me, "Great fun here, isn't it? Every night I try to get away from it and every night I find myself down here getting pissed out of my head. Tenth pint already and I'm just getting warmed up. I went to the doctor before I came away and he said, my boy, your liver is fucked. If you don't stop the drink you'll be dead within six months. But I say fuck it, what the hell do I care? No point in coming to Amsterdam if I'm not going to party, is there?" His beer came and he downed half of it. Smacking his lips in appreciation, he confessed, "God, I love this stuff," and disappeared.

Later, I saw him sprawled out on the floor puking into his glass. He regarded the dark liquid for a moment and drank it down. Then he shouted "YOU HAVE NO IDEA WHAT I'M CAPABLE OF!" before opening his trousers and proceeding to urinate on the floor while still lying down.

Much later, I found myself with a lukewarm beer being asked by a gorgeous Canadian girl wearing a brown sweater riddled with holes, "What will you do when you go home?" John and I had been talking to her on and off in between shots of peach schnapps.

"Get a job, I guess."

"You're not afraid of what people will think of you being gone so long?"

"What do I care? This is my life, not theirs. Besides, you've been gone for two years."

"But studying is productive."

Blinded by drunk lust, I plunged on, "Not everything must be done to further your career. What about living life? At the end will having the biggest house or the fastest car matter? I'm doing this trip to see what the world is, to find my place in it. Improving my soul isn't a waste of time."

"But I think we owe something to the world for living here."

"I have contributed. I earned the money which I'm now spending."

"Most people have responsibilities. They can't leave like you."

"Can't or won't? If they chose to have a family, they chose that over traveling. I chose traveling."

"I like having a nice car and wearing expensive clothes. I like good food and ski weekends. I don't feel guilty for that. I'm willing to earn them. I like being a part of a productive community. I don't like feeling lazy."

"I respect your choices. You've got to do what you want with the one life you get. But don't judge me because my choices differ from yours."

I left.

John was at the bar. "What happened with the Canadian girl you were talking to for ages?"

"She kept asking me to sleep with her and her Swedish girlfriend slash lesbian lover Inga, but I told her I had to finish my beer first."

"You were engaged in very serious discussion. I saw you slapping your hand to make your points."

"I was drunk. Am drunk."

"What was with that torn sweater she couldn't fucking shut up about? Buy a new sweater, you pretentious bitch. You were wasting your time with her, she thought she was too good looking."

"How'd you do?"

"I got too drunk. I told one of the English that I was a volunteer fireman. No, I really was one. I told her I once ran into a burning building too late and came out with burning baby all over me. She didn't like that."

"Baffling."

"She was too small anyway. Big girls are easier to get along with, they don't think so much of themselves. When I get to Prague, I'm going to get me a rather large Czech girlfriend who will roll all over me with no inhibitions."

"Possibly she will let you see one of her breasts, and if you're extraordinarily lucky, two."

"And possibly if I'm a good boy and mind my manners, she may let me touch one of them or even rub my face against them like so." He shook his head vigorously from side to side, wiggling his lips exaggeratedly. "One can only dream. But she must be large. Enormous even. Of a weight sufficient to smother a rutting Siberian tiger." Then he conspicuously adjusted the collar of his sweater and cleared his throat. "Time for a song."

"No."

Shaking his head in disappointment at me, John climbed onto the nearest stool and cleared his throat again. Then he began to sing wonderfully off-key as his skinny white legs swayed in a circular motion akin to the spinner on a decrepit washing machine:

Won't you be my Czechoslovakian lover?

Against your sweet bosom I hope to smother.

You're a large girl, there's no denying

But without your love I'd just be dying.

A roar of apathetic applause greeted John as he stepped down from the bar. He bowed deeply to each of the pub's four corners while repeating to each: "Thank you very little."

"We're in Holland, you know."

"I'm practicing for Prague. First thing I do when I get there is translate it into Czech."

"Lovely."

"Did your friend ever show up?"

"No."

When I woke up in the morning, Emilia's bed was empty. I never saw her again.

Sigmond scowled up from his desk. "What do you want?" He looked back down.

"I think this is wrong, Sigmond."

"Impossible. It's been reviewed and reviewed and reviewed. A snot nose like you comes along and thinks he can find a mistake after ten minutes. Impossible." Sigmond put down his pen and looked back up. With a gesture of his hand: "Show me."

I laid my spreadsheet in front of him. "I was looking at this purchase price allocation for Cocks and Swallows. One million dollars was allocated to Class III when it should have been allocated to Class V. It was capitalized as equipment and depreciated when it should have been allocated to goodwill and never deducted. All the other proportions are right, but one million dollars was arbitrarily added to machinery and equipment."

"Can I have my pen back, please?"

I looked down at my hand. "Sorry. They count them."

"I know." Sigmond studied the sheet for a moment. Then he tore through the file for five minutes. "You're right."

"So the returns must be amended."

"No. The Internal Revenue Service won't find the mistake. The calculation is too complex. Prepare the spreadsheet for the auditors like this. We're not lying, but we're not showing it to them, either."

"That's five hundred thousand dollars in tax."

"No, the company was resold four years later. The only effect is accelerating the deduction. So they would owe penalties and interest on four years' depreciation of five hundred thousand dollars. Who do you think would end up paying it? Net, Block and Tackle, that's who. No, we make it go away. I'll tell Barrington, but no one else. You did good, Peter."

The next day Sigmond invited me to lunch for the first time ever. As I swallowed the first bite of my chicken sandwich, I looked up to see Sigmond had finished his T-bone steak and assorted steamed vegetables in twenty-three seconds flat. His plate was entirely clean, none of the meat remained, no gristle, no fat. He'd even eaten the bone.

"Peter, we're sending you to Century City."

"Oh?"

"Do you want to be a general in this fucking army? Lead troops into battle, determine how and when to decimate the enemy with ruthless intent?"

"What enemy?"

"Any who stand in your way. Do you wish to eviscerate them entirely?"

"Uh, I guess."

"What kind of fucking enthusiasm is that? To be happy in this life, my worthless accounting peon, one must embrace what little it offers. One does not enjoy the succors of our brief, harsh existence by guessing half-heartedly, but by acting with vigorous intent. Achieve with ardor."

"All right."

"Just all right?"

"Fucking all right. Yeah." I raised a fist half-heartedly.

Sigmond stared into my eyes. Ten seconds passed. Twenty seconds passed. Thirty.

I tried the fist again.

"Can I trust you, Peter?"

"Yeah."

Sigmond shook his head sadly. "This is what I've fucking got to deal with… All right. But if you fuck this up, I will eat you alive. You understand me? I will fucking hunt you down and rip out your fucking heart through your asshole."

I said nothing.

More silence on his part. Then: "Do you have a girlfriend, Peter? Well, a nice lady named Julie works there. She's the controller for this client. Maybe she'll roll all over you if you're nice to her. Be nice to her. Very nice. Kiss her ass. Literally, if necessary. It's a big ass, but it's a nice ass. Comes with nice tits. This is very important. They're watching you, giving you your chance. Don't blow it."

"What's the client?"

"Veronica's Secret. The lingerie company."

I'd died and gone to accounting heaven.

The phone rang at work. "Pollack."

"Hello there."

"Hello, Pamela."

"Don't call me that."

"Why not? It's your name."

"Because I'm your mother. I'm not going to respond if you don't address me as such. I earned the title. Eight hours of labor. Eight."

"Last time it was seven, Mom."

"Don't try to tell me. I was there, remember?"

"So was I."

"So you were. For nine hours. Do you want to come to dinner at my mother's house on Friday?"

"Will I know anyone there?"

"One or two people. Your father, me, your grandmother, your sister."

"The names sound vaguely familiar…"

"Dinner's at seven."

"Will the food be good?"

"Goodbye, dear."

Sigmond was standing over me. "Was that your mommy?"

"Don't fuck with my family, Sigmond."

He regarded me silently for a few moments. "About this M-1 schedule…"

My grandmother answered the door. Her hair was pink that week. She was a short woman with enormous glasses that dwarfed her pursed lips and artificially over-blushed cheeks. "Hello, Petra."

"Don't call me that. I'm your grandmother."

"Oh, he's just being a pill," my mother said from behind. "Hello, dear." I hugged her. My mother had been very slender when she was my age but with time she resembled my grandmother more and more. Despite running a mile every day, she was developing a belly and her once very thick dark red hair was thinning. But her vibrant green eyes and ubiquitous smile remained. "I cashed your check by the way. Regardless." She stuck her tongue out.

Whenever I owed my mother money, I would complete the memo section to mess with her. Examples included: thermonuclear missile warheads, huge heaping blocks of uncut brown heroin, mountain gorilla porn, massage services.

Behind my mother and grandmother, I could see my sister and father sitting at the dining table in the kitchen. My father had found a new

128

direction to comb his seven pieces of black hair across his ever-increasing bald spot and was enthusiastically demonstrating this latest technique to my sister.

"Well, come on in and close the door. We don't live in a barn. You can say hello with the door closed. And make sure to lock it. Always lock the door."

"We're going to be right in the dining room, Grandma."

"You never know what might happen. This is the big bad city, this isn't the mountains where everyone lives with the bears and the raccoons. There are crooks here. They steal or worse."

"Okay, Grandma."

"The deadbolt, too. And the bar."

"Yes, Grandma."

"Well, hurry up. The food's getting cold. We've been waiting forty-five minutes for you."

"Mom said come at seven. It is seven oh two."

"Sit down, sit down."

"I'm sitting. Hi, Pen. Hi, Dad."

My dad grunted back. He was eating.

My grandmother said to me, "Why are you always smelling the food? That's the most disgusting thing I've ever seen."

"To check for poison, Petra."

"Now why would I want to poison you?"

"To steal my car."

"That's the most ridiculous thing I ever heard. Why would I want your car when I have a perfectly fine car of my own?"

"Because you're greedy."

"Honestly, Peter, sometimes I don't think your jokes are in the least bit funny."

"What do you want to be when you grow up, Petra?"

"I'm already grown up. And quit calling me Petra. I'm your

grandmother."

"He's just being ornery, Mother. He calls me Pamela and I went through ten hours of labor bringing him into the world."

"It keeps getting longer, Mom."

"Don't argue with me. I'm your mother."

"I hope that one day you can forgive me, maybe not today and maybe not tomorrow, but soon, completely, and to the fullest extent possible."

"I'll think about it. Hard. And I can be bribed. With flowers or a nice dress. But let me pick out the dress."

"Have some more potatoes, Paul," my grandmother said and ladled a giant spoonful onto his plate. "You're running low on salad, Penelope. You're nothing but skin and bones, child. Pamela, you need more gravy. And don't tell me anything ridiculous like you're on a diet. You look perfectly fine."

"Beware the wrath of the food police," my sister Penelope said, smiling. The athlete of the family with long brown hair, a freckled nose and my mother's green eyes, she was captain of her college softball and basketball teams despite her being only five feet two inches tall.

"Violence unfettered and wanton destruction shall be their wont who defies she who ladles," I added.

"Trouble with a capital *T*."

"Honestly. In my day, children were more respectful towards their parents."

"They're just teasing you, Mom."

"So how are they treating you over there?" my dad asked me.

"Long hours, lots of yelling, you know how it is. Next week I'm working in the Century City office."

"Did I ever tell you my story about Century City?"

My mother, grandmother and sister all said in unison, "Oh, no."

"You didn't," I said, ignoring them.

"Have you ever been to the Avenue of the Stars? I think I was one of the first environmentalist persons or people—whatever you call them—maybe

130

you know what they call them… One day I was driving home from the beach, this was back when I lived in Westwood, and I had my towel. It was a beach towel—I think it was blue or maybe white and it was spring and there were these birds I had to move. They were gonna get run over and I had to save them—"

"Dad—"

"Paul—"

"I was late for class and got yelled at, I think. I tried to gather the birds in the towel and carry them… A mother and her babies, all these little ones. Where was it—a field. On the other side of a hill. They didn't want to go, they kept running away. But I got them, I got them all even though I was late for class and they kept running back into the road… I saved them. Your father was a hero. You didn't know that, did you?"

Later, after being lectured for not finishing all sixteen of the rolls (my sister tried and her stomach exploded all over the ceiling in a rainbow of reds, oranges and yellows—it was gross), my father and I sat on the porch watching the Santa Monica traffic rocket by (we had a better chance to see a wild panda bear lumber by than a brake light in that city). "Did I show you my new socks?" he said with a mischievous grin.

"Dad, I'm not happy."

"Why?"

"The job."

"I don't know. There's all this talk today about liking your job. How many people like their job? You just do it, that's all. You have to, you need money, so you do it. That's life. So they give you a hard time, everybody gives you a hard time. People are crazy everywhere. I don't know. You can't wait for the ideal life to come along, you gotta do something. So you make do with what you get."

"But you hate your job."

"What does it matter?"

"Why did you become a lawyer?"

"You know why. At the time, law school exempted me from going to Vietnam. And when that wouldn't work anymore I joined the Peace Corps. Then I married your mother and I needed money. And then you and your sister came along. I always needed money."

"But why didn't you ever change jobs?"

"Jobs are scarce to come by and I had a family to support. I don't know. Having a job I loved wasn't so important to me."

"But I've got no social life. I'm not meeting anybody."

"Don't worry about it. Things will work out."

The Dansen bij Jansen, Night Two. "The Germans are back," I told John. I'd spent the day at the Van Gogh museum and sunning myself in Vondelpark.

"Which do you want?"

"I'll take the black haired one."

"She's all right. A bit strange looking, but then look at you."

"How could any man be so beautiful?"

"I say that to myself in the mirror every morning."

"You've got a picture of me taped to your mirror?"

Beer. Schnapps. "No one gets out alive?"

"No one gets out alive."

"Hello, ladies."

"What's your name?" she asked.

Why not? "My name's Superman. But most people call me Clark Kent."

"You're *The Superman*?"

"The one and only. Man of steel and all that."

She swayed in her seat and eyed me suspiciously. "If you're Superman, where's your cape?"

"Dry cleaners. I may be able to leap tall buildings in a single bound, but I'm a messy eater."

"I've seen your movie."

"Yeah, its slapdash depiction of my superhuman abilities is okay, though, nowhere near comprehensive. However, the actor who played me wasn't nearly handsome enough despite his topping People Magazine's list of the Fifty Most Beautiful People on the Planet."

"Is it hard being Superman?"

"The fame of super heroism isn't all it's cracked up to be. Saving the world is grueling work, sometimes."

"Stressful?"

"Absolutely. If all else fails, I'm the last defense against global destruction. And people aren't too forgiving if I just don't feel up to saving the world that day. Hung over, stomach flu, rain or shine or nuclear storm, I gotta punch that timecard. A lot of people depend on me... And bad guys are always trying to kill me so they can carry out their sinister plans of world domination. They know they won't succeed, but they keep at it all the same. Gets tiresome after a while."

"I can imagine."

"And I've got to wear those tights no matter how cold it gets. Always the same tights with the same colors. And sometimes, those colors clash, baby."

"What about that Lois Lane chick? You guys still going out?"

"I don't want to talk about it."

She reached over and took my beer. Then she sat on my knee. "Does Superman have a kiss for me?"

As I leaned in to oblige her, she stumbled backwards and I kissed her chin. It was a nice chin, I suppose, as chins go.

She finished my beer. "The mouth is a bit higher."

"I noticed."

"You're cute," she said and grabbed my nose to tweak it.

My nose started bleeding. She was gone faster than a speeding bullet.

So ended my career as a superhero.

Much later, at the bar, John turned to me with bleary eyes and said: "You need guidance, young man. Tutelage in the ways of lechery. Lessons in love. Lesson the first is of the most utmost importance. Don't give a shit. Say whatever comes to your head, sink or swim. Be yourself. Don't try to be who you think they want you to be because it's a waste of fucking time. They will always detect your lies. You could be like me and lie all of the time, but only if that is who you are. Do not attempt to be me for I am me and me am I. Everyone else is a mere imitator, a false counterfeit charlatan. I always know I'm doomed when I look down and see one hand slapping the other to make my point. I'm trying too hard. Make them laugh. Any idiot can talk about starving children in Africa or the shrinking rainforest. Lesson the second: always set a time to meet. Women are vague, imprecise creatures, worthy of our love, yes, but incapable of punctuality. Commit them to a meeting and if they show, you know they are interested. Lesson the third will be a phrase that will change your life. It cuts through the bullshit and does so in a nice, polite way. You needed it tonight with your German girl. *Come outside, we have issues to discuss.* But don't overuse it, my friend, or it will be the worst enemy you have."

"It's closing time," the bartender said. He was rather large. Multiple piercings, multiple tattoos, thick sun burnt neck, shaved head, goatee beard and in dire need of lip balm and a manicure. Scary, in other words.

"What about *Come hither and yon and partake in the splendor of my magnificent throbbing cock?*" I asked John.

"Too subtle."

"It's five o'clock in the morning. Go home."

"*Would you care to engage in a rampant sexual frenzy with my lonely personage in the comforting confines of my habitation?*"

"Too much finesse."

Suddenly my stool began shaking as a voice boomed in my ear: "GET THE FUCK OUT!"

"Are you hearing voices?"

"NOW!"

John and I left the pub. Light had just begun to appear as an orange sliver at the horizon. Perfectly puffed clouds dotted a purple sky. The air was clean with the smell of recent rain. "You really told her you were Superman?" John asked from behind me and laughed.

I turned back. "Wow. You're peeing on a church."

"Oh, shit. I didn't know. Sorry."

"Straight to hell shall you go for this sad and grievous crime."

"I swear I didn't know."

"When does the bus come?"

"About six, I think. Find another bar?"

Surprisingly, we weren't successful.

Neither of us could stand up straight on the bus back to the hostel during morning rush hour. A woman in a fur coat holding a small white Maltese (or a Bichon Frise) stared at us with contempt. John began serenading her in French. I stumbled drunkenly from one handrail to the next. The other bus passengers were deathly quiet.

"This is our stop," John said. We both tripped jumping out.

"What were you singing?"

"*I've got a little red crayon in my pocket. Would you like to see it?*"

"You're a sick man."

"Have you got the key?"

"I thought you had it."

"I thought you did."

"The door lady hates us."

"She hates you. I always tell her you forgot the key."

The next evening we started late, not beginning to drink until dark. We forsook the Dansen bij Jansen for the cheaper hostel bar. It was thick with smoke and people when we arrived.

"After you, dear sir."

"Liquid courage?"

"Goes without saying, my inept companion. Bestow bounteous besotting beverages upon our thirst-plagued persons."

Gulp. Gulp. "Another?"

"Oh, yes. And another."

John led the way and with a smile said, "I'll pay you two hundred krowns."

Turning from her two friends, the red-headed girl responded with an Irish brogue: "For what?" Unamused.

"To bathe and bask us blissfully in the exquisite splendor of your peerless beauty by dancing naked on this here table."

Then she laughed. "How much is two hundred krowns?"

"Kingdoms have been bought for less. A veritable fortune in some reaches of this wide, wondrous world fraught with sadness and misery. Peter."

"As your accountant who accompanies you everywhere to aid and abet your any negotiation, I must answer that today's exchange rate translates such a mighty sum to approximately eight dollars of U.S. tender."

Laughter laced her counter-offer of four hundred.

John looked at me. I looked at John. In unison, we cried, "Two hundred!"

"Four hundred!"

"Show pity on a poor wretched soul. People are trying to kill me."

"Who's trying to kill you?"

"Him." Camouflage fatigues, a combat jacket and knee high black leather boots garbed his burly figure beneath a shock of black hair sticking straight up from his melon-like head. Dark, seething eyes above a big, bushy mustache and beard. A Nicaraguan flag embroidered on one arm of his jacket. He sauntered carelessly up to the bar, ordered a bottle of red wine and chugged it down in one long swig. Then he ordered another. As he was bringing the second bottle to his lips, John approached him and asked, "Are you trying to kill me?"

He turned to John with his brooding black eyebrows and asked, "Someone is trying to kill you? Who is trying to kill you? I will kill them!" He smacked his massive open hands together with a clap like unto gunfire. Heads snapped around the room. His head swiveled in our direction. "Are those girls trying to kill you?"

"Hold those proverbial horses. No one's trying to kill me. Chill out and have a drink on me." John desperately signaled the bartender.

136

"Yo soy communista."

"There are no communists left, amigo. It doesn't work."

"What you mean? I am communist."

"I'm sure you are. I'm sorry."

"Every man equal." The Nicaraguan downed his second bottle of wine, spilling much of it in his beard and mustache. His gaze fell on us again. "Who are those girls? I want to meet them. Now."

The unemployed fireman from the Great Land had no choice.

"Everybody, this is…"

"Felipe."

"Felipe, this is…"

"Andrea."

"Andrea." Felipe took her hand as if to kiss it, but instead he bit her. Andrea screamed and tried to pull her hand away. Felipe wouldn't let go. With my help, we managed to pry her free. Felipe fell over the table into the lap of the other two girls. They screamed and tried to push him away. Giggling, he tried to bite their hair.

John and I conferred quickly. "We gotta get him outta here. Fast. This may escalate into an international incident without quick resolution."

John and I each took Felipe by an arm and led him to the bar.

"I want to meet the rest of the girls. Now."

"First a drink, my friend. You wouldn't make us drink alone."

"No, you are my comrades. Somos communistas. Castro vive siempre!"

Felipe was turning his head back to the girls when his peach schnapps came. We turned his head forward and wrapped his fingers around the shot glass. He downed it and smacked his lips loudly. "Yo soy communista." He stumbled from the bar and headed for the door, knocking over two tables and numerous backpackers in the crowded pub. At the door, he stole someone's margarita and downed that, also. He glanced back into the room one last time, his eyes swimming with blood, and left.

On the way up the stairs outside, Felipe crashed into a New Zealander sitting with his girlfriend. "Watch it, man." The Nicaraguan scowled at the couple and stumbled on.

Three minutes later, Felipe reappeared clutching a piece of wood torn off the frame of his bed. He chucked it at the New Zealander's head, missing. "Jesus Christ," the New Zealander shouted, "that guy just chucked a chunk of wood at my head." Felipe stumbled back up the stairs.

Later, at the top of the stairwell, we found the Nicaraguan passed out in a pool of his own vomit with a third bottle of red wine curled in his fist. He was back in the bar the next night.

John woke me in the morning. "Pete, I'm going. This place is becoming too expensive for me. I gotta get to Prague and start on my studying."

I wiped the sleep from my eyes and sat up. "Good luck with getting a large Czech girlfriend and everything."

"Remember: *come outside, we have issues to discuss.*" I laughed. "I'd give you my address, but I'm not sure where I'll be staying."

"And I'll be moving around."

"Take care." We shook hands.

At the travel agent later that day, I bought a round-the-world plane ticket.

A Couple of Wild and Crazy Swedes Rescue Me from the Clutches of the Porn King of Samoa and His Malicious Minions

The following morning I caught a ferry from Amsterdam back to England. Sitting in Vondelpark amid the freshly cut grass and tall green trees in the bright sunshine, I'd asked myself what I would regret not seeing, not doing, if my life ended tomorrow. If I'd had to die on the beaches of Normandy or be slaughtered in the gas chambers at Auschwitz. And the answer was surprisingly simple. It was not to continue my career, but to see the world. From before I could read, it'd been my dream. Not just to visit Europe, but the Himalayas, Machu Picchu, the Serengeti.

Seeing these places was the best way I could think of to honor those who didn't survive to live their own dreams. So I'd bought the airplane ticket around the world. It started and ended in Los Angeles, so that was where I was headed.

Dear Mom and Pop,

I've decided I simply cannot do without a New Zealand T-shirt. So I'm going there. Now.

Love,
Pete

Back in London, I had a day to kill before my flight left back to the States. On a whim, I visited Sir John Soane's Museum near the Holborn Underground station. The three story building was squeezed in amongst similar residences on a tree-lined square. Thinking I had only a residence and not the museum, I tentatively poked my head inside.

A man dressed in a knee length, blue curator's jacket over a droll round belly smiled at me behind thick, magnifying spectacles. Six long black hairs were combed neatly across a wide path of baldness on his dark skinned head.

"Is this the museum?" I asked.

"Come," he said pleasantly. "Relish in the spectacle. Do not be shy, for the shy miss so many of life's pleasures."

He led me into the first room and pointed to a painting on its wall when the tinkle of a small brass bell announced more visitors. The curator popped his head out of the doorway and said: "Excuse me, come in here." A young Australian couple joined me.

"Now, what have we here? An angel, a vision of loveliness. Young love in bloom. And behind them a beautiful wall swathed in ivy. And you think that is all? No, no. Look! A surprise! Another portrait of pulchritude." He reached up and moved the painting aside by means of hinges on its left side, revealing another painting behind. "Methinks I hear others afoot. Ah, yes. Come, come. Join our party. Here is Rome in all its splendor. The ancient haunt of Caesars. But there's much more. This, my friends, my fellow patrons of the arts, is by the painter Henry Howard. It is called *Lear and Cordelia*. It is from a story by someone called William Shakespeare. Perhaps you have heard of our Bard of Avon. His life's story is well dramatized in the motion picture entitled *Shakespeare in Love*.

141

When you return to your country, you should hire it from a video shop. You don't need to go to the theatre, dress up, rent a cab and all these things.

Instead, buy a bottle of wine from the corner shop, perhaps a nice cabernet sauvignon or a merlot, and invite your girlfriend over. Stoke up a warm fire and dim the lights. Snuggle up and make a night of it."

I left an hour later exchanging smiles with the German and Australian couples who'd shared the tour. What most would consider a dismal job: museum curator in a dark, rather cramped museum, this man had turned into a celebration of life. Maybe accounting wasn't so bad, maybe my attitude was.

Afterwards, walking through Hyde Park, I thought of the first time I'd met Belinda.

The night before my first day at Veronica's Secret, I could barely sleep. It was my big chance. I'd finally get to leave the dark recesses of my cubicle and use a bit of my charm. Impress Barrington with my people skills. And maybe meet a supermodel in the bargain. Who'd like an accounting peon with no tan who drove a twenty year old used car. I know, I know, but a man's gotta dream. I spent two hours picking out the perfect tie and another two ironing everything, including my socks. And set three alarm clocks with three independent power sources to make sure I'd wake in time.

Up at five a.m. Shower, scrubbing vigorously behind ears and between toes. Dry. Comb hair. Comb hair again. Apply generously deodorant extra strength. Squeeze unsightly blackheads out of nose while cringing in pain but not crying, definitely not crying. Trim nose hairs. Check for ear hairs. Clip toe nails. Clip fingernails. Shave twice. After-shave lotion. Scream a bit when lotion penetrates shaving cuts. Dress. Tie and retie and retie tie until knot is perfect. Brush teeth. Floss. Mouthwash. Check breath. Brush teeth. Floss. Mouthwash. Comb hair. Brush eyebrows. Polish shoes. Change suit when get polish on trousers. Consider changing tie but don't. Mouthwash. Polish audit bag. Polish watch with wrong rag and abandon watch as eight o'clock has arrived. Leave.

Car starts. Shout in triumph. Remember audit bag left on top of car while unlocking door and slam on brakes. Get broadsided by yellow sports car. Scream a bit more. Exchange insurance information. Kick back tire in frustration and bruise toe. Limp inside. Drive. Get lost. Ask for directions three times. Arrive. Limp through parking structure to building. Return to car for again forgotten audit bag. Limp back to building. Take elevator to third floor.

Wait for elevator doors to open. Take deep breath and step outside. Smile at receptionist and run straight into the invisible glass window, the door being at the far edge of the wall and unseen by my foolish eyes. Fall backwards with broken nose, severely bruised knee cap and no ego whatsoever. Slam back of head into carpet and lose consciousness.

Awake to a vision of surpassing loveliness. Framed by an enormous white straw hat adorned with a red rose and ribbons of white lace filigree. Short cropped brown hair above wide red lips and huge penetrating green eyes. Just over five feet tall and thin. Physically fit but in a feminine way. With concern in her husky voice, she asked, "Are you all right?"

"My noth feelth bath." I was laying where I'd fallen.

"Well, it's the size of a pumpkin."

"Tha small?"

"I think you need to have it set at the hospital."

"Broketh?"

"I think so."

"My nameth Petah Pollack. I Neth, Baa & Tackel."

"Then you'll be glad to know you didn't break the window. Won't affect the fixed asset depreciation schedule."

"I feel so muth betta."

My dad called me that night. "So how was your first day at Veronica's Secret?"

"I don't want to talk about it."

The next day Sigmond treated the tax department of Veronica's Secret to lunch. He appeared at the restaurant shaking his head at my taped nose and then sat among the company's executives. Presumably as reward for my previous day's performance, I was banished to a distant secondary table that held only me and the secretary who had driven me to the emergency room.

"Do you feel a bit unwanted?" asked the secretary whose name was Belinda.

"A tad."

Silence. Then: "Your nose got smaller."

"I've been working out." Me pantomiming lifting weights with my right arm drew a polite smile.

The waiter appeared to take our food orders.

While Sigmond talked in a voice unheard over the restaurant's music, another uncomfortable silence settled upon my table. Belinda said with a sigh, "Ah, I wonder what they're talking about down there."

For the hell of it, I said, "Grown-up stuff, nothing you'd be interested in."

Her eyes lit up. "What are you saying exactly?"

"Not a thing. Really. Don't scold me. Please. I'm on my best behavior."

"I might let it slide this time. This time." She thrust an extended index finger of warning in my direction.

"I'm trying to behave myself. For one day I hope truly to be allowed to sit at the big people's table. I've even been practicing eating without the bib. Carrot sticks now; one day graduating, I *so* hope, to spaghetti with marinara sauce."

"Have you?"

"Hence the dark shirt. Conceals stains better."

"Maybe you've heard of a new invention called the napkin?"

"Progress - ha! First come napkins, then instant decaffeinated coffee with dehydrated, non-dairy, lactose-free, imitation creamer and artificial carbohydrate-deficient sweetener, followed by global thermonuclear warheads. I say fie upon all so-called scientific advancements! For they lead to nothing but deterioration in the morals of our youth, bland homogenization of worldwide culture and dissipation of the ozone layer."

More silence. Then: "And here I thought you were a boring accountant stifled by his environment and doomed by his profession to a life of conformity, unwilling or afraid to do anything about it. When all along, you were one of those brooding intellectual types seething with an inner fury at the world injustices and your impotence to improve them."

Wow and double wow. "That's me."

144

"That's too bad. I was hoping to meet someone a bit funnier."

"My tushy's really cute, though."

"You have a point there."

Sigmond suddenly shouted from the other end of the room: "Peter! Get down here! And bring your chair."

"Looks like somebody's been promoted," said Belinda.

"Don't worry," I responded. "I won't forget the little people who made all of this possible."

"Peter!"

At Veronica's Secret, I was hoping to do my work in the supermodels' dressing room. Instead I was assigned to a cracked cardboard table in a still functioning broom closet with a fluorescent ceiling light that blinked maddeningly. An hour after arriving there on my third day the phone rang at the table in front of me. No one was around. I let it ring once, twice, thrice. No one appeared. I answered it tentatively, "Pollack."

"Do you want to go to lunch?"

"I'm sorry, who is this please?"

"Belinda. You know, the extremely nice girl who drove you to the hospital when you broke your nose."

"I forgot to thank you."

"No, you thanked me. About thirteen times."

"Better make it fourteen."

"Well?"

"Thank you."

"You're welcome."

"I'd love to go to lunch."

"Twelve o'clock." The phone went dead.

Belinda smiled up at me from her desk. "Ready?"

"Born as such. Willing and able, to boot. Who'll drive?" She picked up her hat: a floppy brown saucer with a brim a rhinoceros could camp under.

"I will. But I must warn you, my Porsche is in the shop."

"So's my Ferrari."

"Don't you just hate that?" I pushed the elevator button. "Have you worked here long?"

"Two months. I'd been living in San Diego before that."

"Why the move?"

We boarded the elevator. "My mom lives here. I hadn't seen her for a while and needed to."

"Do you like it?"

"It's okay. I went to high school here. You?"

"I moved here when I got this job after graduation about five months ago. I grew up in Lake Arrowhead."

"It's beautiful up there."

We left the elevator and entered the parking structure. "There she is," I said proudly, pointing to my 1981 Oldsmobile Cutlass Supreme. "A glorious spectacle to behold: the realized product of generations of the finest automobile craftsmanship."

"What happened to your door?"

"Saving a little old lady from a unicycle gang of evil clowns. You know: a typical Tuesday." I inserted said door's key. "It sticks a little." When my gentle approach yielded naught, I yanked with force. But sudden success swung the handle directly into my left kneecap. "Please," I squeaked, "watch your feet," and shut the door. Then I joined her in the front seat.

"Love the fuzzy dice."

"Thank you."

"And the imitation tiger-skin seat covers."

"Classy, aren't they?"

"And it's so neat and tidy."

I gestured towards the backseat which was covered with:

1.   My CPA examination notes

2.   The January 17, 1996 edition of the Los Angeles Times – mint condition

3.   The February 23, 1996 edition of the Los Angeles Times missing the third page of the Sports Section

4.   AAA road maps of every state from California to North Dakota (yes, even Idaho) – some folded incorrectly (I know)

5.   A Rod Carew baseball glove

6.   A broken umbrella – color black

7.   Hiking boots – color brown

8.   The Holy Grail

9.   A map to Atlantis

10.   A stuffed and mounted one-eyed sperm whale

11.   The second rifle used to shoot JFK

12.   Benjamin Franklin's false teeth

13.   The President's brain (Of course, I'm kidding, that doesn't really exist)

14.   A sonnet written by the missing link entitled "The Ooga Booga Blues"

15.   Ivan the Terrible's favorite curly blonde toupee

16.   Jimmy Hoffa's wristwatch

17.   Clark Kent's glasses

18.   Maybe a couple of other things. Maybe.

"Would you like something to read? Perhaps a beverage? There's beer and tastefully done pornography in the trunk, if you like."

"I'm good, thank you."

I turned the key in the ignition. "Please remain seated with all hands and feet inside the vehicle at all times throughout the duration of the flight."

"Flight?"

"I drive fast."

"But safely."

"Of course. No faster than Warp Speed Five. Four, if you insist."

"I insist."

We exited the parking structure and Belinda directed me towards a Mexican restaurant a few minutes away. "What is a sock doing in here?"

"A sock?"

"What scares me the most is the sock's singularity. Where lurks its twin?"

"Your tone of voice concerns me, madame. What are you implying? I'm not sure I like what you're saying or, rather, not saying or saying by not saying that which you're saying. Perhaps you would prefer walking. Personal perambulation, as it were. In other words: hoofing it."

"Having tread most irreverently upon the sanctity of a man's wheels, I do beg a most humble apology, sir."

"Your obvious sincerity has convinced me to let it slide. This time."

"The fullness of your most forgiving heart knows no bounds."

"Don't let that get around. It could hurt my career."

"It will be our little secret. For a fair price, of course."

"You can have the sock."

"I've never seen anyone parallel park as badly as that before. Ever," Belinda said as we sat down in the restaurant. "In all my twenty-seven years."

"It's a gift."

"Can you return it?"

The waitress appeared and took our meal orders. "What would you like to drink?"

"Beer?" I asked Belinda.

"Belinda like beer. Beer good."

"A pitcher of Sierra Nevada, please."

"You didn't order anything for yourself," Belinda said with a smile after the waitress left.

I laughed. "I'll fight you for it. Guns or knives?"

"I wouldn't if I were you. I may be small, but I'm mean. Three older brothers."

"Well, I was raised by wolves. Man-eating wolves. With big teeth."

"Are you a certified accountant yet?"

"I just took the exam last month. Two more months before I get the results. Keep your fingers crossed."

"For the whole two months?"

I stuck my tongue out at her.

"Watch it, buddy. You're treading on thin ice. Latticed."

"Was it something I said? Something I did? Something I didn't say or do? I didn't mean it. Please forgive me. Else I can't go on. The maps, the sock: I can change, I swear."

"You're crazy, you know that?"

"No, I'm normal. Everyone else is crazy… I can't believe you're twenty-seven."

"Thank you."

"No, I took you for eighty-three at the least."

"Never joke with a woman about her age or her weight. I warn you once." Again with The Finger of Warning.

"It wasn't me, it was my evil twin brother Sven."

Her deep thunderous laugh would knock your hat off at thirty paces unless it had a heavy duty leather strap that buckled snugly under your chin to prevent its untimely loss. I liked her laugh's recklessness, its abandonment. And the accompanying infectious smile daring you not to smile back. But underneath, I sensed a forced quality, an artificiality, as if she were trying to convince herself things weren't that bad. Inside, she was hurting. "How old are you?"

"About to turn twenty-two. I graduated high school a year early. Did you go to college?"

"Degree in Communications. But I got sidetracked, that's why I'm working here. I was married for five years. Foolishly, I quit before my senior year to work, so he could go to medical school."

"What happened?"

"Two months after he graduated, I came home from work one day to an empty apartment. No phone calls, no letters, his parents didn't know where he was. Six months later, divorce papers arrived in the mail."

"I'm sorry. Wow."

"So I finished my degree at night school and now I'm studying for my real estate license. My mom's firm is going to sponsor me."

"That's great."

The food arrived.

"These fajitas rock. Excellent choice."

"Thanks."

"So is the real estate exam graded on a curve? Have you considered trying to bring down the average?"

"What are you suggesting?"

"When I took my CPA examination, I dressed up like Superman. The cape, the tights, the knee-high boots. Only I added an A to the S on my chest for *Super Accountant*."

"And why would I do this?"

"To distract the others."

"This worked for you?"

"Actually, no. The proctors just asked the same questions: did I have a driver's license or other acceptable form of picture identification, did I bring a number two pencil. As if Super Accountant could forget his

150

number two pencil."

"Uh-huh." Belinda refilled her glass from the pitcher.

"I was only kidding."

Belinda nodded and drank her beer.

"You're wondering what they're talking about over there, aren't you? And if they have a free seat?"

Belinda laughed.

"Shall we get dessert?" Belinda asked excitedly.

"A foolish question." I scanned the menu. "What are you having?"

"Flan. My favorite. I just hope it's good: quality always seems to vary. Lots of syrup is key."

"Wow. Just wow. All this time we've spent together, all we've been through – the kidney donation, the nuclear holocaust weathered together in the lead-lined refrigerator, the drug-running through the jungles of Panama's Darien Gap – and only now do you tell me you like flan. You look like a crème brulee type of girl to me."

"I get that a lot. Tiramisu as well."

"And peach cobbler?"

"No, never."

Our waiter appeared. "Anything for dessert?"

"This lovely lady would like some flan. And not the factory-made tasteless crap served in most restaurants, but something sublime. Something divine. Something that transcends the ordinary bounds of flan-ness and reaches that elusive gastronomic peak that most people spend a lifetime striving for. This flan must wipe away the tears and heartache of twenty-seven years and herald a new era for this woman, one of hope and happiness and, dare I say, bliss. I know it's a lot to ask out of a dessert, but I think you're up to it. For her sake, I hope so. Oh, and make sure it's got plenty of syrup."

The waiter smiled without amusement. "I'll do my best, sir."

I said, "I think he's going to spit in our food."

"Probably."

The check arrived. Belinda reached for her purse. I said, "I'll get it."

"Are you sure?"

"It's the least I can do. You drove me to the hospital."

"Thank you. For the company as well. My side actually hurts from laughing."

"You're not going to sue, are you? Because my dad's an attorney."

"This I know. You kept shouting it at everyone in the emergency room, remember?"

"Not really. Did it work?"

"They took you first."

Back in the car, Belinda checked her seatbelt three times and then smiled at me. "Next time I'll bring my crash helmet."

"Next time?"

"Uh-huh."

"Okay, then." For the first time in a long while, I felt really good. At peace.

A shaggy-haired young man with a small backpack covered in patches of different country's flags sat down next to me in Heathrow airport as I waited to fly back to Los Angeles before continuing to Fiji. "Been on the road awhile?" I asked him.

"Just starting. But I've traveled before." He nodded towards his bag. "A couple of times for two years each."

"What makes you keep going?"

His blue eyes regarded me for a long moment. "You want the truth."

"Yes."

"You go home and your eyes are all wide open. You see what really matters after observing all this poverty and desperation, people with nothing. And they have hope and happiness. And you're fixed, you're better. But no one wants to hear your stories, really hear your stories. Maybe they'll want to hear how many women you've slept with or how you were nearly eaten by an Australian crocodile, but not the other ones. Not the ones that matter. They're still bigoted with closed minds. They don't see how petty their arguments really are. How precious every minute of life is. How every human being has some sort of beauty to offer. And you try to tell them, but they look at you like you're crazy. So you hate them at first, but you can't live like that and you forget and you accept them and, in doing so, you die a little. Until you go again."

An empty seat divided me from a young British man in the aisle seat of the airplane. His dark eyes were anxious.

"First flight?" I asked.

"Uh-huh."

"It's much safer than before when all those people died. They fixed that problem with the 747 models. A little bumpier now, but just make sure to buckle your seat belt and you'll be fine."

"That's not funny."

"Sorry. I was just kidding. You going to Los Angeles for work?"

"Yes." His eyes drifted forward, signaling our friendship's end. Then he began chugging vodka tonics, hold the tonic. Two hours and six bathroom trips later, he passed out wrapped tightly in two blankets, embracing three pillows, and sucking his thumb. His seatbelt was unbuckled, but I'd teased him enough and left him to sleep in peace.

Over New York, the airplane hit heavy turbulence. My neighbor awoke with wild, terrified eyes as he literally jumped from the seat. Arms flailing in panic, his pillows shot in opposite directions. One boinked a nonplussed six year old boy across the aisle and another caught me in the eye. The *Fasten Seatbelts* sign lit up and his panic increased. He struggled desperately to find the errant buckles, hopping madly in his seat despite the difficulty of being wrapped in two blankets. When he found them: "I can't buckle my seatbelt. I CAN'T BUCKLE MY SEATBELT!"

"Calm down, man. It'll be all right."

His eyes found mine just as the plane dropped five feet. He scrambled into the seat between us and smacked my glasses from my face and bloodied my nose finding the other buckle. After a couple of not entirely painful blows to my midriff, he managed to click the seatbelt together.

"Can you see anything? Are we okay?"

I retrieved my glasses and wiped the blood from my lip. "We're fine. One of the engines is on fire, but we've got three others."

His shoulders relaxed and then, "What!"

"Ha, ha. Sorry. No worries, mate. Hey, look a bird. Oh, no…"

"What? What!"

"Maybe we should ring the stewardess."

"What?"

"The bird. Into engine. Fire."

"We're all going to die. We're all going to die! I'm too young. I'm too young! Please." He grabbed the front of my shirt. "Please!"

"No, I'm just kidding again."

He asked for a new seat.

My father met me for coffee during my four hour layover in Los Angeles. He handed me a flat cardboard box. "Your mother asked me to bring you more toilet seat covers. In case you'd run out."

"The first box had one thousand."

My father shrugged. "I tried to tell her. But you know your mother, once her mind's set, it's best to just go along."

I nodded. "How is everyone?"

"The same. UCLA lost as usual. They're bloody awful this year. Really bloody awful. Enjoying yourself?"

"Dad, I've never felt so alive."

"That's good. Did you see my new socks?"

He loved the Parisian T-shirt.

154

On the flight I met some American missionaries, recent high school graduates full of giggles, on their way to Papua New Guinea. Later in New Zealand I read a young American had been kidnapped there and wondered if it was the blonde girl with glasses who asked me all about my trip and remembered my name to say goodbye at the baggage claim. Her infectious smile devoid of artifice or reserve stayed with me a long time. Where had I lost that? Could it return?

Needless to say, but I will anyway (because I'm like that occasionally), sometime after my seventh cup of free coffee, there was an announcement over the intercom: "Ladies and gentlemen, I have kind of a funny announcement to make. Peter Pollack, your mother says not to forget to buy your pepper spray..."

The Air New Zealand stewardess, a dark-skinned Fijian with playful brown eyes, smiled at me with a mouth full of gold capped teeth. "Are you going to New Zealand or stopping over in Fiji?" she asked.

"I'm stopping in Fiji."

"For how long?"

"I don't know yet. At least a couple of weeks."

"Do you know where you'll be staying?"

"Not yet."

"Well, I'm getting married in two days. If you're staying near Suva, I'd like to invite you to my wedding."

Was this for real? I'd only smiled at her a couple of times and said thank you whenever she handed me a beverage. "You're getting married? Congratulations."

"Thank you."

"I'm not sure... If it'd be okay, I'd love to come. I'm Peter, by the way."

Elizabeth wrote down the details for me.

Stepping from the air conditioned airplane into the sun at the Nadi airport, I began to melt. And entering the terminal didn't help. My clothes turned into saturated rags of perspiration in the stale, unmoving air. Nor was I adjusting, the heat seemed to build and build. If I didn't move quickly, find someplace cool within the next thirteen seconds, I'd be a puddle. Already I could feel my legs starting to liquefy. Mom and Dad would put me on the mantelpiece in a plastic milk jug and tell visitors, "Here's our son, the puddle."

Outside baggage claim, smiling travel agents inundated me with the impossibilities of getting accommodation or transportation anywhere on the islands without them. They followed me to the bank machine offering ever so graciously to help me count the money, followed me to the bathroom door altruistically volunteering to watch my backpack for as long as I needed and then followed me to the glass double doors outside where a blue bus was passing. I raised my hand. The bus stopped.

Harrison Hawk killed Vietnamese soldiers to a chorus of the passengers' cheers, laughter and applause on the television set above the driver's head. I squeezed into an open seat beside the largest woman I'd ever seen and we left. Although made for four people, the seat barely accommodated the two of us.

An instant later, the bus jerked to another stop and the bigger sister of the largest woman I'd ever seen boarded. Of course, she chose to share my seat and I was sandwiched between the two Fijian women. With another jerk forward, the bus resumed its erratic, mostly terrifying journey. I thought that Los Angeles drivers were the worst drivers in the world. I was very, very wrong. But my troubles did not end there. With each succeeding turn, the big sister slipped further and further out of the seat. But she did not go quietly. Using the far wall of the bus for leverage, she shoved herself back into me to make room where there was no vacancy.

"Please, let me take the outside," I gasped.

"Don't trouble yourself, friend," she said sweetly with a smile full of gold teeth.

I grimaced in pain as the air was successively squeezed from my lungs from first the one side and then the other. Then, on a particularly steep curve, I was subjected to the full brunt of the big sister's girth and consciousness failed me in a burst of black and green.

Waking, I thought Satan had me in his sauna in Hell, but, no, my fate was much, much worse. I had been absorbed by the women beside me, becoming one with them, their flesh was my flesh and vice versa. No more Peter, only Senta Peter—a new and separate entity with now three heads, four flabby breasts and one enormous yet magnificent body. Looking down, I saw

156

nothing but brown flesh rolling, splashing, heaving everywhere. Yards of it, miles of it, acres of it. And my pecker had disappeared. Oh, the horror. The unspeakable, unmentionable, unutterable horror. What would this do to my dreams of world domination? Or to my mother, knowing her son had been assimilated into a rather large Fijian mother of four in dire need of a pedicure? How could I go to Christmas dinner – I wouldn't fit through any of the doorways, we'd need to eat in the garage, but we had no garage? My friends would all laugh at me. I would have to buy all new clothes with three neck-holes which would need to be expensively custom-made. Or maybe they'd be cheap in Siam, wherever that is. But how would I get there? I'd have to hire a cargo plane or an aircraft carrier, another added cost of my new and expanded self. All these fears raced through my head as the palm trees whooshed by with whooshing sounds that resembled whooshes.

We rounded a bend and I was given relief: a momentary glimpse of my old familiar body below me. My penis still existed! For now. The women beside me were salivating in their sleep. Like burst fire hydrants. Soon a puddle formed and then a pool. A drool pool, as it were. Engulfing my legs and slowly working up. Why, oh, why hadn't I brought snorkeling gear? Yes, it got worse. Rasping, grating snoring of inordinate volume and magnitude in stereo. Not in tandem, so I could be jostled into one amorphous flab as the other exhaled and back as the first inhaled. (Remember your narrator.) Synchronized, bandying my poor body about like some overworked accordion.

Twice I failed to escape that cellulite death trap. Twice they ensnared me in a noose of absorbing flesh, ceasing their breathing at the very instant of my attempted flight. But on the third attempt, I succeeded in pulling myself up by the overhead baggage rack and threw myself into the seat in front of me. Yes, I hit the heads of the neighboring occupants, but they were Canadians so I felt no guilt. Then I returned to my former seat to sleep on their tummies like a baby, rolling on the most comfortable waterbed in the world, a little wet but very soft and squishy cuddled between, under and through arms like hams and legs like sides of cadaverous beef.

Two hours later, a new passenger carrying a large brown paper envelope awoke me when he asked the man sitting next to me if he could take his place. He tapped me on the shoulder, "Bula, sir."

"Bula."

In nearly unintelligible English, he said, "That is welcome to Fiji, sir."

"Thank you."

"Where from, sir?"

"The United States."

"Very good, sir. Would you be smoking the ganja?"

"I'm sorry?"

"Ganja. You know: happy smoke?" He made the international gesture.

"It gives me bunions."

"Very good price. I get you much."

"My mother would send me to bed without supper. I know it."

"No, good smoke. Good price. I get. You buy."

The bus suddenly stopped at a road blockade. Two policemen boarded leading dogs on thick black leather leashes. The first policeman looked at my drug-selling companion and was met with an almost imperceptible shake of the head. The policeman did not look pleased.

"Passport." I handed it over. "Baggage?"

"On top."

"Show."

I was led out of the bus and the driver climbed up to retrieve my backpack. No other passengers were ordered to follow. The dogs sniffed at my bag. Despite my innocence, I was still a bit frightened. They were obviously looking to frame me. Would they plant evidence or were my shoes just dirty enough that they wouldn't bother? After a long, long glare, the policeman handed me back my passport and said with disgust, "Go."

The bus restarted its engine.

Everyone had warned me how dangerous Suva was, especially at night, but I walked to the hostel anyway. The city was filthy: dirt covered storefront windows, signs were half-broken and the smell of the sea mingled unappealingly with that of gasoline and garbage. People packed the streets, buying or selling or just talking, but I was ignored. Until. A block away from my destination, a policeman on a bicycle asked me where I was going. I nearly panicked. But he was only being friendly. He escorted me to the hostel and told me gently to stay off the streets at night because of thieves. I shared a bunk bed with a surfer from Malibu who'd left the United States to live in the South Pacific, working in bars between competitions. "I'm just tired of all that bullshit, man. Owning stuff, trying to be better than the next
158

guy. Living to make money. For what? This is what it's all about. The sun, the sea, the clean air. The people here are so friendly and when they know you have nothing they can scam, they accept you." When I asked him if he'd found his place and would live here forever, he said, "Man, they're ruining it. Selling out. They don't know what they have. They destroy it for the quick dollar. They sell their land to foreigners who build expensive resorts for tourists and kill off the reef doing it. And they don't treat their sewage. I can't tell you how many times I've gotten ear infections surfing in the filthy water. Near villages. They're accommodating tourists today and ruining their future. They all want to get rich and go to America. This is the promised land, not America. People never appreciate what they have. Soon the Americans, the Germans, the Swiss will own everything and all these people will be working in their hotels, cooking their meals, cleaning their toilets. In ten years, maybe twenty, I'll have to find a new place."

"Bula!"

"Bula."

I shook hands with Elizabeth's father and his six sons, four brothers and two grandsons. Their limp handshakes lacked the challenge and self-assertion in the American greeting. At first I thought it submissive, but these were not small men. They were fishermen and farmers, men of physical labor. The more I talked with them, the more I realized the gesture was one of non-aggression, an acceptance of everyone as they were, not as they were supposed to be. "You must be Peter. Elizabeth told us you would be coming."

"Yes, she was very kind to invite me. You must be very excited for her."

"We are. Come in. We must help you dress for the wedding."

"You don't have to trouble yourselves."

"No trouble at all. But you must wear the proper attire." He led me into the white frame house, proudly showing me the twenty-seven inch screen television and each of the home's four small bedrooms. In the last of these, I was given a sulu, a long skirt Fijian men wore made out of one rectangular piece of thin fabric. Then I was escorted outside where girls with pretty smiles adorned me with necklaces of brightly colored flowers and welcomed me with a kiss to the cheek. After a further tour of the garden which looked out on a quiet cove lined with coconut and papaya trees, one of the grandsons led me to a large woven mat in the center of the backyard where all the men sat cross-legged in a circle. I was introduced and asked to sit down.

The father of the house filled half a coconut shell from a large wooden bowl filled with a milky liquid in front of him and handed it to me. I was instructed to clap before receiving the cup, to recite the word "Dola" before drinking the contents in one swallow, and then clap again once I returned the coconut shell to him. After a few minutes of reflection, another cup of kava was prepared for the next person in the circle.

Marriage. To share a life with someone seemed so impossible, so intimate. Would I ever want to be so close to someone? Would anyone want to be so close to me? A lifetime together. How do you find the right one? So many choices.

After the ceremony, the men reconvened around the kava bowl to continue the ritual until dawn. My own contribution of a bottle of rum I'd bought in town was greatly appreciated and disappeared somewhere around its third revolution.

The world was collapsing upon my head. I awoke to a blur of bright yellow light and streaks of green to find the ground shuddering violently beneath my bed in a back and forth motion. Children's toys and folded clothes pelted me from the shelves above. The room's three other sleeping occupants, only one of who had a bed, were snoring, but not that powerfully. An earthquake! Where were my glasses? To be caught blind in a foreign country during a natural disaster – this was not a good thing. To dodge giant cracks in the earth's crust frothing with molten lava, to elude falling debris: these I could not do without sight. I considered dashing for the doorframe, but it would have been impossible: two enormous Fijian men slept like dead men between the beds blocking the door. So I threw my arms over my head, curled my knees under my belly and waited for the end. The Richter scale 7.2 earthquake ceased ten seconds later, but my companions' snoring continued, unaffected by the offshore rumbling of the planet's tectonic plates. I considered my possible death or dismemberment for a moment and then fell back asleep, wandering amid the Land of Nod with dreams of electing to amortize organizational costs over five years – blissfully ignorant of future legislation that would extend the amortization period to 180 months with a $5,000 first year allowable bonus reduced dollar for dollar for incurred expenses in excess of $50,000. Hours later, after a large breakfast of fruit and bread, I returned to Suva to catch a ferry to Taveuni.

Brisk clean air gusted from a wide blue horizon stretching into the infinite: the promise of any possibility, adventure to be pursued, unknown worlds explored. The lure of the sea: Columbus, Magellan, Drake, Darwin. What lay ahead for me? Challenge? Contentment? Love?

160

I watched the sun set and the water muddy in the darkness from blue to black, then I returned inside to the stench of sweating bodies and a dysfunctional latrine. Choppy unwatchable videotapes of cheap American action movies played on television sets above the blue seats. Stepping over slumbering bodies, I found an unused chair with broken arms and sat to wait out the long night.

Throughout but more so in the morning, each time I made eye contact with a new person, they would engage me in conversation that always ended with an invitation to their village. I felt like a celebrity. As my fatigue grew from lack of sleep, however, I just wanted to be left alone and I sympathized for the first time with those in the public eye.

I hadn't understood why there was such a mad rush to board the boat until later. Then I realized every available inch of floor space had been claimed by one family or another as a place to sleep as the long voyage progressed. I attempted sleeping in one of the numerous broken chairs, but without air conditioning the heat was unbearable. I drank three liters of bottled water and was still thirsty. I hadn't brought any food, hoping to buy some from the cafeteria. Two hours into the voyage, the bathrooms ran out of water and the toilets were swamps of iniquity. I tried not to look at my sandals. I couldn't wash my hands, but then nor could anyone else. I got in line for dinner and hoped for the best. They had no eating utensils on the boat and halfway through the meal, they ran out of clean plates. They had no water to wash them, so if we wanted to eat we had to use someone else's. I skipped dinner in disgust, but succumbed to hunger the next morning and got breakfast on the same unwashed plates from the day before.

Taxis charging tourists fifty U.S. dollars to anywhere on the island greeted the boat. I nearly panicked until I asked a local about a bus and he said if I waited an hour, it would cost one U.S. dollar. I would have to go north first and then wait for the bus to return. That's what I did.

As I sat waiting for a bus connection to the southern tip of the island after visiting The World's Second Most Disgusting Toilet in the back of the station, a man in his late thirties joined me on the broken bench. He wore a baseball cap with a solar powered fan cut into the bill that intermittently would cool his face. "Bula."

"Bula."

"Welcome to my island. You are American?"

"Yes."

"Can I ask you a question? I am a priest here. I have a problem.

161

This American girl, she came to the island with her boyfriend. Then they had a fight and the boyfriend left. Said she could go home, he didn't want to be with her anymore. He gave her the plane ticket home and left her in my sister's hotel. She had no money. She was very upset, crying all of the time. So she calls her mother at home for money. But she does not spend it on a ferry ticket back to Suva. She buys alcohol and spends all day in the hotel drinking until the money is all gone and she has not paid my sister for the hotel. My sister says she must leave, she must go home, but the girl says she has no money. My sister buys the ferry ticket for the girl to get her out of the hotel and because she feels sorry for her. But the girl sells the ticket back to the company and buys more alcohol. My sister asks me to talk to her. I do. The next day, I find her in the church. She has broken into the sacristy and is drinking the holy wine. I don't know what to do with her. She is crazy."

"I don't know either."

The bus was an old American grammar school model. Its original yellow paint had been patched over the years with every color of the rainbow. Half of the seat cushions were broken and what few windows remained had been taped back together over their numerous cracks. The driver smiled widely and told me we'd be leaving in ten minutes. Forty-five minutes later, passengers were still arriving. In a seat built for two seven year old American school children, one teenage Fijian girl sat on her sister's lap keeping me pinned against the wall. Other seats were worse. Goats, pigs, burlap bags of rice, bicycles, giant roots, a generator needing repair: all found places somewhere between the seats. Grandmothers hung from a long metal bar on the ceiling. Everyone laughed as, rounding corners, we were thrown together. The road was atrocious, a rock strewn snake twisting through the jungle. Three hours to drive something like thirty miles with stops every few hundred feet.

A pretty woman in her early forties whose husband had died some years before ran the hostel. She had large bushy black hair which she kept losing her pencil in and a shy smile full of pain. Being childless, she shared the house with her brother and his family who did the washing, cooking and maintenance. The small blue house had four guest rooms, all kept immaculately clean. The mattresses were even remotely soft. But sleep was impossible.

My grandmother's nemesis was her pigeons, mine was the roosters of Fiji. Roosters are supposed to crow at dawn, right? Wrong. These roosters had come from all over the globe -- America, New Zealand, Australia, even England-- and had never adjusted to the time difference. As a consequence they crowed all night long inches from my room's window,

162

announcing dawn at all corners of the world. By Night Three, I'd had enough. After the incident, I was known by all the village for many years as MekeSegaIsuluKeiToa, which roughly translated to "Dances Naked With Roosters." (Or so I was told.) Embarrassed by my loss of temper, I gave up the chase, sleeping when I could, once most embarrassingly at church when I was invited to see a mass.

The hostel sat in a shallow bay on the Pacific Ocean. Cradled by lush jungle and fronted by the sea, the setting was paradise. Before dawn, black water under a canopy of blue clouds slowly faded into obscurity at the horizon. Then shimmering beams bleed through the opaque ceiling, bleaching the water and blinding the eye. Fine sand sifts through my toes as the green hills covered in coconut and mango trees rise behind and a bedraggled fishing boat propelled by a rusty prop patters slowly across the sedate surface in front. Later, sunset is a window of gold through the curtain of clouds, streaking the now dark blue water before fading to crimson striations across the sky's azure palette. The heavens become consumed by a saturation of tangerine, peach and red, swirling in spirals.

The first morning and many that followed, I went snorkeling with the girls in the room adjoining mine. Two were American and the other two were Japanese – all of them taught English in Japan. It was my first time breathing while looking underwater. Dark red and deep purple branches of coral swayed softly in the underwater current, feasting the eye with a surfeit of color. Angelfish, damselfish and grouper darted here and there amid the canyons and crevices below me. A manta ray flapped silently from view while ambient jellyfish pondered the thorny anemone beneath. Schools of tiny, fluorescent blue fish fled from my paddling hands. A gulping turtle spiraled through the dusty blue abyss, its spotted flesh a yellow gold in the filtered sunlight. Waves grated against the sandy ocean floor. The warm sun burned my back. Magical.

When one of the teachers, Heather, joined me on the porch after lunch, I asked, "How are you?"

"Just terrible."

"Oh?"

"No traffic jams, alarm clocks, television commercials, acid rain, smog, credit card bills, mortgage payments, overtime. I can hardly stand it."

I grinned. "Me, neither."

"Nor does it end there. Today I've got to tan my ass. Hard work that. Luckily, I've only got to do the left cheek today. Tomorrow I can do the

163

right."

"Not so bad then."

After a few minutes of watching the waves lap gently against the beach, we'd both fallen asleep, forgetting our assigned tasks for the day and, no doubt, missing all sorts of important meetings.

I was sitting on the porch drinking a glass of crushed papaya juice when the brother of the hostel owner appeared next to me.

He had wide staring eyes and his tightly curled black hair covered the back of his neck. "Peter," he said to me without a good morning, "how long has it been since you sexed up a girl?"

I spluttered in my beverage. "I'm sorry?"

"Do you like women?"

"Absolutely."

"Peter, have you ever licked a woman's vagina?"

"Can we change the subject?"

"Because you shouldn't, you know. Because the smells of the woman's vagina get in your saliva and your breath starts to smell like a vagina. Brushing your teeth doesn't help." He rubbed his gums with his index finger and then sucked the finger dry. "It's a scientific fact."

"You're a sick fucking bastard, you know that?"

He laughed. "Where you go next?"

"Maybe Samoa."

"You know Samoan women like something special when they're having the sex. You know what peanuts are? Put some in your condom when you're sexing them."

"Salted or honey-roasted?"

"Would you like a Fijian woman, Peter?"

"No, thank you."

"So you're with the hand?"

"What the hell is wrong with you? I'm going swimming."

"Because if you keep up the practice you'll be three inches across. And a woman never goes back from that."

After my swim, the brother sat down next to me. "I think Heather she wants the sexing up. I think I'll go into her room tonight and give it to her. She is fierce. Very good for the fucking."

"Don't do that."

"Why not? She wants it, I think."

"She has a boyfriend. And you have a wife."

"Why does she come here to Fiji all alone? I will go."

"If you do that, I'll have to kill you. Skewer your scrotum savagely with this swizzle stick."

"You were in the army, I think."

I laughed. "No."

"You were in the army. This, I know. You have the face of a soldier." I laughed again. "Leftenant Colonel Peter Smith, how many people have you killed?"

"Lost count after seventeen. But it's quite painful and I don't like to talk about it."

"I think maybe you want Heather for yourself."

"She has a boyfriend."

"This means nothing."

"No, she is loyal. American girls, especially with Irish blood, will cut your balls off if you cheat on them."

"Really? So in your point of view, Leftenant Colonel, which are the best women in the world?"

"The Irish."

Evenings I spent playing with the children at cards which they cheated at profusely. When they caught each other, they would fight and then, ten minutes later, be hugging affectionately or sharing a piece of papaya.

165

No one cared what the other one's parents did, no one cared who was the most handsome or the strongest. Everyone seemed equal. So unlike the memories of my own childhood.

The youngest son, nicknamed "Troublemaker" for his torturing of the cat and stealing my glasses when I slept, asked me one day, "Tell me an American story, Peter. Tell me the story of the moon."

Another world. This is all they'd known. And probably ever would. Like I had, they probably ached for the unknown, to see what they'd only heard rumors of: great cities, deserts, Antarctica. So I told him the story of the moon.

A few days later, after we had played rugby in the water at low tide, Troublemaker's fourteen-year old brother asked me, "What is snow like?"

I thought of this. So many things he might never know. Freeways. Skyscrapers. Baseball games. Roller coasters. "Snow quiets the world. It falls without a sound, blanketing the earth in white. Makes the air smell clean, fresh. Unused, virginal. Tasteless as it melts cold and wet on your tongue. Comforting, yet threatening."

"Sounds beautiful. I want to see it."

"If you want to, you will."

"No, it is impossible." He scratched his knee and looked into my eyes. "I want to go to America, Peter. I need a sponsor."

"Why do you want to go to America?"

"I want to be rich. I want to have things."

"You have a good life here. You have enough food to eat, a place to live, why do you want to go to America?"

"Here we have nothing. We work all our lives and get nothing. I want more."

"But your brother tells me you don't even go to school. How can you get these things without an education?"

"In America it's different. Everyone has things. I know."

"Fiji is very beautiful. Why do you think all these Europeans and Americans come to visit? For them, this is paradise, not their own countries."

"You don't understand. Fiji is shit." He walked away.

I could sympathize with his wanting something more. If the longing was real, nothing I could say would help. Maybe he could change his fate, if he really struggled. Maybe. It had been so easy for me to leave. His road was much tougher. Did he have the ability or, more importantly, the luck? Would he give up or struggle to the last, never being happy? Should he accept his lot? Spend a life taking crumbs from unappreciative backpackers so he could feed his family? Should I do the same, accept being an accountant? But I couldn't. Not if I wanted to look at myself. And so how could he?

The one morning the roosters didn't wake me up at dawn, someone knocking at my door did instead. (Life on a beautiful island was tough, I'm telling you.) "What!"

"MekeSegaIsuluKeiToa, come play football!"

"Now?"

"Yes, now!"

I sat up. At home no one had knocked on my door in months.

On my last day near sunset, Kelly, a quiet, very serious young man about my age who'd taken us snorkeling a few hundred yards off the coast in his father's fishing boat, joined me on the porch. After a few minutes, he said, "You leave tomorrow? For home?"

"No, I keep traveling."

The sun dipped below the horizon, flooding the sky with crimson light. "I want to go to America and study to be an engineer. But I need a sponsor."

"I'm not sure what I can do."

"You could sponsor me."

"I'm not an engineer. I don't even have a job when I go back."

"But you must know someone."

"I really don't."

"Well." He reached into his pocket and handed me a piece of paper. "This is my address. If you know someone, could you help me?"

I nodded, not knowing what to say. Ignored at home, in Fiji I was everyone's hope for salvation.

He stood up and extended his hand. "It was nice to have met you."

Besides the English teachers, a fifty-ish newlywed couple was staying at the house as well. The husband's seventeen year old son from a previous marriage accompanied them. Even for a teenager Rand was obnoxious. While cheating the children at cards, he called them vulgar names and often smacked them. The father ignored his son's behavior, maybe hoping it would run its course but I often felt that despite the father's kindness towards me, he expected the family to endure his son's rude behavior because he was patronizing their hotel. I hated them.

After dinner that night, Rand came to me. "Pete, I've got a problem. I need some condoms."

"For who?"

"You know... The daughter. She wants to sleep with me and I don't have any."

"What? I mean, what?"

"The daughter—"

"Have you thought about how the family would react? You're staying in their hotel, after all."

"They've actually encouraged it. Good hospitality or something."

"What have you been telling them?"

"Nothing... So do you have any condoms?"

"Nothing? Leave me out of it."

"Come on, man."

I made eye contact and turned away.

"I gotta be careful, right? You don't think she sleeps around, do you?"

When I didn't answer, he left.

That night young men of the village visited, playing guitars and singing Bob Marley songs. We sat around talking and drinking kava until suddenly Rand rushed out of the house and asked the girl's brother in front of everyone if he had any condoms. I wanted to strangle the boy; when he left in two days, she'd still be here, now walking a different path.

High on weed, the brother laughed before telling his friends in Fijian what Rand had asked. "No, man, I don't," he responded.

"I'll give you twenty dollars."

"I don't, man."

"Forty dollars. And a pack of cigarettes." The brother set down his guitar and was back in five minutes with the condoms.

The next morning, Rand approached me. "I feel really bad." I didn't answer. "I mean, I wanted to and she wanted to, or she seemed to want me to. But she. She was a virgin."

I felt sick to my stomach. "Just go away, Rand."

"But—"

"You're everything I despise about Americans abroad. Leave."

Two days after my lunch with Belinda I approached her desk in the afternoon. She was wearing a florescent orange vest and a white construction helmet over a sleek brown dress. "Not only is she puuurrrty, she's got style."

The Finger of Warning. "Watch who you're talking to. The new fire safety chief. If I want, you burn."

"My tie is fire retardant."

"It's not your tie you have to worry about."

"So your big promotion pay the big bucks?"

Her green eyes flashing, "Get back in your cubby." She turned back to her computer and picked up a stapler.

"Put down the stapler. There's no need for violence."

"Not funny. You really need to work on your material."

"Peter!" Sigmond shouted an inch from my ear. "We don't pay you to flirt with the secretaries. That's my job."

"I am SO lucky." Belinda returned his smile.

I tried the phone next. "This is Belinda."

"Hello."

"Who's this?"

"The charming gentleman who once gave you his kidney. Who rescued your brother from an Icelandic prison. You know, Peter."

"Never heard of him."

"Good looking guy with glasses. Works in the closet with the blinking light and often walks into windows."

"Mom, is that you?"

"Wanna join me in a midday chow down?"

"I brought my lunch today."

"Peanut butter and jelly with the crusts cut off?"

"Weeds with seeds."

"Come on. It's my last day at Veronica's Secret. I promise not to make you laugh once and to tell nothing but extremely boring stories about 1031 exchanges and 754 elections."

"Such a tempting offer is hard for a girl to resist."

"And it's my treat. Cost you nothing more than suffering through the pain and excruciating agony of endlessly amusing accounting anecdotes."

"I never could pass up a bargain. All right."

"Ready?" I asked Belinda at her desk an hour later.

Her phone rang. "Please hold… It's Sigmond."

I shook my head. She left Sigmond on hold and captured my heart forever.

"Why are you running the heater?"

"My car's developed some quirks."

"Quirks?"

I floored the accelerator exiting the parking lot.

"I thought you promised no faster than Warp Speed Four."

As the transmission shifted, I let up on the gas. "I did. But I can't shift into second anymore. Gotta floor it into third."

"And the heater?"

"Prevents the radiator from overheating."

"Nice car this."

"Impresses the babes to no end."

"I did notice an entourage of lovelies clamoring for your autograph as we blasted out of the parking lot."

"I really admire your handling of Sigmond back there."

Belinda reached for the bread in the Italian restaurant. "He's really a pushover." She smiled triumphantly. "I got him to admit he was wrong yesterday."

"Seriously? You should receive an award or something. Have a television movie of the week produced in honor of your victory to inspire and instruct the directionless youth of today."

"Already in the works. Svetlana Swan is playing me. But seriously, you should stand up to him."

"Well, there was this one time when I told him: *To do your job first I don't mind the admonishment of an occasional slap to the head or even the sporadic punch in the eye, but when you threaten my eighty-one year old grandmother with death and unanesthetized dismemberment, I think you're going too far.*"

"Wow. That's really brave of you. Took real courage."

"You don't what it means to me you saying that. Baring your soul

171

so and revealing such naked vulnerability. Dipping that limb so precipitously by going out on it… And I didn't mean that as a weight joke. Crap."

Belinda's eyes wandered across the room. "I wonder if they're talking about 754 elections over there. Maybe I could join them?"

I kissed her. She glared at me. Then she kissed back. "Is that what they call a 1031 exchange?" she said, all smiles.

I nearly lectured her on how the road of accounting humor leads to nothing but darkness, trouble and regret, but I got so busy sucking face, I forgot all about it.

"I can't believe it," Belinda said.

"What?"

"I fell for your old run into a glass window and break your nose to win over my sympathy routine."

"There's a sucker born every forty-nine point six seconds."

"Next you'll try the old get my tie caught in the paper shredder and have the girl save me routine. I fell for that once." The Finger of Warning. "Once. So don't get any ideas, Smarty-pants."

"Never. Every once in a while. The third Thursday of odd-numbered months."

So Belinda and I started going to the movies and dinner Saturdays for the next month. Once we spent an evening composing our letters of resignation together. Hers was: "Fuck you!"

"I want to say *That took you twenty minutes?* but dread the consequences so I'll go with *Terse, but cogent.*"

"Wise choice. And yours?"

I shared with her the following masterpiece of modern literature:

Ladies and gentlemen and other:

A moment of your time, please. For those of you unaware of my feelings on the matter, please be advised that I fucking hate you all. I don't mean I mildly dislike you or that sometimes you really irritate me. No, I fucking hate you all. To the fullest, most comprehensive extent possible. I loathe, despise and abhor your very existence (though not necessarily in that order). I detest the ground you walk upon. I detest the ground you think about walking upon. I hate your teeth, I hate your elbows, I hate your Achilles' tendons. Your Adam's apples sicken me as do your kneecaps. I can't think of your medulla oblongatas without projectile vomiting. From head to toe, fingertip to fingertip, belly button to asshole do I despise. Not an inch nor a centimeter of your being can I tolerate.

With hugs and kisses,

Peter Pollack

"That's pretty good. A tad harsh. Maybe."

"Not too wordy?"

"Well, you wouldn't want to risk not getting your point across."

Another time we visited the mall and handed out tickets as fashion police to offenders (years later, we could have gotten a television show for such antics). Examples: "How can you wear those socks!" or "That blouse with culottes – come on!" But the pain in her laugh never went away and I wondered if I could change that. So I ignored it by never discussing the past, hoping to help her forget. But whenever she kissed me goodnight at her door, she seemed only halfway there.

I didn't send the letter when I left. Of course, I kissed their asses and told them what a great opportunity it had been to work with all of them. Sometimes you must submit. And that's what hurt most of all. For I never had before. My sister had once told me, "You don't just burn your bridges, you dynamite them." And I'd liked it at the time. Then I realized you couldn't always win. Life wouldn't let you. But this trip had me rethinking that.

A second woman from the Taveuni village helped around the house. Large and in her late forties. My last morning as I stood waiting for the bus, she passed by. "You're leaving us, Peter?"

"I'm afraid so."

"This is what I don't like about this business. Everyone is always leaving. You know, Peter, the first time I saw you I thought to myself that I had seen you somewhere before. That you had been in my life before. You have a kind face. And a good heart, I can tell. The way you play with the children and listen."

"That's very kind of you to say, Eleanor."

"Are you married, Peter?"

"No."

"I like working here because I get to meet people from all over the world and they share their lives with me. Even if it's only for a short while, it's a good feeling between people. We talk. It is good for me. You know how I came to work here? I was married when I was very young to my great love, this man I cared for as much as you can care for anyone. I was very beautiful then, very slender, not like now, all the men wanted me. But my husband, his smile was the best. He always made me laugh, even when I was sad. We had two children together. And then he died. Only twenty-four, an accident. I wanted to die I was so sad. I cried and I cried. I wanted to kill myself. I stayed in bed for almost a year. But Feena, she gave me a job and told me the sadness would pass. Her husband had died as well and we helped each other. And I got through it. My life is good now and I have a new husband, a fisherman. He is a good man, but he is not my first love. Even if life takes away what you love best, it gives you something else. I never thought I could be with another man, but now I am and I am happy. I will always love working here." She patted my arm. "I will see you again someday."

"Maybe."

"No, you will return. And you will bring your wife." She patted my arm again and walked down the path, never looking back.

At Kelly's suggestion, I next visited a neighboring island where a small fishing boat spewing noxious gasoline fumes acted as ferry once a week. "They are trying to do something different here. The hotel is owned by a Fijian, not a foreigner. They are keeping the money here, not selling our heritage to the Europeans." The hotel was beautiful, but two hundred U.S. dollars a night, and completely empty. They offered to put me up for one hundred fifty, no less, or let me sleep in an open straw hut on the beach for nine dollars a night. I chose the open hut. Swaying coconut trees, powdery white sand – little did I know that I'd strayed from the path of the righteous and become hopelessly entangled in circumstances iniquitous for I was now firmly ensconced within the clutches of the woefully malicious Porn King of

Samoa whose perverse plots of plunder knew no equal.

The island had no shops, only the restaurant's hotel offered me sustenance. As each meal time approached, the twenty-year old son of the owner would greet me with a menu asking what I would like. (Contrary to what I'd been told, the family was originally from Samoa, not Fiji.) The food was excellent (well, it smelled that way), but expensive – the cheapest meal was a side salad without dressing for fifteen dollars. "The steak is really superb. So is the seared ahi tuna with garlic mashed potatoes." For three times the price. And he insisted on joining me for every meal – always varying his choice of victuals – lobster, roasted leg of lamb with mint jelly, stuffed game hen. I had the salad every day. Once I splurged and got a small dollop of blue cheese dressing for five dollars.

But that wasn't the real trouble. Nowhere near. The toilet in all its fetid glory held that dubious honor. Renters of the open beach huts used an outside commode. The first time I opened it a swarm of mosquitoes akin to a Biblical Plague engulfed me, leaving me a pinkish welt of eczematous flesh with hair. Nor was the outside shower better. Besides the blood-sucking mosquitoes, it also housed cockroaches big enough to kick my fifth grade teacher Mrs. Rubio's ass living amid an unidentified black muck which no doubt had birthed both The Blob and The Creature From the Black Lagoon.

The second morning, I went snorkeling. Gazing out on the quiet bay fronting the hotel, I expected a myriad of virginal coral rarely viewed (the hotel was only one year old). Instead I found a dead reef, teeming with fish but lifeless and a dull brown. While building the completely unremarkable hotel to attract tourists for diving and snorkeling, they'd killed its main draw.

As I exited the water, the owner's son asked me, "How was it?"

"Lots of fish. But the reef is dead."

"Yeah, that's too bad. Did you see any good looking girls on the boat? Coming home to visit my parents is nice and relaxing, but there's no action going on. Except the last time. I must've pulled twelve or thirteen foreign birds."

"I'm the only guest?"

"We're still trying to get the word out. We've been refurbishing most of the rooms. I'm gonna take over management soon. Build a club over there, get all the young hotties here. Pumping music, booze cruises. Oh, yeah. I'll pull left and right. You're traveling for a while? You've got to tell everybody about this place. Help spread the word. Then we'll be drowning in cash." A girl who worked for the hotel appeared. He told her, "Bring me a big coke. And the king crab. Don't burn the asparagus." He turned to me. "You want anything? The lobster's really fresh."

"A large water."

He added it to my tab. Seven dollars. It cost thirty cents in Suva and a dollar in California.

"Hard to get this place started. I'm trying to come up with ideas. All the time. One thing for sure always makes money: porn. Even in a recession. They're two other things that always make money but I can't remember them. Way to get rich on this island would be to do it discreet. Everyone knows everyone else's business here: when you're fighting with your wife, who's cheating on who, everything. If you could keep it secret, you could make a fortune. That's what I did at school to make money on the side. Sold it right out of my dorm room in Auckland. To all sorts of dodgy geezers, real nut cases, some were even homeless. But they couldn't help themselves. If only I could figure out a way to do that here, I'd be set."

I turned twenty-four on the third day. For my present, a privately chartered boat arrived with two bikini clad Swedish supermodel types sunbathing on the deck. They gave me a huge wave hello. Could life really be this good? And what had I done wasting three years of it in a dark cupboard of an office, trying to fit in with (or even just be accepted by) the Robots who occupied the 27th floor? They all looked the same, dressed the same (wearing the same seven variations on suits – blue, blue pinstripe, gray, gray pinstripe, black, black pinstripe, brown – maybe a tan but this was thoroughly discouraged – an anti-pinstripe faction existed, too, but it was nowhere near as extreme as its counterpart in rival firm Hook, Line and Sinker, a California Limited Liability Partnership) and said the same things about restaurants, sports. Their wives looked the same, too. At all levels for generations. And never said a negative word about the firm. Or anything real.

The boat drew alongside the short quay and one of the girls hopped down to secure the boat. The other followed. "Cozy spot, isn't it?"

"Very much so."

Both smiled broadly at me and kissed me on each cheek with soft, warm lips. I nearly swooned.

"Yes, we come here every year with all our friends." More lovelies appeared on deck, brunettes and redheads, all epitomes of feminine exquisiteness to the delight of my pounding heart. And then I noticed most of them were holding hands. As were the four men who emerged as well.

"We're from San Francisco. How about you?"

"Los Angeles."

"How did you hear about this place?"

I hung out with them that night, but as everyone got drunker and they lost their shyness around me, it got too weird and I excused myself to the hard board floor of my open hut. I gazed at the stars for a bit, remembering my childhood dreams of someday exploring their distant worlds, finding a place where I could be accepted – where we all could.

Hours later, I woke up very, very cold to a suffocating silence. Shivering, I removed my sleeping bag and fleece jacket from my backpack.

The shivering continued. I was obviously sick. Real sick. Malaria? Something worse? I finished my only bottle of water and a moment later, thirsted for more. I remembered the health section in my guidebook and rummaged through my bag to find it, disliking leaving the comforting warmth of the sleeping bag. Then I had to find a flashlight. According to page nineteen, I might have dengue fever. But it was three o'clock in the morning – I couldn't do anything.

I counted the hours to dawn, unable to sleep and craving more water. Was my trip to end on such a note? Cut down before it even got started?

Morning arrived. When the owner came down to breakfast, I asked him, "When's the next boat?"

"Not for a week. Maybe ten days. The ferries here run on Fiji time, you know. Go when they want to."

"I'm sick. I need to get back to the mainland."

"Well, I can't do anything for a few days at least."

"I'm really sick."

"Yeah, you look it. I can probably charter a boat in three days if you want. But it'll cost you."

"How much?"

"Not so much. Maybe a thousand dollars. They can be reasonable if you negotiate right."

"A thousand dollars!"

"You don't have to have it on you. They'll take you to a bank."

I thought about asking the girls for a ride, but their boat had slipped away silently sometime during the night. So I was stranded.

Then I heard a loud, gruff voice, "*Ho, ho, ho, a pirate's life so free.*"

Chugging around the corner of our secluded bay, a square-faced fishing boat with flaking blue paint and mewling morbid plumes of greasy smoke from a crooked black pipe running starboard along its uneven roof scudded across the glassy waves into view. Two middle-aged men bedecked in flamboyant pink scarves and poofy white blouses that billowed in the fresh sea breeze manned its deck, their faces obscured by enormous cheap sunglasses and wide-brimmed straw hats. "*Ho, ho, ho, a pirate's life so free.*" It was suddenly obvious they knew none of the other words.

I feared the worst, but these madmen were to become my saviors.

Arriving at the dock, they announced to me, "We're a couple of wild and crazy Swedes looking for cubicle women. Does their kind lurk here?"

"There's a few here of the rather large persuasion, yes."

"Excellent." They tossed me the rope to secure their boat. "We are going to get us some chicks – Fijian beauties. Thomas – he likes them square, cubicles. Those are his, I want the slender ones."

"What about me?"

"All else for…"

"Peter."

"You look terrible."

"I feel terrible."

"You need to go to a hospital."

"Can't. No boat for at least four more days."

They exchanged glances. "We'll take you tomorrow."

"What? Are you sure?"

"Yes, no problem. But now we have dinner." And just like that, I was saved.

As we disembarked the next morning and left behind a pair of weeping Fijian women waving to Sven and Thomas, Sven proffered me slabs of fresh papaya. I had to ride on deck with them because the entire hold was full of beer but I didn't care. Even the pungent mix of suntan oil, perspiration and rotten fish smelled like lilac and daffodils to me. And their erratic driving was a welcome eccentricity. Until they began steering facing me while sitting down drinking a beer.

"Reef," I squawked.

"What did you say?"

"Aren't you worried about the reef?"

"There's no reef around here. Charts say so," Thomas said nonchalantly as he popped open another beer bottle with his teeth, grimacing.

"These are of Samoa!"

"Oh, right." He stood up and surveyed the horizon, suddenly jerking the steering wheel to the right. He winked at me as his companion spilled beer on himself and I got ready to be torn apart on the jagged coral before being devoured by man-eating (and kind of deliberate about it) sharks. "Does that look like Savusavu to you? Or Nabouwalu?"

"I've never been to either one."

"Hmmm... Hope we're not lost."

"We run out of food, we eat the youngest one first. Meat's more tender." Sven winked.

"*Ho, ho, ho. A pirate's life so free!*"

"Where will we take you?"

"A hostel."

"Hospital?"

"No, hostel."

"Oh, yes, those are good."

Sven said, "You don't know what opportunities this hostel thing

179

gives you. It's difficult to meet people as you get older: everyone's married or been married and doesn't want to be again. You get to meet people with the same outlook on life as you. It's so hard to find those people and especially ones that are single. Thomas and I, we've both been married, both been divorced. Me, twice. The second one was such a mistake. I don't know, I've given up trying to find someone who will always make me happy. So this is what we do now."

"Drink beer and chase Fijian women?"

"Yes!"

"Yes!"

What the hell, might as well have fun if I was going to die.

Sometime later, Sven told me, "Those women we met, they were so nice, so innocent and undemanding. Beautiful inside. Crying when we left. But you can't take them from here, it's their world. And you can't live here and leave behind your work and what you are. All you have is moments."

Coming into Nandi the next day, the dawn's sun was bathing the bay the dusky red of congealed blood. Between ruptured shacks and crumbling docks, floating slabs of driftwoods and trailings of various human refuse clanked noisily against the returning boat amid the hum and sputter of the vessel's diesel engine.

Thomas and Sven hailed a taxi and drove me to the nearest traveler's hotel where I shared a room with other backpackers. Along the way, they bought me a gallon of orange juice sweetened with 359 pounds of processed sugar and told me to remember to remain hydrated. As I climbed under the covers, the fever took over.

A blonde Dutch girl with distant eyes was staring at me from a bed across the communal hotel room. "You're awake. We thought we were going to have to take you to the hospital. Your fever was quite bad. You kept shouting *You get the cubicle women, the rest are for me!*"

I laughed. "Did I get them?"

"Sure."

I reached down to drink some more orange juice and found the jug

180

teeming with ants. "Been in Fiji a while?"

"About a month actually. I'm leaving now. On my way to the States. It's time to do something different. It's what I like. Do everything if I can."

"Oh?"

"I've been a bartender, worked in a post office, even was a stripper. Just for a week. For the experience. Life has such possibilities, why do the same thing over and over again? I mean, it's good for some people, they like the sense of familiarity, of belonging, no surprises. Not for me. I get too tied down, I gotta move."

"I'm the same way. Sometimes. Probably not enough."

"Why not?"

"I don't know." I thought about this. "Well, I guess I do."

"We are who we are, not who we think we want to be." She smiled.

"Where did you stay in Fiji?"

"Taveuni."

"Oh? I stayed in the north."

"With those Swedish guys?"

"No, they actually volunteered to take me back here when I got ill. For nothing. Very kind men."

"They kept checking on you."

"How can I be the world's biggest cynic if things like that happen?"

"Don't worry. Someone else will ruin it for you."

"Fingers crossed. You were in Taveuni a whole month?"

"I was staying with someone I met while shopping in the village. Monday I found out something about him and knew it was time to go."

"Oh?"

"Well, he kept staring at me when we met and he was like no one I had ever been with and so I went with him. He was so innocent, childlike even. He was fascinated by my blonde hair. But then I returned to the hostel where I was staying on Monday and a girl was standing in the garden in the middle of the day. Just standing there. I asked her why. She told me that she was guarding the hostel from the boy I was with. He was some sort of gangster who broke into hotels and stole from tourists. He even tried to rape one girl. But they never called the police. Everyone was family there. The tourists would be gone tomorrow, having lost a few dollars, nothing to them, not really, and they'd still be there. With nothing. So nothing happened to him. She told me all this."

"And you left?"

"Not right away. I'd never been with anyone like that before. I'd had a feeling he was like that, but not for sure. Tough guy. When I left, he cried. He said I'd changed him, that no one had ever treated him so well before. I felt bad for him. But... Well."

"You had to go."

She checked her watch. "As I have to now. I'm glad you're better. Take care."

The next day I changed my flight, bought my father the least expensive T-shirt I could find (I ran into a seventy year old man in the street and offered to buy it right off his back — he let me follow him home to complete the transaction. The bright pink concoction had a yellow arrow pointing downward on its front with the caption *One in the Oven*. Perfect for my father. Only cost me two dollars and twelve cents. I threw in an extra dollar and eighty-eight cents because he let me take a photo of him modeling it to include with the parcel to my father.), and, the weather being windy and rainy, went to the movies. Not one seat in the movie theatre was unbroken — it looked like the remnants of a World War II carpet-bombing — and it was eerily deserted. When I returned to the hostel, everyone asked where I was. Apparently there'd been a hurricane warning during the movie and everyone had to evacuate. I could only respond, "It was kinda windy when I went."

In the morning I flew to New Zealand and left Fiji behind.

The Girl Who Runs

From the Auckland airport, I took a bus to the waterfront and walked to the Auckland Central Backpackers hostel. After spending a month on Fiji, seeing American fast food chain restaurants, shopping malls and new cars shocked me a bit.

The hostel was enormous, seven stories with three receptionists and a travel agent. Before receiving my key, I was subjected to a six-minute spiel on how management was not liable for the loss of any valuables stored in the rooms and not in the downstairs safe. The safe that stood wide open behind the receptionist within arm's reach of anyone checking in. I politely declined to leave any of my one thousand U.S. dollars with the receptionist and was pertly rebuked: "Don't come cryin' to us if you get robbed."

A shaggy haired Englishman with a scorpion tattoo on his right bicep was in the twelve bed room. "You're from America? I hate America."

"Why's that?"

"I tried to leave and they wouldn't let me. Put me in jail for two weeks. Stupid fucking country."

184

"They wouldn't let you?"

"I had the plane ticket and everything. Was going home from Japan for Christmas to see my parents. I get to immigration and they arrest me. I was just going to take a couple of days to see Seattle and then get on a plane. Made the American taxpayers pay for me to stay in jail when all I wanted to do was leave the country."

"But what was the reason?"

"They said I'd lied on my traveler's visa about never being convicted of a felony."

"What'd you do?"

"Nothing. Just sold some drugs like ten years ago, I didn't kill anybody."

"That's too bad."

"I fucking hate America."

Six weeks after my first date with Belinda, I had to return to Veronica's Secret to finish up. I went by her desk a few times but she was never there. Then, an hour before I was to leave, I managed to spill coffee on the crotch of my tan trousers. I was able to keep the incident mostly quiet, besides the usual head banging, fist clenching and a few muttered vituperations over the rather extreme temperature of the boiling liquid (and I did collapse the table when I lashed out with my legs, but that's to be expected, I should think). Quickly shielding my crotch with the largest of the scattered files, I prepared for a dash to the bathroom. Trying to will away Belinda by staring down the hall, I ran blindly into Svetlana Swan, the lingerie magazine's cover model.

"I'm terribly sorry," the brown-haired Czech beauty said with a voice that could melt both polar caps and half of Siberia *before* the start of Global Warming.

"No, it's my fault." Fearing she would glimpse my sodden groin, I fled from probably the most beautiful woman in the world, an act I would regret to the end of my days. A very sympathetic "No, it's mine." followed me down the hall. Hearing the voices of the controller and Sigmond approaching around the next corner, I darted inside the bathroom just in time. Sigh of relief and then a slap to the forehead. Following: a survey of the damage. Bad, very bad. A dark stain almost to the knee. I turned on the hot water tap and unfurled wads of toilet paper in an attempt to clean up. Then, brilliantly, I unbuckled my pants to tackle the stain from both sides. Brilliantly because just as I began this operation with my trousers pooled around my knees, Svetlana Swan opened the door. I'd gone into the women's restroom in my haste. And I hadn't used the lock.

"Oh, excuse me."

To perfect my humiliation, as Svetlana shut the door, Sigmond's laughter roared behind her. Even my grandchildren would probably hear a version of this story from complete strangers on trips to Upper Mongolia or the far reaches of the Kashmir.

After the incident, Belinda didn't return my calls for two weeks so I left one last message: "We used to be so close. We used to connect. Now you never call, you never write. I can't even talk to you anymore. We had good times together: going to the copy room, stapling things, changing the coffee filters. Good times. Lots of laughs. What happened?"

My phone rang two minutes after I hung up. "Hello?"

"Has she called?" It was my mother.

"No."

"She doesn't know what she's missing. You're very sweet when you want to be, Peter. If she can see that side of you and she doesn't call, she's an idiot."

"Thanks, Mom. But don't call her that. I think she's still hurt by the divorce. I wanted to help her."

"I know you did, sweetie. And if she can't see that, that's her problem, not yours."

"I know. She just, she makes me want to be better so I can help her. I hope she didn't think I was trying to take advantage of her being hurt."

"She's been divorced, what, a year? If she thinks that, she's still screwed up."

"Mom, I really don't want to talk about it anymore."

"Okay. Goodnight, Peter. I love you."

"You, too, Mom. Thanks for listening."

"That's what mothers are for. It's in our contract, under the changing diapers bit – which clause I could have done without, mind you."

186

"You're not going to start in on the eleven hours of labor again, are you?"

"It was twelve. And don't sass your mother."

"I love you, too." I hung up. The phone rang again immediately. "I'd like to order a pepperoni pizza with extra cheese," I said.

"Word on the street is you had some trouble."

"Belinda." I sat down on my bed. Such an empty apartment: blank walls, one couch, two chairs, a table. I cleared my throat. "Vicious lies spread by the iniquitous. No doubt the progeny of a scandalous, unrepentant rumor-monger of the most unsavory sort."

"You're forgetting I was there when you broke your nose."

"You didn't call me back."

"I had some stuff to work through. It's been hard for me to do that."

"I'm sorry."

"You shouldn't be sorry, it has nothing to do with you. It's my stuff. It's hard for me to trust anyone after what happened with my... husband."

"You can trust me, Belinda." No answer. "Can I see you this weekend?" No answer. "Can I?"

"You don't like your job, Pete."

I nearly dropped the phone. "Yeah. Well, it's only temporary until I get my license. Can I see you?"

"Okay. Come by Sunday. We'll watch the Super Bowl."

When I went by three days later, her apartment was empty. She'd moved out. And her cell-phone was disconnected. I never saw her again.

I spent weeks analyzing our time together, going over and over things she'd told me. Torturing myself, trying to find an answer. But there was no answer. She was gone and there was nothing I could do about it. I drank for a while, trying to forget and feeling sorry for myself. But I thought about how my father had been and what I'd promised myself in those dark nights in my bedroom under the covers with my mom crying next to me and I stopped.

The Auckland hostel bar on the roof was open to the cool night sky. After ordering a pitcher of Mac's Black beer, I sat down at one of the wooden tables where a man with dark features and a shaved head about ten years older than me sat alone. "Peter."

"Murray."

"Been traveling long?"

"On and off for about ten years. I get a job for a year or two and then fuck off again when I'm ready."

"You must have met lots of great people."

"Actually, I met my wife traveling."

"She's here?"

"She's at home with our kid. I'm headed there in a few days. But, really, most travelers are fucking idiots. They spend all of their money on drugs and alcohol. And they pay triple what the locals do. When I traveled Europe, I did it for nothing. Always hitchhike or, if I took a train, I'd jump off just before where the conductors would get on. You just have to ask the locals. And I never paid for food. When I was hungry, I'd go into a supermarket and eat right off the shelf. No one has the balls to say anything. I'd chuck the empty packages in the cart and if they said they'd seen me eating it, I'd say I was going to pay for it. Otherwise, I'd say the empty packages were in there when I got the cart. As for accommodation: you can always get a free shower in a hostel. Just walk right in. Just look like you know where you're going. If you can't find a free bed, you can always sleep in a t.v. room. As a last resort, I'd sleep in my bag on the beach."

More of his stories included how he had paid for his traveling by smuggling currency illegally out of Cyprus in the soles of his shoes. I wasn't exactly sure how you made money doing that, but I found it fascinating, nevertheless (the second pitcher of Mac's Black may have amplified my enthusiasm). When I watched a short Swiss girl with a blonde comma of hair pass by the table, he smiled. "You're too eager, man. Girls can sense it in your eyes. Look like you don't care. If we talked to that one, she'd be throwing herself at me because she'd see your desperation. It'd be easy pickings."

"All right, I admit I'm desperate. But you're married."

"All birds traveling are looking for it. I wouldn't ask, but if it was offered, I wouldn't refuse. Angry if my old lady did the same. But as for
188

me, I'd never tell her."

"Let's test your theory." I stood up and walked to the bar, passing a hungry-eyed Danish girl no more than eighteen sitting at an abandoned table drinking off the dregs of beer in the leftover glasses.

The Swiss girl turned my way as I waited for another pitcher. "How are you?" she asked politely.

"I'm very disappointed, actually. When People Magazine's list of the Fifty Most Beautiful People on the Planet came out this week, I wasn't in it. The competition's rigged, I swear."

Her eyes lit up. "These things are so subjective."

"Easy for you to say – this the fourth time you've made the list?"

"Fifth. But who's counting?"

"What's your beauty secret? Drink lots of water, regular exercise, only eat raw broccoli florets and organically grown carrots?"

She laughed. "Never pay for anything."

"So what did you do today?"

"I had a very, very busy day. Exhausting, really. I bought a toothbrush."

"And?"

"What do you mean: *and*?"

"Nothing. Not a thing."

"How about you?"

"I negotiated a peace treaty between Israel and Palestine, discovered a cure for AIDS, *and* had some calcium-enriched, not from concentrate orange juice all before noon. Before noon."

"*And* after noon?"

"I took a nap. After such a constructive morning, I figured I was entitled."

"You *are* on vacation."

"My point exactly. So you took it easy today besides the toothbrush shopping: no polar bear wrestling, no shark hunting?"

"Well, just a little."

"Which?"

"Shark hunting. Great whites. Anything smaller is not really worth the effort, you know?"

"Not with a spear gun, I hope. Takes all the sport out of it."

"Please. I only use my bare hands."

"Lethal weapons they are."

"Don't mess with me."

"I don't intend to. Well, just a little."

A minute later we were making out furiously.

Twenty minutes in, she stopped kissing me and said, "Do you have a car?"

"Um. No."

She considered this. "Do you want to join me tomorrow then? Try hitchhiking together?"

"Um." I'd never hitchhiked before. But then I'd never made out with a Swiss girl in a bar before. Maybe that was part of the reason why. I had to change that. "That sounds good."

We started kissing again. Then she stopped. "I was in a very controlling relationship for three years before I came away. I had to call him when I went home, to the store, everything. I don't want to be told what to do ever again."

"Um. Okay."

She smiled. "I'm Sara."

"Peter."

"The pitcher's empty."

"I'll get another."

When I came back from the bar, Sara wasn't at the table. I found her playing pool with two Australian guys. And smoking.

"Hey."

"Hey." She took the pitcher from my hands and poured both of us a drink. "You play?"

"Not very well."

"Don't worry, I'm awesome. Wickedly so."

She was. She won game after game for us. Three pitchers in, I went to the bathroom to splash water on my face. When I returned, one of the Australians – a scuba dive instructor – had bought her a rum and coke.

A hand clapped down on my shoulder from behind. "I was wrong," Murray said.

"How are you?"

"Good. Me and a couple of guys are going down to the waterfront to do some more drinking. Join us?"

"Nah, I think I've had it."

"All right, but get her away from the scuba diver."

I turned back to the table and Sara was gone. So were the Australians. Twenty minutes later, I realized they weren't returning and stumbled off to bed.

The next morning, I checked out of the hostel. When I turned from the reception desk, Sara was standing before me with her raggedy blue backpack in hand. "Ready to go?" she asked me.

"What?"

"I thought we could try to hitchhike to Lake Taupo tonight. I want to go skydiving there."

"What?"

"Did you want a coffee first or something?"

"No. Um. Yeah. Okay. Let's go."

We caught a city bus to the outskirts of Auckland and then chose a popular roundabout to begin our journey.

Hitchhiking is not as easy as it seems: stick your thumb out and seconds later someone picks you up. No, it takes patience. People honk at you, shout. Hit mud puddles you hadn't seen and spray you. Throw garbage. Run over your foot if you're not careful. Thirty minutes passed, an hour.

"I've never had to wait so long for a ride," Sara said, lighting up a cigarette.

"I could show more leg."

"You don't want to blind people."

"I'll have you know I was Mr. California runner-up just last year."

"Americans have such bad taste."

A car stopped. A man in his late thirties with long thinning brown hair rolled down the passenger window and asked our destination. "Okay, but first I gotta pee. Do you wanna wait?"

"We'll wait."

When the driver, Malcolm, returned from a nearby restaurant, Sara and I got in his car. "I love this song," he announced and started a cassette. The song was Svetlana Swan's *I Can't Let You Out of My Bed*. As we drove away, he began humming along. It became obvious he didn't know any of the words except the title which was repeated exactly fifteen times in three minutes and twenty-six seconds. The first time Svetlana crooned those eight words that will haunt me the rest of my days, Malcolm glanced at us nervously and sang along tentatively. By the third chorus, his shyness was gone and he was literally shouting them. Sara and I suffered, suppressing giggles, but knowing it could only last for a few minutes. How wrong we were. "I really love that song."

I said, "Yeah, it's nice."

"Nice," Sara echoed.

"You think so? Let's listen to it again, then."

"Um."

Malcolm rewound the tape. He sang along again. His ardor did not lessen the second time. When it ended, he smiled at us. "I love that song! Let's listen to it once more."

"Malcolm, really…"

"Once more." Sara and I had tears in our eyes when "Again!"

This went on for some time. Thirteen minutes and forty-four seconds actually. "Is anyone else dying for a slash?" Without checking over his left shoulder, looking at any of his mirrors or even using a turn signal, Malcolm cut across two lanes of traffic and screeched to halt on the shoulder amid the sound of screeching brakes and flaring horns.

"Let's go," I said.

"Maybe he won't play it again."

"You're kidding."

"Could we throw it out the window?"

"He'll have extra copies."

"I'll ask him nicely."

"It won't work."

"Sorry, guys," Malcolm said as he climbed back in the car.

In a sweet voice, Sara asked, "Malcolm, could we listen to something else for a while?"

"Nah, we'll play it just once more."

"Malcolm."

"Once more. It grows on you, it really does."

Twenty-seven minutes and twenty-eight seconds later when Malcolm had to urinate again, Sara and I ran from the car screaming with our hands clamped over our ears.

We were trapped on a large concrete bridge, miles from the next exit. It wasn't very safe for anyone to stop so they didn't. Sara dropped her pack and sat on it.

I pointed up. "Do you see that streetlamp?" Sara nodded without looking. "I traveled all over the world to find that streetlamp – you can even check my guidebook, I've got it highlighted. World famous it is, people from places as far flung as Burkina Faso and French Guiana flock here in droves to see it. And now that I've found it, I can't take a photo because I forgot to buy film."

"That's sad."

"Tragic, really. A catastrophe of epic proportions sure to go down in history as one of the worst of our generation."

"I just said it was sad. Don't get melodramatic on me."

Smiling, I turned my head and there it was. But it couldn't be. My stolen car. Racing past, ignoring my outstretched thumb. In New Zealand? Impossible. But how many Chevrolets got sold here? Any? Especially silver ones. I tried to distinguish the trademark dent in the rear fender but the car was already too far away.

"That."

"What?"

"Nevermind."

A cold drizzle began.

The drizzle increased to a shower and then a downpour. No one stopped.

"Don't worry. I've got an inflatable raft inside my pack."

"That's not funny."

"And scuba gear."

She smiled. Sort of. "How about dry cigarettes?"

Then the rain stopped and so did a jeep. "They've only got room for one," Sara said from the door. I shrugged and turned around to resume our vigil. The sound of a car door closing turned me back.

I was on my own again.

Five minutes later it began raining again.

I was halfway to the next off ramp when a Japanese tour bus stopped.

The bus driver motioned for me to sit down. "Where to?" he asked in broken English.

"Hamilton, Taupo, someplace not so wet."

He nodded and took a savage bite of the sausage pie in his hand. He shifted the bus into gear and merged back onto the highway. Juggling a bottle of soda, the pie and a microphone, he turned the steering wheel mostly with his supple gut over the slippery road fraught with steep embankments and sharp curves. All the while he never stopped talking in Japanese and gesturing frantically at the passing sights, much to the distress of cars sharing the two lane road as he tended to veer into any direction he was pointing. My fellow passengers seemed oblivious to any potential danger, no doubt pondering the plethora of pertinent facts the guide was ennumerating: the average annual precipitation of the North Island versus the South, the gross national product and reminiscences of the 1983 All-Blacks New Zealand Rugby Team. Nor did the driver shy from passing other vehicles, even on blind curves. Despite the skid-outs and ubiquitous squeal of brakes, I was too wet to care. But I sometimes get flashbacks.

On the outskirts of Rotorua, a town best known for the sulfurous scent of its surrounding geysers and hot springs, the tourist bus got a flat tire, sending us bumping into a ditch and I was able to escape. I spent the night in a hostel and got a ride from a German couple sharing my room the next morning.

I saw Sara again. She was with a sky diving instructor in a Taupo bar. He was buying her a drink.

I awoke from a daze of unconsolidated balances and faulty internal controls to find myself, horribly enough, still at work. Up all night worrying about a column of numbers that just wouldn't foot, checking and rechecking each figure for any transpositions as the night and my sanity trickled away, I'd fallen asleep at my computer keyboard again. A screen full of the letter "r" confirmed this as did the unpleasant dent in my nose. Wondering why I'd ever become an accountant for the 3,023rd time in the past eighteen hours, I began to rise. It was five o'clock.

Making my way through a labyrinth of dark-stained wooden cubicles and then through an outer circle of temporary cardboard ones, I emerged from *The Pit* after getting lost only twice – a new record (I kept forgetting to bring string to map my course). Broken adding machines, open manila files and adding machine tape that billowed softly in the air from the numerous electric fans failing miserably to make up for the woefully inadequate air-conditioning obstructed my path like debris after an aerial bombing. A comrade in arms, a low level peon like myself, lay cradling one of the secretary's computer monitors – no doubt used for its screen size which was double that of entry level staff's – like a child embracing a cherished teddy bear. His arms awry, his legs askew, his jaw slack and lip dribbling onto a page full of numbers that had now blended together into one large ink spot, the sleeping accountant comforted me: others suffered as I did.

Returning to my desk with a cup of coffee that was fresh twelve hours ago, I again tackled the column of numbers in question. No, I didn't leave. I didn't much, anymore. Not since Belinda.

"Are you good at writing, Peter?"

I blinked and there was Cassandra hovering over me, hours or minutes later, I couldn't tell.

"Well?"

"I think so."

"And doing research?"

"I haven't done much of it."

A sigh of disappointment that lasted one thousand years. Then she emitted a belch (with no effort at concealment) redolent of pastrami, garlic pickles and stale coffee. Somehow, someway I maintained consciousness (the other occupants of my quad failed at this behind me). Not apologizing, she said: "Write up a memo on whether or not the CEO of Woodpecker Peaches can deduct the expenses of shuttling back and forth between Seattle and Los Angeles. He lives in Seattle and the business is here on Flower Street. It's for Barrington." She left, her high heels click-clacking across the carpet unevenly but with a grim conviction in her own greatness.

As Wrasse left that night at five-thirty, I saw him glaring at me in the reflection of my computer screen as he passed right by my desk, much closer than usual.

"You're still here, Peter."

"Yes, Sigmond."

Disregarding the possible cataclysmic consequences of such an ill-forethought action, I tore my eyes from the thrilling pages of volume four of

196

the Federal Income Tax Regulations and looked up to "Why?"

"I'm working on your tax return, remember?"

"It's dark outside."

"And it was dark when I got here this morning."

He took a long look at me. "Sit down. I want to tell you the facts of life."

"I am sitting."

"Then I'll sit down... Pete, you seem like a nice kid. I use you not because you're the best guy here but because you're the cheapest billable staff, so I get the best realization on my contracts. It's great that you use the relaxed scrutiny on the cost of your billed hours to learn, but know this firm doesn't give a fuck about you. Barrington doesn't give a fuck about you, I don't give a fuck about you. Never befriend a coworker because they might have to terminate you or you them or a promotion goes to one of you and not the other. Use them as they use you. You're so naive, I think you're actually trying to make friends here. Placate the clients, kiss their fucking asses and tell no one anything. This is war. If you wanna be a general in this fucking army listen to me. I was a soldier in Iran. Life was hell. Life is good here. There is no one shooting at you, there is no sun. This may be bad news but life is good." He stood up and disappeared into the shadows.

Despite swearing I really was going to make it home that night, I awoke again the next morning at my desk but with a splitting headache and a world horribly skewed. While my temples throbbed, the florescent lights overhead kept bursting into fragmented shards and tumbling away across my vision. What the hell had happened?

Sculpin joined me downstairs for a bagel.

"I think Wrasse put something in my coffee last night."

Sculpin shrugged, nonplussed. "It wouldn't be the first time."

"Seriously?"

"Yep."

"If he wishes to do battle, we shall do battle. But, oh, woe is he. For he that crosses blue pencils with me knows not of the pain and suffering that shall befall him. For he incurs a most furious and wrathful vengeance against him. His likeness shall be vanquished from the annual roster of Certified Public Accountants in the state of California. Sorrow unbearable and perpetual inability to foot shall be his fate. He shall pray for death, even via asset-up form division. His pleas for forgiveness will go unheeded, his cries for mercy and sufficient continuing education hours shall be met with scorn. For I will annihilate him thoroughly, strike him from the land of the living, and grind him to pink eraser dust. His hopes, dreams and aspirations will be torn asunder. He will have no future and no past. He will possess not even the ignominy of being only an Enrolled Agent, but just anguish without stop. Ceaseless agony shall be his wont."

"So you're angry?"

"Whatever he wants: guns, knives, staplers at dawn. Halberds, Tommy guns, bazookas. He will plead for my pity and find me the extreme opposite of pusillanimous."

"Sure. Can you pass me a napkin?"

That night I had to stay until midnight to wait for Wrasse to leave. My socks were clammy, pungent sponges, a result of not changing them for three days, and didn't match. I had about 27 black socks at home, none of which had a mate; somehow they disappeared in the washing machine or in my drawer or were pilfered by my grandmother. When Belinda once commented on it, I told her that was how I kept my individuality at work and she looked at me like I was the third most pathetic person alive behind the man who'd been failing for six years to break the world record for stuffing the most number of ping pong balls in his mouth at one time and my Algebra II teacher Mrs. Higgins (the explanation of which would take another book).

I kept passing Wrasse's desk every few hours all day long and his computer was always on. When he wasn't there at eleven, I decided to look for him.

The back conference room affectionately nicknamed by the partners Hog Heaven was empty. This was the venue of choice for all of the firing. The name came from a contest to name all of the conference rooms on the 28th floor – Wrasse wasn't in Cloud Nine or Surfers Paradise, either. (The staff knew them as The Dungeon, The Cell and, for the location of the terminations, The Abattoir. Industrial strength disinfectant was needed to clean up its tears, vomit and blood and, per partner mandate, it was always kept spic and span. No peon ever emerged from its depths alive… Rumor had it a Not-For-Profit Specialist had once blown his brains out in there.)

198

I checked the Employee's Graveyard as well. An unused file room the partners had obviously forgotten had become the resting place for the magnetic nameplates given on your first month anniversary (they didn't bother printing them before that – saved money). Plates covered all four walls and, in some places, overlapped each other.

The bathroom. A place I avoided since the lights out incident, opting instead to use the one at the Lord of the Burgers down the street when I had one of my breaks every three hours. All the stalls were empty. But etched on one wall with what looked like a big knife was the following:

An Accountant's Lament

This firm

Makes me squirm,

Wears me out,

Makes me shout,

Tears me down,

Makes me frown,

Drives me nuts,

Churns my guts,

Rips apart

My lonely heart,

Fires hate

Without abate

Breaks my will.

I've had my fill

Of crying,

Spying,

Lying and other stuff.

Yes, I've had enough.

No pay is worth this shit.

How I long for the day I quit!

But I can't be rash,

I'm short of cash.

So until then I can only ache

For that elusive coffee break.

I spotted Wrasse. Sleeping contentedly with a huge smile on his face beneath Cassandra's desk (I heard the snoring). His face propped against a pillow and covered in a promotional blanket bearing the firm's logo. A well-worn copy of Anglers' Weekly magazine curled loosely in his right fist. Rat fucking bastard. Keeping me here working while he slept.

So I returned to his desk and, after a quick visit to my car for tools, took all the screws out of his chair.

The next morning, despite my exhaustion, I came in extra early to watch my master plan wreak its desired revenge, unaccustomedly grinning the whole elevator trip up.

But my victory was not to be. Wrasse did not arrive at nine. Nor by ten. (And Cassandra, whose job it was to mark who was and was not at their desks in the mornings, was not to be found. Later I did, however, find a notice on my chair asking where I'd been. I knew it was coming, but I didn't care.) Then I heard his repugnant guffaw approaching. Saying hello to this secretary and that, whistling some insipid tune. As he turned the corner heading towards his cubby, he was cut off by Barrington congratulating him on his long hours. Gleeful anticipation grew in my breast. He was at his cubicle. A loud crash. Oh, such a smile came to my lips. A cry of pain. But it was not Wrasse's, but that of the extremely nice, extremely pregnant woman from the Information Technology department who had tried to install a new security program on his computer.

What had I done?

But she was okay (I bought her flowers and chocolate anonymously – yes, it was the cowardly way to apologize). So I gave up on revenge.

I couldn't let it go. Two weeks later I checked out files in Wrasse's name and hid them in the Employee's Graveyard. Barrington congratulated Wrasse ecstatically the following week because he'd forgotten to remove an incriminating memo from one of those files and had avoided disaster with the IRS agent who was conducting an audit in our office the day before.

I tried stealing his keys from his desk and moving his car. A crane collapsed on the old parking space.

Revenge is so futile…

At day's end following a group email announcing the firm would start charging $1.75 for a cup of the always stale, always bitter break room coffee (*10% less than Coffee Cup!* was the sales pitch) to help pay for the elaborate floral arrangements in the 28th floor reception area (phrases in said memo abounded with "one must appear successful to be successful" and "sacrifices must sometimes be made for the good of the firm"), I received another email specifically addressed to me and only me:

We know that you defaced company property with your pornographic manifesto. Confess to the error of your ways and we will let you off with a warning and a mild punishment. Do not admit your guilt and, when proved, we will make you pay for the refurbishing of the entire bathroom as well as terminating your employment. Because of union labor and our accustomed rigorous attention to detail, the best of three estimates is that the price of this is forty-two thousand, one hundred nineteen dollars and twenty-seven cents. All vacation, pension and medical benefits will also be immediately forfeit as a result of your malicious intent. Unless, of course, you repent now.

I was a beaten man that day, I admit it. Please don't tell anyone. Except maybe your crazy cousin Ludwig who talks to mannequins and can't pronounce the word "ambivalent" correctly. But, please, no one else.

I told no one for days of the email and did my best to hide at work (arriving early, leaving late and by the stairway (28 floors worth) – my legs hated me at first and, to be honest, never really changed their opinion later). Then Sculpin cornered me in the bathroom and, after checking under all the stalls for feet, said: "Don't worry. They sent one to everyone." as if he knew exactly what I was thinking (sadly, he did). As I opened my mouth to respond, he said, "Better to talk at lunch."

As we boarded the elevator, Barrington stepped inside beside us. "Where you guys going?"

"Lunch."

"Let's go to my club. I'll buy."

Walking along Flower, we suddenly turned down a deserted alleyway with no exit. Behind an old blue dumpster was a scarred black door which Barrington knocked at three times, paused and knocked twice more in quick succession. The door creaked open and we were admitted to his club – walls paneled with mahogany, white tablecloths, a long oak bar and gloved waiters with slicked back hair and bright red cummerbunds. We ordered and I said: "I heard your wife's pregnant. Congratulations."

"Thanks."

"Is this your first?"

"With Brenda, yes. I was married once before."

"Oh?"

"She died of breast cancer. Our son is eighteen, our daughter fourteen."

"I'm sorry."

"It happened long ago. But now I've been lucky enough to find someone else. Very lucky."

"You're young to have been a partner so long. What: five, six years?"

He took a sip of his iced tea. "I used to live here at the office. Spent my nights reading in the library after work. It's what you have to do if you want it. And I wanted it. But I didn't see her much. I regret that. But you can't change the past. And you can't get it back."

"How come all your managers are new?"

He smiled. "I used to have a temper. I yelled a lot. And maybe I drank too much. But after Betty... Well, the managers before were all horrible to the staff – everyone kept quitting. Cassandra, Sigmond: they're much better, don't you think?"

202

Sculpin warned me with his eyes. "Yes," I answered.

"I know. They have their problems. But the ones before were actually much worse. Much worse. One staff actually tried to kill herself. Twenty-three years old. It was very sad... You're from Wisconsin, Peter?"

So I was a little relieved until a week later when a familiar-looking handwriting analyst was brought in to identify the poem's author. He went from desk to desk reciting his mantra "I'm Mr. Marlin. I cannot be bribed."

When he told my cubicle-mate Gustave "What the hell kind of name is Gustave? We'll call you Gus" Guppy of his immunity to subornation, Gus added: "Probably?" and that was the last anyone ever saw of Gus (including, apparently, his parents).

Two weeks after that, a demand was made for all employees to submit blood, urine and semen (yes, even) samples in order to catch the culprit which was allowed in the fine print on page 14 under footnote 37 of Appendix E of our employment contracts.

Below Taupo, I hiked a trail called the Tongariro Crossing. Volcanic landscape and turquoise lakes under a blaring sun and endless blue sky after a morning of mountains shrouded in mist gave me a beautiful day. I met a pretty American girl in her early thirties named Amy while eating lunch near Emerald Lakes who offered me a ride to Wellington, but I'd bought a bus ticket the day before and I spent the whole ride there the next day wishing I'd gone with her. Perched on the sea's edge, the city's open streets were pummeled by a brisk wind which left the night bitterly cold. I looked for Amy in the hostel bar, but didn't find her. The next morning I caught a ferry to Picton, winding through lumpy green islands radiant in the gorgeous yellow light piercing through the gray heavens. But where I really wanted to go was into the wild again. So I continued to Nelson and met the girl who runs. And everything changed after that.

I first saw Karlijn in the pouring rain. Running barefoot down to the beach clad in only a very transparent white brassiere and underpants. Eight foot waves crashed into the shore of coarse, golden sand. She was going to swim in them. I was shivering under the porch of the Anchorage Hut, the first shelter on the Abel Tasman track in New Zealand. Four hours of hiking in the rain had saturated me.

"That girl's crazy," I said to the nearest person to me, a towering giant with blonde curls, a sunburnt nose and hands the size of Bolivia.

"I think that looks refreshing," he said and went off to join her.

"Everyone else here is crazy, but me. I'm normal." Into the warm, dry hut I went.

In one corner, six men aged forty to sixty-five, some with hair, most without, crowded around a young blonde German girl with glasses. She was one of those unprepared hikers found haunting the huts of New Zealand: no rain gear, no food, and no sleeping bag, all thought to be provided by the hiking faeries. The men hovered over her like lappet-faced vultures around a savannah kill: drool running off their lips and slicking the floor already wet with rain. Each jockeyed for prime position, shoving and scratching to be the one that provided her with some of their steak, Massaman curry or Sunday trifle.

A wave of sound rocked the tiny hut constructed of only wood and reinforced concrete as eight women in their forties entered. Armed with lavish cutlery and crockery to rival the world's most distinguished kitchens, the women inundated us with a laughter whose roar would endure long after the heavens deprived us of their illumination and swaddled all in ultimate darkness. Sometimes, late at night when I'm alone in the dark, I still hear that horrific sound and my screams cannot be stifled. Defying explanation, the walls contained it, rupturing in places but overall staying intact enough to keep out the rain.

I found an abandoned bench to prepare my dried noodle soup and tried to think warm thoughts: a day on the Santa Monica beach, the Mojave desert, the seventh circle of Hell.

"Is this seat free?" an American girl with dark hair asked. "You're wet."

"I hadn't noticed."

"I'm from New York. Megan."

"California. Peter."

"Lovely day for a walk, right?"

"You're a sick girl."

"It's a gift."

"Can't be taught? Stems from birth or is aspired to inefficaciously lifelong?"

"Unquestionably so. You have hit the proverbial nail on the head."

204

"Number me among your most ardent of admirers."

"I'll consider it."

The blonde giant appeared and sat at our table. "I'm Mark."

"You're crazy," I said. "You went swimming."

"It was refreshing."

The swimming girl appeared (now fully dressed) and sat with us as well. "You're crazy, too," I told her. "For swimming in that. Amongst the man-eating sharks."

"It's the octopussies you've got to watch out for." Smiling, she swept her damp dark blonde hair off of her face. "I loved it. Whenever I trek near a lake or the sea, I always take a bath, regardless of the cold. Life must be experienced. Otherwise: why bother? By the way, I'm Karlijn."

We redid the introductions. Karlijn was from Amsterdam and Mark was from Melbourne but he had Dutch parents. Mark began speaking to Karlijn in his broken Dutch and I talked to Megan about the book I was reading: *All the Pretty Horses* by Cormac McCarthy. The book was about a young man who'd been dissatisfied with his life and went on a trip to Mexico to try to change it.

"You're the one with the enormous rucksack," Karlijn said to me suddenly.

"I don't go anywhere without my microwave oven. Or my hair dryer and big screen TV."

"Well, you've got to be prepared."

"Exactly. Just because you're traveling doesn't mean you can't maintain your standard of living."

"But seriously, how much does that weigh?"

"Two, maybe three kilos. Tops."

"My pack really does only weigh three kilos."

"But where do you put your dishwasher and electric generator?"

"See the pockets on the outside?"

"You're shivering. Do you have any other dry clothes?"

"No, my jumper and waterproof trousers are completely soaked."

"Borrow my jacket."

"But what about you?"

"I'm fine with my sweater." I opened the top of my pack and pulled out my Gore-Tex shell.

"You've got everything in there," Megan said.

"Formal dining wear as well. Or a slinky red dress if I'm feeling especially naughty."

"I think purple would go better with your eyes."

"People always tell me that. But purple just isn't me."

"What about walking together tomorrow?" Mark asked.

"Great," Megan said.

"I'm a bit slow," I said.

"We're in no rush. Anyway, I prefer spending time on the trail than getting to the lodge at one o'clock and staying inside the rest of the day."

"I mean I'm really slow."

"How slow?"

"Turtles on crutches passed me yesterday."

"Seriously. How long did it take you?"

"Ninety-three hours. But I did stop twice to tie my shoelaces."

"Not bad, not bad. How about you, Karlijn?"

"Well, I didn't get to the trailhead until four o'clock and I knew there were only two more hours of light so I ran."

"You ran? You are crazy. What if you didn't make it?"

"But I did."

"You ran the whole way?"

"Yeah."

"You always run?"

"Not always. It'd be nice to have some company tomorrow."

At ten o'clock, it was still raining. Mark and Karlijn had reserved beds in the hut's dormitory, but Megan and I foolishly carried tents. At the doorway, my fellow camper and I looked out on a once very inviting bed of dry grass that had been transformed into a vast flooded swampland.

"Are you actually going to pitch your tent?" Megan asked.

"I would but I have trouble sleeping with my snorkeling gear on."

"Isn't that Noah?"

"Standing on the ark waving to us for help?"

"Maybe I'll sleep in the kitchen."

"Maybe I'll join you." We spread out our mattresses between the tables and climbed into our sleeping bags.

An hour later, Megan grabbed my leg. "Stop."

"What?"

"Moving."

"Sandflies."

"If you don't stop, you'll have more than sandflies to worry about. You'll have Megan."

Megan hadn't let go of my leg. I considered this. "Bad?"

"An action full of risk and hazard."

"Fraught with danger and ineluctable peril?"

Megan nodded. "I fear for you."

"I shall cease and desist. From this moment forth until the end of all time. And a few minutes extra, just to make *you* happy."

Bright-eyed and very close, she responded, "Good."

But I did nothing about it and spent the next hour wishing I'd kissed her. When I'd finally changed my mind to try, Megan started snoring.

The morning following, after four cups of coffee, a steaming bowl of porridge deeper than the Indian Ocean and a shower of Arctic temperament, I could open one eye. The second was less cooperative until Karlijn helped it along with vigorous shakings of my person and vociferous encouragements to rise and shine in first one ear and then the other. Murderous threats of prolific violence could not hold her off and slowly, ever so slowly, I awoke, assisted in the end most by our fellow female guests' tsunami of sound, as they arose to cook a breakfast of sausages, fried eggs and buttered toast. Odysseus had not endured such auricular torment at the hands of the Sirens as I did that chilly New Zealand morn. (A boat arrived after the women's meal to transport all their food and equipment to the next hut along the trail which, yeah, I thought was cheating.)

Lovely yellow sand beach followed lovely yellow sand beach between twists of lushly forested coastline laced with freshwater streams feeding a broiling blue-gray ocean. Silt transformed one river to a deep amber color seen splashing on broken trees and gray boulders as we crossed above on a precarious wire suspension bridge.

As I looked at a hill that would dwarf most of the Andes and a few of the Himalayas, I sighed and realized for the first time that I did not need the two extra sets of clothes, the economy-sized bottle of shampoo or the concrete mixer.

Karlijn grabbed my hand, "Let's run."

"You're mad."

"It'll go faster."

It went faster until halfway up when I turned into a giant, quivering bowl of goo. "Save... yourself. You're still young. With your whole life ahead of you. Don't waste it trying to save me. Go... on."

Karlijn stayed with me a while, but my pack was just too heavy. My three companions slowly moved out of hearing and then sight as I lumbered up one hill after another. For an hour I walked alone and then, crossing the third stream from the hut, I found myself the victim of a nefarious liquid assault perpetrated by one Dutch girl. When I splashed back, she fled giggling. Like most of my victories, this one was brief. Upon reaching the comforts of dry land, Karlijn renewed her offensive with a barrage of broken sticks. But I did not give up, I did not go quietly into the dark night. Deprived of like ammunition amid stream and unable to return fire, I commenced with the haka, a native Maori dance used to frighten enemies which involved crude tongue gestures and slapping of the

208

thighs while in a half-crouched position. But Karlijn retaliated in kind. Heroically overcoming debilitating gasps of laughter, I faked a charge, but Karlijn held her ground.

When I reached her, Karlijn suddenly touched my arm and said playfully, "Come on. Let's play, what is it? You catch me." She dashed off through the gray mud left behind by the receding tide. Megan and Mark were nearly half a mile ahead, about to reenter the forest but watching us.

I shook my head as if to say no and then darted after her. Momentarily fooled, she still eluded my first grasp with a duck and a spin. I chased her in circles amid peals of laughter until my second clutch was not so clumsy nor so futile. "Gotcha."

Karlijn suddenly stopped struggling and looked down at my arms wrapped around her waist. She took hold of my forearms and held them there. We stood listening to each other's rapid breath for a delicious moment and then she spun away. "Not for long." When she evaded my next foray, I threw myself backwards into the mud. "No more, no more. I give up." She laughed and came back, putting a boot on my chest and raising a triumphant fist into the air.

After stopping to filter water (which Karlijn commemorated for time immortal with a group photograph, all of us mugging shamelessly without hint or trace of humility) and a brief swim at another beach, we entered a flat valley. Instantly we were set upon by hordes of gruesome blowflies insistent on exploring our every cranial orifice. Karlijn screamed in protest and swatted with wind-milling arms at her airborne assailants. But her cries were all in vain, the flies were not to be dissuaded from their pulchritudinous prey. Covering her head with a red sweater hastily pulled from her pack, Karlijn fled deeper into the forest and was lost to our eyes. Like little Red Riding Hood fleeing the big bad blowfly wolf. Mark, Megan and I soon followed.

"What are you doing?" Karlijn asked.

"My father wants me to bring him a rock from every country I visit. I told him I'm visiting twenty countries. He said make them small. So..." I showed her my trophy, a smooth green pebble the size of a fingernail.

Karlijn pointed to a nearby boulder bigger than a styracosaurus on steroids. "I think you should take that one instead. You could easily fit it inside your pack. Next to Cincinnati." She smiled.

"It *would* go nicely in their living room. In front of the TV."

Mark consulted his map. "There's a pub up ahead, a weekend getaway place. Let's celebrate with some beers."

In between conversations about Mark's days as a sky-diving instructor and mountain guide, Karlijn asked me, "What do you do?"

"I'm just an accountant."

"You're not just an accountant... You're not just anything. You are what you make yourself... Accountants save people money. Money makes the world go 'round. You help make the world go 'round. Everyone has a place, Peter."

I smiled. "You mean that?"

I expected a laugh and a no. Instead she said without a trace of sarcasm, "I do."

It was the nicest thing anyone had said to me in a long time. Instead of having to defend who I was, I was being accepted without justification. Maybe my defending myself had been a waste of time. "What do you do?" I asked.

"I'm a banker."

Not often do I pride myself on my own feats of strength. Many have gone before me and many will come after who will surpass my bravery and endurance one hundred fold. But not this day. The last half hour of our march shall be remembered long and spoke well of for generations. Perhaps statues will be erected in our honor and certainly songs will be written of our daring deeds (fingers crossed: in iambic pentameter). After indulging in a feast of Biblical proportions of guacamole, corn chips and beer (and beer and beer), we rose to our feet like heroes of the ancient epics and pushed on, taking our journey to the level of the Valhalla bound.

Too much? Nah, I'll continue.

Fortifying ourselves with a liter of Australian red wine to take on the wild beasts of the New Zealand forest (lions and tigers and anacondas – the whole bit) and stowing it securely in the pocketed front of Karlijn's blue rain-jacket, we valiantly pushed on. Rocks and otherwise normally inanimate objects materialized to hinder our progress so we indulged in song to fend them off. Karlijn rudely interrupted our boisterous rendition of *You're Way Too Good To Be True* at lung topping capacity for a demonstration of extraordinary dexterity. "Watch this." She somersaulted into the path still wearing her backpack and popped unsteadily to her feet with arms outstretched and smile ablazing.

Ignoring her poor manners and not to be outdone, "Yeah, well, how about this?" I countered and did my best impression of a cartwheel. Torrential cheers rewarded my effort. Mark added an impossible gymnastic double flip and, yes, he stuck the landing, but he took his pack off first (and though I may have applauded like a madman, inside, frankly, I was disappointed).

Megan shook her head sadly. "Kids today."

The competition would have continued long into the night but darkness was afoot and impatient. So we ran (again) the last fifteen minutes to Awaroa hut through a muddy inlet filling with the tide, trying quite unsuccessfully to avoid tripping on mangrove roots.

Karlijn and I unpacked next to each other. Or, rather, I unpacked and she watched. Her bag contained only a sleeping bag, a jacket and a small bag of food. She seemed fascinated by the amount of stuff I had.

"It'll be light soon," she said. "And you'll have to put all that back."

Again I gave her the haka face.

"Oooh. Can I borrow your soap? And your flashlight? Your sandals, too? I want to take a shower."

I made her coffee as well.

During the night, someone began nibbling on my ear. For a moment, I thought it was Karlijn and then was traumatized to discover it was a forty-five year old plumber with halitosis from Wellington dreaming about his Maori girlfriend Mildred.

In the morning Megan shook her head at me sadly and said she was abandoning us. Was I trying for the wrong woman? Asking for too much?

With a heave and a half, I shouldered my pack once more. Turning to Karlijn, I said, "I don't understand it. I eat and I eat and I eat and my pack never gets any lighter."

Smiling, she said, "It's only a three day hike. You could have left the washing machine at home."

"A man's got to be civilized. Come on."

"I'm sorry. Sometimes I speak without thinking."

"Don't let it happen again."

"Or violence will ensue?"

"Especially if you steal my material. That's my damned line."

Across a flat of gray mud, we could see the trail continuing on the other bank into the darkness of a tree-covered slope. Mark and I switched to sandals, tying our boots to the back of our packs, but Karlijn went barefoot. Soon she was yelping in pain and then, a second later, exclaiming "Quit your bloody whingeing, woman!" I nearly laughed when the chill of the water left me incapable.

Karlijn's father was waiting for me as I finished crossing the inlet. He smiled and asked, "Was the water very deep?"

"Back there we had to cross a roaring river with our packs held above our heads with one hand as we fended off flesh hungry crocodiles using only flimsy sticks with the other." He laughed and I added, "Yesterday was tougher."

"Big pack you've got there."

"Well, somebody's got to carry the bazooka. And the waterbed. And one mustn't forget the chandelier."

He slapped me reassuringly on the shoulder. "I like a man who can carry his own weight. So how was your hike?"

Karlijn arrived and I answered, "Good. Except I spent most of the time making this Dutch girl coffee to keep her warm."

He laughed. "And you, darling?"

"Not bad, except for having to drink the American's shitty coffee."

I'd missed my bus back to Nelson because the hostel that sold me the ticket told me the wrong time for the tides despite the usual reassurances. Karlijn offered me a ride in her parents' rented camper van. After a picnic lunch, Mark hiked on and I went to Nelson with Karlijn and her parents, Mr. and Mrs. Kea.

What followed was a nice comforting madness. Karlijn's father, Ken drove like a general leading his troops into one last desperate battle, cigar clenched in his teeth singing merrily with his daughter at his side accompanying and me digging desperately through the glove compartment for a pair of extra-strength ear plugs. Navigation was always changed at the last instant and screeching tires was the norm. Outside the rattling camper van whose cupboards kept spilling open to shoot clanging pots and assorted razor-sharp cutlery around the head of Karlijn's unfazed, always smiling mother, the road was a blur of tall trees and precarious drops, open vistas and lush green valleys. We stopped once: to race up a hill to the Abel Tasman monument where every good Dutch man must visit before he is confined to a bed of earth and worms and I lost by an appalling margin. Myself and the daughter exchanged threats of bodily harm after I claimed that she had cheated. The end result: me fleeing for my life.

Back in Nelson at the Victoria Rose Pub, we celebrated our victory over the Abel Tasman with pitchers of lager and spit-roasted chicken. In the midst of much laughter recounting our courageous exploits, Karlijn's father offered to drive me to the town of Franz Josef where I had plans to scale the glacier. Not wanting to leave Karlijn, I accepted.

The next morning I found it.

"Karlijn, do you want to tell me anything about the six kilogram stone in the bottom of my pack?"

Laughter restrained. "Like what?"

"Like that you put it there and I carried it six miles yesterday in boiling hot weather up a ten thousand meter ascent with a broken leg and no drinking water."

"I thought you said you were collecting rocks for your father."

"Small rocks. His collection is small rocks."

"Oh, I'm sorry. Sometimes my English is not so well."

"I shall have my revenge, Karlijn, and it shall be sweet and ruthless."

Her ensuing laughter betrayed no fear.

After two and a half months on the road and all the doubt that came with leaving, being with Karlijn and her family was very comforting. Karlijn's mother, Karin did all of the cooking and her father all of the driving. Eventually, I broke down and sung with them until they threatened to abandon me roadside unless I stopped. We visited a seal colony at Cape Foulwind (the meaning of which in English I explained to them as "like Cape Fart") and then the pancake rock formations at Punakiki where I bought them Tip Top ice cream in freshly made waffle cones. (The shop didn't have mint chocolate chip!) We camped the night in Greymouth where I slept in a dormitory while they the camper van. Nearby factories pearling flumes of filthy smoke into the grey haze of oncoming dusk, silhouetted like dark evil presences, were an ugly reminder of humanity in this country of such rugged natural beauty.

In the morning, Karlijn woke me with a dazzling smile and invited me to breakfast with her family. (Her mother must have asked six times if the eggs were cooked okay.) Along the way to Franz Josef, we stopped to swim in Lake Ianthe before a lunch of buttered sandwiches and canned beer in the sun while fighting sandflies for our lives. (The shriveled corpses of other not-so-lucky tourists riddled the shoreline, victims of the sanguinary airborne denizens. Despite our foolishness and lack of industrial-strength repellent, we survived, we persevered, we fought the good fight onward, upward and ever forward.)

Karlijn had spent the winter working in Franz Josef Glacier Hotel and wanted to have a drink with her friends that night. I became very anxious driving into town at the thought of never seeing her again. After a last beer with her parents in the street outside the hostel where I was staying, I was on the verge of saying a very reluctant goodbye to Karlijn when she invited me along to the bar.

Karlijn's friends were an English engineering student Nathan and a former Peace Corps volunteer from New York City Honoré who wanted to start a home for troubled youths when he returned.

Nathan was on his second trip abroad – he'd chosen Mongolia for the first after hearing it had no cars or public transportation. So he'd planned a three month excursion on horseback through the whole country and spent the first week buying supplies in the capital. The second night outside of Ulaanbataar, he'd woken at three a.m. to find someone had stolen both of his horses and all of his equipment, including his passport. It took him ten days to walk back to the capital and another three weeks to get a replacement passport ("fucking bureaucracy"). The airline, which was the only international one to service Mongolia, would only change his flight for double the price of the ticket. And he'd lost most of his money in the robbery, so he couldn't visit China. "I was stuck in that city for the
214

remaining two and a half months. I nearly went crazy except for the local birds. You're laughing but I wasn't the only tourist to experience the same fate. I knew a Belgian bloke and two Swiss sisters who had something similar happen to them. They bought a jeep and then spent four weeks looking for a replacement radiator. They searched every single shop in the city, even tried to buy one from a police captain. That one broke as well. Then they had to go home."

"Must have been disappointing."

"So what's your story? Around the world on a unicycle, hitchhiking the hemisphere with a full washer/dryer set, cartwheels to Calcutta?"

"Nothing that interesting, I'm afraid. Just on a crusade to end world hunger in between assassination assignments of totalitarian government officials for the CIA and a juggling job for a Romanian flea circus."

"One of those find yourself trips?"

"Something like that."

"I don't know why people don't call them what they are. A chance to get drunk and try to pull foreign birds for a year. That's what I'm doing, I don't need to find myself."

I turned to Honoré, "You were in the Peace Corps?"

"Two years. In Madagascar. In a small village near Fort Dauphin in the south. Hottest, driest place in the universe."

"How was that? Volunteering? My father joined the Peace Corps to avoid Vietnam. He was stationed in Tonga, but said it was really frustrating after a while. Because you try to help these people by teaching them better methods of agriculture and they don't listen."

"It was frustrating and difficult and, in some ways, extremely rewarding in ways I can't really explain. For instance, something like half of malaria deaths are small children – I think the country has one of the highest infant mortality rates in the world. So we tried to encourage the use of mosquito nets, if only for children under the age of one. In some cases the nets were free and sometimes they had to be bought, but at prices even the Malagasys could afford. But they won't use the nets. They say the kids need to build up a resistance. And so they keep losing children – in some villages as many as half of the children die in the first year. Half. But they won't use vazhaa medicine. It's been done without nets forever and nothing's going to change their mind. Five children died in my village in the two years I lived there."

"That's awful."

"The country is huge in terms of area but only sixteen million people live there. And they can't grow enough rice to feed themselves. Have to import it from Thailand. Because the soil is so depleted. And we try to teach them that the slash and burn way of farming is wholly inefficient as well as environmentally detrimental – the country's lost something like forty percent of its forests in the last twenty years. But they keep doing it. There isn't a place on the whole island you can drive without seeing some sort of fire. They could care less about the environment. Once they burned an entire mountain in the national park near where I lived to protest ANPAC restrictions on cattle grazing inside the park boundaries. An entire mountain."

"Did you ever ask yourself why you stayed?"

"It was really hard on me, especially the food. Because my village had no regular transportation and no money, I had to eat the exact same meal three times a day for months at a time." He paused. "I think I stayed for the kids more than anything else. They still had hope, the adults had mostly given up. The only road through my village had this giant pothole where every single taxi brousse that passed through would break down. I tried to get everyone together to fill in the pothole with rocks and gravel. But no one would help me. Only the children. The adults stood around laughing at us. That's the mentality there sometimes. Another time my neighbor said to me, Honoré, you're the Peace Corps, get your government to fix something else for us. I asked what and she responded she didn't know but that America should think up something to fix for them." He paused again. "I'm being too negative. Sometimes they'd share their whole life because I was an outsider and maybe the only one they'd ever see in their lifetimes. And even though they had nothing, they'd share whatever they had with you. And they were always laughing, always. Something good happened, they'd laugh. Something bad, they'd laugh. I never could understand it. In their way, I've never met a happier people."

"I felt the same about the Fijians – very happy, giving people."

"Says something about our so-called Western civilization, I guess. The funniest thing was their television programs. Their only three channels played these really awful music videos all day long. The singers dress up in cheap rip-off American sports jerseys with bandanas over their foreheads, acting like American gang-bangers and sing cheesy Malagasy love songs by the sea."

Karlijn said, "My sister told me that Vietnamese television shows American movies but they dub the lines in Vietnamese. Only they don't erase the English entirely. And the same woman does all of the translating for all of the programs. She does all of the voices as well, but never

216

changes her tone or inflection, speaking the whole movie in a monotone."

Nathan asked, "Why do American television channels always dub over the original language? Are Americans all too lazy to read?"

Karlijn suddenly grabbed my hand, "Let's play pool."

Karlijn wasn't very good, so I taught her how to hold the cue steady and plant her feet. The touch of her flesh sent charges through my fingertips. And left me hurting knowing I'd have to say goodbye to her soon.

Karlijn said, "I love some of the New Zealand names. You know there is a place called Fuckamama? I'm serious. Me and my parents spent all of last Wednesday trying to find it. You should have seen some of the looks we got from people who didn't know the place when we asked for directions. We laughed the whole day long. There's a Fuckapapa as well. Still serious. I tried to hitchhike there a few months ago. I was laughing so hard holding up the sign saying *Going to Fuckapapa* that no one stopped for an hour. Then a van with six nuns from Milan did and told me what an immoral woman I was."

"England has towns called Middlefahrt and Bad Fart," Nathan said.

I added, "There's a Truth or Consequences, New Mexico. And a village in California named Peter Pollack Is Totally Awesome. I'm deadly serious."

Karlijn countered with, "And some people think all Americans are conceited."

A few beers later when I was alone with Nathan, he said to me, "So you're with her?" I didn't answer so he went on, "But you want to be." He took a drink. "Don't get me wrong, Karlijn is my friend, but she's a bitch."

"You're a fool," I said and rejoined Karlijn at the pool table.

Afterwards, Karlijn and I walked back, giving each other piggyback rides along the way as well as revisiting battles entailing use of the Maori haka and a few judo moves gleaned from my favorite Harrison Hawk movies and that I'd strategically kept in reserve until then. As we turned onto the street where her parents' camper van was parked, I ran out of things to say. But I couldn't keep my eyes off of her. We walked in silence to the door of my hostel. Then she asked, "Are you going to invite me in?"

"You promise not to break anything?"

She stuck her tongue out at me and followed me inside. "Let's sit." She led me by the hand to a couch in the hostel's community living room. I removed the last can of beer from my jacket and passed it to her after popping the top. She took a drink and passed it back. "About three times a day you tell me how beautiful I am."

"Well, your blue toenails are a bit strange. Very, actually. But the rest I could cope with, I guess."

"Cope with?"

"I mean with the help of more alcohol, of course. Lots more." I shook my head no.

Karlijn said, "I wonder what it would be like to kiss you." So I showed her.

Karlijn pulled away. "I don't want to hurt you. You seem to care about me a lot."

"I'll decide what I can and cannot take."

"I'll hurt you."

"I can take it."

"I'm just a bitch, you know."

"I think you're one of the nicest women I've ever met. That's not bullshit, I mean it."

"I know you mean it." She kissed me again for a few minutes. "Your heart is beating so fast. Let me help you."

"Are you sure?"

"Yes."

"Can we?"

"No, just this."

"So you're going home pretty soon?" I said to Karlijn afterward as we lay together on the living room couch.

"Yeah. I'm looking forward to returning to Holland, actually."

"You are?"

"This year's been amazing: one of the best of my life. But now I'm ready to start doing something. Contribute, you know?"

"Contribute what?" Make the rich richer?

"Something I've been trained for, not just working in a bar. Start my life. And see my friends, my sisters again."

"I wish I could have more time with you. You're an amazing woman."

She was touched but not moved. "Well, it's just one of those things about traveling. Saying goodbye to people."

"I wish we didn't have to say goodbye."

She kissed me. "You'll forget all about me when you meet another girl next week in Nepal."

"I won't. Ever."

She kissed me again and sat up. Then she turned away to dress. I pulled on my pants. When she stood up, so did I. "I've got to go."

I nodded. She led me to the door with her hand. "Let's say goodbye here." I kissed her as hard as I could. Whispering, "Remember me in your dreams," she slipped outside and was gone.

Two hours later at dawn, the hostel evicted me to make room for some tour of German schoolchildren arriving that night. I checked into another more rustic (i.e. less clean) hostel across the street and five minutes later boarded the van for my guided glacier hike. I'd booked the tour the day before at Karlijn's urging and paid dearly for my big plans as my exhaustion was nearly complete by the end of its six hours. But it was one of the most rewarding experiences of my life. We wore ice boots and learned how to handle an ice axe (it's all in the grip). Despite the beautiful sunny day, walking on the ice was surprisingly cold and, at times, wet, when I slipped scrambling over some bump or through an ice tunnel the guide had driven screws into so we could pull ourselves up. Smooth-sculpted canyons in the ice revealed layers of coloring, each a different rendering of blue. At the end of the day, I returned to town, devoured every morsel of an extra large pizza and passed out in the hostel for sixteen hours straight.

As I waited for the next bus south the following morning, a man in his late sixties with a spindly nose and bushy white eyebrows under the world's coolest fedora accosted me, "Where are you from?" He had been eying my large orange backpack for some time.

"The United States. You?"

"Czech. What is your surname?"

"Pollack."

"You are Jewish?"

"My father is. My mother's Catholic. I'm not really either one."

"What are you doing here?"

"I wanted to see the world."

He nodded. "I also am of the Jewish race. I lived in Israel for a short time before coming here alone in 1949. Now I live in Twizel. A beautiful place. Mt. Cook is much like the Alps."

"Have you ever gone back? To Israel?"

He shook his head. "I have no one left to visit." He turned his face to the mountains. "I do not blame the Germans, the Arabs, the Christians for what happened to my family. I blame human nature. Why do we have to have these fucking religions? But all that is past, I hold no grudges. I can never forget what was done to my parents, to my friends, to me if I live to be a million years old, but I blame only human nature."

I didn't know what to say. The bus arrived and I got on after telling him goodbye.

He smiled and walked away without responding.

A week later I sent the following email:

Dear Karlijn, I've just finished the Copland trek up to Welcome Flats as you suggested and somehow survived, despite having no Dutch goddess to guide me over the perilous waterfalls New Zealanders call creeks. Nor did the waist deep mud suck me into the bowels of the earth never to return. And, luckily, the rain never stopped, ceased or desisted so I avoided any sunburns. It's easy, huh? After four days of lying in bed, I think I can move one leg now. And the doctors think one day, maybe, after a number of lengthy and painful orthopedic operational procedures, I'll be able to walk again. My armada of attorneys will, of course, be contacting you.

Hope all is well in Australia with your parents. Write soon with an update on your misadventures, mishaps and glorious deeds. Peter

As I hiked the Kepler and Milford tracks, sandflies hunted me relentlessly. (Gangs lurked in wait, stalking me across mountain and sound before catching a cargo flight to Thailand to continue their pursuit – sneakily hiding in someone's checked luggage to save on airfare.) To prove my indifference (and thus achieving the opposite by considering it), I ran naked under Sutherland Falls despite the considerable risks involved. The number one being a possible paparazzi frenzy resulting in my glaringly white buttcheeks splashed across numerous tabloid newspapers in my mother's supermarket back home. I even persevered through the hardship of having one of my boots stolen on the Milford hike. After a near riot, I was forced to leave my rather ripe footwear outside the hut. One of the local birds, a kea promptly stole the right boot despite a rather embarrassing chase over hill and dale and mud, lots of mud. I was not pleased.

Then, after three weeks, Karlijn sent the following two sentence response to my email:

Good to hear from you. I fell in love with this Australian guy I used to know in New Zealand and I think I'm pregnant.

So she was gone. Out of my life. The only woman who'd accepted me for an accountant and still said nice things about me.

In the Casbah that night in Queenstown, I turned from the bar and there stood Megan with a rather large Dutch appendage (not Mark). After we'd updated each other on our travels, she asked, "You were really into that Dutch girl, weren't you? The one who runs."

"Jealous?"

She laughed. "Not when I've got, what's your name again?" But for a moment her eyes winced.

She still went home with the Dutch appendage. I went home alone.

I didn't really want to leave New Zealand, maybe because I didn't know how to say goodbye to Karlijn. But I kept moving, nevertheless.

The next night in Christchurch, I stayed at a hostel above a pub: very clean, very sterile. I talked to an Australian girl for an hour after arriving and then she suddenly left on a date. I couldn't stand to be alone with my thoughts, especially eight o'clock on a Friday night, so I went downstairs where a live band was playing. A blonde girl smiled at me a couple of times going to and from the bar so I sought her out.

"I was just being friendly, smiling at you."

"Oh, right. Thanks very little and have a wonderful life."

I returned to my corner to finish my beer before going to bed. A woman in her late thirties with dark hair done up and puffy black eyes grabbed my shirt lapel and asked, "Do you like to smoke weed?"

Why the fuck not? "Sure."

"Come with us." She took my hand and led me into the street with her red-haired girlfriend.

They put me in the back of her car next to an empty baby seat. Then she lit up a joint.

We ended up in another bar after a short drive. I had no idea where I was or what the two women were talking about. I kept thinking of Karlijn. Suddenly the black haired one started shouting at me, "You just want to go to bed with me and then leave! You haven't even bought me a drink! You're a shit just like all the rest of the world's fucking men!"

"What?"

"You fucking dickhead," the red-haired one said.

I tried to retrace the conversation in my head but remembered only saying, "You girls are nice" before they began chatting about their friends from work. Struggling through the haze, I said, "I think I'll go. Thanks."

Outside, I realized I had no idea where I was. I returned inside.

"Look who's back."

"Can you please tell me which way it is to the bar we met in? I need to find my hostel."

The redhead's eyes softened and she glanced at her friend. "Come on."

"Um."

They paid for their drinks and drove me back. There wasn't much further conversation.

After three weeks of late late (late) nights, gallons of diet colas and stale coffee, on the morning the solution to the tax home question was due, I dropped it in Barrington's inbox and ran back to my desk, expecting a call at any minute praising the great job I'd done finding obscure private letter rulings and arcane tax court cases. An hour passed, two. I called his secretary and asked if he was in. He was. I told Sculpin I couldn't go to lunch, I was awaiting a call from Barrington. A week passed. Two. Then as I was turning off my computer for a three day weekend that I could actually take (my first in two years), Barrington called me into his office.

"You didn't read Revenue Ruling 93-86, did you?" he said and dropped my paper in the trash in front of me.

"Um..."

"How long did that take you?"

"Three weeks."

Barrington shook his head. He picked up the Internal Revenue Code Volume One from his desk. "You see this, son? It's not just a book. No, no. Its power far surpasses such trifling descriptions. The Code giveth and the Code taketh away. It can be a way of life or a way of death. It's a map to the complexities of man's interrelationships. Its intricacies and subtleties mirror those of human beings. To misinterpret it is to suffer. Do not misconstrue its power, nor underestimate its influence. Men have lost fortunes, dreams, lives over its myriad confusions. You must learn to navigate its labyrinthine deceptions, you must be versed in its contradictions or you will not survive. You must understand it. You may not like it, but it's all there is. So you must accept it. You can't avoid it, even outside the accounting profession you're not free of it. There's no escaping. Death and taxes, son, these are the two certainties in life. No man can elude its grasp, no man. Doctors, farmers, lawyers, mechanics, politicians: all men fall within its clutches. But you must not fear it. Or those that don't will take your jobs. Respect it. In its simplest terms it is nothing but a road map so that each man pays his own way and not for that of another. It is a tool, defined and refined by generation after generation, to help people conduct commerce, and even cohabitate the complex world we live in. A living, breathing, constantly changing organism. Without it, we would have no roads, no public schools, no military to protect our homes and families. Chaos would reign. If you get nothing else from your tenure here at the firm, remember this."

"Yes."

He studied my eyes. "Your heart's not in this profession, Peter. I can tell. You're going to have to make a decision, son. Is this what you want to do for the rest of your life? Every day is a gift, remember that. Don't waste it on something you have no passion for."

Oh, fuck. Fuck. "I do want to be an accountant. I do."

"No one wants to be reminded that there may be better things out there, Peter. No one wants to regard their work as pointless. You give that impression, Peter. You're focused elsewhere. I know you think you're smarter than they are. I did, too, at your age. And in some aspects you probably are. But they can sense your indifference. So you must make your decision." He smiled. "Or become a much better actor."

My weekend sucked.

It wasn't the first time I'd felt alone, nor the last. In middle school, my father forced me to join the Boy Scouts. On my first hike, I didn't have the proper rain gear and all of my equipment got soaking wet. It started raining about five minutes after our rides dropped us off in the San Bernardino mountains and it didn't stop all night long. I wasn't strong enough to hike that far either and no one would help carry my gear. Only after I started shaking uncontrollably in the middle of the night with hypothermia (my sleeping bag was wet all the way through) did the father in charge of the expedition do something. He put me in the bag with one of the other boys to warm me up. The next day none of the boys would talk to me – I was too weak in their eyes. But my father made me keep going to Boy Scouts and on the last couple of overnight hikes I was able to hold my own. Even though the fellow boys talked to me during the hikes, at school the next day they acted like they didn't know me. It was an evil everyone's father forced on them and everyone was embarrassed to be a Boy Scout. Only one of the leaders, an Eagle Scout who was also captain of the high school football team would say hello to me when I went to high school. I guess it was better than the other students who talked to me the first few days of new classes and then, a week later, would make fun of everything I

224

said to their friends before completely ignoring me. Maybe.

For years, I couldn't stand school. My mom encouraged me to keep at it, that things would get better and that eventually someone would recognize me for who I was and find value in that. I acted sick to avoid some days, but when I couldn't use that anymore I spent my lunches sitting alone in some secluded part of the high school grounds. Then I started thinking about killing myself. I'm not sure why I didn't except that maybe, in the back of my mind, I believed it would somehow get better. It hadn't. But then I stepped off that plane in Heathrow airport and something changed.

So I was hiking on this trip again, for the first time in almost ten years.

Perverts and prostitutes prowled the sultry streets of Bangkok while drug dealers and CD pirates (who made more money than the country's doctors) plied their wares at every corner. Middle aged European men white haired and balding habited bars with a prostitute on each arm or led small boys back to their hotel rooms. Adolescent tourists laughed in groups at their companions vomiting on street corners between visiting strip clubs. Reverberating techno music haunted dance clubs filled with manic, drug-addled American college students. Everything was for sale on Ko San Road: jewelry, clothing, food, tours, women, men, even children, and drugs, lots of drugs. All that was evil, all that was decadent, was here, encapsulated in one brief half-mile stretch of road. Amid the bustle of a manic Asian city, travelers like debauched Roman senators submerged in every form of the squalor that money could buy. Baser fantasies were indulged, morality discarded. The suffering of Thailand, that had driven its citizens to such depths, was disrespected and forgotten. It made me sad. Oh, how I hated it. Supposed to stay two weeks, I left in two days.

After checking in at the Royal Nepal Airlines desk, I leaned down to tie my bootlace. When I straightened up, the pony-tailed Austrian girl was standing before me.

"You survived the staircase in Paris."

"No thanks to you."

"Why are you stalking me?"

I immediately reached into my pocket, my eyes never straying from her sly green eyes. "You dropped your pen. I thought you'd want it back."

"You followed me all the way from France to return my pen?"

"I thought you might miss it."

She took the cheap ballpoint pen from me to examine. "It's not mine."

"It's not?"

"I've never seen this pen before in my life."

"Are you absolutely, positively, with the utmost certainty, sure?"

"Yes."

"I don't know what to say."

"Sorry would be a start."

We both started laughing. "Where?"

"Thatta way. You?"

"This a way."

She nodded. "Until then."

"Until then."

She turned to go.

"Um."

She turned back. "Yes?"

"Can I have my pen back?"

She laughed. "Of course. Keep it as a memento of our time together."

"I shall treasure it always. Until the sun turns into a cold, lifeless rock, the oceans dry up leaving the fish gasping and flipping in the primordial muck and my days reach their mortal conclusion. Forever and ever."

"Can I go now? My flight leaves in only six hours."

I laughed and we went our separate ways.

A month after I turned in the tax home project (during which I'd stayed late every night in hopes of patching things up and showing I wanted to succeed), Barrington passed my desk one night at nine o'clock. I thought he hadn't seen me, but then my phone rang. "Can you come to my office, Peter?"

I stood up. They'd fired three other people that week (and my uncle the Wisconsin plumber got another lay-off notice).

Barrington stood at his window looking out at the lights in the Los Angeles sky. He did not turn when I entered. "They're thinking of introducing a flat tax, Peter. Think of it. A lifetime spent learning the nuances of a trade and its unspoken subtleties, building a life, giving oneself a purpose, a place on this mad, chaotic planet. A part of everything. All gone." He turned, his eyes full of fear and sadness. "The Code is a cruel mistress, my son." He walked to his desk and sat down to the file sitting there. Without looking up he said, "Go home, Peter."

"But—"

"Be with your wife, girlfriend, whatever. Come back tomorrow."

Kathmandu was my first taste of the true madness. A bit similar, Bangkok so disgusted me that I didn't explore it. But Kathmandu was different and much, much poorer. The filth was ubiquitous, as were the mendicants. Nepal was a country plagued by civil unrest whose sole source of income was foreign madmen intent on scaling eight thousand metre peaks, risking mortality on the ceiling of the world. But the city promised no hope of redemption, no future glories, just desperation and an atavistic struggle to just survive. No one had anything and everyone would kill to possess it.

The district of Thamel was narrow streets lined with shops vying in a life and death battle for the tourist dollar. Westernized restaurants, curio shops, and sporting gear stores bordered its muddy, twisting alleyways waiting for the next European to enter and overpay for their wares so they could go on. False, lifeless smiles backed by resentment everywhere. I laughed once in three days, when a man in a long overcoat approached me in the street and whispered in my ear, "Chess set?" before opening his jacket to display his choices. I left for the mountains as soon as I could.

After a short stay in Pokhara where I stowed half of my pack, I took a very dusty bus ride along a menacing, rock-strewn road winding around devastating drops and the occasional broken-down ox to Besi Sahar to begin trekking the circuit around Annapurna. (More than one fellow hiker on the trail preferred riding on the bus roofs to give them that extra second to jump if the driver made an error.) The next twenty-six days I didn't see a car, a television set or a Lord of the Burgers (Life was very tough, in other words.) Amid the would-be freelance porters and curio shops catering to the foolish tourists who'd chosen to subject themselves to altitude sickness, aching knees and bouts of torrential diarrhea for two weeks or more, was a cozy ramshackle town of restaurants and smiling Nepalese children. And for the first time, looking into those innocent young faces devoid of that hunger for money, I felt Nepal's lure.

I took neither guide nor porter. This was my challenge and mine alone.

The track leaving Besi Sahar was a rough dirt road snaking into the hills. At the first curve, I met a middle-aged couple from New Zealand and an English girl – all of us perplexed as to why a trail that would ascend almost fourteen thousand feet over the next twenty-five miles began with a descent. Craig and Jan ran a tourist hotel in Queenstown and Allison was a hairdresser in Piccadilly Circus. After introductions, they offered to let me walk with them, especially through the section where some Maoists had killed a couple of lone tourists, and so I did.

We didn't go far the first day, just five or six miles along the river as the valley began, but we did pass a couple from Atlanta on their honeymoon. They'd booked a tour at home for what they considered a bargain and now had an entourage of twenty porters, two English speaking guides and a cook (but no sommelier, so…). Despite the availability of tourist hotels in villages only a couple of hours apart, the porters carried tents, sleeping bags and even tables and chairs (not folding tables and chairs, but full-sized wooden ones). The couple admitted their embarrassment at the opulence of it all to us before being abruptly called away to dress for the afternoon cocktail hour.

I noted in my journal to contact the Nepalese government when I returned – which would surely change everything. The bridges we needed to cross were not safe (splintered, squeaking, sometimes shrieking bamboo "held" together with frayed, rotten rope). Each time we succeeded in not dying was a tale worthy of telling the grandkids about over and over again – and Allison always insisted on us posing for a photo on each of them (every single one), often taking minutes and minutes and minutes more in recomposing the shot while she stood on solid ground and we did not, for a more aesthetic representation which I was awfully (awfully) pleased about.

I expected the Himalayas to be cold, but hiking the next morning was a hot, punishing affair – I drank two liters of water before noon and averaged four liters a day the rest of the trip. (By the end, the paper filter of my water purifier was a dark black. But the Nepalese had no filter and no choice. I thought about this while purifying the water in front of them. But I still did it.)

The second night we stayed in Ghermu, opposite a three-tiered waterfall feeding the Marsyangoli Khola. The road, lined intermittently with low stone walls and crumbling bamboo fences, passed sheer-faced mountains of black and white rock. Stone-housed villages at the base of steep cliffs were surrounded by terraces carved from the precipitous landscape for rice and corn fields. Bales of hay covered the rusty corrugated metal roofs for the ubiquitous goats, chickens, mules and water buffaloes roaming the streets, snorting and farting and shitting with no one to clean up after them.

"Going to check my hydration level. Mark my territory as it were," Craig announced and stood to the side of the trail at one point – a phrasing he would repeat often.

The air was clear and crisp except when we passed a house and then wood smoke or the stench of feces overwhelmed us. Prayer wheels, multi-hued tin cylinders mounted on rotating dowels between beribboned slabs of stone, topped some passes and rattled in the whipping wind. Allison treated me to the abridged version of a lecture (total running time: forty-seven minutes – without potty breaks) on the importance of spinning the wheels on the correct side and in the correct direction. When I didn't follow her directions, she shouted "Bad Karma! Bad Karma!" and spent hours asking every Nepalese we passed (even those who spoke no English except "Hello!") how to remedy the curse I'd brought upon us.

"Where did you get that hat?" Allison asked me.

"It's a pretty funny story actually. While my dad and I were preparing to do this ten day hike when I was in Boy Scouts, we went out and bought the ugliest hats we could find. Mine was an oversized hunter's cap with retractable ear flaps that was bright orange – so bright that it hurt your eyes to look at it. I loved that hat. But when we got to the top of Mt. Whitney, this eagle swooped out of the sky and took it right off my head. I guess he liked the bright orange. Well, my dad gave me this hat at the airport in sort of honor of that other hat. And it matches my bag. Pretty cool, huh?" A bright orange band ringed the wide-brimmed tan fedora made of really cheap imitation felt.

"It's ugly."

"But that's the point."

"I don't get it."

In the morning, a Frenchman with wild matted hair and a quivering lip passed us muttering profanities. When we asked what was wrong, he replied he had to turn back at ten thousand feet (3300 metres) because of the altitude and then began a rant about how the Nepalese were nothing but a bunch of filthy thieves who never washed and tried to steal your money every time you went to take a shit. Then he disappeared down the mountain singing "Fuck the Nepalese" alternatively in French, English and German.

"I think he needed a hug," I told Allison.

"I wouldn't hug him," she said. "He smelled."

Then we began meeting mule trains. The animals were overburdened with wooden barrels, pieces of furniture, huge burlap sacks all dwarfing them in size. And the men who drove them had exhausted eyes and lean jaws. Neither backed down at all approaching (and would easily have forced us into the abyss – luckily the beasts wore bells around their necks so we heard them coming) so I scrambled up the sandy incline the trail cut through far beyond where I needed to or leapt up rocks in an exaggerated manner. The men always smiled and nodded their heads in thanks. Sometimes their traffic kept us perched on an unsteady rock or amid a dense and prickly stand of pine for twenty minutes at a time.

At lunch, we met three Israeli girls who'd hired a guide after being told they must by fellow countrymen in Kathmandu. They'd negotiated an all-inclusive price, so he paid the hotel owner for the girls' meals out of his end. But for his own repast, he ate raw rice. The girls had found him on the street in Kathmandu. For a month, he'd been roaming the streets there looking for work. Every few months he would return to his small farm in the mountains to see his sons and young wife. He carried all three of the girls' packs himself, piled one on top of each other and cinched together with frayed rope. He balanced them on the small of his back and used a worn leather strap across his forehead to carry them. He never stopped smiling. Ever. Nor did his eyes. The hotel had a plastic chess set missing two of the castles. When he saw Craig and I playing using rocks for the lost pieces, he watched. So I taught him how to play.

Over the next five days, each time we met he wanted to play me at chess. I'm hardly the best player in the world, but he never got any better. And he never quit smiling. On the last night, I let him win.

Another guide earned the moniker *The Dodgy Geezer* from Allison. A newly married English couple on their honeymoon hired him through an agency in Kathmandu. Despite all the warnings in the guidebooks about alcohol contributing to altitude sickness, this guide drank every night on the way to Throng Pedi. And whenever he cornered one of the white women on the trail, whether she be coming back from the bathroom or on her way upstairs to sleep with her husband, *The Dodgy Geezer* would make a proposition – both Allison and Jan were lucky recipients. Being on a tight schedule, the couple had prepaid for the whole trip so they couldn't necessarily fire him. Or so they thought for a while. On the day we were to ascend to the pass, he got so sick, the husband had to hire a mule to take him down the mountain. Then the husband had to hike all the way back up to his wife on his own – a tremendous feat, especially for a middle-aged man with a beer gut. When he passed us on the other side, he'd been walking for fourteen hours straight.

Two other guides we met got altitude sickness as well, also from agencies in Kathmandu. Obviously they were not regulated. But then, you couldn't really blame them – it was a job in a country mostly lacking those.

About three o'clock I devised the fantastic and, yes, totally brilliant idea to ask "Are we there yet?" at least hourly for the rest of the 24 day hike much to the constant amusement of my companions. What can I say? I'm like that sometimes.

With darkness coming, we arrived in the village of Tal. A line of houses and tourist hotels lay isolated in the middle of a flat grassy plain fenced in on both sides by a jagged ridge of mountains. The hotels listed in the guidebook were all nearly full, promising waits of over two hours for dinner so we chose one run by a smiling woman of indeterminate age who had twenty hoops of gold in either ear. (The harsh sun prematurely wrinkled all girls, making their age impossible to guess once they started having children.) My knee bothering me, I retired early to my room on the second story. The floor was nothing but single, rather giving planks which I stepped on gingerly and with hesitation. In bed, I could feel the heat of the kerosene lamp from the family room directly below me. Unchecked by a glass cover, the flames licked the planks beneath me. I worried at first and then exhaustion took over.

Awake to a loud voice. A shout? Baby crying loudly. Try to open eyes, but smoke stings them shut. Fire? Fire! The lamp. Don't panic. Don't panic. Grab glasses blind off the top of pack, put in pocket. Slip feet in boots. Still can't open eyes. Kick out window and jump through, wrapping sleeping bag over head and using the pack to shield me from shards of untempered glass. Land awkwardly but unbroken eight feet below in courtyard of hotel. Drop sleeping bag from head.

"Hungry, were you?"

Standing amid Craig's runny eggs, left arm bleeding but no crispy parts, I realized the smoke had been from the morning cooking fire.

"I thought the hotel was burning down."

"Excuses, excuses."

Jan said, "You've ruined his eggs."

"Um."

"Kids today."

The Nepalese woman emerged from her hotel, her mouth open wide enough to fit a yak and his brother.

"I'd like some more eggs. He's paying."

I climbed down from the table. "Cup o' tea for me."

Yes, it hadn't been pretty, but then mad dashes from burning buildings never are. Or not in my limited experience, anyway. The important thing was: no videotape existed so people at home could witness the latest of my debacles.

At the next hotel that night, a pair of pretty French girls (blonde and brunette) ate in the restaurant. "See those stairs?" I pointed to the rickety flight twisting steeply up from the road. "I nearly lost my legs there. Glad Craig had bottled oxygen to save me. Close call. Close call."

The girls laughed. "Really?"

"Amputation was almost necessary. Took three skin grafts, a couple of silicon chin implants and an extra large pepperoni pizza hold the anchovies to resuscitate me."

"You're so lucky."

232

"I know, I know. The fifth step was just too much. And the eighth I'll see in my nightmares until I'm eighty. But I can't talk too much more about it."

"We understand."

The blonde asked, "What happened to your arm?"

"I don't want to talk about it. Well, there was this yak…"

"We saw you this morning."

"Right. Right. I might just go to bed now."

"Maria got it on her digital camera. Would you like to see?"

"No, thank you."

"Good night."

In the morning I went behind the hotel to where a black rubber hose piped water down from a spring. A pile of discarded plastic water bottles sold to tourists stood four feet high amid the trees (not an uncommon occurrence along the trail). A smiling boy was using the hose to refill some of the newer water bottles and reapplying a fake seal. I sat down beside him and waited my turn while I set up my water filter.

Just before noon, we came upon those we affectionately nicknamed *The Pole Guys*. Five men dressed in raggedy clothes each carried an eight foot long metal pipe thick as my arm by a greasy strap across their foreheads holding it in place on their backs. Only plastic flip-flops you buy for a dollar back home adorned their feet. At the top of one rather daunting hill, *The Pole Guys* were crowded round a tin can boiling rice over a small wood fire in the only shade for miles. They greeted me with toothless smiles, saying "Namaste." I responded in kind and collapsed next to them in the small remaining shade. One hefted my backpack in hand and nodded approvingly. He reached over and felt my biceps, nodded to his companions, and then slapped me reassuringly on the back. Another gestured towards his pole and then at my backpack, offering to switch. I shook my head. He pointed at the pole and agreed with me brokenly, "Too… easy." We laughed together. Then they offered me some of their rice (apparently, I'd been awarded honorary sherpa status). I showed I was full, but gave them the Snickers bar I'd been dreaming about eating since the day's first hill. They refused at first, but I insisted. Using their filthy hands, they broke it evenly into six pieces and we shared it. Looking at their laughing eyes and bodies smeared with dirt, cinder and dried sweat, emotion overwhelmed me. Here was a life of struggle I could not comprehend. My complaints seemed so petty. These men had no chance at wealth or even comfort, just a cold bed under a thin blanket along the trail before another day of carrying that heavy pole up the Himalayas. What the fuck was wrong with me?

Reaching the next rise, I stuck my tongue out at a pair of water buffalo lazily doing nothing but chewing grass. They were not amused. So much so they began chasing me, their bells ringing madly from their necks. Me: exhausted. Lungs screaming in the thin oxygen. Laughing at first and then running for my bloody life. Then slipping. Clawing at empty air. Twisting in empty space. Falling face first into a great steaming deposit of cow manure.

News headline: *American accountant trampled to death by Nepalese heifer. Deceased found face-down in a pile of buffalo fecal matter, one boot missing.* Mother attending funeral drenched in tears. Father too shamed to leave house, dies of broken heart three weeks later.

Pushing myself up with a grunt to the beautiful face of Svetlana Swan hovering over, last seen when she burst in on me with my pants down around my ankles in the woman's bathroom of Veronica's Secret. "Are you all right?" Me slipping again on the slick grass and tasting shit between my teeth once more.

"Oh, you poor revolting man," Svetlana exclaimed, stifling giggles with little success. Me hoping I never emerge.

I would have killed for a hot shower that night. I didn't get one.

At home, I would have gotten grief about the shit over and over again, but, after the first couple of jokes, Jan and Craig left it alone. That was nice.

As usual, Allison was talking: "I don't know why I know everything I do. I don't watch television. I don't read the newspaper. I think I'm just good at talking about things I know nothing about. I just take other people's theories that I hear and use them as my own." Also as usual, everyone else in the room was ignoring her.

Every night (and all through the day) Allison told long, drawn out stories of her adventures in Sri Lanka of buying bus tickets, booking hotel rooms, and ordering food. All began with "When I was in Sri Lanka" and never lasted one minute less than forty-six hours in duration, reaching no denouement nor conclusion, never emphasizing any interesting details or relating any amusing anecdotes, just going on and on and on (much like this paragraph). They never ceased nor ended and were only momentarily on hiatus when she stuck something in her mouth – but even these pauses were brief as she would start up as soon as the chewing started. You could fall asleep, drop a heavy object on your head, shoot yourself in the ear – be assured that when you came to, she would still be describing the color of her chair in some Colombo curry house or her choice of naan or chapatti for lunch that day.

She continued: "The men there are disgusting. Disgusting. Once in a train, a guy across from me just pulled it out and began stroking himself. Right there in front of everybody. Another time I caught the hotel owner looking through a hole in the wall while I was showering. He was pleasuring himself as well…"

I thought of other things I'd rather be doing than listening to Allison. Like being shot out of a cannon over Lake Michigan. Like drowning in a giant bowl of chocolate pudding. (Preferably white chocolate.) Like being torn apart by a pack of rabid Scottish terriers. Like being put into an industrial sized clothes dryer on the permanent press cycle to be gently spun into oblivion.

I continued the list for another ninety minutes. When I finished, Allison was still talking.

Later, she started showing us her voluminous collection of Sri Lankan photos. (Total count: 4,241. Amount blurred or out of focus: 809. Amount not shown: 0 and/or -6 which may not seem possible, but take my word for it, it most definitely is. Oh, yes.) Hatstands (blue, red, but never green), colorful piles of garbage, her feet (somewhat alluring until you noticed the corns and hideously misshaped baby toenail – that, admittedly, did somewhat resemble Elvis Presley circa 1973): nothing interesting failed to be captured by her lens. And every night she had a new audience of Nepalese to share them with.

As I passed three young Canadian men on an ascent the next day, one of them rushed after me to push money into my hand. "Carry our packs for us! All together they weigh easily only one third of your own. A minor effort for you. Hardly worth mentioning. And we, my fine American friend and neighbor, are smokers. Our damaged, nearly emphysematous lungs are not meant for such trials and tribulations. Take pity on us and help your ally through two World Wars, forgiving the mayhem and madness we brought upon your nation in its infancy. We are willing to pay good money!"

"That's two dollars you're offering me."

"If sick craving of filthy lucre is your reason for reluctance, let me assure you that you will be richly rewarded!"

So, for the hell of it (and two dollars), I carried all four packs to the next hilltop as tourist and sherpa alike looked on in laughter and admiration, but mostly in laughter.

"Well done, young man. Well done." Photographs memorialized the event and I gave my parents' address so copies could be sent to my home to show what a strapping young man their son had become.

"You're forgetting something."

"Yes?"

"My money."

More laughter. "Of course." I could now add *Porter in the Nepalese Himalayas* to my resume. Very good.

That night in Chame, I bought the Canadians a round of San Miguels with my earnings during a relatively short three hour span of waiting for dinner and was nearly deified on the spot – more for the free beer, I think, than the pack-carrying. One of them even asked me to marry him when I handed him the beer, but I found that a bit cheeky and played hard to get.

Later, as we waited for tea after dinner (Years later, I still regretted ordering that tea. Years.), Allison gave a seventeen part dissertation on why marmite was the world's best spread – outdoing competitors such as vegemite, peanut butter and raspberry jam. Someone asked about mayonnaise and the tongue lashing they received, well, it wasn't pretty.

"Pete, what's your favorite?"

"Mustard."

She didn't say a word to me upstairs as we climbed in our respective beds. My ears were glad of the rest.

236

Deciding the borough of Upper Pisang which consisted of square mud huts (many of them abandoned) reminiscent of something out of the Old (Old, Very Old) West would be a better place to acclimatize to the higher altitude than the more luxurious and tourist-friendly Lower Pisang yielded us the choice of two sleeping arrangements. The first was in a straw and feces covered stable with a mule and cow (both of which were excessively flatulent – not that there's anything wrong with that if it's a sort of medical condition, I guess) and voracious fleas. The second (and winner) was a middle-aged woman's living room which she shared with an also flatulent and kind of flirty sheep. But we got a bed so we took it. When we asked for the toilet, she answered with arms spread wide and I found myself unable to shit out of shyness (Too much information? Well, deal with it.)

"This is what the rest of Nepal is like," Craig said. "The people who live along this trail are rich in comparison."

The room stank of smoke and above Allison's bed in the ceiling was the blackest of holes leading we knew not where and were too frightened to check. Allison was not pleased (about the lack of a shower either). We got to hear all fourteen different ways she wasn't pleased that night and, lucky us, again in the morning. She tried to get someone else to take the bed instead via paper, rock, scissors but we all ignored her.

The next day was relatively easy (all up, yes, but only for three hours) to the collection of buildings known as Gharyu. We spent the afternoon playing the card game Shithead while watching avalanches tumble across the face of far-off mountains and waiting for the boom of fallen ice as the sound reached us seconds later.

A pitiless land.

The trees disappeared. Only brown grass and the barest of shrubs replaced them. And even those disappeared as we ascended. The merciless sun parched our throats, cracked our lips and dried out our eyes. The wind's listless whine dulled our thoughts and sharpened our fears. Still we pushed on. With mangled feet, twisted backs, and strained knees carrying our heavy gear needed to ward off freezing from snow and ice. Flea-bitten, ragged yaks starving for food in this empty land wandered aimlessly over the hills. Stone houses with no windows perched precariously on precipices. Dark clouds cast foreboding shadows on the barren white monoliths and jagged shards of gray rock swallowing the horizon in every direction.

Manang.

A cluster of buildings capped by prayer flags flank the uneven muddy path. Solemn brown-faced Nepalese throw rocks at a blind dog running towards us with its tail between its legs. Milky yellow tears of disease course down both sides of the abject creature's gaunt, orange face. A man beats a horse with a whip. Jan asks the man to stop. He nods and whips the horse again. She screams and grabs the whip out of his hands. A crowd of Nepalese who've begun to watch the goings-on begin laughing. The man who lost his whip laughs. "No whip! No! It's cruel!" Jan cries. The man nods in understanding. Jan hesitates, then returns the whip. We walk away. The man whips the horse again and all the Nepalese laugh some more. Jan starts to run back, but Craig restrains her and we go inside a hotel for tea.

Tales of trekkers' woes due to the altitude dominate all conversation around the hotel. Nights of sleeplessness, vomiting, dizziness. A sick Englishman tells of his own illness the night before when his friends had to take him on a mule at three in the morning back down to here. And still we climb. Trying to attain something intangible, to conquer nature, to cheat death, to achieve greatness, to test our limits, to challenge ourselves, to see if we're really alive or only existing in some mindless slog of paperwork in a darkened office hating our colleagues, hating our slow, inevitable future, hating the monotonous doldrums of our lives filled with defeats and disappointments, trying to get what others tell us we want and competing with each other to get it. So we strive for the heavens like others before us and others to come, getting closer to God or beauty or whatever. And then a great calm settles upon us as we witness nature's majesty and fear its power. And everything else means nothing.

That night, the first in two weeks that I felt I could sleep unaffected by the altitude I was serenaded to sleep by the howling of the neighborhood canine population. Luckily, only three feet separated the dogs from my window so I didn't miss a note.

"Sleep well?" a bleary eyed Craig asked me the next morning with an ironic smile.

"Shut the fuck up."

"They're going to build a road here. To Manang," Jan said.

"No," I said. Fill this desolate place with a city? Something great would be lost to the world.

"You can't blame the locals for wanting a better life. You see how they have to carry things here. *The Pole Guys*."

"I know."

"They think the trail will be easier, too. More tourists will come. More money."

The village of Manang had a post office. Sort of. Inside the second floor of a log cabin up a rickety ladder with a missing rung, sat the postman. His garb was typical Nepalese - dirty white button down shirt and brown trousers - except for his very official, very stained, but obviously most beloved blue hat (a glint of pride shone in his eye as he periodically adjusted it on his head when it needed no adjusting). As my face appeared in the doorway for the second time (the missing rung), he smiled at me like I was the sun, the moon, and all the stars except that Adara that no one really cares about (and don't say you do just to be contrarian, I see right through you). I showed him the postcard I'd purchased from a guesthouse where we'd had lunch – the water-stained card had obviously been sitting for years right above a collection of posters advertising toothpaste and 1970s female hygiene products. After I explained in gestures and numerous repetitions of "America," he suddenly became very official (readjusted his hat) and pulled out a huge dusty ledger from a broken down trunk to try and figure how much the postage was. Then he didn't have enough stamps (it cost about one US dollar). After a furious yet fruitless search, he gestured at me to wait and ran out the door. From the window I could see him duck in and out of various homes down the street, every once in a while emerging with another stamp in hand. Ten minutes passed. Twenty. Thirty. I dozed off.

He was back. Stamps now covered my card everywhere except for the address (I guess Mom would have to peel them off to read it.). I paid and signed in the ledger as requested (providing the pen, of course). He smiled triumphantly and said, "Amarica." I shook his hand and left, but not before unsuccessfully trying to trade his hat for mine.

Mom and Dad,

Yeti chasing me. Send help.

Pete

Switchbacks from hell.

Lunch at the Dancing Yak Restaurant which had no dancing yak. No membership discount card, either – even though we'd patronized the Manang Dancing Yak Restaurant as well. Nor an all-you-can-eat buffet. And the color scheme was a joke. Really. How did they expect to keep their customers loyal? Craig did his best to fill in for the missing dancing yak but it became quickly obvious Jan had not chosen Craig for his moves. Nor did I see anything that I could add to my already rather impressive dance repertoire.

More switchbacks from hell.

At a much needed stop for chipped cups of very sugary black tea, a passing storm that immediately became a raging downpour drove us inside the owner's house from his balcony. Despite our protests he forced us to sit on his and his wife's bed and drink our tea while thunder roared overhead. Three small children kept peeking around the door to the house's other room, grinning at us with huge smiles (the fourth child had run away and hid when he saw my big orange backpack – it frightened him so much he wouldn't return).

When the storm had passed, Jan tried to hide in my pack when I wasn't looking and trick me into carrying her up the rest of the mountain. But I was much too clever for her, oh, yes, and totally caught her. Boy, was she embarrassed!

Just hell.

"Gasp. Heave. Vomit."

Allison was not amused: "Very funny."

More lovelies on the trail, this time of the Swedish (!) variety. And another mountain! I said: "The escalator is being put in next year, damnit."

240

"And I guess the elevator's broken?"

"Don't you just hate that? You should come to our hotel tonight, we'll have a disco. I've got an inflatable mirror ball in my pack. But be aware: there's a dress code."

"I have *nothing* to wear."

I grinned, "Even better."

One of them (who wrapped her towering brown legs (think New York's World Trade Center or Kuala Lumpur's Petronas Towers but soft, supple and super sexy) in duct tape as a preventive measure against blisters) said, "You were on the Abel Tasman, weren't you? About a month ago. With the girl who runs."

Yeah, that didn't work.

For the fourteenth time that night in Lower Yak Kharta I had to pee. For the thirteenth time Allison grumbled "Again?" as I stubbed my toe on her belongings she'd conveniently spread across the room's entire floor, my side included. For the fourteenth time, I bumped my head on the top of the doorframe descending the stairs (the Nepalese are short) and added to the headache I already felt from the altitude. For the fourteenth time I had to enter the rickety outhouse perched on the other side of the mountain trail, wondering if this would be the time the squeaking boards gave way underfoot and plunged me into the abyss. For the fourteenth time I left the door open, hoping to make a jump for it if the boards did go. For the fourteenth time I decided not to risk peeing farther down the trail in case my constipated bowels suddenly gave way (I carried only one pair of trousers – any kind of disaster would be just that.) Only this time I forgot my flashlight on my bed, so I didn't see the rock in the road that tripped me and nearly sent me hurtling into the nothingness – a victim of my small bladder. Luckily, my head hit the outhouse roof as I was slipping forward which knocked me flat on my back in the middle of the trail. And, yes, a yak had shit earlier in the area I fell.

The moon was laughing at me, I swear.

"You smell. Did you fall in pooh again?" Allison said as I returned upstairs.

I still couldn't sleep.

In deference to Allison's complaints about my choice in hotels along the trail, I began asking the owners, "Do you have satellite television? Does it show the Los Angeles Lakers?" But they always answered yes and Allison was still mad. She also wanted to speed up. Every time someone passed us on the trail she asked how long it'd taken to get to where we were and every time she stomped her foot in frustration when it was shorter than we'd taken. "We could go further if you went faster," she said to me. "What's the rush? This place is beautiful. It's why we came." "Those Spaniards did this in three hours." "So?"

When we reached Thorong Pedi we had to stop for the day as the next town of Jharkot was on the other side of Thorong La pass, a nine hundred metre ascent to 5,416 above sea level and then a very grueling sixteen hundred metre descent over scree and gravel (pain to the knees – PAIN – Nepalese ran up the opposite way in only flip-flops). The sun shone strongly, it was a beautiful day. We watched in amusement as a female tourist below us went off the trail to pee and thought she wasn't being seen (though she was still a half mile away). But, then, as was recommended in some guidebook by someone and therefore needed to be DONE, she decided to burn her toilet paper instead of carrying it out. She failed, however, to consider the short dry grass covering the hill which quickly ignited. Then, instead of trying to stamp the fire out, she ran back to her boyfriend to tell him. He ran up and tried to stop the fire, but it was too late. Soon the whole hill was ablaze.

"I'm glad there are no houses," Allison said.

"When it rains, the mountain will wash away the trail. These people here will be trapped," Craig said.

"So they'll leave?"

"No."

"But... Oh."

When the couple and their two friends arrived at Thorong Pedi a while later, no one said anything. What could be?

At two in the morning the door to our dormitory room was kicked open. I shot up in bed trying to think where I'd put my Leatherman. Then Craig's flashlight shone on the culprit: a pointy-eared black collie with half a tail. "Shit." I couldn't go back to sleep.

242

At four, it began snowing. We delayed our departure.

At five, it stopped snowing. Heartfelt pleas for five more minutes in the warmth (warmth) of my sleeping bag were cruelly refused and so we started. The dog followed us.

In long switchbacks we ascended the side of a barren mountain. With each step, the air grew thinner. Cresting one plateau, a howling wind pushed us back and bit into our ears. We curled around the base of another saw-toothed peak and past a hut serving tea. No more switchbacks, just up. Every time I saw sky ahead, I thought we were almost done, but we weren't. I fell behind as I needed to take a breath every two steps. The dog regarded me with pity in his brown eyes as he ran ahead a few steps and then skipped back to beg. Craig waved at me from up ahead to hurry, but I couldn't.

And then, the top. With a sign proclaiming the altitude, prayer flags (of course) whipping in the strong wind and a small wooden hut where for a whopping $1.75 (the highest price in Nepal) a man sold Coca-Cola in glass (!) bottles that he'd carried there from Besi Sahar (on top of commuting daily from Thorong Pedi to sell them). A soda at the movies back home sold for twice as much, but then he had no ice (Come on!).

The roof of the world. A broken line of snow-tipped rock cleaved the sky at the horizon, impossibly high above lush green fields so far below as to be somewhere else. Not a cloud to be seen.

Gasp. Gasp. "How... easy... was... that."

"Next time we run," Jan said with a smile.

"Next... time? I'm on... my third... lap."

"Photo," Craig said, directing us to gather round. Checking the view finder, he said to me, "Gotta have the hat."

I donned the fedora heavily stained with sweat and busted out my biggest grin. As Craig clicked the button, a change in the wind's direction flipped my headpiece into the dust, spun it around and then catapulted it from view.

"Shit," I said.

But no. Two of the Pole Guys appeared and one clutched my hat! Smiling, they called me by Nepalese nickname and handed it back. We prepared to re-take the photo, this time joined by the Pole Guys.

"Say formage."

"Queso!"

A tug at my ears and then the hat was gone. I looked up to see a hawk disappearing with it gripped between his talons.

"He did you a favor," Allison said.

Reaching and collapsing at the bottom in a town nestled amid terraced rice fields, irrigation ditches and squawking chickens. In the next days, hiking along a vast stone-covered empty river bed under a dusty drab sky on way to Jomsom. Having snot-faced children with filthy clothes tug at our pant legs when we arrive, asking for money, and telling us in English that they're hungry. Tea and cinnamon rolls (!) at the Jimi Hendrix Café while watching small planes arrive at the one strip airport. Having a hot shower!

Right of the trail lay Mustang Valley – a long rock corridor heading up into the unknown.

Craig said: "I wish we could keep going."

"Keep going?" I gasped. The trail had been especially rocky that day and the heat equally brutal.

"One day you'll understand."

Chirruping birds woke us, the first we'd heard in over a week.

"I hate birds," Craig groaned at breakfast. "I prefer quiet animals. Like fish."

"This coming from a man with the last name Canary," Jan said and smiled at him.

We spent the day scrambling through mud of varying depths and viscosities as it rained and rained and rained. And rained. Heavy grey mists obscured the lush forest as if we traversed a ghost land. The distant peaks remained shrouded and unknown.

"How cute. Inchworms," Allison said.

"Those are leeches," Craig said.

There was some screaming.

The leeches scrambled up my boots every time I stopped moving, so, as I stood gasping for air, I flicked them off or pulled them bloodily from my wet socks. Especially in the rain, they were hard to grip, slipping through tired fingers. All day the ground always seemed to be moving.

In the hut we stopped at for lunch, I shed my saturated shirt to dry it on a stove. As hissing steam rose from the garment, a couple of children who'd been laughing and playing tag ran from the room clutching their noses. They never returned.

Craig took a deep breath. "Ah, nothing like the smell of Hot Pete Sweat in the afternoon."

As our dhal bhaat arrived and I took my first bite of the crunchy yet strangely delicious rice, I felt a pleasant burst of heat on my back.

"Pete!" Jan cried.

I turned and saw that my T-shirt on the stove had burst into flames. Of course, it was the only T-shirt I'd brought on the hike and I couldn't buy another one (not even the *One In the Oven* T-shirt the cook wore was for sale – apparently it was a treasured family heirloom). So I had to hike in my sweater which did its job and added to my stench.

"Is that what I think it is?" I said to Craig as we passed through a field of small, pointy leafed plants with a distinctive odor.

"Yes, sir. Ah, if only I was young again."

"It figures," Allison said.

"What figures?"

"Nothing."

Two of the Canadians offered to buy some of the weed from a farmer standing along the trail.

"I wouldn't do that if I were you," Craig said. "You do not want to get caught with drugs in a foreign country, believe me."

"Who's going to catch us?"

"A couple of years ago I was in Thailand on a boat trip. There was a guy your age on the boat with a black eye and a swollen lip traveling with two Thai policemen. They were taking him to jail for drug possession – he thought the drug dealers turned him into the police for their share of the bribe after they'd sold him the drugs. The police had beaten him for two days before they concluded he really didn't have any money to pay them off. So they decided to take him in. He begged me to get a note to his parents so they could get $10,000. Otherwise he was going to spend thirty years in prison. He had four days to do something. I called the parents when I got to Bangkok – I was leaving for London that night - and gave them the names of the policemen."

"What happened to him?"

"I have no idea."

Jan said, "Pete, why are you still carrying that air mattress? Have you used it once? And your pack is way too big."

A couple from New York passed us, both hiking in G-string bathing suits. Besides the cultural offense to the Nepalese, a forty year old man's sweaty, hairy buttcheeks is not something any person should have to see in his or her lifetime, no matter how evil they've been.

Later that night when I walked back into our room, Allison jumped up in surprise. "You should have knocked."

"What is that?" I said, pointing to the dark brown brick the size of a lunchbox she'd been sawing at with my Leatherman.

"Close the door."

"Is that hash? Where did you get it? And why so much?"

"It was so cheap."

"How long have you had that?"

"Since Kathmandu."

Wow.

Then, after another day of ups contrary to Jan's promises much to my chagrin, this:

"Oh, no," Allison said. "I forgot to take a photo of that bridge. I've got to go back."

"Down?" I asked incredulously.

"Yes."

"Down?"

And she went. Oh, the horror of it, the mind-numbing, excoriating, eviscerating horror of it.

"What are you thinking about?" Craig said as we watched Allison's retreating figure.

"Is it better to adhere to the AICPA rules of independence or the more restrictive ones of the SEC? Is it a cop out to make use of a specialist in auditing the financial statements of an oil and gas syndicate? These questions haunt me."

We watched Allison cross the bridge and take an alternate route away from us. She never looked back.

We never saw her again. Some say the mountain got her, others a homicidal yak. I like to think she found inner peace through the kind and gentle love of a yeti (hopefully deaf) and that they lived happily ever after in some secluded stupa.

Days and days of down (and up!) and down (and up!!) through mist and mud. A sublime interval spent savoring three slices of divinely moist chocolate cake (yes, three and all rather thick) near a waterfall at Rupse Chahara. Passing through villages with houses like Swiss chalets where the streets were slick with yak shit. A sunny day washing clothes (they stunk) and, when the mist returned, hiking five days in wet clothes. More and more frightening rumors of the Maoists killing tourists – a couple being shoved off a precipice, an estate and gift tax expert from Tennessee who'd been masquerading as a Canadian by putting the maple leaf flag on his pack being crucified on a tree. Walking frightened through the silent forests, struggling and mostly failing to keep up with Jan and Craig (my pack was just too heavy) so we'd be more likely to be left alone by the Maoists. Stopping every few minutes to listen for the ominous click of a rifle bolt or a machete unsheathing. More trouble with leeches. Cinnamon rolls at "German" bakeries. No sign of the Maoists. Meeting only smiling Nepalese everywhere. Having my sweat (and my new hat and my socks) smell like dhal bhaat. Eagles soaring overhead: watching, watching. Snow-capped peaks winking in and out of the fog. Wondering what Allison was doing, but knowing the answer (talking). In Tatopani, eating gorgeous lasagna made by a French woman who'd found her place with a Nepalese man. (Raise children here? What if they got sick? And what of their future? But was I happy with what I had? Was her choice any worse than mine?) Rumors of my bottomless appetite grew and grew among the other hikers: "Did you see that American guy with the enormous pack? He eats and eats and eats, he never stops. I saw him eat an entire yak and then have chocolate pudding for desert." "That's nothing. I saw him eat three goats and an entire field of cabbage." "You mean the one with the refrigerator and air conditioner in his pack? Well I saw him eat a rhinoceros, horn and all." "At least the ground shudders when he gets near. Gives you time to run." A day spent lost in a maze of stone walls pursued by the smallest but certainly not the least vicious dog in Nepal first encountered when approaching a dwelling in hopes of receiving directions (initial laughter had turned to fear of the most thorough kind as the day wore on and the chase continued – what diseases lurked in his rather foamy jaws we had no desire to find out and he was extremely adept at dodging rocks and sticks).

In Chomrong, I ate something called the veggie burger and spent the night evacuating fluid from my every orifice at a rate and force to rival Niagara Falls. And it did not stop. I tried not eating, then only eating dhal baat, but neither approach succeeded. For the next week villages greeted me with my new Nepalese nickname "Gophanarana" which is slang for in English "The One With the Orange Mountain On His Back Who Fires Thunder From His Ass." Legend of my flatulence grew and grew. As rumor of our approach reached a village, small children were herded inside to protect them from the fumes. Others ran for the hills. Warnings were etched into the walls of farmhouses and temples: "He eats all our food and then blasts us to infinity with his posterior putridities." (I huffed and I puffed and I blew their houses down – with my ass wind. But not the brick ones. Only the straw and the wood.) Then fear turned to acceptance and laughter. An entourage built. Laughing children began to follow us through the villages, adding to their number as the day progressed. Dogs, chickens and even one rather grumpy yak joined them. (The elephants and rhinoceros had overslept and we couldn't really do anything about that – you know how rhinoceros are.) There were no strewn flower petals nor any red carpet or trumpets (the Nepalese are so disorganized sometimes), but we did have little wooden flutes (sure I paid them, but it was worth every Nepalese rupee). A langur monkey tried to come, too, but then we realized he just wanted to call us names and throw his shit at us.

I tried resting on a pile of corn husks next to a gently rolling stream, but they wouldn't let me. Requests for autographs, hugs, the layman's definition of a qualified covered call...

Multi-generational families stood in the thresholds of their huts watching us pass. (But all carried fans or had clothespins on their noses, even the snotty-faced ones.) I sang "The hills are alive with the sounds of my ass wind." Accentuating my mouthed melodies with cacophonic demonstrations of an emphatic order from the other end. But acceptance did not save them. Structures collapsed, bridges crumbled, crops burst into flames in my wake as the atmospheric emissions hit them, my leavings laying waste their civilization. The U.N. was called. Troops were scrambled, radiation suits dispersed to all personnel, teary-eyed goodbyes exchanged with family and friends.

On the last absolute hill of the hike (Lavender Lad promised and this time he really really meant it) and twelve steps from our last hour long break, I collapsed against a wall gasping for air. As I waited for my head to quit spinning, I watched a hunched over woman with white hair come up the trail from where we'd stopped for lunch. A steady gait. And carrying a basket full of rocks. Yes, rocks. She smiled at me and stopped right next to me, leaning her load against the wall which I sat against. Then she removed a marijuana cigarette from her filthy blue robe and lit up. She smiled and tapped her bag and then mine. Then she offered me a toke. I took it.

A pair of enormous blue butterflies alighted on my boots. I watched their long black tongues lick the blue laces. Then I reached behind me for my camera. The butterflies didn't move. A third yellow one joined them. I took a picture of them on my feet. The old woman and I exchanged smiles.

That night we returned to Pokhara. I gorged myself on cold KingFisher beer, a chicken curry and two Baskin Robbins ice cream waffle cones with chocolate syrup, whipped cream and a cherry – each with four different flavors. Genius that I am, I passed out drunk and shirtless to awake the next morning with a back covered in eighty-seven mosquito bites in places I could reach to count. I continued my eating binge in Kathmandu with pancake breakfasts, Italian style pizzas, and beautiful buffalo steaks in the Everest Steak House. Even considering reincarnation, I'd had enough dhal bhat to last two lifetimes and maybe even a third. In the short intervals I had between meals, I visited the Swoyambhu stupa - finding time, of course to stop twice along the way for snacks – lychees and a small elephant. The pyramid-shaped temple was more like a shopping mall than a place of worship. Amid numerous small restaurants, vendors sold incense, jewelry, prayer beads, wooden masks, khukuri knives, little buddhas, big buddhas, watermelon and coconut slices covered for no extra charge in flies, and *genuine, 100% authentic* fossils. Children slid down metal railings while screaming at their playmates. Beggars in dirty loincloths pointed hungrily at their mouths. Langur monkeys pled for food scraps by tugging at the hem of my trousers, and an old blind lady smoking marijuana tried to sell me a bootleg copy of Svetlana Swan's latest CD. I couldn't find a Lord of the Burgers to calm my rumbling stomach, so I left after taking the requisite two photographs in the obligatory spots everyone else who visited there had. A week later, much fattened and somewhat bored after I'd restocked my reading material in Thamel's fabulous English used bookstores, the police asked me to leave because the city had run out of food.

One night I may have stumbled drunk out onto the street after re-reading Karlijn's last email in an Internet café late and shouted, "Hey, Commie Pinko Scum! I'll fight all of you!"

Someone with teeth and eyes may have come up to me and said, "This is Nepal. They're the oppressed victims of a ruthless dictatorship, not commies. The commies live next door in China."

"They don't fool me. Once a Commie Pinko Scum, always a Commie Pinko Scum."

But this incident may have been just a vicious rumor spread by the iniquitous and not true at all.

All this traveling, was I getting anywhere?

Craig put a reassuring hand on my shoulder, "Cheer up. Look around you. Look at what we get to see."

Two men on bicycles rode by carrying a five-foot high wooden dresser balanced precariously between them. We laughed and then I said, "I know. It's just…"

"So you find another one. Or you don't. Or you get her. Then what?"

"That's not it. It's not the getting, it's the… The back and forth, the looking at something together and just knowing without words…"

"When it happens, yeah, it's great. But it's not perfect, you know. It never is. And you can't make it be everything. You just can't. The things we get, whatever they are, however meaningless and confusing, are all we get. Don't make the mistake of not appreciating them."

I smiled. "What do you suppose Allison is doing right now?"

"Talking."

"Fascinating woman, that Allison."

"Yep."

Jan, Craig and I went for a last drink at Pub Maya together. After a couple of rounds, Jan asked if I'd dropped some money.

"Maybe. I don't know."

She handed me a fist full of bills she'd found on the floor. I forgot all about it until the next morning at breakfast when Jan and Craig appeared carrying their bags. We'd said our last goodbyes the night before - exchanged addresses and phone numbers and hugs. Jan said, "Are you forgetting something?"

"Huh?"

"The money."

"The money?"

"From last night. It was really ours."

"Oh." I instinctively touched my pocket and reached inside but it was empty - all my cash was in my money belt. I'd moved it after paying for the hotel, a bus ticket and a chess set. "How much was it?" I really didn't have any idea.

Jan's eyes were furious. "You don't know?"

"No, I… I paid for a lot of stuff this morning and was, you know, taking all the money out of hiding from when we went through the Maoist area."

Jan said nothing.

"I really don't."

"It was three thousand rupees." About forty-three US dollars.

"Okay." I did my usual routine to access my money belt. Both Jan and Craig's eyes did not soften. "I've got… two thousand one hundred. I was going to the bank to change more before my bus. You want to come with me?"

"We need to go. Our plane's leaving in ninety minutes. We've been looking for you."

"I'm sorry. I only have one hundred dollar bills otherwise. Can I send you the rest?"

Jan said nothing.

Craig said, "Just give us the two thousand."

"Are you sure?"

"Yes."

"I didn't…"

"Have a safe trip." Craig shook my hand and they were gone.

We'd hiked together twenty-six days.

The mini-bus to the village of Sauraha outside Royal Chitwan National Park was cramped with broken seats and a very low ceiling, especially for those in the raised last seat. As we reentered the bus after the first stop on a very bumpy road, a blonde Israeli girl traveling with her tall boyfriend in this last seat approached a mousy American with a scruffy brown beard sitting in the foremost seat of the bus all alone. The conversation began amicably: "Excuse me. My boyfriend is very long. Could he could share your seat? We are in the back and the roof is too low for him."

"I bought two tickets so I could stretch out and relax."

"But my boyfriend—"

"I'm sorry." He smiled at her and turned out the window.

"Meital," the boyfriend whispered and touched her arm from behind, but she could not be called off: "You take the seats in the back then."

"No, I was here first."

"Show me the seat numbers on your tickets." As on all buses in Asia, everyone grabbed whatever seat they could get, despite their assignments.

"No."

"These aren't even your seats!" She had blocked the door onto the bus. Behind her the driver was smiling.

"Why are you making a problem?" the American shouted.

"I'm making a problem because my boyfriend he is hitting his head every time the bus bounces and he is getting a big headache and you are here laying down with your shoes off stinking up the bus while he is in pain. Let me see your ticket because we probably have your seat as we bought our tickets yesterday!"

The American's smugness at beating the Asian bus system had disappeared. "Why are you making a problem?"

"Are you fucking deaf? My--"

A voice of reason interrupted her from another seat near the back: "Don't kill him! Why can't white people get along?" Our Nepalese savior passed his marijuana cigarette to his friend as he stood up. "I will make the peace between the white people. The Nepalis will make the peace. The white man he destroys the whole world with his wars and the Nepalis who have nothing will make the peace. Sit here, my friend. I will sit in back. Only don't kill him or it will take even longer to get there. Calm down, sister. Spare him." So no blood was shed.

And then I realized I'd left my New Zealand T-shirt on the lavatory sink in the Christchurch airport.

Bandying Berating Barbs Most Enjoyable
With the World's Greatest Traveler Before
Getting the Fuck Out of India

I should have worn a cape throughout India. Told everyone I was a super accountant. Footing trial balances for the common man, battling crimes of corporate corruption. Strike fear into their hearts. It might have helped. But read on and soon you'll understand.

The rain stranded me in Chitwan for five days without electricity while I waited for a bus to run. By the end, I was reading shampoo bottle ingredients to help pass the time. Finally, I was told a bus left the next day and this time they seemed to mean it because they actually sold me a ticket.

In the morning, it was raining again. Arriving at the travel agent fifteen minutes early, I found the building locked and seemingly empty. Knocking on the door three times drew no response. Nor did banging. Kicking. Spouting profanities. Seven o'clock came and went and presumably so did my bus at the pickup ten minutes' drive away. Defeated, down on the doorstep did I plunk my posterior.

A woman poked her head out of the next building to ask me "my intent." I told her I was waiting for the shuttle promised when I purchased my ticket to the Indian border the previous day. She disappeared inside.

Five minutes later, the man from whom I'd bought the ticket appeared around the corner. "Jeep gone. You late, you miss. Next bus, three days. Four days. More rain, no bus."

"No, no, no. No. I here on time. Fifteen minutes early."

"You late."

"Bullshit. See that in the street? That's what you say to me. Steaming bovine excretion. A pile of such higher than Sagarmartha. Capiche?"

"No jeep. You miss. You want go, must take motorbike."

"I paid for a jeep. I want a fucking jeep."

"Jeep gone. You late, you miss."

I sighed. "We take motorbike."

"Come, come."

"Yeah, I'm fucking coming."

The next ten minutes changed me as a human being. Every single second lived afterwards was sweet, shimmering bliss in comparison (even those spent eating beets). The man had never driven a motorbike before and the clutch was a concept he found difficult to grasp. Skid-outs were numerous and surfeit with mud and bruises. When he finally did find second gear, he whooped in triumph and did a one-wheeled jump off the next hilltop, which still makes me weep openly when I recall it. Another time he raced the bike across a single wooden plank significantly warped and awfully thin over a stream complete with churning rapids and sharp rocks. (No doubt, infested with crocodiles as well.) At the end, I crumpled off the bike. "Come! Come!" he commanded and dragged me to my feet. "Run! Run!" Oh, how I hated him. We dashed across a broken "bridge" (differentiated from the plank only by the addition of a creaking second board to its width and the significant increased depth to the fierce water beneath) and, yes, I slipped when a support fell out beneath my foot and was only barely saved by the driver's grasp. Nursing my bleeding knee, I limped hurriedly to the other side, expecting to see the bus just leaving. But luck was with me. The bus arrived only two hours later: time well spent huddling underneath a tree with a whole three leaves to shelter out an epic downpour while joined in company by four other backpackers, one of whom hadn't bathed since the Mezoic Era but was blessed with a completely rainproof poncho. The other three chain-smoked and, miraculously, were able to keep their cigarettes lit continuously despite the downpour.

Only three other passengers occupied the bus but of course our bags had to go on top to finish the job of completely soaking their contents. And, thankfully, the driver did not forget to hurl in a manner most markedly lacking gentleness of any kind the bags from the roof into a pool of extremely foul mud when we stopped.

But the trouble did not end there. A flooded river knocked out the road for six hours. But I kept going. I kept going. Laughing, the Indian police received me. As if they knew something I didn't. There was no police station at the border, only a desk on three legs when there should have been four in a murky puddle underneath an outside stairway that dripped on my passport. Trucks lined the swamp-like street that was mostly mud and stagnant water. Rundown shacks with gaping boards and collapsing frames were all the border-town consisted of. As the immigration officer returned my passport, he shook his head at me. "Why you come to India? I spend my whole life trying to leave. And you come here. I hate this country." Then he pressed his index finger against his left nostril and shot a line of mucus into the mud at his feet. As I turned to go, a woman of eighty stepped from her house and threw a pail of unidentified liquid onto the street and my trousers. "What?!!" She shot snot onto my left foot and turned away. In astonishment, I walked on. And then the smell hit me. The smell that was to follow me throughout the entire country, no matter where I went. A mixture of burning garbage, stale cigarettes and the stench of human feces. But I kept going. Into the madness, into the insanity, into India.

Before boarding the bus to Gorakphur on the way to Varanasi, I turned back towards Nepal to see another backpacker: a brown-haired European girl crying and waving her hands frantically to the immigration officials. I stopped at the door to the bus and our eyes met. I was about to head back when she winked at me and began jumping up and down, seemingly in frustration. One of the officials ran back towards Nepal. Another one brought tea and sweet chapattis. She grudgingly sat down and, within moments, had them howling with laughter. As my bus left, the official returned from Nepal and handed the girl some money. I sighed in admiration at who was surely the world's greatest traveler.

The fare collector handed me my change. The one and two rupee notes were torn and bedraggled so badly they were cased in small plastic bags (and, I found out later, perfectly acceptable elsewhere). As he moved down the aisle, he folded each denomination note he received in a different, practiced way (an elephant, rhinoceros and tiger decorated my favorite: the 10) and stuck them between different knuckles on his left hand to help him not make mistakes which I found to be pretty cool.

Ten minutes from the border, police stopped us. I shared the child-sized front seat behind the driver with three other Indian men who, like everyone else on the bus, stared at me the whole journey without once blinking their eyes (not even as they picked at sundry scabs, clipped their toenails or vigorously excavated the contents of every crevice of their noses). After speaking with the driver, the policeman turned to me. "You. Outside." Standing up nervously, I left the bus. A second rather chunky policeman was inspecting the bags on the roof. He stopped at my large orange backpack and turned his eyes deliberately towards me. Then he resumed his search. I turned to the surrounding swamp-like farmland and was nearly stepped on by a water buffalo pulling a farmer's two-wheeled wagon – the farmer had steered the animal right at me even though the road was empty in all directions. I almost said something when the animal spit at me. "Passport." I jumped 0.30 meters (a foot). The first policeman had snuck up behind me. I went through the usual manipulations to get at my identification. He returned it and waved me back inside the bus.

"Excuse me, good sir. Which country?" I was asked as I resumed my seat.

"United States."

"You pay tax? For baggage. Ten rupees every bag." He held up his own: a small duffle holding a few clothes and a broken-spined book.

"No, I didn't pay."

"Everyone on bus must pay. Baksheesh for police." He shook his head. "Thieves. Why my country so poor. Pay money for nothing. But you safe. Government say leave foreigners alone."

"I'm sorry."

"Your watch. How much?"

"Twenty dollars."

"Very nice. In India, one hundred rupees."

A little while later, I bought a coke from a boy selling bottles from a plastic red bucket who came onto the bus at one of the stops. When I finished, I asked the bus driver if he had a trash can or rubbish bin.

"Huh?"

"For the bottle."

He nodded, took the glass bottle from my hands and threw it out the window without looking. We were driving through a crowded village.

When the bus arrived outside the train station in Gorakphur, ten of the male passengers walked three steps from the door, lined up and began peeing in the crowded street. Cars and rickshaws drove by, unnoticing. This was normal behavior.

The driver threw my bag at me from the roof, so I got to fall down in the mud and make some Indians laugh.

Buying a ticket to Varanasi took me two hours. Two hours. Going from counter to counter while Indians constantly shoved in front of me. Until I learned to shake my backpack from side to side with elbows akimbo while kicking at anything that tried to move in front of me. At first I fell for the mothers bringing up babies to inspire enough sympathy for me to let them pass, but I soon realized it was the same baby being passed from hand to hand. (Over the weeks to come, I refined my technique to the point where I could get a ticket in three minutes, leaving a path of stunned and sometimes bloodied Indians in my wake, yes, but always catching my trains on time.)

Having ninety-two minutes before the next train (I'd missed one while purchasing the ticket), I returned outside and crossed the road to have a greasy curry of some unidentifiable vegetable at a café. Coming back, traffic going to the right was stalled but the left was completely clear. I stepped out tentatively in front of a bus, waving to make sure he saw me and then checked both ways twice before stepping into the next lane of traffic. A taxi waiting behind the bus pulled into the open road and came right at me, never hesitating. I had time only to turn my face away.

The taxi swerved minutely and hit my pack instead, sending me spinning back towards the bus. I opened my eyes to find myself plastered against the vehicle's side, hands clutching uselessly at the closed windows, and a group of schoolchildren inside laughing. Unsteadily, I let go and stumbled back into the train station where I collapsed on the nearest platform.

When the train arrived three hours late, the conductor attempted to shake me down for the price of a first class ticket in a second class cabin. I merely laughed in his face, offering to change cars at the next stop. When he threatened with the police, I said "Try it," which, in retrospect, was exceedingly stupid. It did, however, impress my fellow passengers who lamented the corruption of their country. An English teacher translated until everyone had fallen asleep in the cabin but the two of us (yes, they did blow snot out of their left nostrils onto the floor even in their sleep). (We sped through the countryside at the incredible speed of a crippled sloth out for a leisurely stroll, stopping often for hours at a time to savor the sight of a yet another burning heap of garbage in the middle of a field.) My companion was incredibly proud of his country and had traveled widely. He took my Lonely World guidebook in hand and kept exclaiming "And you must go to the Braganza House in Chandor! And you cannot miss the Kali Temple of Calcutta! It is so important." (He marked their pages with upside down stars.) Then he explained the history of each place. His enthusiasm was heartening after my first, rather unappealing hours on Indian soil.

"My country has endured much suffering, much bloodshed. And it still suffers from corruption. But it is a beautiful, beautiful place with much to see, much to learn from." I asked, "Do most Indians dislike the British? Because of their former rule?" "No, of course not. That would be foolish. That is in the past. We must live our lives for now, for the future. They have given us much: medicine, modern machines. And hopefully we will learn from such troubles in the past. To live in anger destroys a man."

Stepping from the train in the Varanasi station was a relief after sitting twelve straight hours to travel something like fourteen miles. And for a moment, quiet, as people rushed to catch a train leaving from a nearby platform. I passed a prostrate man. Looking closer, I saw his eyes were wide open and staring. The conductors ignored the dead man, helping passengers carry their bags to the slowly starting train in hopes of a tip. Then the taxi drivers. I fought through them, somehow. And took sanctuary in a hotel across from the train station. Right up to my entering it, the taxi drivers shouted at me that the hotel I wanted did not exist, had been burned down, stole the guests' kidneys as they slept, trafficked in white slavery, had been shut by the police. And no one in the street would give me directions, looking fearfully back at the taxi and rickshaw drivers following me.

Why had I come to India?

In Chitwan, I had wanted to do a walk through the park for a couple of days. A guide told me: "No, you go on elephant. Like all other tourists. You do this."

"I don't want to do what other tourists do."

"It is dangerous. A tiger may jump out of grass."

"That's the point."

After a day of searching up and down the town's one muddy street and knocking on the doors of many tin shacks, I found a guide willing (or desperate enough) to take me – another man would accompany us and both of them would carry rifles. But the rain never stopped and the grass grew as a consequence, making the walk even more dangerous. So I ended up taking the elephant ride instead. I hated it. The sadness in his eyes tore my heart out. And riding on the back of an elephant when you're suffering from food poisoning (the illness had returned) is not a pleasant experience. Not at all.

But the roar of the rain in that town was captivating. It drowned out every other sound, every other thought. That I loved.

After the week in the Chitwan hotel speaking to no one, I wanted to be near other tourists. So in the morning I asked a rickshaw driver to take me nearer the Ganges to another hotel listed in the guidebook as the most popular among tourists. He swore he knew it and brought me to a bland two story building with peeling white paint and exposed rebar on a side alley. This was popular? But the name was right. Upstairs the price was half what I'd paid at the train station so I took it.

To call the holiest of Indian cities filthy was an understatement of the caliber of saying my tushy was slightly cute. Garbage was strewn everywhere. And it seemed to grow every hour I was there – piles became hills, hills became mountains, whole buildings disappeared. I once saw a rat the size of a brontosaurus and then I met his big brother. People were constantly spitting or hawking up phlegm and propelling it nasally onto the street, onto restaurant floors, onto my leg. And the pervading muggy heat made wearing shoes impossible, so I switched to sandals. Which left my feet black five minutes after I'd washed them. My whole stay in India I never got my ankles completely clean, bathing in cold water just couldn't do it.

When Indians felt the end coming, they started here to Varanasi. By the riverfront, dying old men with frightened eyes sat on stone walls waiting for the unknown. Afflicted with small pox, metastasized cancer, nodular leprosy, lethal snakebites, untreated syphilis, they waited to bathe in the dull gray water with the burning dead and the city's sewage. All as children jack-knifed, back-flipped, or somersaulted in nearby, carrying ringing bells. Dead flowers drifted amid the floating refuse as pockets of yellow light shimmered across the gray hue of the river. Barefoot women in bright orange and red saris slapped their soapy laundry against stones fallen from ancient ghats. All in a country so crowded that if you stretch out your arms, you push one person into Bangladesh and another into Pakistan. (Or into Burma and Bhutan depending on the angle of how you stood.)

Wandering along the Ganges among the ghats (some of which were sinking) and pilgrims, I felt nothing. No oneness with the universe, no calm. Nothing. Only lost in a mass of anger and desperation as each doomed soul clawed and fought and bled for his share of mud and shit.

Faith. A college roommate once told me belief couldn't hurt: if you were wrong you were dead and if you were right you were rewarded with eternal life. And that seemed wrong to me – to believe only to profit yourself. But, then, I was lost myself.

A chorus of "Which country?" pursued me down every road. To which I responded at first with China, Gambia or Pollackania until I realized answering made them even more relentless. So I stopped.

Emerging from an alleyway back at the Ganges, they set upon me - scores of little children with a variety of skin diseases, ragged clothing and running noses all trying to sell me the same ten out-of-focus postcards of Varanasi. I reacted badly at first, ignoring them and then shouting "Get away! Get away!" but that only fed their vigor.

When I'd told Craig I was headed here, he'd smiled and said, "Every man loses it once in India, it's inevitable. When it stops becoming fun, it's time to leave." I'd passed that point at immigration. What the hell was I doing here? Earlier that morning, a taxi driver followed me to the bank from my hotel. When he ignored my numerous polite entreaties to leave me alone, I suddenly threatened to shove his false teeth up the dark brown rectum of his ass and twist with zeal. He backed off, but then returned all of ten seconds later. Exiting the bank, I told him I thought he looked familiar. His response, which he repeated every step of my way back even up to me entering the actual door, was to ask if I needed a ride with exactly the same phrasing each time.

One eager boy selling those same postcards grabbed me the moment I left the hotel in the afternoon so I said: "You're *the* Balou? How extraordinary! I've heard about you. As has everyone in the United States. World renowned, you are. I was warned to avoid your company at all and any costs, no matter how exorbitant or inflated these may at first appear even after taking into account historical cost of living increases. In other words, rather simplistic and woefully trite: to stay far far away from you, shunning your companionship. Told you'll steal all my money and 93.721% of the women. Told to flee from your evil presence as fast as:

A) I could with or possibly and foolhardily without the use of performance enhancing drugs

B) The Wind (in the metaphorical as well as literal sense of the word)

C) Stuff that's really fast, but really two steps faster than that if I could somehow, someway manage it

A really painful hangnail could ensue from failure to follow any of these rather simple guidelines. Or at least a whale of a wet willy. For though some say money is the root of all evil, I know the truth: that it is you."

Grinning magnificently, he answered, "Yes, I am Balou."

I walked on. He tripped trying to keep up with me.

"Are you hurt, dying, on your last legs? Should we throw you in the Ganges? To be devoured by the sharks that may or may not reside there depending on whether or not you believe the legends and/or scientific evidence derived by questionable methods?"

"I am Balou." The same glorious grin.

"Come, Balou." In a nearby bakery, I bought some dough balls dipped in syrup called gulab jamun. We exchanged looks of pain at the sweetness of very intense sugar (Twinkies dipped in molasses could not even come close to comparing).

"What are you doing with my son?" a man shouted from behind me. I turned to see a very angry man glaring at me with murder in his bloodshot eyes.

"N-Nothing. I was buying him a sweet."

"I know what you were doing! You monsters come to my country and think you can commit your perversions. I spit on your money!"

"I wasn't."

"If I see you again, I will summon the police." He took his son by the hand and walked out.

As I stood later at a railing watching a burning body slip into the river, an Indian man in a pristine white suit asked me gently, "Would you mind, good sir, if I ask what you as a foreigner think of my city?"

"This is such a sad place."

"Actually, it is not. They're happy, you know. To be here. To join the eternal. To take their rightful place in the order of the universe. Not many get to die here, it is a true privilege for the spiritual man."

That night around three in the morning, I rolled over and the sheet came off the bed beneath me. My hand brushed something like pebbles. I turned on the light. Rat droppings covered the mattress beneath the sheet. There was screaming.

So I had to find another place to stay. This time I waved down a man pedaling a rickshaw to take me.

He looked old enough to be my grandfather with his withered skin and graying hair. His smile exposed a mouth noticeably lacking in teeth but rich in betel nut stains. He was dressed all in white, though it may not have begun that color, his robe had obviously been washed hundreds of times.

"Can you take me to a hotel?"

"Of course, good sir."

"How old are you?" I asked, expecting an answer in the triple digits.

"Thirty-one."

"Jesus."

"I have two sons and two daughters," he said proudly.

Later I read that the city's pollution reduced these men's life expectancy to less than thirty-five. They chewed the betel nut to feel nothing. In Calcutta, some men pulled the rickshaws on foot.

How good did I have it.

Again I tried to go to the popular hotel listed in my guidebook and again I was taken to a place much like the first except this one was painted pink with lovely yellow trimming. I checked what was under the bed sheet before accepting the room. That night I wished I'd also felt how hard the mattress was.

Later in the day after the usual twenty minutes of trying in vain for the freezing cold shower to get my ankles completely clean of the city's filth (and my fourth shower since the rat droppings incident), I gave up and donned my sandals to change dollars into Indian rupees. The banks wanted to charge me a ten percent commission so I did exactly what all guidebooks told me not to and went on the street. The first man to approach me in the back corridors of Varanasi asked me to follow him inside a seemingly abandoned building at the end of a deserted alley. I didn't. But a moment after I returned to the mayhem of the open street, a cross-eyed man with an obtuse, bald skull covered with flaking skin called to me from one of the stalls, "Change money, sir?"

"What rate?"

He was a shopkeeper, a seller of hookahs, incense and other trinkets. "Dollars? How much?"

"Sixty."

"Forty-two."

"In the bank I get forty-two. You pay me forty-four."

He smiled, exposing a mouthful of rotting, beet-red teeth. "Forty-three."

"Goodbye."

"Yes. Forty-four."

He withdrew money from hidden pockets, desk drawers, pots, a lamp and even a sock. After counting the money twice, he folded it in half and handed it to me. I started to count the rupees myself, keeping my dollars on the carpet between us. When he reached for my dollars, I put my foot on top of them.

"You count away, in hotel. Always do this way. Police come. Trouble."

I shrugged and found the wad of blank paper.

It was his turn to shrug. He handed me more notes from his shirt pocket.

"It is all there."

"I'm sure it is. You owe me ten more."

"I come from poor country. Work very hard, slave away in fields for nothing generation after generation. Nothing to show for all this suffering. Give me the ten rupees, sir. What is it to you? Please, sir. Namaste." He smiled again.

"We split the difference or I walk away. Change my money elsewhere. I very poor man, also. My ancestors slave in rice paddies with blinding sun baking down on their shoulders, scorching their brows and depleting their wills from time immemorial. My brothers have no shoes because we can't afford them. My mother works in a coal mine, my sister a brothel. I sell blood for food. I sleep in the streets hoping to find a fresh pile of cowshit to keep me warm through the night. Don't tell me about poor. Money's money. Five rupees or no transaction. I walk away."

"Ten rupees: baksheesh. Please, sir."

"Baksheesh this, okay, buddy? I'm going." I offered him the bundle of notes.

"I have no five rupees. Please, sir." He produced what he claimed to be his last note: a ten.

"I'll take it," and I did.

He shrugged and picked up my dollars. "You're a hard businessman, sir."

"Evil, too. But you have to be if you want to rule the world. Julius Caesar was no pussy and neither am I. Have a nice day."

I would pay for my insolence. You always do. Especially in India. You never win. The next day as I tried to purchase my train ticket to Agra, the clerk announced, "This no good."

"What?"

"Fake. Need other money."

"No!"

He wouldn't talk to me again.

I went to another window. "No, fake." I tried a third. "Fake." When I returned, the shop was closed, of course.

Since I was stuck there over the weekend until the banks opened again, I decided to visit the ruins at Sarnath.

Surprisingly, twisting-horned antelope grazed on scant clumps of grass surrounding the red bricked remnants of ancient temples. After braving the oppressive heat of the unrelenting sun for a while (and tired of staring at mounds of rubble, attractive as they were), I visited the museum. With no air-conditioning, the attendant had sweated through his suit and jacket, but still he smiled at me. On display were Buddhas, Shivas and Ganeshes galore. All were magnificent and, no doubt, expensive to carve. In such a poor country with people starving on the streets, where had that money come from?

Leaving the grounds, violent rumblings seized my stomach. I dashed into the first restaurant on my left to ask if I could use their toilet. "Why?" the owner replied. "Guess." "No." I received four equally negative responses in the only other restaurants. Then I spotted a snack stand near the fence surrounding the ruins. It was one hundred yards away, but I decided to chance the distance despite the nearing crisis in my bowels.

The answer mirrored those before, and I could wait no longer.

"Excuse me," I said to the only other white tourist I'd seen that day: a brown haired Irish girl sitting at one of the snack stand's tables.

"Hello," she said brightly with the most enormous blue eyes. Light freckles dappled her nose and cheeks.

"Sorry to intrude, but I'm in something of a jam. You see, my breakfast is not agreeing with me so well and no one will let me use their restroom. And I have no paper."

Smiling, she reached inside her daypack. "No problem."

"Now to get a bit of privacy."

"Just shit anywhere. That's what the Indians do."

I smiled back at her. "I shall at that."

In a last effort to save my underclothes from utter destruction, I made a mad dash (which deteriorated into a hobble) for some nearby bushes. As relief swept over me, I realized I had company. Unwittingly, I'd chosen the corner of a playground adjacent to the snack bar for my evacuations. The children were gathered round me in a semi-circle, peeking through the bushes with giggles and pointing fingers. I clumsily waved them away, needing to maintain my squatting position, while shouting "Go away! Can a man not shit in peace?" but they only laughed. To complete my embarrassment, their mothers soon joined them and all basked in the novelty of a white man shitting. They stayed to the very end, watching every single wipe. Applause did not greet my finale nor was one autograph requested, only laughter followed my every gesture for them to leave. They did not part their circle to allow me past nor would they move when I asked, so I pushed through and fled.

"You saved my life."

"All in a day's work."

"Superhero?"

"Close. Traffic engineer."

"Ah. Even more powerful."

"How so?"

"You control traffic, you control time. Time is money. Money makes the world go 'round. You're the most powerful woman in Ireland and you don't even know it."

"How did you know I was Irish?"

"The *Made in Ireland* tattoo adorning your forehead."

"I keep forgetting. Want to sit down?"

"Yes, please. I saw you before. At the border. You winked at me."

"That's right. I'd forgotten."

"What were you doing with those policemen?"

"I'd bought a ticket all the way to Varanasi from Kathmandu, but the Indian leg was fake. I'd already crossed the border, so I couldn't go back. I'd had trouble with Nepalese immigration. So I pleaded and tore out my hair and threatened suicide via drowning myself in Fanta while telling

267

them I had no money and needed a refund to get to a bank in Gorakphur. So the Indian police went back to the bus company in Nepal and got my refund."

"You had trouble with Nepalese immigration?"

"I overstayed my visa by fifteen days and they wanted to fine me two hundred dollars American. When I told them I didn't have it, they threatened to arrest me."

"Shit."

"Yeah. So I started crying, swearing I was very sorry, and they let me go. When I told the Indians this story and played up how I'd fooled the Nepalese, they loved it so much they bought me breakfast."

"You're my hero."

"And the wind beneath your wings?"

"That, too."

As Edith and I walked back towards the Varanasi bus, a half-naked Indian dressed only in a short white cloth tied around his waist and a turban accosted us. "I show you good trick. You take photograph. Pay money."

"Can you make yourself invisible?"

"Good trick. Good photo. I very strong." He flexed his skinny bicep. "You pay big money."

I shrugged at Edith. "Heaps. Millions. Billions."

"More. You pay more." He reached inside a canvas bag he carried for a frayed length of soiled rope. Then he suddenly grabbed at my ankle, or rather, at a fist-sized stone near my ankle much to Edith's amusement as I tripped backwards and stumbled into a camel whom, promptly and with little or no remorse, spat on me.

"You've got a way with animals," Edith laughed.

"Shutup or I will put gum in your hair. And your family's. Your pets', too."

"Some people should be dragged outside through sharp gravel and shot or tickled vigorously. Repeatedly."

"I pity you and, even more so, those forced to endure the presence of your sweetly suffocating beauty."

"Big money, you pay. Good trick." He tied one end of the rope around the rock. When I saw that he was going to cinch the other end around the tip of his penis, I shouted, "Don't!"

He dropped the rock and it swung down between his legs. His facial expression said it all.

"Stop. Stop!" I did the sympathetic male dance as Edith cried with laughter beside me.

The man went through a whole series of contortions as he swung the rock this way and that, grimacing and groaning in what could not be entirely theatrics. But somehow I did not leave.

Finally, however, I had to shut my eyes.

Edith asked, "Should we take a photo?"

I opened my eyes. "Yeah, why not?"

"Something to show the folks back home."

"Grandma will love that one…"

"Big… Money!"

"Do you take credit cards?"

"I don't know which of you looked more in pain," Edith said to me on the bus afterwards.

"Well, you were standing on my foot about half the time."

She laughed. "You should have said something."

"I did. You ignored me."

"I'm sorry. Did you say something?"

A white-haired man wearing a white taqiyah boarded the bus. He was carrying an umbrella, a harmonica and a headless fish. He blew once on his harmonica and then began singing in a deep guttural voice. The tune resembled a Hindi version of *Rudolph the Red-Nosed Reindeer*. Everyone began to sing along with him. As the song ended, he abruptly exited the bus and disappeared into a roadside market, forgetting his fish. An uneasy silence ensued. Caught up in the moment, I jumped to my feet and tried to lead the crowd in an upbeat rendition of *Strangers in the Night*. Nothing.

Edith: "They're not feeling it."

So I gave up after the third verse. And second chorus.

Later the fish began to smell but no one would touch it or allow me to. Bad luck.

Edith said, "Do you want to have dinner together? I know this place that serves really good Indian food... Um, shut up."

We stuffed ourselves on garlic naan, cauliflower and garbanzo bean curries, tandoori chicken, assorted chutneys, fresh samosas and mango lassis for a few dollars and then had to be carried outside as we were too full to move. But there, children who lived in cardboard boxes begged us for pennies before returning across the street to an existence of cooking, doing laundry and shitting all in the same fetid water running from a rusty pipe, waiting for a life that would get better and never would.

"Let's not do that again."

"Agreed."

Had independence from Britain profited these people anything? Were their oppressors now the faceless consumers of the world – those who needed cheap T-shirts, toys, electronic goods that could not be produced for that price in their own nations? And how did we spend that saved money? On essentials like plastic surgery, re-election campaigns, ever more sophisticated weapons of death. But that was the world, right? That's what we wanted.

Coincidentally (Did it mean something? Nothing?), Edith had fallen for the same hotel scam and was in the same hotel as mine. In the morning I left a note on Edith's door as I went downstairs for breakfast: "Dude. So... Um, if you're... like around and not, whatever, doing anything, possibly we could, I don't know, hang out. I mean, unless... you're busy or anything. Have plans, like. I mean: yeah. Right. Totally. Nah, forget it, I mean it was stupid but... Do you wanna?"

When Edith appeared in the hotel's restaurant, she took the table furthest away from mine and avoided my eyes. When the waiter delivered my coffee a few minutes later, he also gave me a folded note from Edith. It said, "You suck."

Suppressing a laugh, I hastily replied in similar fashion: "No, I rule."

Edith's response took much, much longer: "Absolutely and without any equivocation whatsoever, I disagree to the utmost."

When the waiter disappeared, I said, "You're just jealous."

"Of what? Please answer in, knowing you, mind numbing and meticulous detail."

"Me ruling."

"Right."

"So are you busy?"

"Well, the waiter, the cook and the maitre d' all asked me to marry them."

"After that then."

"I suppose."

"Actually, want to go to Agra with me?"

"Sure," she answered. Without a pause.

"So that's the Taj Mahal," I said.

"The guidebook says this king built it in memory of his dead wife. Then he had the architect's hands chopped off so he could never build anything else as beautiful."

"Sounds like a swell boss."

"It says they had a good dental plan and the day off before New Year's."

"Not so bad then."

"The king got his just reward, I guess. His son imprisoned him after it was built."

"Kids yesterday. No respect for their elders."

After we fulfilled requests to pose for photos with twelve different Indian men (two of whom squeezed Edith's ass and one who squeezed mine – suddenly after twenty-four years of being ignored, I had my own paparazzi), I asked my Irish companion, "What do you want to be when you grow up?"

"A pirate. Or maybe a race car driver. You?"

"Good, you're not competition."

"Spill."

"I'd like to be ultimate supreme ruler of the universe. Despot of all dominions. The sun shall never set on my empire."

"Humble aspirations then."

"My needs are few, my virtues a myriad."

"Could I be vice-ruler of the universe?"

"You mean vice-ultimate supreme ruler of the universe?"

"That. Yes."

"I don't much like to share."

"Please?"

"I'll give you Bulgaria."

"Who wants Bulgaria?"

"The Avars, the Ottomans, and, of course, the Bulgarians."

"All right, all right. I'll take it."

We did gut-bustingly, knee-slappingly hi-LAR-ious picture poses by the reflecting pool, tried valiantly to push over one of the walls but met with little success (Why? Just cuz.) and were met with disapproving stares as a result, and paid a guy ten rupees to unravel his four foot long mustache so we could photograph him in front of one of the minarets with each of us holding one end.

Outside afterwards in a surge of goofiness, I shouted, "Which country?" to a group of teenage Indians and we were set upon mercilessly.

A bold girl, very beautiful with long dark hair, answered, "India."

"You don't look Indian. Are you sure?"

They all smiled. "Yes, India."

"Well, I never. For sure I thought you'd say Wales."

"No, India."

"And you're sure? Absolutely? Show me your passport."

"Jaipur," the girl answered with a huge smile. "I am here visiting my cousin."

"Which country?" the youngest boy in the back asked.

"Ireland," Edith answered.

"Neptune," I answered.

The cousin nodded her head towards Edith. "And what is your relation?"

I said, "We've been married twenty-seven years now. It seems like we met only yesterday."

"But you're from Neptune and she's from Ireland."

"Yes, we met during the Peloponnesian War. She was a nurse and I in the underwater cavalry. I was wounded opening a can of tuna. Lost three arms and she saved me. So I fell in love with her and she reciprocated most vehemently despite me being half-bionic and allergic to alfalfa sprouts."

"I don't understand."

"Neither do I. I was hoping you could explain."

Edith said, "He's just kidding. We met yesterday."

"Yes," I added. "And walked down the aisle last night. Romance was in the air. Until this morning when she cheated on me with an Arabian acrobat named Ahmed. Now we're going through aromatherapy and trying to work things out."

"He, the English, is crazy."

"I'm not crazy. I'm normal. Everyone else is crazy."

"You're weird."

"Good weird or stay away from me weird?"

"I'm still deciding."

We passed a taxi stand festering with the usual hangers about. "Marijuana? Cocaine? Heroin?"

I countered: "Kellogg's Corn Flakes? Post Raisin Bran? A small child's head?"

"Why you ask me this?"

"Because I want my doctor's recommended daily intake of dietary fiber and riboflavin, damnit!"

He dismissed me with a hand and resumed the very important business of sitting along the road waiting for tourists to scam.

Edith said, "Personally, I'm all about my folic acid needs."

"Dude. Like totally."

"Did you just *dude* me?"

"I totally *duded* you."

"*Dude*... Thirsty?"

"Yep."

As we approached a place to sit, Edith suddenly let loose with a snot projectile from her left nostril.

"Good to see you're picking up the local customs."

"I can kill a man at thirty paces."

"Yikes."

"Maybe thirty-five. Definitely can wing him from that range."

"Must come in handy. A woman traveling alone. Damned attractive as well."

"Another weapon to wield in my man magnet arsenal."

"Should be taught at all the best finishing schools for young girls."

"That might just be THE WORST JOKE EVER TOLD. If not, a certain runner up. Best of the millennium, for sure."

Suddenly I felt something go into my ear from behind.

I turned around sharply to find the toothless grin of a man in his twenties with wild eyebrows holding a small stick covered in yellow wax. "Good sir! Look how filthy your ears are! Let me clean them—"

For such a skinny man, he was a fast runner.

Gasping for breath, I returned. "What were you going to do once you caught him?' Edith asked.

"You really need to refine your snot projectile aim. I saw what you did to that poor dog, *dude*."

"That's twice you've *duded* me. Three times if you count the note."

We spent the evening fending off touts with water pistols, much to the delight of Indian spectators, as we sauntered/sashayed through the markets.

The next day, Edith wanted to visit a bunch of Hindu temples (if you've seen one typical Hindu temple, you've kind of seen them all...) so I took a daytrip alone to the abandoned city of Fatehpur Sikhri. As usual, the heat was oppressive. And the attention I received even more so. Either tour guides who wanted me to hire them or Indian tourists who wanted me to be in their photos dogged my every step. I left quickly.

The road to Fatehpur Sikhri was typical of the Indian madness. The largest vehicle reigned supreme on the highway, honking at others to clear out of the way. Buses charged head on at automobiles, rickshaws, and camel drawn carts. Motorcycles and motor scooters dodged stray cows, oblivious to the mayhem they caused. Men in red turbans and white shirts stopped traffic to lead chained monkeys into the road to do tricks for tips. Others led woolly black bears with melancholy eyes and backs scarred and balding from continuous beatings.

On the ride back to Agra, a turbaned old man with a wooden cane sat down next to me and smiled. "Too hot," he said and wiped a hand across his sweating brow.

"Yes."

"Which country?"

"I can't tell you that for I am traveling incognito under the strictest need for secrecy. You see, I am Richard Remora's illegitimate bastard child and I am seeking retribution for the trials and tribulations brought upon my head by that software magnate's ruthless abandonment of his offspring. Goddamnit."

Continuing to smile, the man asked, "Your good name, sir?"

"Horace T. Wainwright the Third."

"And your job?"

"I am President of the United States of America."

Sleep interrupted his stare a whole eight seconds later and he slumped against me in all his smelly boniness. I didn't mind the poking elbows or the cuddling, but when he began to drool and the Fijian flashbacks started, I'd had enough. I pushed him away, gently at first and then harder as his skull returned with the accuracy of a guided missile aimed at my head. I'd given in to my fate when he began to fondle my breast and I redoubled my defense. (He hadn't even bought me a drink!) He caromed off the opposite seat and landed in the middle of the aisle. But he did not get up. I ignored him and joined the laughter of the other passengers.

When he still hadn't moved ten minutes later, I grew worried. The bus arrived at its last stop and everyone pushed and shoved each other to be first off the vehicle. Feeling guilty, I nudged him. He did not move. I shoved him. He still did not move. Nor would he ever again.

I stumbled out onto the road. "That man inside. He's dead," I said to the first person I saw.

"Oh. Taxi, sir?"

"No, he's really dead."

"Hotel, sir? Very good price."

Could I risk the police? Indian prison was probably even filthier than it was outside (if that was even possible). I walked away. I walked away faster. Almost out of sight, almost out of sight.

BAAAAAGH!

I dodged a rickshaw and looked back. The bus driver had returned and was dragging the dead man to a garbage heap beside the road. Done, he climbed back into the bus and drove off. I turned the corner.

Back in Agra, Edith asked me: "How was your morning?"

"A man died on my bus."

"What?"

"Yeah. They just dumped his body on the street and drove off."

"Wow."

We didn't say anything for a few minutes. Then she asked: "Did you tell him one of your jokes?"

After visiting the Agra Fort, Edith and I let our rickshaw driver take us to some shops to save the fare (the shopkeepers paid drivers who brought white tourists). The first sold silk garments.

"What about a dress, sir?" the owner asked as we stepped inside.

"She won't let me wear them anymore. Only high heels and only on holidays. She's an iron-fisted tyrant, she is, but I adore the ground she kind of hovers angelically above, anyway."

"A scarf, sir?"

"No, thanks, I'm trying to quit. Years of aromatherapy, electric shock treatment with a rather spotty cattle prod, copious quantities of prescription medication and black market Vitamin D all used to help such. But methinks I've really kicked the heinous habit this time. Keep your fingers crossed. All of them, even the pinkies. Just don't tempt me. Hide that blue beauty. Hide it!"

"You like the blue, sir? I give you good price."

"Honey! The scarves! We must go! We must go!"

"Nice lady, your husband, how is he in bed? He seems very wild. Good for the fucking."

Edith clenched her fists and I had to drag her outside. "I must inflict grievous and unspeakable bodily harm on them. Release me!"

"Let the love back in!" I grasped her shoulders and spoke into her eyes. "Hate out, love in. With every breath you take, every stunningly seductive move you make. Love in. Let it consume you."

"Hate in, love out. Hate in, love out."

"The horror! The horror!"

We started laughing.

"Now take us to our hotel," I said to the driver.

"The owner here, he did not pay me. His grandfather die today, so I get no commission. So no money for my children. My daughter: she needs special medicine – very expensive. Please, one more shop?"

"Okay, okay, one more shop."

Once there: "Not just for this vase, for the whole store. All is so lovely – I want everything. To have less would cause me actual physical pain. And unrelenting acute mental anguish. But my funds are limited. So I will offer twelve dollars. And three cents. For the chairs, jewelry, silk garments... And you must throw in that handsome brother of yours as well." They kicked us out.

The last stop I pretended to be Edith's mental patient throwing a fit because I hadn't received my daily allotment of crunchy peanut butter, so they let us leave to get it. Then we refused to go any further – dead grandfather or no (apparently an aunt, two cousins and a favorite dog named George Washington Lincoln Jefferson had expired today as well – the Patels were having a bad Wednesday).

We couldn't, however, pass up a leather shop which offered a personally signed testimonial by U.S. President Richard Remora as to the unsurpassed quality of its wares - I bought a belt decorated by peacocks that paired fabulously with my third shirt. It fell apart three days later in a rather embarrassing incident I'd rather not share (yes, dwarfing my diarrhea episode).

As we passed a prison on the way to a restaurant for lunch, shouts and whistles greeted us from inside the barred windows.

At the next corner I said to Edith, "You're in a huff, aren't you?"

"About what?"

"Because they asked me out and not you."

Edith lowered her chin dejectedly to her chest. "Well. I only received sixteen marriage proposals today."

"And I got called sweetheart?"

"And schnookums," she pouted without raising her eyes. "And honey bunch."

"And I got twenty-three phone numbers. Digits, baby!"

Edith groaned. "I thought only twenty-one."

I patted her back, "We all have our off days."

"I even showered last week. Or the week prior."

"I know. But not everyone can have as cute a tushy as me."

"But, but, but—"

"You know, it'd really help the day go by faster if you were actually somewhat halfway amusing once in a very long while."

"And your point is?"

Midway through our masala dosas, I felt something enter my ear. "Good sir! Look how filth..."

For a brief moment, the bustling madness of the Indian traffic came to a standstill as a thin mustachioed man catapulted into its midst covered from his greasy hair to the filth of his blackened heels in a green sticky mucus trumpeted from Edith left nostril.

That night I had to switch rooms when the ceiling fan spun off its rod and crashed into the unused side of my bed, nearly decapitating me. Of course, the hotel owner began by accusing me of breaking it and only relented when I threatened having the US Air Force carpet bomb his establishment.

Before leaving Agra, I wanted to mail home my film of Nepal and Edith some clothes and souvenirs. So we hired a rickshaw to take us to the post office. Inside, a three-sided waist-high desk separated the customers from the rear of the room. Above each of the twelve stations (only one of which was occupied despite there being close to thirty people behind milling about looking very busy walking empty-handed from one end of the room to the other and back again repeatedly), a sign read *It is unlawful to give money in the form of bribes to government postal employees. To do so, is to break the law and can be severely punished. If an employee solicits such an offering of money, please do not remunerate any sums and report it immediately to his superior who will severely reprimand any such transgressions.*

When the clerk heard my intentions, he demanded four hundred rupees even though the second class postal tariff for Indians was a tenth that on the chart sitting between us. Nor did he waver when I glanced up at the sign and back. Edith and I had already spent two hours driving to the post office (risking life, limb and sanity braving the Indian traffic) and employing a streetside tailor to sew the packages up in cloth (as was required). Numerous stories in Kathmandu pretty much assured me I'd be robbed sometime in India and so lose all my Himalayan photographs. The clerk could sense this – innate in all Indians is the ability to intuit when you want something which they always exploit. "But the tariff says it's only a dollar," I sort of tried which drew a bored (as in "That's all you got?") headshake. "No, no, no. Postal regulations clearly state all such packages with international destinations be sent with a charge for first class postage. The correct price is eight thousand one hundred rupees." "What! I won't pay that."

The rickshaw driver from our hotel stopped me at the door: "He will take four hundred rupees. No more. He will stamp the package as if it is sent by an Indian." I sighed. "And it will get there? Guaranteed?" "Most assuredly, good sir." I paid him with the counterfeit money.

When the train to Delhi stopped in the middle of a field to take in the local sights, I said to Edith about the mound of burning garbage we'd been staring at for the last six hours: "Cholera."

"Typhoid."

"Bubonic plague."

"Yellow fever."

"Amoebic dysentery."

"Cooties. Atomic cooties."

Seven hours. The garbage fire had gone out. We'd both fallen asleep and woke up again. I nudged her. "Why did the parrot cross the road?"

"No."

280

Eight hours. Someone relit the fire so we'd have something to smell besides the stinky feet surrounding us.

"Why did the toucan—"

"Absolutely not."

"You're just—"

"What?"

"Way too good to be true."

"And some kind of wonderful. I know."

The next time Edith fell asleep was on my shoulder. Her fragrant brown hair, ridiculously soft, tickled my cheek. She cooed and grasped my arm with one hand while pressing her warm body closer to mine, her large breasts rising and falling with each breath against me.

I never wanted to travel any other way. Or for her to wake. It was impossibly perfect.

Weeks, months, years later (Who exactly knew? And whoever did wasn't releasing any hints or dropping any easily decipherable clues.), the train arrived somewhere and we got off. As we stumbled from the station, a voice called: "Where you going, good sir and lady?"

"Sweden. Is it nearby?"

"I take you. Good price. Very fair."

"I always wanted to see the Vasa."

"What's that?"

"A boat that sank about a hundred yards out of the harbor on its maiden voyage because the king insisted on adding another deck of guns to the builders' design. They salvaged it from the harbor just recently (in the cosmic relative sense of that term) and preserved it by transforming the wood to plastic. It's now a national attraction."

"Symbolizing failure? Seems like a good use of taxpayer money."

"Want to share a room this time?" Edith asked me.

Guess my answer.

"This time let me do the negotiation," Edith said. "You're too kind, too polite. Indians see that as a weakness. Blend in, acclimate. Whatever you want, however inappropriate or impossible, ask for it. Demand it."

At breakfast, Edith narrowed her eyes at me. "What's your surname anyway?"

"Pollack."

"You sure?"

"I think so."

"Prove it. Have it tattooed anywhere?" After a moment of considering my possible answers, she added, "Actually... I withdraw the question."

"Check my driver's license, birth certificate *and* past three years of bank statements?"

"Doubtless all forgeries. No, it's Petrel. Or Penguin. As sure as submarine sandwiches on Sunday. Pollack doesn't suit you."

"What's yours?"

"Egret."

"That's the most ridiculous, worstestest, entirely absurd name I've ever heard in all my exceedingly long and varied life."

"Some people shouldn't be allowed to speak."

"Others should be muzzled."

"Or had their tongues chopped."

"Not funny at all. You really need to work on your material."

"As should you: neither parch nor pain my perception's palate with your pathetic palaver, inebriate me with your eloquence, words are to woo and wow, not to woe and weary."

"I have no response to that."

"I have no response to your no response – not that that's any kind of a response."

"Violence is the answer. Violence is always the answer."

If possible, breathing Delhi's air was even worse than Agra's (the equivalent of smoking three packs of cigarettes a day according to the guidebook). And almost none of them could afford to leave for somewhere else.

"Hold on a second," I said to Edith and approached a wooden stand selling bottles of soda from a Styrofoam chest filled with chipped ice. Having learned my lesson before, I asked, "How much for a Thumbs Up?"

"Fifteen."

I laughed. "Ten. Always ten."

He nodded and handed me the bottle.

"I charm them!" a boy shouted six sevenths of an inch from my left ear. "Give me money!"

I looked down. Inches from my sandal-clad, bare white legs lay two woven straw baskets without lids. Inside the baskets were a python and a cobra, both coiled to strike, fangs dripping with poison and looking longingly at my shins.

How I casually paid the soda salesman and walked away, I have no idea, but I did.

"Are you all right?" Edith asked me, touching my arm. "You're completely pale."

"I think they're trying to kill me."

Edith laughed and we entered the Red Fort. As we were paying at the admission booth (foreigners paid one hundred times more than locals), a low boom shook the ground violently from beyond the walls. And then everything became muffled. I looked to Edith who was shouting as she tried to pull me to the ground beside her, but I couldn't hear her.

What was mostly suspicious was the lack of sound. India is full of noises, always present: Hindi music, blaring horns, misfiring engines, screeching brakes, an amalgamate rumble of street vendors, beggars and touts. These had all stopped. Then: a thin, piercing scream. And shouts. Everyone began running outside. Edith and I followed them.

A terrorist bomb had exploded in one of the stands on the far side of the road. Two nearby cars burned as did a few stands. A crowd made it impossible to see, but cries of hysteria called out from behind. Then two men pushed their way out carrying a limp girl, her head dangling disjointedly from her neck. Dark stains streaked their button-down white shirts.

I regretted my joke.

Edith said, "I want to help."

Police cars with blaring sirens began to arrive. "How?"

"I want to help."

A little boy was crying fitfully not far from us. Edith took his hand and led him towards the scene of the bombing. His mother suddenly appeared and pulled him away from us and fled. "Let's return to the hotel. We don't belong here."

A policeman saw us and began pushing us down the street, "No photos. Tourist, go home."

"We want to help."

"Go."

I took Edith's protesting hand and hailed a rickshaw at the next corner. Ten seconds later we were amid the traffic and blaring music again and the driver was telling us how poor his family was and how he wanted triple the fare we had agreed upon.

A seven-year old boy, his left eye filmed over with a cataract, waited for us outside the hotel, begging. As he'd done that morning as we left, he followed us as well as he could to the door of the hotel. With his right leg horribly disfigured, a flat wooden board on wobbly small metal wheels served as his mode of transport.

Inside the room, Edith collapsed against the door. For a long moment she said nothing. Then: "This place…"

"I know."

"Parents blind or cripple their children sometimes. So they'll be better beggars."

"No."

"And the worst part is I find myself wishing they'd just go away. That their poverty is really inconveniencing *me*."

At night, nothing happened. It couldn't.

We went on to the next city. But upon arriving, Edith didn't want to go out, to be harassed. I didn't want to think about the dead girl, so I took a walk.

A man in his early twenties driving a motorcycle suddenly stopped and removed his helmet to talk to me. "You are going to Swargasuli to look at the city, perhaps? As it says in the book, the tower affords the best view of Jaipur."

Never any peace. "I was thinking about it."

"I will show you a place where you can see the view for free and save one hundred rupees. The government, they are always trying to rip off tourists in my country."

"Um…"

"No, costs nothing. You are from the United States, then?"

"Yes, but I don't have much money."

"We just talk. Like one person to another. I like to hear what it is like in other countries. Not everyone is rich there, I know. Most Indians do not know this. They see white skin and think you are all rich. What is your occupation, good sir?"

"I'm a clerk in a hardware store. I sell people paint."

"Are you married?"

"Not anymore."

"I'm single as well. Up here." He led me up the staircase of a deserted building. I went, even though I shouldn't have, but my camera and money belt were back at the hotel. I carried only forty rupees in my wallet and another fifty dollars in the sole of my shoe.

"My parents tried to marry me off, but I want my independence. This is a new India. Ah, look."

Through the polluted gray smoke that masqueraded as air in India, I saw a collection of crumbling buildings with fading paint, collapsing staircases, drying laundry, weirdly fashioned antennae. But this was their home.

"You have a girlfriend?"

"No, I still love my wife. But I screwed up. My father recently died of tennis elbow he caught from a Finnish gopher named Tyrell. I got all depressed and began drinking Pink Ladies with small paper umbrellas by the gallon. My wife left me for the plumber's dominatrix whom she met at a Tupperware party. But now I'm going to community college for underwater communications with a minor in the psychology of house plants. I won't sell paint my whole life. I've got ambition. Well, thank you for the view." I turned to go.

"Wait. I want to talk to you for a moment. Come. We can talk better in my office."

I followed him warily down another staircase into the heart of the building, checking back and forth to see if anyone was lurking with a knife or worse (scimitar, halberd, morning star, meat hook, rusty chainsaw, three-hole punch). He unlocked a door in front of me and walked inside. He took a seat at a desk in a small room with barren walls and gestured for me to sit opposite him. Then he offered me a cigarette.

"Don't smoke."

"Please sit." I glanced back, the door to the office was still open. I sat, despite my misgivings, feeling I owed him. "I forgot to tell you something. There's a way for you to make money. Quite a lot of it. Doing us a favor. You can take gems into your country for us and not pay any taxes."

"That sounds great!" I stood up and left the room quickly, not looking back and dreading what would happen on the descent to the street.

But I made it. I avoided that part of town the rest of my stay there.

When I opened the door, Edith said, "Thank God, you're back. The waiters kept coming up to the room asking me if I wanted tea. Or company. Every twenty minutes. And not once did their eyes make it to my face. The same police came three times to check my passport. From now on, you're my very jealous, very violent husband."

My voice caught. "Deal."

Few cars roamed the dusty streets of Pushkar. Only the ubiquitous shitting cows or half-naked sadhus leading a parade of religious pilgrims garbed in white while trumpets blared, hands clapped and voices sang. Men in bright red, yellow, orange or green turbans sat on overturned crates at every shaded corner smoking cigarettes, drinking hot chai and eating samosas while playing cards as they waited for customers. Young girls in brightly colored saris, many with ornate silver and pearled nose rings, decorated tourists' hands with temporary henna tattoos – swirls, loops and flowers of dark red. At the town's edge, a boy of six with sand in his dark unkempt hair led six burros no taller than my waist. Each carried twin bags of multi-hued soil. The boy's flip flops were a glaring pink. Pigeons rustled softly overhead, fluttering from the rooftop of one ghat to another while casting dead black eyes at me. Dark faced white monkeys leapt from building to building in the shimmering morning heat. Prayers broadcast garishly loud over tinny speakers echoed across the town's central pool. The sun bathed the landscape in a golden yellow until midmorning when the heat came and washed the sky out. A pickup truck full of bananas with two men perched precariously on top (and above the slats holding the fruit in) nearly hit a peacock crossing the road.

"That's a lovely, lovely robe you're wearing. Oleg Cassini or Ralph Lauren?"

"You like gems, sir? Take this crystal as a gift."

"I'd prefer that robe. The craftsmanship is magnificent. The stitching absolutely to die for. Almost as attractive as the extremely fetching physique it teasingly conceals."

He pushed a crystal into my hand. "My gift to you."

"What can I do with a rock?"

"Come, I show you the crystals in my shop. Very beautiful."

"No, I don't buy."

"Why?"

"Do I need material objects? They're just things. To linger on a shelf collecting dust. And use to boast to others of my wealth. I'd rather spend my earnings constructing a big fat ass scarfing chocolate éclairs on the Champs Elysees or Turkish Delight in Istanbul. Didn't Buddha renounce his material wealth? So will I."

Muttering: "Fucking Buddhist," he returned inside his shop to await the next tourist bus.

That night sitting on opposite beds facing each other, legs crossed and under the other's bed: parallel but apart.

"Tell me more about yourself."

Edith smiled. "Like what?"

"Were you ever in the circus? Have you worked for MI-6? Do you like peanut butter? Have you ever dated any US presidents?"

"Yes, no, absolutely not, and yes."

"Which ones?"

"You'll have to buy the book and make me fabulously, obscenely wealthy from the royalties."

"Dude, that joke is so 1991-ish."

She held up her right hand and curled her right thumb into the palm. "Four times you've *duded* me. Four." She stood up.

This was it. With a deep breath, I took her hand as she turned away. "Without you, how will I ever cope with my fear of cancer, stalkers, unfiltered drinking water, defective automobile brakes, the West Nile virus, nuclear terrorism, bio-terrorism, unpasteurized milk, high blood pressure, hormone injected beef, seafood mercury levels, saturated fats, high cholesterol, credit card fraud, a collapsing stock market, rising interest rates, global warming, rabid tree squirrels, malnourished grizzly bears, hammerhead sharks, carpal tunnel syndrome, attention deficit disorder, adult diabetes, rising oil prices, pervasive rosacea, ingrown toenails, adult illiteracy, drive-by shootings, Ebola, avian flu, Mad Cow disease, identity theft, flash floods, earthquakes, tsunamis, tornados and the occasional hurricane?"

"I'm just going to take a shower, I'll be back." But she didn't laugh. Nor did she meet my eyes. Her hand was limp in mine. I let go.

She stayed in the shower a long, long time. Even longer after the water had stopped running. When she came out she was wearing her bright green *I'm Irish!* pajamas. "Hey," she said softly.

"Hey."

"Pete, I have a boyfriend. He's meeting me in Mumbai."

Fuck. "Okay."

"Okay?"

"Okay."

Jodhpur fort. Edith and I spent some time browsing the museum's collection – like castles anywhere else, instruments of torture were plentiful. My favorite pieces were a golden dagger sporting twin muskets attached to either side, velvet lined rocking beds plated in gold, and various howdahs used to transport royalty on elephants. (Sorry, I was late for work, Mr. Maharajah, my elephant wouldn't start.)

I approached one of the policemen in the guard office to ask for directions to the cannons.

"This way, sir. They're very nice."

"Thank you."

"Do you like to smoke opium?"

"What?"

"Opium, sir. I assure it is of the highest possible quality. And for a very good price."

"Um, no, thanks. I quit after it made my left ear fall off one day."

Outside, it seriously considered raining, no doubt going through all the doubts and misgivings all clouds must experience during their tempestuous lives, but at the last minute didn't.

"Heroin then? We have brown as well as white."

"Are you kidding?"

"Kidding?"

"Joking with me?"

"No, sir. I'm serious."

"Well, my cat's addicted to heroin and it's not a pretty sight. I can't end up the same. Thanks for the help."

"Where did you go?" Edith asked.

"You wouldn't believe if I told you."

At dinner, I asked, "Should we risk the meat?"

"Keep an eye on the dogs. If any go missing…"

"Edith."

"Yeah?"

She didn't turn towards me in the other bed. "Good night."

"Good night, Pete."

It took me a long time to fall asleep.

I was drowning in an aquarium as seahorses trickled from the sky to splash through the surface and then spiral down around my descending figure when Edith shook me awake in my bed.

Her enormous blue eyes held mine in the darkness from inches away as some of her stray hairs tickled my cheek. She was on her knees straddling my hips. "Your puerile puns induce me to projectile vomiting," she said and bounded back to her own bed.

"Huh?"

She was already sleeping again.

I woke first and went downstairs to read *Underworld* by Don DeLillo while eating theplas dipped in a mixed pickle yogurt for breakfast. Then I decided. Today I would kiss her no matter what.

Edith appeared with a wide-lipped smile and handed me a parcel wrapped in brown paper she'd been hiding behind her back.

"What's this?"

"A present."

"Goody, goody gumdrops." With vim and vigor, real savage-like I

290

ripped and nearly wept at its beauty – she'd had a T-shirt custom made to replace the one for my father that I'd lost in the New Zealand airport – I'd told her the story. "This is totally fucking awesome. Thank you."

"You're welcome. There's two actually – so you and your father can match."

"You're great, really great."

"Thank you, Peter."

"And we get on so well. Perfect, really."

"I've had a good time, too. Traveling together has been a lot of fun. I'll miss you."

"Miss me?"

"I'm staying here to take a yoga class. I know you wanted to go to Jaisalmer, it sounds beautiful."

"I could stay."

"I know, I like hanging out, too. But you hate India. The sooner you see what you want and leave, the better for you, I think."

No. "I don't want to say goodbye. You should come with me."

"Peter."

"Or I could stay with you. I don't hate it that much."

"Peter, I've got a boyfriend."

"It can't be this special. Can it?"

"It is special. But."

"But."

"I've made a commitment there and I've got to stay with it. He's coming to visit me here, you know that."

"Have a nice life."

"Don't say that."

"I'm sorry."

"We'll write. Who knows what will happen?"

"Yeah."

"I've had a great time with you. You're very funny, Peter."

"Yeah, you, too."

She hugged me, but it was a bullshit hug. Wanting to appear real, but fake.

On the bus, I turned forward and didn't look back. Karlijn had taught me that.

I went on alone to Jaisalmer at the edge of the Thar desert. A sandy hot town where the touts tried to sell camel rides into the abyss. The few other travelers I met asked me if I was going to Pakistan and to my negative reply answered with disdain, "Who wouldn't go to Pakistan?" Some had dressed themselves up as sadhus with fully painted foreheads and revealing (not in a good way) robes, others completely concealed themselves in purdah and adorned their foreheads with bindis, a red dot between the eyes that held religious import for them (for all of the six days since they'd converted upon arrival in the Mumbai airport).

Interlude with an Indian Tobacco Salesman stationed outside my Jaisalmer Hotel

a.k.a. Cigarette Wars

Episode I: The Birth of an Annoyance

"Excuse me, sir. Would you like some cigarettes? Very good price."

"No, thanks. I'm trying to quit."

Episode II: First Inclinations Towards a Response of Violence

(Discarded subtitle - for obvious aesthetic reasons – The Second Time I Passed Him On My Way Back From Purchasing A Bottle of Still and Not Sparkling Water – lacks catchiness)

"Cigarettes? Very good price, sir?"

"Still trying to kick, dude."

Episode III: The Desire for Violence Arrives in Full Force (unused variant – Swells to a Head)

"Sir? Cigarettes?"

Untitled Episode IV (it's an experimentation akin to some modern art – sometimes you just have to put yourself out there, you dig?)

Then it was simply, "Cigarettes?"

"I'm still trying to quit and I don't appreciate you, yes, you chunky Indian hunk of virile manly manhood, trying to hook me again. Like some pusher. A peddler of tobacco, a purveyor of emphysema. Trying to infect my lungs with cancer so I can die after a long drawn out illness, leaving my family heart-broken and bereft of monetary funds spent on my astronomical medical bills because my country lacks a nationalized healthcare plan. Would that curl your cruel lips into a smug smile of satisfaction, you heartless wretch? Fie unto you and your breed! I say fie! And: A PLAGUE UPON ON ALL YOUR HOUSES!!!"

Episode V: A Smallish of the Smalls Type Victory

"Cig—"

I shushed him with a finger to my lips which took after a second emphasis upon turning back.

But as I ordered my third mango lassi to help battle the infernal heat, I heard him utter the word from behind. Stoically, I did not flinch. Nor did I turn back to acknowledge his end to the shushing that, I knew, was just a harbinger of things to come. Instead I just savored my beverage, setting an example that should be followed by many a world leader in the face of conflict. In my humble opinion.

Episode VI: Defeat and Acceptance

"Cigarettes?"

"I don't smoke."

"You should start. Very good for you. Cheap price."

I sighed. "Sure. Why not?" When in Rome…Or Jaisalmer. Whatever.

Fin

(Another experimentation reminiscent of French movies from the 1950s, you're totally impressed and not a bit wowed, I know. When you get over it, if and when you can, please continue.)

After my fourth mango lassi at a stand run by a man who did choreographed and complicated loops, spins, twists and swirls with the spoon, shaker, syrup, and glass as he brewed my beverage (I didn't get the volume discount I SO deserved and quite bluntly asked for. Me not bringing any friends apparently was the deal-breaker. I drank up regardless – he made the best in town (and he fucking knew it) so what was I going to do?), I went for dinner.

A hand clasped my shoulder in the mostly empty restaurant. I turned to see a small Indian man with a large black moustache smiling at me. "Which country?" he asked.

"Uh… Botswana."

"Ah. Good. Want to see Asiatic lion?"

"No, thanks. I'm trying to quit."

"My hotel close to here. We go look at lion. It's stuffed, it's safe. Not alive. No bite. Come now." Grabbing my upper arm, he tried to drag me from the seat.

"I see lion already. My sister used to date one."

"No, no, no. We go hunt lion. Even better. Take home to England. Hang in bedroom. Got gun in hotel. You shoot Asiatic lion. Make you feel better." He tugged at my arm again.

"That's an endangered species, man. I don't want to kill it. Neither should you."

294

"Make great rug. Come."

The proprietor of the restaurant intervened and began talking to the man in a hushed whisper.

Later the hunter vomited into a concrete rain gutter that ran the length of the outside patio. And then he ordered another round of beer. They brought it. (Any customer in India who could afford to drink got served.)

Leaving Jaisalmer, my tuk-tuk driver won my fare from his competitor by ducking under a left jab and finishing with a roundhouse instead of his favored right cross. And then he surprised his second rival completely with a judo *tomoe-nage*. Of course, he got two flat tires on the way to the train station. The first he replaced at a friend's nearby shop we just happened to be passing (he had a drink while waiting and encouraged me to order a meal). At the second he had to forfeit me to some other tuk-tuk driver which he was not pleased about since I'd obviously not negotiated enough on the price. Thus I was late catching the train back to Jodphur. So late that I had no time to buy a reserved second class seat and had to suffer a more easily purchased third class seat or wait four hours for the next train.

Traveling in third class was a shock. I literally had to squeeze through the doors as people were sitting on the ground everywhere. Once inside, a seemingly never ending stream of people kept jostling/shoving/slamming in behind me to fill up every available hint of space on bench, floor and wall. Somehow I oozed through five cars before finally finding room for my pack in a bathroom door swing space. As for the smell: each and every water closet in India contended for the Worst Toilet in the World and this was a definite forerunner. But this did not diminish its popularity or frequency of use starting two minutes after we left the station.

Ninety-one minutes later, a chai salesman took pity and found a berth for me and my pack. Each compartment housed two facing wooden benches made to seat eight people in total. Below a barred wooden luggage rack on either wall, a generous three feet of leg room separated the extremely uncomfortable benches. In that confined space, each bench held seven people, each luggage rack four and on the floor between everyone's legs sat another three. Across the aisle leading down the car were two additional seats. Not only were these occupied but so was all available floor space with five more bodies. The aisle's luggage rack was too narrow for sitting, so people laid on their side there instead. (In my compartment, this extra luggage rack actually served its purpose - this was where the chai salesman had stowed my pack drawing laughter as he maneuvered chicken coops, bed mattresses, unwieldy burlap sacks and an obstinate grandmother to make room.) In all, where ten cramped and grumpy passengers were supposed to reside crowded thirty-two human beings. Each car was like this – discovered when I scrambled to the bathroom not by the floor but atop the seatbacks and luggage racks.

All stared at me. Why didn't they tear me to pieces? I held two or three years' wages in my money belt, maybe more.

Men boarded at every stop (which felt like every five minutes – Third Class Train Time is 17 times slower than Eating Pizza Time) to sell greasy samosas, chapattis, cucumbers seasoned with salt, bananas, soda in glass bottles "chilled" in plastic buckets of water. And they always stopped in front of me and expected me to buy everything – shouting "Samosa!" over and over inches from my face as they wagged one under my nose. ("No, thanks, I'm trying to quit" didn't work and even I tired of my own witty comebacks.) Invariably a fight would break out when someone dropped a banana peel on someone below them and I would suffer collateral damage in the form of a few slaps. Once my glasses got knocked from my face and I suffered another bloody nose. Everything became quiet. Two minutes later they were at each other again, this time over cigarette ashes in the hair or dried mud that had fallen from someone's foot into someone else's curry. I was finally starting to relax and take it all in (my ass had gone completely numb and the bleeding nose had stopped) when a cry sounded from the car's other end:

"Chai! Chai!"

It got closer. Closer. Then before me stood the man who'd found me a seat. He smiled. I smiled. "CHAI! CHAI!"

"It's too hot for chai. You have cold drinks? I buy cold drinks from you."

"No cold drinks. Chai!"

"Okay, okay. For helping me, I buy chai."

Later: "Chai! Chai!"

A sigh. My sigh. "But last one. Last one." 32+ voices of laughter.

Still later: "Chai! Chai!"

"Six cups today. Too much. Chai-ed out."

"Help with bag. No ask money. Chai! Mumbai pinching, Mumbai pinching." He pinched me.

"You know you should rule India? You're just mean enough."

He took my two rupees and handed me the clay cup. "India mine already." He laughed and left.

I heard a door open at the end of the car.

"Your friend is back."

Smiling: "Why me? WHY ME?" The crowd loved it.

He whistled, he shouted and then he turned to me, and whispered, "Chai?"

"Sure... Later, though, you and me, we're going to have to fight. To the death. With, like, flaming chainsaws."

"Okay, no more chai. Now you just give me money." He stooped down on his haunches saying the last bit and rubbed his fingers together accordingly. "Money, money, money."

I checked back at the Jodhpur hotel where Edith and I had stayed together. Despite only three days passing, he didn't remember Edith. Describing her rather distinguishing features didn't help, nor that he'd offered her tea seven times when I'd stepped out for a walk (she got that a lot): all white people looked the same to him.

Arriving in Ahmedabad the next day, I couldn't take it anymore: the bedbugs, the scams, the noise. Time to stop being a victim. To the hotel owner's question of my profession as checking in, I responded, "I'm a writer for Lonely World travel books."

"Oh. Oh!"

I was suddenly showered with amenities I thought did not exist anywhere in the vast miasma of India – a hot, steaming shower that scalded the skin, fluffy soft towels, a thirty-seven inch high-definition television set.

The worst thing was: with Edith gone, I didn't care about any of it.

I went for dinner at a place that seemed to serve students, passing one street where a line of cardboard boxes as far as the eye could see housed human beings. I wasn't through my first bite of naan before a group of them pounced:

"You are English?"

"American."

"Ah! Let us ask your opinion, good sir. What is your thinking on the women of India?"

A specimen of such was shooting phlegm onto the ground next to her at the adjoining table. "They are beautiful."

"And are you desiring an Indian woman?"

A second one chimed in: "We go to train station. Get prostitute. Fifty rupees. In Bombay, only ten."

"Same as a Coca-Cola. Only fizzier."

"You go?"

"No, thank you. Must sleep. I ate a lot." The inedible slop on the plate before me wouldn't even attract flies – they knew better.

"We want American wives. Their skin is so beautiful."

The first added: "And Korean women."

"Korean women very gorgeous!"

"You must get us American wives."

I asked: "Why not Indian?"

"Oh, no, they will not let us touch them. American women are always good for the sex. Wanting it. We see the movies, we know."

"In India, you must marry them. In America, on first day they have the sex," the first said.

A few hours from Ahmedabad the next day (I could still see the station we'd left from – no, it had really crept out of sight five minutes before), a thirteen year old girl sat down to me and asked, "You go to Aurangabad? This Australian man and Irish woman go to Aurangabad. You should go to Aurangabad."

At the other end of the car, I saw the blond hair of the Australian man accompanied by one of those chiseled chins women drool endlessly over. Next to him sat Edith.

"I'm going to Mumbai."

"No! You should go with them and make a friendship with them. I like to make friendships with white people. I make a friendship with Chip from Holland and Sven from Norway…"

"I've always wanted to make passionate love to a suitcase."

She quieted down quite quickly. Then I bit off her left hand.

Sometime later, Edith stood to visit the bathroom. Our eyes met. Her brow furrowed with pain but she came anyway. "Peter…"

"Small world, right?"

"Yeah."

"How was the yoga class?"

"He came early. Surprised me."

"That's nice."

She studied my eyes. "You're alone?"

I wanted to make a joke about Swedish triplets but didn't have the strength.

She smiled. "Want to come play with us? We're trying to sell my water pistol to a used wheelbarrow salesman. He's got us down to five hundred dollars, but I think he's starting to crack."

"I… I don't think I could stand it."

Her response took a few seconds. "Well, if you change your mind…"

On the way back from the bathroom, she watched me watch her, never breaking my glance to seek her boyfriend. She reached out and squeezed my right shoulder. "Come on. We get off soon... Please."

I didn't say anything. She went.

I didn't turn around. I didn't want to see her smiling for him.

Fuck it.

I stood up and reached for my pack.

The train began braking and I saw Edith's smile disappear as my hands dropped. The Australian stood and reached for their packs.

Edith sat watching me.

The Australian said something and she turned to him, then stood to help.

I didn't move. Indians shoved past me, one reaching into my empty pocket. I didn't react.

Edith glanced over a couple of times. She hadn't told him about me. Or he was ignoring me.

They exited the train. I couldn't see them.

Moments passed. Indians swarmed onto the train, two (and a monkey) even taking my seat. I kept looking out the window.

The train began moving slowly. Another one was leaving my life.

Edith came into view looking frantically at the train. The Australian was yelling at her, but she was ignoring him. Her eyes lit up when she saw me.

Fuck this.

I grabbed my pack off the top of a chicken crate and from underneath a bunch of bananas. Indians shouted as feathers and fruit rained down on them. I shouldered my pack somehow, despite the crowd shoving through the aisles. The train was speeding up (Why did it have to work now?). I moved towards the nearest door, stepping on feet and eliciting more angry words. Edith. Only two more seat compartments to pass.

I got stuck.

I thought someone was holding me back when I heard the Indians laughing around me and the hiss of air inside my pack. My air mattress had chosen this exact moment to inflate itself and wedge me between the train wall and one of the compartments.

Indians continued to laugh as I struggled to free myself.

"Edith!" The laughter faded. A couple of men stood up and helped free me. It took long moments for them to get inside the top of my pack, unscrew the nipple and deflate the mattress.

"Thank you. Thank you."

I was at the door. The platform was at the end. I took a step and felt a restraining hand at my elbow.

I turned, furious. My chance was gone.

Kind eyes of a conductor met mine. "Too dangerous. Next stop. Too dangerous."

It went out of me. "Yes. Yes."

I'd lost her. I'd fucking lost her.

"Stop. Stop. Why you hit train? What train ever do to you?"

With Edith gone, I just wanted out. But it wasn't that easy. Nothing in India is easy. Nothing. (See above.) I had already changed the date of my flight to Istanbul in Delhi, paying a fee, of course, when my travel agent had guaranteed I wouldn't need to. But at the flight office in Mumbai/Bombay, the clerk didn't ask for money, he just refused to give me a ticket. Said I needed a visa to visit Turkey. My guidebook said otherwise but he insisted. I nearly tore off his legs to bludgeon his torso with. Nearly.

That was my Friday.

Saturday I visited Elephanta Island on a rather terrifying boat (the Titanic post-iceberg seemed more seaworthy) to see some temples carved out of stone. Ganeshes galore, Shiva fever.

Sunday I visited the Bhau Daji Lad museum. While snacking on greasy (of dripping magnitude) ragda patties, families were picking up artifacts to examine them. And I sewed a button back onto my trousers. Not a story for the grandkids, but close. Damned fucking close.

On Monday began

The Journey

Step 1: Locate Mumbai metro. In rain more akin to a shower (not with the water pressure of an Indian shower, but an American one run amok).

Step 2: Find the right train.

Step 3: Buy the right ticket.

Step 4: Queue for the train.

Miss first train as it is ridiculously full. Catch second train only by wrestling (i.e., eye gouging, tomahawk elbowing, yanking hair, vampire strength biting and dealing out the occasional Atomic Wedgie© – of the both Vertical and Horizontal varieties – the former of which requires use of a jetpack to really get the full effect) multitudes of adversaries to keep my place first in line while having my money belt triple knotted against my inner thigh inside my underwear inside my trousers with both my shirts tucked in. Jump aboard train to be smashed against metal pole in middle of car, bloodying one nostril and kinking my glasses over one ear. Ask every single person (every single person) aboard where my stop was. Claw my way off twice due to misinformation, each time drawing beggars' ire when I am unceremoniously dumped face first onto the concrete platform which is their territory. "Get off my spot!" they shout in Hindi and pelt me with wads of unidentified, cringe-worthy material. Repeat train re-entry bloodying nostril procedure each time. Exit metro station and spend three hours seeking the Turkish consulate. Is always "around the next corner." Woman operating stand with a telephone offers to call the consulate (for money) to receive directions and I tell her, "I don't know where I am, how can they tell me how to get to where they are?" She smiles and tells me no problem, give her money. Search continues. See nice pink sari and decide it's really not me. Get chased by rabid, mangy dogs who are scared off by even larger rats. In final frustration, enter the only visible modern building and ask armed guard if he knows where the Turkish consulate is. "Upstairs," he responds and pushes me away (but gently) when I try to kiss him.

Then the most beautiful man in all of India, middle-aged and prematurely balding with a pot belly and kind eyes who worked for the Turkish consulate, appeared to save me.

When I related my dilemma, he said, "That is foolish. Americans don't need a visa if they are going to visit Turkey for less than forty-five days. They told you the wrong information. It is unfortunate that you have been treated this way."

"Do you have something in writing that I could give to them explaining that?"

"No." I was doomed, I knew it. "But I can give you my card and write you a letter telling them to contact me if they have any questions. Can you wait a few minutes?"

"You beautiful beautiful man, I want to bear your children. Even quintuplets."

He smiled. Ten minutes later, I left with the letter.

A beggar on the street pinched me and held out his hand for money. I pinched him back. He ran away.

When I had tried telling the hotel clerk that I worked for the Lonely World guidebook, he'd shrugged and given me their "deluxe suite." That night returning to my room after a gorgeous chicken curry and the world's best garlic naan at Leopold's Cafe, I saw why. In the stairway leading up to my hotel, two men in rags were smoking crack. They didn't look like they wanted to share (even if I asked nicely and offered to share munchies), so I continued to my room, a smile still affixed to my face from my encounter with the beautiful Turk. (According to the Lonely World, the hotel was "not the best, a little dingy but safe." The next listing in the area I wanted to stay in was ten times the price.) I even fell asleep, despite the heat and the fan's power being shut off by the management at ten o'clock. And then I woke at three a.m. when a rat ran across my naked chest. I spent the rest of the night huddled against the wall clutching my Leatherman tool with the serrated blade extended.

When morning came, I returned to the airline office. This time the clerk was a woman. "Good morning, sir. How may I help you?"

"I want to change my flight to Istanbul to tomorrow."

After studying my ticket, she punched a few keys on her computer. "Do you have a Turkish visa?"

"No. I visited the Turkish consulate yesterday - at your office's bidding, mind you - and they said I didn't need one. As an American citizen, I can visit Turkey up to forty-five days without one. Please change my flight."

"I'm sorry, sir, I cannot do so without you having a Turkish visa."

"Did you hear what I said? See this bloody nose? Mine own damaged proboscis frothing sanguinary milk, the arduous product of my veins and arteries leaking slowly into the vacuous abyss? I suffered such injury yesterday when I was smashed up against a pole repeatedly in the subway. Going to the consulate. And then I contracted a cold in the rain trying to find the building. See?" I put the evidence – a pile of bloodied facial tissue I'd used that morning - on her desk. "But now I want to leave India. Abscond. Escape. Get the fuck out. And I'm tired of you wasting my time."

"Sir, please control your language."

"Here's a letter from the Turkish consulate telling you I can go. And here's the Turkish consulate's phone number. Call them."

She shrugged her shoulders without taking the paperwork. "I don't believe you. Why should I believe you?"

"Take heed and notice of the authentic Turkish consulate stationery upon which the letter is printed."

"Such items are easily counterfeited."

"I'm not bribing you. You understand? No baksheesh." She looked at me blankly. "Get your supervisor."

"I am the supervisor."

"Then I'm calling the police and the prime minister and the American Institute of Certified Public Accountants and my mom. My mom's really mean, you don't want to mess with her. She once kicked the shit out of the offensive line for the Dallas Cowboys. And they were good that year."

"Please wait." She picked up the phone, spoke to someone in Hindi for two minutes and handed me a changed plane ticket.

On the morning before my flight, I had a camel sewn onto my backpack's top flap. The symbol of love. Like Jesus, I was going to turn the other cheek, embrace the world despite how it treated me. Forget the past. Bury it. Be happy. Or try, at least.

Then I changed twenty dollars at the bank and gave it to the most desperate beggars I could along the street of my hotel. As good as the gesture felt, it wasn't enough. And then I felt guilt for feeling good, for owning things, for my opportunities.

In the airport, I went a little nuts.

To the first tourist I saw, a 19 year old blonde hair dresser from Manchester, I said: "What the fuck are you doing? Go home. Enjoy your air-conditioning, running hot water, flush toilets, Mercedes Benz."

When I tired of doing that, I started handing out my list:

Ten Commandments for Survival In India (a.k.a. The Asshole of the World)

(If you really MUST stay. But, please, for your sanity and peace of mind, reconsider and DON'T!)

I.   Thou shalt never trust anyone. Rich businessmen, little old ladies, defenseless babies. Anyone.

II.   Always negotiate a price beforehand. Unless they're screaming about their starving relatives, you're not even close to the real price. And then still threaten to go down the street where you saw it cheaper. Haggling takes time, be patient.

III.   Never talk to strangers. Or dental hygienists.

IV.   Compliment everyone on everything and then tell them how rich they are to afford such luxuries. In other words: spread the love.

V.   Avert one's eyes from this country's version of nudity – it's a bad, detestable thing. Side effects of failure to do so can include blindness, blurred vision and impotency in male adults between the ages of 15 and 72.

VI.   No touching! No touching! You'll thank me later. (Alternate version: Touching, thou shalt not!)

VII.   Carry numerous small bills in different places upon your person. This prevents the phrase "no change" for bills worth as little as two U.S. dollars, makes bribery/baksheesh easier (can't see where and how much your total funds are) and may save you losing everything if you get robbed.

VIII.   Travel with a food-taster. Better to lose an employee than a loved one. And never ever ever order the meat. Ever. If you must (and truly you mustn't), keep an eye on the dogs when ordering a steak to see if any disappear.

IX.   Check your accommodation thoroughly before accepting a room. Rats, cockroaches, Pakistani pole vaulters: any or all may be lurking under the bed.

X.   Go to war, prison, the seventh circle of hell. Just don't stay in India. Exhaust any and all alternatives, however remote their success, before relenting.

Really, however, you should LEAVE. Abscond. Flee.

GET THE FUCK OUT OF THIS GOD-FORSAKEN ABYSS AS SOON AS YOU POSSIBLY CAN!!!!!

Meshugana. A little bit.

I didn't make any friends that day. Which surprised me more than a little, considering what valuable information I'd imparted to all of them.

I was out! I was free! Yeah, baby.

Then I heard on the news in the plane how sixty-eight people had been killed in flooding as huts in slums north of Mumbai collapsed during the rain. I was out. But they weren't. And never would be. And I wasn't sure why I was given this.

Turkish Delight

Istanbul. Constantine had converted the Roman Empire to Christianity here and the world had never been the same. One way or another.

"Come in to my shop."

"Do you sell flying carpets?"

"Of course, sir. I show you."

"With power steering? Must have power steering. And we mustn't forget the anti-lock brakes. Air bags would be nice as well."

"Of course, sir."

"At the last, best, special, once-in-a-lifetime price?"

"Yes."

"Is that the best you can do? Your heart's not really in it, I can tell. You've got to be more assertive, more aggressive. I've just come from India, you'd get eaten alive there. Bunch of cupcakes, you are."

He laughed heartily. "Come inside, drink tea. No charge. You funny man. You make me laugh."

So I went inside for a cup of very sweet tea. At the end, he didn't even try to sell me a carpet. I was going to like Turkey.

I did the tourist things. Visited the Blue Mosque (no one stole my shoes but I did attract more than one admirer of the holes in my non-matching blue and argyle socks – a few of which even resulted in phone numbers received but, unfortunately they were in Cyrillic). Admired the gold mosaics of the Saint Sophia Church which had been converted to the Ayasofya mosque. Tried to count the number of columns in Yerbatan's Cistern but kept getting interrupted around 212 and warned all the other tourists (even the Canadians) not to look into the eyes of the medusa sculptures for fear of turning to stone. Rode a boat up the Bosporus and helped the captain by telling everyone at every single violation to keep their hands and feet inside the vehicle at any and all times. Ate kabobs, humus and Turkish delight at the Grand Bazaar. Tried photographing one of the myriad sets of old men stationed on stools at street corners who played backgammon while twiddling black prayer beads and drinking endless cups of sweet tea, but they weren't fans of that and a chase ensued. Survived. Next tried taking a picture of some children playing while their mother in a black head scarf did laundry by hand behind them. Another chase. Stopped taking photos.

As I stood outside gazing at the Topkapi Palace (and thinking how great it might be to have my own Harem – don't judge, you know you've considered it, too), an old Turkish man approached and said in English, "You need help? No charge."

"No, thanks. I've been here a week: I know my way around. I'm just trying to figure out what to do next."

He narrowed his eyes to regard me carefully. "I think you're maybe ninety percent half-Turkish."

"You think I'm half-Turkish?"

"Yes. I live here fifty years and I still not know how to get around. So I think you are half-Turkish for knowing how in one week."

"So if I stay here three weeks, will I be full Turkish?"

"No. You must stay here fifty years to be full Turkish. One week for half, fifty years for full."

I laughed. He shook my hand and we parted company.

A week of extremely boring traveling conversations passed. Every other backpacker I met asked me: "What's the best place you've been?" or "Are you one of those Americans who travel with a Canadian flag sewn on your backpack?" (I'd answered the latter question a couple of times with "I am who I am, why wouldn't I be proud of being an American?" or "That's a myth." Of course, everyone knew someone who knew someone who knew someone who did it. But then I stopped reacting and just ignored them.) So I got moving again – this time to the country's interior.

"Do you have a girlfriend yet?" my grandmother Bess asked when I visited a month after seeing Belinda for the last time.

"No. I mean I had one, well maybe not a girlfriend... She moved away."

"And?"

"I don't know. How did you stay with Grandpa so long?"

"He didn't understand me and I didn't understand him."

"So how did you end up together?"

"He gave me the soft talk. He came to my sister's party and he was dressed all nice. So he saw me and asked me to have dinner with him. But I was young. I didn't want to be tied down. But then he gave me the soft talk. And that was it."

"Did you fight a lot?"

"Not once in forty-eight years."

"That's impossible."

"I can't remember him ever raising his voice to me. Not once."

I thought of my own parents' hour-long (or much much more) battles over taking out the garbage, not using a coaster for cold drinks or newspapers left in the bathroom. (Seasonal sequels to each were guaranteed.) No yelling didn't seem possible.

"Did your father ever tell you the story of us moving from the East Coast? Your grandfather was tired of the cold in New York so one day he decided we were moving to California. Just like that. We didn't even talk

310

it over first. We exchanged houses with a man who wanted to move back here – he lived in Long Beach. We didn't even know where Long Beach was. So we packed up everything we had and got on a train to Los Angeles. In those days, no public transportation existed to Long Beach. So, when we arrived, we had to find a cab to take us to the house because your grandfather didn't have a car and didn't know how to drive then. Everyone looked at us like we were crazy, Long Beach was many miles from the train station. Well, finally we found somebody who would drive us. We had to go to a hotel for dinner – I had two small children and there were no grocery stores, nothing there. For a week we ate at that hotel until we figured everything out. And your grandfather had to commute to San Pedro – he worked as a controller for a fish-packing plant, a cannery. At lunch hour, he would take the tuna fish sandwich I made him, always the same thing, and watch the gulls eat the refuse out over the Pacific Ocean near the back of the plant."

"Are you glad you came out here?"

She shrugged. "Everyone I knew was in New York. Yes, it's warmer, but I didn't know anyone here."

"If you could've done anything different in your life, what would it be?"

"What does that matter now? Don't ask questions like that."

"I just… don't know what to do."

"About what?"

"My problems."

"Oy. Your problems. You don't know for problems. You're young. What possible troubles could you have?"

I reached into my pocket. "Wanna see my pen? I got it from work. It's a really nice pen."

She laughed. "Whatsa matter with you?"

"Actually it's not my pen, so I most probably shouldn't even show it to you or I could get into all sorts of trouble. Trouble with a capital *T*. I've got to return it tomorrow. In case it's missed. They count them, you know."

"Meshugenah."

"What's that?" I said, pretending not to hear.

"MESHUGENAH! Nuts. You're nuts."

"How sweet of you to say."

The phone rang at work. "Hello?"

"Peter." My mother's voice caught. "Bessie has leukemia."

After the diagnosis, Bessie's health quickly deteriorated. First she had to be helped around the house, the Filipino nurse Anna at her elbow in case she stumbled. Then she would come into the living room only once or twice a day to watch television with her meals. But her mind wandered and she rarely paid attention to the programs. Finally, she stopped getting out of bed.

The first Saturday she refused to join me in the living room to watch the monster truck rally, I yelled at her, "Get out of bed. We're going skydiving!"

"You know how I'm not keen on heights."

"Never too late to confront your fears. Then we'll go surfing."

"You're meshugenah. Nuts." She smiled and struggled up.

The next time she said, "What's the point?" She avoided my eyes. "I'm finished."

"What the fuck do you mean? A brand new episode of McAuk airs in five minutes. He defuses a nuclear bomb and performs open heart surgery aboard a sinking submarine in the middle of a class four typhoon using only his Swiss Army knife and a frayed piece of cinnamon flavored dental floss. In the pitch dark. With the hiccups."

She didn't respond.

"Come on! Dinner is rubbery, overcooked chicken and a flavorless baked potato without butter! A culinary feast of mouth-watering glory impossible to resist, if I ever heard one."

"Finished."

"If you miss McAuk flying across the Grand Canyon with the help of a used condom and a can of pressurized whipped non-fat cream in the opening scene, don't come cryin' to me!"

Anna and I somehow got her into the living room, but she couldn't sit at the table.

I dropped to my hands and knees and squeezed under the coffee table in front of the couch. "Oy! I'm stuck! Schlep me out! Schlep me out!"

"Whatsa matter with you?"

"Tell me how meshugenah I am."

"Uh-uh."

"Say it."

"Uh-uh."

"Say it!"

"Never."

"Stubborn old woman, aren't you?"

"Had to say it, didn't you? Had to bring that up. Every conversation with you. Every one."

"You wouldn't say it."

"No!"

The show began. McAuk employed a series of twirled milkshake straws held together with ABC (already-been-chewed) peppermint gum to breathe fifteen feet underwater amid a pack of tiger sharks.

"Meshugenah. Little bit."

"What was that?"

"Nothing."

"Ha! Ha!"

"Uh-uh. He's carrying on again. Just like his father. I'm gonna call your momma – have her come get you." Despite herself, she smiled.

The paramedics came for her in the middle of the night. I didn't even know she was leaving until I heard a noise and opened the door to my bedroom. Her younger brother followed the stretcher out the door as she left the apartment she'd lived in, laughed in, cried in for the past twenty-

313

three years for what turned out to be the last time.

The end came swiftly. She drifted in and out of consciousness during my visits, each time being awake a little less. The flesh quickly bled from her face, her eyes sunk and darkened. First there was anger, then fear and finally defeat. She stopped listening to me, her listless eyes staring out the window at the approaching abyss. Then she had trouble recognizing me. She developed bed sores and quit speaking or acknowledging the outside world, including my visits.

The last time she spoke to me was out of character for the day. She hadn't said anything for over a week. The morphine rarely lessened its grasp. But suddenly, on this Sunday morning, her eyes cleared and she said distinctly, "I want to die." I remember not being able to say anything. I could only focus on her tongue, so small and white between her chapped lips. I touched her arm and looked out the window. When I turned back, she was back in the morphine coma.

On Wednesday, my parents came and we visited the hospital together, but Bessie looked at none of us. At midnight, we drove back to Lake Arrowhead to spend Thanksgiving there. It was a somber meal, no one laughed at all. Afterwards, my parents went to bed and I stayed up watching a Jack Nicholson movie – *Five Easy Pieces*. Just as he got in the truck to escape his unwanted life, the phone rang. Bessie had just died.

Seeing my father at the funeral, seeing him drawn, beaten was a shock. Just a month before we'd found out his mother was ill, he'd called me (an occurrence usually reserved for emergencies): "I did a great thing today."

"You did?"

"Yes. This guy at work has the ugliest clip-on tie you've ever seen – yellow spots on a purple background with a trout on a fishing line. Just awful. I think it's the only tie he owns because he's worn it to every single manager meeting in the year I've worked there. Well, a month ago, I saw he'd dropped his tie near his parking space. So I picked it up. But I didn't give it to him. I wanted to wear it the next day to work, but I didn't. I bided my time. Four weeks, I had to wait. Twenty-nine excruciating days until the next meeting. He didn't notice at first, maybe not having been able to find another clip-on on such short notice distracted him. The replacement was blue with golf clubs and horribly awry, knotted unevenly, just a shambles. So I asked him a question – to draw his attention, you see. He still didn't notice. So I asked him something else. Again he answered,

314

not noticing. And then, suddenly, he did. I thought his eyes would pop out of his head. He kept staring at it and staring at it. He ignored a question by the boss. The boss asked him again and, instead of answering, he suddenly shouted at me: *THAT'S MY TIE! YOU STOLE MY TIE!* Everyone burst out laughing. I could barely say *I didn't steal it* before he continued shouting *WHAT KIND OF PERSON STEALS SOMEONE'S TIE? AND DON'T TELL ME YOU OWN ANOTHER JUST LIKE MY TIE BECAUSE THAT'S A LIE! A DECEITFUL, UNDERHANDED LIE!* So I told him where I'd found it and gave it to him. He wouldn't talk to me for the rest of the day."

"Thanks, Dad."

"For what?"

"Trying to cheer me up about Belinda."

"That's all right."

Things weren't always so good between my father and I. I was an angry teenager. I resented that I had to do what everyone else told me to. Go to this fucking school that I learned nothing at where idiot teachers droned on, reciting something for an hour it would take me five minutes to read. So I could be trained for a dead-end job shackled to a desk, sacrificing my limited hours of breath to gain sustenance. My father hated it just as much as me. Even at that age, I could tell. Because he drank.

One night he began yelling when I told him I didn't want to go to school again tomorrow. I was sitting in front of the television in my underwear watching some shitty show, knowing the next day at school would be as miserable as the last - maybe someone, just one person would talk to me all day. Maybe. Anyway, my dad just looked at me sitting there, ignoring him. Then he kicked me in the balls. He was wearing shoes. I couldn't do anything for five minutes, only cry, and he'd left the room. It was the first time I'd cried since I was in first grade. My mom came over and asked if I was okay. As soon as I could stand, I went into the bedroom and started hitting him in the back. At first he did nothing as my mom shouted at me to stop. Then he hit me back. And I came back at him. Then my mom hit me, too. And then I realized how alone I really was. I ran up to my room, grabbed my pants and jacket and ran out of the house. But I had nowhere to go (snow covered the ground) and no way to pay for anything. I walked around the block in the dark, shivering with cold and returned to the house. I went into the basement which was accessible only from outside of the house and sat in the dark. I had stopped crying. I didn't know what the fuck to do. Even my mom wasn't on my side. I was alone.

I'd forgiven my father all of that. And he'd forgiven me. I could understand him better now after being in the workplace, seeing what it was

315

like. What drove his rage? Mortality? The layoffs? Us for shackling him with responsibility? Did he envision a different life for himself when he was my age, something more? Did I represent the end of that? And I was not grateful, I never thanked him for this existence and his struggles. Is that what he wanted? Or did he recognize his father a little more in the mirror each morning, thinking what a waste? Should he have done something more, something else? What did all of us become? Did you give up, accept your fate? Fight back? Against who, what? And how? Love, hate, violence? Grab what you can because they'd do the same? No one will save you, no one will give you anything. Never show weakness or let them think they're winning. Because once they smell blood... No mercy. God will save you? Did He save the Jews from Auschwitz, the Armenians from the Turks, the Russians from the Gulag?

And yet there we were: listening to a rabbi talk about God in that temple in the cemetery. Summing up Bessie's life in a few sentences. Trying to make her life seem more interesting than it perhaps was to a handful of people, though she'd lived in the same place for the past forty years. But did that even matter, and why? How quickly it was over and we were heading to the wake at my uncle's house in Beverly Hills. And then the caterers had left and we were again in our cars driving back to our jobs the next day and it was like she never even existed.

At the wake, I saw my father weeping in my uncle's backyard. He was staring at a wooden tree-swing hanging from a rotted rope with his hands in his pockets, oblivious to the world around him. How would I feel when my mother was gone?

I'd only ever seen my father cry three times. The first was at his father's funeral of which I only remembered fragments. One is kneeling next to my mother's bed after we'd driven home and feeling guilty because I hadn't cried. I hadn't felt much of anything at all. Again, it seemed so strange, a person suddenly being gone and the world kept going and me with it.

The second time was when my father called me regarding Penelope.

In the nascent dawn with the sky a broth of shimmering yellows and golds, my bus arrived in Cappadocia at a small desert town called Goreme. Tea houses and carpet shops lined the town's one avenue, empty because of the hour. I followed the map someone had drawn for me in Istanbul and found the Scottish woman's hotel. Too early to check in, I napped on a cushioned lounge chair near the pool.

I hadn't slept much on the bus. In what I soon learned was typical of all Turkish transportation, the passengers were forced to change their seats a number of times over the journey in what appeared to be accordance with some well-conceived and organized plan. At the time I found it frustrating but years and years later after much in-depth consideration, contemplative contemplation and exhaustive, play-by-play analysis, it all became clear why.

After a breakfast of bread, olives, cheese and sweet tea, I spent the day trying to hike to Uchisar, losing myself in narrow canyons shaded by olive trees and twisting grapevines beneath a relentless sun. I kept getting closer and closer to where I thought a tunnel broke through the crumbling sandstone, but each path I took ended in a peaceful grotto or the mountain swallowed, so ultimately I was defeated. But I didn't care too much. And that, maybe, was the point I'd been missing all this time.

Dark haired with the most beautiful face I'd ever seen. Why not?

"Hey, I was just going out for a beer. Wanna come?"

"I'd like to, but I just ordered one from the hotel." I shrugged and started to turn away. "Would you like to join me?"

"Sure. I'm Peter."

"Fiona."

"New York?"

"Don't. Just don't. I know it's not your fault, but I'm so sick of answering the same where are you from, where are you going, what is your major questions. I'm thinking of getting them tattooed across my chest."

"If we hurry, I think there's a place down the street that might still be open. Hopefully, you're not from Pittsburgh, Pennsylvania studying clinical and behavioral psychology of hirsute primates and heading to Antananarivo, Madagascar. A lot of letters."

She laughed. "I'm a communications student at Syracuse headed to Syria."

"Syracuse? Syria? Seriously?"

"Sincerely. This time I'm going for sure. Twice I had to return to Ankara for my visa, the first time to apply, the second to retrieve two weeks later. Twice I had to habit expensive hotels as there are no youth hostels in Ankara – believe me, I asked. Twice I had to pay exorbitant taxi rates as the long distance bus station is not on any of the local transportation routes, according to everyone who spoke English in the bus station. Coincidentally, everyone who did speak English either drove a taxi or had a brother that did. Then, when I arrive at the hotel of their choice as mine is closed for repairs and theirs is the only one open at that hour of the night -- about six in the evening -- it is run, coincidentally, by their other brother. Arriving with a beat-up backpack, I'm treated rudely by snobbish bellhops who think I won't tip them. Then when I try to sleep after being groped by an enormous Turkish man who insisted he was sleeping during the six day nonstop bus journey from Istanbul, I'm harassed all hours of the night by horny, *hirsute* hotel owners wondering if I need room service of a kind reserved for only the most special of their clientele. Twice I did this. Trying a different hotel the second time didn't help. But now I'm going to Syria. I have to. They've tried to stop me, so I can't let them. Syria. Sounds cool, doesn't it?"

I sympathized, relating my own struggle to get the fuck out of India. I demonstrated how the Mumbai train pole had knocked the earpiece of my spectacles across first my left cheek and then, on my return from the Turkish consulate, my right temple, how my face contorted in grimaces of pain and how my arms flailed askew. (She asked, "Should I be taking notes on this? Will there be a test later? Oral or written?" which I answered with the requisite, unrestrained violence. For no matter what they tell you and how many times they tell it, violence is always the answer.) I told her of my two hour search for the building when I was circling it the whole time but no one would tell me. Then I added, "You could not pay me one million dollars to go back. Not two million, not three."

"Four?"

"Don't interrupt me! 'Tis very rude."

"Won't happen again. Unless, of course, it does. Happen again."

"Now where was I?"

"Where you were but not where you were not."

"Exactly and yet, not at all. As I was saying, you could disembowel, quarter and flay me. You could fricassee, sauté, grill, baste or flambé me. Even julienne me. I shall not return. I won't be back. Not if I live to be a billion kazillion years old. Nope."

"That's pretty old."

"From now until the end of all existing existence, wherever I am, whatever I may be doing, whenever I hear mention of that god-forsaken place, I shall cry at the top of my lungs *I HATE INDIA!* I could be buying a toaster, attending a hamster's funeral, even visiting the public library, I will

318

share my feelings most vociferously. The world shall know my pain."

"It's not healthy to keep your emotions bottled up inside. Let 'em out."

"I will."

"Seriously."

"I promise. Cross my heart, hope to die, stick a sharp spear in my eye. Deep-ish."

"Okay. I believe you."

"Trust is the basis of any good relationship."

"What do you do?"

"Rob banks. No, I'm an unemployed underwater fireman by day and caped crime fighter by night."

She laughed again. "No."

"I'm an accountant."

Laughter. Pause, then more laughter.

I continued: "But I'm done now. Seriously. I've had enough of achingly beautiful girls laughing at what I do. You're the 233rd and the last. No more. You've changed my life. If I had never met you, I may have trudged away at it forever. Thank you."

"Glad to be of help." Directed towards me: a cupped hand palm up. "That will be three point two million dollars."

"Plus tax?"

"*Value Added Tax.*"

I nearly swooned. "Do you take cash?" I asked and reached inside my pocket. "What is that? Like a quadrillion Turkish lira?"

She smiled. "How old are you?"

"Eighty-seven."

Shaking her head, she said, "An accountant with a sense of a humor."

"In the interest of shockingly frank but ultimately more respected disclosure, that's actually my evil twin brother Sven."

"I'd like to meet this guy Sven."

"He's a good dancer. Can can-can like a motherfucker: to employ the vernacular."

"Does he own leather chaps? I'm really into guys who wear leather chaps."

"He rents them. And there's no option in the lease to buy so don't even go there."

"Mind if I join you guys?" Fiona and I looked up to see Albert from my room.

"Absolutely."

"Absolutely you mind or absolutely you don't mind?"

I repeated, "Absolutely."

"I don't trust you."

"Nor should you."

Fiona said, "You know: trust is the basis of any good relationship."

Albert regarded us both warily. "I've heard that. I'm Albert."

It turned out they'd both gone to the same school in Edinburgh and knew all of the same people. They chain-smoked the same foul-smelling brand of Turkish cigarettes and he was younger and blonder and better looking. I tuned out and found myself thinking of home, once again the third person in a conversation meant for two.

But then Fiona brought me back. "Where did you go to school?" So I told her.

When I said I was headed towards Jerusalem, Albert told me, "Whatever you do, avoid the Petra Hostel near the Jaffa Gate. They're completely insane there. Two guys from Slovenia who live on the roof worship a deity made out of mud and cowshit up there. Have a little altar built for him. Every morning they offer him a bottle of vodka as sacrifice. By about eleven, they begin to drink the vodka. Straight. It's their own religion, they made it up – wrote down its tenets on all these water-stained yellow notepads. And most people there are like that. Fanatics who have been in Jerusalem forever."

"That sounds awesome." I wrote down the name of the hostel.

"There are women who follow the Trail of Tears – you know, where Jesus was supposed to have carried the cross on the way to his execution. And these women prostrate themselves along it, weeping and groaning and buying trinkets in all the shops that line every step of the way. Some hire their own cross to carry. Fanatics. It's humiliating. Religion is for idiots. So they can surrender to suffering or have an excuse to kill someone with different beliefs. So they can judge others. They can't accept death."

I said, "I don't know. My grandmother lost two husbands and the only thing that gave her peace was going to church. She had a hard life, religion helped her through it."

"But why must we believe we live on, that some greater reward awaits? That each of us is special in some way? We're not. And churches, temples, whatever. Small towns across the world don't have enough money to pay for medicine, schooling for their children. But every one of them has a church or a mosque. And it's always the nicest place in town." Albert was slapping his hand to make each of his points. "If you've been to the Vatican, you know what I'm talking about: all of the best marble in Europe is there."

Our eyes met and Fiona asked me: "Does it get lonely traveling by yourself all of the time?"

"Well, I've got an inflatable Swedish supermodel in the bottom of my pack. And, mind you, she's a real good listener."

"Wow, your jokes are awful. You take them all four steps too far."

"Maybe I should just be quiet then. You two carry on and I'll just sit here saying yes, no, and maybe."

"You promise?"

"Yes."

"Cross your heart and hope to die, stick a sharp spear in your eye?"

"No. Maybe. Yes."

"Good."

Albert changed the subject: "So, Fiona, have you been robbed since you began traveling?"

"Not in the traditional knife-at-my-throat/gun-to-my-temple sense. You?"

"I haven't. But I met this Australian girl who'd been robbed six times. She holds the record – as you Yanks say. Once in Cuzco, Peru, in the Andes, an old man grabbed her purse as she left a bank and just walked away. He was wearing a pink *One in the Oven* T-shirt. You know, like pregnant women wear. And she just started laughing. Then she realized he was getting away. But because of the high altitude, she said she couldn't catch him. He just strolled around a couple of corners and was gone. Was whistling nonchalantly the whole way. How crazy is that?"

A stern look from Fiona kept me from saying I'd probably met her in Amsterdam and, so, both of their lives were inextricably less full and meaningful in consequence. "Pretty crazy," Fiona responded to Albert.

"How about the food? Have you gotten ill?"

I couldn't keep it in any longer (and I was a little bit pissed about him butting in our conversation): "Should I bust out my recording of Travel Conversation #6 and press play?"

"You broke your promise. About talking."

"Then would you write cue cards with what I should say? And prompt me with them across the table?"

With a breathless laugh, she responded, "Suck me."

"Is that the best you can do? You really need to work on your material. Take it back to the drawing board. Vivify vicariously with video-viewing of vicious, virulent invectives. Weary us not with wimpy words woefully without wickedness worthy only of a wuss."

"Stab with spoken salvos smart and smarmy?"

"Yes, and yet at the same time, not at all."

Fiona finished her beer with the requisite flourish. "Let's go have some fun…"

Fiona pushed me playfully as we exited the hostel door and I turned on her in an instant with the dukes up and the foots darting a mesmerizing this way and that so swift they could not actually be seen by the human eye and presented the merest flicker on instant replay. "Bring it, baby. Gloves off, bare-knuckled unfettered fury. Fisticuffs galore."

She shook her head reluctantly. "I can't. Men are so pathetic when they cry."

The night outside was magnificent, the dark sky exploding with a swath of stars begging to be explored.

Fiona ran up to three Turkish men standing outside a restaurant watching us. "HELLO! HOW ARE YOU? I'M FINE! THANK YOU VERY LITTLE!" Then she turned around with a big grin on her face and came back.

"Wait, Funny Girl, return. We want to ask you a question."

But we didn't. Wait, that is. Leaving that question and all its global significance ever unuttered. And thus onto the bar we tread.

At the edge of the dance floor, I asked Fiona, "Are you ready to boogey down, get busy with it, shake that thang?"

"Observe with awe as I strut my stellar surfeit of stuff."

Such a sublime answer stunned me momentarily, but not enough to prevent me from throwing down the gauntlet to the debauching denizens of this tourist town. With dismissive disdain did I declaim, "These Turks. Terrible dancers," before swaggering sultan-like onto the dance floor to give them an eyeful and a half. Walking Like An Egyptian, The Cabbage Patch, Lawnmower, Macarena, Charleston, Moondance, Saturday Night Fever finger shooting, The Karate Kid Crane, the Hokey-Pokey, and my specialty the Chicken Dance – I twisted that tantalizing tushy of mine prodigiously in old school moves the likes of which none of them had seen in many a year and none surely could ever hope to match. (Though I did hold the C.P.A. Dance in reserve for a later encore – its seductive lure is irresistible and something wielding its awesome power should be used only sparingly. And only for good and not for evil, of course. Nor did I have my protective headgear with me, either (for the knee behind the neck fouette en tournant or the newly added second movement's upside down arabesque).) When Fiona could stop laughing, she joined me. Eventually we were slam-dancing to sitars and harpsichords.

Fiona's smile swallowed my heart as her green eyes never left mine. Once she spun me around and then dipped me. Releasing me, she wiggled her ass at me as she sashayed to the other end of the dance floor. I would keep that moment forever.

When Svetlana Swan's song came on, I had to stop for a beer. Fiona joined me. "Come here often?"

I said: "I think that guy over there is giving you the come hither and yon look."

"The one sporting the third eye?"

"No, the young and sprightly one who used to date Stalin's mom. With the pumpkin sized goiter. In the garish yet mysteriously enchanting purple velvet tsarouchia."

"Do you think he likes me? Really, really likes me?"

"That is drool on his chin. And his shirt. And the floor. Don't blow your chance. Fit your footsies with gallivanting galoshes and wade wantonly over to him."

"No, it couldn't miraculously, ever possibly be."

"Chase yer dreams, baby." I left to buy him a beer and then brought him back to Fiona while she scolded me playfully with her eyes.

After I had taught the balding Turk the Polish mazurka and he'd left to show his friends, Fiona said, "You're the funniest dancer I've ever seen."

"You're pretty awesome yourself. Truly."

"I know."

I laughed and then whispered in her ear, "I don't want this night to end. Or you to leave tomorrow." Fiona studied my eyes. I leaned forward to kiss her but she turned her away.

"I'm not sure about this."

"What?"

"What can come of it?"

"Whatever we want it to." Her eyes filled with sadness. "I'll be right back."

Fiona suddenly pressed my hand and asked, "Do you have a room?"

"Yeah."

"Let's get out of here."

"One minute." Dying for a pee, I raced to the restroom. The handle of the steel door was kind of wobbly which I didn't really notice until I wanted to leave and it came off in my hand. I laughed and tried pushing the door open. Nope. I used more force. Still nothing. Then I got violent. Then I shouted for help. The throbbing music drowned out my cries.

By the time the bartender opened the restroom forty minutes later, Fiona was gone.

I tried asking for her in the morning, but she'd checked out at six.

It had fucking happened again.

Stunned by Fiona's disappearance and still a bit hung over, I wandered into town for lunch. As I passed one of the ubiquitous carpet shops, a young man outside said, "Come inside, I invite you."

"I don't want to buy a carpet."

"It matters not. Come."

Shrugging, I followed him.

He handed me a cup of sweet tea as we sat down. "You were the one hitting the girl last night. On the dance floor. Beating her up."

I laughed. "We were just dancing. Having fun. It was a joke."

"No, I saw you. Beat her up. And she was so beautiful. How did you do this? You must have some special power over women. This is what I want to know."

As I passed the next carpet shop, a voice called out, "Come inside, I invite you."

I spent the following three hours drinking tea with carpet salesmen and never once being offered a carpet to buy.

Waiting for my bus on the hotel veranda the following evening after visiting the underground "city" during the day, I noticed a cloth bound journal on the table before me. *Tips For Travelers*. Flipping through the pages covered in where I must go and what I must absolutely and without hesitation do, inspired me to leave the following:

After traversing half the globe these last four months, habiting its ghettoes, sailing its seas and scaling its mountains, my recommendation to the novice backpacker would be to carry a gun. Its versatility is astounding, allowing you to confront and deal with a wide assortment of traveling obstacles: dormitory snorers, overaggressive carpet salesmen, pestering rickshaw drivers, uncooperative travel agents and, perhaps the most treacherous, Canadians. (Those little maple leafs they're so fond of sewing onto their backpacks to identify themselves as not being Americans make perfect targets.) At first glance, a firearm may seem a rather heavy piece of traveling gear, causing undesired perspiration and muscle expenditure, but it really is not, for you no longer have to carry anything else. What you need, you take by force. Money? Rob a bank. Camera? Shoot a tourist, preferably a Canadian. (I know, they may seem harmless at first, chugging Moosehead beer and telling each other to "Take off, ay," but trust me on this: kill as many of their kind as you can. For they will spread their insidious ways until the whole world is consumed unless someone holds them in check. Do not skirt the responsibility, for the duty is each and all of ours.) The larger the caliber of the weapon, the better. Size does matter, as the bigger the bang, the bigger the scare. Yes, larger bullets cost more than smaller ones, but you'll find yourself using less of them which will save you money in the long run. As budget travelers, we need to economize wherever we can. But saving money doesn't mean you have to deprive yourself of the random wanton violence, just buy generic brand ammunition. And be careful in Thailand, the homicide laws are quite strict there. If absolutely necessary, just maim instead. But if you're traveling to the United States, don't bother to buy a gun as the National Rifle Association hands them out at the border.

Peace, Love and Happy Shooting,

Richard Remora's Illegitimate Bastard Child

A few months after I'd started with Net, Block and Tackle, I visited my sister at Pitzer College in Pomona. It was her senior year.

Once we were seated in The Fig Garden for dinner, Penelope asked me, "How's work?"

"Shit."

"Can't you ever be positive? About anything?"

"What does that mean?"

"All you ever do is complain about your life. I've always known I had to work, to be a contributing part of the so-called-system, and I've never had any problems with it. It's you that had them. You always thought you were too good for everything and everyone."

"Nice to see you, too."

"I'm just sick of listening to it. I'd rather spend my time with people who aren't so negative. Who appreciate the world and the brief time we have on it. I'm tired of listening to you criticize everyone constantly. You're no better than any of them. If you want something different, change it. Don't sit there complaining about it."

"Why the fuck did I come here?"

"I don't know. Why did you?"

"I'll take you home."

"Don't bother. I'll have one of my friends pick me up."

I left the restaurant and drove back to Santa Monica. It'd taken me three hours in traffic to get there.

"What happened with you and Penelope?" my mother asked me a week later over the phone.

"She told me she didn't like me very much anymore, so I left."

"You're family. Family. My father and I aren't going to be around forever. I hate to think you won't be together after we're gone. All you've got is family."

My sister couldn't forgive me. For the times I'd hit her when I was younger when I was struggling with the rejection I experienced daily at school? I shouldn't have done it and I tried to make it up, I really did. As I went through high school we didn't really talk but then I went to her high school basketball and softball games, called her regularly when I started working, bought her presents when I began to have some money. I would have killed anyone who hit her at school. When someone in kindergarten put a pencil on her chair so she'd sit on it, I wanted to hunt down the kid and cut his throat.

In high school, we argued a lot because all her friends would walk all over her – ask her to do things and she always did them, no matter how much they cost her emotionally or monetarily. She thought I was telling her what to do, but I was really trying to protect her. But she couldn't see that. It was beautiful, really beautiful, the sacrifices she made for her friends or even for people she'd just met. But she got angry with me when I said they were taking advantage, sometimes to our family's detriment. As if we were secondary to the act. And I couldn't understand that, how that would be more important than family. But for her, it was. And she was as stubborn as me.

My aunt had a similar relationship with my mother. Her husband had cheated on her for years, even before they got married, and she tolerated it. At the end, she'd begged him not to leave her. Then she went through a series of roommates who wouldn't pay the rent on time, would steal from her – and always she took it. She dated men who cared nothing about her, slept with them immediately and tried to make all of them love her. But with my mom who told her not to, with my mom who told her the pain it would cause her later – she argued and ignored and even resented. Because my mom told her things wouldn't turn out the way she wanted, the world just wasn't like that. So my aunt resented her. Though unspoken, she also resented my mother's marriage (though hardly perfect) and her children.

My maternal grandfather was an alcoholic who beat my grandmother which explained some of why my aunt was the way she was. But, except for a couple of isolated incidents, my father wasn't. And my mother was extremely supportive: her whole life she'd helped us with school, talked to us about our problems, immersed her whole existence in helping us. So I figured maybe my sister would hate me, but she'd probably be okay.

She wasn't.

"Pete…" The voice was my father's and yet it wasn't. Never had I heard him sound so beaten. "Your sister… Your sister's run off with Lee."

"Who's Lee?"

"Leanne."

I kind of collapsed against the bed. There was a deep pounding somewhere inside me, sinking me.

Leanne was a high school friend of my sister whose stepfather used to yell at her constantly, make all sorts of threats and tell her how useless she was. The girl was a wreck. Penelope sort of adopted her as a friend – my sister was captain of the basketball team and Leanne was a freshman.

My mother felt sorry for her as well and they ended up taking her to church, all three of them going every Sunday. She came over to the house a couple of times and said nothing but hateful things towards men, which was understandable but not much fun to be around. Especially when it kept going on. And she rarely went to class. Then she started doing drugs and sleeping with another girl on the basketball team. But Penelope and my mom refused to give up on her. My mom said it wasn't the Christian thing to do. I told my sister Leanne was beyond saving and we'd had a fight about it a few months before. Now I understood why Penelope was so mad at me.

"Are you crying?" I asked.

"It's upsetting."

"I'm sorry, Dad."

"And such a bitch. If it'd been Wendy, okay, she has an education, she's a nice person. But Lee... We never should have let her go skiing with your fucking aunt so many times. She never fucking shut up about how awful men are. Fucking bitch..."

I called Penelope. "Why are you doing this to Mom and Dad?"

"Doing what to Mom and Dad?"

"This person isn't good for you. She's an angry person. She's made you angry. You never used to be like that."

"Again you're telling me what to do. It's my life, not yours. Lee is a much better person than you are. You're just a fucking asshole who wants everyone to be as miserable as you are. Everything has to be your way. Well, guess what? It doesn't work that way."

"Why do you hate me?"

She didn't answer.

"So hate me. But don't torture Mom and Dad. Leave them alone. If you want to live your life that way, okay, do it. But don't make them watch. Not Mom. It's killing her."

"Killing her? By me being myself?"

"She's called me every night this week crying. And now you're telling her you might be changing your mind? It's pretty obvious you're not."

"Fuck you. Fuck. You." She hung up.

Whenever my own life had been shit, I'd say at least Pen is okay, at least something is good and pure in this fucked up world, at least something isn't shit.

My sister disappeared after that. My mom would cry, not knowing where she was. Was she safe? She didn't call, didn't write, didn't let them know. And then, after six months, she showed up at my parents' house asking them to take her in. That she'd seen what Lee was and that it was over and she'd go back to school and the church and maybe even have a family. My mom was cautiously happy, my dad more so. But she never called me.

One day when I got home while I was still living with my Grandmother Bess, Penelope was there. It was a shock to see her. She'd put on fifty pounds and all the light had gone out of her eyes. When she talked to my grandmother, it was like she was doing a job interview, nothing she said felt like it came from within. Everything was fake, an affectation. When Bessie had fallen asleep, I said to my sister, "Let's go for a walk."

Down on the beach, we sat in the sand. A chill wind blew in from the grey ocean. "So are you done messing about?"

As her face flashed in anger, I had my answer before she spoke. "Messing about?"

"I don't understand what you're doing with your life and I don't care. Do whatever you want, whatever makes you happy. I don't want to be involved anymore. But stop hurting Mom and Dad. Do what you have to, but don't make them suffer. Live with your choices. And let them go. Mom can't handle it. You can't have everything. She wants so much for you and when you to throw it all in her face, it kills her, more and more each day. All right, you weren't honest to us about your feelings. It hurt a great deal, but we forgive you. But now stop. Mom has never been closer to anyone in her life than to you. She thought you two shared everything: her love of God, her want of children. You shared almost twenty years together. Her life is in us, our hopes and dreams are hers. For her to share all these things with you and for you to dismiss them as nothing hurts her in ways no person should ever be. Stop lying to her. She suffers in your unhappiness. I'm tired of her crying every time I call her. I'm tired of watching her suffer. Leave her alone. Promise me that."

"She's my family, too. She's not just yours."

"You're not a child anymore. You're a grown woman. Take responsibility for your actions, consider their consequences. Act like an adult. If you love her, stop hurting her. If this other love is worth more than the regard of your family, then abandon us for it. You can't have both. Mom and Dad may say they can take it, but they can't. I'm the one who's talked to Mom on the phone every night for six months, listening to her cry as she hopes you change back. Well, that obviously isn't happening. And she can't handle it. So you're killing her slowly."

I stood up and walked back to my car. It was a long time before I spoke to my sister again.

Arriving late in Fetihye along the Mediterranean coast after a long bus ride, the hotel owner ushered me to a bed on the covered porch. Exhausted, I fell asleep within seconds of laying down.

Attacking me. Attacking me. Attacking me! Shit! I came awake to thousands of furry animals crawling over my face and body: legs, arms, feet, everywhere. I sat up sharply in bed and screamed, fearing my end was near. Then I realized the encroaching, consuming carpet of white and black fur belonged to a horde of marauding, ferocious kittens: a roiling mass of meowing, tuna-eating madness. Desperate to survive, I flung them far and wide, catapulting adolescent felines tumbling every which way.

They huddled in the middle of the floor, catching their breath, regrouping, planning their next attack. A flanking maneuver? A frontal assault? Or wait till he falls asleep again and then assail him from above, digging our sharp teeth (and even sharper claws) into his myopic eyes?

The battle went on until dawn. Each time I succumbed to exhaustion and let my eyelids fall, they pounced, enveloping me in their white furred menace.

"Aren't the kittens so cute?"

"I fucking hate the little bastards."

An uncomfortable silence. Later that morning by mutual but unspoken agreement, I changed hostels. They made me pay for the night's accommodation, of course. Full price.

A couple of days later after a visit to the ruins at Ephesus, I took a short ferry ride to the Greek island of Kos. In the small yard of the hotel,

331

the male owner said to me my third morning as I stood at a faucet, "Don't do washing. Are you a woman?" He generally spent his days drinking tea and playing backgammon at the corner with his friends while his wife and daughter did the hotel's cleaning.

"No, but I portray one on television. Have you seen *Charlie's Angels*? I'm the blonde with the rather round shoulder blades and devilishly devastating derriere."

"I wash my clothes once. In the army. In 1966. Never again."

Finished, I went to sit on the verandah. Gorgeous women abounded but they huddled together in groups, mostly speaking some variant of Scandinavian and fending me off with a couple of sentences of small talk in English if I insisted (which I sometimes did, damnit). But then an English girl with short red hair and light blue eyes sat down beside me and said brightly, "How are you?"

Yes! "I'm struggling through, thanks for asking. It's been tough lately, especially yesterday and the day before, but I'm soldiering on. Somehow."

"What happened yesterday?"

"Well, I went swimming, luxuriated lengthily in the hot sun and drank some beers before eating a dinner large enough to feed the population of Nigeria and neighboring Cameroon."

She laughed. "And the day before?"

"Well, I went swimming, luxuriated lengthily in the hot sun and drank some beers."

"Before eating a dinner large enough to feed the population of Nigeria and neighboring Cameroon?"

"No, I was too full from breakfast so I just had a kebab. Life's rough, sometimes, I guess. Sacrifices must often be made."

"Don't know how you do it."

"Strength of character. I'm overflowing with it."

"Amazing, just amazing."

"I know. I know."

One of those big hulking things infested with muscly bits all over and a perfect tan appeared and began mauling the English girl with his lips. "Excuse me," she said and they disappeared.

The rest of my five days there was much of the same: the tanned and beautiful hooking up and me stumbling home drunk alone to sleep on the verandah and often fight the Greek cousins of my Turkish feline nemeses for the mere glimpse of rest.

Nightmares of a giant-sized Garfield disemboweling Big Bird or ripping Flipper's head off haunted my moments of unconsciousness. Nor did Woodstock or Mr. Limpet fare any better at the paws of Sylvester.

On the hilled island of Ios, I tried handing women the following scribbled on a cocktail napkin in four or five bars:

Top Five Reasons to Go Out with Peter*

*Extracted from *List of 1000 Reasons Peter is Great* in *The Encyclopedia of Peter's Awesomeness – A to Z and a couple of letters extra*

1. He's awesome

2. He's totally awesome

3. He's full-on awesome

4. He's wicked awesome

5. He's totally tubular in an awesome-like manner but even more so

Then I tried notes more subtle: "Can we have the band killed?" or "Can you please return my heart?" None worked.

To a rather fetching Italian architect I thought I was making progress with witty sayings such as:

1. I admit I stepped over, on and through many a man to get where I am today: a tax staff accountant intern level one. Woman, too. I meant *man* in the generic non-gender specific kind of way.

2. Svetlana Swan won't stop calling me. And calling me. I really should get a restraining order. It's so sad...

3. Over there a man in the twelfth century, Hans Halibut chopped up his family and made them into a very nice minced stew with cabbage, carrots and green beans. Behind that bush and six metres to the right, nothing has ever, ever happened. Somebody ate lunch here once. You can buy really top quality uncut heroin down that road. I hate that tree, I don't know why, but I do. Abraham Lincoln tripped coming out of that pub one cold December evening and was tragically run over and killed by a herd of albino water buffalo. One of the saddest tales of the Old West, really. Tears me up inside, outside and above.

4. Sometimes I dream of being an acrobat. Or maybe a political cartoonist. Sometimes.

5. I hope you know you haven't got strong enough sunscreen to bask in the glow of my utter magnificence.

during sojourns to the brown sanded beach when she said, "Just because I'm hanging out with you doesn't mean I'll sleep with you. I only wanted some company. You know, you come off like you just want to get the girl in bed. You've got your little travel stories you know by heart with the seven jokes and three points of interest. You're working off a script. I get it. And some girls like that or don't care. Hell, half the guys traveling are doing just the same thing and a lot of them are a lot less interesting than you (but better looking). But I want to be treated as an individual."

My first reaction was to say: "What the fuck makes you so great?" but I didn't. I thought about it. And kept thinking about it. Was that who I was? I didn't think so, but, underneath?

Stumbling back from the bars to Far Out Camping that night to my rented tent (alone once more), I saw an Australian man sleeping on a ledge on the wrong side of the walled road. His right hand dangled over a hundred foot precipice.

"Wake up!"

"What?"

"Look where you are."

"Oh, right. Thanks, mate."

"No! Go left!" I reached out my hand but he wouldn't grab it.

"Right."

"Left!"

He climbed back onto the road. When he stumbled on the uneven wall, this time I could help.

"What the fuck were you doing?"

A couple of dark skinned men passed us and the Australian said, "Look at those fucking Guidos with their greasy fucking hair and their shitty designer jeans."

One of the men turned immediately and came back with rage in his eyes. "What did you say?" His friend joined him.

I kept walking. Some men you can't save.

I kept going, kept moving. There had to be a place I fit, right? And what else could I do? Go back? To what?

Around dinner time on the ferry leaving Ios, I looked up from my soda to see Albert standing before me wearing a wide straw hat. "Pete, wasn't it?"

"Right. Albert?"

"What have you been up to since Turkey?"

"Some of the islands. You?"

"I went to Syria with Fiona."

Fuck. Fuck! Somehow I said, "You did?"

"Yeah. We went on a tour to the underground city in Goreme the day you left and she told me about going to Syria. I had nothing better to do, so I went along."

"Wow."

"She was really funny, you know that? We were in the desert but she insisted on telling everyone her parents were world-famous ichthyologists and that she personally could identify 444 species of fish by their fins alone. Even told kids who probably would never see the ocean their whole lives. And her fish face…"

"She was pretty great."

"Yeah… We got together finally. After your night together, I thought she wasn't really interested. But after a bottle of wine in the middle of the desert and a long conversation about our bad breakups, she said the same thing to me – that she thought I wasn't interested. So… On our last night I broke down, told her a bunch of rubbish. But what can I do? I'm twenty-four years old, I'm not ready to settle down, have kids, a wife. I want to fuck a bunch of women, see the world, experience something of life… When are you going back?"

"I don't know. I really don't."

"If I was you, I'd never stop." He looked at a small island we were passing. "Well, this is me. Tally ho." He opened his black umbrella and dropped over the side of the ferry.

I was stunned for a moment. By the time I got to the railing to look back, I could see only the calm blue water stretching to the horizon. And a seagull perched on a stanchion overhead watching me intently. Preparing to shit on my head as he flew away, no doubt.

Amid the city's labyrinthine old town past all the sidewalk cafes and designer clothing stores nestled the Rhodes hostel. Ornate towers and crumbling arches framed a bleached out sky, roses twisted through stone windows and battlements. The cobblestoned streets were built like a maze to confuse pirates (and inebriated backpackers) so the inhabitants could flee in time.

As I dumped my bag, one of the young backpackers nearby was saying to another: "Look at that ugly old bitch."

A woman in her late fifties with a limp was struggling to move her too large bag.

I walked over to her. "Do you need some help?"

"Yes, thank you. The taxis won't come down this lane." She sounded like my grandmother: a New York Jew.

We headed towards one of the main thoroughfares. "You're very kind to help me. Are you on your school holiday?"

"No, I'm out of school. Traveling around the world actually."

"For how long?"

"Six months now."

A taxi drove up. The driver took her bag. She turned to me: "Don't ruin your life. Get it out of your system and go home."

"I'm sorry?"

"You know what I mean. Don't throw your life away. Have your fun but then go home and work hard."

At dusk, everyone from the hostel went out to a bar. No names were exchanged, everyone became known by their nationality. I was the Yank at first but later dubbed Pogo Boy for my unique style of dancing. There was the Big Aussie, the Little Aussie, the German (usually elaborated with "The Crazy Motherfucking" preceding such title), the similarly elaborated Kiwi, the Englishman and the Spaniard.

"There comes a time in a man's life when he has to do what he has to do."

"I agree with you in no way, shape or form."

We ordered three shots each which we dispatched with much, um, dispatch. The Kiwi shouted, "The point is…" Then he stood up and threw his chair into the street.

The Swedish barmaid approached cautiously after a few moments. "Another round," the Englishman said and tipped generously.

When she brought the drinks, she said to the Kiwi: "I'll give you another chair if you promise not to chuck this one into the street." He took the second chair. "It's one thousand drachmas."

"I'm not paying." He downed his shot. "No, man, they rip you off in this country."

"But. Never mind."

"No, man, they rip you off in this country." He downed his second shot of watered-down ouzo. The barmaid began laughing. "We're all here drinking beer. There. Wherever." He did his third shot.

He stumbled out of the bar and turned down the street towards two couples whom he accosted: "I make more money in a month than you make in a year!" Then he reached into his pocket and gestured at them with a wad of folded cash. Not surprisingly, they stopped moving towards him. He turned his back to them, smiled at us, and dropped his trousers around his ankles, mooning them.

The Englishman said, "Nice one."

He pulled up his underwear, but not his pants. "I'm getting something to eat." Then he waddled away. Passing a streetlamp, he suddenly turned on it and attacked. With his huge hands, he bent the iron in half, smashing the light on the cobble-stoned street. "I hate streetlamps. My first girlfriend died choking on tofu." Weeping, he disappeared into the night.

Later as we sat in the courtyard amid grapevines and molting olive trees, I found myself listening to the Kiwi, "Passion fades, man. The newness wears off. I loved my girlfriend, man, loved her. And she loved me. But after two years, we'd become such good friends, we no longer were passionate about each other. Both of us. We tried to work it out, but it was just that way. We tried pornography, dildos, leather whips, everything. But the emotions were gone and we couldn't force them back. We both cried about it to our families, to our friends, tried to stop it from happening. We couldn't. What you're looking for doesn't exist, man. You think these women you meet traveling are awesome, but they're just traveling. In a distorted sense of joy. It's a skewed reality. If you knew them for a while, the same would happen. You'd get bored, they'd get bored. That's life."

"I don't know."

"No one wants to settle down. They're constantly looking for something better. A better job, a better house, a better fuck, a nicer partner, a less subservient partner, a crueler partner. The unattainable."

"I think settle is the wrong word. You shouldn't settle for anyone. You should be grateful for what you've got."

"You're right. Any time someone likes you in that way is pretty special. It's good to have praise, satiates the ego. Our time on this planet is so brief, so transient, that to want to spend the majority of it with any one person in such an intimate sharing way is quite remarkable. But it won't make you happy."

"You shouldn't stay with people who abuse you or make you feel bad about yourself, but you shouldn't expect too much, either. If you make each other laugh, are attracted to one another, I think that's enough. If she makes you want to be a better person, if just being around her challenges you to become that... Not all of the time, of course, not so much that she doesn't like you for who you are and that you're always needing to please

338

her, but enough so that you feel *something*. Give yourself in every possible way, don't hold back anything. Risk everything. Not with everyone, but, if they might be the right person, why not? That's what it's all about, right? Don't wait until mortality stares you in the face to open up. Live your whole life like that."

"No, man, it doesn't work that way. I tried, she tried. Really fucking tried. You think you can work it out, but you can't. It's not in us as human beings. It's all romantic in movies to give up everything for love, but in reality, you can't. It doesn't work."

"Then what else is there?"

"Why does there have to be something else?"

"So the pursuit is all that matters?"

"No, man, why does there even have to be that? Why does there have to be anything?"

"I'm leaving, guys," the Spaniard announced.

"Every night you disappear. Where do you go?" the Kiwi asked.

"I'm staying in a cave."

"A cave?"

"There's loads of them nearby."

"Why are you staying in a cave?" I said.

"That's fucking awesome," the Kiwi said.

"Want to see it?"

"Of course. When?"

"Now?"

The Kiwi stood up and so did I. The Spaniard looked at me.

"You don't want me to see your cave."

"No."

"You don't like me."

"I don't. You say you're searching, but you're pretending. You'll go back to what you were and perpetuate how things are. You come into my world and regard me with disdain. Fuck you."

I'd had enough of Greece.

Cassandra summoned me into her office the day after my grandmother's funeral. "Shut the door, Peter." I did. "You were three minutes late this morning."

No fucking way was I apologizing. I said nothing.

"You'd better make that time up."

I nodded.

"You don't seem too enthusiastic about that yes, Peter. You know, you should consider yourself lucky. Normally we require employees to take paid time off for any time out of the office during regular working hours. I think we're being pretty flexible and accommodating by letting you make up this time and not take it out of your vacation *allowance*. You should really be more grateful. People, and me especially, don't appreciate a lack of thanks when you bend the rules for them. If you want to move up in this company, Peter, you need to correct your attitude."

I nodded again.

Cassandra waited for me to continue and when I didn't, she added, "You also left two minutes early for lunch. If this becomes a habit, we will really have to reevaluate your utility to this company. Lack of punctuality in the future will not be tolerated. At all."

I nodded for a third time.

"I'm trying to help, you know. I could just have you fired. But I like you, Peter. You work hard, so I'm trying to be frank and candid with you. Some managers would just have you thrown out of the building without so much as a goodbye. But I'm giving you a second chance, a way to keep your job. I'm trying to be your friend."

As much as it pained me, I said it: "Thank you, Cassandra."

The smile came with her victory. Then: "Leave now. I have work to do." As I turned around, she added, "You have to make up the time for this meeting as well, Peter. Peter?"

"Yes, Cassandra. I will."

Cassandra passed me in the hall. "Your shirt's untucked three quarters of an inch too far, Pollack. And I won't even go into the length of
340

your cuff. Did you not read the firm's wardrobe guidelines?"

"They're three hundred pages long."

"Do you not remember the contract you signed on Day One that was duly witnessed and notarized by Mr. Marlin? Or should I send you another copy?"

"No, Cassandra. I mean, yes, Cassandra. One of those."

"Excuse me?"

"I'll go fix it in the bathroom."

"And don't forget that the minimum work week went up to 50 hours," she called after me.

A memo came out the first week in January saying the minimum work week was 55 hours. A week later it increased to 60 hours. By February 1, the minimum was 70 hours. Then 75. On February 10, Cassandra called me into her office.

"You wanted to see me?"

"Do you want to succeed here, Peter?"

"Of course."

"So what's with your hours?"

"Huh?"

"Are you trying to make some sort of statement? To protest your anger over the whole filling of the paper tray incident?"

"What?"

"The memo. You worked only 74.5 hours last week."

"I must've added wrong."

She stared me down. "These hours are only guidelines, you know. And are to be considered a minimum. Do you not like this job? Do you not want to excel?"

On March 1, they increased the minimum to 80. So I made sure to work 81, checking my addition twice. Cassandra still scowled at me when I went home before her (the one time) and said to me in the kitchen (or at least I think she did, at 2 a.m. it could have been the water cooler talking), "You don't really need sleep your first few years, Peter. You're learning."

"And what about doing laundry, picking up dry cleaning, getting a haircut, going to the doctor?" But this time I was talking to the water cooler. A little bit too closely, actually. I stood back.

I was forced to move in with my other grandmother. I still couldn't afford a place on my own, really, and I wanted to save some money for a trip, for a new car, I wasn't sure what. (Despite my first "raise" (and I use that term lightly), the promise of future riches was magnificent and unparalleled if I worked hard and dedicated myself fully to my job, according to Cassandra – 74.5 hours a week wasn't that – it was doing the expected – I needed to do more than the expected. Comments like "You can take your vacation if you want. If that's what you really want." abounded.)

Trouble with my new living arrangements began early. As I finished washing my hands at the kitchen sink for our first Sunday dinner together, my grandmother Petra shouted over the television that was never off and never less than full volume, "That's just about the most disgusting thing I ever saw. Wiping your wet hands on your pants and slopping water all over the place. Why do you have to be such an animal? People would think you were raised by beasts."

After dinner, it continued as we were watching television and I moved a pillow from the couch to the side so I could sit, "I want to ask you a question. Why don't you use that pillow behind your back when you sit?"

I didn't answer.

"What's the matter with you? Don't you answer your grandmother?"

Saturday I worked until midnight. Another eighty-five hour week (they'd increased the minimum again). I passed out as soon as I got home, totally exhausted.

Nine o'clock the next morning, my grandmother woke me shouting, "Why the hell are you sleeping in the middle of the day? Why don't you go to bed at a normal hour?"

Reluctantly I joined her in the living room, not really awake. A moment later she was at me again, "Now why did you unplug the fan? Honestly, I don't know why you always have to screw things up here."

"I didn't unplug the fan."

"Why are you lying to me? I certainly didn't unplug the fan and who else could do it but you?"

"Maybe it was Richard Nixon. Or his evil twin tone deaf brother Heinrich no one knows about. Except me."

"What the hell are you laughing about? I never heard of anyone laughing all by theirselves before."

A minute later she was shouting at me from the kitchen, "What did you do with my red onion? I know you took it. I don't know why you steal my food."

"Mom, I can't take it anymore."

"What?"

"Your mother. Screaming at me."

"Be patient, Peter. She's an angry old woman who's buried two husbands."

"I know, Mom. But this is too much. We sit watching television and every five minutes she criticizes how I sit, where I put my feet. Then I go into my room and turn on the other television to drown her out. She complains that I close the door – that she doesn't like closed doors in her house. She says we can watch whatever show I want in the living room. So I come out and she's at me again."

She'd had a tough life. She'd been raised on a farm in North Dakota and came to California with her two sisters with nothing. Then she'd married my grandfather and had my mom and aunt. He died of a heart attack after he'd beaten her for ten years and she had to raise her children on a cafeteria worker's salary (luckily the house had been paid for). After twenty years, she married my step-grandfather.

Her second husband used to drink water glasses full of vodka every night. And he took prescription drugs. Eventually he got Alzheimer's. He just stopped talking. Then he began playing with himself when sitting on his chair, it didn't matter who was around. But my grandmother refused to put him in a home, she insisted he stay with her long after she could care for him properly. She had bad knees and he didn't help her at all when she had to pull him up from his chair. She didn't want to be left alone. One time, he shoved her away. She fell and broke her hip on the hardwood floor. Only then did she let us put him in a home. I still remember the look on his face when they came for him. He just knew he was never coming out. He died within a month. She'd been alone for five years when I moved in.

The next day I started looking for another job. Using a calling card, I followed up with the companies I'd sent resumes. On the nineteenth call, I actually got to talk to a manager. Just as he was asking why I wanted to leave Net, Block and Tackle, my grandmother started shouting, "Would you get off of the phone? All day long you're on the phone."

"Grandma!"

"Get off the phone! And don't yell at me. Show your elders some respect."

"Hello? Hello?" The manager had hung up. "Grandma, that was a job interview!"

"You know, I pay the bills around here and your phone calls are costing me a fortune."

"That was a toll free number, it's not costing you anything."

"What the hell difference does that make? It's my house, I'll do what I want. And it's my phone."

I went into the bedroom to escape her. She followed me wielding a piece of paper in her hand: the telephone bill. "You see these calls? Three dollars and nineteen cents. Fourteen cents. I paid for these calls. Your calls. Money doesn't grow on trees, Peter. You don't know how good you have it here."

"I always use the calling card, Grandma."

"Then what are these? Huh?"

"All are to North Dakota or misdialing to the same numbers."

"What do you mean I dialed the wrong number? Yes, I called North Dakota but why would I call Hawaii?"

"Look, the numbers are just transposed."

"You're always right, aren't you? That goes both ways, you know."
344

"How do you expect me to get out of here if you interrupt my job interviews for better positions?"

"So it's my fault again? Always my fault. Young people never take responsibility for how their lives turn out. You're always blaming someone else. Always. Since you were a child. Nothing's changed."

I stood up but she was blocking the doorway so I couldn't leave. "Please move."

"I'll move when I want. This is my house."

"I need to get away from you right now."

"Such a cruel boy you are. After everything I've given you. You say these things to me. What an animal you are. I hope you never find anyone and die alone. You're awful. No woman deserves someone like you. No one should have to put up with the likes of you."

If there was something crueler to be said, I couldn't think of it.

"What are you doing coming in at all hours? If you're staying here, you have to live by my rules." It was 11:15 pm. I'd gone for a eight hour walk to clear my head.

"Is this how you want me to remember you?"

"Your mother never taught you to use that tone with your elders. No respect you have. None. How you turned out to be so mean, I'll never know."

The interviews soon developed a theme. More than once I heard: "Why would you leave before getting your certification? You're at a big place now – why won't they give it to you? Are you not that valuable?"

I was going nowhere.

A week after leaving Rhodes, I found myself hitchhiking in Israel's Golan Heights along a paved road lined with barbed wire and signs warning *Danger! Former Mine Field. Do not leave road!* in both English and Hebrew. Cars drove by at full speed, each time getting closer and closer to hitting me as they often deafened me with their horns.

Why I had conceived the rather brilliant idea of trying to get somewhere difficult, I could not understand. Something about achieving

345

the impossible or trying to being the whole point had run through my mind vaguely that morning. Now I realized the bus schedule which required three changes to get here from Akko was not difficult to return on, it was impossible. (Never make a decision without coffee. Never.) After waiting at the now locked gate of a most unimpressive "national park" for two hours, I realized no more buses were coming, the guards wouldn't give me a ride (even after a heartfelt plea), I had no water and no place to buy it, I had a sixty pound backpack on my back and the nearest town with a hotel was twelve miles away. I couldn't sleep anywhere because I couldn't leave the road, either. I was fucked.

A gust of wind blew my hat off and into one of the mine fields. But then you knew that was going to happen.

A small red car laid on the horn rather aggressively and then slammed on the brakes. It backed up. A dark haired French Algerian woman rolled down the window. "What the fuck are you doing in the middle of the road?"

"Trying to get a ride and/or win a gubernatorial election."

"You didn't raise your thumb. You know, that's what you're supposed to do as a hitchhiker. Rule number one."

"I can't lift my arms anymore."

"Where are you going?"

"Anywhere I can catch a bus back to Akko."

"Get in."

I climbed in the back. Another French girl sat up front, this one blonde and very pretty. "How many people do you have hidden inside your pack?" she asked. She was visiting the French Algerian who was volunteering for humanitarian aid in the Gaza Strip.

"Not counting the elephant or the hippopotamus?"

After introductions, the French Algerian answered my question, "How the people in the Gaza are treated: it's disgusting. Horrible. Worse than animals. How the western media just ignores it makes me sick. No one says anything bad about the Israelis, especially the Americans. Jews own all the media in the United States so of course they protect the Israelis."

"I haven't seen what they do, but the Israelis are in a kind of precarious position. Everyone is trying to kill them. They can't afford mercy."

346

"That doesn't justify what I've seen. One atrocity does not excuse another. You know, I had heard about it from my family, but I wanted to be open-minded. So I decided to see it for myself. And it's so much worse than I had heard."

"So what's your solution? How do you stop the terrorist attacks? Every time they gave back this land, they would get bombed again. I don't condone the treatment of the Palestinians, I'm sure it's as bad as you say it is. There's always two sides, right?"

"I don't support terrorism, but what would you do if someone took your land? Gave it to someone else arbitrarily with no compensation?"

"Are those the ones doing the killing? Now, after forty years?"

"They're the ones suffering now. In the Gaza."

"The Jews had to go somewhere. It sucks that it had to be the Palestinians' land, I know that. But why are the Palestinians still living in tents there now, forty years later? The Egyptians, the Jordanians, someone should have let them assimilate. Or maybe they don't want to. Maybe they want to suffer."

"Want to suffer? Who wants to suffer?"

"I think the other Arab countries would prefer to fight rather than give in. To keep Israel as a symbol. Some people just want conflict. It keeps them in power. Gives the people someone to hate. I don't think splitting the country up was a solution. I think it rarely is. Because you can split one smaller and smaller and smaller. People have to learn to get along. But a lot of times I don't think that's what people want. They want someone to hate. Need it."

"Maybe. But right now people are dying in the Gaza. And the world doesn't care. Philosophizing doesn't solve the practical day to day of helping them survive."

The conversation turned to other things: my trip, how clearly awesome I was, how great my hair looked: the usual. As they said good night (lingering hugs as you'd expect – the French Algerian had obviously warmed to me) at the Akko hostel – they needed a place to stay and decided to join me – the French Algerian asked me: "What's your surname, anyway?" At my answer, she flinched. "You're not Jewish, are you?"

The blonde touched her friend's arm and they disappeared.

As I dropped my bag next to a mangy mattress in the Petra Hostel near the Jaffa Gate of old Jerusalem, a blonde German guy with a cast on his arm asked if I wanted to join in a barbecue on the roof.

Across the ancient stone buildings of the old city, the golden dome of the Temple on the Mount shone over everything.

Past a shelter built of garbage fused together with bright purple candle wax by a man staying there for two years, a group of travelers had gathered for Hans' barbecue. He'd collected money from everyone, envisioning a new way to pay for his accommodation and daily intake of three bottles of vodka. (The next morning I witnessed him offering one of these in sacrifice to a mud and cow dung deity housed on the roof's northeastern corner.) But the slabs of chicken breast and leg were hardly cooking over the sputtering charcoal flame. When someone suggested adding more wood to the fire, Hans scowled and waved dismissively while pulling greedily at the vodka bottle in his fist. I gave Hans some money and accompanied the German from my room to the corner shop to buy cans of Goldstar beer.

Two hours later, the meat still wasn't cooked, it was hardly thawed. A Slovenian girl said, "Hans, I'd like my meat a little more well done, thanks." Someone else added: "Could you turn over my piece of chicken? I wouldn't want it to burn." "Anybody got a microwave oven in their pack?" Hans suddenly grabbed the barbecue with both hands (the iron grill was cool enough) and threw it off the roof.

Everyone got quiet.

I said, "Anybody for Lord of the Burgers?"

"I'm game."

Other unusual (well, unique) individuals habited the rooms. A goateed Italian who played the flute with menace and absolutely no skill and who kept 24 five-liter bottles of water in his dorm room. (Once I tried to ask him to stop playing and he started crying.) An African American woman in her late thirties memorizing the Bible who'd got stuck on the Parables and who was especially fond of Exodus. An enormous Dutch man in his late sixties who sat day after day in the common room wearing the same purple T-shirt while he cut out articles from each of the local newspapers to paste in a notebook he was compiling. ("Have you heard of this thing I've invented to help bring my disciples together? The Internet? It's a wonderful thing. Now I can preach my philosophy to all of my followers around the world without actually being with them." He was looking for signs of God in the news – sometimes he cut out furniture advertisements or recipes for chocolate chip cookies. "I first saw God seven years ago when I looked at a hard-boiled egg with open eyes for the first time." He'd left his wife, children and grandchildren six years ago in
348

Rotterdam because God had told him this was what he was intended for.) Bedbugs big enough to have names like Frank and Smithy. No one named Fred.

Most of the "normal" backpackers I met in Jerusalem were German visiting out of guilt at what their grandparents had done during the Holocaust, trying to understand why it had happened, resolved to never let it recur. But they weren't the people who needed to come – they already understood.

Jerusalem teemed with pilgrims paying homage to the creator of their universe, grieving for the past sufferings of men of peace tormented by those of hate. They walked the streets stained by the blood of martyrs, seeking meaning in this cruel, uncaring world. But death in all its various guises, implacable and eternal, lay in wait for each of them. They talked of His pity, His mercy. But what kind of god let children "live" in cardboard boxes, drink water infected by their own feces, die of malaria, AIDS or cholera? Let innocent Jews, Armenians, Rwandans be raped and slaughtered? Let it continue in Vietnam, Cambodia, Afghanistan, Iraq? Let twenty million Russians die by Stalin's hand? What was His greater purpose in that? Why were some people born into wealth and others toiled their whole life for a pile of shit? Why were there pedophiles, rapists, murderers? Why had the Cherokee, the Sioux, the Aztecs, the Mayans, the Incans been wiped out? Why had slavery persisted for almost one hundred years in the "Land of the Free?" Why were Chinese children making tennis shoes sixteen hours a day while American kids played Nintendo, ate Ben and Jerry's ice cream and rode roller coasters?

"Beautiful, isn't it?"

I turned to the man addressing me.

"This city. This city is mankind. In all its sins, its vices, its squalor. And its supreme capacity for love." He touched my shoulder. "I see you doubt me. I see the disdain, the hatred in your eyes. But life is a gift. Every day, every minute, every breath. The taste of an apple, the scent of a daffodil, the curve of a woman's cheek. Beauty is everywhere. You ask why are some crippled, why are some cut down in their youth, but these are the wrong questions. The right questions are why I am blessed with the joy of your companionship, why do I get this moment? Why do I deserve this? And the answer is to try to earn it. If you spend your life doing this, the rest will not matter. You will lose your loneliness and you will have peace."

I visited the Western Wall, the Temple on the Mount (where policemen with cruel eyes chased boys trying to sell postcards), and the church built on the ground where Jesus Christ was supposed to have died. The holiest of grounds for three of the world's most popular religions all within a few yards of each other. So close and yet the bringer of the world's worst slaughters.

This is what we'd come from. This is what we were. Could we change?

Did we want to?

Did it even matter? Or was trying to all that did?

On a tour in the sweltering pre-morning darkness, I ascended Masada where 15,000 Romans had slowly built a ramp to overtake the city and 900 people inside knew each day they were getting that much closer to death. And I thought of the siege of the Edinburgh castle. And the battle of Stalingrad. And a thousand other battles and a thousand other victors of forgotten conflicts. What were we?

But then there was my sister and I. And I couldn't forgive her. Didn't want to. Could I judge?

I know you'd want to know, so, yes, another camel spat at me.

I swam in the Dead Sea. It was oily and icky. Gross. Yuckus.

Back at the Holocaust museum in Jerusalem I saw twelve pages of victims who shared my surname. Amid a book surrounded by hundreds of other such books in a dark room. For worshiping a different god than theirs. And maybe for not even that. Maybe for just a name. And if I'd been born fifty years earlier, maybe mine.

Another building held paintings from the Warsaw ghetto. Murders depicted by the hand of a child. Drawn from their abbreviated lives. I sat down and wept.

How could such things be forgiven? But if we didn't, where would we end?

And it hadn't gotten better. (Would it ever?) After I visited the church in Bethlehem where Christ was supposed to have been born, one of four Arabic men in the street shouted at me as I left (his tone implied the answer mattered): "Are you Jewish?"

But then I'd heard the other side back in the United States. Rants against Arabs, Africans, Asians. Why? Young Israelis in the army had to carry their machine guns everywhere, even to dance clubs. Was religion so important? That one had to live like that? Sacrifice so much. Sacrifice everything you are or could be. Was the sacrifice even intended? Or did you need to? Did it define you? Did you need to give everything? Would you be rewarded? Punished? Did you need to be? Or should you grab what you could: there was no final accounting, no reason for guilt? Was this all there was? This chaos, this madness? And how could it be lived if so? Was that what it was: figuring that out?

It was somewhere, it had to be. It had to. I just had to find it...

I tried the slam dancing at a backpacker club in Jerusalem. Somebody moved and I fell on the drum set. Trouble (with a capital *T*) ensued.

Outside the city at Hadassah Medical Center, I visited the synagogue where Marc Chagall had designed twelve stained glass windows to represent each of the twelve tribes of the Old Testament. Each was a different color of the spectrum with a menorah, doves bearing olive branches of peace, the world. Three had to be replaced in 1967 after injury in one of Israel's numerous wars. It was one of the most beautiful things I'd ever seen.

When I tried talking to the Swedish girls from the Petra Hostel who rode out on the bus with me, they ignored me.

What the fuck was I doing here? Anywhere?

As I waited for a ride back, a rabbi passing by stopped and came back. "I can see the doubt in your eyes. But just look at it all, all the amazing things in the world. Just look at them. If you ever doubted the existence of God... Otherwise it makes no sense. He will help you, son. But you must let Him."

"Fuck off."

"Son."

"Seriously. Fuck off."

He left shaking his head sadly.

I immediately wished I hadn't said it.

Living with my second grandmother waiting for something to change was a dark time for me. Telling Sigmond as I stood in his office one day as he returned and asked what I was doing: "Measuring your office for the Venetian blinds I intend on installing when I usurp your position" and him grabbing the scimitar off of his wall to chase me out while screaming "GET THE FUCK OUT OF HERE!!!" – even this didn't cheer me up.

Evidential matter confirming the validity of my previous statement – excerpts from my journal at the time:

Fuck Valentine's Day.

Fuck the day after Valentine's Day.

Fuck the day after the day after VD.

Fuck the day after the day after the day after VD.

Skipping ahead:

Fuck the 3rd of March. And the 2nd, too. Fuck the whole week. Next week, too. Monday, Tuesday, even goddamned Saturday. Fuck them all. And their mothers, too. And their sisters, first cousins, any and all brief acquaintances.

Fuck the 4th of March. And fuck anybody I left out. Even the garbage collector and newspaper delivery boy. Why should they be excluded? Fuck them, too.

Like I said: a dark time.

Even my mom's story didn't help: "Did you hear, Peter? Oh, I was so proud of myself. I saved a hummingbird! He got entangled in a vine in the backyard and I freed him. Your father is so jealous! Now I have a bird-saving story, too."

As I chugged my fourteenth cup of coffee that day (I'd hit nine by lunch and had slowed down considerably – it was now ten p.m.) and stood toasting a quarter of a three day old bagel scavenged from someone's desk (most restaurants in downtown stopped delivering around nine), two other accountants from the tax department whom I recognized by faces only entered the kitchen from opposite directions.

"Is... Is that shirt pin-striped?"

Proudly: "Yes. Yes, it is."

"You're really nutty, wacky, crazy, out-of-control sometimes."

"Dude. Like totally."

"Living life on that cutting edge."

"Sometimes, I think I take it too far. And... And it haunts me."

"Dude."

A pause preceded what seemed like the continuance of an earlier conversation: "Two-six-three."

A nod. "Four-eight-one?"

"Oh, yeah."

"That's a really well written code section."

"And two-six-seven?"

"Ah, two-six-seven." There was a long sigh. "Use of the word prepaid. So elegant, so graceful. Sheer genius, sheer unadulterated genius."

"Beautifully, beautifully done."

"Brings a tear to the eye each time I pass it by."

"I have a confession to make. I know it's been repealed with the new law, but I still often read section 121."

"Me, too!"

"And the master tax guide of '87."

"I prefer '83."

"People are always telling me that."

"You must read it. Must."

And then I noticed him slumped silently at the far table sipping from an Oceanland coffee mug: the elusive Salmon. All rumors of recent sightings had been unconfirmed and none for months and months. What I was witnessing was something few accountants ever would in their careers – Salmon out of his office.

And he smiled at me! And nodded towards the other two leaving the kitchen (who hadn't seen him).

"What a bunch of dorks."

I was still too stunned to respond.

"If this fucked up, convoluted tax code didn't exist and those guys had to find other jobs, do you think they could? If this country was a true democracy and everyone paid their own share instead of the aristocracy it truly is masquerading as one? But then we'd have to do something more useful with our lives, right? And then where would we be?" He smiled.

Sculpin was never going to fucking believe this. No one was. It was too much. "Probably all end up as taxidermists, right?"

He smiled and stood up. "You know what Mark Twain said was the difference between taxidermists and tax collectors?"

"No."

"Taxidermists only take your skin. See you later." And then he was gone.

Did I have a friend now? Someone to confide in, an advocate

here? Yes, he was reclusive, but he was a senior manager. He outranked Cassandra.

I passed Salmon's office as I left at one a.m. The door was shut. Only a penlight cupped behind a fist illuminated the room. Through the dark shadows I watched silently as Salmon tore page after page from a file before him, crumpled them into perfectly symmetrical balls, and slipped them in his mouth. Every third motion of his jaws was accompanied methodically by a sip from a luke-warm pot of three day old coffee at his elbow (I could tell by the liquid's color). Then our eyes met. He continued to chew.

The following morning, Salmon was not at his desk. At first, everyone was shocked. When that wore off, it was assumed he was sleeping on his floor. The remaining four of the six classic steps of denial followed.

A couple of days later (during the *Anger Step* after the *Abounding of Rumors Step* when it was assumed he'd found another job and his mail was rifled through for stray tax publication coupons), I returned from lunch to find one of the partners, Annabel Anchovy, digging through my waste basket.

"Need some help?"

She swept her brown hair off her face. A stray acco-fastener lingered there behind the left ear. "You took it, didn't you?"

"Took what?"

"You're not fooling anyone with that ignorance act. What a terrible liar you are! Can't even stop smiling, can you? Let me smell your hands."

"Um, no."

"I can smell it all over you – my garlic pesto chicken sandwich from Benny's that I left in the fridge on Friday. Don't think I'll forget this." She stormed off.

I told Sculpin of the incident. "Yeah," he said, "she spent three hours looking for remains of the sandwich in question. Went through all the trash receptacles in the file room, even the locked shredding bin."

"Isn't she the one you said told everyone her husband bought her a forty-thousand dollar wedding ring?"

"Yes."

"Did you eat the sandwich?"

"Yes."

I smiled.

"Put the wrapper in her own trash bin."

"A master stroke."

"That will teach her to change the color code of the files to match her fall wardrobe."

"No."

"Yes."

"Wow."

"Whatever happened with that secretary over at Veronica's Secret?"

"I won't be seeing her on a go forward basis and retroactively I will be making a prior period adjustment to forget every fucking thing about her."

"She broke up with you, huh?"

I tried making the same joke about Belinda with a couple of other people, but no one ever laughed. Or ever asked how I felt about it. And, after a while, I didn't want to tell them anyway. So I didn't mention her again. No one really noticed. But I didn't stop thinking about her.

After two hours freezing in Sigmond's office (my fingers had literally turned blue – and the Hello Kitty pink earmuffs (which Sigmond found endlessly amusing) purchased from the cigarette stand downstairs had only helped marginally) and two hours sweating in Barrington's office (though they shared a wall and, bizarrely, a thermostat), I noticed the aroma Annabel had mentioned. But it wasn't coming from my cubicle. On further investigation I noticed it permeated the entire floor. Others had

356

begun to notice it as well. A crowd soon gathered round its source: Salmon's office.

Knocking drew no response (determining who had to instigate by paper, rock, scissors and, even then (!), an argument still ensued). Nor did pounding on the door. Turning the knob was tried to no avail. After a fifteen minute search for it, the office manager tried their master key. But Salmon had changed the lock.

Building maintenance was summoned, then a locksmith. The door appeared to be welded shut along its entire frame. It being the start of a three day weekend, everyone suddenly gave up at six o'clock and began to leave.

"Wait," I said. "He could be sick inside."

Reluctantly the office manager remained with me as the fire department was called. A battering ram didn't work (Annabel's window shattered down the hall, but not Salmon's), so they got blowtorches.

I feared the worst. Especially when the door shattered as it fell outward and hit the floor (ice covered the inner side). But looking in yielded no body. I held my breath as they entered shivering, their breath clouds before their faces. Long moments passed. Then: "No one's here. Just this." A small scrap of paper with the misspelled word "livrwurst" retrieved from the floor. No computer, no files, no note, nothing else.

"I guess he quit."

"He couldn't have. No way. He hasn't left this building for nine years. Nine years."

"Well, he ain't here now. And we ain't looking in there anymore. It's too freaking cold."

On Tuesday, I implored Human Resources to contact his parents but was told if I tried to violate the firm's privacy guidelines by such a request again, I would immediately be escorted from the building and have my card key collected.

On Wednesday at 9:37 a.m. Pacific Standard Time, I stood outside Cassandra's office. She had summoned me twenty minutes before and not told me who to charge my standing time to. From past experience, I was to make that time up because the client wouldn't pay for it.

She said, "Peter, have you any idea of the magnitude of your fuck-up?"

I had heard it before. The first time, as you can imagine, I nearly wept openly. Then I discovered she never learned the names of any new staff members until they'd been there at least six months since it was a waste of time. Now, since I'd been there six months, every new staff person's name to her was Peter. Even the women. "Do you?"

When some sort of inhuman noise sounded chilling me to the very core of my soul, I knew the new staff had obviously made the mistake of trying to answer the question. As to what magnitude of violence had ensued inside, I was much too cowardly to peek around the corner and find out.

"I told you freshly pressed! Crisp! Look at this crease! Look!"

A mumbled apology, something like "I'm sorry, ma'am, it won't happen again." Another classic mistake.

"What... did you say?" A seething hiss. "You! Fetch me a slice of pepperoni from Johnny's Pizzeria in Pasadena on Fulton Street! I'm not joking. What are you waiting for?" A streak of white and blue flashed by me. "You! Find a green Honda Accord with the license plate TAXGOD in the third lot across the freeway, the five dollar one. Wash it, wax it. Two coats. Two. Check and double check the buffing with a magnifying glass over every square inch. And don't forget to vacuum the interior. Under both seats, not just the driver's side. If I find a scratch... Here are the keys. You have ninety-three minutes." Another streak. This one more gray. "And you! A double cappuccino, soy milk, no cinnamon. Downstairs. Soy-"

A thin scream broke across the cubicles from the direction of one of the floor's smaller storage rooms.

Salmon had been found.

His body was frozen behind a stack of boxes. It appeared he'd gone in there to retrieve a file and the boxes inside had somehow fallen over, limiting his access to the door and shutting it (which you were never supposed to do – the footnote to an amendment to an addendum to a memo had gone out warning of such an action months ago). He'd tried to claw his way out, but the temperature had quickly subdued him.

"Can you believe this? Can you fucking believe it?" Cassandra asked after calling me back into her office. Behind her stood a locked cabinet with her collection of Pez dispensers – behind metal bars reinforcing the display glass alarmed for security Woody Woodpecker, Tweety Bird, The Road Runner, Opus and Chilly Willy regarded me with pleading eyes. (Attempts had been made to steal them – none had ended well for the would-be thieves. Jokes did not go over well, either, but a few terminations later, no one told those.) It being after lunch, a piece of broccoli covered in what looked like ketchup or blood protruded from both sides of Cassandra's lower and upper second molars.

"About Salmon? Yeah—"

"No, the Supreme Court ruled this morning that you can't shackle employees to their desks. Some sort of fire hazard or something, blah, blah, blah. Linking an alarm system so that when smoke is detected the locks are released isn't good enough, apparently. Can't require use of a catheter or a foley to cut down on bathroom breaks, either. Liberal fucking judges. Bunch of goddamned socialists. Barrington is not going to be happy about the deposit I put down on the system." She pounded her desk with a fist.

"Um, what can I do for you, Cassandra?"

She glared at me. And kept glaring at me for some time. Then: "At least we get to link a pressure gauge in the employee seats to a time recording device. *That* they allowed. We think it might be cheaper than video tape surveillance of every desk, but we're still running the numbers."

"That's good news?"

"Sarcasm. You should see what they do at Rod & Reel if you don't like it there. An electric shock protects all the office doors until quitting time so no one can leave early. Of course, we tried that as well, but they've got some sort of grandfather clause with the state so they're allowed."

"Um."

"It is what it is, right? By the way, we've instigated a new policy. Let me see your parking stubs."

"What? Why? You don't even reimburse me."

"We cross check them against your time sheet."

"And if I don't?"

Shrugging, she cocked her head towards the pile of resumes on her desk (at least there was a different name on top this time – but then she was too evil to not of thought of me checking that). "You should be happy here you get six minutes for bathroom breaks and not the average three point one it takes to do your business."

I stood up.

"You know, through ballistics they've narrowed down the origin of where the axe used by the perpetrator of the poetry violation was purchased to a Home Depot in Culver City. Thirty-four employees live within a twelve mile radius of that store. You're one of them. If it's you, we *will* catch you."

Before I left Israel, I had a sublime moment. Snorkeling off the coast of Eilat in the slow, rolling waves comforting like the womb, suspended above the dark blue abyss. It came. Rushing towards me. A long dark body with a sharp dorsal fin. Imminent death. I panicked, gasping into the mask, swallowing water, as it approached much too fast to flee from. No time to watch my life pass before my eyes, no time to pray, no time to see anything but Belinda shaking her head no at me. But it wasn't. A shark, that is. It was a dolphin. Wild. And wanting to play. With me. Inviting me to frolic in the depths alongside. No murderous jaws to tear and rend my soft and pink cherished flesh. He circled me twice, twisting his body playfully, bobbing his head, and sped away. A moment later he was back. And I was touching the infinite and nothing else mattered.

Back on shore twenty minutes later, I wanted to shout with joy, to share my experience with someone. But the beach was empty.

Next came Jordan to see the vaulted tombs carved into the sides red sandstone cliffs in Petra and be harassed by a rather tiny male hotel owner with a rather huge mustache who desperately wanted to sleep with me – I barricaded my door with the bed and two chairs and my pack and the wastebasket (mostly empty) and slept with knife under my pillow. He gently knocked on my door three times during the night and at 4 a.m. whispered: "I will be your banana boy. Very fierce." Needless to say, the blade did not leave my hand until I snuck out at 6:30 (after checking for his heavy breathing in the corridor outside).

After was the stunning desert scenery of the Wadi Rum where Lawrence of Arabia used to live amid orange dunes and towering mesas with sheer-faced cliffs of purple and red rock. Then I crossed the Red Sea in a ferry before catching a mini-van with a bunch of other tourists to the small village of Dahab, Egypt, known for its cheap diving and western restaurants curled around a beach on the Red Sea. I rented a room for two dollars – a straw hut with a mattress on the floor.

After spending the day talking to various shops about a dive course, that night I took a tour to climb Mt. Sinai for sunrise. Besides the camels trying to nudge me off the trail and, yes, spitting at me, I also had to endure the freezing cold at the top. And the crowding. Tourists were shoving each other for a seat, complaining about the cold, and then doing more shoving.

Slowly the sun crept into view, bleeding red across the surrounding peaks through a brown haze. (More shoving as everyone jockeyed for the best photo angle.) Moses had sat here, communicating with his divine. Being told (or deciding?) to take his people to the promised land and, with it, changing the course of humanity. I felt a part of something bigger sitting there. But also that something had been lost. Had that been the start of something great that had been lost through the ages? Or was it the opposite - had time just magnified our faults? Had the complexity of our modern lives made us happier, had there been progress? Or had new ways been found to make each other suffer?

I tried to feel something more. But nothing was there.

Confront your fears. The thought of diving, of being under all that water terrified me. Especially after what had happened. But I had to do it. That's what this was all about.

The diving instructor told me to fall backwards into the water so I did. But he didn't follow right after. And I hardly noticed because a shark at least three times the size of Jaws with even bigger teeth swept past me. And started to slowly circle back.

I realized my tank wasn't working. "Never make any sudden movements near a shark." But I couldn't breathe!

The boat propeller above me started and quickly disappeared.

Movement to my left. Cassandra? Watching me, laughing. And Wrasse. Wearing a T-shirt reading "KISS YOUR ACCOUNTANT. EVERYWHERE." Opus high-fived Chilly Willy behind them. I was in an aquarium. But the sound of the boat propeller lingered. Actually it was getting stronger.

I woke up.

The sound of the propeller hadn't disappeared. It'd grown to a roar. Louder than the dripping rain. Blinking in the darkness, I reached for my trousers. And then it happened.

The hut collapsed around me, smashing timber and straw down on my head. I was thrust into a boiling rush of water. Swept from my feet and tumbled over and over. I grabbed out, my fingers raked along the rough ground for a moment and then I was spinning in the emptiness of water. I burst to the surface for a second as I passed through the hotel gate before being forced down and flipped repeatedly. My hands clutched uselessly at sand. All was darkness. But then I caught something solid and held on. The taste of salt told me I was in the sea. Which direction was up? Purple spots formed behind my eyelids. My lungs pleaded for air. Whatever I was holding began to move, dragging me to the depths, no doubt. But I was powerless to fight it. The swirling currents kicked me back and forth, draining my strength in this airless world. And then, suddenly, I popped above the surface.

I was holding my backpack. Air trapped in its numerous plastic bags had made it buoyant.

My relief dampened as I realized I was being forced out to sea. I needed to get out of this current. Using the bag as a raft, I kicked to the left, trying to escape. I finally did. Barely. But then the bag began to sink, no doubt saturated. I couldn't go on, but I did. My mouth kept filling with saltwater. And then my feet touched sand.

I got to the beach and vomited. When I looked up, an Israeli girl I'd met in a restaurant the day before was standing before me with her mouth open. I touched my backpack reassuringly, picked a piece of seaweed out of my nose and said, "Once I get the jet pack working, it'll be a proper piece of luggage." Then I collapsed.

The mattress hadn't inflated. The one time I needed it to.

Luckily, the earthquake in Fiji taught me to store my glasses in a case inside my backpack before going to sleep so I still had them. And my money. But my journals were destroyed and lost were the email addresses of everyone I'd met so far. As were the New Zealand T-shirts from Edith.

I never told anyone the story. They wouldn't have believed it.

A baptism. Spewed from the belly of the ocean, vomited from the depths, saved. To segregate long term capital gains from short term while keeping in mind the unrecaptured accelerated depreciation on the sale of real estate?

I had to do more.

More.

But not diving.

The Viking Who Loved Me

A new beginning.

Again.

From Dahab, a minibus took me to the sprawling madness of Cairo, a dusty, dirty city of twenty million cradling the Nile River in the middle of the Egyptian desert. The hostel was the fifth floor of a dilapidated brownstone run by a bespectacled clerk. He'd been waiting eight years for a job in law since receiving his attorney's license, going gray and halfway bald in the interim. He spoke impeccable English, one night lecturing me on the proper use of past participles after I'd returned from a visit to the Egyptian Museum where I got to see the contents of King Tutankhamen's tomb – something I'd been reading about since I was six years old.

My second day in Cairo I visited the pyramids at Giza where men in dirty white robes and brown fez caps tried to sell me five minute camel rides for five dollars (the cost of my hostel bed for three nights). One in particular asked me for a cigarette, not for him, but for his camel. I refused, not wanting to live with the guilt of giving a dromedary emphysema.

I tried to catch a mini-bus back to the hostel afterwards but none would stop for me. Egyptians would appear on the road one hundred feet away and wave one down. When I approached waving my arms, they drove off. This happened four times over the next half an hour before being helped by a pilot who'd been in the Egyptian Air Force but now flew commercial jets out of Orange County. He was visiting his parents for the first time in three years.

At the first stop, I had to step out so a woman could pass by. The bus driver floored the accelerator as I was climbing back in. The pilot grabbed me, but not before both my shins were cut open on the doorsill. A few passengers started laughing. The pilot scolded the smirking driver in Arabic, but he was unheeded. "I am sorry for this man. His ignorance brings shame to my country," the pilot said. The bus stopped again. "I have told the driver where to go and paid for you. Please, think nothing of it." He shook my hand. "Goodbye."

Then I got a job.

A large, rather scary looking man showed up at the hostel the next morning asking for candidates interested in pursuing an Egyptian acting career. Of course, I stepped forward, envisioning hordes of fawning groupies of unequaled pulchritude ready, willing and able to engage in an endless Bacchanalian orgy with yours truly. Clearly, I'd been lured by the overpowering temptation of the decadent Bohemian lifestyle, ignorant of its deceptions and destructiveness.

"But I must warn you," I said, "I won't do nudity, frontal nor dorsal. This scintillating skin of mine shall remain a hidden treasure, I will sully not its unblemished legacy by baring it to the masses. And I want that explained explicitly in my contract. In bold print underlined twice."

"If you have any questions, my name is Yasser Arafat."

"Isn't…"

"No relation."

"I'm ready for my close-up, Mr. Arafat."

"Stand over there."

"This is how Harrison Hawk got his start as well," I told the actor next to me on the set in the outskirts of Cairo.

Deciding the natural light wasn't sufficient, the cinematographer erected a couple of high powered lamps to our left. Endlessly (endlessly) entangled cords (two of them) ensued round his feet, his assistant's, the caterer's. Fifty-nine minutes later, all appeared ready.

I said, "Before we begin shooting, let me get into my character. Tell me how I should feel. Give me my motivation."

The cinematographer rolled his eyes, but our casting director indulged me. "You're a tourist leaving a museum."

"I need a moment to prepare. I must give this scene, of all scenes, a sense of authenticity, a truthfulness."

"Yeah, yeah. Buckle your sandal and shutup. We're about to begin filming."

Four men worked in two-man shifts carrying an enormous pink embroidered umbrella for the director, often getting it in front of the camera so we had to re-shoot the scene. The first couple of takes I struggled to find my center, the driving force of the character and, yes, the director was no help. But I nailed the third take, embodying the message of the muse and breathing life into the written page. The epitome of such and so? This guy.

"Did you see me on that one? I was awesome with a capital A-W-E," I said to one of the other actors.

"No. And neither did the camera. The umbrella blocked you out."

"I cannot work under these conditions!"

"Quiet on the set!"

Our involvement in the film ended three hours later. In my final scene our tourist bus exploded, blown up by terrorists. Luckily the lead girl, our guide, was able to jump free at the last moment. The tourists fared not as fortunately.

"I guess we're not in the sequel."

"All right, back in the bus. We're leaving."

"You promised us lunch," I said.

Delicacies overloaded the catering table – smoked meats, olives, peeled grapes and fresh fruit. The main actors picked at the offerings, afraid, no doubt, of gaining weight.

"No lunch, there's no food."

"What's that?"

"Not for you. Cast only."

"You promised us lunch."

He rolled his eyes. "One soda each. One."

"These aren't cold."

"Don't push it."

"Or I'll never work in this town again?"

"Yes."

We each got all twelve of our dollars with no problem (one of my bills was missing a corner but I decided not to make an issue of it – maybe I *was* maturing). And thus ended my Egyptian acting career.

Much later, I did not receive my Egyptian Screen Actors Guild membership card. Nor was I notified of my nomination for an Egyptian Academy Award. Yes, I felt robbed, betrayed and publicly humiliated.

After Egypt, I flew to Kenya.

Consequent to being told over and over again how dangerous Nairobi was, I chose a hostel described in my guidebook as "a bit run down, but clean and very secure." Of course the taxi driver tried to convince me to go elsewhere, claiming the hostel wasn't in a safe part of town and we went through the usual arguments when he took me to two other places first. But he may have been right. In the neighborhood I had selected, groups of young men loitered on every corner drinking beer at one o'clock on a Friday afternoon. The surrounding buildings were ramshackle with peeling paint, warped boards and signboards in misspelled English. Garbage and broken beer bottles strewn the unpaved road. The hostel itself occupied the second floor of a blue building next to a restaurant with orange plastic booths and dark wooden walls. A doorman guarding the entrance had to call upstairs to have a second door unlocked to let me in.

Besides being ill-lit and mildly reeking of dry-rot, it seemed secure.

Checking me in, the clerk recommended using the hostel safe to store valuables. When he repeated himself collecting my money and again showing me the room, I grew suspicious and told him the usual: I had neither camera nor much money on me and then asked where to find the cheapest food and the local bus station.

As I sat at a plastic orange booth eating some indiscernible mass of brown lumps dubbed beef stew while being stared at by everyone else inside, four desperate-eyed women from four separate companies showed up trying to sell me a safari trip – all knew my name, learned from their scouts who had asked it of me as I walked the fifty feet from the hotel to the adjacent restaurant. I tried to be polite to the first one: "My whatever the hell this is is getting cold. As difficult as this may be to believe, I'm afraid it will become even more unpalatable in a cooled and congealed state and I haven't eaten in about nineteen hours. So if you could return a little later I might like to talk then." "Where are you from?" was the immediate response. Repeating "I'm not interested" fifteen times did not dissuade nor disperse them, so, after breaking seven plastic knives trying to saw through the so-called *beef* – a more appropriate designation: UMP – Unidentified Meat Product – *Now on menus everywhere!* - I gave up and left (I know, I know. You're disappointed in me.). They began shouting prices which steeply declined as my distance from them increased. I looked back at mention of the lowest price and the other three women started shouting at the one who'd uttered it, obviously not pleased. One shoved her. She shoved back. I turned away.

As I stepped back inside the hotel, a very fetching Kenyan girl in her early twenties was speaking with the doorman. She smiled at me and we exchanged the usual traveling pleasantries before she asked, "Would you like to go to this club tonight?"

"Sure."

I'd never been out with a local girl before, but I was wary. I went down later to ask the doorman if she was a prostitute and he told me she was a student friend of his. So, at nine o'clock, she and I went to a place called the Florida 2000 disco (though it was three short blocks away, we took a cab at her insistence for safety's sake). I ordered a couple of Tusker Exports and we sat down on a couch. Red lighting illuminated the mirror-covered walls and tacky plastic furniture while atrocious early 1980's disco music throbbed mercilessly.

Halfway through my first beer Beth set her empty bottle down, so I finished mine and ordered two more. She whispered in my ear, "All the women here are prostitutes. Keep an eye on your drink. I mean it. They'll put drugs in it to make you sleep. See how they dance with only their hips? It's to show the men they're good at the fucking."

I shrugged and drank my beer. "So you're a student?"

"I will take classes soon. I've just come back to Kenya." She told me how she'd lived in Japan with a man but come home when he wanted to marry her. "I didn't want to be his, you know, slave. In his world. I wanted to be myself. No master." She lived near Mombasa, a city on the coast, but had come to Nairobi for the weekend to "have fun and drink." "It is not safe in Mombasa, you should not go there. Many tourists get robbed there. They go walking on the beach, they think it is romantic and safe and thieves come with knives or guns and take their money."

As I paid for our third beer, Beth suddenly said, "If you want to be with another woman here, go ahead. I will be okay." Then I saw what was in her eyes and I kissed her. And kept kissing her for the next hour. On the couch, on the dance floor. I kept thinking: was she a prostitute? But she was gorgeous and I'd spent my life being rejected by such women. So I kept kissing her. Every time Beth went to the restroom other women in the club would come up and grab me, asking me to take them home instead. None of them were unattractive.

The next time I went to the bathroom, an Australian guy spoke to me from the next urinal. "Be careful, man. Don't fuck up your life. Not like these old fuckers. The prostitutes here all have AIDS. The truckers from Uganda bring it and pay extra not to use a condom. Don't do it." Then he was gone.

The club was closing. At the door, Beth hailed a cab and pushed me inside, "I'll come later."

"What?"

"Do you want a girl?"

"What? No."

"You should go."

So I went.

The next morning I was awakened by the doorman knocking. "The girl from last night. She wants you to come to her room."

"What? Why?"

"I don't know."

I quickly dressed and followed him.

"I'm sorry about before. I was drunk. I get a bit crazy sometimes," Beth said, letting me into her room. She wore the same jeans and black T-shirt from the night before, but without the bra. Her breath stank of beer.

"That's okay."

"I wanted to see you."

"Here I am and there I am not."

"Come home with me. Visit my village, meet my family."

What had I done? I felt sad. For her, for myself, for the whole country. Whether she was looking to escape this or to rob me was suddenly irrelevant. I'd wanted to experience life. Well, I'd certainly done it. Shit. "I can't," I answered.

"Why not? You could see the real Kenya. Isn't that why you came here?"

I suppose it was. But this was not what I wanted. "I'm sorry, I can't."

She kissed me and grabbed my crotch. "I want you to fuck me."

"I can't."

"Last night you made me so horny. I want your cock inside me. I want to see your face when you come."

Wow. "I've got to go."

"I want to see how big it gets." I went for the door and she grabbed my arm. "Stay. Just for a while." She kissed me again and I had to push her off.

"You can't leave. I don't have any money to go home. Please. I sold my return ticket yesterday so I could go out. I spent it all."

I only wanted was to see how people in other countries thought. I felt like a bastard. "I've got to go. Ask your friend for the money."

"No! He isn't my friend." She was crying.

"How much is the ticket?"

"Two hundred."

Knowing how she would spend it, I reluctantly gave her the money.

"Come with me."

"I can't."

"Why not?"

"No."

"Can you buy me breakfast? I'm hungry. I really have nothing left. See?" She turned out her pockets.

"I can buy you breakfast."

We went outside. Beth led me into a bar across the dirt road. It was already half full at nine in the morning. The waiter approached. Beth said, "I'll have a Guinness."

"I thought you wanted breakfast."

"I don't want food. Can I ask you something? Why do Americans use all this money to fight for oil in Iraq but when people are starving in Africa, dying of disease, we must beg them for money every year? And they never give enough. Don't they care?"

"I don't know."

The beer arrived and I paid. "Blech! God, I hate the taste of it." She took another long swig. "I'd like to open up my stomach and, you know, just put it all in my stomach so I can be drunk without drinking it."

"You should go home." I stood up.

"Why? So I can work some shitty job paying nothing? I want to have fun."

I gave her another two hundred. "Goodbye, Beth."

"Can't you give me more?"

"You'll just drink it away."

"You're a hard man. Hard. I don't like how you're looking at me. Like I'm nothing."

"I'm sorry, Beth." I walked out.

Back in my room the water was running again (everyday by noon, Nairobi went dry), so I took a shower. I scrubbed and scrubbed, but I couldn't get clean of myself.

I saw Beth later that day as I was returning from visiting tourist agencies trying to book a safari to the Maasai Mara. Drunk, she was stumbling back to the hotel. "Hello," she said. Her breath still stank.

"Hello."

"The way you look at me! After last night."

I nodded, not in assent or malice or anything, and went inside the hotel.

She kept walking down the street to the next bar.

A fist banging on the dormitory door woke me at four o'clock in the morning.

"What the fuck is going on?"

The lanky, dreadlocked Ethiopian whom with I shared the room opened the door and spoke to someone outside in Swahili. Then he shut the door.

"The hotel's been robbed."

"What?"

"The boy: he said men came into the hotel with guns and took everything from the safe. They shot the doorman."

"What? I mean, are they gone?"

"I don't know."

We didn't say anything for a few seconds. I looked out the window and could see nothing on the deserted street outside, just smashed beer bottles and a broken bicycle in the winking white light above an all-night bar. If they came to the room... Or was it a scam? A way to show my money? But the Ethiopian was scared. Really scared.

I removed my money belt from my backpack and hid it in a pillow case on one of the unused beds. The Ethiopian removed ten American one hundred dollar bills from his shoe and put them in a sandwich wrapper in the rubbish basket.

Steps hurried on the staircase outside. We exchanged worried glances. Two swift knocks at the door were followed by more shouting in Swahili.

The Ethiopian held out a steadying hand towards me and talked for a few minutes to the man outside. Footsteps descended the staircase.

"Well?"

"They're gone. They took the doorman and left. But everything is gone from the safe. Passports, cash, cameras."

"How did they get inside?"

"I think the doorman let them in. Why else would they take him?"

"And the police?"

"They said they'd come in the morning." He rubbed his chin. "The robbers told the office manager they would come back."

"He told the police that?"

"The police said them returning was a bluff."

I sat down on my bed.

"Did you lose much?" he asked me.

"No, nothing. I didn't trust him." I turned over my hands in my lap. "Do you think the doorman is dead?"

"We should leave here. When it's light. The police can make trouble."

A whole other world. I nodded and began to pack. "I came here because the guidebook said it was very secure." Thinking I shouldn't, I slipped my knife into my boot.

"Nowhere in Nairobi is safe. Even the five star hotels. The Hilton was held up three years ago. And you know about the American embassy bombing."

I laid down on the bed to await sunrise. It was a long wait.

Another knock on the door an hour later. I sat up sharply. So did my roommate. We exchanged glances just as the door opened.

A stout man, his face obscured by shadow, stood in the doorframe garbed in a long black coat and brandishing a sizable pistol.

I didn't move. I couldn't.

"You guys heard about the robbery?" The stout man stepped into the room, revealing his Caucasian countenance.

"Yes," I gasped in relief.

"Apparently they might come back." He raised the weapon in his hand. "I'd like to see them try."

"I wouldn't," the Ethiopian said.

"I definitely and, without further necessity to ruminate on the matter, would not," I seconded, trying to calm myself with the words.

"If they think they can frighten us into submission, they're sorely mistaken. We're made of better stuff than that: we Americans. We shall not let terrorism intimidate us, nor tyranny reign. If they wish to visit violence upon us, I say most emphatically *Bring it!* We won't let them rob us without a fight. What's mine is mine, not theirs. No man will back me down. Especially some petty Kenyan thief."

"You're nuts. Are dirty clothes worth dying for?"

"If we let them take our underwear, where does it end? Where does it end?"

"Um."

"Are you with me?"

"Um."

"Aren't you American? Can't let the savages think they've won. Can't let them think we're afraid."

"They may take our lives, but they'll never take our luggage?"

"This is not a joking matter. We draw a line in the sand now."

I stepped out of bed and walked to the door as if to walk by. "Excuse me." Because of the position of the beds, the man had to step back into the corridor to let me pass. I shut the door in his face and locked it.

At seven o'clock, Mike and I went downstairs. The police were there, dressed in brightly-colored nylon jumpsuits with pink zippers – they looked like they were about to go jogging. Fat and corrupt looking with greedy eyes, only one had a pad of paper and a pen and I think he was taking breakfast orders.

"You are guests here? What did you have in the safe?"

"Nothing. We must go, we have a plane to catch."

He hesitated. "Nothing?" He looked at our clothes, at our backpacks. Someone called to him from inside the management office. "Wait here."

After exchanged glances, Mike and I fled down the stairs.

We zigged, we zagged, we faked right, faked left, stormed up the middle and somehow, someway (amidst much heart hammering and hand sweating) reached the bank a few blocks away where Mike wanted to deposit the cash he was carrying. I stood with the packs in the middle as he waited in line. It was the craziest bank I'd ever been in. People wandered everywhere, many more interested in what others were withdrawing than in visiting a teller. When Mike finished ten minutes later, I asked him, "Did you open an account?"

"They're assholes. Let's get out of here."

"Should we get a cab?" I asked.

"I don't trust them. We'll be there in a minute."

No smile was ever as welcome as the one that greeted me at the reception desk of the Nairobi YMCA and those of the two armed security guards outside. "Hello, sir, how are you?"

"I've had better mornings, but thanks for asking. You have a room?"

"Of course, sir. With or without air conditioning?"

I hugged him.

So Mike and I shared a room where I laid down on my bed, relishing the idea of a swim in the enormous pool after a nap. Mike left to eat something.

I'd just closed my eyes when Mike reappeared in the doorway. "I've got to leave. They kicked me out."

"We've been here three minutes!"

"You can stay."

"What happened?"

"Well, I killed two tourists here. Are you afraid?"

"I strangled five last week. Are you kidding?" He giggled. "What did you do?"

"Well... I used to stay here a lot. But I'd find other tourists and organize a car to go to the parks and not buy any tours. They got mad and kicked me out. One guy even threatened me, but that was a couple of years ago. I thought they'd forgotten."

"They didn't forget."

"No."

"Where will you go?"

"All the overland truck tours stay at this campground that has a hostel. It's safe."

"I'll come with you." I hadn't seen any other backpackers and I didn't want to be alone.

The whole walk to Upper Hill Campground I wished I'd stayed in the YMCA. Everyone we passed stared at us. Cars slowed down as they drove alongside. But we made it.

The next afternoon I wandered into the hostel living room where the television set was playing the news. The screen showed the bank Mike and I had been in the morning before and then a hysterical woman being dragged from a car by three policemen in front of a gas station. Two men were pulled from the other side of the car. The car looked vaguely familiar. Was that a fake tiger-skin interior? It cut away to other news.

Mike sat on a couch with his mouth wide open. "What was that?" I asked him.

376

"Those two men and the woman robbed the bank we went to yesterday this morning at exactly the same time we went in the day before."

"Oh, fuck."

"Exactly."

We didn't say anything for a few minutes. "That woman was really upset."

"If convicted of robbing a bank in Kenya, you get the death penalty."

Mike invited me to join him at an Ethiopian restaurant the next day for lunch where it was "safe. Or as safe as Nairobi can be. And cheap." Even though we'd been cooped up in the walled campground compound for two days, Mike didn't want to walk the ten minutes to get there. "No, the bus is very cheap. Walking burns energy. Food creates energy. Food costs money. Walking costs money."

"Okay."

We ordered the special kifto, a greasy mélange of fried beef on a spongy brown bread used to pick up and eat the meat with – similar to a Mexican tortilla – called injera. Unidentified condiments of the green and white variety were urged upon me by Mike as "delicious and flavorful." I tried them both and paid dearly for such folly later. (Travel Tip #19 – When offered the local version of stinky green cabbage, decline politely but firmly.)

"Do you know much about my country?" Mike asked, twisting a finger in his dreadlocks and then touching the injera that we both shared with the same finger. I really hoped he was Westernized enough to use toilet paper.

"I don't."

"Did you know we're the only country in Africa that was never colonized by the Europeans? Under Mussolini, the Italians occupied us once, but we never gave in. Another battle was fought about a hundred years ago, a great one. The Italians wanted to colonize us and our king, Menelik, he refused. All we had was spears and I don't what you call them even. They're round and... Yes, shields. That's all we had and they had rifles, cannons and all sorts of modern weaponry. But we won. Can you believe it? He was a great man, a great man. He brought the first automobile to our country. There were no roads, just hills and desert. Who would have thought to do such a thing? He was a very forward thinking man. He beat the Italians, he brought us electricity, built hospitals. He built our capital, too. His wife, the queen, came down off the mountains one day and found a nice place to take a bath. As she left the water she saw a beautiful flower on the bank and said they should build a city here. We did and named it Addis Ababa. Means New Flower."

The waiter brought us two very small cups of strong coffee laced heavily with sugar.

"We have a huge market in Addis, the largest in Africa. They sell anything there. See this bottle-cap? Someone there is selling this bottle-cap. For five cents or whatever. If it is cracked and you tell them you have very little money, maybe you can negotiate the price down to only four cents."

"So why Nairobi?"

"Addis has no Australian embassy and I wanted a working visa. I hate Kenya. The crime. It's not safe. All the guns. They kill you for nothing. For nothing. It's not like that in Ethiopia."

"Why Australia?"

"America is impossible and Europe nearly so. But I like their laid back attitude, the Aussies. Take it easy. I had a girlfriend in Addis from Melbourne, she was a social worker. Helped kids who had AIDS. I brought her to Kenya a couple of times."

"You're still in contact?"

"She never wrote back." He shrugged. "Doesn't matter… Not all girls like me, but those who talk to me all want to fuck me. I'm good at talking to them. And once we start kissing, that's it, she's mine. No way I'm letting her stop."

"What?"

"You know that blonde in our room? She wants me. I can tell. Too bad you're there." He smiled.

"What will you do if you don't get the visa?"

"I could try to go to Italy illegally. But it's very dangerous. You have to cross the fucking Sahara desert. Through Sudan – they're crazy there. And then you must take a boat from Libya to Malta. Costs loads. Five hundred dollars, I think. Heaps of Ethiopians do it, though… You know we have a different clock than everyone else in the world? When the sun comes up, that's when the hours begin. Americans can never figure out what time it is when they visit. We have a different calendar, too. From

378

Roman times... Why do you keep looking out the window?"

"It's the craziest thing. No, never mind."

"Tell me."

"It's just... I think there's some birds following me. Ever since I got off the plane. Sounds crazy, right?"

Mike shook his head. "In a small village near Kofele where I grew up lives a species of long-eared owl. I've forgotten its faranji name. Most say it is extinct. But he just goes where people aren't and hides. He is a very wise owl. No one has seen one for many years. Except me. Every time I return to see my cousins, I see him. And no one else does. Just because you're the only one who believes in a thing doesn't mean it doesn't exist."

When the bill came, after a hesitation, Mike told me my share. He put the money in his pocket and walked into the other room to pay. Even though he usually stayed at the Hilton when he visited Nairobi with his parents, I was obviously paying for the whole meal. I would have offered if I'd known he was short on cash, but his assumption that I should pay, when we'd gone through the robbery together and were talking as financial equals, annoyed me.

That night a British man in his late fifties showed up in our room. Sitting outside later with bottles of Tusker, he told Mike and me: "Many, many land mines still remain in Egypt from World War II. Near Libya in the desert. The British government is responsible for about sixty percent of them, Germany thirty and France the other ten. None of these countries want to pay for their removal. Princess Diana found this out and pushed British Parliament to do something about it. I worked with her doing this for about six months. Eventually, the British government tired of her incessant nagging and told her she couldn't return to England. That's why in the last month of her life, Diana was running around from one man with his expensive yacht to the next with his summer villa by the sea. She didn't know what to do, she was a woman without a country. So they killed her."

"You mean they paid the driver to run into that wall and kill himself?"

"No, but they did pay off the bodyguard. And he won't talk. But I know. I worked with her."

"Oh."

"They kill all sorts of people. Lawrence of Arabia, for instance. My grandfather fought in the desert with him – like in the movie. He was inventing all this stuff. He designed a helicopter and the first ever working design of a hovercraft. He was years ahead of his time. Decades. And do you know why they killed him, why they deprived this world of his innumerable gifts? Because he was going to give the helicopter design to the Arabs. For free. Because of the guilt he felt at what he'd done to them, helping end their nomadic existence for a civilization that engendered wars capable of killing millions. An unidentified hit and run on his motorcycle ended all that. A black, nondescript car."

"Oh."

"They even lie about the pyramids. Claim they're tombs for the pharaohs. Come on... I can tell by your face you think it's absurd, what I'm saying. That the men in charge are somewhat greedy, sure, but who isn't. That fundamentally they're good and responsible and looking out for us. And that no one can get away with such behavior. But that's the reason why they do: your incredulity. And it allows them to do whatever they want. And get richer. And because we want our turn at the tit, what scant breadcrumbs they'll give us, we let them. And every once in a while one goes too far and they throw him to the wolves, a sacrificial lamb, to perpetuate the myth of their honesty so they can rob us twice as blind next time. Because what else is there? The anarchy of this fucking place?"

I spent the weekend trying to figure out my next move. Take a tourist truck through Africa – camping along the way but also having someone else tell me when to eat, what to see? And be isolated from the populace. But the stories of other travelers were not promising. A Spaniard's bus had arrived in a South African town later than expected and a group of men chased him down the street into a police station as they shouted "White man, where you go?" A New Zealand girl had rocks thrown at her outside of Fez, Morocco. Africa sounded more dangerous than anywhere else I'd been. And truthfully, I was tired of constantly being on my guard. But then I met an Israeli guy who was interested in climbing Mount Kenya and asked me along – he had all of the equipment. He'd been staying at the hotel Mike and I had fled from and lost his camera and all of his money, but he wasn't going to let that ruin his vacation. His tenacity was encouraging, but another reminder of the dangers involved. Fuck it, I thought. I'll do it. A real adventure. But then I met an Australian doctor trying to sell his overland truck ticket which he'd booked with his girlfriend before they broke up. And he offered it to me for one thousand dollars less than face cost. Maybe I'd meet a nice girl as well. Get to relax for once. So I took it.

The first night I knew I'd made a mistake. We stopped in a "genuine Maasai village" and had a "traditional meal" with the locals. None of the women on the truck would eat the goat killed for our dinner because the Maasai slit the animal's throat in front of us (none, however, became vegetarian). While we waited for the meat to be barbecued, they took us among the village huts and allowed us to photograph the local grim-faced older women who sat patiently while tiny camera flashes went off in their faces. Like visiting a human zoo. After dinner, the brightly-scarved warriors danced for us, hopping up and down higher and higher in their sandals fashioned out of recycled car tires. The great thing was, however ersatz the whole proceedings were, the smiles on the long-legged, long-haired Maasai warriors were genuine.

On the road through flat, endless plains of withered brown grass, we passed other "villages" that were genuine. But really they were just a ring of huts made of black mud roofed with straw, encircled by fences of thorned acacia branches to keep out lions. And each year these and their cattle-raising residents encroached further on the national parks, trying to live in a place with nothing. And each year more of what made Africa wild and visceral and unique was lost. Along with its identity. But then how do you tell Africans their kids aren't as important as a cheetah and get them to listen? Especially when they knew you went home to an air-conditioned apartment in Manhattan with running hot water and a 37 inch television and an affordable drugstore on every corner and every day they had to figure out ways not to starve?

But without solving that, would the world really be worth living in?

Threatening clouds of black hovered at the horizon, concealing and then revealing the elusive peak of Kilimanjaro. Howling winds drove clouds of dust before them, engulfing us in their power. Blood red sunsets blazed across vast, unknowable skies. The fierce beauty of this place, its savagery and starkness, could not be surpassed.

We stopped the truck once to pee at the top of a hill miles from the last village we'd passed and yet, within minutes, gaunt-eyed children dressed in ill-fitting rags with ribs showing over bloated, protruding bellies appeared from the bush selling wooden carvings. Instead of buying anything, we gave them our leftovers from lunch. As the truck started, they renewed their entreaties for us to buy something. As soon as we were all back inside, they gave up on selling anything, and, as they ran after us, instead pleaded beneath tear-streaked cheeks for money. We drove off. No one said anything for a long while.

We passed a couple of other villages that day and each time it was the same: children running after us yelling "Give me money!" Some weren't children. Some were grown men.

Every day that followed was the same: we always had an audience for our meals. When one of my fellow passengers offered the remainder of her sandwich to a dog that had come close to beg (the children kept their distance a few feet away, watching our every bite), the tour guide Veronica snapped at her: "Don't do that. Ever."

"What?"

"Feed the dogs in front of them. Just don't."

She and three of the other girls kept feeding dogs throughout the trip, hiding it from Veronica. But the children saw. They always saw.

I made one friend among the group: a red-haired, goateed Australian named Cameron Cassowary. Six foot two and big, he played Australian rules football back in Perth (sans helmets) – "Not rugby. Better than rugby. Rugby's for tossers. Wankers." He'd driven a truck for a mining company in the middle of the Outback and spent a season working as a busboy at a ski lodge in Whistler, British Columbia. He was kind of an asshole – his humor often relied on making fun of someone to look good in front of the girls. An electrician by profession, he was thinking of returning to school to work in finance.

The tour was well organized so we had to go to Dar es Salaam (not Arusha, not Lushoto) and then Zanzibar before returning to Dar to get a tour to Ngorongoro Crater where we would spend half of the three day tour driving back and forth along distances we'd already covered - this time in a mini-van with broken seats and windows that didn't shut through a dusty landscape which blanketed us in dirt.

Our first morning on what had used to be called the Spice Islands, we spent touring plantations where they grew pepper, cinnamon and saffron. Then we visited the former slave market which had officially closed in 1873, but actually operated until 1993. 1993. I couldn't get over that number. In a space not much bigger than my parents' living room, seventy five people had been confined. A small hole on either end of the fifteen foot long, ten foot wide rectangular room provided the only ventilation. A shallow trough linked to the sea ran through the middle and served as the latrine. Sometimes during the year, high tide would partially flood the room but it was used year-round nevertheless. The conditions were supposed to test if the "merchandise" could survive the voyage to their new "homes" in India, the Middle East and elsewhere. Children were not kept because they couldn't work, they were simply disposed of.

Even with the fresh paint, the smell of the room was terrifying.

1993.

That night in Zanzibar's Stone Town, we went to the fish market for dinner. Men stood before barbecues offering fresh calamari, octopus and kingfish. Nearby a few vendors sold tourist trinkets: wooden giraffes, batiks, salad tongs.

When one of my fellow passengers was about to pay thirty US dollars for a bowl that would probably have sold for one, I told him so.

The salesman said to me, "You're a shit. A no good. You cost me business. Why you talk to that man? You cost me business. Asshole. Why you come to Zanzibar? We don't want you here. You tell us we poor. I should," he unsheathed the blade of a machete he was selling on the table and pointed it threateningly at me, "run this through you. Stab you. We want peace on Zanzibar. We don't want you here. Why you come? You're no good. No fucking good. I should kill you."

"Peace, man. Peace." I stepped back.

He stepped forward still holding the blade.

I slowly turned around. Was this it?

No. He let me walk away. But as I did, I heard my fellow passenger then offer the salesman one dollar for the bowl.

Later in the hotel after listening to the others complain for an hour about the African bugs and how unclean everything was, Cameron and I wanted a drink. Veronica stopped us at the door: "Don't go out. It's not safe." Then I knew it was time to leave. We had a few days free time on the island, so I took a mini-bus alone the next day.

Nwangi Beach, the northernmost point of Zanzibar.

Turquoise water rolled into shore in long languorous waves, gasping gently into the powdery white sand. Junk boats strewn with a medley of floats, poles and hooks cast black nets with quiet splashes into the bubbly depths. Dark-skinned fishermen in cut-off blue jeans and worn-out T-shirts called greetings to each over the grumbling of their vessel's two stroke engines.

The only chair available was one at a table occupied by two young women. The redheaded girl had thin lips, an athletic body and discerning blue eyes. Her blonde companion was shorter with blue eyes as well.

"Is this seat open?" I asked.

"Yes."

"Where are you ladies from?"

"Norway."

"But where are your Viking hats? You know, the ones with the horns on the sides."

"We left them in our room. We don't want to scare off all of the other tourists."

"So you're, what, considerate Vikings?"

"Not really. If we don't wear our hats, other tourists still talk to us. Locals only ask if we want to buy wooden masks and go on snorkeling tours."

"What will people back home think of your improper attire?"

"You can't tell them. You must promise. We wouldn't be able to show our faces in public if it got around we weren't out raping and pillaging the local populace on our vacations abroad."

"It will be our little secret."

The waiter appeared, "Would you like to order something to eat?"

"What have you got?"

"We have fish."

"And?"

"We have fish."

"I'll have the fish."

384

"Good choice."

"So you ladies had…"

"The fish."

"Good choice."

"You two are here alone?"

"Yes. We just left our boyfriends a week ago and are headed back home in another week."

Foiled again by the dreaded nine-letter word! "So you've been in Africa long?"

"Three months. We came up from Cape Town and fly home from Dar es Salaam."

The blonde said, "Tori is writing a book on her travels."

"Is she? Are you?"

"But I'm not going to write about what I saw or what I did. I'm going to write a self-help book for travelers. You know, teach them how to deal with situations they don't encounter back home."

"Such as?"

"Well, one whole chapter will be dedicated to squat toilets. You have to assure people it's okay to use them. People from European countries are scared of doing the squat. I met one Danish girl who was actually psychologically traumatized by the act. You need to tell people like her squatting won't change them as a person. Millions of people around the world use the squat every day and they're the same as you and me. You know, tell travelers the truth that's never revealed in other guidebooks."

The blonde added, "There will be how-to diagrams on proper use of the facilities along with statistical graphs detailing our extensive scientific research on the subject."

"And pie charts?"

"Pie charts a plenty."

"A potpourri, a plethora?"

"Absolutely not. Why would you ever think that?"

Tori explained further, "I met one Canadian boy who got completely naked before he used the squat toilet because he was afraid of not being able to control himself when the moment came. I want people to know that this technique is okay to use, that there is no one right way to do the squat."

"What else?"

"On the last page will be a certificate as a reward for finishing the book. So people feel like they've earned something for reading it. I think people need more encouragement in their lives, too many suffer disappointments and discouragement in our society. Only the best are rewarded. I want to change that, make everyone feel good about themselves."

"Sounds great."

"I want people to feel comfortable with who and what they are. I don't want them always to be straining to be something more: richer, thinner, better-looking."

"You *are* considerate Vikings."

"Do *NOT* mess with us," warned the blonde.

"Or?"

"It's been tried. Always with tragic results."

"Catastrophic."

"Bad, really bad."

"For them, you understand, not us," Tori clarified.

"I understand." I sighed as my food arrived. "I was hoping for a warthog. An entire warthog."

"We had a wildebeest in the Serengeti. Fought off a lion for it."

"Really?"

"We're not lyin'."

"We're Vikings, remember?"

"It wasn't even that filling to tell the truth, the whole truth, and nothing but the truth. We coulda done with a kudu or two for dessert."

"Did you visit the Ngorongoro Crater?"

"Yes."

"How was it?"

"Hot."

"Africa's like that."

"Yeah, definitely on the warmish side."

"And how long were you there?"

"One night."

The blonde continued: "Yeah, it was crazy. We camped in a tent right in the middle. It was so loud and very beautiful listening to all the animals around us. Until the lions came."

"Lions?"

"Around two in the morning, an entire pride began circling our tent."

"Really?"

"We're not lyin'."

"Yeah, we thought, hey, let's be tough, be like the guides and not worry too much about it. But they were shitting themselves."

"Well, they weren't Vikings."

"True."

"Anyway, after an hour, the lions left."

"And Greta went right to sleep. Started snoring immediately."

"What can I say? I'm tough."

"But you left me some zebra to photograph or you ate them all?"

"Um." Greta shrugged guiltily.

"No, there was definitely one. Definitely."

"Can I ask you a personal question?"

"One."

"Are there any ugly Norwegians?"

"I don't know any. Well, your uncle Henrik."

"He was from Chicago."

"I'd forgotten."

"Is this the reason why everyone's always naked in Norway?"

"Who told you that?"

"A Swede."

"Figures."

"So it's not true?"

"No, it is. We're very accepting of our shortcomings."

"Only we don't have any."

Tori elaborated: "Clothes are so confining, so hindering, hiding us from our inner selves. Remember the Bible: Adam and Eve? Clothes are where all the trouble began. In our country, we have no need for such trappings, we shed ourselves of Western civilization's bedevilments whenever we return."

Greta added, "People should be more open to each other. Forget the deceits, the imaginary barriers. People who travel are always lying, pretending to be someone they're not. But when you travel longer, you realize such things are a waste of time. Be yourself, be honest with each other, don't act like how you think people want you to."

"Go naked," I said. "With sandals."

"With sandals?"

"For sharp rocks."

"So you'll do it?"

"Well, we're much more uptight about our bodies in the United States."

"Explains a lot."

"Such as?"

"Why you're always shooting each other."

"I used to, but I gave it up. New Year's resolution. Now I'm into stabbing."

388

"That's kinda scary."

"To a Viking?"

The girls invited me to the beach, so I had to change into my bathing suit. As I was leaving the restaurant, a long-haired Australian guy waiting along the road reached out to shake my right hand while slapping me reassuringly on the shoulder with his left. "Last time I saw you, you were chatting up the girls in Amsterdam. Now I see you in the heart of Africa chatting them up again. Good show."

"Um..."

"Good show." He shouldered the bag he was carrying and boarded a waiting mini-van.

When I returned, the girls were lathering up with sun cream. "We're working on our tans," Tori announced.

"So when you return home people can see how brown your noses are?"

"That's not fair. We had seven minutes of summer last year."

"Five," Greta corrected. "What's your name?"

"Peter. Pete."

"Just Pete?"

"Sorry, all Americans are on a first name basis so there's usually no need for formal introductions and I've gotten out of the habit to tell the truth, the whole truth and nothing but. I'm Pete Pollack. What are your last names?"

Greta smiled mischievously. "Why?"

"I need them if I'm gonna stalk you."

"Oh, right. Grouse."

"Two *s*'s or one?"

"One."

"Tern. With an *e*, not a *u*."

"Wanna go swimming?"

The water was lovely as were the horrific water-fights despite the constant admonitions to "Beware the Viking blood." I tried, I really tried, but I fear I lost every battle. They were Vikings, after all.

"What will you name your book?"

"*The Erotic Confessions of a Dirty Dorm Slut: Hot and Horny Hostel Hookups.*"

"How about *The Whole World Sucks So You're Better Off Staying Home and Watching Coma Inducing Television In Your Underwear on the Couch?*"

"That's a little less positive than I was hoping for. But I did consider *It's Not Easy Being Unemployed and Traveling Around the World For A Year, Staying at Fancy Hotels, Eating Exotic Foods and Visiting Gorgeous Beaches* as an alternate title for a while."

"The first is sexier," Greta added.

"Sex sells. Apparently." Tori shrugged with a smile.

When the thirty-ninth small child approached to invite us on a snorkeling tour, I offered, "You want I should kill him?"

Greta said, "Let me think about it. But remember the law of the jungle: what you kill, you must eat."

"I'll wait for one less stringy."

That evening we met again for dinner and then dancing afterwards. As we sat later on a couch in front of a bar's television ten yards from the sea, Greta asked me, "Does it get lonely traveling on your own?"

"You know, thinking about it, whenever I feel my lowest, I always seem to meet someone. I'm not sure if it means anything, but it keeps happening. I know it sounds lame, but I guess you've got to just keep going and eventually you'll meet a beautiful Viking."

She smiled but didn't say anything, so I kissed her. And then I kissed her again. "Let's get out of here."

We walked out of the bar hand in hand.

After walking along the beach with a couple of stops, we ended up back at my room. "Come in."

"I don't know."

I shrugged. "Whatever you're comfortable with."

"Okay. But keep the door open."

We sat down on one of the beds. "What will you do when you go back?" she asked.

"I've got balance sheets to foot, organizational costs to amortize, furniture and fixtures to depreciate. Baby."

"Huh?"

"Accounting."

"Do you like it?"

"I don't know. Some parts, I guess. It's what I'm good at."

"What else are you good at?" She smiled.

We kissed for a while.

"Close the door," she said.

"You're awake?"

"I'm intrigued by this traveling naked idea."

Smiling, she sat up in bed. "Oh?"

"Well, it has disadvantages."

"Such as?"

"You need to use a lot more sunscreen. That can get expensive over here. Almost prohibitively so."

"And?"

"Mosquitoes can cause trouble."

"Cactus."

"And those thorny African bushes."

"Acacia?"

"Yep."

"You're not finished."

"Nudity is really an open invitation to religious persecution. From those who want you to erect barriers and be like them."

Greta covered herself with the sheet.

Once that was dealt with, I said, "Traveling naked does have advantages, however."

"Such as?"

"No more laundry."

"You speak the truth, the whole truth, and nothing but."

"You can travel lighter. Less time needed to pack."

"Both positives."

"You're forced to stay in better shape, eat healthier."

"There's more."

"You blend in better while traveling in third world countries."

"Anything else?"

"No more worrying about what to wear."

"Do you always have such deep intellectual thoughts?"

"Shutup."

"That's your comeback? I'm surprised you didn't say please."

"Please pause to ponder the retorts I return of a heinous and most prolific nature fraught with scathing acidity that ensue forthwith and henceforth, lacking any delay or quarter, in an unrelenting and deluge-like manner."

"Okay."

"Um."

"I'm waiting."

"Um."

"Still waiting."

"Please shutup?"

"You weren't kidding," she said.

"About what?"

"Your kisses being A Force To Be Reckoned With. That's in capital letters, by the way."

"And?"

"Oh, right. *And* A Miracle of the Modern World. Capital letters again."

After more feats of strength and derring-do while locked in hand-to-ahem combat with the Viking, I still couldn't sleep. So I spent the night watching the lovely curve of her half-covered back and her serene face framed by the scatters of her soft blonde hair. I didn't mind.

The next day was the most perfect of my life.

It began with the girls asking me to cut their pineapple with a borrowed machete. I'd learned how to cut the pieces in spirals from a Malaysian traveling with his girlfriend in Fiji; it wasn't difficult but the girls were impressed. That was nice.

And then I thought it would all come apart. Halfway through eating the pineapple, Cameron appeared. "Aren't you going to introduce me to your jaw-droppingly gorgeous friends, Pete?"

"Ladies, this is Cam. Cam, this is Greta and Tori."

"Please, Pete. Address me by my true and proper name: Super Big Cameron. Any abbreviations or truncations of such title are ardently discouraged."

Tori said, "Hi, Cam." An arched eyebrow from my Australian companion drew a "I'm sorry. Hi, Super Big Cameron." And I knew it was all going to be all right.

Then came [insert dramatic lead-in music of your choosing here, only no xylophones, if you don't mind – but I'm all about accordions]:

The Volleyball Game:

A Battle for the Ages

Sand was kicked at opponents, balls were hit deliberately backwards, into buildings or missed intentionally. Assorted anatomical parts were used to serve - forehead, foot, bottom, right elbow. When things looked grim for us, as if the good fight was lost, destroyed and forever out of reach (the dream being most emphatically over), I took to catching the ball, stomping or goose-stepping to the net and spiking it with both hands over the other side. Shoving matches ensued, most instigated and won triumphantly and with much fanfare by those of the opposite, way way fairer sex. Warnings such as "It's all fun and games until someone loses an eye!" were expressed adamantly and vociferously but were not heeded. I admit that once or twice I dove cowardly for cover with arms protecting my head when a particularly high serve came my way. Taunts such as "You're over, finished, done, through, nothing." were bandied back and forth as was the retort "Your impotent persiflage shits me to tears!" More than one tear was shed over hurt feelings. Blood was spilt, butts were bruised. And yet, and yet, it was perfect.

Greta handed me her collection of shells as we walked along the beach after I'd lost yet another Greco-Roman wrestling match in the sea (a couple of illegal holds had disqualified me - defeat had never been so sweet). "Can you carry these? My arms are tired."

"They are a bit heavy."

"Know where I'm gonna put them at home?"

"Where?"

"On a shelf."

"Shellacked?"

"Surely."

"I need a rest. Shall we sit?"

Greta arranged her towel a little to the left, a little to the right before just so and then sat down. All was for naught as I immediately messed it up crushing her face into mine.

Suddenly a kite crashed into my back and a chorus of barefoot children dressed in rags began laughing. And so did I. They retrieved their kite and more tongue hockey ensued with the Viking. But, like most blissful things in life, it was not to last for it was all too soon raining kites once more. "Little monsters," I laughed. "I might have to kill them all."

"Let me get the one in the blue. He looks tasty."

"Deal."

At dinner, Cam tapped his glass and said, "Pete, don't you have an announcement to make?"

"You promised you wouldn't tell."

"I couldn't keep such joyous tidings to myself."

"I wanted to save it for later... All right, all right. Cam and I got engaged this afternoon." The girls laughed.

"Well, I haven't told the bugger I'd accept."

"You know you'll cave eventually."

"Where's my ring?"

Others: "Yeah, show us the ring. Show us the ring."

I placed the bottleneck beer label on his pinky. "Be mine and you'll make me the happiest man alive."

Greta said, "Pete, would you pass the salt?"

I teased: "What will you pay me?"

"I think I already did."

Everyone around the table burst out laughing.

"Awesome."

"You know, it's getting quite annoying. Don't you know any other words besides awesome?"

"Like splendid, terrific or spectacular? No, not at all. Isn't it—"

"Awesome?"

"Yep."

Later that night returning from the bathroom, I noticed Greta had nicely folded on the opposite bed the T-shirt I'd hung up to dry earlier that day – acquired in Cairo as a replacement for those lost in Dahab, it said "Kiss your accountant. Lasciviously." in 17 languages, including Arabic and, what I was most proud of, Navajo. Innocuous as the act was, its motivation stirred me to the core.

After we made love a second time, Greta slipped to the side and went to sleep, making soft contented noises in her sleep. I couldn't sleep. I lay beside her, watching her beautiful face.

Despite my wishes, daylight crept into the room. Greta opened her eyes and saw me looking at her. She smiled and we said nothing for a long while. Then: "You don't want me to leave, do you?"

"But you have to." I handed her the brassiere off the other bed.

"Not yet."

At the door to the bus, Greta turned me towards her. "This is how we say goodbye in Norwegian." She kissed me softly, cradling my face in her hands. "Du har vakre oyne, jeg vil pule dig na."

"Which means?"

She pressed a folded scrap of paper into my hands, then gently nudged me onto the bus with one hand while the other still clasped my cheek. I nodded and boarded the bus. In my window seat, I unfolded the paper. *You have beautiful eyes, I want to fuck you now.* I looked up laughing but still the bus pulled away and left Greta smiling at the side of the road with tears in her eyes and Tori sticking her tongue out with her thumbs in her ears.

In my pocket, I found another note: *P.S. I will totally kick your ass again in volleyball, I hope you know that much.*

396

Had I lost something? Everything?

Cam placed a reassuring hand on my shoulder. "What was the blonde's name again?" He smiled.

"Can't remember."

He laughed and tightened his grip before releasing me.

Later I asked, "How'd it go with Tori?"

"As expected."

"Really?"

"There's a reason they call me Super Big Cameron... No, but she's a great girl, really keyed in. And what a body. She's a fitness instructor back home. She's even coming to Australia next year. But she's engaged... I've done that before. I had a relationship with a married woman. It was great, I didn't have to try to be what she wanted me to be. She let me be myself, that was the trouble. Then she told me she was leaving her husband. And I kept thinking I really like this girl, will she do it and I kept thinking this is so fucking stupid why am I even thinking about it? Then she really did leave her husband and I didn't really give a shit anymore and I thought what the fuck is wrong with me and yet still I left. So, no, it was fun with Tori but that's it."

Sculpin approached my desk smiling. "You're going to love this." He handed me the latest newsletter of Net, Block, and Tackle: a California Limited Liability Partnership. "Page six."

According to Scientific Quarterly's June issue, "After a comprehensive study conducted over the past three years of the nation's leading 43 public accounting firms, we have found that a professional whose duties focus on audit to be worth 8.0613 professionals whose work focuses on tax. Furthermore, we have found this valuation to be consistent with negligible deviations in all aspects: encompassing personality, intuitive skills and fighting prowess. We may like to think that all men and women are created equal, but according to all of the compiled and thoroughly vetted scientific evidence, this old adage simply does not apply to auditors versus tax accountants. The facts never lie."

Page 96 of Time magazine's February 17 issue stated: "It is common knowledge among the world's educational community that nine out of the ten most intelligent people on the planet are auditors." There was no mention in the article of tax accountants.

At this year's Academy Awards ceremony in Los Angeles, California, actress/supermodel Svetlana Swan (People Magazine's Most Beautiful Woman of last year) said, "I've always wanted to date an auditor. They're super hot." Asked about tax accountants, she cringed and ran away very fast.

Kirk Kite, best-selling author of 1988's "A Brief History of the First Four Dimensions," one of the most highly regarded scientific books of the 20th century said in a January 1996 interview: "I always wanted to be an auditor when I grew up but I just wasn't smart enough. So I became a nuclear theoretical physicist instead. Being a tax accountant just didn't seem challenging enough."

Action movie actor and former Heisman trophy winner Harrison Hawk said, "Auditors frighten me. Truly. I would never fight one of them. I'm not stupid. Ruthless killers each and every one of them, all well versed in the combative arts. Tax accountants I eat for breakfast. As a sort of snack before my Kellogg's cornflakes."

"This is fucking hilarious. Who wrote it?"

"It's not confirmed, but probably Ron Rohu."

"Who's he?"

"An audit manager on the twenty-fifth floor."

"He's going to get fired."

"Nah, they've been trying to prove who wrote it for two weeks now. Somebody hacked into the newsletter, obviously, before it was sent to the printer. Only about half got distributed before it was seen."

"It's still fucking hilarious."

"Last year for Christmas, Rohu gave away action figures of himself to his staff. The year before baseball-type cards of himself in various poses, each named for what he was holding: *The Pen Pose, The Blue Pencil Pose,*

The Red Pencil Pose and another series with an adding machine. All with him wearing the tightest (disturbingly so) yellow T-shirt."

"He sounds awesome."

"He fought Sigmond, you know."

"No! Seriously?"

"Rumor is that two years ago, Sigmond made some disparaging remark about auditors and Rohu tackled him right over his desk. Supposedly, they tore through three offices, knocked down the plaster walls in between, shattered one of the bulletproof windows and dented a structural beam that caused the whole northeast corner of the building to shudder so violently the sprinkler system went off. It progressed to the emergency stairwell, down twenty-seven flights of concrete stairs and then out into the rain."

"Jesus."

"You know that spot above Sigmond's left ear where his hair is combed over the lobe that looks so out of place?"

"Sadly and tragically the craggy contours of his evil countenance are etched permanently on the surface of my corneas."

"Huh? What the fuck are you talking about?"

I shook my head. "What about the spot?"

"Rohu bit off Sigmond's ear in the melee. But they kept fighting – throwing garbage cans, park benches, whatever they could lay their hands on at each other – you could hear the car alarms going off on the twenty-third floor despite the thunderstorm outside. And then suddenly, it stopped. No one knows why. They went into Benny's downstairs and had a drink together. The bartender put Sigmond's ear on ice and Rohu picked shards of his broken glasses from his cheek as they sipped Johnny Walker Blue and waited for an ambulance to arrive."

"You're fucking kidding me."

"Not at all."

"And since then?"

"Everything was good between them – they even ran the potato sack race together at the firm picnic two years ago - and then Rohu slept with Sigmond's mother. Also: he shaved her dog's ass and painted its balls blue. Seriously. He claimed it was retribution for another slight to the audit department. During the Christmas party, Sigmond attacked Rohu's Mercedes with some sort of medieval battle axe. Resultant salvage value: two dollars and forty-three cents. I thought they'd reached some sort of truce, but now..."

Cassandra met me in the hall. "The audit team at Veronica's Secret needs someone to help out. You could get some of those audit hours you've been asking about for a while." Thirteen months of a while.

"That's great!"

"Sigmond says he needs you, so you can't go. Don't ask me anymore about it."

Exiting the coffee room, I came face to face with Sigmond.

"Peter."

I nodded at him.

"What the fuck is your problem?"

Fuck it. "I heard you wouldn't let me get any audit hours for my certification."

"You'll do what you're fucking told and shut the fuck up. Only recently and after much extra blood, sweat and fucking tears from my overworked brow have you become any fucking worth to this company. I'm not about to give all that up so you can waltz out of here with a CPA certification to some cushy job in the private sector and I've got to start all the fuck over on some other worthless piece of shit. Talk to me in two years. How much will all of it mean if someone just hands it to you without you earning it? I'm teaching you a valuable fucking lesson, Peter."

To control myself, I wrote at the top of a piece of paper when I returned to my desk: *Top Ten Reasons Not to Decapitate Sigmond.* For three hours, the sheet remained blank. I couldn't think of a single one. And then I billed one of Sigmond's clients for the time I'd spent on the list. When I caught myself smiling as I logged the hours onto my timesheet, I nearly wept. What was I becoming?

Somewhere to belong. To be accepted. Somewhere.

At 3 pm, when the junior accountants were free to roam from the break room to their desk or from the bathroom to their desk (and nowhere else), I went to get a cup of coffee.

Sculpin appeared in the kitchen. "Check out this memo that's going around."

There have been some recent inappropriate entries in the suggestion box:

1.   *More strippers in the break room*

2.   *Unisex bathrooms*

3.   *Replace water cooler with a beer keg*

4.   *More group hugs*

5.   *More "clothing-optional" meetings*

6.   *Sigmond shouldn't wear his thong bathing suit for casual Saturdays anymore*

7.   *I'd like to share a desk with Melanie and she **should** wear her thong bathing suit for casual Saturdays or, at least, something a little more off the shoulders*

*The suggestion box is for **YOUR** benefit, allowing **YOU** to provide an **APPROPRIATE** form of feedback to upper management and have a voice in the operations and future of Net, Block and Tackle, a California Limited Liability Partnership. The suggestion box is **NOT** a place for jests or other **INAPPROPRIATE** forms of supposed humor. If **YOU** do not take your future of this firm seriously, why should we?*

I didn't laugh, didn't ask if puns and dirty limericks were included in their ban.

"What's wrong?" Sculpin asked.

"Sigmond won't let me have audit hours so I can get my CPA certification."

Sculpin shook his head. "You know, he had to threaten to quit a few years ago when he wanted his audit hours for his own certification.

Rumor was he started swinging some sort of curved sword at Harry Haddock, that old guy on 26, but it was all hushed up. It was right after the fight with Rohu, so between the two incidents, everyone thought he would come back wielding a machine gun if they didn't give him what he wanted. Ironic, isn't it?"

"Yeah."

"Sorry, man."

After a weekend spent trying to figure out what to do with my life, my first voicemail on Monday morning was from Sigmond: "GET IN HERE!"

"What the fuck is this, Peter?"

I took the proffered piece of paper and read:

Mr. Sturgeon,

Please be advised that your reprehensible behavior of last week when you abruptly dismissed our beloved Peter with deplorable aplomb, leaving him abject of asked for assistance in the midst of a crucial crisis, has not gone unheeded. Nor has your repeated failure to return phone calls. For these offenses, you have earned the brand of LELAAD (Lifetime Enemy of the Los Angeles Audit Department). May you rot in hell.

Hugs and kisses and swift kicks to your groin,

Audit God

P.S. Be aware, very fucking aware that a copy of this scathing rebuke has been forwarded to your immediate superiors, competitors in the business community, members of the media and your mother.

P.P.S. To be crystal clear on our feelings with regards to you, I'd like to add the following:

You, sir, are an otter fart.

As well as:

1.   *The unearthed turd of a cadaverous insurance salesman*

2.   *A suppurating pustule in the dark crevice of my rectal cavity*

3.   *A gangrenous lesion on the testicle of a syphilitic pederast*

    In closing, I'd like to add the following wishes for your immediate and long-term future:

    1.   *May the dull blade of a rusty drill bore ceaselessly into each of your teeth for all eternity as someone grates their fingernails across a chalkboard.*

    2.   *May you be forced to eat pig snot and dog vomit for all the rest of your days.*

    3.   *May a hungry badger burrow savagely into the depths of your colon and a marmot shit in your left nostril.   Profusely.*

    4.   *May you drown in the menstrual flow of a gonorrheal hippopotamus.*

    5.   *May you drink the afterbirth of an orangutan mixed with the urinous spew of a kudu.*

    6.   *And most damning of all, may you become a tax accountant.*

    I loved him already. (Yes, he had me at *may you rot in hell.*) He didn't even need to send me a follow up note saying *I've heard of your plight. Come over to the dark side.*

    "Who the fuck have you been whining to?"

    Sculpin? "No one, Sigmond."

    "You'd better learn to keep your fucking mouth shut or I will strangle you with your own tongue."

    "I didn't say anything, Sigmond."

    He didn't respond for a minute. Two. The back of my knees began sweating. Then I noticed the scimitar was missing from the mount on the wall. And Sigmond's hands were hidden underneath the desk in front of him. "Get back to work on Cocks and Swallows." When I hesitated, he shouted, "Now!"

Above a welcome mat reading **Home Sweet Home**, a sign was posted outside Rohu's office:

Now Entering the House of Audit

(Please wipe your feet and nose before entering)

Visiting Hours – 10:00 am to 10:01 am, February 29 in odd numbered years

2:37 pm to 2:49 pm on Blue Mondays & Southern Hemisphere Vernal Equinoxes

NO EXCEPTIONS!

Rules and Regulations of the Realm of Righteous to be adhered to most strictly:

1. First and foremost, no spitting, nail-biting or crying is allowed

2. Banned from entry to the premises those garbed in pink-hued shirts or any garment of the shade chartreuse – each instance of mocha or mother of pearl must be considered separately by The Executive Committee (which meets bi-monthly and gorges itself on Godiva chocolates and Beluga caviar - hint, hint) before access will be granted

3. No frontal nudity – unless done in a tasteful, non-exploitative manner – Barrington, this means you

4. When addressing the erudite, dashingly handsome denizen of this most sacred abode, use of His true and proper title is compulsory and, yes, mandatory. Acceptable forms include: His Supremeness of Audit, the Great One and the less desired Audit Guru. Variations on this theme are allowable on a case by case basis.

5. Pink bunny slippers or clown shoes are perfectly acceptable forms of foot attire and, in fact, are wholly encouraged – they may one day be de rigueur

6. Crop dusting, rectal rumblings and all its myriad euphemistic variations is most emphatically prohibited – Barrington, this also means you

7. Please feed the inhabitants but only with acceptable fare – see the attached forty-seven page addendum for qualifying cuisine – piping hot and fresh is best and only from designated vendors

8. Keep all theological, metaphysical and socioeconomic discussions to an acceptable length not to exceed forty-three seconds

9. Hard hats are not currently obligatory but are strongly suggested – safety in the workplace is our credo and we cannot be held responsible fiscally or morally for any untoward consequence of cranial impairment if such item is not utilized

10. Time spent reading this sign can and will not be charged to any of my clients.

Punishment for any and all transgressions or deviations of the aforesaid Audit House Tenements will be swift, gruesome and truly hideous. No quarter shall ever be considered and certainly never ever ever given. Ever. Insubordination carries a similarly ghastly reward.

I made sure to wipe my feet and then knocked.

"Come in."

I opened the door. "I'm Peter Pollack."

"Wipe your feet and come in." I did so again and entered.

"Ron, you're my fucking hero."

"Please. Call me Audit God."

I laughed.

"I'm fucking serious. And don't you cocksuckers laugh. Respect. Show some fucking respect… Haiku has got some big fucking balls, laughing at me like that." Rohu removed his giant framed dark glasses and stared "Haiku" down with seething beady black eyes. He had the build of a middle-aged accountant – round in the middle and soft around the edges – but the sheer girth of him and vicious sharpness of his teeth made him something I would not want to tangle with lacking full body armor, a riot helmet and a fully-charged electric cattle prod. Above cheekbones as imposing as ramparts, he slicked back his unruly black hair with some sort of designer style grease that went perfect with his two gold chains (one which read "Debit this", the other "Destined to Consolidate"), innumerable thin bracelets and a tailored white shirt with the initials RR stitched on each French cuff (his diamond-studded gold cufflinks were AK-47s).

He put back on his dark sunglasses and turned back to me. "Meet the boys." He gestured at the men surrounding him. "This is The Professor, The Chosen One, The Pimp, and Haiku."

"I'm fucking Korean, you idiot. Haiku is Japanese."

"Oooh. Haiku has got cojones. And no respect. Go photocopy the tax code and all six volumes of the regulations, including the proposed ones." Ron turned to me: "I'm not a racist, I hate everyone equally."

"As do I. Meaning I'm not a misanthrope, misogynist, xenophobe, nor a homophobe. I do, however, hate any and all whose color, creed, sexual orientation, religious disposition or anatomical inventory differs from mine in the slightest."

"Good. That is fucking good. You know what we have here, boys? A good fucking Mugabe. Young, a bit rough around the proverbial fucking edges, but good."

I looked at a photo on the wall above him. "Did you visit the gorillas in Uganda?" Then I moved closer. "Is it wearing a bikini?"

The Professor, The Chosen One, The Pimp and Haiku began laughing.

"What?"

The Professor answered: "That's Sigmond's mom."

"Watch what you say, cocksuckers," Ron said. "She's a classy woman: Mrs. Sturgeon. The epitome of such."

His phone rang. Caller ID identified it as a cute secretary with legs for forever and a day and a half. Ron held up a warning hand and said: "Hello and welcome to Accounting Phone, servicing all your fiscal and regulatory needs and desires. For tax questions, please press or say *One*, auditing queries press or say *Two* or stay on the line for the next available operator." He started singing the Hold Music: "*Your love is so sweet, it makes my life complete!*" "If you think you have a scope limitation, press or say, *One*. If a going concern is your concern, press or say, *Two*. If something is rotten in your statement of cash flows, do the Hokey-Pokey and turn yourself around…"

Laughter from the other end of the line before: "Ron?"

"Yes, my dearest of the dear?"

"Annabel wants to talk to you about the realization on the Audubon job."

"Tell that bitch to fuck off and die. With alacrity."

"I'll say you're in a meeting."

"Whatever your kind heart desires."

The Professor said: "And that's how a short, fat, mostly unattractive Indian gets so much oil change."

Rohu grinned. "The world's a mysterious place."

"Moves and myriad methods beyond the comprehension of inferior intellects such as ours. But deeply wondrous."

"You said it, Professor."

My eye wandered around the office. Against one wall were two lists inscribed by thick black marker. The first (not pinned or even nailed, but driven into the wall by the point of a not entirely legal and obviously well-used butterfly knife):

People We Hate

(the LELAADs)

1. Sigmond Sturgeon

2. Sigmond Sturgeon

3. Sigmond Sturgeon

4. Kobe Bryant (that BITCH has cost me $2,987* to date)

5. Any and every motherfucking Pakistani to have ever lived

6. Tax accountants (those fucking pussies)

*The numbers were interchangeable cards hanging on hooks updated daily.

The second (framed behind museum quality glass):

The Seven Wonders of Net, Block and Tackle

I. The enormous cock of Ron Rohu

II. Cassandra Carp's ankles

III. The coffee machine in the second break room which only rarely breaks, not the one that once poisoned and killed former managing partner, Martin Mackerel in 1981, nor the one that started the horrible fire that burned all the bagels on Free Bagel Day, 1986 – tragically ending Free Bagel Day forever (and not because it wasn't in the budget anymore or anything)

IV. The vast, uncluttered expanse of Harry Haddock's desk

V. The enormous cock of Ron Rohu

VI. The Professor's encyclopedic knowledge of the best changas in the greater Los Angeles metropolitan area

VII. The much cherished, slightly cracked, plain blue coffee mug of Cranston Cod which has been passed down from generation to generation of accountants starting from way way back in the Stone Age when Cranston first invented double entry bookkeeping and gave all of us gainful employment for the next seven thousand years now displayed in a bullet-proof atmospheric modulator at the back of Annabel Anchovy's office (which, when it was given to a woman for the first time in its history back in 1990, created quite the controversy and uproar in the accounting world – with years since, however, many see the event as a New Age to come in accounting and Net, Block and Tackle is truly at its vanguard by holding what is widely considered the most valuable artifact in the accounting world – that whole thing about the abacus of that upstart Evan Eel, who invented the MACRS method of depreciation being more important is complete and utter hogwash despite what they may have told you in grade school)

VIII. The enormous cock of Ron Rohu (yes, I can count)

No mention of the nine foot high balanced files in Barracuda's office? Whenever someone wanted a file from somewhere in its midst, they were required to extract it without moving, and certainly not toppling, the pile or disgrace and remunerative penalties would ensue (the creation of a penalty pot was how money was saved for the Bi-Annual post-April 15th Employee Below the Level of Supervising Senior Thursday Pizza at Super Cheap Pepe's Pepperoni Pizza Afternoon (Try saying that fast ten times. Go on, I dare you.), though most years it didn't happen because someone stole the pot – usually when it got above a Venti-sized Coffee Cup brew of the day. Once it was fourteen dollars before it got stolen. Once.). For fun some late nights, staff would dare each other to take files from one place in the pile and move them further up the pile. But usually the dares were never acted upon, certain risks in life just weren't worth taking was the general consensus on why.

Barracuda had never noticed the pile was even there.

Below the lists, a laminated SCUBA license (Ron dived!) and a painting of a bald eagle decapitating a sturgeon gripped in its talons, a mahogany cabinet displayed plastic action figures of Ron (and his not inconspicuous beer belly) in various poses.

"I heard about these," I said, reaching for *The Blue Pencil Pose*.

The Chosen One held my arm as Ron thundered "No touching!" A second later, everyone in the office laughed except me. Then I joined them.

"So, Ron, about your email and my audit hours—"

The phone rang. "Hold on," Ron said and picked up. "Thank you so much for returning my call… What can you do for me? Get rid of that bitch Kobe. Yeah, that fucking one. There's a guy we like to call Baby Shaq… Cuz he's better than Shaq, you dumb fucking idiot. Baby Shaq's got skills, baby. Talent. *The* proverbial fucking moves. He's an artiste of the dribble, a layup virtuoso and, yes, a wonder at the pick and fucking roll…" Ron turned to us. "Lakers are looking at a thirty win season this year and the fucking guy hangs up on me. You!"

"Me?"

"Your first mission, should you choose to accept it, is to get our friend here… Where the fuck is Baby Shaq by the way?"

"Vouching the schedule of investments for the Madoff Management Partnership."

"First things first. Get his ass in here. All the securities are publicly traded, how wrong could he be regarding valuation? If we're going to get him to be the first ever Indian to play in the NBA, he'd best fucking be here to witness this historical event."

"How tall is he?" I asked.

"Five six," The Professor answered. "But with the shit he puts in his hair, six five."

"All right, Mugabe, get Baby Shaq a try-out, I don't care what it takes, whose gonads you've got to grease, what wanton dalliances and torrid maulings of an erotic persuasion you must endure, make it happen. Fake right, fake left, then go up the fucking middle. Call the General Manager, the Head Coach, the daughters of both. Here are their numbers. Both have some really nice changas. Ooooh. Very nice. Perky, succulent, bra bursting – everything a young Mugabe could want in a changa and more. Suckle their cunts, toy lovingly yet persistently with their clitorises. Show me just how dedicated you are to this firm. And then get Baby Shaq to work on his fucking free-throws. Put up a net in the file room if you have to. Now get out and take the Pimp with you, The Professor and I have important matters to discuss."

Shit. Still no audit hours.

The phone calls went as expected. And so I had nothing to tell Ron. So I stayed away.

I decided to become more proactive, to change my unhappiness and quit relying on others. I began purchasing lottery tickets. I wrote letters to Forbes' List of 100 Most Powerful Women in the World asking them to adopt me. Neither worked. Nor did trademarking the expressions "Closest out the door" and "It is what it is" – Ron already owned them.

Outside I stood in the sun and watched the cars pass along Flower Boulevard. A pigeon flew by, smirking at me. "What the fuck is wrong with Young Mugabe?"

"Hey, Ron."

"Well?"

"Nothing."

"I fucking asked you the question. On the rare occasions in this

410

life when someone asks you this question and actually means to help, I strongly advise you fucking answer."

"Sigmond won't give me audit hours so I can get licensed."

"I'll get you your fucking audit hours, don't you worry. But you gotta do something for me. Quid pro fucking quo."

"What?"

"Get me Ankles, man."

"Ankles?"

"Ankles. What the fuck's her name? Cassandra. You have no idea what those lean, lustrous lines do to me. Tomorrow. I want her waiting for me. Snip, snap. Handcuffed upside down from the ceiling with her steaming wet pussy wide fucking open in all its fragrant splendor while her velvety tongue twists sinuously around my prolific prick as she hums a melancholy melody. So I can burrow my nose like a curious badger into the perfumed folds of her juicy cunt. Make that big wrinkled ass of hers wriggle in perverse delight. Right here, right now. Shackle her wrists to the desk, man. And her bony, oh-so-delicate ankles to the chandelier."

"Deal."

"Good. That is good. A good fucking young Mugabe." He hitched up his belt over his considerable gut and we started walking back towards the building entrance. "Did I ever tell you about the fight I had with Sigmond? He pushed me too far. Too far. So one day, I just had to regulate him. We knocked down the fucking walls, went through an office, down a fire escape. Then we kept going in the street. Afterward we went inside some bar, all covered in blood, and had a beer together. Like men. We got it out of our system. None of this bullshit, complaining behind people's backs behind closed doors. Intrigues and plots to bring about others' downfalls. Just the pure, unprejudiced pursuit of ass." He gripped my shoulder. "I'll talk to him."

And then somehow, someway: success! I was scheduled for an audit job with Ron, The Professor and Haiku (Kory Koi) at a slaughterhouse.

At the door to the corporate office on the first day of field work, Ron said, "We've got some really good changas inside. Fair to middling ones as well. And one or two magnificent asses. Hotcha! But behave yourself, young Mugabe. Don't do anything stupid." He opened the door and began his introductions, beginning his teaching me of The Way.

"This is Clarice, the controller. She won her sixth grade spelling bee on the word *irrelevant*. She wants to be a singer and dancer when she grows up. She's also the reason Harrison Hawk dumped Svetlana Swan and yet she can't help endlessly toying with his affections. And mine. Her most annoying attribute, as you can clearly see, is that she never stops smiling. But I must live with it. She did, after all, take a bullet for me in Vietnam. And again in Encino." By the end, Clarice was gasping with laughter.

"Myriad methods," the Professor whispered to me.

"This is the CFO, Michael. He played badminton for the North Korean Olympic team as an alternate and enjoys long walks on the beach, candlelit dinners for two and honest, genuine people. He was raised by Muppets and spent a bit of time living in a hockey net. He's also a Veronica Secret supermodel. Looks spectacular in a leather bustier."

"Ron, you promised never to tell."

"Well, now that the video is on the Internet, I figured it no longer mattered."

"Too true, too true. How are you, Ron?"

"You know. Faking right, faking left—"

"Storming up the middle?"

"You said it."

"And last, but certainly not least, is Ivana, the assistant controller. She used to play small forward for the Los Angeles Lakers until her cosmetic elbow surgery. Now she's a brain surgeon on the weekends and does accounting just for fun. She's truly sick."

"You forgot to mention my time in the Green Berets."

"I thought it was the CIA."

"That was before."

The Professor, Haiku and I were herded into a small room with possibly dried blood on the walls (it was really too dark to tell for certain). And despite the abattoir being across the street, the whole place smelled worse than a skunk's asshole. Ron was given his own air-conditioned room down the hall with a view. Before disappearing for the week, he said to me:

412

"Now to fucking work. First, foremost and without fail, this is what I fucking want out of you and your workpapers. Tell a little story. Give it characters, dates, times. Context and color. Breathe life into these flat paper panels pounded from the pulp of forgotten forests once habited by now murdered bird and beast. Imbue them with delicious details, indisputable facts and circumstances that can be used against the other guy in a court of law. Give them soul. Document your innocence, even if guilt is your sin. For in this litigious society fraught with fraud and seekers of the free ride, chances are the enemy acted likewise but hopefully not as thorough, nor as devilishly eloquent. Arm your attorneys with an arsenal of your guiltless acts and honest inquiries. For instance: Donald Dolphin, insidious agent for the dreaded Internal Revenue Service, grinning with greed, robustly boasted with much aplomb that the partnership allocations lacked substantial economic effect in every way, shape and form until I proved him to be wrong, wrong, wrong with a deft stroke of my wrist, displaying to him the qualified income offset provision of the current agreement that was written and approved years and years and years before the utterly unfounded dispute in question. Oh, how his countenance collapsed, tears welling in his weary eyes and victory, both intellectually and remuneratively, was assured. He fled, absconded with much swiftness and his humbled superior assured us the client's refund would be forthcoming.

"These are your footprints in the sand, my friend. These are the relics you leave behind, your legacy. Make them epic, grandiose. Inundate them with magnificence and love. Do not dwell on the paltriness of your compensation, for one day, millenniums from now, you will get a cost of living two percent wage increase accompanied by an ever so slight as to be almost not worth mentioning cut in benefits and a demand for you to increase your billable hours threefold. You will see the wealthy pay no taxes, corporations destroy the environment and dissolve before ever having to pay the paltry fines, pension funds deficient in their due diligence invest in non-existent companies. Do not trouble yourself with such trifles. Do it for yourself. Magellan circled the globe, Stanley sought Livingstone, Mallory scaled Everest. Not for fortune, not for fame. For themselves. No one else. Because it was there, God Fucking Damnit. Everything you do in your brief lives should be for the same reason. Never go half way, give it less than your full, concentrated effort. Because if you do, what will your life mean, how will you feel at the point of your empty, dissatisfied death if all you can say is: I sorta tried? Of all the paths you could have chosen to traverse in this whole wide world, you chose this one. No one forced it upon you. No one held a gun to your head and said, be an accountant. What reflection is it of your choices, of you, if you don't like it, if you don't give it everything you've got, guts, blood and shit? Your pride and dignity demand nothing less.

"Patience, son. All that will come, don't you worry. Too soon, too

413

fucking soon. Because with great money comes great responsibility. Enjoy your freedom now, for youth is gone in the blink of an eye, never to return. You'll get all those things: the luxury car, the house with the 15% mortgage interest payment, termite infestation and perennial water damage, the bloodsucking three ex-wives, just make sure you lived in the meantime. For the automatic transmission will fail, inflation will skyrocket, your ass will fall and your belly swell, and all those things your ex-wives don't take will become worthless."

As Kory and I walked/waded(!) through the abattoir in high rubber boots and stained white coats counting the sad-looking animals while breathing the wretched air, Kory said, "I'm pissed at my parents." (I'll spare you the description of what I waded through. I didn't eat red meat for almost a year afterwards.)

"Why?"

"If they'd worked harder, I wouldn't have to."

"Nice."

"We need to figure out a way to embezzle some of this money our clients are bilking from the IRS. Like that chick who worked for the IRS for only two years. She just changed the names on some of the checks to hers. Iris Ibis. Added an *I* and her last name. They never caught her, she just disappeared. Even claim it never happened to keep from embarrassing themselves. But my buddy in the Portland office says she's the most wanted woman in the United States. She was smart, not trying to do it too long. Got her forty-two million and got out."

"Forty-two million? Are you kidding?"

"Can you imagine? Never having to listen to Bob talk about his pigeons again?"

"Who's Bob?"

"Pray you never find out. Pray."

The second day of field work, the phone rang in our small office. "Fucking get in here!" Ron hung up. I'd just given him my work from the previous day.

What had I done? Was he another Sigmond?

414

"What the fuck took you so long?"

"I—"

"Young fucking Mugabe." He laughed. "I need your help. Someone without an accent. I have a bet with Haiku and The Chosen One I need to win."

"A bet on what?"

"You want audit hours, I'm getting you audit hours. Don't ask so many fucking questions! We need to ever so gently massage the odds in my favor. You know this reality t.v. show: *The Catch*? Where this doctor chooses which of fifty women to marry?"

I started laughing.

"I'm dead fucking serious right now. I bet these motherfuckers five dollars."

"Five dollars?"

"Victory or death in all that you do, Mugabe. Have you not been listening to everything I've been telling you, taking notes and studying them all hours of the night until they become your motherfucking mantra?"

"What do you need me to do?"

"I found some of the women's phone numbers, those that are competing for this guy, on the Internet. I need you to talk them out of trying to marry him. Tell them you're his buddy and he'll just cheat on them, that you think they're a nice girl and don't want to see this happen to them, some fucking thing. I don't care. They won't fucking listen to me, keep hanging up. What did I say about the fucking laughing? Then later you have to show me how to use this new program I got: Photoshop – we need to cut and paste this guy's head onto other guys' bodies and post the new photos onto the Internet. Show him at strip clubs and the like."

I saw the photos on his desk. "With your body?"

"What the fuck are you saying about my body? Yeah, all right, they may not believe that. We'll find other photos."

When I returned to the room after lunch, Kory said: "Ron got you to help him try to sabotage their bet, didn't he?"

"Um."

"I knew it! He did the same when Audrey kept winning the NFL pool. She knew nothing about football and kept winning week after week by just picking teams at random. After she'd made her choices he tried to start rumors of steroid abuse, coaches being fired – all against her picks - psychological warfare he called it. Once he even got on the air on a sports channel. He was actually getting somewhere until he started calling the interviewer one smart fucking Mugabe – he didn't know the names of any of the enhancement drugs – he just made up names. Said Reds, Blues, Speed-Them-The-Fuck-Ups. They cut him off about one second into one of his rants. After that, he banned Audrey from the pool. She was winning for the season overall. Paid her 120% of the entire pot out of his own pocket just so she'd be disqualified and made her sign something like a covenant not to compete so she wouldn't make any choices for the rest of the year – hence the 20% bonus. Then he paid her not to join the basketball pool, either."

"Who's Audrey?"

"Cute redheaded receptionist. She quit to join the Peace Corps in Peru."

"I met her my first day."

"She was way too nice to work here. She even cared about her job. What's that all about?"

"What is this Mugabe that he calls me?"

"Ron told us once it's some professional wrestler who lost an ear during a title bout in Calcutta. But no one's ever heard of him except Ron." He laughed. "Did you know he calls the Jewish managing partner Abdul behind his back? Anyway, one day, he slipped up and called him it to his face not once, but twice. The Professor and I nearly fell out of our chairs. We think he got away with it just because he talks so fast no one's ever sure what the fuck he's saying."

Ron handed a large flashlight to Ivana, the assistant controller. A dollar sign crafted from Lord of the Burgers straws was Scotch-taped to its center so that a dim shadow of a dollar sign would appear on the surface of where the light was directed. Ron said: "This, my dearest of the dear, is for whenever my services are desired." When she opened her mouth to protest, he continued with: "Whenever an IRS agent is questioning whether or not your business falls within the Los Angeles Revitalization Zone and therefore a portion of your payroll qualifies for the employment credit, I'll be there. Whenever your costs of developing an Internet website need amortizing for Massachusetts tax purposes, I'll be there. Whenever you're

416

not sure whether to annualize your income for purposes of estimated tax payments or use the safe harbor method—"

"You'll be there?"

"Smart girl. Very smart girl."

Spotted hyena galloped soundlessly with low-swinging heads while leisurely pursuing a terrified wildebeest through the dead brown Serengeti grass. Overhead against a burned yellow sky, lappet-faced vultures circled in ever widening spirals while others perched on desiccated trees along with marabou stork watching, waiting for death. Bateleurs with vibrant red breasts dove at unsuspecting hare amid the undergrowth. Lilac breasted rollers, green-backed bee eaters and plain doves (that resembled pigeons) twisted from the talons of martial eagles, giving flashes of color to an otherwise empty landscape. No calls of distress, just the beating of wings. A pair of massive white rhinoceros regard us with haunting expressionless eyes as they pause from their persistent grazing. Clouds of flies swarm along the back of a long-necked giraffe while a bright-beaked ox-pecker picks fleas from its host's left eye, oblivious to the long slithering gray tongue rending leaves from the acacia tree. Islands of dark gray boulders rising from the plain. Herds of zebra or Thompson's gazelle emerging from the simmering desert floor at the edge of our vision, slowly popping into view one at a time. Hippopotamuses honking and moaning as we pass a rare waterhole. Two crouching cheetah with curled tails drinking nervously, one always watching for approaching peril. A yellow mongoose darts across the track, the left side of its face marred by a long jagged scar and lifeless eye.

A cruel, violent land of unrivaled beauty.

A warthog with his hair all a-mess and genuinely not caring stood in the middle of the track, preventing our truck from passing.

"Roadhog!" Cam shouted.

He snorted contemptuously and moved when he felt like it.

"We haven't seen a leopard," one of the English girls complained.

"They're really hard to spot. Watch the trees."

An hour later, someone screeched from the back of the second truck: "STOP THE FUCKING TRUCK!!! LEOPARD!" Slammed brakes much bloodied this narrator's nose on the truck's dashboard.

"Where? Where?"

Minutes passed as fingers were pointed and the vehicle maneuvered. Then came the guide's ominous proclamation: "It's a branch."

I said: "And for six hours, the intrepid explorers sat and watched a stick." The comment had no fans. Nor did my follow-up: "Do you think the guides use inflated replicas of the more rare animals like leopards to fuck with us?"

Then Cam broke the silence with: "I'm hoping we're among the privileged few to see a silver-backed mountain gorilla making sweet sweet love to a Bengal tiger."

"I heard that," I seconded. The rest of the truck did not concur.

On the steep, sandy bank of a dry creek bed, flies buzzed above the remains of a zebra, its yawning rictus a frozen scream. Nearby, the killers, four tawny lionesses, lounged carelessly in the shade of an acacia. Their blank green eyes, empty of malice, watched us with a deceptive laziness. Even waving at them for a better photo couldn't detract them from their current vigorous undertaking: lounging around scratching themselves. They ignored us, giving themselves tongue baths and soaking up the sun's rays with bleary eyes, preoccupied with farting and discussing Nietzsche and the deductibility of a reserve for contingent liabilities if held in escrow by an independent third party. They didn't care that I'd braved a flash flood in Dahab, escaped a super close to burning hotel in Tal, Nepal and done furious battle with a multitude of Indian taxi drivers to be there.

So I shouted: "Kill somebody else for Christ's sake! That zebra couldn't possibly fill you up, not with those skinny calves of his. Come on! There's a big fat, somewhat daft red hartebeest just around that tree. Aren't you hungry?"

They yawned at me, besotted with indifference.

As we came upon a stand of trees, suddenly a swarm of hand-sized birds dropped from the sky and alighted on its every branch. Moments later, in a flurry of activity, they vanished as fast as they'd appeared – some even darting through the open canopy of our truck. "What were those?"

"Red-billed quelea. Some flocks number almost a million. Can wipe out an entire crop in moments. Legend has it they will hunt a human who is not pure of heart."

"No worries there, right, Pete?" Cam smiled.

Near a bend in the river, we were allowed out of the truck. And suddenly our guides were carrying rifles.

"For the hippopotamuses."

"Oh."

"Number one killer of humans in Africa. My wife's cooking is number two."

"Not lions?"

"Lions are lazy. Well, unless you leave the car to get a group photo with one. Happened last week."

"It's better to weed out the stupid."

"Have you ever had to fire the gun?"

"Very rarely. Once a week. Tops."

"How many trips do you make here a week?"

"One."

I never wanted it to end. But it did all too soon. And so we headed south.

Excepting Cam and I, the rest of the tour group was pleased about leaving the park. They spent the following two days engrossed in yet more complaining about the bugs and often polluting the air of the truck with outbursts of canned insect repellent. In the middle of one such hour-long tirade about how much a bite on one girl's knee really really itched, Cam asked: "Anybody been to Angkor Wat in Cambodia?"

No one had.

"My guide somehow survived the Vietnam War intact. If you

didn't know, lots of Cambodians were killed besides the Vietnamese. Anyway, he's not home a week before he steps on a mine and loses his leg. Five years later, despite it all, he finds a woman and they marry and have a kid together. When the boy is three, he is with his mother in a rice paddy when she steps on a mine and both are killed. Now the guide is in his late forties on crutches, waiting for who knows what, teaching the history of his country, hoping it won't happen to anyone else but knowing it will. But he never stops smiling." Cam smiled and placed a knowing hand on my shoulder.

They stopped complaining. Until after dinner.

In the hills near Zomba, Malawi, the truck needed to be worked on by the driver Simon. The surroundings were lush and very green; ferns overhung both sides of a faint dirt trail nearby. No one was in sight and we hadn't seen a village for two hours. "You can go for a hike into the mountains up there," the guide Veronica said. "A small waterfall feeds a pool at the top."

"Is it safe?"

"Yes. Just go with someone."

The rest of the group never ever (ever) left the truck so Cam and I went by ourselves. Rounding the third bend, we passed two men standing beside the trail. They looked at us with angry eyes and didn't acknowledge our nods. Cam and I went on as if nothing had happened. At the next switchback, I whispered without turning around, "They're following us."

"I know."

"They've got machetes."

"I know."

"One's got a nasty scar."

"I know."

"What are we going to do?" I had everything with me: camera, both lenses and, stupidly (stupidly, stupidly), money belt with my remaining cash.

"I'll offer them a joint. See if that works."

"So we let them catch up to us?"

"Yep."

420

"Fuck."

"Just stay calm."

When we stopped at the trail's next turn, so did they. The machetes looked even bigger and sharper up close (I failed not to stare – especially at the bigger man's blade which was covered in some black sticky substance of suspect origin.). Cam calmly lit up his marijuana cigarette and offered them a toke. When they offered it back, he shook them off and handed them an extra from his shirt pocket. Then he pantomimed wiping his brow with fatigue and we headed back towards the truck.

We walked in silence for a few minutes. Every moment I expected to feel a prick in my back - they were barefoot and soundless. Finally, I could stand it no more, "Are they following?"

"Wait." We crossed a slight rise and Cam glanced back. "No. But they're watching us."

"Let's get back to the truck."

Around the next bend we ran as hard as we could. And then some.

Back at the truck with a second beer in hand ("Why were you guys running?" "Beer." "Did something happen?" "BEER!"), Cam said: "You know, it's kind of lucky I'm still alive, I guess. That married girl I was telling you about, her husband was in the Russian mob. The funny thing was he didn't threaten me like you think he would, he actually encouraged it. Maybe to get rid of her, I don't know. Maybe he couldn't take the sex anymore. She was a nympho, wanted to fuck in all sorts of crazy places and screamed her head off while doing it. Made me take Viagra just to keep up with her. I had to go to three different doctors to keep up the prescription. She liked to watch pornos of really ugly people doing it to get in the mood. Like people missing limbs, midgets, people with tumors. I got nothing against people with disabilities, but seeing them fucking, that's another story."

I said: "I had a great uncle Sammy who lost his driver's license because he kept causing accidents – he never obeyed stop signs or looked before turning. So he got this young guy from Croatia to be his driver. But Sammy didn't have any money to pay him, he was always broke. He was in his early seventies at this time. He financed everything with credit – had 57 different cards which he proudly showed off at family gatherings. Somehow he talked the Croatian into buying a car and that he'd reimburse him. Well, he tried paying the Croatian first by giving him one of the credit cards. Of course, it was max-ed out. Then he wrote a bad check. A few days later the Croatian showed up asking for his money, really politely. Sammy started yelling (he was always yelling, always) and threatened the Croatian with the mob – this was in Las Vegas – if he didn't leave him alone. Sammy didn't know the mob, he didn't know anybody. Three days later, two guys with baseball bats showed up saying *they* were the mob, that the Croatian was a friend and that Sammy had better pay. My grandmother had to wire him money."

"Funny how visiting a waterfall can be more dangerous than fucking a mob boss' wife... Africa Rule #1: never get out of the goddamned fucking truck without a grenade launcher."

"What are those wires?" I asked of the unconnected ends poking out from under the schoolhouse roof in the village we camped in next.

Veronica answered: "A German NGO raised some money for this village's school. Around ten thousand American dollars. But they decided how the money should be spent. They mean well, but they don't really understand how things are here. They bought a speaker system for the school. Only there was no electricity and no money for a generator or the fuel to run it. And with only enough students for one classroom, they don't need an intercom system. The first weekend someone stole the speakers and tried to sell them who knows where. I don't know who would buy them around here. So the NGO came back and tried to install an air conditioner, said that would get the kids to attend school. But the teacher, who was from Britain, argued otherwise and convinced them to use their money more wisely. Even more money was raised. Then they spent it right – flush toilets and showers so the students could wash. Hoped to decrease disease and sickness. But the students never used the toilets, not once, and instead shit in the showers. Soon the plumbing was broken... It's pretty hard to change things here. Almost impossible, really, when the parents aren't receptive."

"Do you like it here?"

"I love it. Love it. When I left Britain, no one could understand why. My father asked me why I would want to spend my time with a bunch of poor people. And it's tough to connect with them, really connect, because I can always leave and they can't and they know that. So I'm always an outsider. But the children are so open and there's less artifice than in the adults back home... It's hard to explain. I used to go every day to an office and it was all the same. No one ever said one real word to each other. And I came here and it was all different and so fucking beautiful. But I've seen what it does to the people who came here to escape. The drugs, the pushing people to do extra tours so they'll get a kickback or have

422

a party at a certain bar, encouraging a driver to crowd a hunting cheetah so the photos are better and the tip is bigger... Seems too much like the race back home to me."

"Will you go back?"

"Yes."

"To your office job?"

"I guess I will. Money, right?"

"Will you come back?"

"I don't think so. This place, this whole continent is collapsing. Everything is being destroyed. Even in the short time I've been doing these tours it's gotten worse. I'd rather have the memory of what I've seen than return in twenty years and see even less."

We next took a cruise on the second of the three days required to drive the length of Lake Malawi, home to hundreds of different types of fish found nowhere else. "Nice lake, isn't it?" Veronica said to me.

"Yeah."

"Want to go swimming?"

"I didn't bring my suit."

"I'm just kidding. See those guys casting nets from the shore? Three or four fisherman get eaten here every year. Crocodiles."

"Don't they know it's not safe?"

"They know. About the bilharzias, too. But how else will they eat?"

"Excuse me," I said to the nearest girl not on our tour. "Would you mind jumping out of the boat so we could take a few action photographs of the crocodiles feeding?"

"Not at all. Could you use my camera as well?"

"No problem. It's autofocus?"

"The flash is automated, too... Actually, could you?" She handed me her camera and posed by the railing.

"Did you want to be in it?"

"Yes, please."

I raised the camera to my eye and then shouted, "Oh, no!"

Panicking, she spun around. "What? What?"

"Nothing."

She scowled.

"Except—"

She was from Wellington, New Zealand and her cuteness factor was well into the 13 digits. We liked the same American television shows, a couple of the same books (she'd even read *A Confederacy of Dunces*), had done the same hike in Nepal. Everything was going great. We sat drinking beers while the sky filled with red and everyone paired off in their separate corners, many to smoke marijuana. Then I stood up to get us a couple of more beers from the cooler. When I returned, the driver Simon was making out with her.

I joined Reuben, a Kenyan hired to do all the physical labor required on our truck. He would start the fire for cooking, chop wood (which he loved to do – shirtless, mostly: often we left piles of unused wood behind when there was no room in the truck for them), help those who couldn't close their tents tight enough to fit in the limited stow space (this happened a lot).

Reuben was very drunk – the truck kept a cooler stocked with beers which cost $1 each – Veronica allowed Reuben to drink free out of the profits and since we were staying in a hostel that night instead of camping he had little to do the next day. As I joined him, he looked over at the girl kissing Simon (that bastard) and asked: "Would you prepare a meal, do all the chopping, slicing and cooking, set a nice table, open the wine and then let someone else eat it? You should have... kicked her. Not with your leg. With your thing. You understand?"

"Reuben, go chop some more wood."

He laughed, showing the whitest teeth I'd ever seen.

"Beer?" I offered.

"Uh-huh... Did you know that beer originally comes from Malawi?"

"No."

"So does electricity, computers, atomic energy, carbonated beverages, Velcro, potatoes, tomatoes, chewing gum, cotton candy and the G-string bathing suit. Some people call it a thong."

Reuben spent three months at a time away from his newborn son and wife, but he never complained about it. That night, however, because we shared a hostel room with him, Cam and I witnessed the extent of his loneliness. He stumbled in later than either of us and scrambled into the bunk above me (kicking me only once (with his foot) and falling off the ladder merely twice). An hour later, in the midst of his sleep, he began masturbating quite loudly, muttering endearments in Swahili which gradually became violent commands.

"Reuben, wake up."

He kept at it.

"Reuben!"

He kept at it.

"The sneaky bugger can really go on, can't he?" Cam said to me.

When he climaxed, the bunk quit shaking and he immediately began snoring. It was the sickest, funniest and saddest thing I'd ever seen (well, heard – no way, no how, did I open my eyes during the whole proceedings).

"How was your weekend?" Ron asked me on a Monday morning. I held a memo announcing that Carlton Cod, forensic accounting partner for 17 years and father of five, had blatantly disregarded the company dress code by violating the specific ban on wearing apparel with avian elements found on page 17 clause 45 by donning a sapphire blue tie bearing doves and the word *Peace* to the company Christmas party four months before. The transgression had been discovered by the Marketing Department as they were compiling publicity photos from the evening for the quarterly newsletter. Cod had been escorted from the building under guard and his bonus, due to be paid in three days, forfeited. A lesson to us all.

"I was here."

His dark eyes regarded me intensely. "By your jest, I do not think that you see. You are young and lack understanding. Guidance is what you need. You think you need a purpose, a reason for all this. That accounting lacks those. But you're wrong, very wrong. Debits, credits, incomes, expenses: all have meanings. All contain the answers. You only must see them.

"There is a beauty to numbers, a wholesomeness. They are a constant, irrefutable fact. What they are is what they are, there is no deception inherent in their nature. When they fit, when they finally balance, their essence approaches the sublime. Like a changa and a black lace, see-through brassiere, like an engorged penis nestled snugly in the comforting juices of a well-lubricated vagina: their match is perfect. A sense of accomplishment, a sense of purpose comes when they are right. Joy will consume you, only you must let it. Let life embrace you with its rapture. Strip yourself of the hatred.

"Most accountants never see that, never embrace their vocation for they lack the vision. Desperation and boredom fill their lives. Do not make that mistake.

"I've been working with numbers all of my life and a pattern is emerging. A grand scheme to it all. They're starting to make sense. The same numbers keep reappearing. 78, for instance. It can't be just a coincidence. There must be a plan, an objective."

After a moment, I said: "But it's not just about the numbers. Or even your ability with them. I don't understand why you still do this shit. I heard you have plenty of money."

"Actually it's my wife's money. And you can't just travel all the time. You need to keep your mind sharp somehow. Or you'll just spend all your time drinking. And the job teaches you things. Ways."

"Ways?"

"To fake right, fake left—"

"Storm up the middle?"

He clamped a hand on my shoulder. "Young Mugabe. A good fucking Mugabe. What sign are you?"

"Leo, I think."

"I thought so. I'm a Pisces. You should get your chart done. Remember Ivana?"

"The brain surgeon who used to play for the Lakers?"

"Yes! She's an astrologist. You should have her do your chart."

Days later, I received the following invitation from Ron on pink construction paper decorated with stickered gold stars:

As we have survived yet another season of tax return madness, eluding its numerous pitfalls and death traps, we would be most remiss if we did not indulge most copiously in the decadent splendor of imbibing delicious beverages of the alcoholic and non-alcoholic persuasion – most decidedly the former in my case. For betwixt and between debits and credits there is only one noble pursuit – that of the female heart and alcohol does aid that errand most effectively. We could, of course, partake prolifically in the consumption of appetizers but such pursuit is entirely voluntary and, in no way, shape or form, mandatory.

Please feel free and quite welcome to bring wives, husbands, children of all ages shapes and sizes (assuming they can fit through the door), girlfriends, boyfriends, significant others, insignificant practical strangers, random hook-ups, rentals, lipstick lovers, blood brothers, your attorney, my attorney, your rather hot personal trainer/pool boy, your BFF (Best Friend Forever, duh!), anyone who will buy me a drink, fugitives from justice, political refugees who just want to get out of the top secret safe house and have fun for once, Svetlana Swan, anyone but my wife, pets, barnyard animals you're thinking about dating but haven't yet mustered up the courage and are thinking a little intoxication will be just the thing to push you in the right direction...

If you RSVP or casually tell me in an offhand way that for sure you'll totally drop by, you are hereby and forever summarily disinvited.

Of course, I RSVP'd ASAP through email, voicemail and a notarized letter (as did everyone else – Kory even sent a singing telegram of which we were all completely envious). When I told my dad about the party, he said: "Be careful, they're watching you."

"Even after two years?"

"They never stop."

I promised to heed his warning, but apparently, like always, failed to do so. Kory told me the next day I'd given out my business card to every single man, woman, or child within three hundred yards of the party: my co-workers, waitresses at the bar, even a couple of homeless people in the alley outside. None knew Svetlana Swan, either, and could not, as it were, "put in a good word for me."

Did a man, a real man, live in fear?

At the party, Ron gave out blue baseball caps and matching velour wristbands with his nicknames stitched on them: *The Professor, The Chosen One, The Pimp.*

I lost mine, *The 2nd Mugabe*, on a trip to SeaWorld with the company at the Jackass Penguin Tank. But I'm getting ahead of myself again.

Zimbabwe. Where a ruler named Mugabe reigned. Despite being voted out a number of times by their so-called democratic process. He just never left.

Luckily my country's electoral process was immune to such corruption.

Much of the trip had been through farmland, miles and miles of grass or crops more resembling central California than my preconceptions of what Africa looked like.

An incident occurred during a visit to Rhodes Matopos National Park – known for its leopards (of which we saw none), boulders precariously and often impossibly balanced at the tops of wooded hills, and white rhinoceros. At one point we were allowed out of the jeeps to try and see some of the latter on foot. A few minutes later, three of them emerged from a cluster of trees only yards away. One of the girls from the truck insisted on getting a photo in front of the horned beasts. But she failed to turn the automatic flash off on her camera which wasn't good. Even less good was that she insisted on getting closer and yet closer to the weak-eyed creatures. On the third picture, the rhinos were startled and charged forward. The guide, relatively ineffective with a puny rifle against the three ton creatures capable of sprinting up to thirty miles an hour, shouted at us to get down. Which we did without needing to be told twice (the guilty girl tried to run and the guide tackled her to the ground and held her beneath him). The rhinos glanced in our direction but luckily ran off in the opposite. No one talked to the girl on the way back to camp. Or the next day, for that matter.

"Watch and learn as I perform the world's most perfect haggle," I told Cam as we approached the handicrafts market at Victoria Falls, a town pretty much owned by said Mugabe and mostly frequented by white tourists some of who would lose their ranches to his repossession policy a few years later before the country's economy entirely collapsed. Despite my experience in Zanzibar, I was going in again. Why not? "First you must show interest. But with complete indifference." I demonstrated: "Wooden elephants! No way!"

"Sir, have a look."

"An absolutely stunning miracle of modern craftsmanship! Despite that seemingly contradictory validation of profound eloquence, words fail me." I kept walking.

And that's just a nibble, more of my magnificence will follow. How had I become so great, you inquire? Experience. My first haggling opponent: my grandmother. I didn't know much, but I knew to start high: "I'll sell you some salad dressing for twelve dollars."

"It's my salad dressing. Why would I pay you for my own salad dressing?"

"Okay. Eight dollars." Her facial expression told me I needed to try another tack: "I'll play you at basketball for $500."

"You know I don't play basketball."

"Okay, $400 and a five point lead."

"I don't understand why you're laughing. I never saw anyone ever laughing at theirselves like that before."

Three hours later, I broke her down. Persistence is key. Persistence.

A second look at the merchandise and then: "Pay me to take that piece of crap off of your hands."

"Only fifty US dollars." Item: a Malawi chair decorated with a herd of oryx carved into the wooden back and actually very nice – my mom would love it.

"One thousand rupees."

"Rupees?"

"No, ten thousand rupees. No, ten thousand dollars."

He smiled. "Okay, ten thousand dollars."

"No, twenty thousand dollars. One million."

Another smile. "This is too much. Fifty thousand dollars."

"No, I couldn't rip you off so. Six million dollars. No, six million pounds. And the shirt off of my back. And my watch. And my first-born child. This is my last bestest price."

"Okay."

"I'll be right back. Wait for me. Preferably naked."

"Come into my shop. I have nice animal carvings. Anything you want, I've got." Though it was only eighteen hours later and the market was mostly empty, he'd forgotten me: all white men look the same.

"A nice ironwood kangaroo?"

"Yes, come."

"And echidna having carnal relations with wombats? Something truly lurid and a bit illegal: a real bestial turn-on?"

"Yes, come."

"And I'd like a Swedish girl: blonde hair, about yea high, penetrating blue eyes, giant heaving…"

"Yes, come."

"After I my date with this hippo. Can't keep a woman waiting, especially one who weighs two tons. Then I'll come back. And bring all of my rich and rather stupid tourist friends so you can rip them off."

"You promise?"

"You have my solemn oath."

As we walked away, Cam said: "How you've traveled the world for six months without being stabbed is beyond me."

Day Three.

"I'm back. Like I promised."

"You are most welcome."

"That's very considerate of you. Polite as well as damned good looking. Bet you have to fight them off with a Maasai club. How much for the chair?"

430

"How much do you want to pay?"

"Nothing. Give it to me free. As a token of friendship between our countries." To pay a higher price was to miss the whole point. This is what needed to be sought. Not necessarily achieved, but sought. This or something similar.

He laughed. "Okay, twenty-five dollars."

"Zimbabwe dollars?"

"No, American."

I considered this. Pursed the lips, took off my baseball cap and studied it. Stirred the dirt at my feet. Took a deep breath and another. Looked up, looked down. Looked up again. "I'll give you nothing."

"I'm sorry?"

"I'll give you nothing."

He laughed. "Okay, okay. Twenty-four dollars."

"No, no, no. No. I'll give you nothing. Zero. That's my best, last, special price. Take it or leave it. But I guarantee you, it's the best price you'll get."

"Okay, that is your starting price. Twenty-three dollars I give you, but I am losing money."

"No, this is my starting and my ending price. Not open to negotiation. Nothing. And for that price, you should throw in one of those wooden bowls as well. I'm giving you a bargain you're not likely to see again. In this lifetime or the next."

"Twenty dollars is my cost. Make it twenty dollars and one cent. One cent. That way I know I am not working for free."

Cam approached with a bowl he'd bought. I ignored the salesman and asked the Australian: "What did you get it for?"

"One dollar."

"You got ripped off. You should have paid nothing. That's the right price, the fair price. They're going to sell me that chair for nothing. And they're going to throw in a bowl. I don't really want a bowl, you can have mine. Try returning yours. I hope you kept the receipt."

"Eighteen dollars. But truly I can go no lower."

I smiled. "You have change for a hundred? Just kidding, my friend. Just kidding." You couldn't always achieve the impossible. But so fun to try. Haggling as a sport.

"Fuck, that was beautiful," Cam said as we walked away.

In between haggling, I did other things. One was hiking to a BaoBab tree, thousands of years old and over forty meters in circumference. To prevent vandalism, evidenced by carvings beginning in the late 1800's, a uniformed guard with far-off eyes and immaculately combed hair was stationed beneath it.

"How long have you worked here?"

"Five years, good sir."

Watch leaves grow. For five years.

"It is a good job, good sir. My country is very poor."

On another hike along a dirt path that passed by one of the rivers that fed the top of Victoria Falls, I came upon two eighteen year old Brits carrying beach towels. Both wore bathing trunks and were bare-chested. "Is there a good place for swimming along here?"

"You're kidding?"

"No, we heard there's a nice place."

"Didn't you see the warning signs? About the crocodiles?"

"But they'll stay off the path, right?"

The second Brit seconded: "Yeah, there's a pool surrounded by rocks which keep out the hippos. It's supposed to be perfectly safe."

"And the crocodiles?"

"They said it was fine."

"They?"

"Didn't see it, huh? Well, cheers."

Some men you can't save.

As I sat in the shade waiting for the return bus to Victoria Falls after a failed attempt to get to Hwange National Park (for three hours no one took the turn-off to the park so I gave up – twenty miles was too far to walk), I began talking to a coal miner headed home for the first time in six months to see his twin children. Earlier, two ten year old girls had approached me and asked if, for money, I wanted to watch them kiss and have sex together (they'd giggled but only half-heartedly – what did other tourists do here?).

"I'm trying to get away from this terrible affliction that is decimating my country," the miner said. "This HIV, AIDS. That's why I've married. Did you know that you're a very lucky man in Zimbabwe if you live to be forty? Very lucky... Do they have a vaccine for AIDS in America yet?"

"No."

"So they're not keeping it from us? And it'd be very expensive, wouldn't it? We couldn't afford it."

When I told Cam of my conversation on our way to the cheap bar in Victoria Falls (we were the only tourists who went there, most went where the beers cost too much for the natives to afford – effectively there were white bars and black bars – Mugabe owned most of the town's former even though a few years later he would seize all his country's land owned by whites and give it to the blacks, a justified move in some ways but one which would essentially destroy the country's agricultural industry and cause widespread starvation and the destruction of all the national parks which were overrun by people needing food), he said: "You know about the Three Gorges Dam they're building over China's Yangtze River? It's going to displace something like a million people and wipe out all these villages that have existed for centuries. Progress, right? Well, the story is that to help facilitate the relocation, the Chinese government is going around to these small towns and giving AIDS tests to the inhabitants under the guise of trying to isolate the epidemic. However, the rumor is that they keep re-using the same needle so everyone becomes infected and then no one has to be relocated because they're all dead."

"I don't know. That seems pretty far-fetched."

"I talked to aid workers when I was there who know all about it. But no one else wants to discuss it. Not with the Chinese economy doing so well. And with their military growing in strength. How could we justify western investment in an economy run by genocidal thugs? Remember when China opened up to US investment? All the high and mighty language about only giving money to a democratic country which had no

433

human rights violations was forgotten for the promise of future wealth. AIDS is a lot worse than anyone knows. You know that, right? Even what we've seen here. Most countries in Asia and South America don't even do testing so there are no statistics. One day there's going to be a hell of a reckoning."

We passed the men selling tours, those who couldn't afford handicraft stalls at the market and others peddling black market currency transactions. I said: "Did you see that guy selling one pair of sunglasses? And they're broken?"

"He's not begging."

"Yeah."

Then Cam had to leave and I continued south with the second leg of the tour I'd bought.

As Cam's shuttle bus to the airport pulled away, he stood in his seat and mooned me.

I called after him: "You know that I will always love you."

No one else on our tour laughed. It was going to be a long five weeks going through Namibia.

Four English girls and an Australian accountant named Wayne joined the tour in Victoria Falls. I decided to start off right with them and coordinated a group discount with the only rafting company that would give me one (yes, I know). It took some convincing to get all of them to come as well – something I would regret almost immediately.

On the morning that we were to whitewater raft down the Zambezi River below the falls, our guide Nicholas introduced himself in the truck beforehand and told us we had to make two decisions.

The first: "Do you want to paddle or have it done for you?"

I said immediately, "Life is not a spectator sport" and the others somewhat begrudgingly agreed.

The second: the easier or harder route through the rapids, some Class IV and even a Class V.

I wanted to say, "Are we not men?" but waited for their response this time (not wanting to offend with the gender specific comment, either).
434

Doubt clouded the brows of the girls and the young South African couple not on our truck tour.

Wayne said: "You'll wake up in tomorrow or in five years and ask yourself why didn't I do this or why didn't I do that? And your whole life will become like that and you'll die a dissatisfied soul. And then it will be over anyway and what will you have done and what will they say about you. Nothing. Fuck that noise. Aspire to greatness, I say. Bite life in the balls. Till the flesh puckers and tears between your incisors, gushing bounteous bouts of blood. It's time we learned there are no limits, but those we impose upon ourselves. Come. Release the fear. Become immortal."

Fear had replaced the doubt.

"We all end as dust and are forgotten. Dwindling away, memory fading in a room somewhere attended by strangers who probably don't speak our language and certainly don't care as they try to eke out their own miserable existences and feed their broods of mewling ungrateful brats. Stewing in our own feces until their next shift, our lusts now ridiculous, our torments now meaningless, discarded for the next set of television-watching, paper-pushing, factory-working clones. Do I want to end like that? The ones who are remembered are not the ones who clung to life so. It's those who didn't. Not that any of us are really remembered, but to waste away in some home, watching my hair fall out and my skin wrinkle: no, thank you. Join me. Let us take the hard route."

He had my vote.

Thirty-six year old Wayne was a huge man - six five and weighed over three hundred and fifty pounds – and he had a deep booming voice to match. His green, expressionless eyes were sunken between flabby pouches of flesh that flanked his dour face beneath his rigidly square, closely shorn temples which, along with the rest of him, were eternally sunburned after the rafting trip. Originally from Brisbane, he'd spent the last ten years since his divorce following the Australian cricket team around the world between accounting contracts in London. He spent the first few days in Africa trying to get everyone to call him Dingo, but no one ever did.

Lush vegetation draped the gorge's purple and black rock cut deeply by the tumultuous brown waters of the Zambezi. Wearing only sandals, the descent into the sun baked canyon to start at the fourth rapid below the falls was a slippery, precarious affair full of the expected yelps, screams and lamentations (I held back a couple of times most stoically, thank you very little, but three of the rickety ladders were just too much.).

"Are those crocodiles?"

"Don't worry, the water is too swift for them to come in. I think."

Where we launched the raft, the water was not swift at all.

"They let you back?" the guide for another rafting company asked Nicholas as we pushed out into the current.

"I'm back, baby. And better than ever. 6 ½ times so."

The other guide turned to us: "Are you all crazy? Viva Rafting? Look at your dodgy equipment. All patches and tears. And your guide just got out of prison yesterday."

Glares of the ferocious hatred sort aimed at yours truly, the ringmaster of the big white water rafting group discount. So I dove in: "But it was clearly self-defense. I believe him. Anything can happen in the heat of the moment, even triple homicide with malicious intent. And they were mimes, damnit!"

Amused, Nicholas asked me: "What was your name again?"

"Just call me American if it's easier. Or bloody American if you prefer."

"How about if I call you asshole?"

"Only if I can call you fuckface."

Mutual laughter and backslapping.

Our raft did, however, have inordinately more patches than any of the other companies' we saw.

Nicholas rehearsed the various commands he would give on which way to row with our oars (it's all in the grip) and we practiced backpedaling, going right, going left, storming up the middle. He also explained the right way and the wrong way to hold on and to stay with the boat if it capsized, if at all possible. "Everyone got it?"

I said: "Anything you say, I do. Anything. You hold my precious life in your hands. You are my protector and my savior. I'll just call you God. And I will name my first born son Nicholas. And he will name his first son the same and so will his son."

We navigated the first couple of rapids a little ineptly (the girls from our truck apparently were still learning the difference between left and right), but only the South African girl fell out. Two rapids later the guide was finally able to pull her back into the boat (she wasn't really strong enough to do it herself) after chasing her back and forth across the river.

She asked, scared: "What was that one called?"

"*Stairway to Heaven.*"

"Was that the worst one?"

"No."

"*Express Elevator to Hell* would be more appropriate, don't you think?" I said.

Nicholas laughed and then, as we rounded the next bend, grew tense. "This one is *Midnight Diner*, a Class V. We have to get out of the boat before we reach the next one which is a Class VI. Whatever you do, don't fall out now."

The South African girl jumped out of the boat.

"What the hell are you doing?"

"You said fall out of the boat," she called through a mouth of water and then the burgeoning rapids swept her under.

"Oh, shit."

To be heard over the suddenly fierce white water, Nicholas had to shout his commands. As we plunged into what seemed an endless drop, my surge of exhilaration was cut short as the boat completely flipped over and cast us airborne.

There was nowhere to grasp, no way to direct my landing. Suddenly I was thrust deep beneath the churning water with no chance to hold my breath. My legs bounced against something solid.

Wrasse was there at the bottom, smiling. In his arms, he held the limp body of Ron, dressed in a *Sodomize your accountant. Gently, ever so gently* T-shirt. Chilly Willy and Opus reached up and tried to grab my arms with their beaks.

I popped above the water, shouting. My life jacket had worked. Feuding currents buffeted me in opposite directions as I caromed off a couple of rocks and tried to keep my legs together and in front of me as instructed. Where was everyone?

I saw Nicholas and Wayne holding onto the upturned raft thirty feet away. I kicked over to them, swallowing water and struggling to keep my head above the surface.

Just as I grasped the boat, totally exhausted, Nicholas said, "I'm going to flip it." I kicked away again to give him room, submerging my head to move swifter.

I swam the wrong way. He flipped the boat on top of me and when I came up for air, there was none to be had. I'd also let all the air out of my lungs in anticipation of surfacing.

Understanding what I'd done and that the boat was holding me down took a second I probably didn't have. I started kicking for one of the sides. Reflexively choking, I began swallowing water. Purple and yellow spots appeared before my eyes. Wrasse was laughing. The colors began to fade to black. All black.

Oxygen! I cleared the boat and re-surfaced. The guide and the South African boy helped me into the boat. I was so exhausted they had to pull me in. But we didn't have time to talk about it. The South African girl was still missing. And the Class VI rapid was swiftly approaching.

The girls from our truck were missing, too. And Wayne was too big to pull himself back aboard, so he was holding onto the rope lining the perimeter of the raft.

"You okay?" Wayne asked, looking at my face.

"Not really."

"I could hear your feet kicking against the bottom of the boat."

We spotted the four girls from our truck in the shallows on the right side of the river. Then we saw the South African girl trapped in a whirlpool on the left, being bumped against rocks on three sides. Up ahead other boats were being pulled out of the water in anticipation of *Commercial Suicide*. To retrieve everyone and exit the river in time was going to be a tricky move.

I'm not sure how, but we did it. As we walked overland to avoid the rapid, the obviously frightened South African girl tripped a couple of times, skinning her knee in the red dirt. Her boyfriend, also 18, did not reach down to help her so I did. "It's character building, right?" I said and she actually smiled.

The fun had drained from everyone's faces except Wayne's and mine. We had ten more rapids to go – *Gnashing Jaws of Death, Overland Truck Eater, Three Ugly Sisters, The Mother, The Terminator, Oblivion* – and they counted down every one. The South African girl fell out again on *Gnashing Jaws of Death* and when we pulled her back in, she smiled at me. "Character building, right?" But when it reoccurred on the following rapid, she didn't say anything and I knew not to.

438

Wayne and I had to help the South African girl up the ladders leaving the canyon because her boyfriend went on ahead. She screamed at him at the top, but, a few minutes later, she still sat on his lap.

"The river was a monster that day. But it could not tame us," Wayne said and no one smiled but me. The rest were verging on tears of relief from being finished. Though that was not the story they told in the weeks to come. And who could blame them?

I was done with water sports. Done.

That night back at the campground across from where I lay in my tent, I heard Wayne ask: "What was your father's name, Reuben?"

"Reuben."

"And your grandfather's?"

"Reuben."

"And your great grandfather's?"

"Fred."

"And what will you name your sons?"

"Reuben."

"Never Reuben the First? Or Reuben the Second?"

"Just Reuben."

"And your daughters?"

"The same: Reuben."

"How will they know when you call Reuben who should come?"

"They will know."

"Reuben, do you know about secret names? Mine is Wayne Warbler."

"But that's not secret. That's just your name."

"But, you see, I'm adopted. My biological mother didn't want me. She didn't love me. She gave birth to me and then she gave me away. Do you know what adoption means, Reuben?"

"Yes, it's when a mother cow dies and they take the baby cow and give it to another for the milk."

"I am that cow, Reuben. I am that cow."

On the road to the Okavango Delta of Botswana the next day, I asked Wayne what he was reading.

A dog-eared paperback biography of Victor Hugo. "There was a great man. He changed his world. Today, there are no great men. Only artists driven by greed, masquerading as our national conscience when it's convenient, when it turns a profit. Our politicians are corporate puppets oblivious to what their greed engenders, our religious zealots are indifferent to the less fortunate's suffering. Western civilization is deteriorating – the triumphs of our forefathers and civil rights leaders are being squandered by the superficial greed of the television and videogame generation."

"Kind of the negative type, aren't you?"

"You have this skewed vision of life from this traveling experience. The world is not good, it is shit. At any time your wife can leave you, your children be killed in a car wreck. There is no permanence, no assurances, and all your struggles and sacrifices can be for naught. Look at these people, Peter. Look at them. Starving, shoveling elephant shit for a living, begging for a fucking penny to get medicine for their sick kid or drink away their miserable existence. Really fucking look at them, don't give me that liberal shit that you care. You don't care. Nobody cares. If someone did, they'd help. But they don't. And those that really try have no power. Everything good and pure in this world is destroyed. They killed Jesus, didn't they? They whine about it now, but at the time, no one gave a shit. Debs and Mandela spent most of their lives in prison. Gandhi got blown up, King got shot."

He opened a beer. His third of the day. It was eleven in the morning. Barely. "Notice people. No one is a minor character, Peter. Everyone counts."

6 wildebeest.

12 water buffalo.

14 interesting tree stump sightings (two of which were almost leopards).

½ a zebra (the back half).

3,272,106 mosquitoes. (Plus or minus 3.)

Sun, lots of sun.

The Okavango Delta was a labyrinth of murky waterways cut through high grassed marshland. We spent three days going in circles and seeing not much wildlife – the water was too high – but constantly being reminded to keep our hands and all other valued limbs inside the confines of the cramped, rather narrow canoes (crocodiles).

Back in Maun, Botswana, Wayne stocked up for the trip through Namibia by purchasing twelve bottles of vodka. He asked me to help him carry them back to the truck.

"How much cash are you carrying?"

"All of it. I don't bother with a money belt. It's fucking uncomfortable. Look at me, Peter. I'm the type of person people cross the street to avoid late at night."

"Are we having a party?" I asked as we filled his locker.

He waited until we were seated to say: "I'm an alcoholic, Peter. I know what I'm doing. My wife left me because I couldn't stop drinking. I didn't want to. But I still love her. I'll always love her. She is the only woman for me. But I can't stop drinking. Not for her, not for anyone. I'm not stupid, I know I'm killing myself... I see the judgment in your eyes, but you should know: I didn't always used to be such a wreck. They all wanted a piece of me. I've made women squeal with pleasure, so much so that they peed in my mouth as I gave them head. One after the other they lined up to see what all the fuss was about... You must give yourself completely to life, to them. Hold nothing back. Let go of your ego, your inhibitions."

"The whitewater rafting was my idea, remember?"

"You're still clinging. Fleeing what they want you to do but ultimately you're going back. You need to let go. Embrace now who you are. Cease being their sheep. You're still pursuing a life destined to disappoint. Stop. See how things change. Stop letting them dictate your future."

Wayne continued: "If you never look into the abyss, never risk it all, embrace the chaos, suckle it to your bosom, are you alive? A man? The safe path, follow the rules. Their rules. Why do they get to make the rules and do you want their fucking rules or what you get when you follow them? Their scraps, what they'll throw to you? You'll never become as *good* as them because you're not them. Is that the life you want? Dwell in your darkness, eschew their schoolboy moralities. Most never do. Most give up hope, give up the fight, and let the bastards win. And they always win."

"Men used to wander from place to place seeking adventure, strange pieces of ass and telling stories – now it's all about accumulating shit. Kerouac, Cendrars, Bukowski, these men understood. Fuck it all."

"Kerouac died pretty young and Bukowski almost did. It's pretty hard to live that way. Especially without money."

"So? Consider what we do, Pete, as accountants. Is it essential? If someone killed us all off, would others spring up in our place? Are we helping move the world in the right direction? Is there a right direction? Is there a plan, are we going someplace as a race? And is it good? Think about it, it's kind of interesting. If you killed off one half of the population – the conservatives or the liberals - would some of the remainder become the opposite to compensate? Would their children? Is it in our DNA or the product of our environment? Does the population need both to function? Is that the driving force of civilization or does the conflict keep it in check? What will stop us from destroying the world, end our parasitic presence? Or does it even matter? Would we never have enough time before the sun explodes? Does creating the technology to be able to leave Earth take so much waste that it destroys the planet? Or can we beat it, begin exploring the universe? And if so, will there be accountants in ten million years? And why the fuck do we even care? Live for today. Today. A wife, family, it's all bullshit. Women all want one thing. One thing. And you'll squander your days away giving it to them."

The bottles of vodka lasted only four days. No one drank them but Wayne.

A pair of elegant oryx, black and white faced antelope with long straight horns rising parallel from the front of their oval heads, cresting a sandy ridge as the dark yellow sun descended. A quartet of bat-eared foxes wrestling playfully among a cluster of pinnacled termite mounds in the burgeoning dawn. A jittery ostrich floating across a salt-encrusted dune, never seeming to touch down as its powerful legs scissor past us. A honey badger darting jaggedly across a plain at the sound of our truck. A caracal watching us suspiciously from the brush, only the pointy ears of his light brown head visible. A four metre black mamba snake, half coiled in lazy loops, obstinately refusing to leave the track in front of us. The deep imprint of a leopard claw near a leaky pipe outside a toilet.

Etosha National Park in northern Namibia.

The first night, I woke to the flapping of wings outside my tent. The quelea? Scramble for glasses as flapping intensifies, closing in. Where the fuck?

Sudden quiet.

Watch. 2 am. Thinking I probably shouldn't but wanting to see what it was (there's nothing worse than the waiting inside where you're blind – until, of course, a leopard tears out your throat), with my flashlight I checked right, left and then right again for scorpions and snakes and other sinister eyes. (Were yellow eyes or green bad? I couldn't remember. And what was the range of this flashlight?) Left again. I climbed out with my camera.

Yes, I tripped.

A pearl-spotted owlet was perched on the tree above me. Just as I got the camera focused, he flew to the next tree. And he did the same again, drawing me further away from the truck. And again.

Each time before following, I'd check my surroundings. Each time.

Really, what was the flashlight's range?

After the fourth tree, the owlet disappeared over the electrified fence surrounding the camp. I plucked a couple of barbed thorns out of my foot and headed back.

My tent had been torn to shreds. So, too, my sleeping bag. But not my mattress.

I hadn't even heard it happen.

The girls had. They slept in the truck from then on and made Reuben station his tent right outside the door when he refused to share the furthermost back seat with them – it wasn't comfortable. But that night they didn't go anywhere, one peed in her water bottle and cared less about mostly missing. (Towards the end, it was probably more about not wanting to have to set up the tent more than anything. But it was good for security – apparently thieves had been known to sneak into tourist trucks during the night.)

I tried sharing Wayne's tent. That was a rather unpleasant mistake. Afterwards, there were plenty of extra tents (though a couple of times by accident I set up the one that smelled like pee, damnit).

The next morning I found out a spotted hyena had gotten into the camp. What if I hadn't left my tent? Or I'd gotten the first photo?

(Okay, okay, not technically *chased by a hyena* as I had first promised way at the beginning of this tale. But, in my opinion, close enough. And, yes, admittedly, I was trying to get you interested. You made it this far, so I'm guessing it worked.)

We wind through crumbling plateaus of red stone, wide open expanses and then vast collections of smooth-faced boulders and shattered brittle plates underneath towering overhangs of rock on route to the Skeleton Coast. Short but intense rainstorms pelt the sides of the truck and, despite the plastic sides, soak everyone inside as a roaring wind rattles the stanchions holding them down. Jagged teeth of crimson rock line the horizon, ominous looking beneath the dark grey sky. And there's nothing. No towns, no villages, no roads.

Shallow gullies of hard packed yellow sand precede the coast where occasional rusted skeletons of ships are pounded by an intense surf. At the top of a dune, I see a lone old man, his leathery face atwinkle with a luminous grin, garbed in a threadbare white suit riding side saddle on a white mule shaded by a bedraggled blue umbrella decorated with pink flamingoes. "Look!"

But when Wayne turned, the old man was gone.

We started down the coast, Simon edging the truck closer and closer to the water as he increased our speed. I drove up front with him, watching as his grin grew and grew and grew. Thirty miles an hour, thirty-five. Forty.

"You're getting too close!" Veronica shouted from the rear.

Simon kept grinning, ignoring her. Fifty miles an hour.

"Hey!" She started pounding on the roof of the cab.

The truck suddenly wrenched forward and drove deep into the sand before completely stopping a hundred feet later.

"Shit."

The wheels were half submerged in sand. We were fucked.

The truck was equipped with long metal sand tracks for just such an event. Only to use them, you had to maneuver them under the tires. The front tires.

The only shade in 130 degree Fahrenheit heat was a sliver on one side of the truck.

When it became apparent it would take more than Reuben, Veronica and Simon digging to get out quickly (forty-five minutes), Wayne and I joined in. And even the girls (!).

I couldn't wear my sandals. The pads inside were so hot they were burning my feet.

Ninety minutes later, the truck was ready to back up on two sets of the sand tracks. Simon had to get the truck rocking back and forth before it would go, but it finally did: slowly at first and then gaining speed. And then, as soon as it left the tracks, the truck sunk just as deep into the sand as before.

Hours passed in similar failed results. The girls gave up after the first failure and sat around drinking water and complaining in whispers. Wayne, Reuben, Simon and I dug and dug and dug, with each failure trying to direct the truck further from shore and closer to where the ground was more compacted.

No one responded to the truck radio.

"How much water do we have?" I asked Veronica during a break. Sand covered me in all sorts of places you wouldn't want to know about.

"Plenty, we filled the tank in Etosha. Enough for a couple of weeks, if need be. Food, too. Though we'll get sick of canned goods. But don't worry. When someone comes by, we'll go for help."

We weren't on a road. "And if no one comes?"

"Someone will come… They'll start looking."

"When?"

"It may take a week. Hey, Jane, let's not use the water to wash up for now."

When it was completely dark, we stopped digging. We were so exhausted we slept on the truck without setting up our tents. I didn't even notice Wayne's snoring.

As I stepped out in the middle of the night to pee, Veronica mumbled, "Stay close. There's lions around here."

I put off going. But two hours later, I had no choice.

I walked fifty feet from the truck and unzipped, nervously scanning the darkness for any movement.

Bright shining lights flooded the sky behind me.

I swiveled around and there was nothing.

There wasn't a city for miles. I waited for the sound of a car, an airplane, but neither came.

Aliens?

God?

I returned to the truck.

"Why is it called The Skeleton Coast?" I asked Veronica the next morning.

"Lots of ships wrecked here over the centuries. And, as you can see, there's nowhere to go. If you made it to shore."

The truck nearly tipped over as one of the six sand tracks suddenly snapped in two lengthwise.

The second day was hotter than the day before.

"Jane, please! Can't you wash up in the ocean?" Veronica asked near sunset.

A trio of gaunt figures carrying what looked like bows and quivers of arrows with braceleted arms crossed the crest of a dune at the far edge of my sight. "Hey!" I shouted. "Hey!"

"See someone else?" Wayne asked.

"I did, actually." Every inch of me ached but Wayne looked worse: his face was wan and his lips blue. "You need to drink some water."

"No, I just ran out of booze. Well, except for the last bottle. That I'm saving."

I didn't need to ask him what for.

The next morning two of the women shouting at Simon about driving into the sand awoke me. He let them yell for five minutes and then walked off. A half hour later he returned and we continued digging. This time the girls helped.

Six vultures circled over us for hours as we dug. The ground kept feeling like it was solid enough under our feet but it wouldn't hold the truck. Unloading the tents and crates of food to lessen the weight didn't help.

"Guys, I hate to do this, but maybe we should start rationing the water," Veronica said to us over lunch.

No one argued. Not even Jane.

Around three, there was a rattling from behind one of the dunes. But it didn't fade out. It got louder and louder and then a small blue truck appeared.

Our savior was a jolly round fisherman from Swakopmond who looked like Santa Claus and had the beard, belly and rosy cheeks to match. To fit everyone in the truck filled with shucking knives, fishing rods and reels, nets, buckets and lobster traps, Wayne and I had to share the cab with him. The girls piled in the back amid the gear and smell of fish. Simon and Reuben stayed with our truck (yes, despite its failings, I'd started to think of it in the possessive sense).

Random note: I'd once thought of traveling dressed as Santa Claus.

"You're a fisherman, Roy?"

"Yep. Jesus was, too, you know?" He winked.

"Thank you for saving us."

"Well, a couple of the Himbas happened upon my campfire last night and said there might be some tourists up here having trouble, so I figured it was the neighborly thing to do. To come see if I could lend a hand. Would have been here sooner, but ran into some trouble of my own in a spot. Never drove this particular beach before. Thought the ground wasn't made for it."

"We're all glad you did."

"Yeah, this land is nothing to trifle with. Foreigners don't always understand that. It's a hard land and it takes a lot to make a life from. But I wouldn't live anywhere else."

Four hours later in Swakopmond, Veronica tried to give Roy some money for cutting his trip short by driving us and he refused it. Wouldn't even let Wayne or I buy him a beer.

Wayne made up for lost time by visiting the pubs aggressively and I joined him as we waited four days for the truck (though the third day I did a horseback ride offered by the hostel we were staying in).

The morning of the fifth day the truck arrived and Reuben leaped down from the cab smiling. When we came outside with our packed bags, someone new stood with Reuben and Veronica: Simon's replacement.

A shout turned us across the courtyard. Simon galloped past on one of the hostel's horses. With a whoop of "Yippee-kai-yay, motherfuckers!" he rode out the gates, laughing.

"Where the hell is he going?"

"He mentioned once he'd like to ride a horse from Cape Town to Perth."

"But that's impossible," Jane said.

I thought it was awesome.

After the giant red dunes of Sossusvlei, the diamond mining capital of Luderitz (miners used to be force fed castor oil to insure they hadn't secreted away any of the merchandise) and the ghost town of Kolmanskop, our last stop before South Africa was Fish River Canyon. Since Wayne was in no shape to leave the truck and everyone else seemed to be counting the minutes until the end, I climbed down by myself. It wasn't as deep as the Grand Canyon, so the descent didn't take long, but it was equally as beautiful. At the bottom, I stripped down and somersaulted into a beckoning clear pool. Coming out, I gave three elderly French ladies eating their egg sandwiches a show (I hadn't seen them there). Then I started the hot ascent.

Halfway up I saw it. My car with its distinctive blue?/green? paintjob perched on an escarpment near the top, gunning its engine menacingly. It couldn't be and yet it was. I raced to finish.

When I reached the top, the only vehicles were our truck and that of the French women. My car had vanished.

The ghost town of crumbling buildings filled with sand was visited weekly (at most) but had a permanent guide: a black man in his early thirties with a lazy eye who never stopped smiling. "So what were these two white basins used for? Do you know? To do laundry is one answer. Clean dishes is another. Maybe use as an icebox to cool beers is the right one. Cooler or esky are other words which also mean icebox. Each can be used interchangeably, but rarely are – which continent you call home usually being the determining factor of which term you prefer. But we really didn't know until an Italian tourist, a man of much age, came here two years ago on a Thursday and said the basins were used to cook spaghetti. Do you know what spaghetti is? And then a Japanese tourist three weeks ago said they were actually used for baths where the water is heated from below. A Dutch woman once suggested they were used to perform human sacrifices. But what's the real answer? There are many answers in life. The answers are not difficult, they are easy. What is hard is finding the right questions. And asking them."

I wished he would have been my guide throughout all of Africa. Although Reuben's pancakes could not be beat.

And yet not done. Never fucking done. That was the point, right?

It wasn't challenging, but we canoed down the Orange River anyway. It did, however, present its problems. Not from the rather tame Class II rapids, but mostly in the form of Wayne who shared my canoe and did the steering. Right into a bank of reeds once and into the shore another time, both of which resulted in capsizing the boat into supposedly (supposedly) crocodile-free waters. The second time resulted in me losing another hat as Wayne knocked it off me turning the canoe back over.

Knowing it was coming but still kind of ticked off about the hat so I didn't enjoy it as much as, looking back on it now, I should have: Wayne said, "The river was a monster that day. But it could not tame us."

Modern houses with air conditioning and satellite dishes all protected by electrified fences filled the cities of Namibia and South Africa. In contrast to Kenya to Malawi, grocery stores were fully stocked with all sorts of meats, vegetables, processed foods, and kitchen supplies. But black people did all the manual labor jobs and every white person I saw seemed to be giving someone orders. And many of the former still lived in mud huts or aluminum sided lean-to's outside and sometimes even inside the cities. Sometimes it was hard to tell that Apartheid and colonialism were over.

"What are all these private reserves we keep passing?" I asked Veronica.

"For hunting. Some tourists will pay fifty thousand dollars to shoot a cheetah… For that kind of money on this continent you can do anything. Anything."

In the university town of Stellenbosch, known best for its surrounding vineyards, Wayne drank so much that when he tried to pat the back of a woman on the dance floor in a friendly way, he missed and palmed her face instead. In a flurry of limbs and shouts, he and I were thrown out of the bar.

"What the fuck, man?"

"I didn't mean to do it."

"I know. But you've got to get a control of yourself. I don't want to tell you what to do with your life, but you're going to kill yourself."

Sadness filled his fleshy face. "You can't help me, Pete. No one can. I don't want them to." He shook my hand. "Goodbye." He turned and walked off into the darkness.

In the morning, Wayne's hostel bed was empty and his bag was gone.

I never saw him again.

The truck tour had two more stops and then I was free. I was looking forward to it and yet I wasn't. I'd be on the watch for my stuff all the time again. Organizing things.

The first stop was the Cape of Good Hope, the southernmost point in Africa. Arriving, I stepped away from the parking lot to a small winding path through the purple-flowered heather, happy to get away from the crowds and the girls who were reveling in Wayne's disappearance. After a few hundred feet, I stopped to photograph the curve of the winding shore framed by billowing white clouds and the luminous blue sea. As I pressed the shutter release, I heard movement to my right and turned.

A baboon, certainly five times my size and, therefore forty times as strong (picture King Kong's older brother), was rushing right at me – no doubt drawn to the promise of food in my camera bag.

If I had thought I probably would have run (completely forgetting the first rule of all animal encounters as it brings out the preternatural predator instincts). Instead I yelled at him with all my lungs could muster. I expected him to keep coming and rip my throat out with his rather large fangs and that my shaky falsetto half-shout, half cowardly cry was to be my epitaph. Instead, he stopped dead and looked at me. So I yelled at him again. He sat up on his haunches ten feet from me and hissed, showing me all of his fangs and nearly emptying my bladder. I yelled again, encouraged now in my madness and half-congratulating myself for not running, but the baboon had grown bored of the whole operation and began playing with his genitals while facing me.

Movement to my left turned my head towards another baboon approaching, this one twice as fast and at least seventeen times as big. I yelled again.

This one stopped, scratched its head, and immediately began picking berries from nearby shrubs, forgetting all about me. I turned back again to the first baboon to find he'd snuck two steps forward, but still had a firm grip on himself. Fearing all sorts of further sexually traumatizing experiences – already ten years of psychotherapy beckoned – I shouted while backing up, trying to keep both baboons in sight. But they both ignored me.

Fifty feet up the path, I bumped into a group of Portuguese tourists with video cameras rolling. I was the star, no doubt, of some news blurb that night in Lisbon, the headline being *American accountant molested by monkeys in South Africa goes mad.* I returned to the bus and sat in the back until the remainder of the tour group returned. A couple of the Portuguese passed the bus later, pointing at me, and I hid my face away.

"How was your walk?" Veronica asked.

"I don't want to talk about it."

The second stop was to see the jack penguins in Simon's Town. As I was trying to get a better photo, I put my hat (this one a South African *billy* purchased in the Citrusdal campground shop) on a rock. Indifferent to my presence, the penguins allowed me to get extremely close. But then I realized why. One of their companions had hopped over to inspect my hat. I laughed, watching how slowly he moved as he tried to flee with it. When I realized he was actually in earnest and quickened my step, he was just one step quicker and able to disappear into the water with it clamped in his bill.

Veronica handed me a beer on the second story deck of the hostel overlooking the lights of Cape Town. "I like to commit random acts of kindness."

"Are you trying to get me to fall in love with you?"

"What shall we talk about, Pete?"

"The meaning of life?"

"What meaning? There is no heaven, no hell. Just be happy. Without hurting others."

"Amazing how different things would be if people just followed that tenet. Really followed it without pretending to."

She nodded and put down her beer. "This job can get really lonely."

I thought of her firing Simon in the middle of Namibia, stranding him there. I turned away and smiled. "But look at what it gives you."

"Too true."

But, again, I hadn't forgiven Penelope.

I visited Robben Island where Nelson Mandela had been imprisoned from 1964 to 1982 (he spent 9 more years in other prisons) along with other future South African presidents and admired the views of Table Mountain which I was to climb the next day. That night at The Long Beach Club, a white South African tried to start a fight with me by

452

shouting: "Americans are the most bigoted, hateful people on the planet!"

I tried to visit the aquarium, but I realized at the entrance that I wasn't ready – I needed more time.

I passed a division of Net Block and Tackle on Main Street so I bought a postcard and wrote:

Dear Cassandra,

I think you're just the bestest accountant ever. I read about you and when I grows up I wants to be just like you! I loves you much and the bestest.

I mailed it unsigned.

As I waited for a bus in Cape Town headed to the Drakensberg mountain range where I wanted to do a four day hike called the Giant's Cup Walk, a white woman in her late fifties with a bubbly smile, twinkling green eyes and enormous coiffure of white hair said, "I'm so glad you're visiting my country. Such a beautiful place, yes? Too bad most of the world hasn't seen it. Isn't Cape Town gorgeous? And the Wild Coast."

"Yes."

"The only problem is the crime. You're very brave to travel around on your own. You've got to be so careful. They tried to carjack my sister twice."

"Really?"

"Isn't it terrible? Once at a robot with guns, but she just ran through the red light and went. Another time they were waiting at her gate. She's so lucky to be alive." Her voice dropped to a whisper. "The blacks are so lazy. Don't want to work. Want to steal everything. Ruining the country."

"Yeah, Apartheid, now that was a glorious time. Friday night lynchings, always a beheading to attend after a Sunday barbecue. Those were the days. Now who do you persecute? Taxi drivers? Bisexual botanists? White people? It's just not the same."

She didn't appreciate my sarcasm.

1993.

I had wanted to do a hike along the Wild Coast, but no public transportation served either Port St. Johns or Coffee Bay. Other travelers told me how taxi-drivers had shot up the bus of the hostel shuttle service because they wanted the business instead, that the trail was hard to follow and none of the villages along the way would help you without you having to pay for directions. So I skipped it.

That made my last adventure in Africa the Giant's Cup Walk. On the third night my boots expertly repaired by the *Finest Shoe Craftsman in Cape Town* came completely apart, forcing me to cut the hike short. (The second night I'd tried using my entire supply of crazy glue – originally purchased to attach flag patches of the countries I'd visited to the outside of my pack - to weld the bottoms back on. It worked beautifully until I took my third step of the day into the smallest of puddles on the trail. Then I had to use compression straps to hold the boots together – flip, flap, flip, flap – and walked in an always wet sock.)

Besides vultures, I also saw a couple herds of zebra and a family of eland, the world's largest antelope. Most of the hike cut through grass along contours of vast open hills offering no shade. Huge flat-topped mesas lined the horizon.

The second night I gave my second nude revue of South Africa when I exited the river and the hut caretaker, an enormous black woman in her late thirties, stood waiting for my registration. (She made no attempt to avert her eyes, none, which kind of creeped me out. Again I slept with my knife unfolded.) Thick plastic covered the mattress making for a night so hot I sweated through my entire sleeping bag. Not so fun.

No warden attended the metal-roofed third hut (or rondavel). Inside, the metal grilled bunk bed lacked mattresses (locals often stole them, I heard later, since they could afford nothing better) and the ground was concrete. As it also reeked terribly of kerosene with little ventilation, the night ahead promised pain.

The setting could not be beat, however. Nothing separated the hut nestled in one corner of the huge valley from a collection of buildings barely visible at the other end – no trees, no buildings, no hills. Just a long, long expanse of grass. Save the cut I came in through, green mountains rimmed the enclosure.

Lightning interrupted my not quite done dinner of chicken noodle soup as I drank in another glorious African sunset. I watched with pleasure white streaks crease the distant darkening sky until a drizzling rain reached

454

me. Then I went inside and laid down on the metal cot. It was painful. But the ground covered in unidentified droppings was even more so (yes, I checked). I began counting marabou stork to fall asleep.

Booming thunder woke me. I opened the door to pouring rain. The storm had moved into the valley right above my hut. Then I saw the lightning.

The whole valley lit up like it was day. I watched for a few minutes and then climbed back onto the cot.

Just as my eyes closed in exhaustion, I suddenly realized the rondavel's peaked roof was metal. As was the bed frame. And the structure was the highest point in the entire valley for miles.

I leapt off the bed. Who the hell had designed a hut with a metal roof and a metal bed in a place where these storms probably happened all of the time?

I considered going outside. I'd be the target instead of the hut. And I'd be wet, too.

I yanked my pack off the top bunk like grabbing a hot pan from the oven.

The storm went on and on. I couldn't stand any longer. I found the spot least covered with droppings and curled up there on my bag.

The storm continued. Even through the tiny barred window the lightning lit up the inside of the hut.

And then suddenly I was no longer afraid. Of anything. I didn't care. It was an amazing feeling: transformative, liberating.

The storm passed on. Lightning never struck the hut.

I passed out on the bed.

In the morning, I abandoned the hike. Every ten steps I had to reach down to adjust the straps on my boots (though you couldn't really call them that anymore).

I had to hitchhike back to Sani Pass where the remainder of my gear was stored (including my sandals!) and forego the prepaid shuttle at the trail's end. No one picked me up for three hours (the what-felt-like-permanent indentations from where I'd slept on my face against the metal grill of the bed may not have helped my chances for a ride) and I was envisioning another dread-filled night in the hut, when a pickup truck stopped. The white driver told me to get in the back when I told him my destination.

After the third hairpin turn, I realized the truck bed was covered in grease and unidentified blood which soon saturated my shorts and pack. The hostel where I'd stowed my gear wouldn't let me inside because of the smell.

As I sat waiting in the movie theatre for the midnight bus to Johannesburg from Pietermaritzburg, one of the ushers approached me. I'd left the bus stop earlier when the fifth person to pass by told me it was unsafe to wait there after dark. I'd tried staying in the local hostel after the place in Sani Pass had said I could, but the Pietermaritzburg owner wanted to charge me a night's stay to just store my bag (myself excluded) for five hours, saying "You've come from Sani Pass? Well, they take all of the business and if I keep your bag here, what benefit do I receive?"

After the preliminary questions, the half-Indian, half-black usher told me, "I don't like the new South Africa. It used to be first came the whites, then the coloreds, then the Indians, then the you-know-who. Now it's hard to get a job if you're not black. I hate them. They're destroying the country. I want to get out, go to the States. I get nine rand an hour. Nine! That's less than one English pound. Won't even buy you a bag of crisps in England. I'm going to be a civil engineer. I wanted to be an electrical engineer, but things don't always work out the way you want. The problem here is the crime, man. South Africans are stupid. Stupid, I tell you. I'm from South Africa, but I still say this. You know, I got stabbed? Came this close, this fucking close to getting my spinal cord severed."

I was cornered. So I asked, "What happened?"

"It was just one of those things."

"What things? People don't just stab you to stab you."

"You want to know? I'll tell you. These guys were hassling a girl, tugging her shirt and that. My cousin and I told him to stop. Then later he drove by me and stabbed me. Luckily I beat him off or I would've died. For what? Now I've learned never to interfere. As soon as I can I'm getting the fuck out. You can't change this place, man. Mandela, all them, won't help. Why? Because they don't want it to change." My disbelief must have shown because he lifted his shirt to show me a deep puckered scar near his left kidney.

Turning to a group entering a tour bus outside the Johannesburg airport after the grueling twenty hour ride to get there, I shouted the following (Taking my first steps towards becoming a prophet of perambulation, an elocutionist of love. Becoming immortal.):

Be not a messiah of misogyny and misanthropy

Love thy neighbor

To any and all extremes

Go perpetually naked if necessary

For it is the artifice that separates us

We are all the same: penises, vaginas, nipples, knees

Shackle yourselves not with the trappings and boundaries of Western civilization

Become one

And let the hate

Dissipate

I needed to leave Africa, so I went. But I wouldn't be able to stay away. It was in my blood now.

Bolivian Border Bustin' Blues

As I sat in the Santiago bus station in the early morning sipping a large coke (*coca grande*), a young man wearing two gold hoop earrings and with long hair tied up in a ponytail said to me, "Don't drink that."

"Why not?"

"You'll regret it. The buses don't stop in South America. For anything. Locals always dehydrate themselves so they don't have to pee. They never tell you that."

"Why not?"

He shrugged. "They like to watch tourists squirm." He smiled. "I

458

am Manuel. I am from Colombia."

"Peter. Estados Unidos."

"I know."

"You knew my name was Peter?" He smiled. "I'm thinking of going to Colombia. To visit the Ciudad Perdida." The ruins of a city in the jungle near Santa Marta only reachable by foot. You couldn't go alone, you had to use an official guide – part of the money you paid was spent on bribing the drug dealers who used some of the fields you passed through.

"You should not go to Colombia. Your life will become a tale of two circles. You understand?" I shook my head. With the stub of a pencil, he drew two circles on the bench, one small and one much larger. "The guerrillas do not like Americans – your country funds the fascist government, perpetuating an oppressive aristocracy, under the banner of battling drug production. The first circle is your asshole before they stop your bus and see your passport. The second is your asshole after they finish with it." He laughed.

"Well, that's encouraging."

"Yes, I left as soon as I could. Now I just travel around South America. Do work here and there."

"Work?"

"I come from Colombia, yes? So I know good drugs. Cocaine. What is shit and what is not. So I take it across borders and make money that way."

"You swallow it in plastic bags?"

"Of course not. I put it in my backpack. But not in the pockets. Behind the belt. They never look there. Especially if you fill your backpack with filthy clothes and spilt shampoo. That is the most important thing. By the time they're finished with your stinking underwear, they want you out of there as soon as possible, believe me. Never look at the rest."

"That's good advice."

"We travelers must look out for each other. Something else – where to carry your money. Mine is sewn in my pants. Where's yours?"

So that was it. "I don't carry much. Use the money machine to get more. Carry my card in my shoe."

"Not such a good idea. Colombians will take your shoes." He

laughed again. "Will you watch my bag? I need to use the restroom."

"Sure."

He was good. Upon returning a few minutes later, he said, "Thank you. You cannot trust many people here."

"That's true."

"Where you headed?"

I considered lying, but there was no one else around. It was too early. "San Pedro de Atacama."

"Me as well. You want to travel together?"

"That's okay."

"You speak Spanish?"

"Not much."

"It would be easier with someone who speaks Spanish. I could show you things. Get the real prices. Not the gringo prices."

"Thanks, but if I travel with you, there won't be much challenge." I wanted to add how I enjoyed ordering chicken by flapping my arms and going "Bawk, bawk" or asking for beef by dipping my head to "Moo" or trying to find the train station by saying "Choo-choo," but I figured he wouldn't understand. Even when I learned the words *pollo, carne asada* and *ferrocarril*, I didn't always use them. Making people laugh was more fun. At home, I wouldn't have done that – was I changing? For the good?

"Okay. Want me to watch your bag while you use the restroom?"

A minute before leaving, a woman carrying two crying babies sat next to me to prevent my sleeping after a night of fleeing hordes of fist-sized cockroaches (I kid you not) around my hotel room when the electricity went out at two a.m. I would meet her kind again (they ALWAYS sat next to me but the infants didn't ALWAYS kick me for hour upon hour upon hour – only sometimes).

Manuel was not on my bus.

An hour into the ride, the ticket collector handed out BINGO cards. I prematurely proclaimed my victory and was banned from the remainder of the games, being branded *The Gringo Who Cried Bingo*. My shame knew no end.

Somewhere near Los Vilos (or *Where is This Godforsaken Place?* in English – we didn't pass a Coffee Cup nor a Lord of the Burgers for *miles/kilometres*), the woman with the crying babies left the bus and, unbelievably, was not replaced by a twin cousin (she waited to show until the train leaving Uyuni, Bolivia and, I admit, I thought I was safe – little did I know and all that) but by a French girl. Flowing dark hair, playful eyes and possessor of a sublime example of my favorite feminine physical attribute, i.e.: super duper (duper) sexy.

"You are American, yes? Teach me how to say the bad things to someone in English. If they enrage my anger." Her accent: even more irresistible.

I had to try something different. "Well, you could call someone *the pungent pudenda of a koala bear. Or a llama testicle.*"

"What does this mean: *pudenda?*"

"Another favorite of mine is *You tube of toothpaste, you.*"

"These are ridiculous, yes?"

"Which is their appeal. What would make you angrier: a second-rate, nearly dispassionate *Fuck you* or the more inventive *You stink like a menstruating elephant's vagina?*"

She smiled. "Teach me more."

"Um, *I've seen prettier assholes on a warthog than your face.*"

"This is the best traveling conversation I have ever had."

Despite having bought a ticket all the way to Colama, I was about to ask her if I should get off the bus with her at La Serena (I had to know, right?) when she asked, "This trip you're doing, it's a bit like running away from your problems, no? Instead of staying to face them?" and I knew not to.

He who sired me and she who birthed me:

Arriving in South America, I embarked upon The Saga of a Dog

461

Named Stinky and My Chilean Modeling Career. *Santiago was cold and polluted so I headed north by northwest by southeast by north towards the least wet desert in the world, the Atacama. Along the way, I passed through Antofagasta – also cold and polluted and not anywhere near as spectacular as the name promised. In the desert town of San Pedro I met a pudgy canine with above mentioned soubriquet and a nine-necklaced Australian hippie named Darrel who taught me the beauty of bald women, spouting such sage advice as "There is nothing more erotic or sensual than a woman with a smooth shaven skull." Stinky loved romantic comedies, the Seattle Seahawks, and chasing crickets and, occasionally, his rather wispy tail. As the guidebook recommended, Darrel was intent on blending in to the extent that he renounced all other endeavors except that of acquiring a fossilized axe-head along the desert floor – keeping his head and eyes down whenever we walked anywhere much to the consternation of anyone else in his way. On an excursion to do just that, we headed into the hills where we were accosted in a valley of fire by four men driving a pretty white and super shiny SUV. After choking us in a cloud of their not inconsiderable dust, they requested our and the dog's services as photographic models for their cellular phone billboard advertisement. We declined as they could not afford our fees. But then they upped the ante with a half a Snickers bar each and a free phone call home – hence the voicemail of heavy breathing in the middle of the night – no, it wasn't Uncle Sammy out of prison once again. We capitulated.*

Then we began preparations for our triumphant entry into Bolivia. A motorcycle pushing a blue railed cart was to be our mode of transport. Stinky was to come as well (his nickname earned by his bathing habits, or lack thereof). But then, in an unexpected turn of events, one day Darrel blended in so well, I turned around and he'd disappeared.

So, solo I journeyed to Bolivia on a jeep tour across the Andes where I encountered pink and white flamingoes fishing in shallow salt lakes at fifteen thousand feet – an otherworldly landscape of snow-capped peaks and weird rock formations devoid of any other life. The sunsets were brilliant explosions of red that stirred me to the core. Our guides were an elderly couple who never left each other's side even outside the jeep and who were constantly canoodling or giggling at each other's jokes. And they would never let me carry my own rather enormous bag into the hotels we stayed en route. Our last stop before arriving in Uyuni was a hotel made entirely of salt where pepper was forbidden. Yesterday, I visited the nearby graveyard of locomotives and stole a rock. The rock was ovoid-shaped and brownish. Tomorrow I'm headed towards Tupiza where Butch Cassidy and the Sundance Kid met their untimely demise and where no one knows how to correctly pronounce "petunia."

The world's greatest, most caring and best looking son

I stood next to Heinrich Herring (a.k.a. The Professor) at the Oceanland puffer fish tank on Employee Appreciation Day. "Where's Kory?" I asked.

"Kory?"

"Haiku."

"Oh. He took a job at an insurance company. Did you hear about what happened to Saul Sole, Sculpin's replacement?"

"Saul got fired? He was really nice to me. Even asked me my first name and where I was from. Remembered the answer. Promised to treat me to lunch one day at a sushi place he liked."

"You're lucky. That restaurant serves one type of poisonous fish that if cut wrong, you die. Well, they cut it wrong."

We didn't say anything for a few minutes. Then I pointed up: "It's unusual to see a Bulwer's petrel here. Really unusual. You know that many birds are losing their migratory routes? There just isn't a place for them to land anymore. A place to be free. The world is becoming too developed. So they're dying off." Then the bird cut my comment short with one of his own.

"What happened to young Mugabe's shirt?" Ron said, appearing beside me.

"I don't... want to talk about it."

"When I moved here to work at Bait and Hook before the merger changed it to Hook Line and Sinker, I forgot to bring any of my dress pants from my parents' house. I brought only the jackets. I didn't realize this until a few moments before leaving for work on my first day. Well, I drove to three stores before finding one open. But it didn't carry my size. Just trousers three sizes too large or ones much too small. I took the too large. Met the heads of two departments and the managing partner of the Los Angeles office." He looked at my shirt and placed a reassuring hand on my shoulder. "Every great man must face adversity before his day in the sun." Then his eyes lit up. He approached two brightly garbed Oceanland *Fish Friends* of exceeding loveliness. "Is it true that some types of fish will follow the fish in front of them right into the mouth of a predator such as a Pollock because the one before it does? And that, like their brethren humans of the ever so enchanting and much fairer sex, they can't resist a tantalizing worm on the end of an exceedingly long and curved hook?" He grinned.

One said: "I have no idea what he said but I think it was gross. Let's go."

"Jesus. Changas like that don't grow on trees, you know. A rare and wondrous sighting... Chosen One, what the fuck are you laughing about?"

"Sigmond has been handing these out to everyone."

Printed on a pink sheet of paper was the following:

How to Reduce Your Rohu Gas Emissions - A Survival Guide for the Delicate of Nose

More and more people these days are wondering how they can do their part to help reduce the emission of RAG (Rohu Anal Gases) into the atmosphere. While change won't happen overnight, here are six easy steps that you can take that will help mitigate their disastrous environmental impact.

Six Simple Steps

1. Plant a rose garden. Plant a lot of rose gardens. Whilst alive, the flowers will store nitrous oxide that would otherwise linger in the atmosphere. If strategically placed to provide shade for your cubicle, rose vines will also help it stay cool in the summer. Better yet, make it a fruit or a nut tree. Planting perennials that yield food, including berry bushes and garden vegetables and herbs, will help you eat locally while 'fixing' more unwanted gas emissions emitted by work colleagues into the air that you breathe. Introducing these plants in public places, by the sides of roads and in parks, is another way to benefit the community and the climate.

2. Regimen Rohu's diet to be strictly bean-free. Band together to make this a reality. Work in shifts, if necessary, to assure twenty-four hour coverage. If you need to make an important call during your shift, inform your co-workers so they can watch him. Never leave Rohu unattended – don't forego use of a leash if necessary. Make him purchase lunches with the official "Non Rohu Gas Emission Food" labels and don't be fooled by cheap imitation labels. With communication and teamwork, we can make this work and have a RAG-free future for us and our children.

3. Just say "No" to his flatulence shenanigans. Do NOT encourage his behavior in any way, shape or form. This includes laughter, giggles or even something seemingly innocuous as a smile.

> *4.   Purchase a hermetically sealed glass cylinder which Rohu must stay in at all times.   Use an airlock to pass him documents, food, and other sundries so no debilitating gases can escape.   As tempting as it may seem at times, do not fall for the trap of Sphincter Plugs – all scientific studies conducted in recent years have shown these to be totally ineffective and may, in fact, further perpetuate the problem by causing irritation in the rectal area which could result in more potent emissions.*

> *5.   Post a copy of these steps along with his photograph at all your local bars, restaurants and shopping malls to help your community so that they too will not suffer the harmful effect of Rohu gases.*

> *6.   Keep a heavy (heavy heavy) duty fan on hand in case you are unable to prevent exposure.   Despite the difficulty inherent in using a keyboard with it on, the U.S. Surgeon General actually recommends wearing a gas mask at all times to be 100% safe.*

Use wanton, unrepentant violence to enforce these steps.   Do not turn the other cheek or he will.

If you should enter an infected area unawares, stop, drop and roll and, for God's sake, cover your nose as soon as is humanly possible.   And know, our prayers are with you.

Should you miraculously survive, be sure to incinerate your clothes and visit an accredited decontamination center immediately.   As a safety precaution, it is recommended that you stay away from children under the age of 11 for at least 72 hours after exposure to prevent collateral damage.

"D-E-D.   Dead.   He is fucking dead."   Ron removed his glasses and folded them neatly in the breast pocket of his bright pink polo shirt embroidered with the question *HAVE YOU KISSED YOUR CPA TODAY?* Then he took off running.

From where he stood near one of the aquariums, Sigmond looked up from his triple olive martini to see an accountant built like a rhinoceros excessively fond of jelly donuts charging.   I hated Sigmond, don't misconstrue that, but his look of fear – the fount of terror he experienced in that instant – I could not wish upon any man.   And then I noticed his left hand rested on a sign saying *TIGER SHARK TANK.*

"Ron! No!"

But I was too late. Rohu tackled Sigmond mid-chest and they went tumbling over the edge into the water.

When I reached the tank, the liquid's surface was completely still. Then Sigmond's head popped above the surface. A moment later, so did Ron's facing Sigmond. They went for each other's throats.

Then I saw the fins converging upon them. "Get out! Now!" Again: too late. A flurry of activity followed, the water broiling with a violent scissoring of arms, blood and fins. And then they went under again.

A long silence. I noticed a torn pocket holding Ron's glasses had drifted to the edge below me. I retrieved it.

Others joined me beside the tank. Still nothing.

Herring's "What—" was cut off as an air bubble broke the surface and Rohu's voice squawked "Cock." Then all truly was silence.

"Wait." Wrasse reached down where I was about to step. His fingers came up with an olive pimento. He plopped it into his mouth. "Bummer, dude."

"I mine for diamonds," the red-faced South African man with an unruly white beard and curly blonde half-eyebrows said to me on the train to Tupiza, Bolivia. "Just came from Madagascar. But don't tell anyone. I wasn't supposed to be there. Didn't have a permit or whatever. Didn't own the land. Fuck them. Just because they were born first and didn't move. Like some slug, some fungus. Just went into the jungle with some men I'd hired. Didn't cost much. Labor's cheap there, real cheap. A day's work for two or three dollars American. Even negotiate it down for longer projects. But they wouldn't stay in the bush. Complained about the heat, the digging. Took my money and run off. No respect, nothing... Now I'm here. To do mining, maybe. I love traveling. It affords such freedom. Freedom to do whatever you want. Freedom to kill if desired. Who would know? By the time it's discovered you're already gone. And no one ever knows your name – these hotels never check the name you give against a passport. You could just walk down the street and disappear. Never get caught. Ever."

"I'm going to check if there's a dining car."

"I'll join you. I'm famished."

"Señor, shoeshine?" said one of two filthy faced boys in Tupiza's main square.

"No, thanks, I'm trying to quit."

"Señor, shoeshine?"

"No, gracias, but if you know any good crack dealers..."

"Shoeshine!"

"If you insist." I guided him to the nearest bench and kneeled in front of him to shine his shoes. "Dos bolivianos."

He and his friend exchanged giggles.

"Un boliviano. No menos. Mejor precio. Es verdad."

"Why aren't you in school?" I asked in my awful Spanish as I polished his torn and dirty tennis shoes three sizes too big for him.

"School is for rich kids."

Shit. I held out my hand for the money and smiled. "Un boliviano."

"No tengo."

"Sigame. Tu amigo tambien."

They shook their heads. "Si. Insisto."

I led them across the street to a barbershop where I bought them haircuts and shaves (they loved my insisting the barber lather their chins with shaving cream) and told them they were *muy guapo* and were going to steal all of my women. Then I left, feeling really good about myself until the next corner when three more even dirtier boys in rags asked to shine my shoes as well.

Near midnight, I found myself at a wobbly three-legged table in a run-down karaoke bar with glaring pink neon lights everywhere and a cracked glass of pisco sour in hand. The walls were covered with flaking blue paint (that I was washing out of my hair for the next three days) and gaudily hued Madonna and child drawings ripped not so successfully from some children's book. There was no heating: my breath blew out in plumes of white smoke.

In one corner the South African was passed out on a bench

elevated at the opposite end like a teeter totter. What the hell, there were almost no tourists around and my Spanish was terrible. (I'd asked an Israeli girl in the hotel if she'd like to go for a drink and she'd told me she'd hung out with enough North Americans when she lived in New York, she didn't come here to do the same. She wanted to hang out only with locals.)

Wherewith had I gone to ponder the wretchedness of my days at the bottom of a bottle in a Bolivian bodega where a bearded transvestite in pink miniskirt and fake pearls lisped in my ear a soft, off-key rendition of a Panamanian dirge?

I skipped Potosi. Its main backpacker attraction was a tour of the notoriously dangerous mines. I was starting to feel like I'd seen enough of that.

In Sucre, a package awaited me from my mother.

"What's that?" the tall, mustached hotel owner asked me.

"My mom sends me disposable toilet seat covers."

"Would you like to hear a story? If you have time."

"Sure."

"Before this, I ran a hotel in Nicaragua. I'm not sure how he found my hotel, but there was this American guy, twenty-nine years old, looked sort of like you, who came. I thought he was okay, a normal guy, and then on the second day the phone calls started. His parents were checking up on him. Twenty-nine years old. He wasn't allowed anywhere by himself, he had to go in a group and always in the middle. Like the rest of us were protecting him. And he'd always carry his gas, his pepper spray, to keep the robbers off of him. Every day a big, I mean a really big, Fedex package this size would arrive. His mother was sending him cornflakes and mineral water, the ten liter ones, in the mail. She didn't trust any of the food down here. Either her or his father called every day: I got to know them both. They always asked me what he was up to and how things were going. One day he told his mother he wanted to play basketball and the next day two pairs of expensive Reeboks - you know, top of the line - came in the Fedex. His family was very rich, owned the biggest funeral parlor in Chicago, I think. He ate in nothing but the most expensive restaurants in Managua. Again, he couldn't go by himself so he would invite me along, never letting me pay. Sometimes he'd treat everyone in the hotel. He was studying Spanish, but he had a dream. To climb the nearby volcano. From the road, it was only one and a half hours to the top. Every night before he went to bed he told me, *Tomorrow is going to be the great day of my life! I am going to climb the volcano.* His mother forbid him to go. So did his father. And his cousins. Each called him and said, *It's too dangerous. Don't do it.* Despite their warnings, he got in the shuttle the next day and drove to the trailhead. But he couldn't make himself leave the car. We did the walk without him and he drove back with us."

"That's very funny. How did you end up in Bolivia?"

"See this scar on my leg? I was shot fighting in the war. Fighting your government. The American government that tried to come into my country and tell us who our leaders are, who we should elect to power. I was a fool. I thought I could change the world. I nearly died. For what? No one even remembers anymore. All they care about is Coca-cola and DVD's and Nike basketball shoes. Only one person cared. A woman. She saved me, took me from that filthy hospital into her home and loved me. Brought me back to life. I would've died, I know that. I was sick a long time. But she took care of me. And so I loved her. But she was older than me, much. Seventeen years. Too old to have children. And this is what I wanted. This is always what I wanted. What is a man without children? I told her this, even when she was loving me, but she didn't understand. Didn't listen. And so, at the end, I told her I must leave. And so I did. She followed me here, told everyone that I was her husband. She threatened to suicide. So I took her back for a while. She saved my life. But I couldn't... Can you spend your life repaying a debt? If you're not happy? I tried, I really tried. But. I don't know. You only get one life to get it right." I touched his shoulder. "You're a good person. For listening."

A couple of days later, he threatened to kill a couple of dread-locked Argentineans who had been trying to check in accompanied by the girl who worked for him. Afterwards, he told me: "This is my business, this is my life. I worked damned hard to make enough money to own it. It is very hard to save money here. I am an honest person, but if they come again I will get my gun and kill them dead. They're thieves, they don't work. I work for what is mine. I have to help my brother. Let them earn their way like me. I won't give it to them. They'll have to kill me to take it."

I thought I'd made a real connection with a local until I checked out. Then he tried to charge me extra for taking too many showers (one a day) and I realized I hadn't.

Dear Mother and Father,

After six months on the road, I finally got my first ever green hat stand in the room. Photographs, though painful to wait for, are forthcoming. Even more exciting news to report: this hotel also had a parrot that said, "Fucking Gringo" every time I passed.

Saw a UFO (actually in Namibia, please excuse the break in chronology – spewing me forth dictates you must deal with it, regardless). Passed myself off as a talking mime – yes, I am a Master of Disguise. AND, while enjoying empanadas of dubious origin in a deceptively quiet square in Sucre, escaped an onslaught of Bolivian children wielding firecrackers – surviving only by the hair of my chinny chin chin when I leapt onto a lice-ridden llama (or it could have been a vicuna) to flee through the cobblestoned streets.

   Peter

What the fuck had I done?

In an attempt to achieve something more and stop feeling sorry for myself, I'd booked a bus to Coroico on the aptly named *Highway of Death*. Drivers who never took breaks navigated antiquated buses with squealing brakes along a one-lane mud track dropping off into thousand meter chasms from La Paz to a mountain jungle town perched on the edge of forever. And then they kept going and going and going over similarly treacherous roads into the beginnings of the Amazon basin, arriving more than twenty-four hours later at Rurrenbaque where I was to first glimpse the enormous jungle rodent capybara and the distinctive dark blue plumage of the blue hyacinth macaw. Crosses lined the oft mist-obscured road right outside La Paz amid countless waterfalls soaking the track. (It was also a tourist attraction – bikes could be rented to ride down the steepest parts – after my Amsterdam incident I was wary of such endeavors, especially when who knew how safe/suspect the brakes were or how many of those crosses were those of tourists who'd found out.) To stay awake, the drivers drank caffeine-packed mate or chewed cocoa leaves and played music louder than any disco. When buses met going opposite directions, it was often a duel of wills and horns as to which would back up and hang precariously half a wheel or more over the edge to let the other pass.

On my journey, a French judo enthusiast (he took lessons in every South American city he could – salsa classes, too) who kept asking me how far the drop was (I had the window seat) needed to pee – he'd obviously not gotten the valuable advice I had from Manuel. At a crucial moment after two skids and an extended, exceedingly violent wobble, he clawed up from his seat and asked the fully concentrated driver to stop so he could relieve his bladder. The other passengers badgered him back into his seat.

Later a squealing piglet, brought onto the bus in a burlap bag, bumped up and down the aisle, coming steadily closer and closer to the

470

driver and the truck's stick shift while still in the bag. I got a serious talking to when I returned it to the back of the bus.

Towards the end, the driver was shaking his head to stay awake. After he had to jerk the wheel back a couple of times to avoid ending us, the passengers made him stop and drink another mate.

A second two-laned road with asphalt and tunnels lay half built and abandoned on the next mountain over. Money donated by European governments to construct it was insufficient to pay all the bribes and so a truck a month on average was lost (at one point we passed a trail of debris leading down to a bus that had gone over recently).

At a junction, the bus slowed down and a woman with short red hair boarded. Rather than sitting down (which I immensely hoped for – she was supremely not unattractive), she stood in the aisle and reached into her bag for something. A banana. Rather than try to sell it, however, instead she next removed a condom from her pocket and proceeded to show the bus how to sheathe the piece of fruit, lecturing the whole time in Spanish.

When she was done, she offered me the banana.

"No, thanks, I'm trying to quit."

"Please pass it on. I want the women to see how to use them."

"Oh, sorry."

As she took back the banana to show the next bus, I recognized her: the secretary who'd greeted me my first day of work.

"Wait. You used to work at Net, Block and Tackle, a California Limited Liability Partnership."

She looked me up and down. "Didn't I tell you?" Then she stepped off the bus.

Sigmond was gone but then so was Ron.

However, Cassandra's cruelty knew no bounds: "You'll now be working for Bob."

It was the first time I'd heard her laugh. It wasn't a pleasant sound.

Her laugh warned me but the reality of it was not something I could imagine.

There had been hints around the office. Once, when choosing which books on international insurance companies I wanted from the many piles in Ron's office, Herring had said *sotto voce*: "Bob Alert! Avert your eyes. Don't make eye contact for any reason whatsoever, ever ever." When I smiled and was turning towards the open door, he grabbed my arm. "For the love of God, man, heed my words! All else is folly!"

My eyes landed on a sign whose number had been rewritten a number of times: *It's been 876 days since Bob made me laugh.* Underneath was another: *It's been 9 days since Peter made me laugh.*

"He had three kids," I said.

"They'll be fine. Her family is rich."

Another time in the kitchen, I heard: "I interviewed with Rod and Reel and everyone there was named Tuna."

"No fucking shit."

"No fucking shit. They weren't like even related. It was like... *a coincidence.*"

"That's some serious shit, man."

"Like totally."

"What are we gonna do about Bob?"

"If we put a GPS tracking device on him, we could pinpoint his location worldwide 24/7. We could even link the doors to electrically lock whenever he's near. Have a blue light flash in warning. Give people time to swallow the cyanide tablets when he needs staff for new assignments."

"But who will do it?"

"Therein lies the rub."

Answering his phone calls was known as "taking one for the team" and was usually the result of a lost rock, paper, scissors contest or when the letter opener was just too dull to slit one's wrists and the window's glass just too strong to hurl oneself through. Sometimes people paid others to visit his office in their place, but then a lottery system was started in hopes of ending that practice (too often rent money was being used). It didn't work: the bribes continued.

As I walked towards his office that first morning, people approached me with earplugs, sample-sized bottles of alcohol and a noose fashioned from an extension cord while muttering heartfelt "Go with God" or "May the gods smite your hearing!" before whispering to each other as I passed: "He seemed such a sweet guy. It's too bad." (Even Wrasse patted my shoulder consolingly.)

I'd dealt with Sigmond. I'd dealt with Cassandra. How bad could Bob be?

He was.

"They showed this city market in Iraq on the news last night," Bob was telling a secretary named Leah as I rounded the corner. He was tall, over six foot, with slicked back brown hair, a grey flecked goatee and enormous veined hands. "On the top of the tents of where people were selling stuff, perched these pigeons. And they looked exactly like the pigeons they have in Union Square. And the stuff they were selling looked like the stuff they sell in Wal-Mart. And I started thinking about how pigeons are the same everywhere. They fly the same. They eat the same. They look the same. And if pigeons are the same, maybe so are people? 'Cuz they buy the same stuff we do. Maybe they're the same as us except that they have darker skin. And don't use toilet paper. Maybe people are the same world over. Maybe we're not so different. It makes you think. About pigeons and everything, you know?"

I just couldn't do it. I wasn't even close to capable. I turned back.

"Pete. Peter Pollack, where are you going?"

"Um." I should have run, but sometimes man is self-destructive for no reason. Not that he doesn't regret it to the end of his days.

"I'm Bob. We're going to be working together. I've heard you like to mix it up. So do I. Working together is going to be great fun. Come into my office and let's get acquainted. I've got to tell you about this show I saw last night."

Unlocking his office door (though it was 11 am, he'd just arrived), he went through a myriad collection of keys before he found the right ones to open the two extra deadbolts he'd installed himself. Then, as he turned on his light, he said, "They think it's funny. Just so immature." He grit his jaw as he moved around the office removing the signs that read "Bob's stapler," "Bob's hole punch," a chair labeled "Desk" and a desk labeled "Chair," "Not a chair," and "Maybe a chair, maybe not." Then he dumped into his garbage bin from his desk the book *Accounting for Dummies* with his company portrait superimposed over the face of the cover model with a typed message below: "You should read this."

"How... How did they get in? Erhh!" He scanned the room (thoroughly) for any other irregularities and then sat down. He readjusted the angle of his keyboard just so. And then his eyes relaxed.

I pointed to his nameplate. It read: *Martin Marlin* who had retired rather abruptly to somewhere in Costa Rica last week. (The next week it became *Michael Minnow* who'd been fired for forgetting to lock his desk drawer at night when he passed out on it – a clear and shockingly blatant violation of firm security policy.)

"Let's get out of here. Let's just get out of the office. Come on, we'll go to Lord of the Burgers. My treat."

He didn't want to go to the Lord of the Burgers right near the office so we walked to Pershing Square (he would not cross the street unless the light changed, even if no cars were visible in either direction on the narrowest of side-streets and then with checking both ways twice before stepping away from the curb). But when he saw one of the servers scratch his head, we had to walk back to the restaurant on Flower. It was about 98 degrees Fahrenheit out with a humidity level to match.

"Order fries and a drink if you want. Whatever you like. My treat. Go on, get a cookie, too. Don't worry about it." He recounted the bills three times before handing them to the cashier. "I'll need a receipt."

"It'll come with your food, sir."

"I'll need a receipt."

"If you sit down, sir, the server will bring it to you."

At the table: "I'm just so glad you're here with me, Pete. I'm swamped, just swamped. You'll be a great help to me."

"That's what I'm here for."

"I just have no time. None. Never enough time to do things."

"You have a lot of responsibilities as a senior manager." I looked at my watch: we'd been gone for 97 minutes and still didn't have our food.

He smiled. "Exactly! And they don't see that... Peter, I sense I can trust you, you seem like a nice guy – do you know if any of the partners have been talking about me?"

"Not that I've heard of."

"Even secondhand, you haven't heard anything?"

"Um, no."

"And you're sure?"

"Um, yes."

"You should listen to me. This is invaluable advice. The partners wouldn't like to hear me saying this, but, for me, it's not about the firm. Firms come and go, it's the people that matter, the relationships. And I'm hoping and I'm getting the vibe that it's mutual that this between us is going to be a career-long, nay lifelong, relationship. Am I right?"

"Um, yes."

"You may think I'm over-cautious, but only the paranoid survive this business, Pete. Like Kurt Cobain said, *Just because you're paranoid, doesn't mean they're not out to get you.*" Little did I know, but hearing variations of those two sentences would occupy literally hours upon hours of my life over the next couple of months. "Did you wash your hands? You really should wash your hands before we eat. Go wash your hands."

I made it back to the table. Somehow.

I spent the rest of that afternoon helping him fix his outgoing automatic email response. Each time I did, it was immediately replaced with (shown in chronological order):

1.   Napping (2:09 pm)

2.   Still napping (2:42 pm)

3.   At the beauty parlor getting my hair done pretty with the girls. Feathering! (3:17 pm)

4.   I'm disgruntled and unapproachable today, suffering from fulsome fits of sulkiness over the UNBELIEVABILITY of what happened on last night's semi-final episode of *Svetlana Swan's Superhot Chicks You Never Noticed Living on Your Block*. Go away! (4:32 pm - change delayed because the head partner received this reply and immediately appeared)

5.   No fun at all this afternoon. Hard at work trying to look busy (4:59 pm)

Despite a consolidated corporation's return being due the next day which paid us $1.3 million in annual fees (including the audit) and which we'd been caught in a bidding war over such fees and timeliness of deliverables with Rod and Reel a few months before, the fifth change was the last of the day because after that Bob left to go to his son's Little League baseball game, though he told Barrington it was to take a very important client out to dinner. No doubt, the rather frantic owner of the privately held corporation received the sixth variation a number of times throughout the night.

Thursday Bob called me into his office at 9:39 am. When I arrived (even the baby-est of baby steps eventually brought me there), his computer wasn't on yet. He immediately shut the door behind me and asked, "Did you hear anything about me this morning?"

"No—"

"I thought I heard someone say something. You know, I didn't actually take a client to dinner last night." He sat down and stared past me through the window looking back into the office.

"Yes, you told me."

"I feel like I'm in a fishbowl here. Everyone always watching me. And saying nothing to me. Nothing!"

"Did you tell anyone besides me?"

"Just Leah. And Skate in estate planning. But they wouldn't say anything. They like me."

"Then I don't know."

"They don't see how slammed I am lately. I'm literally working my fingers to the bone. To the bone. See? I'm just so tired. So very, very tired." Not one file topped his desk nor his credenza. All that did was a collection of button-eyed fabric dolls that I was to learn later represented his most hated clients. He would stick pins in the dolls during endless conversations disputing the billing (and sometimes pricking himself – I'd have to bite my fingers to keep from laughing as he'd thrash and grunt from pain). Figuring out what to bill for he and the two staff he had working under him would take up two weeks of every month as he endlessly drafted and redrafted each and every invoice for sometimes as small as 1/12 of an hour. Clients like Safeway and Trader Joe's were not so pleased about receiving current bills for $16 of time instead of larger more rounded figures in the future, but Bob diligently and without qualms fought to collect such sums as soon as the time was incurred.

He left that day at 4:46 pm.

A week later, a huge brass gong and accompanying rubber-headed sledgehammer was delivered to the Professor's desk from a company in Kathmandu. A skewered, hooked and gutted burbot (Bob's last name) was engraved on its shiny surface.

The day Ron had ordered the gong to announce Bob's approach, he said to me: "You can sit back and watch him destroy the ones who came after you. You can be amused by their struggle and be glad you don't have to relive it. That's the easy way. Or you can face up to it, do something about the iniquity you see." He didn't regret the $1,813 price tag, only that he'd waited too long to make the purchase and seen too many good men suffer under Bob. At the time, I thought he was joking, but no longer.

Envisioning my trip into the jungle near Rurrenbaque to be a somewhat similar experience to that of the African truck (listening to other tourists' meticulously detailed complaints about the bugs, bouts of diarrhea and not being able to see anything), I talked four other tourists into hiring an independent guide with me, including the French judo enthusiast who I met on the street.

He wasn't so independent in terms of transportation. The jeep which crammed all five of us, our packs and the driver joined a long line of such jeeps on a deeply rutted muddy road that led out of town towards the jungle. The guide rode on the roof.

"Is it safe?" I asked.

The Frenchman translated the guide's answer: "If problem, I jump."

"Problem?" I wasn't sure the brakes were fully functional, let alone the lack of airbags, seatbelts or working windshield wipers. If the road was half as dangerous as the one getting us to Rurrenbaque...

"No problema."

My pack was especially hated and seventeen times conspired against to be abandoned alongside the road – even more so than the Frenchman's whose bag was full of sharp corners (he traveled everywhere with a framed photograph of Bob Dylan and approached predicaments with the question "What would Bob do?" which I knew to be folly, knowing all about the perils of Bobs) and smelled much like a koala bear's pungent pudenda (See? The phrase is useful in real world applications. Though it hardly rolls off the tongue.).

How I knew what a koala bear's pungent pudenda smells like is a whole other story I don't like to talk about.

We spent seven hours reaching the jungle, much of it consumed with the driver exiting the vehicle to manually switch the car to four wheel drive and then switch it back after navigating especially muddy patches which he would always unsuccessfully try to steer through in two wheel drive first – often violently careening us to one side or the other (and getting us intimately acquainted with each other in a much too physical way inside – I soon knew the Frenchman's body better than a few ex-girlfriends') and nearly tipping over. He insisted on keeping the wrench that helped him perform the duty underneath the backseat – retrieving it the first 63 times was okay, but the 64th was kind of tedious. The duct tape holding some of the sides of the car together which undoubtedly would have given way to aid in our crushing didn't bother me too much because I got a middle seat (with no leg room) that kept any of the tape from sticking to my clothes like the others.

Every break for a cigarette or a pee ended with a race back to the jeep to be the one not sitting in the middle. International Rules of Shotgun were thrown out around five hours into the drive – also about the time we'd all given up hope of ever arriving. Such hope had not been dashed an hour in. Independently, we'd each felt it was too late to turn back, that we'd all muddle through somehow, and, therefore couldn't say anything. So not one of us articulated his or her fears at the ride's safety. Two hours in, we actually did speak it aloud but were assured we were "almost there." Four hours in, it was only *dos minutos mas*.

We completed *100 Bottles of Beer on the Wall* in all six languages available to us in the jeep. Again no one went for my *Strangers in the Night* (Not one hour in, not three hours in, nor at five – such grumps!).

The English couple were doctors who studied human stool samples given at hospitals. At the Frenchman's request, they treated us to a lengthy dissertation on quantity, coloration and frequency of their subject with much enthusiasm despite my protests.

I so wanted it to end and then we had to stop for someone to pee. And then we had to stop again for someone to pee. And then…

The driver smoked in the car, but courteously exhaled 4.63% of it out the top of his window.

The Frenchman was suffering from food poisoning. Yes, there were flatulence issues.

The guide's idea of "independent tour" meant setting up tent about two hundred feet from the other companies' permanent camps (which had framed mosquito screens around the sleeping and eating areas – we, of course, had none) and doing pretty much all the things you HAD to do when going on a tour in the Amazon: looking for climbing "parasitic" vines in the primary forest, fishing for piranha, shooting a blow dart gun.

Our guide looked exactly like the action movie actor Harrison Hawk – even had the same black handlebar mustache. He did everything with his machete – cleared a way through the vines, hacked down trees we could easily have passed, opened tin cans, chopped vegetables, shaved his chin. At night I caught him staring at the blade longingly by the fire's light.

He'd been in the Ecuadorian army but had left because everyone fell asleep at their posts during the night. He hated the Peruvians – if he had his choice, they'd invade Peru and kill everyone there. We asked him about war and how he would feel if his son were forced to go – he thought his son should and die if need be.

He was genuinely disappointed when we didn't want him to track down an anaconda and wrestle it so we could take photos. ("Would you like it if someone broke into your bedroom and put you in a headlock?") He did it with a cayman before we could stop him but that was because when we opened up the tent flap on the second morning, there he stood with the many, many toothed reptile. Yes, shenanigans ensued.

The trip was split into two sections. First was a tour of the pampas where we rode around on a longboat and saw birds, an occasional monkey (howler, white-faced capuchin, spider or a small species that traveled in packs and came down to the water to take bananas from the guide), and the backs of pink river dolphins when they surfaced for air and sometimes called out greetings. Second was a visit to the jungle after the same drive back. We didn't see a jaguar or a tapir, but did see plenty of capybara – a large brown rodent that traveled in packs and squealed if surprised.

The Frenchman banged his chest with both his fists and grunted/hooted after every monkey sighting. "Ever see Greystoke, the Legend of Tarzan? I love that movie. My brothers…"

One of the doctors said: "This is a lot better than the jungle in Ecuador. We drove pretty much to the end of the roads there in hopes of getting deep into the primary rainforest. We did a four day hike and not once could we not hear chainsaws or the roar of some oil company's tractor. And we didn't see anywhere near as many animals, even birds."

If the trail was clear, the guide would hang back and let one of us go first to knock down the spider webs or catch the leeches hanging off branches waiting all day for something to pass. He added a warning, too:

"Watch your step. Very poisonous snakes here." In places where grass alongside was high, we asked him to go first just in case. "No worry. Be okay," he said in English.

Yes, I was once chased by herd of tusk-bearing peccaries when going off-trail to relieve myself and led them right back to our group. Shenanigans again ensued.

The Frenchman wanted to hike through jungle so thick you had to use a machete to make your way. So, after the second day of his nagging, the guide led us to such a place. The guide demonstrated the proper technique and handed his blade to the Frenchman (though it was obvious by his covetous eyes he hated relinquishing the weapon). "Not you?" "You." After five minutes, the Frenchman's arm tired and we went back the way we'd come.

Back in the La Paz bus station, I glanced up from perusing my guidebook to see a middle-aged woman dressed in what looked like her bathrobe dragging my backpack very unsuccessfully towards the exit. "Hey!"

"You come with me. I have hostel. You stay there. Very cheap, very good. These girls come, you come. They very beautiful, you alone."

"Wait."

"No wait. You come. Include breakfast. Very good. Girls very beautiful. You come."

I had no retort so I went.

At the door to her hotel, the woman withdrew the key from the pocket of her robe, but not before taking a swig from the wine bottle that also resided there. "Nice rooms. Beautiful girls. I am Patricia."

"Peter."

"You open door."

"Huh?"

"Open door!"

I tried, but the door didn't budge.

"You must to shove. Shove!"

480

I did. My third attempt succeeded, though my shoulder could have argued regarding the degree of which.

She blocked my entrance. "Pay me now. Quince bolivianos. Fifteen."

"Can I see the room first?"

"Pay now. Stay room later. When sleep."

"But—"

"Buenas, Patricia," the beautiful girls said and slipped past us into the hotel.

I paid.

"For breakfast, you can have two pieces of bread, no more. Two pieces, no more."

"Can I have three?"

"Two. No more."

The showerhead dripped so loud you could hear it down the hall, around a corner, up a flight of stairs, down another hall and over a trio of barking neighborhood dogs (off-key, of course). None of the cardboard doors fit the frames. Bats flew in and out of holes in the ceiling. Broken pieces of linoleum (all of different designs) decorated the walls in non-geometrical, non-uniform designs (which was more than a little jarring aesthetically, lemme tell ya). A stuffed pigeon with evil (evil) glass eyes loomed over my assigned bed/hard metal cot.

I didn't leave. One of the two beautiful girls, a redhead with freckles, had beamed the most amazing smile at me when entering the hotel.

The second morning Patricia would not give me breakfast. A German engineer who had left on an early morning bus to Potosi had taken four pieces of bread. "He took too much, so none for you. I have only so much bread. He is a very bad man. A very bad man. If I see him again..." She shook her tiny fist threateningly. "Sit, sit." Patricia went into the kitchen to get the galaxy's oldest, weakest and least palatable instant coffee. "And Fernando and Marcus are not here," she said, returning. "Where have they gone? Why does everyone keep leaving?"

When I put the chipped *World's Sexiest Mom* mug flat on the table, it began to slide towards me.

After the third day of only brief glimpses of the redhead and still no bread for breakfast, I decided to leave La Paz. Only it wasn't that easy. The President of the United States chose that week to tell the Bolivian government he'd cut off aid unless something was done about the coca farmers. Their crop could be used to produce cocaine. So the Bolivian government had begun burning fields. The farmers and their families were left with nothing. But they could start over with money they didn't have and grow potatoes or coffee for a fraction of the yield. To protest, they'd blocked all the roads out of the city.

I'd read somewhere that 90% of hundred dollar bills in Washington D.C., where most of our lawmakers lived, carried traces of cocaine.

My daily routine soon fell into a pattern.

Wake at dawn. Freeze nipples off putting on shirt, freeze ass off putting on trousers, freeze toes off putting on socks. Finish packing. Check out of Hotel Austria. Stagger in chilly air (freezing off nose and reattached nipples as well as any other body parts that may still remain) to main bus terminal. Purchase ticket to Peru. Wait. Wait more. Wait still more. Get told bus is not going. Argue for refund as change has mysteriously disappeared. Be told other bus is going. Search frantically for the kiosk selling its tickets as its departure is "immediately imminent." Repeat ticket purchase and above mentioned waiting process. Get tourist police involved this time in acquiring refund. Catch minibus to other bus terminal outside the cemetery. Search for another bus. Fight locals for seat on second bus after being pushed out of the line for boarding the first. Keep Leatherman tool with serrated blade handy. Watch out for pickpockets and Communists distributing propagandist literature capable of corrupting my weak mind. Keep thinking capitalism, exploitation of cheap labor in inhumane working conditions and Western domination of third world countries is all for the best. Have a saltena. Drive out of La Paz dodging rocks scattered across the sealed road. Answer always in the affirmative fellow gringo passenger questions of "Do you think we'll make it? Do you really think we'll make it?" Hear comments such as "I think I see Peru. Do they have trees in Peru?" Watch the jagged line of snowy peaks at the edge of a light brown plain before a bleak gray sky. Scratch elbow if it requires scratching. Think fondly of pizza. Observe cattle trucks and other vehicles returning with shattered windows and drivers shaking their heads. Do a bit of my own head shaking as my bus turns back. Tell bus driver to commit uncouth acts with filthy denizens of nearby chicken coops as he drops us seven miles beyond the middle of fucking nowhere. Continue my tirade when he throws my backpack off the roof and crushes a small child. Ask local to take my photo with my camera holding a sign with an arrow pointing down saying *Middle of Fucking Nowhere*. Be accosted by taxi drivers who wish to drive me back to La Paz for double the Bolivian Gross National Product. Squeeze into minibus grinding my pack in parts of my anatomy I didn't know I had. Ooze out of said vehicle like a finely squeezed fruit pulp stinking of rank feet and pisco sour miles from the hotel. Walk up, up and more up, gulping the high altitude's thin air in a futile attempt to fill my lungs with oxygen. Think fondly of pizza. Check back into Hotel Austria. Go out for Chinese food as there is not one decent pizza place in all of Bolivia. Try calling place in Peru to deliver, but they can't get past the blockade, either, and certainly not in thirty minutes or less. Shower, savoring the ten minutes of warmth in the day while suffering occasional electric shocks trying to keep the electric showerhead adjusted to the correct temperature setting. Do nothing. Do more nothing. Contemplate shaving, but don't. Watch toenails grow. Consider going to a terrible American movie starring Svetlana Swan as a beautiful nuclear physicist with a crush on a lowly tax accountant played by Earnest Eagle which I've already seen thirteen times but don't. Get in bed because it's too fucking cold to do anything else. Dream of heat. Sleep. Wake at four in the morning due to lack of exercise and read the washing instructions on my sweater to help pass the time (they didn't have a telephone book - a favorite of my father for bathroom reading material). Repeat day after day after day.

The third time I was stranded, neither a minibus nor a taxi passed for hours.

It wasn't possible. And yet, there it was. I somehow managed to wave them down. Each of the four men inside was huge and hulking with mean eyes. "Speak English?"

"What you want, mister?"

"This is my car."

He laughed and then translated what I'd said. The three other men were equally amused.

"Let me see your driver's license and proof of registration!"

"Aqui." He reached onto the seat beside him and showed me a gun. I couldn't tell you which kind.

"This is my car," I insisted. "You stole it from outside my

483

grandmother's house in Santa Monica, California."

He cocked the gun's hammer.

"Perhaps I was mistaken. It appears all your paperwork *is* in order. You're free to go."

"Loco gringo." He questioned his companions with his eyes. One in the back slightly shook his head. "Be glad we don't rob you, pendejo." They drove off.

Knocking at my door at 2 am.

Nairobi.

Instead: "Wanna go for a beer?"

Why not?

Ten minutes later I was wandering through the streets of La Paz with a group of tourists from the hotel.

"How do you like South America?" I asked a Danish girl. Yeah, she was only eighteen but you know how I feel about Vikings.

"It'd be better if I spoke Spanish."

A carpenter from Dublin said, "You only need two phrases for traveling here. *Does it look like I need a fucking taxi?* And: *if I wanted a fucking coke, I'd ask you for one.* One or the other pretty much handle 97% of situations where you need to talk."

The poetry of the Irish.

"Where's the fucking bar?" Again: same source.

Our guide, an anthropologist from Montreal who had roused myself and others from our beds at 2 a.m to go on this tour, stopped us in front of a dark, indistinguishable building. "This is where the Bolivian government held Simon Bolivar prisoner... He escaped through that window... And that's the corner where the revolution started. Did you know it all began with a shattered vase?"

The Danish girl said: "I thought Bolivar was held prisoner in Colombia."

The carpenter said: "I just came from there."

"Didn't a backpacker just get killed there?"

"An American actually."

"Did you know him?"

"Everybody did.   There aren't that many backpackers in Colombia... He was a fucking idiot. He deserved to die. Everyone told him if you go to this place and try to cross the Darien Gap you will die. But he went anyway. And he got caught in a crossfire between the police and some guerrillas who were trying to rob his bus. So now he's dead and everyone says it's a tragedy. But everyday Columbians die there because they have no choice, they can't leave. And some fucking idiot American goes where no one wants him and everyone tells him not to and he dies there. And it's a big fucking tragedy. Bullshit."

I kept at it with the Viking: "Over there, for three and fifty-seven years, nothing of any significance whatsoever happened. But seventeen inches to the left, Cortes and Pizarro once shared two halves of the same pastrami sandwich. You have four point six three two minutes to visit this vitally important historical site. Please take a photo standing here with camera pointing in that direction at a ten degree angle from the horizon. Also: here, here and over there as you and roughly three million seven hundred twenty-six thousand one hundred forty-five other tourists do each and every year. But not there! Definitely not!"

You gotta try, right?

We did get to see where Bolivar grew up, where beer was invented (!) and where our guide was thinking of building a tourist restaurant sometime in the next few years if he could find some international backing. My "wink, wink, nudge, nudge" went ignored by the Viking as the guide began to argue the merits of the spot's location and his knowledge of the area and connections to the town's backpacker scene (we obviously weren't the first, nor the last, of his 2 a.m. victims). All without ever reaching a bar. When a cab drove past at 5 a.m., the carpenter hailed it down and offered triple the normal fare to get us (the fuck) out of there.

In the hostel courtyard, a dark haired man sat drinking a cup of wine. I took the chair opposite. "I'm Pete."

"Pancho Terromotos de Amor. It used to be different but I changed it when I got my Canadian citizenship. It means Earthquakes of Love. It describes my passion, my heart. See my passport? I'm telling the truth." He was. "I'm on my way to Paraguay to meet my girlfriend. She doesn't know I'm coming. She's left me twice at the altar but I got her face tattooed on my belly." He lifted his shirt. "See? The bitch has to marry me this time. Because I can't go through life with a woman's face tattooed to my belly that isn't my wife. People will laugh at me."

"Well, good luck with that. All the best." I stood to go.

"Mock me and I will kill you!"

"I think possibly, and forgive me if I'm mistaken, you may be plotting my imminent and most gruesome demise. Well, be aware, be very aware and cognizant that I work for the CIA, the NFL and PBS."

He jumped up and I ran away.

Later I found out he'd punched a German girl from a room down the hall who had unwittingly fallen into conversation with him trying to practice her English. They kicked him out into the street. He came back the next morning to pick up his stuff. He'd been beaten and robbed – his face was bruised and still bleeding - but no one really cared.

Another day passed. And another. My sympathy for the farmers' cause began to wane.

The fifth (sixth?) day of the siege another traveler in the market told me about a tourist bus leaving the next morning at six for Puno. The redhead and her sister, Marcella and Melanie, had tried going with me to the cemetery bus terminal the day before, so I asked them if they wanted to come along. They did.

Needing to change twenty dollars for the bus ticket, I visited the bank in the afternoon. As I munched away at a typically dry flavorless pastry, I thanked my luck when only twenty-nine people preceded me in line – a rare treat in South America. Suddenly a loud boom rattled the windows. I hit the floor. Outside, a double column of miners wearing their helmets walked by, some holding canvas banners with words of protest while balancing bright red popsicles in their other hands. Another loud boom. They were exploding very small amounts of dynamite to make their message clear. People laughed nervously and lined back up. Shouting outside. People, then miners running back in our direction. Police in full riot gear holding shields and batons giving chase. The guards began to roll down the bank's metal shuttered storefront with everyone inside. A few customers ran out into the chaos and a policeman bludgeoned one. I stayed inside the bank. Then just as the door was nearly down, a tear gas canister rolled to my feet.

486

Not good. Never again would I believe an action movie which showed people fighting after being tear-gassed. Your eyes water terribly, you can't stop gagging. And the taste is pretty horrific as well. I think some people would have screamed if they could. Nor could they open the door. It's said you haven't been to South America unless you've been tear-gassed. Well...

Luckily, my paparazzi had missed the moment of me not looking my best – a rare occurrence sure to make them kick themselves the next morning for having missed out.

When I finally recovered and went outside, a vendor had set up selling pickets and rocks to throw at the riot police. His spiel: "This one's roundness gives it a long trajectory. And this one's sharp edge is ideal for drawing blood. Special today: two for one."

Melanie said as we walked to the travel agency in the morning, "The weirdest thing happened at the hotel yesterday afternoon. A couple of guys in business suits showed up looking for a traveler who calls himself Richard Remora's Illegitimate Bastard Child."

Marcella said, "We thought it was a joke and began laughing, but they didn't. Laugh, that is."

"That's definitely weird."

As we crossed Calle Sagarnaga, snow began falling, making the streets slippery underfoot. But we made it. And the bus even looked respectable: cushioned seats, air-conditioning, even a videotape player and television set. It was late leaving, but that was to be expected.

"Do you mind taking the window seat?"

"Sure," she said and then hesitated. "But why?"

"To shield me." I smiled and slipped past her into the window seat.

As I unzipped my jacket, Marcella asked, "What's with the priest's collar?"

"In case we're taken. They wouldn't kill a priest."

"And what about us?"

From my daypack: "Nun's habits."

"Those look like dinner napkins."

Shrugging, "I did my best. Sorry about the pizza stains."

Melanie said, "Is this pepperoni? We're vegetarians."

Her sister said, "I really hope this works. We don't have the money for a flight. Even if they stop barricading the road to the airport."

"There are alternatives."

"Such as?"

Peter's First Suggestion: "We could dig a tunnel to the border. Like the movie *The Great Escape*."

Marcella's First Counter-Argument: "Well, I've got my nails to think of."

"I'm morally opposed to physical exertion," Melanie added. "Though how long could tunneling three hundred kilometers take?"

Peter's Second Suggestion: "We could rent some alpaca and go through the mountains. Or even better: dress like llamas and hope we don't meet any lonely Bolivian shepherds."

Marcella's Second Counter-Argument: "I'm not sure I could go without television for that long."

"Likewise my hairdryer," Melanie said.

"Disguise ourselves as farmers, join the protest and then silently slip away? I saw a place in La Paz that rents pitchforks."

Marcella shook her head. "I left my *Fuck the Police* T-shirt at home. I couldn't possibly attend a protest without it."

"Wouldn't be fashionably sensible," said Melanie.

"Paddle a raft across Lake Titicaca?"

"Sounds tiring and wet. Both of which I'm not big advocates of. To tell the truth, I don't like either one," Marcella responded.

"And I was serious about my moral opposition to physical exertion," added Melanie.

"Well, I'm out of ideas."

Marcella said: "Don't worry, you'll think of something. In the meantime we'll be able to do more shopping."

Melanie's eyes lit up. "Shopping, yes. Shopping."

"Good morning, ladies and gentlemen. Today we'll be attempting to circumvent the coca farmers' blockade outside the city by taking alternate roads to Desaguadero on the Peruvian frontier. Light refreshments will be served during the in-bus entertainment, a presentation of the motion picture prison drama set in a futuristic New York - *Escape From Manhattan* starring American actor Harrison Hawk. On your right hand side as we pass the first barrier, you'll be seeing llama herders wielding genuine pitchforks and on your left the protestors will be armed with more traditional weapons—hoes and round stones as were used in the Santa Cruz blockade of '86. Please notice the mob's multi-colored garments, which are indigenous to this region. For your own safety, ladies and gentlemen, keep your hands and feet inside the vehicle at all times. The use of imprudent hand gestures or flash photography is strictly prohibited and may result in your immediate ejection from the vehicle into the bloodthirsty maw of the mob. Buckle your seat belts when prompted and don't panic if we experience a bit of turbulence running over some of the more persistent farmers. This is a nonsmoking vehicle. Thank you for driving with us and I hope you enjoy a pleasant journey."

"Do you think light refreshments include cocktails?"

Marcella: "Why didn't you ask?"

"Why didn't you? I mean, bringing you along has proved useless!"

She smiled. "A Pisco Sour would be nice."

"Or a martini with green olives."

"Yuck."

"You prefer yours with onions?"

"I don't like martinis."

"I knew there was something deeply, fundamentally sick and twisted about you the first time we met, but I couldn't put my finger on it. Until now."

"Ah, there goes the cemetery."

"Fond memories?"

"Well, based on how our escape was going, I kind of figured I was

489

going to be buried there."

"Whatcha doin'?"

Marcella answered, "Writing a postcard home."

"All about me, I suppose."

"No, just the usual complaints about how badly my sister smells and what an evil bitch she is." When Melanie laughed, so did I. "Yeah, we write to our friends not about all the great sights we're seeing or the fantastic food we're eating, but only about how much we hate each other."

Melanie said, "I tell them we haven't spoken in months and that she's trying to kill me."

"I describe each of the 16, no, 19 ways her hair looks bad."

"I complain she steals the covers off my bed in the middle of the night."

I said, "But I thought you had separate beds."

"We do."

Minutes later, a group of policeman stopped the bus to talk to the driver. I told Marcella, "Apparently the protestors will let us through if we give them two Dutch girls."

Laughter. Melanie: "You and your shitty Spanish."

Marcella: "Actually they said they prefer eating Americans."

"Not with all that American junk food in my system. I'm too fatty."

An English tourist behind us said: "Keep it down about being American - we all don't want to get shot for your fucking President."

I let it go. But it was the closest I came to killing an Englishman. That day.

Up ahead, a group of angry (and armed!) farmers stood blocking the road at the first barrier. With them was a small boy with a T-shirt
490

reading:

I EAT AMERICANS FOR BREAKFAST.

AND ENGLISH AS A LIGHT SNACK BEFORE LUNCH.

His father's shirt read:

**THE ONLY GOOD EXPLOITATIVE CAPITALIST
AGGRESSOR IS A**

DEAD EXPLOITATIVE CAPITALIST AGGRESSOR.

"Got your machine gun handy?"

"Swiss army knife."

"They have rocks, machetes and pitchforks."

"Did you see my serrated blade?" It was one and three-quarters inches long.

I nodded in agreement. "And don't forget your tweezers."

"I'm surprised they're not running already."

"You have to stop cowering in fear behind me long enough for them to see the knife."

"I'm not cowering. I just, uh, dropped something." Big smile.

The man who had collected the money for the bus tickets climbed out to speak with the farmers. The farmers shouted for a while and threatened with their rocks, but the man from the bus exuded calm (oozed oodles of such) as he talked with them. It was an odd moment. I didn't know if I should be scared or not, but I wasn't. Finally, our man from the bus offered some money to the farmers. They shook their heads vehemently and pointed back at La Paz. Someone threw their hat into the dirt (a move I would later have to incorporate into my haggling technique). Our man shrugged and offered the money again. They took it and he calmly got back on the bus. The farmers moved the overturned cart from the middle of the road to let us through.

At the next barrier during the negotiations outside, an Englishman and an older Italian couple moved to the front of the bus to photograph the farmers.

"Did you get the guy holding that bottle?"

"He moved. I bet he'd take two dollars to pose."

"Probably get it for a dollar and a half."

"If he'd just step a little to the left. Better light."

The driver turned, "No fotographia. No!" He was ignored.

The men outside saw the cameras and intensified their shouting. A couple even banged their pitchforks against the window.

The three tourists quickly *cowered* back to their seats.

The rest of the bus was quiet.

The negotiations went on.

This was not good. I was going to become the accountant with the tale of two circles.

"Really should have made you sit by the window," I said to Marcella.

"That isn't right, taking their photos," Marcella said. "They're trying to change their lives."

"I would agree," Melanie said, "but I might be too busy being raped and pillaged."

And then twelve miles further than seven miles beyond The Middle of Fucking Nowhere, I saw the one thing we hadn't thought of: a tall Scotsman with a scraggly red beard and wild unkempt hair walking westward. It wasn't the rucksack on his back that made him stand out, but the kilt he wore and the bagpipes he was playing. He smiled at me through the window, despite the dust and falling snow, and then was gone. "Did you see that?" I asked the girls but they had dozed off in the middle of our dangerous border run.

Leading a string of alpaca along the road, two small boys clutching glass bottles of Coca-Cola smiled toothlessly at us.

At the Peruvian border, we switched to a local bus (and the woman with the crying baby boarded to share my seat). Minutes after our three hour wait for its departure, the vehicle was waved to a stop by a man who climbed on carrying his eight year old daughter. Her foot was bleeding heavily, but she wasn't crying. The driver turned off the main road.

"This isn't the right direction," the English guy said.

"Shut up," Marcella told him.

Over the next twenty minutes of bumps and dips on the way to a filthy local hospital, the girl never cried out once.

"What will you do in Peru?" Marcella asked me.

"I'd like to do some hiking but I don't have a tent."

"You can have mine," the Englishman said from the seat behind the girls. "I was just going to throw it out anyway. I don't even know why I brought it."

"Do you want some money?"

"Not at all. Like I said, I was just going to chuck it."

And that's how I got a tent.

At the hotel in Puno (Peru!), Melanie asked me, "Should we share a room together?"

"As long as she," I hooked a thumb in Marcella's direction, "doesn't snore."

"I do," Melanie said.

"Well, I sing Broadway show tunes in my sleep. You prefer *Fiddler on the Roof* or *My Fair Lady*?"

"*West Side Story*."

Cutting into her recent purchase, Marcella said, "This avocado isn't very ripe."

"How can you stand her constant complaining? You should ditch her."

Melanie sighed. "I try but she keeps turning up in the same hotel room as I."

"Television!" I tried pushing the power button, but the set was unplugged. And the room had no electrical outlets. "South America."

"Running border blockades is dusty work," Marcella said. "I *need* a shower."

"Do you need some privacy?"

"I'm Dutch. Do *you* need any privacy?"

"We're just going to change some money. Then we can have dinner. Unless you have other plans," Melanie said a while later.

"My dinner with the Presidente is tomorrow night, remember?"

"We'll see you later then."

"Do you mind if I try on some of your underwear while you're gone?"

"Just the dirty stuff."

"Melanie doesn't feel well, so we're eating by ourselves," Marcella said when they returned. "If you're okay with that."

Well, well, well. "I suppose."

Restaurant-bound, we passed through the market to get snacks for tomorrow. The more upscale butchers' stalls defended their meat with mostly ineffective small electric fans, the others let the flies do as they willed.

"If that meat's less than three weeks old, I'm not touching it!" I said in passing.

"It might upset your stomach?"

"Exactly and yet, at the same time, not at all. And I'm kinda, sorta, totally flabbergasted and not a bit put out that you'd go so far as to suggest something vaguely approximate to that."

In another section tourists had gathered at a stand serving meats of endangered species. Today's special: deep fried white-winged guan aged a premature three days in the sun. "Come, come. Muchas turistas se gusta," they beckoned when they saw me looking. And that's the closest I ever came to killing a Peruvian.

A German ordered seconds of the guan. And though it wasn't the closest I ever came to killing a German, it ranked among the top fourteen times.

"This place has chicken *and* beef."

"I know where we're eating."

"I love what they've done with the place."

"The headless plastic Jesus really makes the room."

"So what's your plan after Peru?"

"Maybe the Galapagos and then home via land through Guatemala and Mexico. You know, just show up on my mom's doorstep and say hello."

"You won't like Guatemala."

"Why not?"

"Everything tastes the same there. Bread, chicken, bananas. Everything."

"I'll bring pepper."

Marcella shrugged. "Won't help."

"I've only got room in my brain for five things. Now that you've told me something new, I've forgotten one of them. Thanks a bunch."

"I hope it wasn't anything important. Like how you should never run with scissors. Even with the direct supervision of a responsible adult or parental guardian."

"You did it again."

"Go for another beer?" Marcella asked.

"That goes without saying so I have no idea why you said it or even had to contemplate the possibility of asking such." I pushed her playfully out the door.

"I will fight you," she said.

"You won't."

"Oh?"

"Not even with that useless Dutch army of yours would you dare to threaten my mother's son. For at my request, she will fly here most expeditiously and kick your adorable Netherlandian arse."

"I'm shaking in my, uh, flip flops. Not!"

"That joke is so 1985-ish."

"As is that T-shirt of yours."

"Absolutely. Without a doubt. Unequivocally. Yes."

"Keep that up and people will think you repeat yourself."

"What did you say?"

"Keep—"

"Sorry. Never mind… This place looks good, right?"

A couple of jumbo-sized Cusquena's later (served in chipped porcelain vases of curvy naked women – comments were unnecessary), Marcella said, "Is accounting your passion?"

"I'm good at it."

"That's not what I asked."

Suddenly everything felt all wrong, but I continued anyway, "You have to make money somehow. Sometimes you don't have the luxury of doing what you want. I've lived without money and it was suffocating. I saw how it affected my parents – the constant fights, the repetitive arguments. I mean, they found that special other person. If I ever do, I don't want money to be an issue."

"I understand. I do. But I think you're wrong to do accounting."

"I don't really know any other way to make money. And all the things I don't like about my job, I don't think are unique to accounting. I think they're just results of human nature. Everyone only wants to use each other."

"I try to stay away from people who aren't happy with what they do. Our time here is too short to waste with people who aren't happy. And

496

it rubs off on you."

I smiled. "So you're saying I'm doomed?"

She didn't return the gesture. "Do you really want to change your life? Or do you just want to talk about changing it without really doing anything? When it's gone, it's fucking gone."

"It's kind of what my trip is about. But I'm coming to realize that there is no special end place. It's what you bring to it. Your attitude. Your friends. The journey, not the destination."

"But, still, it's not your passion. If you ever want to share your life with someone and have both of you happy, you're going to have to fix that... I'm sorry, I shouldn't have said that. Maybe it's just a dream. My parents were hippies, Dutch hippies. They had an open marriage. But my father couldn't really handle it or his job or maybe both and became an alcoholic. So my parents got divorced when I was about ten. It did something to me: made me tough, I think. Maybe too tough. And I say what I think. And do what I want. Because you have to sometimes. No else is going to look out for you, not even family. And the traveling I've done: while it's been awesome, made me kind of more selfish. Because I can essentially do whatever I want whenever I want with no one to answer to. I don't know."

"I think you're pretty great."

"I've done some bad things, terrible things."

"Like what?"

"I used to be kind of wild... My first boyfriend I dated for four years. He really loved me and I broke his heart. I left him for another guy. With this other guy, it was more. So much more. He really changed the perception of what I want, what I need. It was true passion. But it was a crazy time. Six months of tumultuous ups and downs. It shattered me... At some point, though, you just say: stop the pain. But do you really stop if you love that person? Truly love them? Is there a limit?"

"I think there is."

"Me, too."

"What happened to your father?"

"He got better in a few years and stopped drinking. My mom just remarried the guy she's been living with the last ten years."

"My father was an alcoholic, too. But my mother stayed with him.

He'd probably be dead if she hadn't. I think she made the right choice. But for a couple of years it was really hard... My parents have been married thirty-one years and they scream at each other constantly. I once said to my dad I don't understand why they're together. He complains to me about her and she does the same to me about him. And then one day last year she'd just yelled at him about watching sports or something and I saw his face as he left the room. He was smiling. He loves it. Such a difference from my grandparents. Before she died, I asked my grandmother how her and my grandfather got along through fifty years of marriage. Did they fight a lot? And you know she told me they never fought? Not once. Never even raised their voices to each other. I asked her how that could be and she answered, I didn't understand him and he didn't understand me. I think that's why we got along..."

"What do you want?"

I didn't answer.

Her blue eyes held mine for a long moment before she said, "So, um, what kind of music do you like?"

"Rock mostly. Alternative, classic. Some jazz, bebop mostly. You?"

"Eagles, Black Crows, the Byrds. But my favorite band in English is the Counting Crows."

"That's the saddest thing I ever heard."

But she didn't laugh. She just got quiet. Then: "Have you visited any of the small villages here in South America? Where the tourists don't go."

"Not really."

"My sister and I spent some time there. The women were really open and friendly. But it was difficult for me. I like to think the world is moving in the right direction, that things are getting better. I need to, I have to. Because the alternative, to give in to negativity, it's such a draining force. It can just deeply affect your whole being. If you're positive, it just makes you feel better and everyone around you, too. It's very, very important for me. And these women living here in the twentieth century need to marry or they'll starve to death. There's no alternative for them. Unlike for me, there's no opportunity. And so they stay with these men that cheat on them or beat the shit out of them... I asked them why and they tell me they have no other choice. It really got to me. That and that I could just leave. Poof. Like that. But then I saw how close the women in these villages were, how it drew them together. And how we don't really have that in Europe anymore. I mean, I have girlfriends and my sister, but their bond seemed something more. I don't know. What does it all mean, right?" She finished her beer and smiled as her finger lingered on her vase's left breast. "Should we go?"

At the door, she shoved me out.

"*Now* we're definitely fighting."

She feinted jabs left and right. I whipped out the haka. When she did a spin fake kick in super slow motion accompanied by mouthed sound effects, I ducked under but then had to grab her from behind to keep her from falling when my foot slipped. She quickly pulled away and kept her face hidden.

"Hey—"

"Do you have any brothers or sisters?" she asked me in a small voice.

"A younger sister."

"Are you close?"

"Not anymore."

She turned her eyes to me. "What happened?"

"She became a lesbian."

Her shoulders tightened. "Became? Maybe you discover you are a lesbian, but you don't really become one... You don't like homosexuals?"

"It's not that. It's how she treated us. My parents especially."

"It's a tough time coming out. People say stuff they don't mean when they feel attacked or at their most vulnerable. You need to forgive her."

"I tried. Yes, I was really angry at her for a while. She'd lied to us for months and months. But now it's not about that. I think I could forgive her. I'm pretty selfish myself sometimes. But she doesn't want to be forgiven. She doesn't think she's done anything wrong. Relationships must be built on trust. And when I see her now her at my parents, she just makes sniping remarks at me. It's not fun to be around her."

"She's probably very hurt and alone. You should call her. She's your sister, right? I can't imagine going through my life without Melanie.

It's not like we never hurt each other… You will go back to your sister. Eventually. You will. You'll have to. You won't be able to live with it if you don't."

Maybe that's why Belinda had left. I was angry and bitter and she didn't need that. No one did, I guess. Maybe that's why I was alone. And maybe always would be. But maybe I didn't have to be. Could I become the person Marcella thought I needed to be?

"I shouldn't have told you this."

"You don't have to apologize. Everyone needs to talk."

"What the—"

We'd entered the Plaza des Armas. The square was lined with boxwood hedges carved into first unidentifiable shapes. But the longer we looked at them under the light of the full moon, the clearer their outlines became. A shark with two heads. A hunchbacked man with a square body and Sigmond's smile (The horror! The horror!). An eagle wrestling with an octopus. A goldfish with half a head and a snake's tail.

"Where are you going next?"

I'd fucked it up. "Maybe a tour of Lake Titicaca. You?"

"We're meeting some friends from home in Cuzco… But maybe we could meet up there after you're done. Or further north. You really need to see the lake. I went a few years ago and it's truly worth it. We'll email."

Outside the hotel door, I said, "Good night, Marcella."

"I'll wake you before we go."

"Good."

"You don't have to walk me to the bus station."

"I want to."

At the door to the bus, Marcella said, "Maybe we'll see you in Cuzco or Ecuador."

"I truly, full on hope not."

Marcella reached for her camera. "Make yourself look pretty. And for God's sake, fix your hair."

I shook my head. "You can't take my photo. It might infringe on my exclusive modeling contract with Calvin Klein as you are not one of their designated representatives and clause six paragraph two of said contract clearly and definitively forbids such an action by a non-designee."

"Shut the fuck up," she said. I nearly wept at the beauty of it. But still she went.

A hug and three kisses each and they were gone. I returned to my hotel alone.

I thought it was over and I'd never hear from her again. But I did. Not that it was any better for that. Knowing it was coming didn't make it hurt any less.

The email that night:

I'm sorry, I think that I led you on. I have a boyfriend in Holland. He's a singer for a band, a Dutch version of the Counting Crows. They're called the Tallying Toucans. The name's a joke, obviously - they met working in an accounting office. Kind of funny, actually, in a weird ironic kind of way, though you probably won't think so. I had a lot of fun hanging out with you. Marcella

I went to a bar. I shouldn't have, but I did anyway. I should have just tried talking to someone new, moved on, but I figured she'd just leave like everyone else, so I concentrated only on drinking. After a while, I couldn't stand it any longer.

He turned towards me with that smirk they all seemed to have. Looked me up and down. "Hello."

"What kind of fucking piece of shit are you?"

The surrounding people at the bar got quiet. He turned from me and drank from his beer. The ten year old boy accompanying him didn't look at me, didn't look at anyone, just sipped his soda.

"I asked you a question, fuckhead." I touched his shoulder.

I expected him to swing at me. Instead he caught the eye of the bartender and raised his eyebrows.

"I asked you--" Suddenly I was lifted from both sides and dragged outside by two men of a size I couldn't have fought even if I was sober. They shoved me out the door without bothering to open it first and, as I struggled to stay on my feet, one of them kicked me in the balls. I collapsed in the street.

"*No regrese*." He poured a beer on my head.

No one helped me up. After a while, I struggled drunkenly to my feet, having failed to start my one and only fight as an adult. The one who'd kicked me stood watching, ready to continue. Wanting to continue.

There it was. Right in front of me. And I couldn't do a fucking thing to stop it. A superhero I was not.

I staggered back to my hotel to a night of vomiting.

I may have shouted at poor, defenseless strangers on my walk home: "I know more about Internal Revenue Code section 321 in my little finger than you know in your whole body!" Yes, I'm like that sometimes.

The next afternoon, a travel agent enthusiastically showed me photos of the *traditional* reed boats we would ride across Lake Titicaca that had added manufactured yet "authentic" dragon heads for the tourists. He explained I would even get to taste the reeds comprising the boats and sample *traditional* life on the lake's islands where men and women wore different colored hats depending on their marital status. I could give a shit about any of it (Is this what I'd been doing for six months?), but I bought the ticket anyway. I didn't know what else to do.

In the morning I fell asleep waiting outside my hotel for the mini-van that would start my tour. Still waiting two hours later, I turned around to see a dog peeing on my backpack. "Of course."

I returned inside and told reception not to disturb me if the van ever showed up. I didn't bother to get a refund.

The road to Cuzco ascended through barren valley after valley with ever closing glimpses of snow-capped peaks.

I needed to talk to someone. Anyone. So I asked the tourist sitting across from me for the time.

He regarded me for a moment. In his left hand he held an Australian aboriginal didgeridoo, a musical instrument fashioned from a long, hollowed out eucalyptus tree stem. "Imagine throwing this watch away. You can't, you'd go crazy. We see life as segments, as fragments, that are completed one after the other. It gives us order. A Bedouin in the desert, they see no beginning, no end, they just are. They sit in the desert and have no conception of time. They feel no need to accomplish anything, they have no concept of aging, of regrets, they just are. There is no progression, they live only for the moment. And they are happy."

Okay. "You're Israeli?" I recognized the accent.

"I was born there, I lived there for a while, but, no, I'm not Israeli. Because I'm never going back. They're fucked. Fucked. This, this, is my home." He waved his arms around.

Fucking hell. "You live in this bus?"

He didn't answer me.

No one went to Sigmond's funeral. His family moved back to Iran.

How many women Ron had worked his charms on became evident at his funeral. Excepting Ivana from the slaughterhouse who was away on a bird-watching world cruise, at least one woman (sometimes two!) from each of Ron's clients showed up at his funeral tear-streaked and/or wailing. His widow did not take too kindly to their appearance and threatened them with a flamethrower (apparently one was conveniently located in the limousine trunk). Assistant controllers, accounts receivable clerks and Fedex delivery girls toppled memorial wreaths as they trampled each other with stiletto heels in the cemetery grass trying to escape.

Besides his now evident flagrant infidelities, other reasons for Mrs. Rohu's rage became apparent.

Sculpin was laughing inside Salmon's old office. No one else would go in there, not since a state and local tax expert waited all of three days after Salmon's death to claim the office as his own. Envy burned in all the other supervisors' eyes as they passed the now occupied desk. Until a few screws popped loose (it was later discovered the extreme temperature changes had cracked all the threads) and the overhead light swung down from one end and clubbed the man sitting at the desk below in the right temple. Now even maintenance wouldn't enter to do anything about the exposed octopus of wires or the flickering light.

I hadn't seen Sculpin since our lunch when I'd said, "In those huge lots, I can never find my car," and he'd laughed. But it'd gone on too long. "What's funny?"

"They take your keys when you're not looking and move your car." He laughed some more.

I said nothing.

His smile disappeared. "You chew really loud," he'd said and then there was an awkward twenty-six minute silence as we waited for the check followed by a second twelve minute silence as we waited twice for them to correct errors in the bill.

Sculpin held a cell phone to his ear. He was rolling a broken owl figurine back and forth under his left foot. As we made eye contact, he beckoned me inside.

I considered going on but joined him instead, trying not to look at the smudge darkening one end of the dangling light.

He gestured for me to lean shut the slab of prefabricated wood temporarily acting as the blow-torched door's replacement. Again, I hesitated but did it. The room smelled of instant coffee and onion bagels. So this was where accountants went to die.

Sculpin moved the phone from his ear and pushed a button activating its speaker.

The deep voice of a man said, "What do you know about Pisces Insurance Company?"

A woman's voice responded: "Never heard of it."

"And Smart Girl Management Limited?"

"Same."

"We'll need copies of all your bank statements for the past three years as well as details on any incoming or outgoing wires."

"I don't have to give you those." Then I recognized the voice: Cassandra!

"Read your employment contract."

"What's this about? Something fishy is going on here."

"You're not fooling anyone with this little ignorance act, you know that."

"I have no idea what you're talking about. I think I'd like my lawyer present."

"You really should have read your employment contract." Rustling of papers. "You almost got away with it. Almost. But you got greedy."

"You're making a mistake."

"We saw the Allstate policy. Otherwise, we might never have caught you."

"Doing what?"

"We know about the other policies, Ms. Carp. Oh, you're good, we'll give you that. At first we suspected Mrs. Rohu. Then there was the flamethrower incident when she found out about the other women at the funeral right after she'd been told the three million dollars of policies she did know about had had the beneficiary changed and we were less convinced. After she tore apart the interrogation room's steel table with her teeth when we told her about the additional fourteen million dollars Mr. Rohu's life had been insured for, we turned our suspicions elsewhere. And then we found the Allstate policy. You almost got away with the full seventeen million. But then we saw your sloppiness. And all for a seven hundred dollar pay-off."

"I still have no idea what you're talking about."

"You forgot to name that policy's beneficiary one of your shell companies! We caught you, woman! We caught you! The others were untraceable: first paid to a Cayman Islands limited liability company which was in turn owned by a Luxembourgian charitable foundation owned by an Oman shipping corporation. Then our trail went cold… Your structuring was masterly, I'll concede that. It took us weeks to navigate the labyrinth of privacy laws and red tape involved in finding out the ultimate owner. Each entity's officers were pseudonyms, their transactional history completely fictitious. We lost hope. But then Allstate told us they'd sent you a check for $700. And everything fell into place."

"Even if I did do it, which I didn't, what law has been broken here, anyway?"

There was a long pause. When the voice continued, the volume had decreased: "You know that the moneys were disbursed based on reports filed with the various insurance companies claiming that the cause of death

505

was not what further investigation has shown to be the case: that Mr. Rohu was complicit and even, perhaps, fully responsible for his death when he attacked Sigmond Sturgeon with the intent of inflicting bodily harm. The reports told another story: that Mr. Sturgeon had tripped and fallen against the glass surrounding the tiger shark tank of Oceanworld and that Mr. Rohu attempted to stop his fall, but that he, too, had slipped on the water slick near the tank and the added momentum of both of their bodies had propelled them over the lip of the glass into the tank. Those reports were notarized by a member of your firm, a person who, despite an exemplary career of thirty plus years, has subsequently disappeared. A person you have worked with in the past and have obviously interacted with on a day to day basis. A Mr. Martin Marlin. Are you denying you had knowledge of this?"

"Yes."

"And what about the insurance investigator—"

The phone went silent.

"The battery died."

"How?"

"Planted a second phone in The Abattoir. There's like six cops in there but none of them bothered to look around the first corner of the ceiling air duct."

Bob never completely deleted an email: sent or received. He printed and filed them in meticulously organized manila folders with specially created labels in an intricately locked coffin-sized cabinet that involved levers, pulleys and dials to open. In the heat of a dispute over past correspondence, however, he could never find the paper he sought because either it didn't exist or, in his agitated state, he couldn't manage the requisite maneuvers to open the cabinet.

The mahogany cabinet was actually the second one he'd purchased, each time he'd had to wait four months for it to arrive as it was custom built in Indonesia. The first he'd assembled at home. For months before its appearance in the office, he told me he was "swamped" and his favorite: "tired, just so tired." He'd been pretty regularly putting in seven hours days barely broken by only two hour lunches and six coffee breaks during that whole time, so I figured later that his state of being "swamped" was somehow related to the cabinet's assembly.

Unfortunately, when he brought the first assembled cabinet to the office in a rented moving van, its length prevented it from fitting in the freight elevator. So he requisitioned three staff members (me among them) to carry it up twenty-eight flights of stairs. Twenty-eight. Standing it on end at every landing was involved. Then it wouldn't fit inside his office door.

"I guess I should have listened to the maintenance guy at the building entrance," Bob told me. "He insisted I couldn't fit it inside my office door. Apparently he was right."

For two days, the cabinet sat outside his office blocking the northwest exit to the elevator bay and the bathrooms.

It was sort of good that no one could access his office for those two days. Sort of. Bob was hard of hearing, though he insisted that he wasn't, and would increase the volume of his speakerphone to the maximum. Since I got tired of climbing over the cabinet to reach his office and he made me switch cubicles to be closer to him after we started working together, screeching feedback often punctuated our phone conversations.

For two years, I'd shared only grunts and nods with my cubicle neighbors until the week before Bob forced me to change seats. Then the honey-haired Sally Sardine - a hot tamale and at least a third, probably a half and it wouldn't be exaggerating to say an additional 3/4 - had moved in next to me, said hello and started laughing at 93.6% of my jokes.

But my efforts to duck Bob's proximity proved futile, most of our phone conversations ended with him exclaiming: "I can't understand what you're saying. You lost me." So I was forced to scramble over the cabinet, attempting to avoid its sharp points and protuberances and once, most embarrassingly, failing at which just as Sally Sardine walked by and I was standing with torn trousers in Bob's office doorway in a scene reminiscent of my bathroom encounter at Veronica's Secret. (A year later, I heard Sally had married the guy who took my vacated cubicle – he also wore glasses, was shorter than me and couldn't match his socks, either.)

On the third night, the cabinet was found hacked to pieces with the remnants piled up in front of Bob's door. The murder weapon? Thought to be a combination of bare hands and acco fasteners, but that was just conjecture as I had no knowledge whatsoever of the most heinous crime. None.

"Do you think it was Barrington--" Bob whispered to me in the elevator that night as I was going to pick up dinner for the office and he was headed home, but was cut off by Barrington stepping in just behind us.

"What was that?" I said.

Bob shook his head vehemently and stared at his feet. When the doors opened at the lobby, perspiration drenched his brow.

He never mentioned the first cabinet again, but would occasionally make vague references to *The Crime Against Humanity* which took me a while to figure out he wasn't talking about the Holocaust or the Vietnam War.

Thirteen days before the first income tax return deadline of April 15 and when the minimum weekly hour requirement reached 85, Bob began assembling the second cabinet. It took him 16 hours over two days. Near the end, he realized he'd forgotten to measure if it would fit inside his office. It did, but only diagonally. Our daily marathon meetings, when he regularly veered off into dissertations about the greatness of the San Francisco Giants and Barry Bonds, excellent uses for duct tape and the importance of enough protein in one's diet, went as you'd expect in the now cramped space.

Some thought it was a ploy by Bob to get a bigger office, especially when he'd try to unsuccessfully close his door any time a partner passed and then would continue to try for minutes upon minutes upon minutes. (There were kitchen conversations such as "Want to go watch Bob try to shut his door again?") But when it worked, they thought him quite the Machiavellian mastermind. (The bigger office was across the floor which not only necessitated me moving again, but his desk. Getting the desk across the labyrinth of cubicles was an exercise no mergers & acquisitions specialist or tax accountant should ever have to witness, let alone perpetrate. It was brutal.) In reality, it was probably a human resources solution. Bob had grown tired of scrambling over the desk and had it leaned against one wall in his office, knocking out all the cardboard panels in his roof in the process. Just as I was asking if that was safe the next morning, it toppled over and I had to dive to avoid being crushed (ripping my trousers again). The glass wall of his office shattered behind me – which eased getting the desk out of his office and into the new one. A note announcing his new office arrived shortly. He thought, of course, this was a sign from the partners that all was forgiven and his time had come. His gloating and fatherly advice to everyone he came in contact with (a three hour discussion with the copy machine repairman on the importance of using a firm handshake while networking) didn't end until someone (again – I have NO idea who) locked a bicycle chain and padlock around the cabinet in its new location. Bob spent two hours hacking at the padlock with a three-hole punch (!) before calling a locksmith.

Monday morning Bob called me into his office a moment after he arrived at 10 a.m. (He'd missed the daily department ritual imposed by the office partner in charge – a group chant nine times at 9 a.m. of the mantra: "Bill, bill, bill." Some liked to hold hands during said ritual, but I wasn't really into it – Flounder, the nose picker, was. As a reminder, the mantra was also the standard phone ring, engraved in brass above each conference room doorway and embossed in gold at the bottom of all internal memorandums.) "Pete, do you have a minute?"

"I had the worst weekend of my life," he told me as I sat down.

"What happened?" I asked with concern.

"You know we live on a street with a hill nearby. Well, my fourteen year old son and a few of his friends stole a shopping cart from the local Safeway and were taking turns riding it down this hill. Only it got away from them."

"Did someone get hurt?"

"No. But when one of the other boys was riding in the cart, it hit my neighbor's car and caused over $800 of damage. All his friends ran away, but my son knocked on the man's door and let him know what had happened. The police came and everything. Luckily, my neighbor didn't want to press charges: he said when he was young he did some crazy stuff, too. I just had to pay for the damages. Luckily. I don't know what I would have done if he had pressed charges."

This was the worst weekend of his life. "But your son did the right thing by accepting responsibility for his actions?"

"He's just so wild. I don't know what to do with him. We sent him to military school last year and it doesn't seem to have helped at all. I really think he's going down that wrong path and there's nothing I can do to correct it."

"Yeah, it's tough raising children and letting them make their own choices. Did you want to work on the J&J tax provision?"

"I don't know. I can't even think right now. I didn't sleep at all for two days worrying about this."

"I'm sorry. But really all there is to this provision is the nondeductible portion of meals and entertainment expense for tax purposes."

"All right, all right. You know me, I'm the first to jump right in and help out whenever anybody needs it. Even a day like today. Like my father used to say, I'll just have to knuckle down. He was in the military, you know."

"I didn't."

"A retired colonel when he died. That's when my mother began eating herself to death. She became fat and disgusting. You know what's the worst thing about America these days? How fat everyone's become. And how much money it costs us in increased medical insurance. Not that I don't love America, I do. I spoke too harshly and I hope you'll forgive me because I didn't mean it. Like I said, I had a really tough weekend and I let my emotions take over when I said that. When you move up in the ranks, Pete, you're going to have to remember that: you can't let emotion rule your decision making process or affect the way you treat your employees."

Eleven o'clock came. Eleven o'clock went. Twelve o'clock came. Twelve o'clock went.

I blacked out. When I came to, I tried to focus on what he was saying (I did, I really did), but I just couldn't. But then, somehow, someway, I did (though I regretted it later, of course).

"...That was my friend Jim who went to Iowa that one time. He didn't even know anyone there or anything. He was one of those really adventurous types, always doing crazy, adventurous things. He'd never been to Iowa before, you see. It was all unknown to him. Now that's courage. I met him at the firm I worked at before here. That's where I did nothing but FAS 109 provisions. I did hundreds of them, I was the country-wide expert. I was very good at them."

Totally ignored went my "Speaking of which—". I didn't know yet to wait for the lulls.

"Most accounting firms are Jewish, but this one was Italian. Pigeons might be the same everywhere, but Italians are notoriously cheap. Everyone knows that. Not like the French who are all cheats. And South Africans are just arrogant. I knew a couple at the firm before this and they were both just so arrogant."

"You can't make such generalizations about people."

"No, they are. I want to show you an email one of them sent me." He turned to his cabinet and, after consulting its user's manual (which he had to do every single time he tried to open it), started looking through the drawer for his 1982 correspondence. (He had his sick notes from second grade in there, too – a later thrilling and in no way shortened episode of *Bob's Show and Tell*.) "I know... Here! Look: *Bob, do the Wingman return first*. Arrogant, right?"

I blacked out again.

"Pete! Do you want to do this provision or not?"

12:16 p.m. 136 minutes I would never get back. "Yes. As you can see, the only adjustment is for 50% of the meals and entertainment expenses. The client even confirmed the amount in this email."

"Where?"

I soon learned that even if I put the paper directly in front of him and pointed, Bob couldn't always follow and punctuated such failures by throwing up his hands in exasperation. The reason? He insisted his eyes were perfect and always had been. Once he told me I shouldn't wear glasses because doing so prevented my body from getting better by accommodating its imperfections. Most of our conversations included this exchange: "What is the answer? Tell me the answer." *"It's right there. On the paper. In front of you."* "I can't see that. How can you expect me to see that? You don't put your full effort into this."

I started using a smaller and smaller font for every printout I gave him. (He insisted on seeing all documents and spreadsheets in hard copy no matter the size or unwieldiness to formatting and, despite how few pages he actually looked at, required I properly label, margin and number each page uniformly or I would have to entirely reprint. Yes, there is an empty field northeast of Seattle the size of Luxembourg where the trees cut down for Bob's print jobs once stood.) When he pricked himself removing a heavy duty staple from a three hundred page printout (of a two row spreadsheet) and cursed/whimpered before demanding I use acco fasteners, I used only the heavy duty stapler from then on, even to bind only two sheets. I prepared returns in fluorescent yellow crayon (okay, I never turned them in). It wasn't enough.

I hid an egg in one of Bob's cupboards. It didn't make me feel any better and I had to smell it for two weeks before he found it. Well, I found it. He tended to give up looking after all of ten seconds every morning. Probably couldn't differentiate the smell from his own eggs and protein shake.

I tried exchanging his nameplate for those of people who had been fired from the thousands in the Employees' Graveyard. At first, he didn't notice and I'd forgotten I'd done it. It was a female name – Charlotte Chard - and everyone laughed about it for a while. Then Barrington noticed and laughed, but told Bob about it. Afterwards Bob screwed his nameplate in (a process that somehow took him three hours and, yet, he remained, according to him: "fully billable this week."). Of course, we screwed it out – even pooled our money to purchase an electric screwdriver in a rare moment of office solidarity to better be able to make the switch when he went to the bathroom (pretty much everyone on the floor had a copy of his office keys – including the two additional deadbolts he'd installed himself (speedily)). He bolted it in, soldered it. We figured out ways to combat them all. Then, one sad, sad Thursday morning, we came to work to find the nameplate housing missing.

I changed the CD in his office's player to *Svetlana Swan's Greatest Hits* – had even burned something like a hundred extra copies to replenish those he found (and stored in his cabinet as "evidence.") If he forgot to recheck the machine or its much increased volume in the morning...

We changed his computer's screensaver to a picture of Ron and password protected it. He was not pleased.

I figured out his tie cycle (not a difficult feat) and combed the super discount bins at Marshall's and JC Penny's to copy it (hardest to find was his *Flotsam and Jetsam* Friday selection – moray eel cartoon characters from the film *The Little Mermaid* – I always assumed a gift from his daughter until I found out he only had a son). Then half the floor aped his outfit for a week (including some of the women). He didn't notice.

Nothing helped. Not even the day Sculpin guided me to the remotest of filing rooms where a copy of Bob's employee picture had been affixed to a punching bag (not that I didn't enjoy that – exchanging his picture for Cassandra's was kind of fun, too – I had troubles making a fist the rest of that week).

After two interminable days spent fixing a comma on the Schedule K-1 being issued by a real estate partnership because it was, in his words, "terrible, not at all professional, and, to put it bluntly, completely unacceptable – I'm sorry sometimes I just have to be this way but it is, after all, my job," I made the grave (grave) error of passing Bob's office on my way to the elevator and my first weekend off in four months. (If you're interested, tech support told me the computer program experienced a "glitch," so I had to reenter everything somewhere else. My sigh drew one of Bob's "You've got to catch these things, Peter, if you want to move up" which always made me nervous.)

The week before he'd adorned a return I'd done with a bright pink sticker *You're tops!* and written next to it in green crayon *No. 1 Worker* beneath a smiley face. I am serious.

A grunt, a cough, a tentative start and then, in a voice not to be ignored, "Pete, do you have a minute? And when I say a minute, you know that I'm not like those other people who ask if you have a minute and then ramble on about nothing for half an hour."

"I guess."

"That's a really nice shirt. Really nice." He leaned across his immaculate desk – scrubbed, scoured and ultra-sanitized by cleaning supplies he brought from home and kept neatly organized on a portable tray in one of his cupboards: "I don't want to catch anything. People here are so filthy. Filthy." – and pinched my shirt at my belly to rub. "Great material. I love the color." He grunted. "Where'd you get it?"

I tried not to cringe, as did everyone entering his office. Some sort of bright red rash covered his elbows – and only his elbows, he insisted. He'd supposedly caught something from someone at his last firm and been unable to get rid of it. During the summer it was easily spotted as he wore tight (tight) short-sleeved shirts that showed off well-sculpted arms that he was very proud of – he often spent a whole conversation with a client watching himself flex and asking over the speaker phone set to the highest possible volume to continually repeat their entity structure we'd set up for them for tax efficiency until they got frustrated and hung up. To maintain his physique, throughout the day he ate regimented portions of microwaved eggs (the stink of which won him fans among the cubicle dwellers nearest the kitchen) and putrid protein shakes which he would leave in the middle of client meetings to consume at the exact required minute and then return with breath redolent of a panda bear's asshole.

"I don't know. Sears, maybe." I'd thought I was safe. As I was leaving my desk minutes before (though it now felt like hours – staff called it *Bob-time* – a minute with him was like an hour without), I'd heard him rehearsing part of a voicemail to Barrington which included the phrasing "I keep giving Pete the same comments over and over again and he never seems to get it" in reference to the missed comma which was a big bonus after spending twenty-nine of the last forty-eight hours fixing the problem and completely annihilating the budget. Bob always rehearsed his voicemails never less than eight times before actually hitting *SEND* and always had his wife proofread a script beforehand. Emails, memos – he gave all a similar treatment – even for something as simple as accepting a meeting time. The Holy Grail of the office (besides that damned three-hole punch) came from a time he'd tried to improvise a voicemail to Ron a few months before and accidentally hit *SEND* before any revisions. A copy of the voicemail circulated the office electronically for weeks before it completely clogged the system and took the IT department four days to clean out. Supposedly a few copies survived but, yes, possession of such was grounds for immediate dismissal.

"They have this really good presentation at manager training - when you make manager which I'm sure one day you will because you really seem to know what is going on or at least that's my perception which may or may not be correct. Regardless, the presentation is entitled *The Art*

513

of Leaving a Conversation and I've found it immensely helpful lately, almost too valuable for words to express completely and to my satisfaction. You know, when someone is wasting your time talking about something utterly meaningless, going on and on and on about absolutely nothing for what seems like days and days without end. Seemingly weeks. Interminably, as it were. The class teaches you how to extricate yourself without rudeness and even leave them smiling with a positive impression of you."

"I'm really looking forward to that class. But I must, unfortunately, go into the bathroom and chop off my pinky toe with a letter opener rather than continue this extremely dull conversation. Such digit, by the way, happens to be my favorite among them."

Shock, then laughter. "That's what I like about you, Pete, always kidding, keeping it light, not making it seem like a job at all. Reminds me of myself when I was younger. Mixing it up, staring authority in the face - DEFIANTLY. Tossing convention and conformity to that proverbial wind. We're much alike, you and I." He touched my arm affectionately.

"Touch me again and I will be forced to pummel you profusely into a squishy pulp. Or, at the least, bludgeon and batter you bloody."

A nervous laugh. "You know, Pete, I'm sculpting you. Honing you so that one day when you're ready and experienced enough you can move up to the level of senior. You're like a rough rock and I'm polishing your sharp edges. Filing you with finesse. You know?"

"I'm a rock?"

"I'm grooming you like a stable horse who one day will run the Kentucky Derby."

"I'm a horse?"

"A bucking bronco about to have its first jockey. A tax virgin about to be deflowered on the Code's spread pages."

"Jesus."

"Please don't take the Lord's name in vain." I said nothing. "The period looked terrible, just not at all professional. It had to be a comma, you get it?"

"I got it the first seventeen times you told me."

He gritted his teeth. "I try so hard, so very hard with you. One day you'll thank me for it. You have no idea what leniency I give you, how nurturing I am. What sufferings I take upon myself, what I endure, so that

514

you can grow and stumble your first baby steps out into the accounting world without fear of attack. That first day with you when you so obviously, so… so… cavalierly did not care about the comma, I must say, was one of the most difficult of my professional career." He waited for me to say something. I didn't. "So the K-1's are ready for my review now? You'd feel comfortable mailing them out as they are now?"

"Well, except for the mistake I always leave in each of my returns so you have something to do."

"You do that?"

I couldn't even have that. "No."

"Always joking." He smiled, "You get me. Uh-huh. We understand each other. Like peas in a pod. Two sides of the same coin."

I wanted to drive a red pencil through my skull. Instead I said: "I complete you?"

He pointed an enthusiastic finger at me. "I couldn't have said it better myself! You know."

"Know what?"

"We speak the same language. Sometimes we don't even have to say anything – we just know."

And that's the closest I ever came to killing myself.

Monday morning my voicemail-box was full. Seventeen messages from Bob.

The first from three minutes after I left the office on Friday: "I thought about what you said about leaving a mistake in your returns and that's not right. You shouldn't do that. And that thing you said about beating me up. You shouldn't say that. It's not right…" The message rambled on (and on (and on)) in a similar vein. The others were variations on the same theme at regular intervals throughout the entire weekend, day and night.

The phone rang. "Come to my office, please." Bob.

I went after first visiting the bathroom. And getting a cup of coffee. And taking ten minutes to scratch my ass most thoroughly in the hallway. I thought again about driving the red pencil through my skull.

His whole body was rigid with anger. "Sit down, please. Well, do

515

you have anything to say?"

"I'm thinking about starting a band called *Accumulated Depreciation*. I've already written one song. Would you like to hear it? *Debits and credits! Debits and credits!*"

"What?"

"I prefer the name *Bad Debt Reserve* but with the new language in the SAS mandating the term Allowance for Doubtful Accounts, I can't really. Doesn't have the same ring to it."

"What?"

I stood up and walked back to my desk. I didn't open any files, I didn't read any emails, I didn't answer my phone. I waited for Cassandra to come and fire me. And waited. And waited. At five thirty, I went home.

I woke and there was nothing. So I went to work. What else was I going to do?

There was one road in South America I would not attempt. I'd visit the lawless mountains of Kashmir or the war-torn country of Congo first. Cuzco's Gringo Alley.

Irish, Equatorial Guinean, Upper Voltan (Voltish?) – all fell victim (though, mysteriously, Finnish seemed immune – something in the water?). The consensus, even among the intrepid and the foolhardy (and even Canadians agreed with Americans on this point): it was folly to try. But.

In the dark corners of the dance club Mama Africa and around the somewhat level pool tables of Cross Keys, a rumor was being whispered that a Frenchman proficient in judo (and perhaps with a penchant for Bob Dylan?) had successfully traversed its length. Envision it:

Do you want to hike the Incan trail?

Waahh!!! (A cloud of glossy two-sided promotional pamphlets mushrooms into the sky.)

Whitewater rafting?

Hatcha!!!

Mexican food?

516

Hi-YAAAH!!!

Popcorn and (unbelievable as it may seem) sweets salesmen scatter (often their kind could be seen playing soccer in the adjoining Plaza de Armas with the latest tourist's head).

A query of "Internet?" draws a fist of fury to the chest followed by tearing the heart out.

"Cigarettes?" attracts a flying kick to the face.

"Pizza?"   Bodies crash through windows.   A defense of defenestration, as it were.

At the time, I didn't give the Frenchman enough credit. But upon later contemplation, I realized he'd done a great, great thing. A monument of the age, even. But it's always like that...

An open-armed stone Jesus beckoned at Cuzco's gates while behind *Vive El Peru* was etched in the barren mountainside above. The congested city, on a plateau four thousand metres above sea level, was the center of urban activity for the surrounding highlands. Gringo bars, handicraft markets, and tourist agencies were sprinkled around the Plaza des Armas next to magnificent old churches and drafty hotels. An array of bars serviced the visitors, offering free drinks and local girls to dance with as enticements. I sampled the former (doing the equivalent of a pub crawl as each bar's specials were timed differently – which actually worked out much to my ever shrinking wallet's advantage) but stayed away from the latter, earning myself the sobriquet Gringo Barracho within a couple of days of arriving.

On my way home after one such night of overindulgence while thinking I shouldn't be out at that time, I heard a shout just as I entered a narrow passage between two lines of houses I had thought not to go down but did anyway because it would save me five minutes of walking.

"Espera, espera!"

A woman wobbling on a scooter crashed it into a building to my right, trapping me between the vehicle and the concrete wall. "We fuck. Good price." After smiling, she suddenly lurched forward and vomited on my shoes.

She wiped her mouth and looked up, again smiling. "Si?"

"Tempting. Awful tempting."

"Bueno!"

"No, gracias." I maneuvered around her.

She backed the scooter unsteadily away from the wall and trapped me in again. "We fuck. *Very* good price."

"No, gracias."

She trapped me six more times until I was out of the alleyway. Then she drove off, mumbling, "Faggot."

After suffering my sixth or seventh (or eighth?) hangover from the cheap, free alcohol (and not really wanting to leave the warm bed in the morning – my hotel had no heating and the shower had a very temperamental electrically heated tap which would always turn icy cold during mid-shampoo – Wrasse somehow, someway controlled it, I knew – part of his job being my arch nemesis and all that) I finally got around to what I'd come there for: the Incan Trail – a hike of three days through the jungle and past a couple of minor ruins to Macchu Pichu. I wanted to do it on my own, but that was impossible since they wanted to regulate the number of visitors. So once again I booked a tour.

We had to meet the bus at 6 a.m. so, of course, ten minutes after departing the driver stopped at a restaurant in The Middle of Nowhere (not The Middle of *Fucking* Nowhere which was someplace in Bolivia) and announced we would be staying two and a half hours for breakfast.

But that was only after we'd left Cuzco. Which took time. The driver forgot his cigarettes. He bought new ones, but only after a thorough (thorough) search. He didn't take the first price offered. Nor the seventeenth. For cigarettes. How did anyone do anything all day but negotiate here in South America? Then he remembered his cigarettes were in his coat pocket, of all places. So he had to get his money back from the street salesman. There was arguing. Then he realized he'd forgotten his lunch. And he needed the newspaper, air in the tires... It went on. Twelve thousand two hundred and forty-one years (including three thousand sixty leap years) to be exactly precise.

A note of interest before we continue with the story:

Some people think The Middle of Nowhere is somewhere in the Mojave Desert, others along the I5 on the road to Stockton, California and one travel agent some field in Belgium – they're all wrong (both objectively and subjectively).

518

(Resuming) At the breakfast stop, I glanced at the menu – double the price of a room in Cuzco for two runny eggs and burnt toast. South America: inflated prices and no quality. Not that you could blame them.

Close by, three British girls were worrying for the twenty-third time how they would finish the trek with no shower on the second night.

Angry (and stupid), I left the restaurant and bought ceviche (cubed river fish marinated in lemon juice, but not cooked) from a cart along the road for the normal price after the usual negotiation.

Two hours into the hike I paid for my defiance: the **Vomiting** began.

As I stood hunched over for the fifth time, my very kind guide offered to carry my backpack to the first camp, but I refused, telling him I couldn't let him. He stayed with me, even though it took us until after dark to reach camp, arriving two hours after everyone else.

Then the French Canadian with whom I shared a tent with had to carry a plastic bag of my vomit from the tent as I could hardly stand. Poor guy. Even worse, I think the bag had a tear at the bottom.

He didn't come back to the tent.

The hike's second day was especially brutal as I couldn't eat and it was all up along the side of one mountain to a pass. Tourists ran past me, many carrying nothing at all, having hired porters. At one point, a porter carrying four packs asked me for water (there was none *en route*). Though I sympathized with him, I couldn't give it. Then two other porters asked the same and I felt better about saying no. But not completely. It was a very hot day.

Peeing on the trail was a public affair. But I'd had practice.

The Incans must have had extremely small feet because my boot would not fit completely on any of the trail's many stone steps which made descents particularly precarious.

The easier third day took us past a couple of smaller ruins, really just collections of crumbling roofless walls perched on the edge of verdurous cliffs beneath a wide open blue sky. Parakeets, toucans, and howler monkeys called to each other in the dense jungle below over the buzz of mosquitoes.

Moss now covered what had once been palaces, churches. Forgotten men and women had struggled, loved, and died here. Fought against the tyranny of the Incas or then the Spanish. Or aspired to build empires that would last forever. The Crusades, the Spanish Inquisition, two World Wars – all had come after. More would follow. I wanted to do more, so much more, but what? It couldn't all be about achievement. But its pursuit... That was something. Right? Or was it, like Wayne said, voluntary enslavement to the men who never left their offices? Who made all the rules so they could tell everyone else what they had to do if they wanted to fail to be like them, but, if they were lucky, take their scraps?

A life to choose.

Someone suddenly shouted at a Canadian scratching himself like a monkey and pursing his lips (you know how Canadians are – or you should, for your own safety and those of unaccompanied minors under the age of fourteen who might be in the general vicinity): "Don't make fun of my brothers! I mean it. Ever see Greystoke, Legend of Tarzan? I love that movie." He banged his chest like a gorilla and stomped his feet in place.

It was the French judo enthusiast.

We avoided each other's eyes. It'd been that way ever since being so close physically to each other on the seven hour jeep ride to the Bolivian jungle. I was unsure of the protocol in situations such as these and he, too, appeared confused. Should we shake hands and laugh it off, go for a drink and talk about it, hug it out? Being men, it was never really resolved, and, in some ways, I'll regret that always.

The camp where all groups stopped had been turned into a disco where hikers partied almost until dawn with loud music playing and a bar served beer. (There was, no doubt, a salsa line going on somewhere, but, no, I didn't take advantage of that to fix things with the Frenchman.) Not my idea of a hike. I went to bed early in anticipation of a pre-dawn departure to see the first light on the Gate of Dawn.

No one today knows Machu Picchu's purpose. A temple or a vacation spot for the Incas? Me: a gourmet hot dog stand. (Just kidding. Really. To think that would be silly.)

The ruins saddled a ridge below a ring of green coated peaks that spread until the horizon in every direction. The jungle had been cleared from the topless grey stone buildings and replaced by a lawn of freshly cut grass. Colorful flowers, many in vibrant blossom, had been planted amid the restored walls, architraves and cornices. Traditionally dressed natives looking for modeling fees led ornamented llamas bearing ringing bells through empty doorways from one terraced level to the next. Other locals led cantankerous (and not amenable to knock-knock jokes of any sort or kind) burros while trying to carry hikers' packs (we'd only carried them three days to get there and needed someone's help for the last few feet). But, despite the continuous arrival of tourist buses at the entrance below and the hikers swarming everywhere, I found a quiet spot to seriously bask in the glow of my accomplishment (and it was pretty, too). Until an Italian showed up and tried to use his cellphone. But that distraction was momentary (I snatched it from his hands and chucked it into the gorge).

My trip was coming to an end. But I needed something more. I just wasn't sure what.

"Police stole my camera in Cuzco!" someone said on the train back from Aguas Calientes early the next morning. I'd spent the evening before soaking in the thermal baths with a beer in each fist (and one in reserve often replenished).

"Did they speak English? The real police don't."

I was tired of trying to blend in, so, against my better judgment, I chose a heavily recommended hotel when I returned to Cuzco. (I hated that hotels recommended in the Lonely World were all rich and treated their guests with indifference while the rest of the town's hotels starved.) It was located off a side alley near the Plaza de Armas named (seriously) *Camino 1 7/8*.

As I inscribed *lactose intolerant beekeeper* as my occupation on the hotel register, I noticed every other guest was Canadian. (My other favorite occupations for hotel registers: fallen idol, professional eraser of blackboards, omniscient deity, underwater fireman suffering from acute hydrophobia, political assassin, talking mime, door-to-door vibrator salesman, rotting corpse, banana imitator, useless shit, dirty tent slut, jellybean enthusiast of the first order, and the oldie but goody retired matador with perverse proclivities prone to bouts of bestiality. At one point I had used parachute stuffer but then stopped, wanting the women of the world to fall in love with me for who I was and not what I did.)

"Dude, where's your Canadian flag?" a hairy guy with too tight a blue *Amsterdam!* T-shirt said to me.

521

"I'm American."

"So is everyone else here. Doesn't mean you should go unprotected. You do not want people knowing you're an American. John over there didn't have it and they took his kidney in a hosteleria in Istanbul. Now he doesn't go anywhere without it. The flag, I mean, the kidney, well, he lost that. But so I mentioned. Even uses the flag in Salt Lake City. Everybody thinks Canadians are so nice – no more paying in advance for rooms, towel deposits... Shitloads of drinks on the house... Brenda's bus got stopped in Paraguay and they robbed everyone but her. She had two thousand dollars in her sleeping bag but they never opened her pack. The flag, man. Such wonders it shall work... Come for a beer later at the bar, they have the craziest shit going on here."

I took a local bus to the Valle Sagrada and hiked to the ruins at Ollantaytambo and then Chincero through terraced fields cut into the face of dramatic inclines – every inch of available land was used. The farmers lived in uneven adobe huts with corrugated metal roofs – many of which were painted with the name of the next presidential candidate or Coca-Cola advertisements. (I made sure to avoid all eye contact with the local cows and listened intently for any sound of prowling dogs.) Pigs were everywhere acting pig-like. One trail ended at a set of low walls on a precarious spur jutting into a wide open gap between two walls of mountains under a bright yellow sun. A lovely day, though disappointingly, no pagan sexual rituals were going on (they took Thursdays off apparently, depending on what was showing on TV).

I may have passed a family dancing to a frayed accordion on the roof of a newly built house while drinking plastic cups full of Pisco Sour and I may have joined them at their urging and done a jig until I fell through said new roof and landed with my head in the new toilet bowl. But then I may not have.

In Cuzco, tourists come and go

While I sit thinking of girls I used to know

Beer in hand, I sat in the Plaza des Armas watching two little boys attack a tourist's taxi with paper airplanes while crowing victoriously. Red-headed turkey vultures spiraled overhead. The cathedral's bells chimed out six o'clock.

But then I saw the tourists giving money only to the children beggars, encouraging their families to keep them out of school and limit their future.

It got worse. A thirteen year old boy dressed in rags snatched at a local woman's purse a few feet away. But she wouldn't give it up. A crowd quickly converged. A man shoved the boy down. Another kicked him on the ground. And then others joined in, shouting. A policeman looked on indifferently.

"Hey! Hey!"

No one heard me, but then they slipped away of their own accord. The boy wasn't moving. With all the blood I thought he was dead. Until I saw his chest move. Still the policeman did nothing. I began to walk towards them. But then a crying woman appeared with another boy and they carried him away.

I needed something stronger than a beer. I returned to the hostel bar and, after recovering from the temporary blindness instilled by the flashing pink neon disco lights, noticed the least attractive women in the world standing among the stools. Then I realized they were all men in drag. Closer, I noticed they'd all gone a little much on the makeup side, had very short skirts, and, much to my chagrined chagrin and dismayed dismay, none wore underwear.

"Hey, how was your day?"

"Actually, not the best—"

"Good shit, man. Crazy. Get a beer. Beer him! Dude, we got some beer pong going in the corner. Larry fouled!" In the corner, "Larry" was being punished by his fellow player for his sin by being whacked (after a running start) with the thick rubber hose of a beer bong on his bare back. A huge red welt instantly appeared and he ran into the adjoining hall. A moment later he returned with tears in his eyes and ordered a shot of whiskey from the bar. Those standing around the table cheered. "Fucking awesome! That one's almost as good as the one John gave me last week. That fucker left a scar… Oh, that is some funny shit. Chicks love it, man. Love it! We're all getting laid tonight. Every last one of us!" Then I noticed the floor behind the bar was covered in empty grape soda bottles.

"What's with the skirts?"

"Dude, it's hilarious. We do this every night. I keep wanting to go see the rest of South America or whatever, get culture and shit. See that Macco Pacco thing nearby. But I can't leave. It's too much fucking fun. Been here three weeks. Drunk every night. And Larry's been here six months. Ever since he got gassed in a Spanish train. Didn't have the flag.

This place is unbelievable! You know, rich people are just better looking than poor people. Smarter, too. It's just a fact. I'm not being a bigot or something, I'm only stating the truth. That's why we get all the best pussy. Larry, I'm next! Dude, get another beer. Join us. Get laid, we're all in this together... I don't even know where Canada is, man! How awesome is that!"

Later, during a momentary lull in the deafening 1970s disco music, Larry suddenly shouted "I HAVE THE SMALLEST PENIS IN THE ENTIRE WORLD AND I'M DAMNED OKAY WITH THAT!"

John countered with: "MINE IS SMALLER AND I'VE TOTALLY ACCEPTED IT!"

I said nothing.

"Dad, I'm still not happy."

"So what do you want to do?"

"I've got some money saved. I was thinking of going traveling."

"You should. You haven't had a vacation in a while."

"I mean quitting. Leaving my job."

"What will you do when you get back?"

"I think that's something I've got to figure out."

"Are you sure?"

"I kind of am. But it may hurt my career quite a bit. Bosses don't like to see that."

"How long would you go?"

"Until I figure things out. Or run out of money. I don't really know."

There was a long pause. "Fuck it. Why not? Go. If it's something you think you need, you have to do it. You can't not."

"But what if I don't find what I'm looking for?"

"You'll figure that out then."

"Do you think I'm making a mistake?"

"There are no mistakes. There's just what you do."

"Thanks, Dad."

I wore the same shirt and clip-on polyester tie for a week. No one noticed.

"Barrington, you got a minute?"

"Bigger fish to fry, is it?"

"How did you--?"

"I've been at this a while, Peter."

"I'm going traveling."

"You see this Code? There are pleasures in its secrets, its mad machinations, its depths, nuances and intricacies. Its treacheries for the uninitiated. The original issue discount accretion of preferred stock buried in the 305 regulations. Whether or not non-periodic payments of a notional principal contract designated as a total return swap should be treated as ordinary income and not as capital gain, possibly long term depending on the holding period. Only a few people in the world know these things, glimpse their secrets. And understand them. It is something special to be among these elite. When you return, you have to decide if you want to be among them."

"I really don't know what I'll do when I get back. If I even come back."

"When you're young, you always want to do something more. Different. Flee the comfort of the same routine, not be like everyone else and live lives already lived... We all carry something inside that makes us want to tear down what's come before and start anew – that that's the only way to remain sane... Except with age, you realize it's almost impossible to do. But other rewards come with conforming. You'll see in time. Just be careful, don't ruin your chance for those figuring that out. Keep the illusion, yes, it's necessary to have that. But don't let it destroy you." Barrington stood up and extended his hand. "You'll come back to it."

"I—"

"I'll walk you out." Barrington walked over to his coat closet and

525

removed his raincoat. He paused a moment with the door open before closing it, letting me see inside.

Behind the array of sport coats and tailored suits was an axe. That maybe was used to carve a poem into the stall of a men's restroom and help along the demise of a manager's filing cabinet.

"Whatever you choose, enjoy it. This. This is all we get. And it's all over soon enough."

In the coffee room the next morning, Sculpin said, "I heard you're quitting to travel."

"Yeah."

"What the hell would you do that for? Waste your money like that? You're lying, right? You're going to Hook, Line and Sinker instead?"

There really wasn't any point in answering.

I had to meet with someone from "Human" Resources. "You'll need a pass to take your stuff out of the building. I'll have to inspect it first, of course. And so will someone else not related to me by blood or marriage. For security. Neither one of us can be bribed so don't be so foolish as to try: I am not Martin Marlin. My advice? Be extremely careful you don't take any office supplies by accident. Not even a paper clip. There would be consequences."

I surveyed all the personal effects I had accumulated in my desk over three years of my life (i.e., 12.456%). Two brittle slices of Big Red gum, a battered can of Dr. Pepper, a Rohu action figure (the "limited edition" adding machine pose initialed personally by the model), and my most cherished possession from a year ago:

Certificate of Merit

*The recipient of this award, one **Peter Pollack**, aspiring Certified Public Accountant and resident of the Greater Los Angeles metropolitan area is hereby acknowledged by all and sundry (Auditors, taxation specialists, those guys who sit near the copy room who no one knows what they do all day. Even hot dog vendors agree. And, of course, all the leading experts in the field – again whoever those people are.) as the most deserving of lavish*

526

and unrelenting praise for his rare and wondrous achievement without precedent in the history of human endeavor for getting Sigmond Sturgeon to admit orally and in writing that he was wrong, wrong, wrong. Words fail us as we try to articulate the measure of our admiration for such a feat.

Signed on the sixth day of the third month of the year nineteen hundred and ninety-nine

[Despite a coffee smudge obscuring the remainder of the date, this does not lessen its validity!]

by **Belinda Bonita**

Resident of Huntington Beach, California in the United States of America and all-around super-duper hottie

Duly Notarized and Verified on same date as above by **Mr. Martin Marlin**

Licensed Notary Republic
since before the dawn of time

[A post it note] - Don't let this go to your head...

Fuck. I really was leaving with nothing.

As I boarded the elevator, I handed Cassandra my security card.

Her goodbye: "I knew you wouldn't last the moment I met you."

The doors shut.

A moment later they reopened halfway between floors 26 and 27 to an enormous room never seen before.

Affixed to one wall stood a line of illuminated TV screens showing all corners of Net, Block and Tackle, a California Limited Liability Partnership. At their base were scattered empty two liter bottles of grape soda before a six foot high pile of three-hole punches in one corner. Against the other wall, metal wheels, pumps and pressure gauges measured by hundreds of cracked and melted thermometers spewed clouds of noxious steam. Facing the televisions in a mechanized chair with dual bottle holders for the grape soda and a hanging intravenous drip filled with a milky white fluid, sat an old man wreathed in lariats of cigar smoke. Hundreds of spiraled cords and elbowed hoses attached to the back of the chair were obviously manipulated by the leather gloved joysticks on the chair's armrests or by the dialed monitors before him. His gnarled, yellow feet with purple liver spots and long spiraled toenails rested askew on what looked like a stuffed dodo.

This was where the office's thermostats were controlled.

As the doors immediately began to creak closed again, the man turned to leer a smile. Between his pencil thin mustache and a cracked glass eye, a purple scar in the shape of an ampersand marred his left cheek. But that's not what I noticed.

With less hair and only one ear, he was Salmon's twin.

But then, at the last moment, a second man appeared on the other side of the room. He, too, was Salmon's twin.

I couldn't go back. Security was waiting for me at the lobby.

In Lima after a two day hike to the bottom of Colca Canyon, I signed the hotel register with one of my aliases and the clerk smiled.

"Mr. Remora's Illegitimate Bastard Child, we have mail for you."

What the fuck? I began to sweat and look at everyone in the lobby. The clerk handed me three postcards.

The first was a picture of my dad grinning while wearing a glaring pink *One in the Oven* T-shirt, lemon yellow shorts and mismatched flip-flops. The caption read: *$4.98.*

On the back:

*They said breaking the five dollar barrier couldn't be done. Not here in the United States, nor even in the Western Hemisphere. Not in the 20th century and certainly not in the one to come. Not now, not ever again. That **The Trousers Dilemma** could not be surmounted. But I found a way. Achieving your dreams is possible. (A flea market in Phoenix. Who woulda thunk it?)*

The beast misses you. The beast is very lazy. The beast just eats and eats and sleeps and sleeps all day. And shits more than she eats in never the same spot so I have to clean it up. (I mean the dog, not your mother.)

Love, Dad

The second was of an office with cubicles where parrots sat at all the desks.

We play Where in the World is Peter Pollack when you're not here. Best answers: In a Bolivian Prison, Crashing an Ethiopian Wedding, In a Liquor Store, Passed out on a Pool Table, Passed out under a Pool Table – there's a whole series on pool tables, then another on places you've passed out... Then, well, we get bored and mislabel the furniture in Bob's office again – or go back to filling his office with thousands of very thin water balloons tied together. Remember him?

Da Boyz

The third was of a naked woman covered in sand. With Cassandra's face superimposed over that of the model's and a postmark in Arabic. On the back it read:

His Magnificence:

I have heard tell of your erotic European escapades as the rambling roads of Rome run rampant with the rumors of your thunderous thrusts on the Spanish Steps - stabbing and spearing ceaselessly the saucy, salacious Slovakian sluts as they bellow beastily for more and more and yet more of your jolting, jerking, Jewish jism javelin. I do beseech thee to cease and desist yer lurid legacy of lust herewith, focusing foreto upon luring the lovely, leggy Leah into your lair of libidinous lechery. Do take pity on an old man such as myself and give me a chance with even one of these Latvian lasses, French fillies or Danish debauchees, be she grotesque, gangrenous or possessing a gargantuan goiter before the sperm so long unspewed doth surge and shoot from my eyes.

P.S. My friend asks how you will ever be a general in this fucking army while following only the whims of your woefully withered cock but, deep down in a place no one ever ever wants to go to, see or, in any way whiff – his love bubbles and stews for you.

With or Without Shoes: To Go Or Not To Go Naked With Sandals

Without shoes, without clothes, into the wilderness, into the depths of the soul, without barriers, without defenses, no pretensions, no lies, naked to the world, naked to myself. Be myself. Be true.

The travel agent at Puerto Ayora in the Galapagos Islands told me the tour started at: "Eight a.m. Sharp. Unlike the rest of Ecuador, we pride ourselves on our punctuality. To an almost perverse degree. If you're late, we leave without you. Don't be late."

So I showed up early. The office wasn't open. It began raining, of course, and there was no place to shelter. But then appeared the Austrian girl with the pony-tail.

"I told you it wasn't my pen."

"I wanted to be sure."

We both laughed. "Are you on this tour then? Too late to get my money back probably."

"You should feel privileged and honored that I'm even here. I was offered another more expensive tour at an extremely outrageous, once-in-two-lifetimes discount, but it was filled with people in their sixties, many of them single. And chances are, I'd fall in love with one of them. Lucky for you, I just can't put myself through that again."

She and her companion, a slightly older blonde but of equal loveliness and obviously related, laughed as if surprised at their own laughter. "Again?"

"I don't want to talk about it."

"Keeping your emotions bottled up inside is very unhealthy."

"I've heard that."

"Look at him. Suddenly without a word to say. Sulky even."

"What's come between us? We don't even communicate any more. After having been so close," her companion added.

"Don't shut us out. We're willing to work things through."

"Whatever it takes."

Was this really happening? "I apologize. Sometimes I can be so selfish. When I'm not busy thinking about how good my hair looks, sometimes all I think about is how good my hair looks. I'm truly, deeply, sincerely sorry."

"Yeah, okay, I guess. I guess."

"I'll entertain you with traveling tales of intrigue and suspense fraught with intriguing suspense and suspenseful intrigue."

"Cash is better."

"No collateralized debt obligations, preferred stock warrants, or second tier corporate debentures. Cash," her companion clarified.

"As much as it pains us not to—"

"Excruciatingly so."

"To our very cores."

"In there. Somewhere."

"We're not going to tell you how fabulous your hair looks even in this veritable flood from the sky."

"We don't fall into such traps. We're wily."

W. O. W.

The tour guide arrived. Forty-five minutes late. Luckily the heel of my left sock was still moderately dry.

Me on the way to the airport where we were collecting the rest of the tour group: "Pssst… Yeah, you. I'm over my morose stage."

"I'm *so* relieved… What's your name then?"

"Peter. Peter Pollack."

"Peter Peter Pollack, may I present my sister Rita Wren? I'm Rhonda."

"Quite a coincidence for us to keep meeting. It must mean we're destined to get married and have forty-three children together. You're already hopelessly in love with me, I'm sure."

"Not quite yet." Her wide smile pulverized me. "Maybe after a little more time together."

I counted to five on my fingers. "Now?"

"Of course. But will we have a May wedding or a June? Are you a morning person or a night? Which side of the bed do you prefer? Will our parents get along? Have you considered these pertinent points in your proposal?"

"May, night, right, yes and yes. Okay?"

"Oh, absolutely."

"Joyous tidings! But you must laugh at 29% of my jokes."

"And not one child more than thirty-three."

"Deal." We shook on it (including the thumb lock, fist bump and knocking elbows upside down to make the contract official and binding according to Statute 7, Clause 43 of international law). "Seriously, what have you been up to?"

"Well, I was studying English in London when we first met. Then Rita—"

"That's me!"

"That's her."

"We met. But only too briefly."

"How sweet."

"Rita joined me in Paris to celebrate finishing and we left for Cannes. Then I went to Quito to study Spanish for three months while I worked in a bar. That's when we, meaning you and I and not Rita and me… or Rita and I, met in the airport."

"Rita and I."

"I just love it when people talk about me."

"Now I'm done—"

"Not talking about me?"

"Not talking about you. We're going around South America for a little bit before I go home."

"And you?"

"We have known each other twenty-five minutes now. The time has come to bare our souls and become completely open with one another, hasn't it? End the lies, the deceptions, the concealments."

"It's certainly a start."

"With the impending nuptials and resultant wedded bliss, most assuredly. Before I begin all that autobiographical where I am from, where I am going stuff, which could go on for quite some time – days even, certainly hours – you'll want to study the transcript later to be sure you didn't miss a word of my subtle yet clarified phrasing – please tell me what you're going to do upon returning home. I did, after all, confess to you my weakness for older women."

"I'm opening my own café in Vienna."

"Really?"

"End the lies, the deceptions?" One of the many wide smile's sequels, each no less candescent than the first.

534

"And Rita, what will you do?"

"Go back to my job. I organize trips for companies that want to reward their employees. I get to see the world for free."

"I'm immensely jealous." I resisted the temptation to tell her this was my immensely jealous face that she'd now be able to recognize on me in the future. I don't know why, I just did.

"Yeah, everybody's going on vacation basically for free. They're all happy. My last job everyone was angry all of the time. Made going to work every day miserable. I couldn't stand it."

The plane arrived with the rest of the tourists who'd paid full price for the Galapagos tour so there were more introductions to be made as we drove the short distance to the dock.

"Must I laugh at that joke to meet my 29% quota?"

"Yes."

As I shouldered my bag to carry onto the boat (the "tourist class" Yolita), Rhonda asked, "Have you ever thought about getting that enormous orange tumor on your back surgically removed?"

"So what's in this bag then? Two sperm whales, the Taj Mahal, a thermonuclear intercontinental ballistic tactical missile?"

"Um. Shoes."

"We like shoes."

"We like shoes a lot."

"A lot."

I shared a cabin with Ralph, a financier from Frankfurt. When shaking my hand, he said, "Yes, I know my name means vomit in English," I knew we were going to be friends. "Do you want the upper bunk? Or the lower so I can *ralph* on you when I get seasick and kick you repeatedly in the face while I try to scramble onto the top bunk in a drunken stupor?" "I'll take the top." "Very astute and street savvy of you."

Then we had to start shouting to be heard over the engine. "Think it will quiet down when we get going?" "Of course." "What?"

Over the next week, Ralph told me his story. He didn't talk as if I was already gone and so was he, just filling time. When he asked a question, he wanted the answer and not only his turn to speak. He'd done a bit of traveling, mostly with his girlfriend of eight years – he was thirty-two - but now was on his own. They'd broken up because she wanted to get married but he wasn't completely happy. She wanted him back, but he couldn't decide. "Something's missing and I'm not sure if it's fair to either one of us to not have that," he said. "Or maybe I just want too much. She's a good person, a sweet woman, I don't know what I want. But it's something more."

In case you're interested (And who wouldn't be?), the engine didn't quiet down once we got started. Just the opposite. Day and night, night and day, the pistons banged and rattled and guffawed to keep the electricity going. It was the loudest boat in the Galapagos (and, almost certainly, the Pacific Ocean I can say, sadly and tragically, with little exaggeration) – all other vessels moored as far from us as possible at each of the permitted stopping points to avoid our noise. And the toilet broke twice a day, usually when I had to go or was going. But the sights were sublime.

Also: the two-storied boat had only one tape of music which was played a total of twelve times a day for six days to help dampen the cacophony of the engine. You know which song was featured prominently on each side.

Later that afternoon, we were sitting on the deck in the sun watching the swallow-tailed gulls fly along with the boat, drifting silently within arm's reach often, accepting us. I stood up.

Rhonda said, "Where are you headed?"

"I go where the wind takes me. Freedom is my song, unfettered by the shackles of responsibility or propriety, I move ever onwards."

"I just wanted to know if you were going inside because I wanted a soda."

I put the cold unopened can down the back of her one piece bathing suit.

536

Rhonda: "You like hiking? Isn't that hard? Would you get dirty? Like sweat and stuff? Yuck!"

"Do I get to answer now?"

"Yes. No. Maybe. Sometimes. Never. Every once in a while."

"And they say women have trouble making up their minds."

She stuck her tongue out at me. "How did you pay for such a trip? Are you rich or something?"

"Hardly. I rob banks along the way."

Rhonda considered this. "Can you teach me? Like a summer internship?"

"Only if you concede that North America is mine. Stay outta my 'hood."

"I promise," she said, crossing eight of her ten fingers behind her back. "But is it difficult, this bank robbing? I'm lazy."

"'Tis a fine art whose nuances and subtleties take a lifetime of larceny to perfect. You have to know who to shoot first, when just to maim, how to dispose of the bodies…"

"Seriously and to be a little less gruesome: what do you do?"

"Well, I gave up a very lucrative career as an exotic dancer to become a tax accountant. Had this whole routine with a frilly pink tutu and a live anaconda. Every once in a while I flash some of this (I wiggled my right ankle in the appropriately lascivious manner despite the obvious dangers involved. Could her heart take such excitement? Despite her youth, not many women's could…) just to tantalize the crowd and leave 'em begging for my triumphant return to the stage."

"I think I believe you. No one ever lies about being an accountant."

"I almost said I was an unemployed astronaut. Or an unemployed matador or an unemployed beekeeper."

"But you didn't. How does that make you feel?"

"I'm okay with it. Really. I don't even need to talk about it. Which surprises me a little."

Around two, Ralph stood up and put on his shirt. "Where are you going?"

"I go where the wind takes me – without a plan, without a guide. Rudderless on this grand, chaotic river of life. Anarchy is my anthem, circumambulation my creed. To have a map, a destiny set and laid out for the years to come, is to be already dead. Conformity is suicide for the soul. I strive to live a life less ordinary, shunning the bonds and shackles of responsibility. A steady job, a marriage, children, a home mortgage – let these traps fetter other men, strangle their souls – for I will not let them take me."

"You and Pete make it really difficult for somebody to ask for a soda."

At our first dinner, Ralph appeared sporting a huge straw sombrero like the ones they wear while singing to you *Happy Birthday* in Mexican restaurants. (I thought his "Shall we dress for dinner?" meant something else. He'd also busted out with the black socks and sandals which epitomizes class, I always say when I'm not busy saying something else.) After everyone received their plate of food (which was consistently great) from the ever-smiling chef, Ralph rose and made us all hold hands. Initially we laughed, but he insisted.

"Heavenly father, bless us ignorant tourists for we are doomed to wander the earth abject with traveler's diarrhea taking underexposed photographs, writing illegible postcards and eluding ubiquitous pick-pockets in drip-dried underwear.

"Give us the divine guidance to choose our accommodation well, have our reservations not be lost, swaddle us in sheets clean, crisp and bug-free and have hot, scorching water emit forcefully from every tap. Muzzle the roosters and gag the dogs in our hotel's environs, especially in the wee small hours. May telephone operators speak our tongue and the connection always be strong. Forgive us for tipping too little out of ignorance or too much out of fear. Let the locals see us for who we really are and not for what they can steal from us, for to covet the possession of worldly goods corrupts a man's soul. Imbue not our meals with artificial flavors or chemical preservatives, but do cool our beer and Coca-Cola to an icy chill.

"May we visit each and every museum, palace, castle, cathedral, or temple defined as a *must-see* by the Lonely World guidebook. But forgive us if we miss one to take a nap after lunch, for mortal flesh is weak..."

Later on deck as the sky exploded with stars, Ralph was dancing a jig and singing with perfect pitch: "I'm a lumberjack and I don't care. I've got hairy nipples and a pint of beer."

Thick brown stands of cactus overrun far reaching stretches of broken black rock. Charcoal and red backed marine iguana scamper over slick rocks in front of steep black cliffs while the murky blue water pounds their base in a spray of foam. Between brackish lagoons, skeletal gray trees plead for the heavens' mercy atop crimson domes runneled from the flames of the world's forgotten battles. The wild call of finches, magnificent frigate birds and brown pelicans are the only sounds above the whipping wind in this harsh land. A perched Galapagos hawk regards us indifferently as the salty air dishevels his brown feathers. Galapagos fur seals greet us with flippers and guttural cries. Here everything is stripped away with no grass, no shade, no cities of man. All is stark and isolation. And slowly man destroys even this. A couple of years after I left an oil spill killed half of the island's marine iguana.

Would I ever get to see any of these things again?

On deck.

Rhonda: "I forget. What did we descend from? Birds or fish? One of those, right?"

Rita (interrupting): "Why did the ostrich cross the road?"

Rhonda: "You promised!" A Finger of Warning extended in my direction, even more emphatic than Belinda ever busted out with. "You must never encourage her! Ever! No matter what she promises you. Not even Austrian chocolate. Or Austrian beer. Or wild monkey sex with no strings attached and no need to even call the next day. Promise!"

Lunch.

Me: "What are you doing? Sitting on my side."

Rhonda: "Your side? What is this with sides? Why do we all need sides? Why can't we all be on the same side?"

"I'm never ever ever talking to you ever ever again. Ever. Unless the Chicago Cubs win the World Series."

"Yes!"

"Did you notice the distinctive bright red gular pouches of the magnificent frigate bird today? Also: were you aware that they are monogamous, have an average wingspan of up to 91 inches and raise their young the longest of any bird?"

She feigned a sigh. (Believe me when I say I can identify a feigned sigh regarding ornithological miscellany better than anyone else alive. Just do. For your own safety.) "Promises, promises."

"Can I ask you a personal question?"

Smiling (and without hesitation): "Okay."

"Does this annoy you?" I asked as I pushed the brim of her baseball cap down over her face.

With squished nose, "No, not at all."

"Is she –

1) Extremely and thoroughly disgruntled at my taking that last piece of gloriously pungent cheese – so much so she will inevitably inflict wanton heinous violence upon my most pacific person?

2) Momentarily dazed into a state of extreme bliss by my shimmering, unequaled beauty – a condition which could easily gestate into one of permanence if we were spend further time together?

3) Both of the above?

Or, in a similar vein, contemplating in minute detail all of the myriad facets of my wonderfulness?"

"You do go on a bit, don't you?"

Failing to keep from laughing, I said, "You think you're so funny. You think you're freakin' hilarious."

"Even got a certificate to prove it." She handed me a napkin: *The bearer, one Rhonda Wren, is freakin' hilarious. Affectionately, the President of Austria.*

"Why didn't he sign his name, only his title? I think this is fake, counterfeit, not real at all."

"You're wrong."

"Oh. Sorry."

"Doubt me not."

"For he who doubts you suffers unspeakable horrors?"

"Yes. That."

"I hope one day you'll forgive me. Maybe not today and maybe not tomorrow, but soon and to the depths of your most merciful heart."

"The two napkins in your collar at lunch clearly didn't help."

"I outran a killer two-toothed hamster in Huntington Beach, swam goldfish infested waters in my aunt's inflatable backyard pool, and survived three assassination attempts by bipolar three–toed sloths to take this abuse? I think not."

"Well, I did the *Australian* crawl through piranha-infested waters in the heart of the Amazon, evaded two avalanches by snowboard in the Himalayas, was chased by a homicidal heifer in Rajastan and ate dhal baat for 27 days straight to give it to you. So you'll take it and you'll like it."

There it was. Wow. So I went for it: "That's a really good story. You should get it published, sell the movie rights for a billion bucks, retire and drink extra-foam cappuccinos on the Italian Riviera while your chauffeur attends lovingly to the racing green Bentley with a chamois cloth."

"I prefer the color gun-metal blue."

"Forget what I said then."

"To tell the truth, the whole truth and nothing but, I never listened in the first place. I was too busy thinking about my hair."

"Don't mess with me: I'm mean, but my mom's meaner. If I ask her she'll fly down here and kick your Austrian tushy. She's taken on Navy Seals, Green Berets and once thumb-wrestled a state and local tax expert – I would not mess with her."

"I will beat you to the point where the only means of identification will be carbon dating. Neither dental records nor DNA will be of the slightest assistance."

"Yeah, well, I will fight you to the death and way, way beyond. Like really far. Far."

"That's not very nice. Threatening a girl."

"You're a girl? I had not noticed."

"What will you do when you go back?"

"Be an accountant again, I guess. I may not love it, but it's what I'm best at. To make money. You can't always do what you want."

"It seems such a waste. With someone of your imagination. You should start a talk show like Lonnie Loon and tell your jokes there."

"But who would watch?"

"I would."

"That will justify the television studio paying me millions of dollars to host the show. I'll have a guaranteed audience of one."

"I'll get my family to watch, too."

"In Vienna?"

"We get cable."

"Well, then. I'll have to ask for tens of millions of dollars."

"Don't short change yourself. Ask for more. Always. Don't even ask, just take it. I've got three friends who might watch if I asked them."

A sudden lament from the Austrian echoed across the water: "It's been five days since we shopped. Five days!"

Rita nudged me: "Hey, why did the blue-footed booby cross the road?"

"I can't. I mustn't. I promised."

That evening when we moored, we spent the time before dinner diving off the top of the second story of the boat. There were sidewise landings, belly flops aplenty (though artistically done) and a cannonball of Homeric scale perpetrated by one unemployed matador. At the end a group of Galapagos seals approached to see what we were doing.

"Look!" I pointed, abrim with excitement after our first wet landing the next morning. Wet or dry designated how our feet would arrive on the beach. The guide would also tell us if we needed to wear shoes or not, if we wanted. Whenever I could, I didn't.

Rhonda turned eagerly, drawing her camera as she moved.

"A rock!"

A wide smile creased her lips. "Thank you. I almost missed that one."

"Another rock!"

"Wow. And they're so rare here."

"Just wait until tomorrow. There's a whole colony endemic to Santa Cruz Island. Two are mating! That's very rare to see in the wild. You should feel honored and privileged."

"I do."

"Such a photo opportunity comes along once in a lifetime."

"If you're lucky. Doubly so that we have you along to spot it with your expertise in rock breeding. Is there anything you don't know?"

"I don't think so. Wait. No, nothing."

Rhonda stumbled forward over a lava rock.

"Are you all right?"

"I'm fine."

"No need to amputate? I've got my Leatherman."

Rita added, "And I could assist with my Swiss Army knife. Run an I.V. or put in a central line, if necessary. Even if the procedure is completely elective, if you catch the general gist of my drift."

Rhonda did her bunny rabbit you're so funny look. "You're really annoying, you know that?"

I nodded my head vigorously. "I'm captain of the American Annoying Olympic Team. Medaled silver in Sydney, hoping for the gold in

Seoul. Boring Stories are my best event, Awful Singing my second."

"I'm sure you'll win."

"I don't know. Led by their captain Rhonda, the Austrian team presents real competition this year in the Bad Joke event."

"I didn't think it was remotely possible, but the jokes are actually getting worse." Then she tripped again and giggled.

"So despite having the 23 pairs of shoes, not one is suitable for actual walking?"

"Who gave you permission to talk again? We're definitely buying you one of those things they have for dogs – what is the word in English? Muzzle."

"Ouch."

"What?"

"I scratched my knee."

"How bad is it?"

"I can't look. Would you?"

"Ugh!"

"What?!"

"Well, you'll probably be hideously deformed for life, carrying this horrible disfigurement and stain upon the eyes to your grave, no doubt being ostracized by all and sundry as this base defilement of the senses blinds each with its rank repulsiveness. We'd better amputate."

"No, I'm fine."

"It's best to take the whole leg in these situations, just to be sure. Can't be too careful. Minimize the risk of infection and all that."

"Really, I'm fine. Absolutely and without reservation."

"Suit yourself. But don't tell me later that I didn't warn ya."

"Ya?"

"Ya."

At the cave mouth, Rhonda forged ahead in her sandals with her flashlight, leaving the barefoot Rita behind. I had to help Rita navigate the sharp rocks to the cave's pool.

Photographing a yellow-faced land iguana chow down on a prickly pear cactus on the way back to the boat, I was suddenly left all alone in the rear of the path. And then I saw something that made my head spin. Topping a tree sixty feet away, a red breasted frigate bird kept watch over his nest. In the nest, hung all my lost hats. The fedora stolen from me in Nepal, the bright orange hunter's cap lost as a Boy Scout while summiting California's Mt. Whitney, the imitation New York Yankees hat swept down the Orange River in South Africa. Even the bright pink Mardi Gras capuchon.

There was a Turkish fez and a Mexican straw sombrero, too. They weren't mine. I'd wanted them, though.

Without really thinking I headed towards the nest. Jumped a small but jagged ravine. Cut myself on numerous thorny bushes. Twisted an ankle on a loose rock. But the tree had no lower branches capable of supporting me and I could just barely brush one of the hats with my fingertips.

I couldn't get them.

"You have to help me," I told the guide when I returned to the path.

"We must go."

"With a boost—"

"We must leave."

"It will only take a minute."

"No, we'll lose our license. You're lucky we don't kick you off the tour."

I had to let them go. "We have to go back."

"I don't like the police. Even more than I don't like you. And then there's the paperwork. So you're lucky. But no more. No more."

Rita: "What happened to you?"

"I can't really explain."

"Stranger than pigeons eating a man in the Rizal section of Manila? Or a school of Sockeye salmon leaping from one swimming pool to another through a southern suburb of Seattle?"

"Huh?"

"Both I've seen. He was just feeding them breadcrumbs and they were landing on him and then, suddenly, they flew off and he wasn't there anymore."

"No, I meant: you've been to Seattle?"

Her eyes narrowed. "I'll be watching you like a rufous-necked sparrowhawk."

"You're into birds, too?"

"I spent one summer trying to find out what the mating call of the kookaburra sounded like."

"Because they're from Australia. Not Austria."

"Yep."

"Actually, one day I came out to my car in Los Angeles and found the parking lot filled with Canadian geese."

"Everywhere birds are losing their spots to stop in the midst of their migration patterns."

"And they *never* will ask for directions."

"I know. Right?"

Rhonda interrupted: "I once saw a waddle – yes, a waddle - of Emperor penguins hitchhiking in the Atacama Desert with the sign *Somewhere the fucking humans haven't melted with the use of chlorofluorocarbons, nitrous fuels and weapons grade plutonium.* Just so you know."

I turned to Rita: "Do you know any more knock-knock jokes?"

Rhonda said: "Always remember—"

"And never forget?"

"Recognize you have violated the Third Key to a Lively Conversation. The first being to read a newspaper a day and the second is to maintain eye contact while noting facial expressions and body language. The third which you have so callously disregarded with little attention to normal human convention is to use humor to lighten the situation, especially where events have become intense or heated."

"I have an annotated, indexed, and thoroughly cross-referenced list of fifty-seven reasons why you're wrong, wrong, wrong."

"Oh, how your antiquated articulation bores me to suicidal distraction."

"Do you wanna talk about it?"

"Not in the slightest."

"May I add this advice? Never listen to any story that begins with, *Guess what happened after I pulled down my pants?* My dad once began a story thus and no one had imparted such recommendation myself-wise. It still haunts me to this day: that story."

"The Fourth Key to a Lively Conversation, in case you're interested and, no doubt hanging on my every word and/or dangling participle is: make and retain eye contact, though not in a creepy, stalker-like way. Sometimes such a course of action requires the walking of that clichéd fine line."

"I concur most whole-heartedly. For as that well-known ancient Chinese proverb dictates: He who doubts Rhonda is like a man drowning in his own bathtub who refuses to swim."

"Arabic has 47 words for love. I can think of 29 more than that to express the way I feel about that comment."

"I'm pretty mad at you," I told Rhonda later.

"What? Why?"

"You haven't once remarked how awesome my hair looks today. And it's been pretty spot on perfect for the duration."

"Peter."

"Yes?"

"Your hair looks awesome."

"How sweet of you to say."

"Just so you know: I'm becoming immune to your bad jokes. I only hope I can develop a serum potent enough to save the rest of the world from your weapon of mass destruction."

Rhonda: "I've thought long and I've thought hard, contemplating it this way and that and sometimes the other and I want to tell you something of grave and worlds-shattering importance. Super-duper gargantuan stuff, in other words."

"That beer really comes from Ecuador but that you tell everyone it comes from Austria? That you and Rita are going to wear home leg casts and eyepatches just to mess with your mother? That you're an expert in blindfolded synchronized swimming and/or juggling flaming swords while riding an unicycle across a tightrope, also blindfolded?

"Maybe. But in this instance what I wished to elucidate (this is correct English, yes?) in reference to your earlier comment, was of the difference in how women give directions to men."

"Please do illuminate me."

"Your photographs are probably of monuments and castles. Ours are of the little boutique that had sublime yet unaffordable leather boots (though, if you ask me, no boots of such magnificence are truly unaffordable) or of the shop with the snakeskin purse to die for in a most horrific way but so extraordinarily worth it. And by a horrific way, I mean, like without eyeliner and wearing a blouse the color of chartreuse."

"And so your directions include *past the place with the divine silk skirts in the window* or *next to the store with the hideous yellow hats*."

"Exactly! You *so* get me."

"I think I do."

Rita interrupted: "I have detachable breasts."

"NO!" Rhonda fled with her hands clamped over her ears.

"This is something I must hear more of."

Ralph said to me in the room that night, "So what's happening with Rhonda?"

548

"I don't know. Fuck, if nothing happens... I'll always regret it, I know it."

Ralph shook his head. "It's not the ones you sleep with you remember, it's the ones you didn't. The ones who got away, who still had mystery to them. Because the others all become the same and not much to them because you're always there and you're always the same."

As we sat on another amazing beach the next day, Ralph asked me if I'd been to Jaipur in India and then said, "My brother went there about six months ago. Some guy on the street offered to show him around and, I don't why, he accepted. He said he wanted to see how the locals lived and the guy seemed pretty genuine, as if he wanted to share the difference in their cultures. The guy brought along his two cousins and they showed him all the tourist spots. Then, at the end of the day, the guy asked my brother if he'd like to make some extra money buying jewels that he could re-sell to a buyer they had an arrangement with in England. My brother suddenly realized what was going on and told them no."

"What happened?"

"They wouldn't let him leave. He said it was weird at first. There were no threats of violence, it was all kind of implied. But then the guy had a gun and my brother couldn't do anything about it. For three days, they made him withdraw the maximum money he could out of the ATM and then would take him back to the room and beat the shit out of him. Eventually the bank caught on and stopped the account withdrawals. They made him call home and authorize more withdrawals. When the account was completely empty, they put a hood on him and took him out to the desert someplace and made him get out of the car. He said he thought this was it, he was dead. But then they just left."

"Fucking hell. That could have been me. Somebody on the street there asked me if I wanted to sell jewels."

Another tourist on the boat, a redhead from Delft said to me: "But that can't be your only close call, staying in hostels?"

"Actually, I really like hostels. You meet people from all walks of life. But, yes, you do meet some crazy ones as well. You've had problems? Like violence?"

She rubbed her right arm. "Yeah." I waited and she continued, "I met this American when I was in Cancun, actually. Normal guy, he could be you, real casual, no signs of violence. He was in the bed next to mine. So we went out for drinks, went dancing, spent some time on the beach and we ended up getting together. We got a double room and I thought everything was great. Anyway, one morning the hotel door gets kicked in. All these cops come rushing in pointing guns and tell us to put our hands up and not move." She rubbed her arm again. "He'd murdered his wife and their three kids in Seattle and run off to Mexico. The kids were three, four and two months old. But he was taking me to disco-techs and restaurants and not trying to hide. I think he was trying to get caught. Maybe he knew he'd done something wrong, I don't know."

"That must have scared the hell out of you."

"It really freaked me out for a couple of weeks. I just sat there going ah, ah and shaking my head. My mom desperately wanted me to go home, but I knew if I did I'd just sit in my room reliving it and it would suffocate me. So I went to Guatemala and tried to work it out on my own, do other stuff so I wouldn't think about it too much. I think I'm over it now. You never know who people are when you meet them traveling, do you? I could have made a lot of money out of it, but I didn't want to share my private life with the whole world and affect the rest of my life." She smiled. "I'm still e-mailing some of the FBI, it's supposed to be about the case but really it's about surfing. They've lost interest lately. Have a new case. Looking for someone calling himself Richard Remora's Illegitimate Bastard Child. Apparently Richard is not pleased."

Was she lying or wasn't she?

After lunch, sitting back on that beach watching the marine iguanas, the brightly-colored Sally Lightfoot crabs and blue-footed boobies interact without malice, it came to me: what I could do, be. I didn't have to try to be someone I was not. I could be myself: this was my place. To do accounting, to exploit my strength. But for good. This was my purpose. I had such opportunities, it was a waste to feel miserable. I could do what I was best at. Because it would help. Help keep money out of the government's hands. Hands that used the money to exploit poor countries through economic sanctions or violence. And then I was at peace, really at peace. For I had found my way.

We kept exploring the islands for the tour's two remaining days. I discovered that the way Rita and Rhonda distinguished their clothes was that Rhonda's invariably had a food stain on the left breast, usually incurred in the meal's final minute whenever she thought she'd almost made it and then took that final and one too many bite. Said blemish was really helpful to me in distinguishing the two girls myself, or so I joked to much amusement (or, at least, I thought so – especially when Rita wore one of

Rhonda's shirts by mistake and all sorts of shenanigans of mistaken identity ensued). I learned that Ralph had seen stuffed Mao and pickled Ho (or was it the other way around?) when visiting China and Vietnam a few years before and wondered how I would end up after my misadventures of mischief and mayhem. Rita told us her first job was with a swimming pig in some sort of aquatic show – she explained it would try to drown her any time she let her guard down (subsequently, she loved bacon).

Back in Quito, Rita insisted on taking me to an Internet café to show me something. "Have you ever heard of a lyrebird? It's from near Melbourne and can imitate pretty much any sound. And it lives longer than most species. But it has no voice of its own."

"That's sad."

She found the website. The bird mimicked a chainsaw, cell phone ring, a honking horn. "This is the best," she said, giggling. A deep guttural voice emitted from the bird's beak: "HEY, YOU FUCKING IDIOTS, GET IN HERE!"

I didn't agree.

We each had a couple of days before our respective planes onward. Ralph and I decided to share a room next to the girls in a hotel near the Old Town. As Ralph and I left it to meet the girls for dinner, we suddenly heard screams.

"Rhonda."

"Rita."

How quickly one's heart fills with dread.

We raced over to the girls' room and threw open the door, expecting the worst.

The sisters stood embracing in the middle of the bed, hiding their faces in each other's shoulders. The room was otherwise empty.

"What's wrong?"

"There's… a *frog* in the bathroom."

The hotel staff were even more amused than Ralph and I.

We were to meet in the morning. Morning became afternoon. So I went up to knock impatiently and without relent on their door: "What!"

"Wanna join a polka band?" I smiled and handed her two coffees each rivaling the Atlantic Ocean in size.

Suddenly blinding me with her grin, she took the coffee. "I play a mean accordion."

Rita shouted something in German from behind.

"What did she say?"

"If we don't shut up already, she'll start singing."

"Fate worse than death?"

"And then some… I was dreaming of my clothes back home."

"And your shoes?"

"And my shoes!"

The girls appeared downstairs. I narrowed my eyes at Rhonda. "I've seen you before, you know."

"Oh, really?"

"On the cover of *Cosmopolitan* and *Vogue* last month."

"Yeah, *Elle* wouldn't pay me enough."

"They have big regrets?"

"Huuuuuge! I look pretty much absolutely ravishing in lederhosen."

"Not a man, woman, child or small farm animal alive could argue with that in any way, shape or form."

"We're going shopping!"

Rita nudged me. "Need to. Without an hour a day, we get ill. Can get by on such, barely, but two or even three hours are better."

Rhonda said to me: "You're wearing the green shirt again. That's a nice change."

We entered the first shop.

"We're going to be a while."

"I'm not very good at shopping."

"Most men aren't."

"I'll leave you to it. But first…" I approached the salesman. "Do you speak English?"

"Of course, señor."

With one hand each, I presented the sisters to the salesman. "Okay, now I want you to go find something in the back truly worthy of these two women's peerless, unsurpassed beauty. Something that can set off their flawless eyes, enhance their already stunning figures. Drive men panting through the streets with tongues awagging for one briefest of glimpses of their sublime saunter. Enrage other women into violent fits of jealousy so that they tear out their hair and weep rivers of regret. Don't bother us with accoutrements and attire of marchionesses and contessas, we want the stuff of queens and empresses, nigh unto the blandishments of angels. If they deign to grace the humble interior of your shop with their deific presence, grovel at their feet, heaping upon them prolific poems of praise futilely attempting to capture the tiniest smidgen of their miraculous loveliness. Indulge their every whim, tire not at their demands. Enslave yourself to their needs for they are beauty defined and you should feel sanctified to serve it."

"Of course, señor."

"I'll see you later."

Of course the girls were late, so I laid down on the bench to wait for them and draped an arm over my weary eyes. Almost immediately, I felt the tapping of a police blackjack on my forearm. I opened my eyes. A man garbed in mall security regalia hovered over me with a menacing smile, hard black eyes beneath fat eyelids regarding me contemptuously. He shook his rather swollen head at me in disdain and gestured for me to sit up. I questioned him with my eyes. He cocked his head to one side and half closed his nearly invisible eyes, then he moved the index finger of his right hand side to side in admonishment.

Clasping my hands before me in a penitent manner, I pleaded with the utmost sincerity, "Truly and with much veracity and even more contrition, please (please, PLEASE) accept my humblest and most profuse apologies." He glared back at me without comprehension and walked slowly away, his fearsome black eyes never leaving me. But our battle was not to end there. Nor may it ever end. I keep dreaming, fearing he'll appear one day in the future still garbed in his mall police uniform, draw his automatic pistol, and empty his entire clip of ammunition into my fragile frame for treading on shopping mall grass I had no right or business treading upon. Criminals of my sort, blatantly disobedient to the laws of a civilized world, should be exterminated, wiped out, had bad, evil things done to them.

Rhonda appeared first, gripping an ice cream cone (chocolate chip) and smiling at me. I stood up and she sat down. She stood up and I sat down. This continued for some time – empires expanded and expired, mountains rose and crumbled, some poor soul inserted the updated pages in all 89 binders containing the Federal Tax Reporter in the file room of Net, Block and Tackle (a California Limited Liability Partnership) for the 117th straight month before moving on to the same task in the file room of Hook Line & Sinker – and then my legs gave out as I simultaneously was fooled by her most cunning of cunning fake-out. With a triumphant smile she sat down. "Rita's just finishing her cigarette. You'll never believe what this mall cop did when she tried to enter the building smoking."

"I might."

"I thought he was going to draw his gun and shoot the cigarette from her lips."

Hearing deep, heavy breathing behind me, I turned. The Guardian of the Mall glared down at me, pointing at my lap. Without considering the consequences of my actions, I had sat cross-legged on the bench. I grasped the top of my head with both hands, covering my face protectively with my arms. "Don't shoot! I'm an innocent man. My evil twin brother Sven did it, not me. Or my conniving clone Claudio. I hadn't taken my medication." I pointed an accusatory finger at Rhonda. "It was the heartless Austrian enchantress. She made me do it! You wouldn't believe the threats she's capable of. She's mean, really mean." Rhonda licked her ice cream cone indifferently. "Take my money, the clothes from my clean-shaven back, my navel lint, only don't shoot. Take my arthritic aunt Ada instead. I'm a young man, for Christ's sake!"

Rhonda licked her ice cream cone again.

Leaving, Rhonda suddenly clutched my arm. "No."

"What?"

"There's an escalator. I don't like escalators… Don't laugh."

Rita: "She's serious."

"Oh."

"Let's go around."

"But. Okay."

"There have been incidents. And no, I don't want to talk about them... Ever."

Momentary separations were punctuated by me shouting "I'M OVER HERE!" when three feet from ear or whispering it at inappropriate times.

"I've decided something."

"You have?"

"It's big. Huge. Tremendous. Will drastically change the course of all our lives and our progeny, alter the destiny of nations, and, quite possibly determine the fate of the universe."

"Big."

"Will you help me?"

"Does it involve danger?"

"Yes."

"Reckless disregard for the laws and morals of civilized man?"

"Yes."

"How can I aid and abet your errand of anarchy?"

At the police station's front steps, a sentry stopped Rhonda and me. "Tell him we wish to speak to the chief of police."

Rhonda translated: "Queremos decir a el jefe de policia... He asked us why."

"Tell him I want to run for Miss Ecuador. In the beauty pageant." She laughed. "Tell him. And that I want to run, not you." He laughed and lowered his rifle. "Tengo mucho serio." He laughed again. "What? My face not pretty enough? Breasts too small? This is discrimination, I tell you. Blatant and vile. Look at my legs, damn you." I lifted the hem of my trousers over my ankle suggestively yet tastefully. "I would totally kick ass in the evening gown competition."

"He said that the joke is over now and if we don't leave he will shoot you and take me as his second wife."

"That doesn't sound good."

"Yeah, my thirteen husbands might get jealous."

"You should have worn something that accentuated your calves more. High heels."

"*Now* you tell me."

Then for a while (I won't tell you how long, I just won't) we walked around fixing the spelling of all the English signs in town. As we left one store, Rhonda suddenly stopped and frowned at her reflection in the front window.

"What's wrong?"

"These pants make my butt look wrinkly. My butt isn't wrinkly!"

"It certainly isn't."

"Behave yourself."

Back at the hotel, Rhonda went upstairs. I ordered a coffee and sat in the lobby writing my journal. A while later, she reappeared sleepy-eyed and asked, "Whatcha doin'?"

"Writing a poem."

"About what?"

"It's called *832 Things I Love, Adore and Cherish About Rhonda's Left Knee.*"

"Only 832? Actually, I'm going to get plastic surgery on my knees when I get back. See the scars?" I couldn't. "When I was a kid, I was a what-you-call-it in English, a tomboy. I always was scraping my knees on the ground. Now I hate them. They're so hideous." She wasn't kidding.

For the first time, I felt something missing between us. "If it will make you feel better."

"Want to go dancing with Rita and I?"

"I do have kind of a heavy schedule…"

"Shut-up. Go upstairs and make yourself more pretty. Not that it's humanly possible." She smiled.

As I returned downstairs, Rhonda said, "Wow. I feel honored. You got out the third shirt."

A man accosted Rhonda as she bought the next round at the bar.

When she returned, I asked, "Did you get engaged again?"

"Yes."

"Isn't thirteen husbands enough already?"

"I don't think so."

Rita said, "I have sixteen. And two lovers."

"Well, la-de-da."

"And you ask yourself seriously with much introspection and not a little soul searching, why is he still talking?"

Rhonda nudged me in the bar, "I think she's looking at you."

"She's a bit young for my taste, actually."

"Now's your chance. Go!"

"Don't tempt me. I told you about my vow not to date older women. The pain was too much. And your designee for my future affections and molten hot kissee-kissee sessions is a heartbreaker with a capital *H* if I ever saw one."

"But she's not too old. Maybe fifty?"

"I can't."

"What's your age limit? Give me something to work with."

"Twenty-four."

She studied my eyes. "Old age discriminator type person." Her sister returned to the table with another round of drinks. "I want to ask you something."

"What?"

She hesitated. "I'm not sure that I can."

"Say it."

"Well, you're really great, a lot of fun to be around. But anyone who has all these real high moments... They tend to have great sadness as well."

"Uh-huh."

"Maybe you don't want to answer me."

"No, I do. I guess I've had some rough times, but I mean I've seen how some people live on this planet now. I've seen some of the suffering and, though it's not my suffering, I know how privileged I am to have grown up in the country I did with my opportunities. And I can't complain. So I guess, yes, I suffer some times, but then everyone does. And to each of them, their suffering has meaning because it's real to them. So we've just got to be grateful for what we've got."

When I returned with another round, Rhonda said, "We were just talking about how many times you have to make mistakes before you find the one."

Rita added, "So many. So many."

"The thirteen husbands."

"Sixteen. Not including those I've divorced."

I took a long drink. "But that's all going to change? Now that you're dating only men off the list of the world's most eligible bachelors?"

Rhonda answered, "Exactly."

Rita said, "I met this guy when I was in Australia six years ago. An American. For a year we wrote back and forth and then I said, enough is enough. I have to see him, I have to know. So I visited him in San Francisco, all the way from Vienna. He was kind, polite, but he wasn't happy enough to see me. I knew it almost right away when he picked me up from the airport. I don't know what it was. Writing our emotions back and forth instead of living them? Being in this heightened state of happiness when we met because we were traveling and all the world was new? Something. I was ready to commit, to take that jump and see where I landed. Who cared, right? Well, it seemed he wanted the world to change to make him happy, but he wasn't ready to change to make it do so. I don't know. I was really bitter about that for a while. It'd cost me a lot of money and I'd basically had these really heavy feelings for a guy for a year all gone to waste. It hurt a lot. I think it may have even been easier if he'd been cruel or turned out to be a bad person, but he wasn't. Our differences were much, what is the word in English, yes, more subtle. That's why I made sure, really sure, that he loved me before I let those feelings form for Klaus."

"Your boyfriend."

"Yes. I mean, I love traveling, the new experiences and spending time with Rhonda, but I'm really beginning to miss him."

"And not having to look for new accommodation every two days."

"Or sit on buses."

"Having a warm towel."

"A soft bed."

"My music."

"Toilet paper not made out of industrial strength sandpaper."

"No frogs."

More Rita: "What I really hate is having to be so upbeat all of the time, especially if you've just left someone you may never see again that probably changed your life. Sometimes you just don't feel like being cheerful. You want to just be quiet and think."

Rhonda added: "And you especially don't want to talk in English."

"Way to go. Way to rip my heart out of its skeletal cage, throw it on the filthy ground, dig your stiletto high heel in and twist."

Rhonda said, "You know what I mean. It's tiring thinking in

another language all of the time. You don't know how nice we are to you."

Wow.

As Rita stood up to go the restroom, Rhonda studied my eyes. Then she said, "I don't believe in long distance relationships."

"Because of what happened to Rita."

"And some of my own experiences. Why be miserable or not even miserable but alone when you don't have to be? Yes, he's gone, but there's probably someone else close by you can be with who will make you just as happy. And who might be different in some way that opens all types of new experiences."

"But what if you're perfect for each other?"

Ralph appeared at the table wearing his sombrero: "Who wants to see my blue-footed booby mating dance?"

Rhonda responded, "I'd gladly give my left arm and second least favorite toe for such a privilege."

"Well, then." Ralph proffered his arm to escort Rhonda back to the dance floor.

We danced and we danced and we danced. It was too hot to wear shoes so we didn't and the girls never stopped smiling the whole night long. Ralph did a kick-ass Robot and I showed them the Maasai warrior jumping dance, but it still wasn't the right time for the C.P.A. dance. Always keep some hidden strength in reserve. Or don't. Lay it all on the line every single time. What the fuck was I waiting for? But I still didn't.

At the door to the hotel around three, I handed Rhonda the following scribbled on the back of a Galapagos map during a break (Rhonda was cool and everything but her Macarena sucked. Really sucked. Not that I would ever tell her.):

An American-English Primer for Rhonda (of Austria):

An Illuminating Lesson in Slang Stylings of California Speak for the Traveler, or

Verbal Variations of Vernacular for the Verbose Vagabond

Lesson the First: "Dude, like totally awesome!" (Note: "Dude" is commonly considered the best all-around, most utilitarian phrase in the language – good in nearly any context. Successful use of which phrase, however, is predicated on deft eyebrow manipulation as well as proper vocal intonation culled from years of experience and rigorous field training at all the best finishing schools and in the mean streets of eastern Pasadena. Some argue "Man" or "Homey" is a better word, but empirical scientific evidence as well as my vast, unsurpassed knowledge in this area of expertise lead me to argue most emphatically to the contrary.)

__Lesson the Second__: "That's so phat." Acceptable substitutes for "phat" include, and are certainly not limited to, "sick"(or its more robust and laudatory cousin "super sick"), "dope," or the even more old school (and personal favorite) "radical."

__Lesson the Third__: "Fer sure" – which is a more cool, hip, happenin' way of saying "Yes!" "Right on" or "Solid" can also be used, but these phrases are starting to show their age and should be employed only as a last resort.

__Lesson the Fourth__: Phrases to be avoided at all costs – use of which shall inevitably result in being labeled a Loser of the First and Unequaled Magnitude:

1. "Not!" – Popularized by a movie in the late 1980's as a way of expressing dissent in an attempted humorous manner, it is hopelessly dated in today's world.

2. "Word." – A supportive snippet which has gestated into something quite annoying, now not a little repugnant through over-use. This is a common conclusion for all slang stylings and should be considered when utilizing such phrases. To preserve their poignancy and retain their freshness, please practice discretion, for as the Greeks did say most eloquently "Moderation in all things."

3. "You go, girlfriend!" – Another expression of encouragement that now makes the ears smart with distaste.

__Lesson the Fifth__: "Don't be buggin'." or "Don't be trippin'." or "Just relax." Another phrase "Settle down" is showing some promise, however, it's probably best to see how it's accepted before incorporating it into daily usage.

__Lesson the Sixth__ (and one which you, of all people, need no guidance on): "I'll be back."

The next morning Rhonda opened the door in only a dark red

towel, her brown shoulders bare.

"I brought you coffee one last time."

She smiled. "I can't say goodbye naked."

"Best way to say it."

"I'll put something on."

I rethought about bringing the sombrero Ralph had given me.

Was I a bird or a fish? Both? Neither?

The door reopened. She said, "You went all out, didn't you? Wore the green shirt again and everything."

"I try."

"Well, it's been great meeting you. You're a lot of fun. That English Primer was hilarious."

"You're pretty amazing yourself."

"Good luck with the rest of your trip. And be sure to write me about it." She reached up to hug me.

I didn't want to, but somehow I let go. And then I turned to leave.

Too much living for tomorrow.

"Rhonda."

"Yes?"

Without really needing to think about it, I said, "I know we just met. I know that... I'll just say it and then it'll be said." She waited. "I don't... I don't want you to leave. Come to America."

"Are you... asking me to marry you?"

"No. I don't know. I mean, we've got something. We connect. You get me. I don't want to leave that. It's so rare."

She kissed my cheek. "You're sweet."

"The last year I've spent saying goodbye to amazing people, hurting at never getting to see them again. The last time it happened, I swore that if I had a chance to ask someone to stay, I would. I don't want to regret never having asked. And you're so right to be the one I ask."

562

She took my hand. "I always meet amazing people. It'll keep happening to you. Don't worry. You'll find someone else."

"Which somebody else would that be? Because I've spent twenty-four years looking and found only you."

She sighed and then said, "He gave me fifty thousand dollars for my café. I mean, seriously, you're just like every other backpacker. Just because I like hanging out with you doesn't mean I'm falling in love with you. You're all right, but just not that good looking."

Well, I asked.

"Mom."

"Well, hello! So you finally decided to call your mother."

"I did."

"What's wrong?"

"I'm coming home." What I hadn't seen, hadn't done, no longer mattered. I'd accomplished what I needed to, filled that empty space in my soul. What I hadn't done, I couldn't do here. It was time to go home.

"What happened?"

"I know what I want now."

"But she's gone."

"Yep."

"I'm so sorry, honey."

"Yep."

"I know it doesn't help you right now, but there's plenty of other fish in the ocean... I love you, sweetheart."

"Even after the fifteen hours of labor spent giving birth to me?"

"Sixteen. But, yes, even after that. Especially after that."

"I love you, Mom."

I had realized there was no point going on.

I didn't want this to keep happening. I wanted to meet someone and be able to say stay and be able to offer her something if she did. Yeah, it was old-fashioned, but I wanted to provide for her and maybe even have a family (something I'd never thought of before). I wanted to be able to take it easy, not rush things because she was going to Botswana or Syria the next day. So I bought the last ticket home.

The woman with the two crying babies appeared to take the airplane seat next to mine. We took off.

And, yes, before you ask, the plane radio played that song. On every freaking channel. An electronic glitch, they said. But I knew better.

On the first flight to Mexico City, two travelers were talking in front of me. "I heard about this guy whose ideal for traveling is the extreme. You know, no luggage, no accoutrements of any kind, not even clothes. Just sandals. The ultimate lightweight. Well, I'm gonna take it to the next level. That's right. Just naked. None of this sandals shit. For pussies. The only reason I'm wearing clothes now is they wouldn't let me on the plane otherwise. Aviation regulations or something. But I'm going to change all that, man. Spread the love…"

Whenever you think you're the best, that you excel at something, there's always someone better. What had I accomplished? I was just going to be another guy in shorts and a T-shirt walking into LAX needing a job.

In Mexico City, a connecting flight.

"I'm Fredericka."

Fred. "Are you telling the truth, the whole truth, and nothing but? The truth, that is."

"Not in the slightest. I prevaricate perpetually."

"I must admit I've just fallen madly, deeply and without reserve in love with you. Just like that."

"You're not the first. I'm tremendously attractive and not a little charming. And, well, my ass is quite divine."

"You do speak the truth, the whole truth and nothing—"

564

"But?"

"Exactly, and yet at the same time, that squared. Trebled. Whichever is mathematically more in earnest."

"Well, I can lick my elbow, have never eaten peanut butter and can name at least three independent European countries with very little prompting. I even raise my pinky when I drink tea – be it Oolong or Earl Grey. Oh, yeah, I kick tuckus and take names."

"You must have quite the fan club."

"Like grains of sand in the Saharan desert. And you are?"

"Peter. I'm just finishing a six-month trip around the world."

"Did you find what you were looking for?"

Sunrise over the silent, mossed walls of Macchu Picchu.

Cresting the pass at Throng La at fifty-four hundred metres above sea level to an infinite horizon.

Karlijn wondering what it would be like to kiss me.

Edith sleeping against me on the train to Delhi.

Fiona wiggling her ass at me across the dance floor in Goreme.

Greta's goodbye note: "You have beautiful eyes. I would like to fuck you now."

Rhonda's smile in the pale morning light.

"Yes."

"And what was that?"

I said nothing.

"Good answer."

When it had begun, I was just looking for girls and to see the world. I realized now that it was something more. And that searching, that was everything.

Maybe I didn't need Rhonda waiting for me at the LAX airport.

Maybe I just needed my parents. Maybe that was enough.

Fredericka began laughing.

"What?"

"The stewardess said if the cabin is depressurized, secure the oxygen mask on yourself first and then on your children, starting with whichever one you like best... Now she's asking for all the trash, so she can be the trashiest stewardess in the sky."

"So you speak Spanish?"

"And French, German, Italian, Japanese and a light, light smattering of Xhose. But not Inuit. Just so you know."

"I'm taking thorough notes in case there's a test..." What the hell did I just say? Fuck.

Fredericka nudged my shoulder with her own. "I'm not ambidextrous. Essential information for your edification."

"But you do have a tattoo."

"Yes." She slipped down the shoulder of her jacket. Three interlaced green vines with dark blue irises surrounding a scrolled number: seventy-eight.

"Does the number mean anything?"

The first round of airplane beverages arrived. She opened her honey-roasted peanuts and ate two. Then she looked into my eyes. I waited. She kept looking at me. And looking. Then: "My first year of school there was a fire in my apartment at Berkeley and two of my best friends died, but I got out. They died but I didn't. I don't know why. And I had these burn scars. I didn't want to get plastic surgery because it felt like then I'd be forgetting them. But then I had a friend who was a tattoo artist and he said why not transform this loss I suffered into something beautiful. So I did. Seventy-eight was the apartment number."

"How can you not have tried peanut butter?"

She smiled. "Some people are just born lucky."

"Not you. You must to listen to my jokes for the next four hours, sixteen minutes and twenty-six seconds. And I'll probably stand in line
566

next to you at baggage claim as well."

She reached into her leather handbag and removed a pair of air traffic worker's industrial strength earphones which she put on. "Did you say something?"

"You know, I'd already written my *List of Top Ten Reasons to Love, Worship and Adore Fredericka*, but with those earphones, it's now eleven. Reasons, that is."

"Eleven seems a woefully inadequate number for the tremendous undertaking you have assigned to yourself. Rome was not built in a day, I hope you know that much."

"So you're saying I'll need more paper?"

"Most emphatically."

"Humble also goes on the list. Perhaps I'll even set it to music."

She smiled. "Excuse me." She stood up. "Could you?" She offered me her handbag to hold.

"Sure."

As she turned to go to the restroom, I glimpsed a second tattoo on the back of her left leg through the slit in her black skirt. It was a long limbed white bird with a downward curving yellow beak and a red face. I recognized it, but couldn't remember its name.

A moment later, turbulence sent a brown notebook slipped from Fredericka's bag into my lap. As I picked it up, I noticed its thick parchment pages held charcoal sketches of birds. The first page depicted a wren. An emu followed. I flipped past a finch and an egret. The last page was of the long limbed white bird with the downward curving beak that was tattooed on the back of Fredericka's left leg. What the hell was going on? Then I saw the bathroom occupied light go off and quickly put the book back inside.

"You gave me your purse."

"Of course. If you don't risk it all, how will you ever know?"

"Know what I like most about traveling?" I said.

"The food? The shopping! The openness? The ability to reinvent oneself, meet people you would never meet otherwise who live a world away and see they're like you?"

"All that. But also the signs."

"The signs?"

"Yeah, like: *Toilet – No Occupation While Stabilizing*. Or: *Allow the Police to Molest You At Their Request For Your Own Benefit*."

"*Be Aware For the Fire*."

"Exactly. Another favorite: *Respect the Relic, Don't Relieve Yourself*."

"Pizza!" Fredericka exclaimed.

"Great. Just great. I was having an idea on how to cure world hunger, cancer and heart disease but then you say *pizza* and I've totally forgotten it all."

"Who cares? We get pizza!"

We both asked for seconds. And thirds. Fourths. Fifths, too, but they said we'd have to split up and sit on opposite sides of the plane because of weight considerations if we kept eating so we passed. Grumpily and not a bit disappointedly, I might add. Or I might not. I haven't decided.

As the food coma of all food comas kicked in, I turned to the window. And nearly screamed. On the wing sat a horde of birds. The red-billed quelea. About thirty of them. Glaring at me. With menace.

How?

I couldn't find the button to alert the stewardess. My hands wouldn't work. But I needed to tell someone. Warn the pilot. Do something.

I turned back to the window. And the birds suddenly took flight. As I began to scream, they flew ahead of the wing and suddenly plunged into the engine. An explosion rocked the plane. We began to fall.

A gentle hand shook me awake. "Pete. Hey. Your nose is bleeding. Here. Press it."

568

The plane's wheels hit the tarmac at Los Angeles International Airport. And there was Belinda's favorite bar – in the control tower – where I'd left it nine months before. A woman, her features indistinguishable, sat on Belinda's favorite stool looking out at our arriving airplane. Was it her? The funny thing was: I no longer cared.

Fredericka said, "So we're here. You have checked luggage?"

"Yep."

"Me, too. Walk together?"

"Yep. I--"

"Keep your head tilted back till we stop."

"You live in LA?"

"My mom does. She's sick."

Her shoulders tensed as we reached immigration. "That desk over there is free," she said as I waited behind her.

"I… Okay, thanks."

"You've been gone a while," the stern-faced immigration officer said to me.

"Yep," I said, preparing for a barrage of questions.

"Welcome home." He smiled.

Fredericka had disappeared. I stood just beyond immigration, looking. Had she?

Fuck.

After a couple of minutes, I gave up and went down the escalator to collect my luggage.

She wasn't in the baggage claim area, either. But my cousin who worked security part-time was (as were all the part-timers – there must have been a security alert). I avoided his eyes – I wasn't ready yet.

The conveyor belt began delivering the luggage.

Still no Fredericka.

My orange bag popped out. As I reached down, a voice from behind me said, "Can your pack be seen from space?" It was her.

I suddenly remembered the name of the bird. "Your real name isn't Fredericka."

Amused smile. "No?"

"What if I told you that this poor backpacker veneer is just a cover. And that, whether by design or by fate, my trip had one purpose: to track you down. To help you escape. Because there are two types of people in the world, two that matter – us and the rest of them. And the rest, each and every single one of them, don't matter at all."

"You're cute. Crazy, but cute." She glanced quickly at the police officer near the exit.

"I don't fit. I don't give a damn about owning a Mercedes Benz, which Italian restaurant serves the creamiest tiramisu, who is going to win the Super Bowl next year… And neither do you."

"I'm actually kind of particular about my tiramisu. Or any ladyfinger-based desserts."

I said nothing.

"What?"

"You know."

"I know."

"Well?"

Made in the
USA
Columbia, SC